Contents

Yun Lili
雲璃

Chapter 1: The Golden Bird's Express Delivery

Yun Lili, an utterly ordinary peasant girl from a backwater village, had never in her life imagined she might one day be entangled with the lofty realm of immortals.

Her daily concerns were simple enough: keeping her hens from freezing in winter, keeping the ducks out of the vegetable patch, and occasionally shooing Auntie Zhang's goose away from bullying the neighbour's children.

Immortal sects? Heavenly destinies? Those belonged in the wild tales told by storytellers at the teahouse—never in the life of a girl who perpetually smelled faintly of chicken feed.

Yet for three nights in a row, she had been plagued by the same dream.

A sea of fire raged across the heavens, rolling waves of flame that seemed to sear her very skin even through sleep.

From that inferno descended a bronze mirror, its surface veined with cracks of molten gold, crashing down as if hurled by some furious deity.

In its fractured depths stared out a pair of bloodshot eyes—anguished, accusing, and so piercing that her heart clenched tight as though caught in a fist.

Each time she woke, sweat drenched her hair and collar, her pulse still galloping like she had been chased through a battlefield.

The dream was too vivid to dismiss, its details etched into her mind with the clarity of lived memory. And those eyes… oh, those eyes were the worst of it.

They stirred a pang of familiarity that was sharper than the fire itself.

She was certain she had seen them before, intimately even—but no matter how she ransacked her memories, she could not place when, or where.

If one wished to trace the start of Yun Lili's absurd, lifelong entanglement with poultry, however, one had to go back eighteen years, to a thunder-slashed night that changed everything.

According to old man Yun, who she called Grandfather Yun, he had been returning from a house call that evening when, beneath the old locust tree at the edge of the village, he stumbled upon a swaddled infant wailing at the sky.

Squatting protectively beside the child, glaring at the rain as if it could be packed into submission, was a rooster of truly majestic presence—so tall and broad of chest it looked as though it had survived ten lifetimes of cockfights.

Only later did they realize it was Auntie Zhang's missing patriarch rooster, the one she had been mourning as though widowed.

The infant carried no token save for a tiny handkerchief, embroidered with a single character: Li, therefore, they named her Lili, and she took the old man's surname, Yun.

Grandfather Yun, being a man of compassion, scooped up both child and rooster and brought them home.

From that day forward, the whole village knew there was something unusual about little Lili. Chickens, ducks, geese—every feathered creature within a mile seemed to trail after her wherever she went.

Auntie Zhang's goose once even "helped" her sweep the yard by clamping the broom in its beak and dragging it about, honking furiously as though scolding the dust for insolence.

Now grown, Lili carried with her a small bronze mirror, its surface hazy and veined with a crack down the middle.

They said it, too, had been tucked into her swaddling cloth that stormy night. She often stared at it, half wondering if it would someday tell her who she really was.

But before she could get too sentimental, the wind above her head suddenly shifted.

"Gaaaaawk—!"

A massive bird came plummeting out of the sky, its feathers blazing gold like a sun newly risen.

Its tail streamed crimson light as if ribbons of dawn, and with a dramatic cry it dropped something shiny—smack!—straight onto Lili's head.

She staggered, blinking. A square of golden-edged parchment bounced off her scalp.

Looking up, she saw the source: a colossal shadow wheeling in the sky.

"Woooow." Lili tilted her head back, jaw falling open in awe. "That's a huuuuuge bird—"

And golden!

The magnificent creature swooped lower, hovering right in front of her nose. Its eyes, scarlet and glowing like twin lanterns, scanned her up and down, lingering far too long at chest height.

Then it gave a deep, rumbling *coo,* and the tone—Lili swore—was suspiciously excited.

"Such a presence… and you're living as a chicken-herder in the mortal realm?" it muttered, sounding downright scandalized.

Lili, feeling extremely ogled, instinctively clutched her collar. "Hey! What's with that look? Planning to molest me, feather ball?"

This bird… did not seem particularly wholesome.

And then, to her utter horror, the golden giant actually spoke.

"Mortal realm: Immortal aptitude detected."

"Generating invitation scroll…"

"…Error: insufficient ink supply. Please wait."

Lili: ",,,..."

A moment later, the bird spat out a crumpled piece of gold-foil paper, which landed squarely on her face with a wet *slap.*

"Congratulations, young lady," the bird intoned with exaggerated solemnity. "Your spiritual root is glowing. Please familiarize yourself with the Immortal Realm's premier sect, the Lingxiao Sect."

"Ugh! Filthy!" Lili shrieked, peeling the sticky foil from her nose. On it, bold characters announced:

Dear Candidate,

Our divine scanners have detected you possess the rare constitution of spiritual roots! Congratulations—you are hereby selected as a lucky potential disciple of the esteemed Lingxiao Sect! We warmly invite you to attend our Free Spiritual Root Testing Assembly. Complimentary starter elixir bundle awaits you!

Note: The first hundred participants will also receive an exclusive autographed portrait of a Celestial Lord!

At the bottom was a crooked red stamp: Lingxiao Sect – by order of Sect Master Yun Wuntang (stamp applied in proxy).

P.S. The Sect Master is currently in closed-door meditation.

"What on earth...? This scam is ridiculously over the top," Lili muttered, rolling her eyes. She was about to crumple the parchment when a line of tiny print caught her eye in the corner:

Disclaimer: Should you decline this invitation, your village of Green Radish will be automatically subscribed to the 'Immortal Gossip Weekly' for one hundred years. To unsubscribe, please call 8888-8888 (hotline managed by the East Sea Dragon Palace). Current estimated wait time: 34 years, 8 months, 9 days, 3 hours, and one quarter.

Lili's lips twitched. "That's... one hell of a threat."

Before she could finish the thought, the gold foil combusted with a sharp *fwoom!*

Ash swirled upward, reassembling itself into a radiant golden staircase that rose straight into the clouds.

On the first step was a neat little sign: "Watch Your Step."

On the second: "No Spitting."

"......"

Without realizing, Lili had already placed one foot on the stair. To her surprise, it was solid beneath her weight.

A cool mist curled around the steps, and with every rise came a refreshing breeze that brushed against her skin.

Just then, three chickens came charging from the yard, wings flapping as if mad, squawking as though the world were ending.

"Huh? Why are all my chickens running here?"

"Cluck cluck cluck!"

"Cluck cluck cluck!"

Lili sighed, bent down, and scooped the lot of them into her arms. "Fine, I'll bring you along. If they starve us up there in **Lingxiao Sect**, at least I'll have some emergency rations."

"Don't go up there! Come down at once—!"

"Relax, Grandpa, I'm just going for a peek—"

"I wasn't talking about you, I was talking about those three chickens! Put them down, I still need their eggs!"

"...Grandpa, they're *roosters*."

"...Bah. Fine, then off you go. But be careful out there!"

Suppressing a laugh, Lili tightened her hold on the squirming chickens and climbed higher.

Somehow, her steps felt steadier, her back straighter, than before.

The three roosters clucked solemnly and followed her every step, as though they had rehearsed this ascent a hundred times already.

The wind roared. Clouds churned and broke into splintered light.

Behind them, the golden bird spread its wings wide and murmured under its breath, "So… perhaps the Phoenix's return… is true after all."

Above, the golden stairway stretched toward the gates of the immortal realm's foremost sect—the Lingxiao Sect.

And hidden deep within the clouds, an ancient bronze mirror floated silently, its surface fractured yet glimmering.

Within its depths, it reflected the small figure of Lili climbing step by step into destiny. Beyond the mirror, a voice whispered, low and shivering with long-suppressed emotion:

"At last… you've come."

* * * * *

With a heart snagged between excitement and reluctant farewell, Lili set her foot upon the radiant stair and began to climb.

At first, it was a steady trudge. But as she ascended, the surroundings became increasingly… peculiar.

On the 17th step, a crane hunched, eyes half-lidded in a nap, one long leg tucked beneath it. Hung crookedly from its neck was a badge that read, in proper formal script: *Reception Officer*. The bird nodded to no one in particular, dozing so hard its beak clicked against its breast every few breaths.

On the 24th step, a white-robed vendor drifted by at waist height as if this were an ordinary street market and not, in fact, a sky ladder. He twirled a little pennant and bellowed in the sing-song cadence of a seasoned hawker, "Lightning rods for your heavenly tribulations! Buy two, get one free! Bonus thunder talismans with every purchase—step right up, don't step away!"

On the 32nd step, a cherubic child immortal crouched beside a bamboo basket piled with tiny porcelain bottles. He waved so enthusiastically his sleeve nearly flew off. "Beauty Elixirs! Guaranteed to make you lovelier than the Moon Goddess—one dose and you'll glow!"

Lili nearly missed a rung. "This immortal realm," she muttered, "is surprisingly… down-to-earth."

The golden bird—coasting lazily alongside like a very smug escort banner—yawned wide enough to swallow a peach pit. "The Heavenly Court's incense supply's in a slump. Budget's been slashed. Everyone's taken up a side hustle to keep the clouds paid."

"…Pardon?" Lili's face filled with question marks. Side hustles. In heaven. Very practical. Alarmingly practical.

She continued climbing until her legs began to ache. By the time she'd counted a hundred breaths, she had to purse her lips and mutter to herself that the heavens were really laying it on thick with the altitude today.

Then, without warning, the stair shuddered.

It was not the delicate tremor of a well-mannered cloud. The whole golden ladder jolted like a great beast rousing from a nap, and—without so much as a polite warning—sped up. The steps beneath her transformed into a shining slide, whisking her upward toward the vault of the sky.

She had just enough time to clamp one arm around the chicken that had somehow burrowed into the sash at her waist, and her startled scream was carried clean away by the wind. Her other two roosters flapped for dear life at her heels, their wings snapping like flags in a gale as they skittered up the moving steps.

The world fell away beneath her. Light streamed past in rippling bands. She squinted into the brilliance and, for a heartbeat, thought she saw a figure turn within thunder and flame—someone standing perfectly still inside the storm, gaze fixed on her through layer after layer of blazing light.

She almost heard a voice call to her from within that fire. It crossed the clouds soft as a hand, so gentle it made her skin break into gooseflesh. She would have sworn her name rode that breath of sound.

Then, far ahead and above, the slide levelled out, depositing her onto an immense jade platform.

A palace reared above her, magnificent, severe, and so tall it seemed to continue into the cloudbank without end. The walls were panelled in a marriage of white and gold that made her eyes water.

Across the lintel, three characters blazed with unsubtle pride: Lingxiao Sect. They gleamed so fiercely she had to blink at them through her lashes.

The doors themselves were over three zhang high: sheets of bronze overlaid with beaten gold, with door rings shaped as twin dragons rearing to the sky, pearls clamped between their fangs.

They looked seconds from dropping down and slithering off for a quick prowl.

Lili sucked in a breath. "Wow… that gate's at least three times taller than our village shrine."

Her three birds puffed to maximum roundness, chests out, beaks politely shut.

She patted their plump behinds one by one, stage-whispering, "Stick close. Everything here looks expensive. If you break anything, we can't afford the apology, let alone the bill."

Then she squared her small shoulders, hugged her chickens tighter, and walked toward the main gate.

Against the vastness of that edifice her shadow was tiny—but her back was straight, and she went without flinching.

She knew perfectly well she was here only for a spiritual-root test.

With luck, she would be sent home tomorrow to resume her honourable career of arguing with geese.

And yet—standing there—her heart thumped twice, loud as a drum in a quiet hall. It felt, unreasonably, as if stepping through that door would tip her life onto some entirely different track.

While she stared, a white-bearded immortal dozed upright in the shadow of the gate, leaning against the wall with a jade ruler dangling from lax fingers.

At the sound of approaching feet (and the unmistakable whisper of chicken claws on stone), he jolted, blinked grit out of his eyes, and squinted at her.

"Root testing?" he asked, voice hoarse with sleep. He fumbled in his sleeve and produced an entire stack of papers. "Fill out a form first."

"…A form?" Lili echoed, appalled. Bureaucracy—here too?

"Of course," the old immortal yawned. "Entry to Lingxiao Sect requires proper procedure. Procedures are the rails upon which heavenly order glides." He glanced down, just then noticing her entourage. His brow twitched. "And these… chickens?"

"Oh, my rations," Lili said, completely earnest. She gave the rooster in her sash an encouraging pat. "First time entering an immortal sect; didn't know if they'd feed me. So I brought the whole coop."

The immortal: ",,,..."

"They're very well-behaved," Lili went on, glowing with pride. "They nod hello."

The immortal lifted his eyes to the rafters, as if appealing to any god not currently livestreaming. In the end he merely said, with the patient resignation of a man who had seen stranger things this week, "Girl, put them down. Hard to write with your arms full."

"Oh." She set the trio carefully on the flagstones. They arranged themselves at her ankles like a living footstool and *clucked* twice in genteel greeting.

Lili accepted the form and scanned the first question. She nearly sprayed laughter across the paper.

How did you learn about this Spiritual Root Testing Event?

□ *Immortal Times* advertisement

□ Shared by friends on the Celestial Moments feed

□ Awakened past-life memories after being struck by lightning

□ Other (please specify): ___________

She tossed the sky a theatrical side-eye and muttered, "What kind of nonsense…"

A prickle speared her temple—sharp as flint on steel.

For a breath, an image ripped through her mind with lightning's clarity: thunder roaring around her ears, golden feathers turning black at the edges, a pair of red, red eyes searching through a wall of flame.

Annoying. That would be the nightmares again, bleeding into daylight.

She set her jaw, crossed out the listed options, and wrote neatly in the blank: Warmly invited by a very large golden bird.

On to the next. It was worse.

What elemental attribute do you wish your spiritual root to be? (Multiple choice allowed.)

□ Fire — Perk: cafeteria leftovers may be packed to go

□ Water — Perk: free bathhouse / hot spring access

☐ Wood — Perk: permission to pilfer from the Pántáo Peach Orchard

☐ Metal — Perk: commission bonus when helping the God of Wealth count money

☐ Earth — Perk: none for now; please look forward to updates

Lili read the list aloud, incredulity rising like yeast. "Leftovers to go? Free bathwater? Even the God of Wealth is running loyalty programs now?"

The old immortal gave a delicate cough into his fist. "Only a preference survey. Actual attribute determined by testing. Choose as you please."

"Oh, so it's a wishing well," Lili said, brightening. "In that case—I won't be shy."

With a flick of her pen like a commander surveying a map, she placed decisive check marks beside each item. "Food, water, peaches, funds… and Earth," she added with a playful nod. "No perks at present, but we mustn't let it feel left out."

Down the page she went.

Have you ever dreamt of a past life?

☐ Dreamt I was the orphaned remnant of a celestial clan

☐ Dreamt I loved a Sword Immortal and came to a bad end

☐ Dreamt I was struck by lightning and reincarnated as a chicken

☐ Dreamt I filled out forms until I ascended

",,,…"

Lili stared at the paper until the ink seemed to wobble. Quietly, reverently, she said to the air, "Immortal brains… truly not something mortals can comprehend."

Her three roosters nodded solemnly, as if in scholarly agreement.

The old immortal pretended not to see any of this—girl, chickens, existential paperwork—and flicked his jade ruler against his palm in a steady *tok, tok, tok…*

The universal tempo of bureaucrats everywhere.

Behind them the gate breathed a faint metallic sigh, the dragons on the rings throwing long, curled shadows across the stones.

High above, the words *Lingxiao Sect* went on glittering without shame, as if they hadn't just subjected a mortal to a survey that included "reincarnated as a chicken" as a perfectly ordinary option.

Lili dipped her brush again, lips quirking despite herself. Whatever this was—scam, destiny, budget-cut carnival in the clouds—it was happening.

And judging from the weight in her chest, from the way the wind on the ladder had smelled like thunder and old bronze, from the eyes she thought she'd seen in the fire, it had been happening for a very long time.

She set the tip of the brush to the paper and kept writing.

Chapter 2: The Phoenix Feather in the Hall of Jade

A veritable **farce** was playing out in a certain floral hall within the Lingxiao Sect compound.

"This single strike can cleave the Heavenly Thunder itself, do you truly doubt it?!"

A figure of slender build, with a remarkably **effeminate** countenance, clad in robes of deep red embroidered with subtle dark patterns, stood with one foot planted firmly upon a purple sandalwood console table.

The keen tip of their azure sword pointed directly toward the ceiling.

A wine goblet had been overturned; the precious nectar flowed across the priceless, golden-threaded carpet, catching the light of the luminous night-pearls and shimmering like a miniature silver river.

"My esteemed Young Master!" Old Nanny Li clutched desperately at her chest, her voice trembling like a candle flame guttering in a profound gale. "That, that rug is woven from the finest **Golden-Mist Brocade**…"

"Magnificent swordsmanship!" A disciple from the opposing Immortal Sect across the room applauded with genuine admiration, then froze abruptly as a belated realisation struck him. "Wait, you just referred to yourself as…?"

Yun Zhou tilted his head back, draining the remnants of the wine.

His Adam's apple bobbed prominently with the swallowing motion—a minute detail that plunged everyone present into a palpable, awkward silence.

"The legitimate eldest son of the Yun Manor, and the current frontrunner to succeed as Sect Master of the Lingxiao Sect," she—or rather, he— used the tip of his sword to flick up a jade wine pot, before pouring himself another brimming cup. "Is there some manner of objection?"

The hall instantly grew quiet enough to clearly hear the dripping of the gilded water-clock.

Three days prior, this individual, known throughout the Immortal Realm as "Miss Yun, the Eldest Daughter," had publicly undone the restrictive binding around their chest during a grand ceremonial gathering.

It was rumoured that the Young Master of the Great Primordial Sect, observing the rites, had immediately crushed the jade sceptre in his hand.

"Preposterous!" an elderly figure roared, followed by the violent crash of porcelain. "The Spiritual Assessment Ceremony is upon us, and the Young Master still behaves with such moral dissipation, being neither man nor womanly…"

"What manner of commentary is the Elder speaking?" Yun Zhou frowned, his pair of inherently virile eyebrows knitting together in displeasure. "What do you mean, 'neither man nor womanly'? I am simply honouring a lost wager, which requires me to wear feminine attire for one hundred days."

He wore an expression of utmost arrogance and self-satisfaction, adopting the air of a young master who upholds his promises above all else.

The assembled guests: ",,,…"

"Do not let the Young Master Yun's frivolous demeanour deceive you; he defeated that one from Jade Spire Tower in under three hundred moves back then, the one they called… what was his name again?" one Elder whispered softly, only to be silenced by a sharp elbow jab from his neighbour.

"Rest assured, Elder," Yun Zhou executed a casual flourish with his sword, the resulting *qi* sweeping a decade of dust from the rafters. "Your young master here is blessed with abnormal talent. A mere Spiritual Assessment is hardly a challenge."

From a quiet corner, a sudden soft meow sounded.

A maiden in white robes leaned against a pillar, her fingers playfully teasing the snow-white spirit cat nestled in her arms.

Her presence was normally so ethereal it resembled a watercolour painting, yet the cat's purring was astonishingly loud.

"Yara is going as well?" Yun Zhou raised an eyebrow playfully. "Did you not claim that the cultivation world was a polluted mess, and that you preferred merely stroking your cat at home?"

He intentionally extended a fingertip toward the cat. The snowy creature instantly bristled, its fur standing on end, and with a sharp —*Meow*.

It leapt onto Yun Yara's shoulder, its back arched like a drawn bowstring.

Yun Yara lifted her gaze, her eyes so cool they could quell the summer heat: "The Sect Master stated that if I refused to attend, he would immediately cut off my supply of the premium Fairy Fish Flakes."

Now that, to any cat owner, is truly a threat of devastating proportion. These flakes, it must be noted, are exclusively supplied by the Dragon King and cannot be acquired anywhere else.

Just as the atmosphere reached a delicate point of subtle tension, a clear, sharp voice pierced the air:

"It seems this Sword Immortal has arrived at a most opportune moment."

A man in azure robes entered, stepping in beneath the moonlight.

His gait appeared slow yet was deceptively fast, allowing him to glide silently into the hall like a draught of clean wind.

The longsword at his waist, still sheathed, cast a chilling sliver of light under the lamps.

His steps were so light they seemed to skim across the surface of water; not a single fallen leaf on the ground was disturbed.

With a flick of his sleeve, *Pah!*

Two rectangular invitation scrolls embedded themselves into the floor by Yun Zhou's feet, striking the polished stone with a resounding *Clang* that immediately sent a small cloud of light smoke billowing outwards.

Someone in the crowd trembled in genuine fear, believing the Sword Immortal had lost his temper. Xie Wuchen stood with his hands clasped behind his back, his face as calm as spring water seen through severe frost, the corner of his lips slightly upturned—a look of sharp intelligence, like a blade that revealed its edge before leaving the sheath.

The person was none other than **Xie Wuchen**.

He was famously known as the **"Sword Immortal Sovereign who Slices Dragons and Punishes Demons from the Ninth Heaven and Shatters Star-Rivers and the Ten Continents with a Single Querying Strike, Unbeatable in Half a Step."**

(Phew. One truly needs a cup of water after reciting that title.)

It was said that this title had been personally penned by him on the Sect's registration roster during a bout of heavy intoxication, and upon waking the following day, he adamantly refused to alter it, citing the simple reason: "Wherever I go, my name must resonate." He served as the Chief Disciple of the Lingxiao Sect's Sword Pavilion and was widely acknowledged in the Sword Immortal circles as the man "whose sword strikes are so handsome they automatically generate a heroic *Swoosh* sound."

"Senior Brother Xie, is something the matter?" Yun Zhou used his sword sheath to flick open one of the scrolls, then suddenly burst into laughter. "Two invitations?"

Xie Wuchen's lips curled into a gentle smile: "Your esteemed father specifically instructed me. He was concerned that a certain eldest son, being neither entirely masculine nor feminine… er, forgive me, being equally masculine and feminine, might inadvertently monopolise his sister's quota. Therefore, two invitations were prepared as a precaution."

Before his words had fully faded, a loud *CLANG* sounded from outside the main doors.

Everyone turned to look. Standing frozen in the courtyard was a young woman with a medicine basket strapped to her back. Her foot was planted firmly upon a severely deformed threshold of golden *nanmu* wood. She looked first at the gilded, magnificent hall, then finally fixed her gaze upon Yun Zhou.

"Ahem… that is to say," she scratched her head awkwardly, pulling a crumpled golden invitation from her bosom. "Heh heh, might I ask if this establishment is the Mortal Realm branch office for the Lingxiao Sect? I have arrived to register. The old man with the white beard advised that mortal applicants must first complete their procedures at the Mortal Window."

She stood by the entrance, clutching her medicine basket, looking precisely like a lost village courier attempting to file a tax return.

Witnessing this utterly bizarre entrance, the wine goblet in Yun Zhou's hand *clattered* and fell to the floor.

No one noticed that the sword in Yun Zhou's sheath was letting out a faint, clear dragon's cry. The sound was not piercing but rather resembled an ancient phoenix song travelling through the Ninth Heaven.

Simultaneously, the bronze mirror hanging at Yun Lili's waist flickered with a thread of golden light, vaguely illuminating a tiny red mark on the centre of her forehead.

* * * * *

The hall glittered with shimmering jewels and **luminous pearls**. Amidst the swirling celestial *qi*, the maiden's smiling face shone with a jarring, almost blinding brightness.

She stood rigidly by the doorway, clutching her medicine basket. A single strand of hair at her forehead had been flipped up by the wind.

Her expression was a peculiar mixture of naive expectation and utter foolishness. Her eyes scanned the various individuals arrayed within the hall, finally settling upon the spot where Yun Zhou's wine goblet lay in pieces on the floor.

"I am Yun Lili!" Her voice was clear and bright, and she added, enunciating each word with exaggerated clarity: "I have… arrived… to **register**?"

Her tone was precisely that of a small-town primary school student who had accidentally stumbled into the wrong examination venue and was desperately trying to confirm the address.

The assembled Immortals had barely recovered from the sight of the mud streaks clinging to her coarse cloth robes when they saw her shake out a gold-embossed envelope from her satchel—identical in form to the prestigious invitations Xie Wuchen had just delivered, save for the suspicious grease stains marring its corners.

Just as Yun Lili was about to launch into a clumsy explanation, a loud *Cluck* sounded. Three enormous, gorgeously patterned roosters brazenly strutted into the floral hall. The largest of the three hopped onto her shoulder, affectionately pecking at a loose piece of grass caught in her hair.

"Are those... are those actually **Spirit Pets**?" a white-robed cultivator asked, his voice trembling with sheer disbelief.

"They're my **rations**, naturally!" Yun Lili casually pulled a handful of feathers from the rooster, without breaking stride. "I heard that the Immortal Sects live a rather abstemious, hard life, so I even prepared the goji berries for the stew." As she spoke, she genuinely shook out a small cloth bundle from her sleeve, scattering a few shrivelled, dried red berries onto the polished floor.

"Pfft—"

Someone, somewhere, broke the dam of restraint first, and the tightly controlled expressions of the gathered Immortals instantly crumbled. Even the most ancient and **pedantic** of the disciplinary Elders nearly choked on his tea.

The statement plunged the hall into a fresh, awkward silence, which was immediately followed by a cacophony of stifled laughs, polite coughs, and hands clamped over mouths. Even the notoriously stern, humourless Elders couldn't prevent their lips from twitching uncontrollably.

Yun Zhou, who had been deep in discussion of swordsmanship and wine with a Celestial Sword Cultivator, was startled back to the present.

He whipped his head around to look at her, laughing so hard that he nearly spat wine through his nose: "What remarkable **gall** you possess, Maiden. You are the first person to openly propose the immediate consumption of chicken broth right at the entrance of my Yun family manor."

Even the Nanny in charge of the household turned her back, her shoulders shaking like a faulty automaton, clearly fighting internal injuries from suppressing her laughter.

Everyone was amused, save for Yun Yara, who stood silently in the centre of the hall. Her white robes were like snow, her expression cold as the frost that had yet to thaw outside the window.

She glared subtly at Yun Lili, the corner of her lips curling into the slightest, sharpest arc.

Yun Yara's gaze was frigidly clear, and her voice was low, like a cold wind sweeping over snow: "'Have you, perhaps, come to the incorrect establishment?'"

Her voice was neither loud nor soft, but it was perfectly audible to the disciples closest to her. The atmosphere, which had been on the verge of collapsing into mirth, instantly turned complex and slightly awkward.

But Yun Lili was entirely oblivious to the subtle tension. She remained squatting, attempting to coral the chickens, muttering incessantly: "You must all be very well-behaved, alright? This is not our thatched hut at the foot of the mountain; it's all gilded and magnificent. If you accidentally step on a tile and break it, I certainly cannot afford the reparations..."

No sooner had the words left her mouth than a thread of golden light, like the morning sun bursting through clouds, descended from the heavens outside the hall.

The air in its path vibrated, and the petals on the ground fluttered gently, as if all creation were bowing its head in reverence.

Celestial music resonated in the high air, sounding like bells and chimes, like a divine edict descending upon the nine continents, shaking the earth. " **Lingxiao Sect Immortal Gate, Spiritual Assessment Ceremony—Commence.**"

As the golden light fell upon the hall, the assembled Immortals rose in unison.

Their spiritual senses automatically gathered, and the primal *qi* of heaven and earth converged instantly. All traces of laughter vanished, replaced by an air of profound solemnity.

Only Yun Lili remained looking up at the golden light, her eyes sparkling with excitement. She whispered a single, awe-struck sentence: "…Wow, it genuinely glows, doesn't it?"

* * * * *

The Spiritual Assessment Ceremony was, ostensibly, simpler than one might have imagined—it merely required the subject to stand upon an ancient bronze mirror, intricately carved with runes and inlaid with gold and precious jade, and place both hands upon its surface. The resulting colour of the emitted light would determine if a spiritual root existed, or what specific type of spiritual root the subject possessed, based on the hue.

Yun Lili stood there, gazing down at the mirror, her expression one of profound subtlety and discomfort.

She had been distracted by the observation that the seven gemstones embedded in the mirror's frame were clearly forced into a rough semblance of the Big Dipper constellation.

Their **lustre** was uneven and patchy; the sixth stone, noticeably smaller than the others, was clearly a piece of makeshift glass, crudely patched in, and bore a faint, sticky watermark from the residual adhesive.

The frame itself was encircled by divine beasts in a tail-biting posture, and the seven jade stars should have been radiating boundless glory. Yet, they merely flickered erratically, like cheap lanterns outside a local temple, betraying an embarrassing awkwardness, as if someone had forgotten to activate the actual formation.

"This mirror looks decidedly odd," Yun Lili muttered, instinctively rubbing her hands vigorously on her clothes.

An elderly Immortal, who was overseeing the assessment, noticed her prolonged inaction. He frowned and urged her impatiently: "Be quick about it. This old Immortal must return to his nap shortly."

Yun Lili offered a slightly embarrassed smile: "But my hands… they are quite filthy."

"Nonsense." The old Immortal dismissed her concern with a wave of his hand. In an instant, her mud-patched, coarse robes were replaced by a pristine, moon-white silken tunic.

A profound sensation of cleanliness immediately enveloped her.

"Wow…"

"Hurry along now, my shift is nearing its end. No more dawdling," the Immortal grumbled, clearly displeased.

"Er, right then."

After a final, brief moment of hesitation, Yun Lili placed both hands onto the mirror's surface.

The instant her palms made contact, the entire bronze panel began to flash wildly, switching haphazardly between seven distinct colours like a broken streetlamp suffering a catastrophic electrical fault.

"This is strange," the old Immortal scratched his head in confusion. "The last time this precise anomaly occurred was five hundred years ago, when we were assessing the spiritual root of the Third Prince Nezha."

Just as the assembled Immortals held their collective breath, the mirror emitted a loud, rattling *K-r-r-a-c-k!* and shuddered violently, as if someone inside were furiously shaking a celestial lottery machine.

The seven-coloured light flashed chaotically, until finally, with a loud **"POOF!"** a plume of grey smoke erupted. The entire bronze mirror surface went dark, save for a few small, wavering words that flickered erratically:

—Mirror Model Obsolete. Current User Format Not Supported. For repairs, please contact: Celestial Lord Jì-Míng (寂明仙君).

A final, smaller postscript was appended to the corner:

—In case of dispute, please report to the Heavenly Court. Final interpretation rights reserved by the 'Celestial Apparatus Bureau of Lingxiao' (Heavenly Firmament). (Mirror Code: Alpha-One).

—This mirror has served multiple Immortal Masters; this version was authorised and sealed by the current Sword Venerable, Celestial Lord Jì Míng.

Yun Lili: ",,,..."

Is this Celestial Lord Jì Míng, this 'Jì Míng Xiān Jūn'… some kind of divine artisan or mirror repairman?

"…Shouldn't someone immediately send word for Celestial Lord Jì Míng?"

Someone whispered the question, and the surrounding Celestial Officials instantly fell into a suffocating silence, as if the very air had congealed.

"Are you insane? That individual… why would he possibly concern himself with a trivial matter such as this?"

"But he is the recognised Master of this generation's Celestial Mirror, and the Chief of the Sword Dao. Should this anomaly escalate out of control, surely only he possesses the power to suppress it."

"Do you truly believe he would condescend to heed the summons? He has been in closed-door cultivation for three years without uttering a single word. Even Vice Envoy Sang's simple advice once caused him such spiritual fury that the Vice Envoy coughed up blood… do you truly dare to disturb him again?"

At this anecdote, the surrounding figures all adopted expressions of profound sympathy, looking towards Sang Li with a noticeable increase in pity.

Sang Li stood there, his dark robes whipping in the unfelt wind. He simply rubbed the bridge of his nose with an air of utterly defeated resignation.

Well, who is one to blame? That man is the Sword Venerable, the most unfeeling, living King of Hell in the entire Azure Heavens and the Lingxiao Sect.

Chapter 3: The Mirror's Hidden Light

Since "Ji Ming Immortal Lord" Yu Sord was the sole maintenance provider—no—the sole designated person, the gathered immortals had no recourse but to turn to him for aid.

With a low *rumble*, a luminous array manifested in the center of the main hall.

Within its glow, an ancient bronze mirror materialized, its surface undulating like water and shimmering with a faint auroral light. Spiritual power swelled, drawing winds from all directions.

The arriving figure was clad in robes of profound black and gold, standing tall and poised with hands clasped behind his back. His features were elegantly sculpted, radiating an immortal's grace.

Yet, a faint blue vein pulsed at his brow—a telltale sign of one who had just been compelled to repair thirty spirit-measuring mirrors without respite before being summoned to extinguish this new fire.

This was Sang Li, Vice-Commander of the Lingxiao Sect's Law Enforcement Division.

Yun Lili stared wide-eyed at the dazzling, golden spectacle of his arrival, utterly astonished. "Wow."

The chicken in her arms let out a soft "cluck," as if in agreement.

The sound pierced the previously tense atmosphere. The man in the black-and-gold embroidered robes glanced sideways, his gaze settling upon Yun Lili.

She beamed with radiant innocence, her face a picture of naivety, all while cradling a plump chicken.

"…" After a prolonged silence, he finally spoke, his tone mild. "This young lady, have you come for the spirit measurement?"

"Yes!" Yun Lili nodded briskly, adjusting the chicken in her arms. "I came as soon as I received the summons. It was such a long journey— my feet are nearly worn out… but I think I might have broken the mirror by touching it!"

As soon as the words left her mouth, many disciples below lowered their heads, shoulders trembling subtly as they stifled laughter, their faces flushed.

Yun Yara's mouth twitched, her eyes rolling almost imperceptibly.

Beside her, Yun Zhou chuckled heartily. "How amusing. Today's spirit measurement is nearly a comedy, bringing in such a… vibrant character."

"Trouble not. A simple repair will suffice."

Scarcely had Sang Li's words fallen when his foot lashed out against the mirror.

A sudden, violent burst of multi-coloured light erupted, swirling around the mirror's frame like a frantic rainbow before abruptly ceasing.

An odd silence blanketed the surroundings. Then, Sang Li declared impassively, *"Repaired."*

"…" A collective speechlessness hung in the air.

"Huh? It's fixed already?" Yun Lili was dumbfounded.

Did the immortal simply kick it, and that was all it took?

Sang Li gave a slight nod, the faintest ripple of emotion finally crossing his features. He opened his mouth to speak, only to be interrupted by a light cough.

From the crowd emerged a silver-robed man of middle years, his posture upright and demeanour steady. He bowed respectfully before speaking clearly:

"Vice-Commander Sang, your esteemed self need not labor over such a minor trial."

He turned to Yun Lili, his tone even. "This humble one is Jing Yu, an outer hall steward and seventh-rank celestial official of Lingxiao Sect. The spirit measurement shall proceed under my guidance."

Sang Li lowered his gaze, offering no objection—a tacit consent.

Official Jing Yu nodded towards Yun Lili and gestured towards a simple bronze mirror. "This mirror is named 'Spirit Reflection.' Simply place your hand upon it, and it shall reveal whether you possess a spiritual root."

"Really? That amazing?" Yun Lili widened her eyes, leaning in with keen curiosity. "But my hands are full with this chicken… can I put it down?"

"…By all means," Jing Yu replied, his voice catching slightly as it rose in pitch.

A wave of muffled laughter rippled through the hall.

Finally setting the chicken down, Yun Lili approached the mirror hesitantly. She rubbed her hands together but delayed placing them on the surface.

"Young lady, do you have concerns?"

"Uh… hehe, I'm a bit nervous. Maybe someone else should go first?" Yun Lili scratched her head, somewhat abashed.

Sang Li inclined his head. "Very well." He looked towards Yun Zhou and made a courteous gesture. "Please."

As Yun Zhou stepped onto the platform, his tall figure stood poised, the light-blue robes of his attire stirring as if touched by a preternatural breeze even before he moved.

The moment his palm met the immortal mirror, dual spirits of wind and fire roared in unison, and extraordinary phenomena erupted between heaven and earth.

A colossal pillar of flame churned like a dragon, while fierce winds howled like a tiger. Crimson light shot skyward, piercing the ninth layer of clouds. I

immortal cranes and spirit birds took startled flight; thousands of spiritual beasts prostrated themselves. Even the guardian stone beasts at the gate gnashed their teeth as if ready to bow in submission.

Within the hall, the celestial officials paled in unison. Some stood, only to hesitate and sit back down; others muttered under their breath. One even dropped his spirit fan to the floor with a clatter, utterly unaware.

The immortal mirror trembled with a deafening hum. Ancient seal script blazed forth, revealing four characters: **"Dual Spirit Destiny."**

A collective gasp swept the assembly—

This was the Dual Spirit Destiny, unseen for a millennium! Legend held that only one capable of opposing the Demon Sovereign could possess such a fate!

The celestial officials were visibly moved. An elder whispered hoarsely, "If this one does not fall, a divine seat surely awaits… but should he fall, calamity may befall the world."

Yun Zhou merely curved his lips slightly, an aura of peerless arrogance emanating from his brow and eyes.

As he stepped down, he called out to his legitimate younger sister, Yun Yara, "Go on, don't be afraid. At worst, it's just a lightning strike!"

Passing by Yun Lili on his way, his gaze fell upon the plump chicken in her arms, and his eyebrow arched faintly. Yun Lili grinned, giving the chicken's foot a little wave.

He, however, turned his eyes away with a seemingly amused yet dismissive glance, a light *hmph* escaping him as his sleeve fluttered—aloof and proud, just as he had arrived.

The phenomena from Yun Zhou's test had yet to fully dissipate, spiritual energy still churning in the air. As the assembly remained immersed in awe over the "Dual Spirit Destiny," the old immortal who had been dozing earlier called out loudly,

"Second Young Lady of the Yun family, Yun Yara, step forward for the spirit measurement!"

The crowd quieted, their gazes sweeping in unison toward the young woman clad in moon-white robes, her features carrying a spirited dignity. She held a sword in her arms, paused for a silent moment, then stepped forward as instructed.

"She is Yun Zhou's sister, and has been clever since childhood. She shouldn't be bad, right?"

"Perhaps another Dual Spirit? The Yun family might produce twin prodigies!"

Yun Yara shot a cool, fleeting glance at Yun Zhou before advancing. Slowly, she placed her hand upon the immortal mirror.

Everyone held their breath. The mirror's surface first flickered with a faint light, then a flash of fire, a hint of water, a wisp of wood energy… all chaotically intertwining before a violent tremor shook the mirror. With a final hum, its radiance abruptly dimmed.

—No phenomena, no spiritual resonance.

Seeing this, the old immortal suddenly became alert, his expression shifting as he muttered apprehensively, "Mixed… mixed… poor spiritual root."

As these words fell, an uproar erupted in the hall.

"What?!"

"How is this possible? Yun Zhou possesses a Dual Spirit destiny, yet she has a poor spiritual root?"

"Has the immortal mirror malfunctioned? Should we test again?"

"How could a poor spiritual root ever enter Lingxiao Sect?"

How could it be… a poor spiritual root?

Her fingertips trembled slightly. As she withdrew her hand, she didn't even notice her nails digging deep into her palm. She could barely hear the surrounding commotion, her mind ringing as if struck by a sudden blow.

—Since childhood, she had been exceptionally clever, the focus of everyone's attention, the genius her master called "equal in fame to her elder brother"… How could she have a poor spiritual root?!

In that moment—she refused to believe it!

She felt her entire body ignite, not with spiritual fire, but with overwhelming shame and… resentment.

Yet she had no choice but to believe, for her cultivation journey had indeed always been forcefully aided—by "metal" attributes.

Naturally gifted and brilliant, she always lagged a step behind her brother. Thus, her father, the Sect Leader, filled her storage pouches and private treasury with all manner of rare treasures and spiritual pills— anything that could boost her cultivation.

Voices clamouring for a retest surged like waves. Just then, someone spoke coldly, "If you doubt the mirror's accuracy, retesting is futile. Better to have someone else try; then we'll know the truth."

With that, whether intentionally or not, the crowd collectively pushed forward Yun Lili, who had been standing to the side.

She froze for a moment, a flicker of panic crossing her eyes, yet she still steadied herself and took a step forward, approaching the immortal mirror. Softly, she responded, "My turn now? Oh… well, I'll give it a try."

Yun Lili hesitantly walked up to the mirror, rubbing her hands together, and even turned back to ask, "So… just a touch is enough?"

Jing Yu barely suppressed the urge to massage his temples. Just as he was about to speak, Sang Li's voice, as light as wind through a bamboo grove, drifted from behind:

"Close your eyes, focus your spirit, clear your mind of distractions."

"I'll try… but my chicken seems to have gotten stuck in the spirit array…"

"???"

The immortals exchanged bewildered glances. For a moment, the atmosphere atop the spiritual platform eerily froze.

Yun Lili secretly scooped the chicken back into her arms from the edge of the array, muttering under her breath, "Sorry about that, won't let it run off next time."

She turned back to the immortal official and blinked. "Really, just placing my hand on it is enough? No need for incantations or anything? I just learned the multiplication table the day before yesterday—should I recite it for courage?"

A hint of amusement seemed to flicker in Yun Zhou's eyes, but it vanished in an instant, his expression returning to its usual calm detachment.

The moment Yun Lili's fingertip lightly touched the mirror's surface—

"BOOOOM—!!!"

Heaven and earth's spiritual energy surged like a tidal wave. The ancient mirror trembled violently as a pillar of golden light shot toward the sky, accompanied by the phantom image of a spirit crane spreading its wings with a long, resonant cry. Celestial music echoed, as if the very heavens were singing!

"That's… a Heavenly Spiritual Root?!"

"And accompanied by a bloodline phenomenon?! How is that possible?!"

"This girl looks like she hasn't even entered Qi Refining… how could she…"

The cultivators present were struck speechless with shock. Even the usually unflappable Official Jing Yu wore a look of utter bewilderment.

Yun Lili stood within the column of churning spiritual light, clutching the still-clucking, **bristling chicken** in her arms, her mind utterly blank."

The immortal officials: ",,,…,,,…"

Sang Li, however, gazed calmly at the lingering phantom light within the mirror. Lowering his eyes, he said nothing. With a flick of his long finger, the wildly surging phenomena receded like a tide.

His voice, clear as jade dropping into a tranquil pool, rang out across the surroundings: "The Heavenly Spiritual Root phenomenon has manifested. This girl may ascend directly to the inner sect."

—Never in the thousand-year history of spirit measurement at Lingxiao Sect had it been so… eventful!

* * * * *

The light gradually faded, the phenomena dissipated, and the immortal mirror lay quietly in place as if the earth-shattering spectacle had never occurred.

Yun Lili stood dazed, her palm still pressed against the mirror's surface. It took her a long moment to regain her senses before she murmured, "But it was said... there was nothing special about it?"

"*This young lady is indeed special.*" Jing Yu's voice held an unprecedented gravity, his gaze carrying a hint of indescribable complexity as it rested upon her.

Not far away, Yun Yara clenched her teeth tightly, her fingers hidden within her sleeves balled into white-knuckled fists, nails nearly digging into her palms. She was the legitimate daughter of an immortal sect, the one naturally burdened with great expectations—so why had the mirror revealed a poor spiritual root for her, while this rustic girl… was granted an omen of the phoenix's cry?

Sang Li remained silent as ever, yet a trace of icy clarity flashed deep within his eyes. He seemed to have understood something, but chose not to voice it.

Before the crowd could recover from the shock, the surface of the Heaven-Reflecting Mirror suddenly shimmered with an extremely faint, gentle halo. That light, soft and delicate, pierced through the sky above the spiritual platform, painting the horizon with hues of twilight.

"This is no ordinary spirit-measuring mirror light..." an immortal official murmured under his breath, "Could it be… a remnant echo of the *Spirit Reflection Realm*?"

"What?" The assembly stirred in alarm.

"Impossible. The Spirit Reflection Mirror is an ancient divine artifact, long since destroyed. This is merely a replica, how could it..." Another voice trailed off mid-sentence, for he too saw it—the faint, indistinct silhouette of a pair of golden feathers hovering within the twilight glow, silently circling the highest heavens.

It was an ancient, familiar aura—the aura of Phoenix bloodline.

The immortal officials fell utterly silent. For a moment, the entire great hall was hushed, save for Yun Lili clutching her chicken as she cautiously took a step back and whispered,

"Um… maybe I should go back and wait for the news?"

The crowd: ",,,..."

"I meant no harm… really just a touch… please don't break, I'm begging you…" She secretly stroked the corner of the bronze mirror as if coaxing a sulking porcelain doll.

The chicken clucked twice, seemingly in agreement.

Sang Li withdrew his gaze, his tone unchanged yet imbued with an added layer of indisputable authority:

"*You may not leave. You shall remain in the sect for temporary observation.*"

In that moment, everyone understood—this chaotic, chicken-scattering spirit measurement was not merely a farce. It was the beginning of a destiny ordained by heaven.

Chapter 4: The Crane Reveals the Bloodline

At this very instant, within the rear hall of the Lingxiao Sect, the smoke of incense curled in lazy spirals.

Before the celestial markings had chosen to manifest, the silence was quite uncanny; the air held nothing but the faint, rhythmic chanting of scriptures drifting from the prayer cushions.

All of a sudden, a totem of a crane soaring towards the heavens surfaced upon the Spirit Reflection Mirror.

Golden light cascaded down like sunbeams cleaving through cloud and mist, illuminating the entire spiritual platform with a dreamlike, almost hallucinatory quality.

The Old Matriarch of the Yun family had originally been sat cross-legged upon her cushion, eyes slightly closed, a string of prayer beads in hand as she chanted *sotto voce*.

Yet, at the precise moment the celestial marking abruptly appeared, her eyes snapped open.

A physical jolt ran through her entire frame; the prayer beads in her hand snapped in response to the shock, scattering across the floor with a distinct clatter.

She rose trembling, leaning heavily on her dragon-headed cane as she staggered a few steps forward.

Raising a hand, the scene upon the spiritual platform was reflected into the void—the golden crane totem upon the Celestial Mirror was glittering with brilliance, crying out softly as if possessed of its own sentient spirit.

The Old Matriarch fixed her gaze upon it for a moment, her eyes instantly flooding with a heavy layer of shock and hesitation.

"This pattern... it is the Ancestor's mark..."

She murmured in a low voice, her tone almost quivering: "How could it appear on her? Could it be... that *she* is the one..."

Before she could finish this sentence, several elders had arrived in a hurried fluster. Seeing the Old Matriarch's expression was far from ordinary, they hastily enquired: "Old Matriarch, this mark... what is its origin?"

The Old Matriarch's gaze remained locked upon the Celestial Mirror, silent for a long while. It was only when she clearly beheld the maiden standing before the mirror on the platform—features delicate yet possessing a spirited aura—that she slowly opened her mouth:

"A century ago, as the Yun Ancestor sat in meditation passing into ascended beyond the mortal realm, he concealed the sole seal of true inheritance within the very marrow and blood. This seal... only the direct line may inherit it; collateral branches haven't a ghost of a chance of obtaining it."

She paused, her gaze turning sharp as a knife: "This maiden—what is her name?"

A small attendant at the side hurriedly replied: "In reply to the Old Matriarch, her name is Yun Lili. She hails from a side branch of a side branch of a side branch of the Yun family. She originally dwelt in a small village, Green Radish, at the foot of the South cloud Mountains. Her background... is hardly illustrious. It is merely that... somehow or other, she received a golden invitation to come and have her spirit measured."

Upon hearing this, the Old Matriarch's gaze froze like coagulated frost. After a long pause, she enunciated every word: "The Spirit Reflection Mirror does not err... Come with me."

With a sharp shout and a sweep of her sleeves, light and shadow surged, and she led the throng of elders to manifest directly atop the spiritual platform.

"The Old Matriarch appears in person!"

"She has actually come for a girl from a side branch?"

The entire venue erupted in uproar; cultivators whispered amongst themselves, the atmosphere suddenly pulled taut.

Old Matriarch Yun stood before the Celestial Mirror, looking quietly at Yun Lili for a moment, before suddenly announcing in a clear, ringing voice: "Gentlemen, hear me, this girl... is very likely the true bearer of the Yun bloodline, the authentic descendant of the direct line!"

As these words were spoken, the crowd in the hall felt as though they had been struck by a thunderbolt; all were greatly shaken.

Yun Yara's face drained of all colour in an instant, as though struck by a heavy blow. Her body swayed; she could scarcely keep her balance.

A faint tremor ran through her frame.

The blood had fled her lips entirely, yet she forced her spine to remain straight. Hidden within her sleeves, her fingers curled tight—so tight they dug into her own palm, sharp enough to nearly draw blood.

Under the gaze of the multitude, she could not collapse, nor did she dare to; she could only bite down hard on her lower lip, forcing herself to remain composed.

Yun Zhou looked up in bewilderment, his eyes written full of disbelief: "What? Yun Lili... is my true sister? Then... then who is Yun Yara?"

The Matriarch gave a cold harrumph, her voice deep as a great bell: "The true inheritance mark of a century ago has finally reappeared after eighteen years. Alas, on the day the Yun direct daughter was born, it coincided with a raid by the remnants of the Western Ridge Demon Clan upon Yunzhou. Beacons of fire engulfed half the city; the Lingxiao Sect was rife with internal chaos, and the spiritual platform shook."

Her voice lowered a few degrees as she slowly continued: "At that time, a maid from the main courtyard fled for her life clutching a newborn infant. *En route*, she collided with a family of mortal refugees. In the bedlam, both infants were stained by smoke and fire, their clothes mottled with blood, making them indistinguishable... It is rumoured that the maid hurriedly scooped up one of them and hastily delivered the child back to the Sect."

She paused, her eyes burning like torches: "For many years, I assumed this was merely a mistake made in the chaos. Yet now that the Celestial Mirror has revealed the truth, not only verifying the Phoenix Shadow Spirit Mark but also the reappearance of the Ancestor's legacy seal... how could this matter be a mere coincidence?"

A deathly silence fell over the hall.

Her gaze swept over the various elders, her voice low: "Perhaps... the chaos of those years was not entirely a natural disaster. Someone, utilising the fire to further their own layout, secretly swapped the Mandate of Heaven."

"As for who that person might be—" She did not continue, merely tightening her grip on her cane until the wood emitted a subtle creaking sound. Her voice halted, her gaze falling back upon Yun Lili, her tone possessing an unprecedented firmness and certainty.

"Today, with the Spirit Reflection Mirror as witness, the Phoenix Seal has re-emerged, and the bloodline is beyond doubt—the true direct line of the Yun family has finally returned to its rightful seat."

The crowd fell silent, rendered speechless. Only upon the Celestial Mirror did the golden crane shadow linger, refusing to disperse, circling above Yun Lili's head as if crying out spiritually.

She stared blankly at the Old Matriarch, as if some nightmare sealed away for eighteen years was prying open the doors of her memory; she wanted to say something, yet found she could not utter a single syllable.

For a time, it seemed impossible to reconcile this earth-shattering realisation of identity with her own self, feeling only a voice deep within her soul slowly awakening:

"This woman shall inherit the Yun orthodoxy and succeed the responsibility of Heaven's Mandate."

* * * * *

The emerald waves of the water mirror flowed in perpetuity, shimmering with a faint luminescence as they reflected the myriad anomalies occurring before the Spirit Measuring Platform—

Yun Zhou's spiritual light rushed to the heavens, a phenomenon that startled the skies. Yun Yara was measured to possess Impure Spiritual Root, causing the entire venue to erupt in uproar.

Yun Lili manifested the shadow of a crying crane, its clear call piercing the clouds.

The Old Matriarch rose in shock, the hand clutching her cane trembling slightly, shaking the entire hall.

Before the water mirror, Xie Wuchen stood with arms crossed, a grin of a rogue playing upon the corners of his mouth.

He gave a tut of appreciation and said, "This show is quite the spectacle. This drama of the real and counterfeit daughters flips the narrative more wildly than any play script. Were it not for this Immortal Lord seeing it with his own eyes, I would truly believe some arbiter of destiny had gone stark raving mad."

Yu Sord's scabbard hummed with a light tremor; a glacial sword aura forced Xie Wuchen to retreat three paces.

The water mirror reflected the subtle shift in his gaze—that maiden standing before the celestial mirror, looking entirely at a loss.

The moon-crescent gown of the Immortal Realm's standard issue set off her small face, making it appear white yet flushed with a rosy hue.

Xie Wuchen turned his head to look at the man beside him, whose expression was as cold as frost, and raised an eyebrow in a teasing manner: "That future fiancée of yours... went from the Yun manor's legitimate daughter to a possessor of Impure Spiritual Root overnight. Are you surprised? Is it not unexpected?"

Yu Sord withdrew his gaze indifferently, his voice sounding like cold spring water dripping onto stone: "I would advise you to hold your tongue."

* * * * *

In point of fact, this was not the first time he had laid eyes upon her.

In his previous life, the manner of her death amidst the lightning tribulation remained branded upon his heart to this day.

She was haughty, brimming with confidence, and had never cultivated with proper diligence. The lightning tribulation arrived with abrupt suddenness.

When he arrived, he saw only a bolt of lightning swallowing her figure whole.

She fell from the firmament, even her protective spiritual light shattering into streaming sparks.

He was too late to save her; he only managed—by virtue of his cultivation—to protect a wisp of her remnant soul, guiding her into the cycle of reincarnation and leading her towards rebirth.

That year, at the tail end of autumn, he travelled to the mortal realm's Southern Ridge to investigate a disturbance in a spiritual vein.

Upon reaching the Cloud Water Ravine, he spotted a slight, nimble figure from afar, weaving through the forest in the col of the mountain. Though her footsteps were rapid, she was staggering from side to side.

And now, she squatted in the mud, pouncing towards a medicinal herb, smiling at him with a face covered in mud, looking for all the world like a wild little beast that had rolled in from the mortal realm.

She crouched upon the ground, staring with delight at a fuzzy blade of grass, muttering to herself: "You look terribly like that rabbit's ears from next door... Come, come now, let Big Sister pluck you to take home for a medicinal primer."

With that, she pounced upon it, resulting in a resounding *thud* as her foot slipped. She flipped entirely into the ditch, her posture bizarre, four limbs pointing towards the heavens, head covered in fallen leaves.

"Oh dear, oh dear... is anyone there? I seem to have... stepped upon my own foot and fractured a bone..."

Her tone was aggrieved and utterly bewildered.

He walked over, looking down at this girl whose face was caked in soil yet whose eyes were startlingly bright. He felt it was simply preposterous, yet felt a pang of—heartache.

The time was not yet ripe; he could not yet take her back to the Immortal Realm.

She tilted her head back to look at him, saying with a dazed and muddled expression: "Are... are you an immortal? You are dreadfully handsome..."

He remained silent for a long while before replying, the corners of his lips hooking up slightly; his handsomeness seemed to gain a touch of human warmth. "Is that so?"

Within his lowered gaze, there was a fleeting warmth.

He was unwilling to admit it, but when she had pounced into the grass and smiled at him with a head full of mud, his heart had actually moved, lost in a trance for a moment.

That smile, and the image of her falling amidst the lightning tribulation, were like memories from two different worlds, yet both were etched into his very marrow.

* * * * *

Xie Wuchen clapped his hands together, laughing with wanton abandon. "Right-o. Your reaction is truly a living billboard for the Path of Ruthlessness; the heavens could collapse, and you wouldn't so much as bat an eyelid. A faerie pampered by a thousand affections tumbles from the divine altar in a single morning, and yet you harbour not a shred of tender feeling for the fairer sex?"

Yu Sord offered no word. His fingertips tapped lightly against the stone balustrade, yet his gaze remained fixed unshakeably upon Yun Lili within the water mirror—tranquil as a mountain, the depths of his eyes rippling without a trace. Yet, at the corner of his lips, the ghost of an arc seemed to flit past.

Xie Wuchen, sharp-eyed as ever, immediately leaned in a step closer. "Am I seeing things? The Jade Sword Venerable, legendary for severing the galaxy with his blade, is actually capable of smiling?"

He shook his head with a sigh, his face a picture of regret. "Now the heart of the Faerie Yun Yara shall truly be shattered..."

Yu Sord's brow furrowed slightly, his tone carrying a distinct chill. "Shut your mouth."

Xie Wuchen laughed uproariously. His fingers had not yet reached Yu Sord's shoulder when he saw the other's figure flash like a phantom in the wind; in the blink of an eye, he was already three feet away.

"Keep your hands to yourself," Yu Sord said coldly.

"Fine, fine, fine. I understand, I understand," Xie Wuchen shrugged. "The Path of Ruthlessness: cultivated well, cultivated wondrously, cultivated to absolute screaming perfection."

"Get lost."

* * * * *

Upon the spiritual platform, Yun Yara's face was the colour of parchment.

The three words "Impure Spiritual Root" struck like a thunderclap, shattering her mind and spirit.

The sounds of discussion buzzing in her ears were like a rising tide, every sentence a knife, peeling her away from the clouds and casting her down into the mire.

Never had she imagined that she herself would be the counterfeit.

Yun Zhou strode forward rapidly, his hand half-extended. "Yara, fear not, I..."

Yun Yara stared at him blankly, yet her feet instinctively took a step back. That single step seemed to carve out an abyss ten thousand fathoms deep.

She looked up at the stage and below it, at those faces both familiar and strange.

Shock, pity, suspicion, disgust... they interlaced into masks that seemed carved by a knife. Her lips moved slightly, yet she could not utter a single sound; she felt only that the entire world was suffocating her.

In a trice, she gritted her teeth and unsheathed her sword. With a flash of her figure, she rose upon the blade. The sword-light was like frost, skimming the very clouds.

Before the crowd's gasps could cease, they saw only her robes fluttering in the wind, a solitary shadow shooting violently into the firmament, her momentum like a rainbow, unreachable by any other.

At this moment, Yun Lili remained the picture of befuddlement, her brain still stalled in a blank state of *Who am I? Where am I? What just happened?*

Her mouth was slightly agape as she watched the retreating figure of Yun Yara, flying away on her sword with such dash—ink-black hair flowing, white robes and broad sleeves billowing in the wind.

She could not help but be filled with admiration. "Wow... how dashing..."

She turned her head to the disciple of the sect beside her and whispered, "If I were to have Impure Spiritual Root, I also would wish to fly away with such dash; the aura was simply pumped to the absolute maximum..."

The sect disciple wanted to weep but lacked the tears. "Miss, are your priorities not a tad eccentric?"

What was there to be smug about regarding Impure Spiritual Root? Surely that anomaly of the soaring crane and a flood of golden light was the truly formidable existence?

Yun Lili, however, nodded with a face full of seriousness, her tone actually betraying a hint of reverence. "You don't understand. That is a kind of... tragic yet dashing aesthetic."

The corner of the sect disciple's mouth twitched, his expression utterly complex. "But... do you not feel that the Crane Soaring to the Heavens is a point more worthy of study?"

Yun Lili's eyes lit up, as if she had automatically filtered out the other's retort, and she suddenly leaned in close. "Tell me, that angle of take-off just now—was it three parts *qi* manipulation, two parts sword control, plus one part... emotional explosion?"

The sect disciple: "...Miss, could you please stop researching such strange things?"

Yun Lili tilted her head, thinking for a moment, extremely earnest. "I was merely thinking, if one day I must suffer a blow and fly away, I could at least look a bit dashing... so as not to be humiliating."

The sect disciple: "...You win."

This train of thought was simply too bizarre; he could only blame his own lack of wisdom roots for being unable to keep up.

Just then, a senior martial sister nearby could not help but interject. "I feel this young lady makes a rather valid point. That sword-flight take-off by Faerie Yun Yara... truly had a cinematic quality."

Yun Lili's eyes immediately sparkled, as if meeting a kindred spirit. Excitedly, she grabbed the hand of this unknown senior sister. "Right? Right? It was simply too poignantly beautiful!"

The senior sister's eyes reddened slightly, resonating with the emotion. "Indeed. A bit broken, a bit heartbroken... our Yun Yara..."

"Wuu..."

The surrounding sect disciples covered their faces in a breakdown. "What manner of people am I cultivating immortality with...?"

* * * * *

Within the precincts of the Lingxiao Sect, the atmosphere inside the Great Hall of the Yun family ancestral shrine hung heavy, as if a thunderstorm were on the very brink of breaking.

The expressions of the assembled crowd were far from benevolent, a cacophony of dissent rippling through the air.

"Impure Spiritual Root! And yet she dares to style herself a legitimate daughter—it is nothing short of a stain upon the century-old reputation of our Yun clan!" A kinsman elder of straightforward and fiery temperament slammed his hand heavily upon the table, the sound exploding like a clap of thunder.

"As I see it, we ought to immediately abolish her immortal arts and expel her from the Yun manor, that we might rectify the family ethos!"

"Quite right. The shame of this day stems entirely from her imposture; if she is not dealt with, with what face shall the Lingxiao Sect continue to stand within the Immortal Realm?" another voice chimed in agreement.

"Enough!" A white-bearded elder suddenly barked a cold command to desist, his brows knit tight in a frown. "Yun Yara has been diligent in her cultivation since childhood.

Her techniques are without deficit. Though her disposition is strong, she harbours not a half-penny's worth of malice. The events of this day were hardly of her own volition; how can we, upon the singular revelation of the truth, negate her worth in its entirety?"

"Indeed. Though Yun Yara is not of the blood, she was nonetheless raised within the Sect. Specifically, during the battle at Spirit Beast Mountain last year, she used her own body to shield the disciples, achieving great merit."

Another elder of the moderate faction also spoke up. "Regarding the chaos of the war in those years, who can guarantee it was not the machination of Fate itself? The true fault does not lie with her."

"Yet she is not of the Yun bloodline; that is an immutable fact!" The kinsman at the fore refused to yield. "Are you suggesting we allow a woman of Impure Spiritual Root to continue sitting comfortably in the high seat of the legitimate daughter?"

"Who says she *wishes* to sit there?"

A cold, clear voice rang out from a corner. It was Yun Zhou, his expression solemn. "She has never once vied for it, yet you lot seem to be vying with distinct enthusiasm."

The crowd was momentarily struck dumb, the atmosphere plunging into sudden silence.

"As the Master of the Lingxiao Sect remains in seclusion and has yet to emerge, all matters shall be deliberated only after his retreat has concluded."

Inside and outside the Lingxiao Sect, the winds rose and the clouds shifted; a storm had already, quietly, begun to sweep in.

Chapter 5: The Spectator in the Shadows

Beyond the hall's threshold, the shadows of the flowers swayed gently, stirred by a whispering breeze.

Yun Lili was crouched beneath the flower-laden wall of the Lingxiao Sect, clutching a warm packet of butter-crisp pastries freshly pilfered from the kitchens. She munched away whilst staring unblinkingly at the narrow fissure between the window shutters, her eyes gleaming with the predatory delight like a cat guarding a fish basket.

Beside her, her newly assigned maid, Moony, lay flat against the window ledge, her eyes as round as saucers. She whispered through her teeth, barely containing her shock:

"Miss, look! That ruddy-faced, bushy-bearded elder slapped the table again! *Aiya*, even the teacup went flying!"

This little maid had been shoved at Lili barely an hour prior by the house matron, with the solemn explanation: *A daughter of the Yun Clan—newly confirmed at that—cannot be without a personal attendant.*

Lili had been delighted. Before the sentence was even finished, she had accepted the girl on the spot.

"Shhh, keep it down." Lili deftly stuffed a piece of osmanthus cake into the girl's mouth without diverting her gaze from the half-open window. "I hear them saying they intend to expel Sister Yara from the clan, and even abolish her immortal arts... *Tsk tsk*. This plot is more clichéd than a street-corner storybook!"

"Is it not just..." Moony mumbled around the cake, her words muffled and indistinct. "I can practically guess the trajectory: first the family betrayal, then the revenge arc, then 'you kill me, I kill you', and finally all the messy, unmentionable bits—"

"No spoilers." Lili shook her head, stopping her with a face full of solemnity. "This is my first time witnessing a live-action drama of an aristocratic cultivation clan. We must respect the artistic integrity of the performers. Let us not interrupt the flow; after all, they are acting with such dedication."

The two were watching with deep concentration when a furious roar suddenly burst from within:

"Who is sneaking around out there?"

Lili froze. In an instant, she grabbed Moony and bolted, muttering frantically as she ran: "Run! Run! We haven't finished this scene yet! Remember to bring drinks and dry rations tomorrow; we shall return to catch the next instalment!"

They had barely taken two steps—had not even managed to scramble over the wall—when a streak of sword-light flashed across the courtyard like lightning. Immediately following it, a figure in azure robes descended, elegant and imposing, blocking their path.

Yun Zhou stood with arms crossed, handsome brows raised high, wearing an expression that clearly read: *I have already seen through you.*

His voice was cold. "You two, sneaking about outside the window— what were you eavesdropping on?"

Lili's heart plummeted with guilt. She hurriedly plastered on a smile, waving her hand as if playing the fool. "Aiya, What do you mean, sneaking?? Was I not merely... ah... inspecting the window boundary seals for breaches! Yes! The maintenance of Sect property is the basic duty of every disciple! Everyone has a responsibility!"

Moony: "???"

Zhou's brows knitted even tighter, his tone freezing. "You are a daughter of the Yun Clan. Why must you behave without a shred of decorum? Were it not for the gravity of today's events, would you mistake this for a theatre stage?"

Lili nodded with the utmost seriousness. "Eh? Now that you mention it, I honestly think it is. The character roles are distinct, the plot is ridiculous, and the emotions are pumped to the heavens—if this were performed in a mortal teahouse, it would play to a full house every night."

Zhou let out a disbelieving laugh, cold and sharp. "Oh? Then why do you not simply set up a hawthorn skewer stall at the entrance, selling snacks whilst offering live commentary?"

Lili's eyes lit up instantly, sparkling as if she had just discovered the meaning of life. She immediately seconded the motion: "That is a splendid idea! I could shout: 'Roll up, roll up! A grand drama at the Yun Manor today! The True versus Counterfeit Daughter battling for Immortal Destiny! Three copper coins a skewer—if the show bores you, it's free!' Hahaha..."

Moony looked as though she might die on the spot. She tugged at Lili's sleeve, eyes brimming with despair. "Miss... have you forgotten that you are also one of the main characters in this play? In the drama of the True and False Daughters—*you* are the True Daughter!!"

"Oh. Right. I forgot." Lili scratched her head.

Zhou's eye twitched violently. A vein throbbed visibly upon his forehead as he sucked in a deep breath, gritting his teeth as he spoke: "If you utter one more word, I shall hang you from the highest tree on Wind-Chime Cliff and make you sing into the gale for an entire day!"

Lili instantly folded, mimicking the motion of zipping her lips shut. She clasped her hands together and bowed with exaggerated obedience.

"All right, all right, Young Master Yun, calm your heavenly temper. We shall return immediately to reflect behind closed doors, meditate earnestly, rethink our lives, rethink our spiritual roots, re— Anyway, I shall shut up."

"Shut up."

Zhou flung the words over his shoulder without looking back, turning to leave, his sleeves billowing in the wind.

Lili stared at his retreating figure and muttered softly: "Why is that man so fierce all the time... If he weren't so good-looking—with that pointy little chin that is actually rather cute—I wouldn't bother dealing with him."

Moony nodded silently. "Yes, yes... the Young Master gets by entirely on his looks."

The two exchanged a look of mutual understanding—and slipped away to their next gossip vantage point.

Meanwhile, the so-called 'gets-by-on-his-looks' Zhou halted mid-stride. The tips of his ears turned a shade of red. He gritted his teeth, thinking darkly:

That chin... in what way is it pointy?

* * * * *

The Abyss of Chaos—a nexus where the Immortal and Demon realms converged, a forbidden zone across all planes since time immemorial.

Mists coiled in endless spirals; a mournful wind keened through the gorge. Jagged stones jutted upwards like the piled bones of prehistoric beasts, whilst the ground was strewn with withered vines and bleached skeletons. The air hung heavy with the stench of death, so palpable that not a single bird or beast dared tread half a pace within.

Since fleeing upon her sword, Yun Yara's mind had been adrift in a trance, her breath in disarray. Her flight-light swayed like a lantern carried by a drunkard on a stormy night, pitching and yawing until, quite by accident, she strayed into this forbidden territory—a place whose very name even the High Immortal Lords shunned to speak.

She touched down in a desolate expanse where spiritual *qi* was thin to the point of non-existence, replaced by a rampant flood of demonic aura. The silence was absolute, pressing against the eardrums with heart-palpitating weight. She had not yet managed to steady her breath when the fog ahead roiled violently—

Swish! Swish! Swish!

Several sharp, ear-piercing sounds tore through the air. Then, a squad of demon soldiers burst from the shadowy mist. Clad in pitch-black armour, their eyes glowing with a blood-red light, they exuded a chilling aura, resembling vengeful wraiths returning from the underworld.

Their long halberds glinted with frost as they barked in unison:

"State your name! All who trespass upon the Abyss of Chaos shall be killed without mercy!"

Yara's heart gave a violent lurch; her breath caught in her throat. Instinctively, she formed a seal, attempting to conjure a technique in defence. Yet, the spiritual light at her fingertips had barely sparked before it was extinguished—snuffed out like a candle in a gale.

She froze, staring at her own hands in disbelief.

Her spiritual energy... had it been severed?

Her throat felt parched, her chest constricted. A reality she had desperately tried to evade flashed in the depths of her mind. For years she had cultivated, yet her progress had been painfully sluggish. It was not that she possessed peerless talent; rather, she had relied on her status as the legitimate daughter of the Yun Manor, propped up by mountains of elixirs and protective artifacts to barely maintain her footing within the sect.

Now that the truth of her poor spiritual roots had been laid bare, her immortal arts had deserted her, and her artifacts lay silent. she was nothing more than someone abandoned by the Immortal Path.

She bit down hard on her lower lip, the light in her eyes dimming.

So it seems... I was never worthy of the title of Immortal?

The demon soldiers advanced step by step, their blades wreathed in demonic flames, their presence radiating malice. She could not retreat; there was no road of escape. She could only grit her teeth and brace herself, prepared to go down fighting in a desperate bid for mutual destruction.

The Abyss of Chaos was a place where ten thousand magics failed; immortal *qi* was stifled whilst demonic *qi* thrived. With her spiritual roots already unstable, she had not a shred of advantage here.

She swept her gaze around, making a rough assessment of the tactical situation: she was alone, whilst the demon soldiers numbered a dozen or so. This would be a brutal skirmish.

She flipped her hand, palm facing upwards. A streak of azure light flashed, and a longsword instantly materialised in her grip.

With a sharp *shing*, the demon soldiers brandished their own weapons, rapidly splitting their formation to engage her.

Just as she squeezed her eyes shut, ready to gamble her life on a final, broken resolve—

A voice, cold as the frozen springs of the Nine Underworlds, abruptly rang out from the mist:

"Stand down. She is mine to deal with."

The moment the voice spoke, the black fog instantly contracted. A tall, lithe silhouette walked slowly out from the vapour. His cloak of black gauze embroidered with crimson sigils snapped violently in the yin wind; his ink-black hair fell to his waist, his eyes were as cold as stars, and his aura was boundless.

Demonic energy surged like a tidal wave—it was the Demon Prince, Mo Han.

Upon hearing his voice, the demon soldiers dropped to one knee in unison, heads bowed low, not daring to breathe.

A look of fear and trepidation washed over Yun Yara's face; her gaze locked onto that figure. An inexplicable tremor rippled through her heart. She forced a façade of composure and asked coldly:

"Hmph. So, it is Prince Mo. Have you come to watch me make a fool of myself?"

Mo Han's thin lips hooked into a faint curve. His eyes held a measure of interest and mockery as he closed the distance step by step, his tone cool and thin:

* * * * *

"A joke? Looking as you do now... it is indeed quite the farce."

Yara gritted her teeth, her anger flaring. "If you wish to kill me, then strike. What need is there for this charade?"

Mo Han lowered his gaze to look at her, his eyes dark and abyssal.

"Had I truly intended to kill you, do you fancy you would still draw breath at this moment?" His tone was light, indifferent even, yet every word landed with the weight of stone upon her heart.

His gaze seemed to sweep over her casually, yet it felt as though he were peering through to the most fragile recesses of her soul.

"Little faerie of the Impure Spiritual Root, your audacity is considerable. To think you would dare trespass even into the Abyss of Chaos."

Yara's face went rigid.

Impure Spiritual Root.

So, even the Demon Realm knew.

In that case... the entirety of the Four Seas and Eight Wildernesses, the whole of the Immortal Realm from high to low, must surely view her as a laughingstock.

A violent tremor shook her heart; her cheeks grew inexplicably hot. She turned her face away hurriedly, gritting her teeth to spit out two words: "Shut up!"

Mo Han gave a low chuckle. With a casual wave of his hand, the demon soldiers dissolved into the mist. He spoke dispassionately: "Had I not intervened; you would already be a target practice dummy for the Demon Realm. Furthermore... for a future ally, I am never stingy with a helping hand."

"Ally?" Yara raised her head, her brows knitting together tightly.

Mo Han offered no words, only a shallow smile. It was like a wisp of fire beneath a cold winter moon—chillingly wicked, yet possessing a certain unspeakable magnetism.

A thread of unease rose in her heart. She forced herself to maintain a cold front. "You wish to ally with me? Do you intend to exploit my grievances against the Lingxiao Sect, or... do you assume I would beg you?"

"No." Mo Han halted his steps, meeting her gaze. His voice was low but crystalline in its clarity. "It is that I wish to offer you a path."

"A path?" Yara scoffed. "The path of your Demon Race is paved with blood and fire, is it not? I would sooner perish and have my Dao dissipate than wallow in the mire with you."

Mo Han stared at her for a moment before suddenly leaning in closer, his voice dropping a few degrees lower. "But that Immortal Realm... for what, exactly, do you still yearn?"

Yara was struck dumb.

Mo Han's voice was soft, like a murmur in the wind, yet akin to some dark enchantment: "Just now, who was it that forced you to abolish your immortal arts? Who cast you out from the sect gates, discarding you like a worn shoe? That world you are breaking yourself to protect... does it truly merit your devotion?"

Her throat felt as though it were blocked by something; she could not utter a word.

Mo Han's gaze was scorching. He suddenly leaned his body in, his presence looming, his breath nearly brushing against her ear. His voice was deep, carrying a trace of terrifying tenderness:

"Yara, you know in your heart: without me, had I not appeared today... not even your bones would remain."

She turned her head sharply, the tip of her nose nearly colliding with his. The tips of her ears flushed red as she feigned composure: "D-Don't come so close..."

Mo Han chuckled lightly, his tone so low it was almost teasing. "You fear me?"

"I merely... have no desire to inhale the stench of your overwhelming demonic aura!" Yara retorted angrily, though she unconsciously inched sideways.

Mo Han blocked her retreat with one arm, caging her back against the rock wall. His tone was lazy, almost indulgent:

"Where is the fire? I told you, I am not here to force you. I am merely... offering you a choice."

As he spoke, his fingertips lightly brushed aside a stray lock of hair on her forehead. The gesture was unexpectedly gentle, utterly incongruous with his status as the Demon Prince, yet it inexplicably caused her heart to skip a chaotic beat.

"When you have thought it through clearly... I shall wait for you to come and find me yourself."

"You will wait in vain." Yara turned her face away. Her voice was ice-cold, yet she could not hide the tremor at the tail end of her words.

Mo Han's smile deepened, his eyes darkening. "Then let us... wait and see."

Before his voice had even faded, his fingers twitched in a subtle incantation. Yara's body suddenly went limp, collapsing like a puppet with severed strings. Mo Han was quick of eye and hand; he caught her in a single arm, preventing her from striking the ground.

He looked down at her unconscious form nestled in his embrace. His expression was inscrutable, yet his voice softened unconsciously.

"Why remain so obstinate? See, this is much more becoming."

He lifted her slowly, cradling her horizontally in his arms. The mist roiled and demon shadows crisscrossed the air as, step by step, he walked deeper into the valley.

"Do not fear. Very soon... you will understand. This path is one only I can grant you."

Chapter 6: The Wonton Soup Sect Master

The great bells of the Lingxiao Sect Main Hall boomed, their deep resonance shaking the very heavens. Ten thousand rays of rosy light cascaded from the firmament, illuminating the entire palace in a bath of celestial glory.

Inside, a thousand immortals stood in solemn formation, holding their breath, daring not disturb even a wisp of air.

Amidst the radiance, the great palace doors slowly parted. From the depths of the Hall of High Heavens walked a solitary figure.

He was clad in snow-white robes, his hair—white as flying frost—cascading to his waist. His temperament was transcendent, like an immortal stepping upon clouds. His pace was neither fast nor slow, his expression indifferent, yet he carried with him an invisible, crushing pressure.

The assembly held their breath in anticipation.

And then, unexpectedly, the Sect Master of Lingxiao, Yun Wuntang, who was rumoured to have been in a life-or-death seclusion for a century—and whom many suspected had long since sat in meditation until petrification—had truly returned!

Just as the crowd prepared to perform the Grand Prostration, the white-haired Immortal Lord swept his gaze across the hall, suddenly pausing at a specific spot.

The crowd followed his gaze, landing upon a young woman of clear and lovely features standing amongst the outer disciples—Yun Lili.

Everyone expected him to utter words of profound Daoist wisdom or heavy, solemn decree. Instead, in the very next moment—

He suddenly flashed a mischievous grin, utterly incongruous with his lofty appearance. The corner of his mouth hooked up as he remarked:

"Aiya, this daughter of mine is actually quite good-looking. She looks exactly like I did when I was small... though her smile lacks a bit of that 'empty-headed' charm."

"???"

The immortals froze in place, exchanging bewildered glances.

This is... Sect Master Yun Wuntang?

Not... Yun Wonton Soup?

Lili, who had been standing with rigid spine, nervously preparing to bow properly alongside the other disciples, felt as though she had been struck by lightning. She stunned for a moment, then suddenly clapped a hand over her mouth, a stifled *pfft* escaping her lips.

"Won... Wonton Soup... Hahahaha!"

Moony's face turned green with panic. She yanked frantically at Lili's sleeve. "Miss! Stop laughing! That is your father! The Sect Master of Lingxiao!"

Lili was laughing so hard she was doubled over, gasping for air.

"No, no... I'm really not laughing at him, I'm laughing at... at that... Soup... no, wait, Tang! Hahaha... sorry, sorry, I can't control it! I just keep picturing that bubbling pot, sprinkled with chopped spring onions..."

The faces of the surrounding disciples twitched collectively. Some were desperately holding back laughter; others were swallowing their guffaws so hard their teeth ached. The air in the hall froze in sheer awkwardness.

Zhou's face, meanwhile, had turned as black as charcoal. He took a swift step forward and—*thwack!*—slapped a palm against Lili's forehead, roaring:

"Can you not have a shred of decorum, you wretched girl? That is your biological father! The Sect Master! The Lord of High Heaven!"

Lili staggered from the blow, rubbing her forehead and wailing,

"Ouch! Go easy on me! My head is going to explode... I was just laughing at the name! Yun—Wun—Tang... doesn't it just sound like... Wonton..." *Soup?*

"Cough, cough, cough!"

Moony looked ready to stuff her sleeve into Lili's mouth.

At this moment, however, Yun Wuntang had already descended the steps. Far from being angry, his expression was one of immense relief and delight. Hands clasped behind his back, he beamed:

"Not bad, not bad. A sense of humour this low—definitely my daughter. Your mother used to laugh at my name back in the day, too. She said if you say it fast, it sounds like a pot boiling over. This is truly a heritage passed down the bloodline!"

The Immortals: "......"

Is this Immortal Lord truly not a comedic character who wandered out of a street-corner script?

Before the crowd could recover their wits, Yun Wuntang added another remark:

"I knew it. How could I possibly have sired a daughter as stiff and serious as Yun Yara? Clearly, there was a mistake. But now that we've matched up—this air of goofiness cannot be faked. She is my seed!"

Lili laughed until tears nearly streamed from her eyes.

"Dad, now that you mention it, I really kind of want a bowl of Wonton Soup to celebrate..."

"Splendid! Have the kitchens boil a pot!" Yun Wuntang laughed heartily. "But you must add chopped spring onions, or the flavour isn't right."

"And a dash of sesame oil, plus two sheets of seaweed..."

"Done. Come down later and cook a bowl yourself; I want to see if your skills are up to scratch!"

The two of them, one word after another, had actually begun discussing the recipe for wontons in front of the entire assembly.

The hall was dead silent for three seconds.

Then, a muffled laugh could no longer be contained—*Pfft!*—and exploded.

Then a second, a third... until the scene collapsed completely.

The sect elders held their foreheads in helplessness; the young disciples stared with glazed eyes, feeling as though they had walked onto the set of a comedy play.

This Grand Recognition Ceremony, which should have been solemn, ritualistic, and overflowing with immortal gravitas, had been forcibly turned into a slapstick farce by this father-daughter duo.

From that day forth, the Lingxiao Sect was crowned with a resounding new reputation:

—Since then, the artistic style of the Lingxiao Sect has not remained serious for more than three days.

* * * * *

The Water Mirror Realm was a place of secluded tranquillity. Ripples of light shimmered across the surface of the pool, reflecting two silhouetted figures—one in motion, the other still—both possessing an aura of extraordinary transcendence.

What manifested within the depths of the water mirror was the utterly farcical Recognition Ceremony currently taking place in the Main Hall of the Lingxiao Sect. Within the reflection, Yun Lili was grinning like a blossoming flower, while Yun Wuntang was speaking solemn nonsense with a perfectly straight face.

Below them, the gathered assembly of immortals were holding back their laughter with such exertion that their faces had turned crimson and the veins in their necks bulged.

"Hahahaha... *cough, cough!*"

Xie Wuchen laughed until he rocked back and forth, completely losing his composure. His raucous laughter vibrated through the air, causing the entire surface of the water mirror to tremble with fine ripples.

He laughed so hard his stomach cramped, forcing him to slump over the jade table, unable to straighten his back, nearly grabbing the sacred immortal scroll before him to use as a handkerchief for his sweat.

Beside him, Yu Sord's brows furrowed ever so slightly. His countenance maintained that signature look of the Emotionless Path—cold, joyless, and devoid of grief—yet his gaze fell upon Xie Wuchen as if he were observing a complete simpleton. His tone was faint, laced with disdain:

"Wuchen, you are truly... a sight to behold. Astounding."

Yu Sord glanced helplessly at Xie Wuchen. This fellow possessed an exterior that was handsome, aloof, and elegant, yet the moment he opened his mouth, he transformed instantly into a chatterbox who simply could not cease his prattle.

Xie Wuchen wiped tears of mirth from the corners of his eyes while struggling to suppress his remaining laughter. "Haha... that Yun Wuntang... no, no, wait. The moment I heard that name, my brain was instantly filled with the image of a steaming hot... 'Wonton Soup'! Heavens above, I am suddenly starving."

He grew more animated as he spoke, his eyes shining with the gleam of a fox that had successfully pilfered a jar of oil. "Tell me, honestly—this Sect Master's name is simply too flavourful. If Yun Lili hadn't said it herself, my thoughts wouldn't have strayed in that direction, but now that I think about it—ha, it is simply delicious! Fragrant and savory!"

Yu Sord: "......"

Xie Wuchen was still overcome with delight, unable to stop. "You know, I have practiced *inedia*—abstaining from earthly grains—for so many years, but this time my appetite has truly been roused. One of these days, I really must descend to the mortal realm to seek out this legendary Wonton Soup. Who knows? I might accidentally achieve enlightenment and realize a 'Dao of Flavour'!"

Yu Sord finally spoke, his tone biting and glacial. "You would descend to the mortal realm merely to drink soup?"

"To cultivate the Dao!" Xie Wuchen patted his chest with righteous solemnity, as if defending a sacred truth. "Cultivating the heart, cultivating the nature, cultivating the appetite—only when these three are united can one become a true immortal."

Yu Sord glanced at him sideways and said indifferently, "If you rely on *that* method to become an immortal, I fear the path you ascend to will not be the Celestial Heavens, but the 'Path of the Gluttonous Beast'."

Xie Wuchen laughed heartily, a mischievous glint dancing in the corner of his eye. "Well, look at you. You cultivate the 'Path of Emotionlessness,' yet after a thousand years, you still only wear this one frozen face. Are you not tired?"

Yu Sord remained silent, looking away, clearly having no intention of debating him further.

Xie Wuchen, however, had already fallen deep into his own culinary fantasy, his eyes sparkling with anticipation. "Wonton Soup... a steaming little pot, the broth clear and rich, sprinkled with chopped spring onions and a dash of sesame oil, perhaps accompanied by a few spirit-beast meat buns—tsk, *that* is the true flavour of the Immortal Realm!"

Yu Sord uttered a low threat, his voice dropping an octave: "Say one more word, and I will throw you into the Imperial Fire Pool and boil *you* into soup."

"Hahaha! You say *I* have a wild imagination, but *you* are the one painting such vivid pictures!"

Amidst the shimmering water, one cold, one hot; one rowdy, one quiet. The path to immortality was long and endless, but with such a chatterbox for a companion, it was, at the very least, not lonely.

* * * * *

The sun set in the west, casting long shadows across the grounds.

Yun Lili, clutching a massive pile of "greeting gifts" that everyone had stuffed into her arms moments ago, smiled until her eyes curved into crescent moons.

"I'm rich, I'm rich!" She hummed a cheerful little tune, her steps light and bouncy as she traversed the courtyard.

Thinking back to the "Wonton Soup" incident, she couldn't help but burst into laughter again.

These "treasures" were of all sorts—exquisitely embroidered purses, several bolts of fine silk, a box of pearl powder rumoured to beautify the skin and restore youth, and even a bag of candied fruits from heaven knows who.

Especially the *Buddha Spirit Beads* her biological father had given her, which were said to greatly enhance one's cultivation base when worn on the wrist.

Although she didn't quite understand why everyone was suddenly treating her so well—hadn't they said earlier that they looked down on her for being a girl from the countryside?—Yun Lili had always been an optimist. If it was free stuff, why not take it? Rejecting gifts would be a waste!

She had just pushed open the wooden door of her small pavilion when the three chickens raised in the backyard came rushing up, clucking excitedly—*cluck, cluck, cluck*—as they circled her.

"Aiya, why are you three so enthusiastic today?" Lili smiled and squatted down, intending to pat their little heads, but suddenly she discovered something odd—

One of the chickens was holding something in its beak. It was black, dark, and fluttering softly in the wind.

"Eh? What is this?" Curious, she reached out and grabbed it, lifting it up for a closer inspection—

...A pair of men's breeches—undergarments, to be precise. They were pitch-black in colour and cut with a generous width.

Lili: "......?"

She blinked, unable to believe her own eyes.

She shook the underpants; the fabric even carried a faint, fresh scent of soap pods, looking as if it had been washed not long ago.

"Who threw their underpants in my yard?" she muttered in confusion. Just as she was about to toss them aside like rubbish, she suddenly sensed a scorching, intense gaze burning into her back.

She slowly looked up—

By the courtyard wall stood a man of tall, imposing stature. His face was dark—alternating between a flush of red and a shade of black—as he glared at her.

He was dressed in ink-black combat gear, a sharp sword hanging at his waist, his features handsome as a painting. Only at this moment... he was staring dead on at the underpants in her hand.

The air solidified for one second.

Two seconds.

Three seconds.

Then—

"Female. Hooligan!"

The man gritted his teeth, enunciating every syllable. He lunged forward like an arrow released from a bow, snatching the underpants with a sharp chop of his hand. In the next instant, moving as fast as a sword leaving its sheath, he was standing right in front of her. He snatched the underpants so quickly she didn't even see the movement clearly.

Lili: "......???"

She was stunned for a moment, then bristled like a cat whose tail had been stepped on. "Who's a female hooligan?!"

She was completely bewildered, scolded for no reason whatsoever.

"My pan... er... how did they end up in your hands?" The man swallowed the rest of the word "pants," his expression a mix of mortification and rage.

"It seems that *my* chicken was holding *your* underpants whilst running about in *my* yard. Given that my chicken belongs in my yard, how is it, pray tell, that *your* underpants came to be in my yard for *my* chicken to snatch in the first place?"

Her words were like a tongue twister, winding around until she nearly confused herself.

The man's ears turned bright red.

He roared, "You are a young maiden! How can you casually pick up a man's intimate clothing and... and hold it up to look at it?!"

Lili laughed in anger. "Ha! Who cares to look at your underpants? They have no style, no pattern, and they've been pecked full of holes by the chickens—I wouldn't take them if you gifted them to me wrapped in silk!"

The man: "You—!"

Lili: "You what?!"

The man: "How can you be so utterly lacking in upbringing?"

Lili: "My chickens are very well-behaved. They never run wild. They followed me all the way from Cloud Village to here, a journey of half a month, without ever straying. Why would they peck your underpants the moment we arrive? Clearly, it was your underpants that fell into my yard first!"

The man: "......"

The two stared each other down, eyes locked, neither willing to yield an inch.

In the end, the man took a deep breath, stuffed the underpants into the lapel of his robes, and turned to leave with a face as cold as ice.

Lili shouted at his retreating back: "Hey! Keep a better eye on your underpants! Don't let the wind blow them over here again!"

* * * * *

Moony stepped lightly into the small pavilion, balancing a tea tray with practiced care. "Miss, tea is served."

Lili whipped the curtain aside in a flash, beckoning wildly with dancing eyebrows and a face full of gossip. "Moony, Little Moon! Come here, quick! You will absolutely *never* guess what just happened!"

Moony blinked, her curiosity instantly piqued as she leaned in closer. "What is it? What happened?"

Lili cradled her forehead, looking caught between laughter and tears, her expression one of utter absurdity. "I don't know what kind of madness possessed my chickens, but just now, they actually dragged back a pair of... of men's large underpants!"

Moony froze, the tea tray in her hands nearly tilting over in her shock. "Huh? Large... underpants?"

Lili nodded furiously like a pestle pounding garlic, her eyes filled with the despair of the wrongly accused. "And then, out of nowhere, a man darted out, snatched them back, and had the gall to call *me* a female hooligan!"

"W-What? Truly? Such a thing happened?" Moony's eyes widened to the size of saucers, her voice pitching up half an octave in disbelief.

"I found it completely baffling too!" Lili spread her hands in a gesture of helplessness. "Aside from you and me, where did a man pop out from in this pavilion? Do underpants simply rain from the sky in this sect?"

Moony suddenly slapped her own forehead, as if recalling something vital. "Ah! Miss, you might not know, but that person... is likely General Xiao Yan!"

"Xiao Yan?" Lili stared, her face written with disbelief. "The War God of the Immortal Realm, *that* Xiao Yan?"

"Precisely!" Moony nodded, lowering her voice to a conspiratorial whisper, as if fearing the walls had ears. "He is a close friend of Young Master Zhou. He recently returned from a dangerous trial and is staying at the Lingxiao Sect for a few days to recuperate. The side hall nearby was arranged specifically for his stay."

Lili stood dazed for a long moment, processing this information, before finally muttering in a trance, "So, you're saying... I fought General Xiao Yan over a pair of... underpants?"

Moony was already shaking with suppressed laughter, but she couldn't resist adding a little salt to the wound. "And were called a female hooligan..."

Lili's face went dark as the bottom of a pot. Just as she was about to explode, Moony added with a face full of seriousness:

"Miss, you really must be careful. General Xiao is invincible in battle, and he is as handsome as he is cold. Countless immortal maidens have swooned over him, their souls turned upside down with longing."

Lili sighed deeply, glancing at her maid with a speechless expression. "Moony, your face is already turning red, yet you lecture me..."

Moony gave two dry laughs, gently patting the back of Lili's hand comfortingly. "It truly isn't me... I'm just saying, a man like General Xiao is not someone we can afford to provoke casually."

Lili couldn't help but roll her eyes towards the heavens in utter resignation.

Chapter 7: Salt and Tears of Parting

Lingxiao Sect – Hall of Deliberation

Upon the jade steps, wreathed in immortal mist, a figure clad in robes of dark green with sweeping sleeves paced back and forth in evident agitation.

The atmosphere within the hall was leaden; several elders stood with eyes lowered and brows submissive, daring not to breathe too loudly.

The usually composed Sect Master Yun now had his brows locked in a tight knot.

His silver hairpin was stuck askew in his hair, and his entire face seemed to have four large characters written across it: I Am Currently Very Annoyed.

"Where is Yun Yara?" He suddenly slammed his hand upon the table and rose. His voice was not loud, yet it cut like a sudden gust of bitter wind, chilling one's spine. "How many days has it been? And you still cannot find a single person?"

Elder A shrank his neck into his collar, answering with extreme caution, "In reply to the Sect Master... ever since Fairy Yun Yara departed the palace on her sword the day of the spirit test, there has been no news whatsoever. We have dispatched disciples to search the four directions, yet... we have found nothing..."

"Cannot find her? Then what of the Grand Immortal Sect Tournament?" Sect Master Yun roared, slamming the table once more. The jade artefacts throughout the hall vibrated with a faint hum.

Elder B reminded him in a hushed voice, "If we lack Yun Yara, the Lingxiao Sect's combat power will decrease by thirty per cent. I fear retaining first place will be difficult..."

"Do you think I don't know that?" Sect Master Yun was so incensed his moustache quivered as he rolled his eyes heavenward.

With that, he stormed out of the hall aggressively.

Just as he stepped across the threshold, his gaze swept across the grounds and landed upon a lovely silhouette in pink robes squatting in the flower garden, teasing a chicken with a smile of utter, harmless innocence.

Yun Lili!

His biological daughter, whom he had only recently recognised.

Sect Master Yun's footsteps halted abruptly.

A flash of inspiration struck his mind like a bolt of lightning cleaving the skull, blasting open his roots of wisdom.

"...It is merely a shortage of personnel, is it not? I have it!"

His eyes lit up. He slapped his forehead, waved a large hand, and bellowed in a voice like a great bell: "Yun! Little! Li!"

Yun Lili jumped violently at the sound. The little chicken in her arms, equally startled, let out a *cluck-cluck* and fluttered into the air.

"Dad?" She stood up blankly; the hem of her robes still stained with grass clippings and chicken feathers. "Why are you shouting so loudly?"

Sect Master Yun strode forward quickly, placing a heavy hand on her shoulder. His tone was steady and resolute: "For the Grand Immortal Sect Tournament, you shall take Yun Yara's place."

"...Huh?" Lili felt as though she had been struck by lightning; her hair practically stood on end. "I-I don't know anything! I only know how to feed chickens, pull weeds, and collect Spirit Eggs!"

"You possess the Heavenly Spiritual Root. Your wisdom root is not poor, and you are of the direct Yun bloodline. With proper training, you will certainly suffice." Sect Master Yun's face was full of certainty.

"But..."

"I have specially arranged the strongest master for you—Yu Sord of the Sword Pavilion." His tone carried a hint of pride, as if to say, *Look how capable I am at arranging things.*

Lili's eyes lit up. "You mean that legendary 'Immortal Lord Ji-Ming'— the one who comprehended the Dao at three, built his foundation at five, and couldn't even be struck dead by heavenly tribulation?!"

"Precisely. On the day of your spirit test, he was standing right there."

She tried hard to recall... a face, handsome and flawless, with an aura that transcended the mortal dust, floated into her mind. *Hmm... he really was handsome.*

"Him..." The corners of Lili's mouth began to rise traitorously.

Seeing this, Sect Master Yun seized the opportunity to add the final blow: "He is currently cultivating in seclusion at the peak of Mount Alioth. I have just sent a divine message to request his aid."

"And then?" Lili's eyes sparkled. "He agreed?"

"I kowtowed three times and even gifted him a bottle of Snow Spirit Pills refined by the Grand Supreme Elderly Lord himself. He said..." Sect Master Yun lowered his voice, imitating that cool tone, "—Barely teachable."

Lili beamed with joy. "Hehe..."

Sect Master Yun smiled and patted her shoulder, his tone gentle yet carrying a suffocating pressure: "The Grand Immortal Sect Tournament is in three days. Remember, do not make our Lingxiao Sect lose face. Otherwise, your little chickens... shall be expelled from the chicken registry... oh, slip of the tongue. I meant the Immortal Registry!"

Lili: "......"

Three days? No, wait, did she hear correctly?

Moreover, to think that the three chickens she brought from the mortal realm had truly—as the saying goes—ascended to heaven alongside her.

Yet before they could enjoy their celestial status for two days, they were already at risk of being expelled from the chicken... no, the Immortal Registry!

The fireworks of joy that had just sparked in her heart were instantly extinguished. Lili waved her hands frantically. "No, no, Dad, stop joking! You should hurry and find Fairy Yun Yara back!"

She wanted to live to farm and raise chickens! Not be dragged off to fight for her life!

That so-called Sword Sovereign... no matter how handsome he was, he wasn't worth losing her little life over.

Sect Master Yun glared at her with disdain: *If I could find her, would I need you?*

"The matter is settled." With those words, he pinched a seal, and his figure vanished abruptly from the spot.

"Dad? Dad? Don't go!" Lili shouted at the empty air, but received only a gust of clear wind in return.

Was this really her biological father?

She stood blankly in place, looking toward the hazy Mount Alioth on the horizon.

The sword qi at the peak was ethereal as a painting, and as the cold wind blew past, it felt as though heaven and earth had begun a countdown.

Hellish Training Countdown: Three Days.

Yun Lili squatted on the ground, clutching her head, her face the very picture of despair.

Just as Yun Lili was racked with trepidation, bracing herself for the oncoming storm, the days drifted by with a tranquillity that was entirely undisturbed.

The surface of her life remained unrippled.

She tended to her chickens and gathered herbs in accordance with her usual routine, occasionally taking her small basket to wander idly through the mountains.

In truth, her existence had become almost excessively comfortable.

On this particular day, she and Moony were in the Spirit Beast Garden, tasked with collecting a few spirit beast eggs.

A gentle breeze brushed through the treetops, causing the leaves to whisper, and the sunlight slanted down in golden beams.

The garden, overgrown with lush spirit grasses, wafted with a faint, ethereal fragrance. Everything seemed strangely, almost suspiciously, quiet.

"How utterly peculiar..."

Yun Lili squatted beside a clump of weeds, her fingers lightly stroking her temple, her expression slightly suspicious. "Wasn't it said that Immortal Lord Yu of the Sword Pavilion was going to teach me some spells? Why has there been no movement at all? Has he forgotten?"

Moony walked behind her carrying a small bamboo basket, smiling with a cheeky cheerfulness. "Miss, if you ask me, perhaps the Sword Immortal feels that teaching or not teaching makes no difference. Perhaps he thinks your aptitude is so poor that he simply couldn't be bothered to manage you."

"What do you mean by that?" Lili immediately glared back, her eyes widening slightly, her cheeks puffing up in indignation. "Are you insinuating I am dim-witted?"

"Hehe, this servant wouldn't dare." Moony deftly placed a dusty, palm-sized spirit beast egg into the basket, a smile still playing on her lips. "It is because Miss is uniquely gifted—the kind of person who will achieve enlightenment and become an immortal entirely on her own, whether taught or not."

Hearing this, Lili finally let out a satisfied "Hmph," the corners of her mouth turning up traitorously as her eyes curved into happy crescents. "That is more like it."

She bent down, brushing aside the tall grass at her feet with one hand. Suddenly, a faint glimmer flashed past.

Curled within the dense foliage was a round, rolling ball-like creature. The thing was a brilliant, shiny purple, resembling a cluster of gigantic grapes. Its skin surface was even bubbling with a wet *plip-plop* sound. It actually looked somewhat cute.

"Eh? This bunch of grapes... it actually moves."

Her face lit up with interest. She leaned in closer, extending a finger to gingerly poke the mass with cautious curiosity.

The instant her fingertip touched the skin—

"GWA-WAH—!"

The purple ball exploded abruptly, emitting an ear-piercing shriek that tore through the peaceful garden. Bubbles shot everywhere, splashing wet foam all over her face.

"Aiya!"

Lili was so startled she stumbled backward three steps, her foot slipping on the grass, sending her sitting down hard on her bottom.

The purple ball's form swelled instantly. Bubbles gurgled out madly, and in moments it had expanded to a towering height of three *zhang*.

Its limbs grew thick and sturdy, its eyes turned blood-red, and its aura became terrifyingly imposing.

"M-Moony, why did it get so big!" Lili stammered, eyes wide.

Moony turned pale with fright, recognizing the creature instantly. "Miss! That is a Third-Rank Bubble Beast! Once startled, it becomes enraged. The bubbles all over its body are toxic; if they burst on you, they can disfigure your face! We must run!"

Just as Lili tried to scramble to her feet, a rustling sound came from the grass to her right. Out darted a creature covered in fur, shaped like a small sheep. It walked out unsteadily, wobbling left and right, before opening its mouth in a grin to reveal a maw full of teeth so black they shone like obsidian.

"W-What is *that* now?!"

"A Black-Tooth Beast!" Moony's voice trembled with terror. "That thing specialises in bewitching the soul with phantom sounds. One laugh can invert the five senses; even a Nascent Soul Patriarch cannot withstand it! Miss, whatever you do, do not listen to it laugh!"

However, it was too late. The Black-Tooth Beast's eerie laughter drilled into her ears like fine silk threads. Lili felt her eardrums itch, her vision went dark, and her head began to swim with dizziness.

"Ahhh, I can't take it..." She clutched her head, attempting to flee, but her foot landed squarely upon a mound of softness. She looked down—

It was a round, soft grey spirit beast, curled up asleep on the ground like a fleshy cushion.

"A Rolling Beast!" Moony's face went white as a sheet. "Miss, you stepped on it!! That thing seeks vengeance the moment it wakes!"

"I don't want to know *how* it seeks vengeance!!!"

"ROAR—!"

Sure enough, the Rolling Beast opened its mouth and roared furiously, the sound shaking the forest canopy. A blast of hot air nearly sent Lili flying.

The entire Spirit Beast Garden instantly descended into chaos. The four spirit beasts seemed to go mad, lunging toward her in unison.

The Bubble Beast spewed toxic bubbles; the Black-Tooth Beast grinned and laughed maniacally; the Rolling Beast leapt up to ram her with brute force.

And that wasn't all.

A gust of wind-swept past, and a small bird covered in golden feathers descended from the sky.

Its wingspan was no more than an arm's length, yet it landed with exquisite precision directly on top of Yun Lili's head and gave a triumphant *chirp*.

"Who did I offend to deserve this!!"

Seeing the four beasts lunging at her face, Lili felt as though doomsday had arrived. She curled up on the ground clutching her head, tears nearly springing from her eyes.

Just then—

Pop—

A golden light blossomed from thin air three inches above the crown of her head.

Brilliant as the blazing sun, it exploded instantly, slicing out a circular arc of sword radiance that swept in all four directions.

HUMMM—!

The Bubble Beast was blasted back several *zhang* by the sword qi, exploding a dozen bubbles on the spot; the Black-Tooth Beast's laughter cut off abruptly as it stumbled back, looking bewildered; the Rolling Beast froze in mid-air, eyes vacant, as if it had forgotten what it was doing; the yellow bird atop her head was so scared it flipped over to play dead, wings splayed, falling *plap* into Lili's lap.

The entire Spirit Beast Garden fell abruptly silent.

In the distance, several patrolling disciples watched, jaw-dropped. Their baskets fell to the ground; they had forgotten how to speak.

"Who... is she?"

"That just now... was Immortal Lord Silentstar's Sword Seal."

"It seems so. Uh... but why would she have a Sword Seal protecting her?"

"Did she just... call a Third-Rank Bubble Beast a 'grape'?"

Lili slumped on the ground, staring at the sky above, her face blank.

"I... I just wanted to go back and feed the chickens... who wants to be gang-beaten by spirit beasts here..."

Lili remained sitting on the ground, her face full of shock and existential doubt.

The little yellow bird poked its head out from her lap, trembling: "*Chirp...*"

Lili sat dazedly on the ground. The yellow bird beast lay belly-up in her lap, still shivering, while Moony clutched her basket, looking as if life had lost all meaning.

She blinked, looking ahead at the spirit beasts that had been aggressive moments ago but were now as docile as if struck by lightning, then looked at her own sleeves and hem, soaked by foam. She couldn't help but mutter:

"What is this... I was just collecting eggs, and I nearly lost my little life."

"Miss, *woo*... let's hurry back."

Just as she caught her breath, a familiar voice drifted slowly from above—steady as jade, carrying that consistent tone of cold distance—

"The spiritual roots responded, automatically protecting their master. It seems... you do indeed have some destiny with the Way of the Sword."

"Eh?"

Lili raised her head blankly.

She saw Yu Sord standing atop a distant rock peak, white robes whiter than snow, sleeves fluttering in the wind. Wind rose and clouds were born around him.

The Spirit Beast Garden fell into a sudden deathly silence; even the wind seemed afraid to move recklessly.

The sunlight was perfect, golden threads falling strand by strand upon his white robes. He stood with hands clasped behind his back beneath a nearby spirit tree.

He looked as though he had walked straight out of a painting—brows handsome and clear, temperament cold and sparse. His long hair was bound by a jade crown, his robes snapping crisply as the breeze brushed past.

Moony's complexion drained of all colours, leaving her face as pale as a sheet of rice paper. She recognised the creature instantly.

"Miss! That is a Third-Rank Bubble Beast! Once startled, it flies into a violent rage. The bubbles covering its entire body are highly toxic; if they burst upon you, they can cause permanent disfigurement! We must run, immediately!"

Yun Lili attempted to scramble to her feet, but before she could regain her balance, a rustling sound erupted from the tall grass to her right.

Out darted another creature—this one covered in fluff, shaped uncannily like a small sheep.

It walked out with an unsteady, wobbling gait, lurching left and right, before opening its mouth in a wide grin to reveal a maw full of teeth so black they shone like polished obsidian.

"W-What is *that* now?!"

"A Black-Tooth Beast!" Moony's voice trembled with sheer terror. "That creature specialises in bewitching the soul with phantom sounds. A single laugh from it can invert the five senses; even a Nascent Soul

Patriarch cannot easily withstand it! Miss, whatever you do, do not listen to it laugh!"

However, the warning came too late. The Black-Tooth Beast's eerie laughter drilled into her ears like fine silk threads, bypassing all defences.

Lili felt a maddening itch deep within her eardrums; her vision went dark, and her head began to swim with a heavy, intoxicating dizziness.

"Ahhh, I can't take it..." She clutched her head, attempting to turn and flee, but her foot landed squarely upon a mound of peculiar softness. She looked down—

It was a round, soft grey spirit beast, curled up asleep on the ground like a fleshy, breathing cushion.

"A Rolling Beast!" Moony's face went white. "Miss, you stepped on it!! That thing seeks vengeance the moment it wakes!"

"I don't want to know *how* it seeks vengeance!!!"

"ROAR—!"

Sure enough, the Rolling Beast opened its mouth and unleashed a furious roar, the sound shaking the forest canopy and sending tremors through the earth. A blast of scorching hot air erupted from its throat, nearly sending Lili flying through the air.

The entire Spirit Beast Garden instantly descended into absolute chaos. The four spirit beasts seemed to lose their minds, lunging toward her in unison.

The Bubble Beast spewed a barrage of toxic bubbles; the Black-Tooth Beast grinned and laughed maniacally; the Rolling Beast leapt up to ram her with brute force.

And that was not all.

A gust of wind swept past, and a small bird covered in brilliant golden feathers descended from the sky. Its wingspan was no more than an arm's length, yet it landed with exquisite, military precision directly on top of Yun Lili's head and gave a triumphant, high-pitched *chirp*.

"Who did I offend to deserve this!!"

Seeing the four beasts lunging at her face, Lili felt as though doomsday had arrived. She curled up into a ball on the ground, clutching her head, tears of frustration nearly springing from her eyes.

Just then—

Pop—

A golden light blossomed from thin air, exactly three inches above the crown of her head. Brilliant as the blazing sun, it exploded instantly, slicing out a circular arc of sword radiance that swept outwards in all four directions.

HUMMM—!

The force was absolute. The Bubble Beast was blasted back several *zhang* by the sword qi, a dozen of its bubbles exploding harmlessly on the spot; the Black-Tooth Beast's laughter cut off abruptly as it stumbled back, looking utterly bewildered; the Rolling Beast froze in mid-air, its eyes vacant, as if it had suddenly forgotten what it was doing; the yellow bird atop her head was so terrified it flipped over to feign death, wings splayed, falling with a soft *plap* into Lili's lap.

The entire Spirit Beast Garden fell abruptly, eerily silent.

In the distance, several patrolling disciples watched, jaw dropped.

Their baskets slipped from their hands and fell to the ground; they had forgotten how to speak.

"Who... is she?"

"That just now... that was Immortal Lord Silentstar's Sword Seal."

"It seems so. Uh... but why would she have a Sword Seal protecting her?"

"Did she just... call a Third-Rank Bubble Beast a 'grape'?"

Lili slumped on the ground, staring blankly at the sky above, her face emptied of all expression.

"I... I just wanted to go back and feed the chickens... who wants to be gang-beaten by spirit beasts here..."

Lili remained sitting on the ground, her face full of shock and existential doubt. The little yellow bird poked its head out from her lap, trembling: "*Chirp...*"

Lili sat dazedly on the ground. The yellow bird beast lay belly-up in her lap, still shivering, while Moony clutched her basket nearby, looking as if life had lost all meaning.

She blinked, looking ahead at the spirit beasts that had been aggressive moments ago but were now as docile as if struck by lightning, then looked down at her own sleeves and hem, soaked through by the strange foam. She couldn't help but mutter:

"What is this... I was just collecting eggs, and I nearly lost my little life."

"Miss, *woo*... let's hurry back."

Just as she caught her breath, a familiar voice drifted slowly from above—steady as jade, carrying that consistent tone of cold distance—

"The spiritual roots responded, automatically protecting their master. It seems... you do indeed have some destiny with the Way of the Sword."

"Eh?"

Lili raised her head blankly.

She saw Yu Sord standing atop a distant rock peak, white robes whiter than snow, sleeves fluttering in the wind. Wind rose and clouds were born around him.

The Spirit Beast Garden fell into a sudden deathly silence; even the wind seemed afraid to move recklessly.

The sunlight was perfect, golden threads falling strand by strand upon his white robes. He stood with hands clasped behind his back beneath a nearby spirit tree.

He looked as though he had walked straight out of a painting—brows handsome and clear, temperament cold and sparse. His long hair was bound by a jade crown, his robes snapping crisply as the breeze brushed past.

Chapter 8: The Hellish Training Countdown

It *was* Yu Sord!

"...Master?"

Yun Lili froze for two breaths before the horrifying realisation of her own dishevelment crashed down upon her—her skirts were crumpled like dried vegetables, her face was splattered with the foamy residue of the Bubble Beast, and nestled in her arms was a yellow bird beast feigning death.

It was over. Her image... was completely, utterly ruined!

She planted a hand on the ground, scrambling to stand in a panic, only for her foot to land squarely upon the Rolling Beast, which had not yet fully swooned. Instantly, her footing gave way.

"Ahhh—!"

Her centre of gravity shifted; just as she was about to become intimately acquainted with the dirt, a wisp of sword *qi* gently buoyed her up by the waist. To her surprise, it was warm. She stood up, bracing herself dazed, her heart beating in a chaotic rhythm.

Yu Sord stood not far away, his robes spotless, resembling a deity walking upon the wind, untouched by mortal dust.

"...Many thanks, Master."

She spoke in a low voice, daring not lift her head, feeling her entire face burning with heat.

He merely swept a cool glance over her, his tone as calm as ever:

"If you are to be this rash next time, do not enter the Spirit Beast Garden."

Lili faltered, then muttered a small, aggrieved protest, "It wasn't that I was rash; it is that these spirit beasts are too bizarre."

"They cannot abide the scent of blood; naturally, they became agitated." He offered this explanation with an air of lightness, as if discussing the weather.

Lili's heart gave a small jump. *He had arrived early?*

Then... how long had he been watching?

"That stomp just now... did it intend to trample me to death?" she asked again.

Yu Sord lowered his eyes, his gaze resting upon the muddy hem of her skirt. After a long moment, he spoke:

"Yes."

A single word, concise and powerful.

The tone remained faint, yet for some reason, it sent a chill down her spine.

Lili shrank her neck. Just as she was about to offer thanks, she heard him suddenly say:

"You are too noisy."

She froze, staring at him wide-eyed, stunned into silence for three full seconds before slowly turning her head to look at him. "I... I am... noisy?"

He did not look at her, but turned slightly in the wind, severing the line of sight between them.

She looked at him in confusion, but suddenly realised his gaze was not upon her face, but rather falling upon the yellow bird beast curled into a ball in her arms.

"This beast," his tone was neither cold nor hot, "did you pick it up?"

"It flew here on its own!" Lili defended herself. "It even chirped at me atop my head. It was especially cute, so I..."

"Chirped?"

He finally revealed a trace of a smile, imperceptible, which was swiftly suppressed.

He lifted a palm and brushed the air; a formless pressure of divine sense pressed down gently. The yellow bird beast shuddered instantly, let out a strange squawk—*Cheeep!*—leapt from Lili's embrace, and fled without a trace in a puff of smoke.

Lili: "Don't scare it!"

That little yellow bird was quite cute; she had intended to keep it as a pet.

Yu Sord gave a cold laugh. "It is good that it knows its place."

She did not see it, but he saw at a glance: that yellow finch spirit was a *male*. And it dared nestle in her arms?

Lili mumbled, "What a pity."

Yu Sord's gaze fell upon her disappointed face, his tone carrying a note of admonishment. "Do not bring anything by your side simply because it possesses a slight degree of good looks."

She stood frozen in place, momentarily unable to discern the meaning behind the Immortal Lord's words.

Lili: "......"

Hearing her silence, Yu Sord seemed to give a light cough, yet his tone remained calm: "The Grand Immortal Sect Tournament is tomorrow."

Her heart gave a jolt. She opened her mouth to speak, but heard him continue: "Do not be late."

With that, he turned and departed. His white robes moved slightly, like a solitary crane amidst the snow, silent and without trace.

"Ah, wait! Wait! Immortal Lord, you haven't taught me anything yet! I haven't learned a single thing..."

Wasn't this tantamount to sending her to die in vain?

* * * * *

Pengying Terrace

Clouds and mist coiled in thick, ethereal ribbons around Pengying Terrace. The disciples of the various immortal sects had gathered in a veritable sea, for the first round of the Grand Immortal Sect Tournament—the Trial of the Illusionary Mirror—was imminent.

High upon the cloud thrones sat the Sect Masters and Elders of every faction, engaging in spirited discussion. Below them, the disciples were rubbing their fists and wiping their palms, eager to try their luck and prove their mettle.

To put it simply, the Grand Immortal Sect Tournament was a grand contest occurring once every century, where every sect in the Immortal Realm dispatched their most outstanding disciples to compete. The sect that claimed victory would be crowned the premier sect of the Immortal Realm.

The rules of this competition were straightforward, akin to a mortal hunt. The disciples of all houses would enter the Illusionary Mirror Trial together.

Slaying monsters and hunting beasts yielded points; the one who accumulated the highest score would emerge the victor.

Yet at this very moment, in a secluded corner far removed from the fervor.

Yun Lili was squatting on the ground, lazily shelling melon seeds with a rhythmic *crack-crack*. Beside her sat a small pot of plum wine.

"So many immortal disciples... it is even livelier than a mortal market on festival day..." She tossed a kernel into her mouth, chewing slowly. "I wonder if one can merely watch the drama from the sidelines in this Illusionary Mirror Trial? Let us hope they don't actually expect me to go up and join the fray. I, for one, cherish my little life."

Scarcely had her voice faded when a soft sound chimed above her head, accompanied by a wisp of refreshing breeze.

Yu Sord had descended from the heavens, seemingly out of nowhere. His boots remained untouched by the mortal dust, and his sweeping sleeves were as white as snow.

"Yun Lili."

"Eh? Ah?"

Her hand trembled in fright, scattering the handful of melon seeds all over the ground.

He raised a hand and tapped lightly upon the center of her brow. A warm, lustrous rune of light sank into her skin instantly, vanishing like a drop of moonlight concealing itself between her brows.

In that split second, Yun Lili seemed to hear the rolling of distant thunder from the mountains and the gurgling of spiritual springs, yet in the next heartbeat, there was nothing. She felt only a faint heat in her heart, while conversely, her forehead felt cool as snow.

Yun Lili was stunned for a moment, unable to process what had just occurred.

"I... why does my forehead feel cold? Immortal Lord, you... uh? What did you just do?"

Yu Sord's tone was faint, as if discussing tomorrow's weather. "The rune is cast. You shall participate in the trial."

"...No, wait, you must be mad! I am not a cultivator! Although my spiritual roots are..."

Before she could finish her sentence, Yu Sord gently raised his palm.

Whap.

Heaven and earth spun violently.

Before she could even utter a single curse word, her vision went black, and she was blasted straight into the Illusionary Mirror by a single, decisive palm strike.

Crimson gauze draperies cascaded down from the high ceiling like blood-coloured mist. Amidst the flickering candlelight, the entire hall appeared as a lotus of hell in full bloom, beautiful yet ominous.

A chill mist lingered in the air, while in the shadowed corners, gilded beast motifs shimmered with a faint, predatory light, as though they too were quietly spying on the occupants within.

Yun Yara, clad in Daoist robes of icy cyan, sat in solitary pride before a carved rosewood table. Her brow and eyes were sharp as blades quenched in snow, cold to the point of appearing devoid of human warmth.

She swept a single glance over the table full of so-called "delicacies" before her: Blood Lingzhi stewed with Dragon Tendon, Black Ice Bass from the Nine Nether Cold Pool, and spirit meat roasted with the heart of a Thousand-Year Fire Fox. Steam spiralled from the dishes, yet to her eyes, they possessed not a shred of vitality.

"The hospitality of the Demon Realm," she sneered coldly, "is apparently this vulgar."

"Mo Han!"

She flung down her jade chopsticks. The silver-tipped utensils struck the black jade table, emitting a crisp, sharp clatter that echoed through the silent hall.

The hall doors swung open at the sound, and a tall figure strolled in with leisurely grace.

His dark robes were unfastened and loose, his gait languid. Mo Han possessed a lithe, long-limbed frame, his features cool and handsome as a blade's edge. At his collarbone, a dark red demonic sigil wound downwards, seemingly pulsing with flowing malevolence.

Soon, he leaned against the doorframe, a smile playing on his lips, his gaze fixing on her like that of a wolf in the night.

"What is this? This Crown Prince personally ordered these dishes prepared for you, yet Eldest Miss Yun remains ungrateful?"

Yun Yara cast him a faint glance, her eyes rippling with not a trace of emotion. "I have practised *inedia* for many years."

"That is your affair."

He raised a hand and waved it lightly; the flames in the hall instantly dimmed, and the temperature sank several degrees. "But since you have come to the Demon Realm, you naturally must abide by the rules of my race. Courtesy demands reciprocity; food must not be spurned."

"What do the rules of your Demon Race have to do with me?"

"Since you are here, you are a guest." He stepped closer, his tone lazy yet carrying a hint of steel. "If I do not entertain you thoroughly, I fear I shall be mocked for losing my sense of propriety as Crown Prince."

Yun Yara's gaze was like frost. "You speak with honeyed words, but in truth, this is imprisonment."

Mo Han's eyes darkened slightly, yet his smile grew even more languid. "Imprisonment? If I truly wished to trap you, do you fancy you would still be sitting here conversing so comfortably?"

He cast a sidelong glance at the table of dishes, the corner of his mouth hooking up to reveal a roguish charm. "And be served with such a table of fine wine and delicacies?"

Yun Yara's lips curled slightly, her tone ice-cold. "No one asked you to prepare them."

Mo Han's gaze paused, then he laughed softly. His steps were like the wind as he swept close to her, lowering his head to look down upon that face as cold as glacial ice.

"What is the rush? What is so good about returning to the Immortal Sects? A flock of sanctimonious hypocrites—can they compare to the liveliness I have here?"

"Impudent." Yun Yara spoke coldly. "I am a disciple of the Lingxiao Sect, an enemy of your Demon Race. For your conduct today, you will sooner or later pay the price."

"Alas," he reached out, winding a strand of the hair by her ear around his knuckle. His smile was as lazy as resting one's head upon an afternoon breeze. "I am treating you with kindness, yet every word you speak cuts to the bone. It truly chills the heart."

Yun Yara slapped his hand away, rising to glare at him, her voice like the edge of a sword. "What exactly do you want? Keeping me under house arrest here... you merely wish to borrow my name to suppress the Immortal Sects? Mo Han, stop dreaming!"

Mo Han took a half-step back, raising an eyebrow at her. His tone remained as roguish and unconcerned as ever.

"Do not speak so harshly, Eldest Miss Yun. You were the one who trespassed into the forbidden grounds of my Demon Realm; you walked into the net yourself. What has that to do with me? Furthermore, I have said it before—I keep you here only for cooperation."

"Cooperation?" Yun Yara's brow twitched. She spoke coldly, "You think I would associate with demonic cultivators? Why do you not go directly to the Four Great Immortal Sects to discuss cooperation?"

"The Four Great Immortal Sects?" Mo Han wore a smile that was not quite a smile. "Those hidebound old Daoists? If they beheld you fallen into my hands, I fear they would not so much as change their expressions before abandoning you outright."

Yun Yara's expression darkened, flames of fury churning within her eyes.

Mo Han, however, seemed long accustomed to her reaction. He merely paced leisurely to the edge of the jade steps and sat down, propping his chin in his hand as he gazed up at her. "However, when all is said and done... your urgency to return is merely because you wish to clarify matters regarding that country wench from the mortal realm, is it not?"

Yun Yara's brow twitched; her pupils contracted slightly.

"You... have investigated her?"

"Heh." Mo Han seemed to see right through her thoughts, laughing lightly. "This Crown Prince has always enjoyed a good spectacle. For instance—a counterfeit heiress struggling to cling to a nobility she *thought* was hers; and a true legitimate daughter, unwittingly stepping onto a throne that never belonged to her. Is this drama not far more intriguing than some Grand Immortal Sect Tournament?"

Crash!

Yun Yara shattered the jade cup beside her with a strike of her palm. Porcelain shards flew through the air as she rebuked him coldly, "Cease your prattle!"

Mo Han hooked his lips, slowly rising to his feet. He approached her step by step, his aura oppressive and suffocating. "I insist on speaking. What are you afraid of? Are you afraid that once your status is gone, your nominal fiancé—Yu Sord—will have a change of heart?"

"You—spout nonsense!" She gritted her teeth, her voice as cold as fractured ice.

Mo Han had already taken a step closer, his fingertip tilting her chin up, his eyes holding that ambiguous smile. "That fiancé of yours... outwardly cold as frost, but in his bones, he is the most sentimental of men. If Yun Lili is truly the biological daughter of the Yun family, how will he choose? You... have no confidence in your heart, do you?"

Yun Yara violently threw off his hand, her chest heaving unsteadily. She could not speak; her face was pale, as if she had been stripped of all her armor.

"Do not speak utter rubbish. Immortal Lord Yu is a paragon of noble virtue; he has no relation to me."

"Is that so?" He raised an eyebrow.

Mo Han finally stepped back, turning to stride away. Just before exiting the hall doors, he spoke without looking back:

"Tomorrow, switch the menu to plain porridge and side dishes. Do not let my honoured guest go hungry; it would sound terrible if word got out that this Crown Prince slighted a prodigy of the Sword Path."

With a wave of his hand, the hall doors closed silently.

Only Yun Yara remained standing in the vast hall, fingertips trembling. The longsword within her sleeve hummed softly, echoing the fury she suppressed at the bottom of her heart.

Her gaze grew firm.

One day, she would draw her sword and strike this cunning, frivolous Demon Prince dead beneath her blade.

Chapter 9: The Sword of Stars

Yun Lili lay sprawled on her back in a patch of wet mud, as if a salted fish who had just gone through a breakup.

"I can't do this, I really can't do this…"

Before the words finished, a deep beastly roar echoed from afar.

She lifted her head tremblingly—only to see a tiger demon, two zhang tall, leaping through the air toward her. Three eyes blazing red, fangs gleaming, its bloody breath hit her face.

"D-d-don't come over here!"

Lili hugged a small stone and shrank backward, shaking.

The demon's shadow darkened the sky; it was about to lunge—

Suddenly, the sigil on her forehead flared.

A column of pure white light descended from above, striking the tiger demon and blasting it into charred ashes—gone without even residue.

Lili stared, dumbfounded, her ears full only of her own rapid breathing.

The forest was dim, thick fog swirling.

Next came a three-eyed demon ape, roaring as it burst from the undergrowth, fangs bared, its scream shaking the air.

Before it even reacted, a thin line of blood appeared across its chest.

A heartbeat later, it crashed to the ground, tumbling motionless in the smoke.

Mist drifted through the illusion realm; cold winds whistled.

In the gloom of the forest, pairs of crimson beast eyes flickered.

Lili stepped on a slick vine and almost fell.

"Aaaaaah! Something moved!

There's something moving!!"

She screamed and squatted with her sword hugged to her chest, trembling all over.

"Did I enter the wrong dungeon?

Why is it suddenly… all demon beasts?!"

Wasn't the mirror supposed to be *fake*?

Why was everything here so *real*?

A giant wolf with flaming-red fur lunged out of the mist, claws gleaming as it dove for her head.

Lili squeezed her eyes shut, hugging her head, nearly dropping her sword.

"No!! I didn't come here to fight you!!"

In the next instant—

A soft hum vibrated.

The faint golden light at her forehead burst like morning glow—gentle yet sacred—spreading instantly.

The giant wolf didn't even touch her.

It shrieked as though burned, its body twisting as golden fire devoured it.

Within a breath, it dissolved into a curl of black smoke and vanished.

The other demon beasts in the forest caught sight of it.

None dared approach.

One after another, they whimpered and fled into the mist.

Lili cracked open one eye cautiously.

Seeing the empty clearing—no demon shadows—her jaw dropped.

"Huh? Th-they… left by themselves?"

Clutching her chest, still shaken, she muttered,

"Could it be my aura was too intimidating just now and scared them off?

…No way, I was about to cry myself!"

Not far away, Yu Sord hovered quietly in the air.

Seeing the faint glow flicker at her forehead, his gaze darkened slightly, and a soft laugh slipped from him.

"What is this thing? Why is it so powerful?"

She murmured to herself, even poking experimentally at her own forehead.

"Wow… this thing is kind of insane?"

* * * * *

The disciples and elders of every sect were staring fixedly at the huge suspended Spirit Mirror leaderboard.

A young girl in plain robes had just stepped into the mirror realm—

yet within only a few breaths, she had already slain three demon beasts, broken through two formations, and her points were soaring, shooting straight into the top twenty.

"Who is that? Why is there no spiritual fluctuation at all?"

"She just… seemed to shout 'don't come over here' at the demon beast, and it exploded?"

"Could she be using some ancient artifact? Or maybe a sect's secretly raised favourite disciple?"

"Heavens, she's in the top fifteen!"

"She's actually being *chased* by the demon beasts? She isn't even hunting monsters—she keeps hiding?"

The crowd erupted in noisy speculation, eyes glued to the real-time updates on the leaderboard, expressions frozen in disbelief.

"Top ten now…"

"What did she just throw—was that… a stone?

You can get points with *that*?!"

Yu Sord stood beneath the leaderboard with his hands behind his back, expression cold as frost.

Someone ventured cautiously,

"Immortal Sord… that young woman is…?"

His gaze darkened slightly; his tone was with cool indifference:

"Lili."

After a pause, he added,

"The sect master's trueborn daughter of Lingxiao Sect."

Realization dawned among the onlookers.

Everyone remembered the recent spiritual-root testing:

the true daughter returning, the fake one fleeing the sect on a sword.

"So… that is your newly acknowledged fiancée?"

Yu Sord was silent for a long moment.

His eyes drifted to the spirit mirror, falling on the little face inside—
frightened, reckless, and annoyingly bold.

When he finally spoke, his voice was cool and measured:

"Mind your own business."

The questioner flinched, immediately retreating three steps.

——He didn't deny it?

Then isn't that basically admitting it?!

* * * * *

Meanwhile, inside the mirror realm, Lili had already opened an entirely
different… well, a path that no one before or after her would ever tread.

She used a *roasted chicken leg* to lure away an entire nest of fire
serpents, used a few pieces of biscuits to coax a black fox inside a cave
to sleep, and even picked up a glowing spirit beast egg around a corner.

On the scoreboard, her ranking shot upward like a rocket, steadily
climbing to seventh place.

But she was completely unaware—only wandering forward with a blank
face, muttering to herself:

"Am I sure this doesn't count as cheating…? I'm literally the most
ordinary person ever—

AIYA, DON'T BITE ME!!"

She had been trying to pull up a spirit herb, only for the little spirit
mouse she fed earlier to suddenly clamp onto the hem of her robe and
burrow desperately into her arms.

Covered in tiny tooth marks and slobber, she jumped in frustration:

"Hey hey hey! I came here to cultivate immortality, not to become all of
your foster mother—!"

* * * * *

Outside — Pengying Platform, the trial just ended

The moment the mirror trial ended, Lili felt her brain buzzing; her mind
was filled with only four words:

I was tricked. Badly.

That burst of white light that flung her out of the mirror hit her so hard
she spun three full circles in midair like a ragged cloth bag thrown by the
wind.

She landed dizzy, legs unsteady, vision spinning.

When her eyes finally focused, the culprit, Yu Sord, was standing under a pine tree beneath the stage—

elegant, snow-white robes floating lightly, looking exactly like he had stepped out of a painting.

…the infuriating part was that his immortal face actually made her heart beat a little faster.

"You—YOU YOU YOU!" Lili puffed up, charging toward him.

Her hand almost reached his collar—then jerked back as if burned, and she could only kick a stone while grumbling:

"Did you do it on purpose…? I—I had *just* stood steady and you slapped me right inside!"

Yu Sord lowered his gaze at her, tone calm as clear spring water:

"If I were you, I'd save some energy instead of complaining."

"What did you say?!"

"The next trial—sword combat."

Lili froze on the spot, expression collapsing.

"I… I don't know how!"

He nodded lightly, voice still smooth and emotionless:

"Don't worry. I will teach you."

She had just let out a breath of relief—

when she heard him add, just as calmly:

"Since you are someone brought in by me… you are not allowed to embarrass me."

The tone peaceful, yet every word struck the heart.

Lili's ears turned scarlet in an instant.

A breeze swept through the bamboo forest on the back mountain of Yuheng.

Sunlight spilled in broken patterns across the sword training platform.

Lili slumped on a stone bench, her face full of despair.

"I'm serious—I really can't practice this stuff."

Yu Sord stood before her, a long sword strapped diagonally across his back.

He extended a sword toward her and said, voice as calm as ever:

"Hold the sword."

Lili wanted to refuse, but her eyes refused to leave the sword in his hand.

No other reason—this sword was tooooooo beautiful.

The blade was dark as the night sky, flowing with shifting light, dotted with starlit gleams.

"But these hands of mine are for grinding herbs, not holding swords."

She said it righteously—yet her hands still betrayed her and took the sword.

The moment her fingers wrapped around the hilt—

Smack.

She hit her own knee.

"Ow… that hurts…"

Yu Sord's gaze lingered only on the newly forged sword in her hands, showing not the slightest sympathy for her poor knee.

Lili forgot the pain and stared in awe at the unbelievably beautiful blade.

A rather evocative description of a blade, though perhaps a touch too heavy on the 'starlight' metaphor initially. We shall elevate the diction and refine the rhythm to achieve that requisite published quality.

The blade possessed a profound, abyssal blue, a shade so deep it seemed to capture the very essence of the night sky itself.

Its cold illumination pulsed subtly, faintly traversed by the phantom shimmer of drifting stars—as though the weapon held within it the accumulated, fallen argent radiance of the celestial sphere.

With her slightest motion, the sword responded, stirring silent, languid waves of light.

Yu Sord raised a single finger, tracing a delicate line along the sword's spine and his touch was almost reverent, extraordinarily gentle—like one deciphering a sacred poem that had been inscribed without the impediment of written words.

He spoke, his voice measured and low:

"The luminescence of this blade is akin to a **cosmic ocean** of stars; its inherent spirit, as aloof and remote as the heavens themselves. This sword—it is named *Starveil.*"

He did not say aloud that this sword was forged after he alone quelled the northern demon crisis,

venturing into the ancient ruins of the Northern Cold, retrieving metal formed from a fallen primordial star—*Star-Submerged Iron*—

and commissioning Heavenly Craft Pavilion to temper it in violet flame for forty-nine days.

On the day the sword was completed, starlight filled the sky, and every sword within three miles resonated.

An old master had exclaimed:

"This sword shall be called *Starveil*—only one with a clear and unclouded heart may wield it."

Yu Sord's tone was faint:

"This sword suits you."

Lili blinked, stunned.

She lowered her head, and the silver light in her palms shimmered lightly as if answering his words—

a soft ripple spreading outward.

A fleeting warmth flashed in Yu Sord's eyes, hard to notice.

But his voice remained as cool as always:

"*Starveil* makes no sound, yet it can cut through all illusions."

He paused, letting his gaze fall to the center of her forehead.

In his heart, he added a silent line:

Just like you.

Outwardly, he was still composed and solemn.

"In the sword trial, they test basic sword forms and footwork."

His voice was calm as still water, showing no mercy.

"Today I will teach you *Cold-Frost Form.*"

Lili's eyes widened instantly.

She shook her hands frantically and shoved the sword back at him:

"W-wait, wait! How am I supposed to learn this in time? I can't even hold a sword without hitting myself!"

Pretty sword or not—this was impossible!

Yu Sord tilted his head slightly, placing the long sword horizontally before her, his voice low and calm:

"Hold the sword. Don't be afraid."

Lili nearly threw the sword in frustration.

But one look at his cold, impossibly handsome face—she swallowed it back down.

"…Then tell me," she grumbled, "how is someone like me—this level of trash—supposed to learn?"

He stepped closer, coming to stand behind her, and placed his hand over hers on the sword hilt.

His voice was soft yet emotionless:

"Do not belittle yourself. You possess a Heaven-grade spiritual root, and the bloodline of the Yun clan."

"…"

"Raise your hand. If you don't know how, I will teach you."

His tone remained cold, yet he was so close he was nearly brushing her ear, his voice low like mist winding through a forest.

"I was entrusted with this task, so I will carry it out."

Lili froze like a wooden post.

"…Huh?"

"Why are you standing so close to me?" Her ears flushed red.

"No—I'm not close. You are short."

"You! Who are you calling—"

"Raise the sword."

His tone allowed no argument. His fingers guided hers, and she felt the wooden sword—previously heavy and awkward—settle firmly and securely in her grip.

"Tip upward. Straighten your waist—

No, that's not straightening, that's locking up."

"…"

"Focus. Stop letting your mind wander."

His tone was still calm.

Lili's hands trembled with anger, yet she didn't dare actually strike him—looking very much like a salted fish called fat but unable to refute it.

After two moves, her arms were sore and she could barely hold the sword.

"I can't. I think my hands are about to fall off."

Lili took a deep breath and reached out again to hold the sword hilt.

Instantly, a chill seeped through her palm; she reflexively jumped back half a step.

"So cold… like grabbing an ice pop."

Yu Sord's expression didn't change, but there was a hint of amusement between his brows.

Without a word, he demonstrated the first stance, "Condensed Frost."

His toe lightly tapped the ground; his figure drifted like smoke.

Then "Flowing Light Returns"—the sword light arched like a rainbow streak, sweeping through the bamboo shadows without a sound.

Lili watched, entranced—

but her limbs refused to cooperate, moving in complete disarray as she tried to follow along.

Her steps swayed like a drunkard's, her sword angle was as crooked as a handcart, and instead of releasing sword qi…

she sliced up an enormous patch of grass.

"Oh no!" She panicked and tried to withdraw the sword.

But losing her balance, the tip pointed skyward while she herself fell flat on her back.

Yu Sord immediately stepped forward, catching her with one steady motion.

His touch was gentle, yet carried an unshakable firmness.

"Your strength is too forceful, but your heart is too timid," he said quietly, correcting her grip.

"Relax your fingers. Bend your elbow slightly… like this."

Lili felt a faint warmth spreading from his palm into her elbow, then all the way to her heart.

Her heart skipped a beat—something felt wrong, vaguely, but she couldn't say what.

Following his instructions, she swung out *Flowing Light Returns* once more.

Though there was no killing intent, the sword energy had faintly taken shape, drawing a pale arc through the air.

"Good." Yu Sord nodded slightly.

"Practice it a hundred more times, and you will have entered the basics."

"A hundred times?!" She was stunned, shouting aloud.

"Endure three more forms."

"I really can't."

"Then endure one."

"…I'm a girl, you know!"

(Subtext: show a little pity for fragrant soft jade, will you?!)

"I am helping you because you are my…"

At those words, Lili froze entirely.

She jerked her head up at him:

"What did you say?"

Yu Sord's expression did not change.

"My disciple.

Win or lose, you must make others dare not look down on you."

She narrowed her eyes suspiciously.

"Is that so?!"

He didn't answer—only lowered his head to adjust her posture again.

Lili tried not to let her thoughts run wild,

but her heartbeat refused to listen, pounding chaotically in her chest.

She rubbed her forehead, the lingering warmth still there,

while across from her Yu Sord had already drawn his sword and stood ready, his figure tall and straight like bamboo, his sword intent cold and spotless.

Then Lili repositioned herself into the *Condensed Frost* stance, forcing her trembling hands and weak knees to cooperate, and began practicing one move at a time toward the bamboo grove.

Not far away, Yu Sord stood quietly in the wind.

His body like a sword, his sword like the wind.

He said nothing, but silently observed each of her strikes.

When the training finally ended, she collapsed onto the grass outright, like a salted fish that had just run a marathon.

"Next time I'm signing up for the talisman array class!

At least… I won't have to move my hands!

Drawing talismans has got to be easier than swinging a sword, right?!"

Slowly, Yu Sord leaned down.

His long fingers brushed aside the sweat-dampened strands sticking to her forehead,

his tone as soft as a feather:

"If you can master even one-tenth,

I won't make you touch a sword again."

"Really?" Her eyes lit up instantly, as if she had just drawn an SSR card.

"But if you fail—"

"W-w-what now?" She shrank her neck back in full alert,

terrified he might say something like *"Copy the sect rules three thousand times."*

His expression remained calm.

With a light flick of his fingertip against her brow, he said,

"Then for the rest of your life, you will only be able to keep learning…

swordplay from me."

She shot upright instantly, as if three enormous question-mark emojis had popped up above her head.

"W-what?!"

The corner of his lips lifted slightly.

His long eyes hooked at her, wordless yet teasing.

",,,..."

She *suspected* he was playing word games again, but she had no proof.

"In swordsmanship—who else surpasses me?"

…Alright, it was her overthinking.

On the Cultivation Realm Sword master Leaderboard, the golden *TOP 1* glowing behind his username hadn't budged for… who knew how many centuries.

To be bound to the server's number-one boss as her instructor didn't sound like a bad deal at all.

"That's enough for today.

We continue tomorrow."

Before the last word had faded, he had already turned and walked away, steady, composed, exactly as always.

Lili stared at his departing back, her heart suddenly thudding in a strange rhythm.

Just as she sank into some inexplicable emotion—

Behind her came a burst of… chicken cries.

The three spirit fowls had already gathered at her feet, chirping insistently, as if urging her to get up and continue training.

She hugged her sword, rubbed her head, and let out a long sigh.

Under the fading sunset glow, the blade trembled faintly.

She gritted her teeth, a fierce resolution burning in her chest. "The sword trials have only just begun," she thought. "I can't keep falling like this. If this continues, even my chickens will strut past me with disdain!"

With that thought fuelling her, Lili settled once more into the Condensed Frost Step stance. She forced her trembling limbs to steady themselves, took a deep breath, and resumed her practice, moving with renewed determination toward the bamboo grove.

Behind her, Yu Sord's silhouette stood like a cold, solitary blade, rooted among the clouds,

watching quietly, guarding her in silence.

Chapter10: The Sword Trial Turns Upside Down

The illusion realm that had run for several days in a row were finally dissolving bit by bit in the glow of dawn.

In the swirling rosy clouds and drifting mists, the last two figures slowly stepped out.

"It's Xiao Yan! And Zhou!"

A cry of shock burst from the crowd like a pot boiling over.

The two of them had their sleeves and robes billowing, their bearing otherworldly and aloof, standing there in front of everyone as if they truly were immortals descended.

Their breathing was steady, their auras calm and controlled—it was clear they had walked out of the illusion realm with their whole bodies intact, not even ruffled.

The steward elder's voice rang out as he announced the rankings:

"In this illusion trial, Xiao Yan takes first place, Zhou is second, and those ranked from third to tenth are…"

Before his words had even fallen completely, the crowd below was already in an uproar.

"Xiao Yan got first place?!"

"But Zhou is the legitimate son of the Yun family, the seed disciple personally chosen by Lingxiao Sect—how did he end up only second?"

"Even so, the two of them are simply too strong… At this rate, we probably won't catch up to them in this lifetime."

"Even Lili managed to grab seventh place—"

Voices rose and fell, layered over one another.

Everyone was talking at once, eyes full of admiration and awe as they stared at the two of them, as if looking up at true immortals in the clouds.

Zhou, for his part, wore his usual cultivated smile. His expression was gentle, his gaze warm as he inclined his head and gave the crowd a small nod of greeting.

On his face there was not the slightest shadow of defeat; instead, his composure and steadiness only made him seem even more gracious and admirable.

Outside the sword arena once the trial was over, the place was still buzzing with noise and excitement.

Lili stood on the outer edge of the crowd, holding the small packet of dried fruits Little Yue had just shoved into her hands.

She was staring at it with great interest, completely absorbed, when she suddenly heard a clear, bright voice call out to her:

"Lili, over here."

She lifted her head and saw Zhou waving her over.

Standing beside him was a youth whose brows and eyes were as sharp and cool as a drawn sword—sword brows, starry eyes, a presence that was anything but ordinary—yet his expression looked faintly stiff and ill at ease.

"And this is…?"

"Eh?" Lili blinked. She hadn't even gone all the way over yet, but she clearly felt that young man look at her.

In the very next instant, his entire body went rigid where he stood, his ears turning from pale to crimson in the space of half a breath.

Just for a heartbeat.

Then he reacted as though a bolt of lightning had struck him from the sky—his whole figure locking up, the tips of his ears burning, and the next second he spun around and bolted, taking off at a dead run with the resolve of someone fleeing for his life.

—This was the champion of the illusion trial.

The cold, aloof genius admired and worshiped by thousands?

Yet the instant he laid eyes on her, he detonated on the spot, couldn't even force out a single word, acting exactly as if she were some calamity-level monster.

Lili: ",,,...?"

Zhou: ",,,...What exactly did you do to him?"

"N–Nothing… I didn't do anything…"

He had only just barely lifted his gaze to look at her, and the moment their eyes touched, he reacted like facing a mortal enemy, like staring down certain death, almost fleeing in panic.

Clearly he could stand in the middle of a sword formation with ten thousand blades and not bat an eye, but now he suddenly looked as if he'd seen a ghost.

And then that person… actually turned around and left!

Left?!

Was her face really that terrifying?

"Xiao Yan!" Zhou called out instinctively to the retreating back, disbelief written all over his voice. "How could you…?"

…run away?

Xiao Yan did not look back. He only left them a view of his back as he strode away faster and faster, like a man running for his life.

Lili stood there, completely at a loss, and turned to look at Zhou. "What… happened to him?"

Zhou looked just as baffled. "I was about to ask you the same thing."

He thought back to that fleeting flash of fear and flustered embarrassment on Xiao Yan's face just now and only felt that it was all extremely strange.

Was this really the same cold and arrogant genius who had remained unmoved before a sea of swords and blades, the one who took first place in the illusion realm?

Could it be that… he owed this little girl money?

Lili, however, rubbed the bridge of her nose, her voice dropping as she spoke with a guilty conscience:

"I think… last time, when his, uh… underpants got blown into my yard… I scolded him for a while…"

Zhou: ",,,,..."

He silently lifted his head to look up at the sky, and suddenly felt that today's breeze…

was quite a bit chillier than usual.

* * * * *

The Sword Trial Tournament had finally begun.

On the martial arena, sword-qi crisscrossed the air, the atmosphere so tense it seemed capable of tearing the sky open.

Young disciples from all major sects gathered together, their swords all unsheathed, sharpness overflowing.

This year, Lingxiao Sect had performed quite well—victories and losses mixed, yet they had remained steadily within the top three.

Now, only the final match remained.

If they could win this last battle, they would secure the championship of this year's Sword Trial.

The problem was—

the one going up for the final match was Lili.

The same girl who'd only arrived a few days ago…

who had just barely learned how to *hold* a sword.

Her opponent was Xiao Yan.

First place in the illusion trial.

Possessor of a Heaven-rank sword bone.

Began sword training at three, rode his sword at seven, and by ten could slice an ox in half with a single strike.

Recognized by all major sects as a once-in-a-century sword prodigy—a future Sword Immortal.

The spectator stands erupted instantly:

"Why send that village girl up?!"

"Isn't this basically handing the championship over to Sky-Sword Sect?!"

"What a pity… Lingxiao Sect is going to lose everything at the very end."

Lili held her barely-summoned **Starveil Sword**, standing in the centre of the stage, feeling unbelievably hollow inside. She knew her chance of winning was extremely low—but she still stepped onto the platform, because she did not want to disappoint everyone.

Xiao Yan walked onto the stage at an unhurried pace, calm and composed.

But the moment he saw Lili's face—

He froze like someone struck by lightning.

His step halted, his expression twisted.

"You again?!"

Images crashed through his mind:

Wind blowing—robes flying—underpants soaring through the sky…

Worst of all, that pair of underpants *just had* to land in Lili's courtyard, where her chickens pecked several holes into them.

And she even picked them up in front of him.

And looked at them.

Xiao Yan's face instantly flushed red like a cooked shrimp. His ears steamed. His sword nearly slipped out of his hand.

* * * * *

The match began.

Lili also recognized her opponent as the owner of that ill-fated pair of underpants.

She even tried to greet him politely:

"Hi~"

But Xiao Yan's handsome face instantly lost all color, and he backed up three full steps.

"Uh…"

Lili held her sword with both trembling hands. Since he clearly had no intention of exchanging greetings, she politely said,

"So… shall we begin?"

Xiao Yan subconsciously retreated again.

His sword trembled.

His breathing fell apart.

The entire arena fell into a terrifying silence.

The audience stood there stunned.

Even the referee wondered whether the sword formation on the stage had malfunctioned.

"How strange… why do both sides look terrified of each other?"

"Yeah, it's the war god versus a total newbie—shouldn't the outcome be obvious?"

And then—

Because Xiao Yan was mentally collapsing the entire time, his moves erratic and chaotic, he was caught by Lili's clumsy trip and—fell straight out of bounds.

Defeat.

The entire arena exploded.

"Xiao Yan lost?!"

"Are you kidding me?!"

"Lingxiao Sect actually won the championship?!"

Xiao Yan lay sprawled on the ground, golden stars dancing before his eyes, his mind filled only with the traumatic image of underpants fluttering in the wind.

When the referee asked if he conceded, his lips trembled.

At last, he muttered softly:

"…Forget it."

Back at the spectator stands, he sat in the farthest corner with a devastated expression, head lowered, hugging his sword as if trying to hide inside the scabbard itself.

A disciple tried to speak to him—

but he coldly snapped,

"Shut up."

…while the tips of his ears were still burning red.

* * * * *

Meanwhile, high up above—

Yu Sord stood silently, wide sleeves drifting lightly, his brows and eyes cold and distant. His expression was calm, as though this shocking reversal meant nothing to him.

In truth, he had indeed risen to act—

planning to intervene and protect her.

But in the end, he didn't move.

He simply stood there watching.

Lili glanced up at him from the stage, her eyes shining with gratitude and certainty:

It must have been Immortal Sord secretly helping me—just like in the illusion realm.

Yu Sord, however, frowned slightly.

He had not helped her. Not even a little.

But he had sensed Xiao Yan's abnormality.

That boy should have had sword-qi like a rainbow, killing moves flowing like a dance, yet his steps were chaotic, his sword intent scattered, like a kite whose string had snapped in the wind.

And especially when his gaze met Lili's—

That flicker of panic and disorder.

That evasive, guilty look.

Yu Sord's gaze deepened.

This was not Xiao Yan

And what unsettled him even more was that when Lili looked at Xiao Yan…there had been a flash of something familiar.

Something like… nervousness? Or recognition?

Her slight bow as she whispered "thank you" was so sincere it made something tighten sharply in his chest.

A strange emotion, thin as mist, yet clinging like vines, slowly curled around his heart.

He could not tell whether it was annoyance, or…

He lowered his eyes.

She had won.

Lingxiao Sect had taken the championship.

It should have been a joyous moment.

Yet his gaze kept drifting—again and again—toward her and Xiao Yan

How did the two of them know each other?

Or rather… was it more than just "knowing"?

Why did she have past dealings with him?

And why …in that boy's panicked gaze… did she show not the slightest fear?

Yu Sord's fingers tightened around the jade fan in his hand.

He prided himself on not being someone ruled by emotions, yet this sudden surge of possessiveness was impossible to ignore.

And this feeling…

He did not like it. Not one bit.

* * * * *

Yun Yara had just arrived at the Nether Palace, and everything in the Demon Realm felt utterly unfamiliar to her. She had originally believed that the demon lands were nothing more than barren, gloomy, filled with slaughter and shadows—but unexpectedly, the sight before her was a completely different world.

Mo Han said, "Since you're here, let's walk around and take a look."

Yara kept her face cold, wanting to refuse, but he directly dragged her onto the back of the demon roc, lifting her into the air.

"You don't think I'd let you rot inside the palace all day, do you?"

"Don't push me."

"Just think of it that way." He shrugged, a careless, roguish look on his face.

Their first stop was the Scarlet Flame Valley.

There, the cliff faces glowed like fire, lava flowed in streams—scorching but not burning—and clusters of rare Fire Phoenix Blossoms bloomed among the heated rocks, brilliant and dazzling.

She stood at the edge of the cliff and lifted her hand to touch the petal of a Fire Phoenix Blossom. It was warm, soft—completely different from what she had imagined.

She froze slightly—

The demon realm was not what she had known.

A giant red bird she had never seen before rose from the bottom of the valley, its wings shining like flowing light, letting out a pleasant, ringing cry.

Yara exclaimed in shock, "This fire… why doesn't it burn?"

Mo Han said indifferently, "This is the fire of the earth's core. It responds to people. If you weren't brought here by this crown prince, you would've already turned to ash."

He tilted his head to look at her. "Well? Not grateful?"

She gave a short snort, not a trace of sincerity in her voice. "Many thanks, Prince Mo."

Mo Han raised a brow and didn't answer, but the corner of his lips curved slightly.

When she turned around, she found Mo Han leaning lazily against the roc's back, looking at her with a half-smile.

A jolt ran through her heart; she instantly withdrew her hand and restored her cold expression. "Enough. Take me back."

"Ah, you're touched, aren't you?"

"You think too much."

"I never think randomly. I only guess accurately."

* * * * *

Their second stop was the Endless Sea.

Though called the Endless Sea, it was actually an inland sea—one could also call it a vast lake stretching so far that its boundaries could not be seen.

The Endless Sea lay in the far west of the demon domain. Its thousands of miles of black water reflected the heavens above, and within the water floated countless ethereal stone isles that drifted slowly with the sea breeze. When the tide rose at night, dots of light appeared upon the surface, like stars falling into the mortal world.

Yara wore the cloak he had draped over her shoulders and stood on a drifting stone skiff, letting the wind gently lift strands of her hair.

She could not deny that the sight before her… was breathtaking.

She had always thought the demon realm was nothing but blood and fire, yet she had never expected a place like this:

Starlight fell into the sea, scattering like shards of gold across the black water, turning and drifting with the waves. The sea breeze lifted the hair at her temples, coolness seeping down to her bones.

She paused slightly in surprise.

If she had remained in the Lingxiao Palace, she might never have been fated to witness such a scene in her entire life.

Even that part of her heart that had been frozen for many years… seemed to be brushed lightly by one of those drifting lights in the wind.

"Beautiful, isn't it?" Mo Han asked with a tone of claiming credit, reaching as if to wrap an arm around her shoulders—only for her to slip aside in an instant.

"Keep your hands to yourself." She frowned, displeased.

Mo Han took no offense. The corner of his lips lifted slightly as he stood behind her, watching the faint upturn of her face. His voice was low. "What difference is there between demons and immortals? Both are creations of heaven and earth. What your immortal realm sees is nothing more than prejudice."

Yara gave him a sidelong glance. "You do see things clearly."

He answered with a small smile. "I only want to show you that the place you're so eager to escape… is not entirely a hell."

* * * * *

Soon after, he also brought her through the Vine Forest, where countless green-violet vines draped from the skies, swaying gently with a person's breath. They bore strange blossoms capable of drawing one into dreams and released a unique fragrance.

They had also travelled to the Moonless Marsh, a still lake at the border of the demon realm where no moon or stars ever appeared throughout the year; yet the lake surface glowed on its own, reflecting the deepest images hidden in one's heart.

Yara stood by the lakeside, watching scenes of herself in the Lingxiao Sect flicker upon the water, a faint ripple rising within her chest.

She abruptly turned away, refusing to look anymore—only to bump straight into Mo Han's arms.

He caught her with one hand, his brows barely furrowing. "The demon marsh shows the heart. Are you afraid?"

She replied quietly, "It has nothing to do with you."

He smiled lightly. "Since you are already here, there is no way back. Your path is not to return."

It was to move forward—together with him.

That night, he did not force her to look into the lake again. He simply sat beside her in silence and kept watch for the entire night.

After that, he and she had also leapt across the Duanba Mountain Range, a stretch of dozens of floating peaks. White mist coiled around the mountaintops, ethereal like illusion; the peaks were connected by suspension bridge that wound between them, and when the wind blew, they produced a sound like a celestial flute.

She could not help murmuring, "Higher than the Bixu Mountains of the immortal realm…"

Mo Han heard her and said calmly, "Heh, so even you immortals have times when you are amazed."

She shot him a glare. "Shut up."

He half-smiled. "Otherwise, would you rather hide in the Nether Palace all day weeping? I don't raise lost little birds."

She retorted, "Who are you calling a bird?"

"You, of course." He stared at her, eyes carrying a hint of amusement. "Just a little bird with wounded wings. Since you've fallen into my hands, I have to raise you properly."

He brought her to Jiuji Peak atop the Duanba Range, the highest mountain in the demon realm. The winds at the summit were as sharp as blades, and among the jagged rocks grew a kind of Phoenix-Feather Grass—born once every thousand years, dying every ten thousand.

He said, "This grass only blooms on the night of a lunar eclipse. When it opens, it sets the entire mountaintop alight like flame."

Yara asked him, "Have you seen it?"

He shook his head. "I don't have the patience to wait ten thousand years. But I can be kind enough to wait with you for this one night."

If you are willing—

She paused, for some reason feeling a strange emotion stir within her chest.

Snow-laden wind rose suddenly. She coughed lightly, and Mo Han, without a hint of hesitation, draped his cloak over her shoulders. "Be strong. There's nothing more important than making yourself live happily."

She looked up at him, her eyes flashing with a rare trace of a smile. "You actually know how to care about people."

He gave her a sideways look. "If you're unhappy, then all the trouble I spent on this journey would be wasted, wouldn't it?"

After that, she had no choice but to admit: though Mo Han was the crown prince of the demon domain and acted with outrageous dominance, the places he took her to… allowed her to see a world she had never imagined.

The demon realm was not only a battlefield of slaughter and blood—it also held vast grandeur, mysterious wonders, and magnificent landscapes.

Upon that deep, boundless land, her understanding of the world slowly shattered and reshaped—and the outline of his figure gradually, little by little, grew clear in her heart.

Yu Sord
玉玄溯

Chapter 11: The Fool's Choice

The Grand Immortal Sect Tournament had drawn to a close.

Atop the summit of Mount Wanxiang, ten thousand rays of rosy light pierced the firmament, while multicoloured clouds rolled and surged like a celestial tide. Three resonant peals of the great bell tolled, declaring to all under heaven—the Lingxiao Sect claimed the crown!

Cheers erupted from the disciples like rolling thunder; even the elders of the Lingxiao Sect could barely conceal their beaming smiles. Who could have fathomed that this grand competition, determining both glory and the allocation of resources, would be snatched from the jaws of defeat and claimed by a young girl who had barely stepped through the sect gates?

She stood upon the high dais clad in simple robes, the spiritual light around her yet to dissipate. Amidst the churning spiritual energy, rain composed of pure light drifted down from the sky, as if heaven and earth themselves were applauding her.

"Yun Lili—well done! You have performed a great service in protecting our sect!"

"To defeat Xiao Yan at such a young age... she is simply the Chosen Daughter of Heaven!"

"Come, come! Bring forth the treasures from the Sect Vault for her to choose!"

Three treasures had long been prepared upon the jade pedestal, floating amidst the clouds and shimmering with light.

The first was the 'Demon-Slaying Cold Light Sword', capable of slicing through iron as though it were mud, slaying demons and breaking formations; it held a distinguished place upon the Ranking of Famous Swords.

The second was the 'Nine-Turn True Gold Pill', capable of aiding the ascension of one's primordial spirit and breaking through cultivation boundaries—a treasure dreamed of by countless cultivators.

The third was... a round, warm, nameless object. It was a pale yellow colour, possessed a few spiderweb cracks upon its surface, and was roughly the size of a coconut—a Spirit Egg.

The Spirit Egg lay quietly in the jade dish, silent and still, looking even... somewhat cute?

Yun Lili was captivated by it at a single glance.

She tilted her head, pondering for a long while, before clasping her hands in apology to the sword: "I do not walk the path of the sword cultivator..."

Moreover, she already possessed the exquisitely beautiful sword, 'Star-Mist'.

She then looked at the brilliantly glittering golden pill and blinked: "If my mana grows too strong, I shall have to fight in more battles, won't I? I have no desire to become a brute warrior."

Finally, she pointed a finger at the egg and spoke with determination: "I choose this one. I feel that it... is calling to me."

For a moment, a hush fell over the audience below, followed immediately by—

"Ah! Waah! Has she gone mad?! That is the Cold Light Sword!!"

"If not the sword, at least choose the pill! You chose an... egg??!!"

"At most, that egg will hatch a spirit beast! Hey!"

"They say fortune favours fools, but this is simply *too* foolish!"

"Alas..."

The crowd chattered all at once, wringing their hands and sighing, wishing they could rush up and re-select on her behalf. Even an old elder on the judging panel could not help but slap his thigh in frustration: "Little girl! That is the sword *this seat* yearned for in his youth but could never obtain!"

Yun Lili, however, remained unmoved. She merely cupped the Spirit Egg carefully with both hands, as if embracing a future hope.

Standing not far away, Yu Sord had not uttered a single word from beginning to end; he simply watched her quietly.

He had long discerned that the Spirit Egg possessed a peculiar spiritual energy; it was no ordinary object. Yet such a choice was not one a rational cultivator would make—and yet she had chosen it, without hesitation, and even with a measure of... tenderness.

He looked at the egg nestled in her arms, then at the expression of satisfaction upon her face. His cold brows finally softened ever so slightly, and the corner of his lips hooked up imperceptibly into the faintest of arcs.

Yun Lili had chosen the Spirit Egg, and after the initial uproar of the crowd had subsided, the first person to jump to his feet in protest was, predictably, her "cheap" brother—Yun Zhou.

He pounced forward with a look of utter exasperation, as if wishing he could transmute iron into steel by sheer force of will, nearly snatching the egg from her embrace.

"Did your brain get knocked senseless by that egg?!"

"That is the Demon-Slaying Cold Light Sword! Even if *you* don't cultivate the sword, *I* could have kept it!"

"That is the Nine-Turn True Gold Pill! Even if *you* don't want to eat it, *I* could have eaten it!"

"And you chose *this*... this thing that might hatch into heaven knows what kind of mess?!"

Lili guarded the egg with her life, turning her body away while shooting him a warning glance. "You stay away from it! It will be afraid of you!"

Zhou was so angry he nearly ascended on the spot. "I'm afraid of *it*! Do you believe me?!"

To the side, Xie Wuchen watched with immense amusement, cradling his tea and remarking airily with a smile, "I actually find it quite interesting. That egg looks... rather cute."

Zhou immediately whipped his head around to glare at him. "Have you gone mad as well?"

Xie Wuchen raised an elegant brow. "In any case, your Lingxiao Sect has won the championship. Whatever you choose is your prerogative."

Just then, the Spirit Egg in Lili's hands seemed to sense the chaotic atmosphere. It grew slightly warm in her palm and emitted a soft *pop*, releasing a faint glimmer of light. The crowd instantly fell silent for a beat; even Yu Sord turned his gaze slightly sideways.

At this moment, the noble Wonton Soup... er, no, Sect Master Yun Wuntang also appeared beneath the high dais.

Standing with hands clasped behind his back, his face beaming with smiles, he announced: "Since it is the object Lili has chosen, it is naturally her destiny. Men—add a gift of a pure gold spirit cage! Let her raise the egg properly; we can't have her hatching some four-unlike beast with nowhere to put it!"

With a flash of spiritual light, a cage of golden wire descended from the sky. Encased in glazed glass and wreathed in an aura of treasure, it was so opulent that Zhou nearly choked. "...I've raised spirit beasts for three years and never had such a setup!"

Before the crowd could recover their wits, a hearty laugh rang out.

"Good! Good! This little doll is truly interesting!"

Old Matriarch Yun had arrived as well. Clad in a cloak of cloud-patterned crane feathers, her steps were slow but her presence was imposing. She beamed with the kindest of benevolent smiles, chortling happily.

"My granddaughter has chosen well. We have plenty of pills and swords, but this egg... is a treasure amongst treasures!"

Having spoken, she waved her sleeve without allowing room for argument. "Men! Fetch that Small Blazing Red Lantern from my Treasure Pavilion! Give it to her to keep the egg warm!"

Upon hearing this, the crowd gasped in unison, sucking in a breath of cold air.

What was that? That was the legendary spirit lantern capable of hatching even an Ice Phoenix egg!

Zhou's face turned green.

"Great-Grandmother, please calm down! If this continues, this egg will rank higher in status than I do!"

The Old Matriarch patted his head with a beaming smile. "It was already higher than you. Stop making a fuss."

Xie Wuchen lowered his head to sip his tea, laughing until the tips of his ears turned red. Yu Sord gazed at the Spirit Egg, a hint of indescribable depth surfacing in his eyes.

—*This egg truly possesses no small destiny; to think it has such fortune.*

Meanwhile, Lili was squatting in the corner, whispering to the egg: "You be good, don't be afraid. With me here, you definitely won't turn into egg drop soup. You must be... what are you? We can chat slowly later."

The egg flashed with light, actually rolling once in her palm, as if responding to her.

The Crowd: "????"

* * * * *

The Nether Palace. Black mist coiled in suffocating tendrils, and the air was permeated with the faint, acrid scent of sulphurous fire.

A Netherfire Mirror hung suspended in mid-air, its surface glowing with a ghostly green light as it reflected the final scene of the Grand Immortal Sect Tournament—

Yun Lili stood amidst the gaze of ten thousand eyes, cradling a Spirit Egg in her arms. Her face was bathed in a soft, gentle light, as if she needed to do nothing at all for the entire world to automatically bow its head to her.

The members of the Lingxiao Sect clustered around her, faces brimming with pride, kneeling to cry out:

"Senior Sister Lili possesses the appearance of a jade immortal! Invincible in battle! The egg holds a spirit! Her merit is boundless!"

Yun Yara stood in the shadows, clad in black robes. Her brows and eyes were as cold as trackless snow, her lips pressed into a line of extreme frigidity. She spoke not a word, merely staring at the image in the mirror, the depths of her eyes seemingly crusted over with a layer of frost so deep the bottom could not be seen.

Mo Han leaned back in the bone chair of the Nether Hall, idly toying with a demonic bone bead in his hand. He cast a glance at the scene in the mirror and suddenly burst into laughter.

The sound was unbridled and flamboyant, shaking the empty hall until the very earth veins vibrated beneath them.

"Hahahahaha—"

He laughed until he rocked back and forth, nearly falling from his chair, slapping her shoulder as he did so. "Truly astounding. One can be deified for this? The intellect of these people in the Immortal Realm is truly touching."

He turned his head to look at her, his tone roguish and arrogant: "In the past, you risked your life, carving out glory sword-stroke by sword-stroke. Yet now, she needs only an egg and an innocent face to effortlessly grind you into dust."

Yun Yara: "......"

She did not speak, but her fingertips tightened slightly, her knuckles turning white.

Mo Han, acting as if he had seen the funniest thing in the world, continued to laugh ceaselessly. "Look at you, look at you. Back then, you considered showing mercy under the blade a shame. And the result? Yun Lili couldn't even be bothered to draw her sword. A single move of 'I don't know how,' and she clears the entire field! This operation... I nearly ascended on the spot from the sheer absurdity."

"Especially that match against Xiao Yan..." He drawled, the corners of his eyes lifting with amusement. "The War God Xiao Yan. That brat stood there like a terrified spring chicken, not daring to move, not daring to speak a word too loudly, for fear of scaring that country girl."

"Do you not find it absurd to the point of hilarity?" He narrowed his eyes, his tone slowing down like a blade sliding across a throat. "How did you put it before? 'Only those with a flawless Dao Heart can win without fighting.' And now? She didn't fight, nor does she possess any Dao, yet she still won a hall full of applause."

Yun Yara slowly raised her eyes, her gaze cold as a frosty blade. "Have you laughed enough?"

Her voice was low and cold, like a sudden surge from a freezing spring in a dark valley. "Do you believe I can make you unable to laugh right now?"

Mo Han raised a brow, the tail of his eye lifting with innate, roguish mockery as he shrugged lazily. "If you don't try, how do you know I don't enjoy being beaten?"

Her eyes darkened. Just as she was about to strike, he suddenly leaned in, his entire body almost pressing against her brow, his voice so light it barely registered in her ear.

"...Indeed, I am sick."

He paused, the smile remaining on his lips, but he did not speak the latter half of the sentence.

—*Sick enough to bind you to my side, like a prisoner, yet also like... my only obsession.*

Yun Yara did not notice, assuming he was spouting nonsense again. She turned her head away coldly, disdainfully replying, "You are sick."

Mo Han smiled and did not argue further. Instead, he retreated to the bone chair, hooking one leg over the other lazily, lowering his eyes to toy with the bone bead, his finger joints distinct and elegant.

"Xiao Yan could not possibly have lost," Yun Yara said suddenly.

His movements paused slightly, but he did not look up. His voice rang out slowly, carrying an unsettling composure:

"Of course he didn't lose. He simply saw clearly—what is worth winning, and what should not be touched."

"You are too high up, your killing aura too heavy; no one dares approach. Yun Lili only needs to feign weakness, cry a little, smile a little, and a whole crowd paves the way for her."

His gaze held a smile that was not a smile as he whispered against her ear:

"So, you did not lose in strength. You lost because—your face is too cold. Cold enough that no one dares to cherish you."

Yun Yara's expression finally shifted, her gaze so morose and cold it seemed ready to strip bone from flesh. She raised a hand; though the bone sword did not appear, the sword intent surged forth.

She silently recalled the words her Master had taught her when she first drew her sword:

The sword strikes as the heart dictates. If the heart is already dead, ten thousand blades cannot harm it.

Only it was a pity... her heart was not yet completely dead.

Mo Han neither dodged nor retreated. He extended two fingers, pointing vaguely at his own forehead, his tone suddenly dropping low. "Come. Thrust the sword in. See if you can kill me."

The two remained in a standoff for several breaths before Yun Yara suddenly withdrew her hand and turned away in silence.

Mo Han gave a harrumph, his smiling tone returning to its roguish nature. "Don't look at me like that. Keeping you here is out of the kindness of my heart. If you go back, I fear you'll be stepped on as a stepping stone, unable to even die a clean death."

He stood and walked to her side, his tone carrying an unquestionable arrogance:

"Yun Yara, you can lose a match, but you cannot lose with such a lack of style. By staying with me now, at least you retain your backbone."

Yun Yara said coldly, "To speak of kidnapping with such high-sounding excuses... the Demon Race truly has skin thick enough to shock the world."

Mo Han laughed loudly. "Thank you for the compliment. I knew you didn't truly wish to leave."

At this moment, Yun Yara really, truly wanted to smash that Netherfire Mirror.

Chapter 12: The Livestream of Shame

Just as Yun Lili was swelling with indignation, prepared to voice her grievances regarding these three roosters who were becoming increasingly lawless with each passing day, a crisp *ding* suddenly resounded from the heavens above.

A semi-transparent mirror surface seemed to split open from the very air itself, floating before her eyes and emitting a soft, gentle glow.

It was a livestream window from the Heaven-Illuminating Mirror, hovering exactly three feet above the crown of her head.

"...What in the ghostly hells is this?" Lili was half a beat slow, still not realising what was transpiring.

But Moony had already let out a shriek: "Ahhh... Miss... look! We... we are being livestreamed!!"

Moony immediately fished a mirror out from her robes. With a flurry of frantic tapping and swiping, the mirror displayed the entire process of their recent great war with the chickens, and furthermore...

[Bullet Screen Barrage Incoming]

"Ahahahaha, that Spirit Egg is too cute! I'm absolutely in love!!"

"Is this... a female cultivator of the Lingxiao Sect? Why have I never seen her before?"

"The chickens are so fierce, the egg looks so fragrant, I desperately want to see the sequel!"

"Is the one with feathers stuck in her hair Fairy Yun Lili? Does anyone have her account handle? I want to follow her."

"Begging for a follow-up!!"

"......"

The comments surged like a torrential rain, flooding into Lili's personal page on the Immortal-Demon Net at lightning speed. Within a mere quarter of an hour, she was trending straight towards the top three of the monthly hot list.

Lili's mind went completely blank. She stared with a face full of bewilderment at the small, consciousness-formed round mirror floating in the air.

It was small, dark and inconspicuous, semi-transparent, with edges like smoke and mist—clearly not a physical entity.

Then she looked at the one Moony was holding. It was larger, physically tangible, and oval-shaped.

Moony stared unblinkingly at the mirror, her fingers flying as she tapped and swiped, the image on the mirror surface changing accordingly.

"What is this? Let me see?" Her curiosity surged, temporarily overriding her confusion.

She vaguely remembered that when she was climbing the Heaven Stairway back then, she seemed to have spotted two little immortal maids holding similar gadgets, reading storybooks or something of the sort.

She subconsciously reached out, wanting to switch off the mirror in Moony's hand. Unfortunately, this image was being livestreamed by someone else; she had no authority to terminate it.

"Tell me... if I were to slaughter these three chickens right this instant, would it still be too late?" She took a deep breath, yanked the chicken feathers from her hair, her expression a mix of ferocity and helplessness.

The bullet screen responded instantly:

"Dying of laughter! Are these two female cultivators really fighting chickens for an egg???"

"When she had three feathers stuck in her head, I nearly spat out my spirit tea!!"

"I could watch this egg-hatching livestream for a year!"

"I don't care about the egg, I just want to know what hair-protection spell they use. Pecked by chickens and still looking so fairy-like?"

"Isn't this Fairy Yun Lili? The one who angered Fairy Yun Yara into running away... Woo woo, I can't believe her persona is like this. So down-to-earth!"

"May I ask when the Spirit Egg will hatch? I want to make a reservation to spectate."

Moony had already collapsed on the ground with laughter. "Miss... you're famous. You are truly famous..."

Yun Lili hugged that Spirit Egg, her face the very picture of windswept chaos.

She grabbed Moony, pointing at the hazy black mirror surface in mid-air, then pointing at the obviously much prettier mirror in Moony's hand. "Moony, Little Moon, what the devil are these two things?"

Moony kindly explained. "This is the Immortal-Demon Net. Its full name is the 'Spiritual Consciousness Void Network System'. It was established by the Supreme Elder of the Tianxuan Sect using three hundred and sixty-five Heavenly Heart Divine Runes to lay out a Void Divine Web, connecting the Four Realms. Cultivators of all realms, as long as their spiritual roots are qualified, can operate the Heaven-Illuminating Mirror with their divine consciousness to open accounts, browse information, and even earn Immortal Qi through livestreams."

She added a supplementary sentence at the end. "Oh, right. The Heaven-Illuminating Mirror requires Spirit Stones to purchase."

Hearing this, Lili's mouth, which had been about to open, closed helplessly. "......"

She had been just about to ask how to get a Heaven-Illuminating Mirror.

She had no Spirit Stones!

At this moment, the bullet screen was still scrolling madly:

"I know that maid helping to protect the egg. Her name is Moony. I swept the floor with her in the Lingxiao Sect garden fifty years ago. By the way, she is too brave. I dub her the Sword Cultivator of the Poultry Realm!"

Lili: ".........."

What kind of nonsense was this?

* * * * *

Lingxiao Sect – Main Hall

Yun Zhou slammed his palm heavily upon the low table.

The bronze incense burner sitting atop it vibrated violently from the force, scattering fine grey ash all over his satin-patterned luxurious robes, yet he remained utterly oblivious to the mess.

"To think it has come to this... all over a single Spirit Egg!"

He spoke through gritted teeth, pointing a shaking finger at the suspended Heaven-Illuminating Mirror and roaring: "A legitimate daughter of the Yun family, making a spectacle of herself before the masses with dishevelled hair and chicken feathers stuck all over her head? What manner of propriety is this!"

The image in the mirror had long since shifted to the trending list of the Spirit Net.

The bullet screen comments on the video titled 'Chaos and Chickens: The Egg Protection Scene' were scrolling by at a flying pace, a blur of text mocking the dignity of his clan.

Zhou's face was an iron-green hue; spiritual power surged chaotically within his sleeves, seemingly on the verge of a violent eruption.

Beside him, Xiao Yan looked rather uncomfortable as well.

He lowered his eyes to look at that frozen frame: the girl with skewed clothes, two golden feathers stuck haphazardly in her hair, rolling all over the ground while hugging a Spirit Egg for dear life, while those three spirit chickens flapped furiously beside her...

He pursed his lips and said softly, "...Actually, it cannot be considered shameful. It is merely a little... undignified."

"You tell me... does that appearance befit the legitimate daughter of the Yun family? She doesn't even possess ten per cent of Yun Yara's grace."

Zhou was dressed in robes of silver gauze that flowed like smoke.

His aura was naturally sharp and imposing, and now that his anger was roused, he resembled ice blades hiding needles, condensing the air in the hall with a suffocating pressure.

As he spoke, he stood up, turning furiously toward the door. "No, this won't do. I'm going to grab her back right now and give her a good beating. Let's see if she dares to run wild again..."

"Wait." Xiao Yan finally spoke, reaching out a hand to block him.

Zhou paused, frowning. "Why do you stop me?"

Xiao Yan shook his head. His gaze was calm as water, yet his tone gathered a measure of seriousness. "Now that her fame has risen so sharply, if your actions are too heavy, it will backfire and burn you instead. Furthermore, rather than beating her, it would be better to find her a master who can suppress her temperament. Let her be properly educated and cultivate the Dao with a focused mind. It is surely better than you venting your anger like this."

Zhou froze. His brow slowly relaxed as the logic sank in, as if his mind had been awakened. He pondered for a moment, then gave a cold laugh. "You make it sound easy. With that kind of unbridled temperament, who can possibly suppress her?"

Xiao Yan paused slightly, a thought-provoking smile revealing itself at the corner of his lips. "In the Grand Immortal Sect Tournament, was there not someone who managed to suppress her just recently?"

Zhou's eyes lit up. As he came to his senses, he murmured to himself, "...Yu Sord."

"His sword strikes are steady and ruthless, his Dao Heart is firm and cold, and he is untouched by lust. He is exactly the right person to subdue her," Xiao Yan added faintly.

Zhou gazed at the girl's face in the mirror—covered in dust yet fiercely protecting the Spirit Egg—his emotions inexplicably complex.

It took a long time before he huffed, "That wretched girl has audacity that reaches the heavens. Indeed, she truly ought to be ground down properly by that Immortal Lord Yu..."

Xiao Yan sighed inwardly, daring not say more.

Naturally, he too had watched the livestream with heart palpitations.

He had never seen anyone force an immortal chicken to retreat again and again, only to be pecked until covered in chicken feathers in return. That scene... was indeed rather undignified for a cultivator.

But having said that, his impression of Yun Lili was actually not bad.

Although the girl was flighty and eccentric, she possessed great spiritual energy and her nature was not malicious; she simply lacked a master who could... suppress her wildness.

Zhou added a final sentence, his tone brooking no argument: "...Since it is so, I will have her enter the mountain immediately. She shall not refuse."

Xiao Yan sighed softly, whispering under his breath, "Let us hope she doesn't pack up and run away immediately."

* * * * *

The news of Yun Zhou's personal arrival at Mount Alioth had startled the entire Sword Inquiry Pavilion even before it manifested upon the Spirit Net.

Clad in robes of profound black and gold, with cloud-patterned embroidered sashes brushing the ground as he walked, Zhou stood before the mountain gate.

Although his expression was placid, his aura was so imposing that it forced the disciples guarding the gate to hold their breath, daring not to breathe too loudly.

Although the cultivators of the Sword Inquiry Pavilion did not involve themselves in worldly affairs, everyone knew—this Head of the Yun Family was never one to be trifled with, and he certainly would not ascend the mountain without grave cause.

"Immortal Lord Yun has arrived. The Pavilion Master awaits at the Cloud Terrace," an inner sect disciple announced, bowing respectfully.

Zhou nodded. His steps were swift as the wind; in mere moments, he had arrived at the Cloud Terrace. Mount Alioth was a place of high winds and cold moons.

Upon the clear terrace that stood ten thousand fathoms high, Yu Sord stood amidst the gale, his robes fluttering wildly like drifting clouds and swirling snow.

He offered no word of greeting, merely nodding slightly to Zhou before turning to take his seat.

Zhou dispensed with empty courtesies. With a brush of spiritual energy from his sleeve, he sat himself upon the jade couch opposite. He poured tea, drank a cup, and actually began to scrutinise his host first.

Yu Sord's expression was as calm as stagnant water, his brows and eyes cool as the distant, frost-laden mountains.

Only the green jade brush turning idly between his slender fingers paused occasionally, betraying a trace of faint impatience. It was an unspoken resistance, yet he did not flick his sleeves and leave.

Zhou suddenly laughed. "What? Am I annoying you already? If I don't speak, do you intend to sit like this until the end of time?"

Yu Sord did not speak. His gaze swept over the expression between Zhou's brows, and for some reason, he suddenly recalled a similar expression that had appeared in that livestream footage he had glimpsed.

He thought to himself, *They truly are biological siblings.*

He raised his brow slightly, his expression unchanged, yet the subtle movement caused Zhou's heart to pause.

This man is meticulous as dust, his thoughts deep as the abyss. Impossible to guess.

Zhou put away his smile and spoke directly. "I came up the mountain today for only one matter..." He paused, then continued, "Presumably, Immortal Lord Yu also knows that wretched girl, Yun Lili. Although she is the legitimate daughter of the Yun family, she was raised in the mortal countryside since childhood. Her nature is flighty and unbridled, and recently she has caused quite a stir... You have surely seen that farce of a livestream as well?"

Yu Sord neither nodded nor denied it, merely lifting the corner of his eye slightly, clearly a tacit admission.

Zhou paused for a word, a few degrees of gravity flashing in his eyes. "This halfway-found sister... I imagine I cannot control her. However, Xiao Yan offered me a reminder; presumably her immortal roots are tenacious, and it is time for someone to suppress her temperament."

"Since this girl received your guidance and protection during the Grand Immortal Sect Tournament, suppressing the various factions... if I were to hand her over to your tutelage, whether in cultivation or in tempering her nature, she ought to learn a thing or two."

Yu Sord finally moved. The brush landed on the table, his fingertip tapping it lightly with a soft sound.

He raised his eyes to look at Zhou.

There was no refusal in his eyes, nor acceptance; only the silence of mountain rocks beneath unmelting frost and snow.

Lonely, quiet.

That single glance was akin to winter water reflecting the silent mountains—ten thousand miles without a ripple—yet it silently weighed the sincerity and gravity of the request.

This time, Zhou did not push.

He merely smiled and said, "With that virtue of hers, if you are unwilling, I shall seek someone else. Only it is a pity... others may not be able to suppress her. You, on the other hand, have won her heartfelt admiration."

Yu Sord remained silent for a long while, the green jade brush in his hand turning no more. He suddenly thought of Yun Lili's appearance that day—covered in mess and dirt, yet fiercely protecting the Spirit Egg with her life. Foolish, laughable, yet also...

Stubborn to the point of pitifulness.

The wind blew from the corner of the terrace, ruffling the hair at his temples. He finally spoke, his voice cool as the moon: "Acceptable."

Zhou seemed to turn a deaf ear, continuing to speak to himself, "If Immortal Lord Yu is busy, it is understandable, or... *Uh?*"

"The matter entrusted. I... accept."

Zhou's eyes lit up. He rose slowly, shaking his sleeves to straighten them. "Excellent. Then I shall trouble Immortal Lord Yu."

He walked a few steps, then suddenly turned back, his tone shifting to one of profound meaning: "Since the Immortal Sovereign cultivates the Path of Emotionlessness, then I need not worry that you will be vexed to death by that girl."

Yu Sord did not reply.

He watched the figure in wide, fluttering sleeves depart into the distance. At the corner of his lips, an arc that was barely there suddenly revealed itself.

Chapter 13: The Sentencing of the Lazy Disciple

Following the spectacular success of the **"Spiritual Egg and Three-Chicken Fiasco"** that had gone viral across the Immortal and Demonic web.

Yun Lili was enjoying a period of immense, widespread **acclaim**, effectively serving as the living promotional image for the younger generation of the Immortal Sect. Yet, after only a few brief days of basking in this ephemeral glory, disaster crept stealthily upon her.

This day, she was in the secluded thatched hut behind the mountain, innocently discussing the intricate secrets of egg incubation with Moony, when a flash of golden light suddenly illuminated the sky.

 A gold talisman plummeted down from the heavens, instantly igniting upon arrival and coalescing into a voice imbued with chilling, undeniable authority:

"Yun Lili, cease your current caprice and scurry back to the Main Hall. There is urgent business requiring your presence."

—It was Yun Zhou's voice, and his tone was as cold and unforgiving as severe mountain frost.

Yun Lili's face instantly drained to the colour of ashes, and her demeanour clearly articulated the four words: *Life is entirely devoid of all meaning.*

Outside the Main Hall, Yun Zhou stood rigidly upon the steps, his hands clasped behind his back, his face as still and dark as deep water.

Xiao Yan was leaning against the stone balustrade nearby, his expression deeply awkward and nuanced, like a man who had just been struck by celestial lightning and was too traumatised to comment.

"Ahem…" Yun Lili drew out her voice, attempting a long, tentative approach. "Might I politely enquire if your summons pertains to offering commendation for the absolutely sterling performance I put on during the Grand Immortal Tournament?"

"…I summoned you because I intended to shave away your spiritual root and simultaneously amputate your lower limbs."

Yun Zhou's voice was utterly calm and level, yet his words were chilling to the bone.

Xiao Yan couldn't help but let out a dry cough. He was keenly aware that his ignominious retreat during his bout with her had rendered him the persistent laughingstock of the entire Immortal Sect.

Yun Zhou merely offered him a severe, sidelong glance: "Is your throat experiencing some form of profound discomfort?"

Xiao Yan: "…Ahem." He immediately retreated three full paces, as if avoiding an infectious disease.

Yun Lili sensed the dangerously sharp atmosphere. Her feet subtly edged backward, preparing a discreet exit, only to be stopped by Yun Zhou's icy command: "**Halt.**"

He approached her step by slow, deliberate step, his voice compressed like a chilling wind sweeping through a snow-laden mountain pass: "Do you now believe that merely because your paltry spiritual power has marginally increased, you are suddenly authorised to indulge in unbridled caprice?"

"What grievous act have I committed, I ask you?!" Yun Lili cried out in protest, feigning utter innocence.

"Enough," Yun Zhou flicked his sleeve, his spiritual **pressure** surging outward. "From this very day forward, you shall formally take a master, enter serious, rigorous cultivation, curb your reckless nature, and cease all idle commentary."

"I refuse."

Before the word could fully leave her mouth, the **Spirit-Sealing Jade** had appeared in Yun Zhou's hand: "If you dare utter the word 'no' one more time, I shall seal your spiritual mouth for three full days."

"…" Yun Lili was momentarily stunned into enraged silence, her teeth grinding audibly: "And whose unwanted tutelage must I endure?"

Yun Zhou coldly delivered the three words: "**Yu Sord.**"

At this stark statement, the profound stillness returned, as if the very air had crystallised.

Xiao Yan let out another, very genuine cough—this time, it was authentic—and discreetly turned his back, too cautious to witness the spectacle of her profound shock.

Yun Lili violently lifted her head, her eyes wide with shock and pure, burning disbelief: "…You utter scoundrel, Yun Zhou."

Yun Zhou raised his hand, halting any further protest: "You need not speak further. This is not a request for consultation; it is a direct order of notification."

Yun Lili bit her lip, knowing she could not argue her way out of the decree, yet unable to resist a final, weak retort: "I refuse. Learning the blade under his tutelage… is simply too utterly exhausting and arduous."

Her 'Star Vapour' sword, she reasoned, was perfectly adequate for purely aesthetic purposes and occasional, light-duty intimidation.

Yun Zhou raised a sarcastic eyebrow, a faint, mocking curve playing on his lips: "Are you not exceedingly talented at the aerial hug-and-egg-protection manoeuvre? And you have the **gall** to harass three chickens simultaneously; why, then, can you not muster the strength to lift a sword and apply yourself?"

Yun Lili was struck dumb by his accurate summary of her behaviour, lowering her head in defeated silence. The atmosphere grew increasingly oppressive.

Yun Zhou slowly descended the steps, his tone placid, yet the weight of his command felt like a crushing mountain: "Remember this: Yu Sord does not condescend to teach just anyone. His willingness to continue guiding your cultivation and swordsmanship, already a public spectacle, is a massive exception to his rule. To refuse further would be simple arrogance and a failure to recognise your immense fortune."

"I merely… merely felt that…" Yun Lili's voice was weak, still clinging to a thread of lingering reluctance.

Yun Zhou coldly interrupted her: "Do you perhaps feel that his tutelage during the Grand Tournament was too cold-blooded, too ruthlessly unfeeling, and devoid of common human courtesy? Then why do you omit mention of your own contributions? Sleeping five times in three days, mastering one sword form only to instantly forget three others— and then daring to blame the master for your profound shortcomings?"

Yun Lili's lips moved slightly in a futile attempt at defense, but she offered no further protest.

Her hands, which hung at her sides, subtly clenched into fists, her brows tightly furrowed, and her eyes darkening like dust settling in a shadowed corner.

Yun Zhou, seeing that she had no further substantial objection, turned to depart, but suddenly paused and looked back, as if recalling a vital detail:

"You claimed just now that he was unfeeling and cold-blooded, did you not?"

Yun Lili nodded reluctantly.

Yun Zhou's gaze was deep and knowing.

His tone softened marginally, yet the implication intensified: "Splendid, then. You shall witness, with your own eyes, how he maintains his celebrated emotional detachment towards you to the bitter end. Only then will you truly commit to studying the blade and finally excise that debilitating root of sloth."

He was relying entirely on Yu Sord's infamous reputation for being unfeeling and unyielding, confident that this forced hardship would forge her.

Yun Lili: "……"

Her face fell, her entire being deflating like a punctured spiritual egg.

Seeing her profound dejection, Yun Zhou finally softened his tone slightly: "The air on Mount Yuheng is cold as a blade. If you cannot endure it, return quickly, lest you freeze the excellent **honour** of my Yun family door and embarrass us further."

"…" Yun Lili's mouth twitched uncontrollably. *She mentally cursed him: This is surely not the standard behaviour of a genuine blood brother.*

Yun Zhou flicked his sleeve, turning to stride quickly away, his silhouette as resolute and unyielding as a mountain peak.

Yun Lili was left alone in the hall, her shoulders slumped, her face etched with profound misery. She looked out the window. The immense shadow of Mount Yuheng loomed in the distance, stained gold and red by the sunset, standing like an insurmountable, formidable heavenly chasm.

* * * * *

That very night, Yun Lili began the urgent process of packing her meagre luggage, meticulously preparing for an immediate, secret **bolt** from the Yun Manor.

The moonlight washed the outer bamboo grove with a stark clarity. The space outside her small loft was extraordinarily quiet; even the slightest breeze seemed utterly reluctant to make a sound.

Yun Lili tiptoed and pushed open the side door. She wore her ordinary casual clothes, only a slightly ill-fitting, rough vine served as an improvised belt around her waist, giving her the distinct, pathetic look of a refugee fleeing a sudden, devastating famine. She stole a final, hurried glance back at the high palace walls, a look of grim, defiant resolve flashing in her eyes, and softly muttered under her breath:

"I shall simply renounce this entire family, if need be! Lingxiao Sect, Celestial Lord Yun Zhou, the whole lot of you can collectively go straight to blazes..."

She had only managed to take a few tentative, cautious steps when she felt a sudden, profound chill travel down her spine; a wave of icy coldness shot straight up from her neck to the crown of her head.

"Miss, where precisely are we headed this evening?"

The voice detonated like a sudden, chilling whisper of a phantom directly behind her ear.

Yun Lili spun around violently, her soul almost leaping out of her body. In the pale moonlight stood a small, familiar figure, burdened by a bundle significantly larger than she was, clearly bulging with contents, signifying a carefully premeditated plan.

Her face wore an expression of utterly innocent enthusiasm, as though she were merely enquiring about the best roadside inn for the night's lodging.

"Moony?! Are you, by some chance, attempting to give me a fatal fright!" Yun Lili hissed in a low shriek, so shocked that her own small bundle nearly slipped from her grasp, ready to be deployed as an improvised weapon.

"Miss, you are running away, are you not? I have already packed everything! Five days' worth of dry rations, the three prize chickens, and the highly essential Spiritual Egg are all secured inside," Moony said, patting the bulging pack with a proud, self-satisfied look, as if she had just executed a masterful espionage mission.

"You..." Yun Lili was too stunned to formulate a coherent sentence, managing only to clamp her hand over Moony's mouth, glancing around in paranoid terror. The night air was cool, the bamboo shadows swayed, and even the moonlight seemed to be silently observing her criminal endeavour. Her heart hammered wildly, and a fine, cold sweat began to prickle her skin.

"Are you deliberately trying to scare me to death! Why do you walk without making a sound, and why did you prepare the luggage beforehand, without informing me?!"

Moony emitted a muffled "Mmmph," her eyes wide and staring beneath the covering hand.

Yun Lili bit her lip, finally releasing her hand. She spoke in a strained whisper: "Since you already know, I cannot possibly, in good conscience, leave you behind to face punishment… Come, run with me!"

"Where does Miss intend to run to?" Moony asked, her enthusiasm bubbling uncontrollably.

"Anywhere at all! Anywhere that is not frigidly cold, as long as it is not Mount Yuheng," Yun Lili declared, her teeth grinding audibly. "I would sooner willingly return to the backward Yun Family Village than ascend Mount Yuheng to take a master."

Moony blinked slowly: "Mount Yuheng? The Hall of Heavenly Sword? Is that not Celestial Lord Yu Sord's highly sought-after immortal abode?"

"It is," Yun Lili sighed softly, her voice barely audible, as if she feared disturbing some deep, immutable destiny.

Moony frowned faintly: "Is that not an immense stroke of fortune? Countless serious cultivators dream of such an opportunity…"

"Silence!" Yun Lili laughed hysterically out of sheer frustration, thinking: *Who, exactly, is the mistress and who is the maidservant here, giving unsolicited life advice?*

"Fine, well, let us just make a quick escape, then." Moony stopped arguing, hoisting the large, cumbersome pack onto her shoulder, poised and ready for immediate action.

"…" Yun Lili was speechless. She knew this path was destined to be utterly arduous, yet her maidservant seemed far more capable and confident than she was.

She looked hard at Moony. A sudden, unexpected warmth welled up in her heart, though it was quickly followed by a fresh wave of panic regarding their impending capture.

Regardless of the danger, she could not allow Moony to face punishment by association. Since her companion was already present, the plan simply had to be drastically upgraded.

She lowered her voice and delivered her instructions: "We take the small, winding forest paths. Do not alert the night patrols. We must traverse the Sunset Glow Slope, then discreetly bypass the Flying Star Pool. We will take refuge in Yun Family Village first, and only then shall we make further, more detailed plans."

"Awaiting your command!" Moony was brimming with more frantic energy than her mistress.

The two slipped into the night, one after the other. Beneath the pale, spying moonlight, a single, distressed silhouette and a small, excessively cheerful maidservant were quietly fleeing down the mountain.

Neither of them realised that shortly after their hurried departure, a single thread of cold, clear divine sense swept silently and efficiently through the deep bamboo grove, like a frosty star falling into the soundless night rain.

One from Mount Yuheng, after all, rarely needs to condescend to descend the mountain in person.

* * * * *

No sooner had they stepped beyond the Cloud Gate than the heavens and earth shuddered violently. A spiritual barrier, etched with intricate azure runes, suddenly roared to life and unfurled, blocking their entire escape route with a blinding flash.

Then, a snow-white silhouette emerged slowly from the heavy mist.

Yu Sord, clad in pristine, snow-white Immortal robes, his long hair secured by a crown, stood perfectly still outside the barrier. His expression was utterly placid. A subtle breeze passed behind him, his robes flowed majestically like cloud-mist, and his spiritual aura was frigid as frost.

He did not utter a single word. He merely raised one hand towards Yun Lili.

An invisible surge of spiritual energy instantly enveloped her, lifting her clean off the ground. She was forcefully "escorted" upward as if being retrieved like a small, spiritual cat, in a posture that was deeply undignified and completely out of her control.

He lightly waved his sleeve. The barrier shimmered once, and in an instant, he had bundled her up and teleported away, leaving behind a completely stunned, bewildered, and wide-eyed Moony.

II. The Viral Sensation

Just as Yun Lili was moodily squatting on a stone platform atop Mount Yuheng, sighing profoundly at the endless, cold sea of clouds, the cultivation world below had erupted into utter, joyful chaos.

The residual image in the Spiritual Mirror had not yet faded. That single scene—the Celestial Lord Yu personally intervening to "escort" the

Cloud family's legitimate daughter up the mountain as if she were a small, struggling cat—had been witnessed in excruciating, meme-worthy detail by the elders and disciples of every major sect. It instantly spread, becoming the single biggest piece of gossip in the entire Immortal Realm.

The comments section of the Immortal Web immediately exploded. The scrolling text rained down like spiritual droplets, layer upon dense layer, scrolling at impossible speeds:

Hahaha, she was actually hauled away! Is Celestial Lord Yu accepting a disciple or capturing a rogue spirit!

I wish someone would haul me like that, just once… Celestial Lord Yu's aura, ooh, why is he both cold AND incredibly alluring!

That moment when Yun Lili was hauled up the mountain is utterly epic; who has the screen capture? I need it for a meme!

Aaaah, this is forced cultivation; I am insanely jealous of her misfortune…

——

Many cultivators were equally sour and envious:

I'm utterly green with envy… Celestial Lord Yu never accepts disciples. How on earth did she acquire such profound good fortune?

It's simply because she's born with a Heavenly Spiritual Root; naturally, she's different and entitled to special treatment…

——

And of course, those who couldn't resist fanning the flames:

These two, one a firecracker, one an iceberg—a perfect cosmic collision! The sequel is guaranteed to be excellent drama.

Celestial Maiden Lili probably still doesn't realise she's become the number one trending topic in the entire Immortal Realm, has she?

——

In just half a day, the keywords **#CelestialLordYuHaulsMaidenUpMountain**, **#TheCloudDaughter'sDiscipleship**, and **#IcebergAndKitten** dominated the top three spots on the Immortal Web's trending charts.

Furthermore, idle cultivators who had nothing better to do cropped and edited the Spiritual Mirror footage, adding voiceovers, subtitles, and narration. A short video titled **'Immortal Realm Famous Scenes: Yu Sord's Hauling Compilation'** quickly soared to the top of the Spiritual Light Billboard, garnering over a hundred thousand views in a single hour.

As for the main perpetrator—

Yun Lili, hugging a handful of spiritual fruit, was squatting miserably on a stone platform on Mount Yuheng, her face etched with profound gloom.

She was completely oblivious to the fact that her grumpy little face had already been screenshotted into countless spiritual pictures, captioned with phrases like "Grumpy Kitten" and quickly circulating across major cultivation forums, inner disciple networks, and gossip **sections**.

Her entire "forced discipleship" spectacle had instantly become the Immortal Realm's viral meme of the year:

——

Over ten thousand likes, comments overflowing, memes currently in production.

——

Yu Sord, finally receiving a tentative spiritual slip from a disciple, silently viewed one of the notorious screen captures:

The image showed Yun Lili, clutched by the spiritual sense he had dispatched, her small face frozen in shock, her legs bicycling wildly, her robes flapping, looking precisely like a small, indignant wildcat being retrieved from a tree. The captions read: ***'Celestial Lord Yu Personally Captures Rogue!'*** and ***'Even Icebergs Haul Cats?!'***

Yu Sord: "……"

He remained silent for three full breaths, then slipped the spiritual slip into his sleeve. His expression unchanged, he rose from his seat and walked away. No one was privileged enough to witness the faint, almost imperceptible curve of self-satisfaction that touched his lips.

Meanwhile, on the Immortal Web, the discussion surrounding "What sort of spark will this peculiar Master and Disciple pair generate?" had only just begun.

Chapter 14: Candied Hawthorns on the Precipice

Mount Alioth – The Summit

The peak of Mount Alioth was wreathed in ethereal clouds and mist, an island floating in a sea of white.

A small pavilion stood perched precariously upon the precipice, bathed in the rosy hues of dawn that dyed the fog in layers of soft colour.

Yun Lili stood within the pavilion, her brow furrowed with palpable anxiety. She paced back and forth like a trapped beast or a caged bird, her entire face practically screaming the words: "Let me out immediately."

She muttered under her breath, "Does this Immortal Lord Yu intend for me to dine on the wind and sleep in the dew here for three years, relying on breathing mist to become an immortal? Before I've even mastered a single Daoist art, I'll have practised my soul right out of my body!"

Suddenly, she halted.

She scratched her head, smoothed the creases on her cuffs, and attempted to sit down, only to spring back up instantly as if a thunder talisman were hidden beneath her buttocks.

Her mouth moved in a ceaseless stream of complaints: "No, no, this won't do. If this continues, I shall surely suffer internal injuries from sheer boredom... Is there no one coming to save the scene?"

The mist shifted slightly. A light chuckle drifted from the forest, the voice warm as jade yet carrying the distinct, languid air of a noble scion, like a pebble cast into a clear spring, creating faint ripples.

"Tsk, keep your voice down. You're so noisy; if you keep making such a ruckus, the mountain ghosts will invite you for tea."

Yun Lili spun around violently, narrowing her eyes in vigilance. "...Who is there?"

The mist gradually dispersed, revealing a figure treading upon the clouds.

The youth was clad in robes whiter than snow, carrying a green-edged longsword on his back. His brows were picturesque, yet the corner of his lips held a smirk he made no effort to conceal.

"So you really are here." He raised a brow slightly, walking into the pavilion with natural ease. "I thought Immortal Lord Yu would have locked you up at the foot of the mountain, yet here I find you in the spot with the finest scenery."

"Xie Wuchen?" Yun Lili blinked, a look of suspicion on her face. "Why have you come as well?"

She recognised him—the Chief Disciple of the Lingxiao Sword Pavilion, ranked within the top ten of sword cultivators, a genius and famous to boot.

However... compared to the rumoured image of a cold, solemn sword immortal, the person she saw before her was clearly an idle, wealthy loafer.

Xie Wuchen spread his hands. "I heard you were hauled up the mountain by Yu Sord to become his apprentice. As I count as half a senior to you, surely I must come to offer my condolences—ah, I mean, comfort—to the little fairy?"

Lili rolled her eyes. "Just admit you came to watch the show."

"I am wrongly accused." Xie Wuchen raised an eyebrow, fishing a bundle from his sleeve. "I even brought a greeting gift."

As he spoke, he skilfully unwrapped the cloth, revealing a stick of crystal-clear candied hawthorns, still emitting a faint spiritual mist.

"...What kind of divine operation is this?" Lili's gaze was hooked; she couldn't help but reach out. "Where did this come from?"

"The market at the foot of the mountain," Xie Wuchen said as if it were the most natural thing in the world. "Originally, I wanted to bring a pot of wine to liven things up, but it was confiscated the moment I entered the mountain gate. Alas... I had to make do with candied hawthorns."

Yun Lili took a bite, half-believing and half-doubting. Sweet and sour intermingled, wreathed in spiritual qi; it was actually rather delicious.

She mumbled around the hawthorn, "If you want me to apprentice, you'd be better off finding that Fairy Yun Yara. Immortal Lord Yu said he'd teach me, but I haven't seen even a shadow of him. What kind of immortal am I worshipping here..."

Xie Wuchen glanced at her and laughed. "That is no ordinary immortal; that is the Iceberg Immortal Lord, the most un-provokable being in the entire Immortal Realm. Do you know how many people would break their heads squeezing in just to bow at his door? And now that it's your turn, you complain that he has evaporated from the mortal world?"

Lili's eyes were full of resentment. "He isn't human; he is a god—"

"Mind your words, Little Junior Sister," Xie Wuchen mumbled around his own candied hawthorn, smiling vaguely. "If this reaches his ears—"

Before he could finish, a wisp of azure-patterned sword intent suddenly descended from the sky outside the pavilion. It was extremely faint and light, yet it caused the wind of the entire mountain to congeal, akin to frost descending from the Ninth Heaven.

Xie Wuchen shut his mouth immediately and gave a dry cough. "...He heard that."

Yun Lili, with the candied hawthorn still in her mouth, looked as though she had lost the will to live. "I want to go home."

Xie Wuchen silently patted her shoulder, speaking with grave earnestness: "The only thing you can do now is finish the candy quickly to replenish your blood and save your little life."

He paused, then added the final blow: "Once he appears, there won't even be candy to eat."

* * * * *

The Demon Realm, Outside the Nether Palace

The night wind cut like a blade, and the mountains behind the Nether Palace were devoid of light. Yun Yara leaned against a rough tree trunk, gasping for breath, the longsword in her hand still dripping with fresh blood. Behind her, black shadows surged like a tide, crashing towards her in wave after wave.

Her eyes were a desolate void of cold silence.

Gritting her teeth, she hurled a talisman light; seizing the brief gap created by the explosion, she leapt atop a rock face, climbing the vines and darting through the forest.

This was already her third escape attempt from the Nether Palace.

She had long since memorised the *Soul-Chasing Curses, Bone-Crushing Seals,* and *Absolute Earth Nets* laid out against her, stepping precisely upon their flaws to depart, all for this single gamble today.

If she did not escape now, she would truly never leave.

Her figure was dishevelled, the corners of her robes torn to shreds, her breathing erratic and shallow. Finally, she halted before a mountain forest shrouded in thick fog.

* * * * *

The Demonic Mist Forest.

She had once heard the elders say that this forest was hallucinogenic to the extreme; of those who entered by mistake, not one in ten survived.

Yet at this moment, she had no other path.

The mist was dense as a cocoon, roiling like the sea. She took a single step inside, and the face of heaven and earth instantly changed.

The wind whistled in her ears like a weeping ghost.

Shadows flickered indistinctly through the trees—one moment taking the form of her childhood bosom friend, the next transforming into the sneering elders of the Nether Palace. Familiar faces floated in the mist one after another, their eyes filled with anguish or hatred, seeming both real and illusory.

"You killed us."

"You shouldn't exist at all."

"Kill her!"

Roars rose from all sides as countless demonic shadows lunged from the trees.

Yun Yara's gaze remained clear. With a cold shout, her sword light flashed like a halo as she swung a horizontal slash.

"Get... out!"

The sword light flashed like snow, cleaving through three shadows, yet five more immediately rushed in to fill the gap.

Blood splattered across the wild grass. Demon creatures with claws like iron lunged from the darkness, tearing open her arm and staining her sleeves red with blood.

"Tsk..."

Her breathing grew heavier, yet the depths of her eyes grew colder and more condensed.

She retreated step by step, yet no matter how she moved, she could not see the end.

Finally, she retreated to the forest's edge.

A sheer cliff cut across her path. Below the cliff, a deep valley churned with black clouds; ghostly wails and the howling of wolves rose from below as if ascending from hell itself.

"One step forward lies the destruction of body and soul."

A voice drifted down from high above, low and cool, landing with the weight of cold iron.

Yun Yara spun around abruptly.

A figure in ink-black descended slowly from the heavens, his long hair brushing the wind.

His features were handsome, yet piercingly cold. He stood in mid-air, the depths of his eyes sinking like a deep pool.

"Mo Han."

Yun Yara gritted her teeth, fury erupting from her, completely unsurprised by his appearance.

Mo Han gave a faint smile, pointing to the cliff below. "Fallen Mist Valley. Do you know that beneath this cliff sleeps the Ancient Demon of Absolute Void? It has not woken for ten thousand years. If you jump, I fear you will be reduced to ash, bones and all."

Yun Yara huffed coldly. "So?"

Having spoken, she raised her hand and struck with her sword, the momentum fierce and sharp, without a shred of hesitation.

Mo Han said nothing. He merely raised a hand to block, his wide sleeves fluttering as spiritual power flowed into a shield, dissolving her offensive completely.

Yun Yara struck again and again, yet he remained purely on the defensive, never attacking. There was even a look of forbearance and pity in his eyes.

He had thought that after a period of touring the mountains and waters together, she would stay for him...

"Cut the chat, fight if you want." Yun Yara unleashed a continuous barrage of sword techniques, yet she could not touch even half an inch of Mo Han.

The black figure dodged her attacks easily with a few flashes of movement. His physique was elegant, his ink-black hair scattering in the wind.

His long, narrow eyes were wicked and charming, staring at her tightly like prey, yet he was in no hurry.

"Why do you not strike?" She was attacked by anxiety and rage.

"There is no need to strike." Against her, he had no desire to use force.

Yun Yara did not appreciate the sentiment in the slightest. "Get out of my way."

"Return with me." He reached out a hand towards her, his wide sleeves snapping in the wind, looking both bewitching and wicked.

"In your dreams!" Yun Yara launched several more moves at him, shouting, "Don't even think about taking me back to the Nether Palace."

Mo Han gave a low chuckle, speaking heavily, "If you were not Yun Yara, if you had never come to the Demon Realm, I could have..."

"Silence!"

Yun Yara shook violently.

The blade of her sword abruptly veered, the tip turning to point directly at her own heart.

Mo Han's expression changed instantly. "What are you doing?"

He recognised that sword. It was no ordinary blade, but a Divine Sword capable of slaying demons and devils, named **'Frost Sorrow'** (*Shuang'ai*).

"Do not come closer." Yun Yara pressed the sword a fraction deeper against her own fair neck, her face solemn and cold.

"You are mad!" Mo Han's eyes widened enormously. One hand instinctively reached forward, attempting to grab her.

Yun Yara took a step back in tandem, threatening coldly, "If you do not retreat, I shall be buried with this demonic cliff!"

Suddenly, Mo Han fell silent for a moment. Then, he laughed lightly, an expression that could topple the masses. "Don't be foolish. Come here quickly, come back with me."

"You and your demon soldiers, stand back!" Yun Yara shouted loudly.

"You..." Mo Han seemed to be gradually losing his patience.

His long fingers were just forming a seal in the air, intending to pull her back to his side by force, when the scene before his eyes changed abruptly.

"Forget it!" Yun Yara roared in rage. With a turn of her hand, she threw her body backward in a leap without a shred of hesitation!

"Yun Yara!"

Shock and fury mingled in Mo Han's voice. He moved instantly to pursue, but was held back in a death grip by a guard behind him. "Your Highness, absolutely not! Below that cliff is..."

"Scram!"

He struck with his palm, sending the guard flying and vomiting blood. Mo Han hesitated no longer. Spreading both sleeves, his long sword curling the wind, he hurled himself down after her without a moment's delay!

The mountain wind howled, and the demonic fog roiled. One black, one white—the two figures vanished abruptly into the abyss of the ten-thousand-fathom deep valley.

* * * * *

The light of day lingered on the precipice of dissolution, the dusk beginning to settle heavily.

Shadows flickered across the surface of the bronze mirror, reflecting the urgent reports held within.

A disciple clad in silver robes strode hurriedly into the hall, dropping to one knee with a voice that trembled slightly. "Reporting to the Sect Master. At the intersection of the Immortal and Demon Realms—Fallen Mist Valley—scouts have used secret arts to sense the aura of Fairy Yun Yara."

The hall fell into an instant silence.

Upon the high seat, the Sect Master of Lingxiao, Yun Wuntang, who had been sitting as steady as a mountain, knit his brow into a tight frown upon hearing these words, shedding his usual air of jovial nonchalance.

He asked in a deep voice, "Is it confirmed to be Yun Yara?"

Yun Wuntang rose slowly.

His cloak shifted like dark clouds pressing down upon a night sea.

His gaze was deep and abyssal as he looked toward the Cloud Screen Immortal Map in the distance, as if attempting to pierce through the barrier and gaze directly at the borderlands of the Demon Realm.

"The scouts dare not speak falsely. There are indeed residual traces of Fairy Yun Yara's aura. She appears to have left the area within the last two days, and following that..."

"...Entered the Demon Realm." Yun Wuntang completed the latter half of the sentence lightly, yet his voice was already heavy as the calm before a mountain storm.

The deacon remained prostrated on the ground, daring not to breathe loudly.

For a time, the hall was so silent that even the sound of incense ash falling was clearly audible.

Yun Wuntang stood before the window, watching the drifting clouds in the high heavens, silent for a long while.

He had once established the palace rules: no mortal attachments, no favouritism. Yet at this moment, it felt as though the bottom of his heart was being slowly sliced open by a fine, keen blade—

That was the daughter he had raised with his own hands; to say his heart did not ache would be a lie.

Now she had trespassed into the Demonic Mist Forest and penetrated deep into the Demon Realm... What he feared was not that she had been abducted by someone, but that she had walked in *herself*.

It was her own choice.

She had chosen to turn her back on the Immortal Path, chosen to be disappointed in him, her "adoptive father," perhaps even to hate him.

"The Dao Heart loses its balance; a single thought becomes a demon," he murmured low.

He exhaled slowly, his voice dropping. "Fallen Mist Valley... it is already the critical limit. Exiting the Demonic Mist Forest leads directly to that cliff; ten *zhang* further lies the intersection of Immortals and Demons. With the slightest carelessness, both realms could be shaken."

Whispers began to ripple through the hall.

"Could Fairy Yun Yara have been abducted?"

"That day she left on her sword in a fit of anger; perhaps it was a moment of impulse..."

"Impossible. Fairy Yun Yara is the pride of our Lingxiao Sect..."

"Indeed, she has slain so many demons in the past. How could she possibly..."

Hearing this, Yun Wuntang shed his usual amiable facade. His gaze turned abruptly cold as he shouted to stop the voices: "All of you, hold your tongues."

He turned, speaking heavily, "If she has truly lost her way... then that would not be an abduction; it would be a fall from grace. As an inner disciple of the Lingxiao Sect, her status is special. If a single thought turns to evil and her Dao Heart is dyed black... she will not be the only one destroyed."

In this moment, fear surfaced in the bottom of Yun Wuntang's heart for the first time.

He did not fear her wandering into the Demon Realm by mistake; he feared that once the Heart Demon took hold, she would no longer be willing to turn back.

To the side, a Deputy Palace Master asked coldly, "Shall we select men to descend into the valley and retrieve her?"

Yun Wuntang was silent for a moment before finally shaking his head slowly.

"We must not act rashly. That is Fallen Mist Valley; we cannot startle the snake in the grass."

He frowned, puzzled. Since Yun Yara was so close to the Demon Realm, it was impossible for the Demon Realm to be unaware of it, or even to have no reaction whatsoever.

"First, probe the attitude of the Demon Realm. If she is truly within their borders, it is impossible for them to be completely silent."

Now that she had revealed her tracks in Fallen Mist Valley—the most bizarre zone at the intersection of the two realms, where day and night were impermanent and demonic mist bred freely—it was known as the "Valley of Illusions."

If one's mortal heart was not steadfast, one would fall into the illusions of the Heart Demon and lose oneself.

Of course, he feared she had been taken, but he still held onto a sliver of hope.

"Summon Yun Zhou, Xie Wuchen, and Elder Ling Yu to come for council immediately."

His voice was steady as thunder, finally setting the tone with a single command.

The disciples outside the hall received the order and departed, their footsteps hurried as the wind.

Yun Wuntang remained standing motionless.

Gone was the joking demeanour of ordinary days; his brow was furrowed, his hands gently clenched into fists.

It was the most silent anxiety of a father.

He gazed toward the East, his eyes unable to hide the exhaustion and pain within.

"Yara... if you are still willing to return, as your father, I will spare no cost... but if you have truly fallen to the devil..."

His voice cut off abruptly. After a long while, he let out a low, deep sigh.

Chapter 15: The Heart Demon in the Fog

Deep within Fallen Mist Valley, here, heaven and earth were bereft of light.

Shadows loomed in ominous clusters, the fog was black as ink, and the wind howled like the shrieking of ghosts—biting and sharp as a blade, chilling one to the bone.

Yun Yara stumbled through this dense, suffocating fog.

The world before her eyes flickered between dimness and darkness, teetering on the boundary of a nightmare.

Twisted branches reached out like ghostly hands, hooking and tearing at the hem of her robes.

The ground was muddy, wet, and cold; her footsteps fell without a sound, swallowed by the mire. Beside her ears, the low weeping of women and children mingled with the soft chuckling of malicious spirits.

She could distinguish neither distance nor direction, truth nor falsehood.

Her arms had already been torn open by sharp claws.

Blood mixed with the mist, staining her fingertips crimson. Yet those demonic shadows surged forward like an endless tide.

A slash of her sword would shatter them into nothingness, only for them to coalesce anew behind her—more of them, and closer than before.

Her breathing grew ragged and chaotic. Her knees went soft, and she nearly collapsed.

The longsword in Yun Yara's hand was already coated in dark red blood mixed with unknown slime.

Her robes were tattered, her hair wet and dishevelled, and a mixture of sweat and blood trickled coldly down her temples.

Her breath came in short gasps, yet before her eyes remained endless black shadows, moving with terrifying speed.

They surged in wave after wave, ceaseless and boundless, like vicious waves threatening to swallow a lone boat.

"Die!" She gave a low roar, swinging her sword in a horizontal slash, the light of the blade flashing like snow.

But what she struck was merely a phantom.

Amongst those demonic shadows, some were enemies she had slain in the past; some were strangers she did not know; there even appeared her own cold reflection, the corner of its lips curled in mockery: *"Heh... you can protect nothing. So what if you kill?"*

She gritted her teeth and attacked again.

The sword in her hand danced without pause, sword *qi* tumbling and whistling as it broke the wind, yet it was all in vain.

Those demonic shadows were like mist, like water—slashing did not disperse them, driving them did not banish them.

As the ones in front vanished, those behind surged forward.

She felt as though she had fallen into a cycle of reincarnation; with every strike, her mind grew weaker by a fraction, her steps heavier by a degree.

Finally, her knees gave way.

She collapsed into the thick fog, the tip of her sword hitting the ground with a sharp *ding*, trembling uncontrollably.

She lowered her head, her vision blurring, and murmured, "How can this be..."

The surrounding demonic shadows did not stop.

Instead, they circled around her, whispering and murmuring, seemingly intent on swallowing her last shreds of will.

In Fallen Mist Valley, the fog grew heavier.

A solitary shadow, caught between illusion and demon, was on the verge of collapse.

Suddenly, a familiar figure emerged from the mist.

Dark robes, silver hair, brows and eyes cold and stern. It was the person she was most familiar with. A surge of joy rose in her heart, only to be quickly cooled.

The Sect Master of Lingxiao, her... adoptive father.

"Dad..." She spoke dazedly, her voice trembling slightly.

Yun Wuntang stood amidst the mist. His expression was as she remembered, yet incomparably cold and indifferent.

"Shut your mouth. You have now fallen into the Demon's Den and are no longer a disciple of the Lingxiao Sect. What does your life or death have to do with me?"

"No, I haven't!" Yun Yara's voice pitched up, almost a scream.

"I can now only barely be considered your adoptive father." His voice was faint, like a light slice from a blade. "You are no longer of the Yun bloodline."

Yun Yara jerked back a step, her face as pale as paper.

"I..."

"Admit it. You hate this world. You hate that you should not have been abandoned; you hate that girl from the countryside, which is why you turned into the Demon's Den in a fit of pique. You also hate me; you hate yourself even more; you hate everyone... You possess poor spiritual roots. On the path of cultivation, you will ultimately achieve nothing."

Every word struck her heart like an iron hammer. In the mist, Yun Wuntang's figure drifted near and far, flickering between solid and void.

She struggled to cover her ears, yet those voices already echoed at the bottom of her heart, impossible to escape.

"No! You are not my father; you are a demon!"

Although her father was the Sect Master of Lingxiao and was often unreliable, he had doted on her since childhood.

Her current magical power and cultivation base had largely been built up by her father using countless rare treasures and miraculous medicines to supplement her roots.

"Heh heh. Heart Demon. I am the 'him' within your heart." The phantom Yun Wuntang reached out, striking with a palm that carried a powerful gale.

With a thunderous boom, the ground cracked, and the demonic mist surged violently. She was blasted to the edge of the cliff!

"No..."

Her foot slipped. Gravel tumbled down into the abyss of ten thousand fathoms.

She was left with only her fingertips hooking onto a sliver of stone ridge, watching as she was about to fall into the bottomless depths.

Just at this moment...

A streak of shadow, painted in hues of black and crimson, plummeted quietly from above like a colossal ink-black butterfly fighting against the wind.

Mo Han rushed forth from the dense fog, his black robes fluttering wildly like the beating wings of that dark butterfly. His eyes burned with rage, and his voice was cold enough to freeze the very air into shards.

The figure moved with a lightness that made no sound, yet in a split second, it expanded, enveloping her entire being within his embrace like a pair of protective wings.

A surge of powerful spiritual energy instantly stabilised her crumbling, teetering form.

She raised her head. Her vision had not yet fully focused, but she had already discerned that familiar aura.

"...Mo Han?" She spoke his name instinctively, disbelief colouring her tone.

His face was dark and overcast, the bottom of his eyes filled with an uncontrollable mixture of fury and terror.

"Are you mad? You dare to barge into a place like this alone?"

Yun Yara widened her eyes, gazing into his long, narrow pupils, seeing her own reflection clearly within them. "I..."

"Do you think your life is too long?" He was flustered and exasperated to the point of rage.

"How are you... here?"

His tone was vicious, yet unconsciously, he pulled her tighter into his arms, his fingertips trembling slightly. "You are simply looking for death!"

Seeing the bloodstains mottling her shoulders and sensing her chaotic breathing, the anger in his eyes intertwined with a deep, aching pain.

"Are you crazy?!" he roared low, his voice trembling with suppressed emotion. "You would rather jump into this Fallen Mist Valley and awaken that damned Ancient Demon of Absolute Void than return to the Nether Palace with me?!"

Yun Yara held her body stiffly as he embraced her. She said nothing, merely biting her lip lightly, her eyes filled with stubbornness.

She wanted to push him away, but she was too exhausted. Every single bone in her body screamed with pain.

Mo Han glared at her, his chest heaving, appearing as though he wished to press his fury down into the bottom of his heart, yet failing to contain it.

"Do you not know? Once you fall here, it means the complete dissipation of body and soul! I chased you all this way not to imprison you, not to trap you, but only to..." At this point, his voice caught, his throat seemingly blocked by something.

He suddenly tightened his hold, pressing his forehead against her messy hair, speaking in a soft voice that sounded like weeping, like a plea: "If you truly fall to the devil... how could I...

" *...ever forgive myself?*

She lowered her eyes, murmuring, "Don't be like this. I only wanted to..."

Mo Han gritted his teeth, pushing her into the protective healing array generated within his embrace. "Nothing is worth throwing your life away like this."

Having watched helplessly as she turned and leapt down without hesitation, the pain in his heart had been added to until it could increase no further, his reason swept away completely.

Just as Yun Yara moved to push him away, the spiritual energy in their surroundings suddenly underwent a drastic change.

The air surged backward like a reverse tide; the colour of the fog flickered between red and black.

She jerked her head up. In the distant demonic mist, four ghostly red pupils emerged—burning like fire, malicious like ghosts—flickering and jumping as they approached like a hunter closing in!

Simultaneously, the illusion collapsed abruptly. The image of Yun Wuntang dissipated into the void, replaced by waves of shrill, mournful ghostly wails, accompanied by the sharp, piercing sound of iron chains dragging across the ground—a sound that scraped against the bone.

A blast of yin wind howled towards them, causing dead wood and broken branches to dance madly, withering every blade of grass and tree in its path.

Mo Han's expression changed instantly. The azure sigil between his brows lit up, and his hand was already gripping his sword. He whispered in a grave, condensed voice:

"Not good... The Ancient Demon of Absolute Void has awakened."

* * * * *

High upon Mount Alioth, cloud waterfalls hung suspended like white silk. As the first light of dawn broke, celestial mists wrapped gently around the mountain peaks like a lover's veil. Within the Cloud-Light Pavilion, Yu Sord's lesson was set to begin as scheduled.

Yun Lili, harbouring a hundred kinds of unwillingness, followed the little immortal maid up the stone steps.

She sighed and groaned the entire way, her heart filled with resentment:

How can there be such a cold and heartless person in this world? To toss a person up a mountain and force them to apprentice—he is no different from a demon lord.

Yet, who could have known that the moment she stepped into the cloud-island immortal pavilion where the class was to be held, she would freeze in her tracks?

Pine winds rustled softly on all sides; the flying waterfall descended like a white ribbon.

The small pavilion was hidden within the smoke and mist, appearing as if it were suspended beyond the mortal heavens.

Inside the pavilion, a pot of spirit tea had long been prepared. The spiritual steam curled upwards, carrying a moist, sweet fragrance that assailed the nose.

Yu Sord was already seated formally within the pavilion.

He was clad in simple robes of pale moon-white, the lapels spreading out like frost and snow, with only a simple white jade hairpin securing his hair. He did not open his mouth to lecture, but merely spoke a single, faint word:

"Sit."

Lili took her seat, her belly full of suspicion. She was still wondering if she would be required to hold her breath and circulate energy, or perhaps sit cross-legged without moving for three days.

But the result was just... drinking tea?

She took a sceptical sip of the spirit tea. It was clear upon entry, sweet with a moist aftertaste.

The spiritual energy coiled around her, feeling like wisps of spring breeze brushing against her face.

The gloom that had been knotted in her chest inexplicably dissipated by more than half.

Her mind, surprisingly, quieted down.

Amidst the floating smoke and mist, the person opposite her remained a man of few words. His side profile was handsome to the point of unreality.

The bridge of his nose was high and straight, his eyelashes casting a slight shadow; the whole of him seemed to merge as one with the clouds and mist—aloof from the world, yet impossible to ignore.

Lili had originally intended to steal a bored glance, but that single look caused her heart to skip a sudden beat.

She subconsciously averted her gaze, then quietly stole another look.

How can someone be grown so good-looking...

He simply sat there quietly, yet he made one feel as though time itself had slowed by half a beat.

The wind brushed the corners of his robes; his eyes did not move, save for when he occasionally raised a hand to pour tea for her. That instant of elegance was as if a figure had walked straight out of an ink-wash painting.

For no reason at all, a sudden palpitation seized her heart; it was as if a fawn were crashing around inside her chest.

After sitting down, she stared dazedly at the clear spirit spring tea before her. Before she could react, the person opposite had already reached out without a sound to refill her cup.

His finger joints were long and slender, his palm steady.

As the spout tilted, the pale green tea water created a circle of spiritual steam in the cup, filling it just to the brim. In the process, the side of his hand inadvertently brushed lightly against the back of her fingers.

In that split second, she felt as though she had been electrocuted; her body trembled slightly, and her heartbeat accelerated inexplicably.

Yet Yu Sord seemed entirely unaware, merely lowering his eyes and saying faintly, "This tea must be taken while hot; that is when the spiritual *qi* is most abundant."

Lili was a little flustered. She lowered her head to take small sips of tea, stealing glances at him through the rising steam.

He still sat with extreme stability, his brows and eyes calm, seeming to have blended into the light waterfalls and flowing clouds outside the pavilion.

The lines of that handsome face were cold and severe, yet softened by the moist light of the mist.

Occasionally, he would lower his head in thought, his eyelashes casting faint shadows, a calm flowing across his cheeks that defied description.

Suddenly, he raised his eyes, colliding head-on with her gaze.

Lili's heart jumped. She hurriedly lowered her head, unable to stop the roots of her ears from burning hot.

Just as she was trying to find a topic to diffuse the awkwardness, she saw him lift his wide sleeve and gently brush away a plum blossom petal that the wind had carried onto her shoulder.

In that instant, she held her breath, daring not even move.

The pads of his fingers grazed the fabric at her shoulder and neck, feeling as though they were brushing across her heart, stirring up wave after wave of ripples.

"Don't move." His voice was extremely low, yet it held a gentleness that left one with nowhere to flee.

Lili's heartbeat was already in complete disarray.

Her eyes darted about aimlessly as she tried to drink her tea as if nothing had happened, but she found she couldn't swallow a single drop.

In the distance, immortal cranes called out long and clear.

A layer of thin mist obscured their surroundings, leaving only the two of them in the pavilion, close enough that they could almost hear each other's heartbeats.

Why is this atmosphere... a little incorrect...

She scolded herself in shame and annoyance, yet she could not help but quietly look at him again.

Yu Sord, however, merely turned to gaze at the cloud waterfall, his voice drifting from the mist: "If you sit quietly in this place daily, you should be able to sever distracting thoughts and quell the floating heart."

He spoke lightly as the wind and clouds, unaware that on this day, the floating thoughts and distractions in her heart had already tangled into a chaotic knot, leaving her no escape.

She couldn't help but curse her own lack of resolve, then she hurriedly lowered her eyes, only to discover that even the tips of her ears were scalding.

The mist drifted leisurely; the spirit tea gradually cooled. Yet the resistance and annoyance she had harboured were, in this moment, melted away bit by bit by the gentle wind and the quiet scenery.

Yu Sord finally spoke: "Today's lesson is concluded."

Lili froze, only then realising she had been sitting there for two whole hours.

The corners of her mouth twitched as she muttered softly, "This counts as... a lesson?"

Yu Sord replied faintly, "Calming the heart is the beginning. Without a heart, it is difficult to cultivate."

Lili watched the view of his back as he rose and departed, and the tips of her ears, traitorously, turned red once more.

Xiao Ya

Chapter 16: The Original Sin of Penury

Deep beneath the chasm of Fallen Mist Valley, at the bottom of that abyss where no sunlight had touched for countless years, a surging tide of black mist roiled and churned like a living, breathing organism.

The thick, sticky demonic qi clung to the jagged crevices of the surrounding cliffs, threading through every crack and bone pit as if seeking escape, releasing shrill and piercing screams that grated like metal against bone.

The Primordial Void Demon had awakened.

It was a creature without a solid body, an ancient monstrosity whose existence predated entire sects and dynasties.

Its form seemed forged entirely from demonic miasma and the bound hatred of innumerable vengeful spirits—shaped vaguely like an enormous shadow-soul, its outline flickering with an unstable, ghostlike wavering, and its aura colder than a thousand-year glacier.

Its four limbs were thick as aged wooden pillars, every one of its steps landing with a ground-shattering impact that sent tremors through the abyss. Its tail stretched impossibly long like a demonic serpent, only to split at the very end into three separate branches.

Each forked tip curved like a bone-forged blade, writhing and angling in slow, serpentine arcs, exuding a chilling scent that was the very breath of death itself.

Draped over its massive form were fragments of withered bones—layers upon layers of accumulated remains, the remnants of countless lives crushed, consumed, and absorbed.

The bones clattered faintly as the creature shifted, as though a host of spirits still lingered within them. In the swirling black fog, four blood-red eyes burned with a hellish, eerie flame.

It had no mouth, yet its very presence echoed like the collective wailing of ten thousand tormented souls.

Sometimes it moved like a beast on all fours, its claws crushing stone into dust; sometimes it rose upright like a grotesque mockery of a human form.

Merely standing before it was enough to freeze even a Golden Core cultivator's mind—shattering their spiritual sea, disrupting their breath, and plunging them into a despair that could annihilate life itself.

This was no creature.

This was a calamity that had crawled up from the deepest layer of hell.

Yara's sword trembled violently in her hand, the fractured shards of its blade embedded deeply into her palm.

Fresh blood seeped through the tiny gaps between her fingers, dripping onto the pitch-black ground below.

Wherever the drops landed, they sizzled into thin white curls of smoke, as though the earth itself rejected the very warmth of her life.

Her breathing was laboured, chest rising and falling sharply. Her back pressed against a jagged rib of some colossal beast's ancient remains.

Her gaze was fixed—unyielding and unfaltering—upon the monstrous figure towering before her, its four burning eyes glaring down with murderous hunger.

The massive skeletal body, pieced together from the bones of thousands upon thousands of dead creatures, slowly rose into full height.

In the hollow sockets where eyes should never have existed, four clusters of blood-coloured ghost fire ignited with a sudden flare.

The creature opened a maw that existed only through force of demonic will—within it, a blade of pure demonic qi condensed, sharp enough to tear apart spirit, soul, and flesh.

Its razor point aimed directly at Yara's brow.

"Little girl of Lingxiao Sect..."

The ancient demon's voice was the overlapping howl of endless dead souls, layered and warped.

"Your blood... carries such an exquisite scent."

Yara clenched her teeth, forcing herself upright despite the tearing pain in her palm.

The shock that this creature knew her origin flashed through her eyes.

"Mo Han!" she suddenly shouted, her voice echoing through the abyss with fierce determination.

"Get back to your damned demonic domain! This is my mess—I don't need you meddling!"

A cold, mocking laugh drifted in from behind her.

Mo Han stepped forward slowly, his dark robes billowing as demonic qi coiled around him like serpents awakening.

The movement revealed at his waist the narrow blade he had never once drawn. He seized Yara's wrist in a single swift motion—his grip so vice-like that it felt as if he would crush bone if he willed it.

"Playing the hero, are you?"

His voice rumbled low, threaded with a dark amusement.

"Yara, have you forgotten where you're standing? This abyss, this valley, this entire stretch of cursed land—it's *my* domain."

Yara yanked her hand but could not break free.

"Let go! I caused this disaster. I'll deal with it myself!"

But the black mist surged again.

The colossal demon loomed larger, its four blood-red eyes flaring as a wave of murderous cold swept across the chasm.

Yara inhaled sharply.

She drew her sword again—the remnant of its blade still trembling—and flashed forward like a shard of pure winter frost.

Sword-light streaked across the darkness toward one of the demon's glowing eyes, tearing open the void itself.

But her blade sliced only mist.

The backlash force slammed into her, sending her stumbling backward several steps as her chest churned violently with chaotic qi.

"Stop forcing it!" Mo Han roared.

A burst of crimson spiritual power exploded from his palm.

With a thunderous strike, he knocked aside the demon's sweeping bone-tail.

His body twisted midair with impeccable precision, landing before Yara like a wall of living shadow.

His cloak billowed behind him, rippling like dark wings caught in a wild tempest.

His expression hardened. Both hands formed a seal, and a tidal surge of killing intent erupted from him.

The demonic qi twisted and condensed into thousands upon thousands of scarlet chains, which snapped forward like serpents to bind the ancient creature.

The demon shrieked violently.

Its tail-blades swept across the ground, shattering the earth, sending a maelstrom of ghostly wind spiralling through the abyss.

Yara seized the brief opening.

She leapt upward, sword gleaming like a streaking comet. From midair, she slashed downward with all her remaining strength.

Her sword-light merged with Mo Han's crimson chains in a dazzling explosion.

A deafening boom cracked through the valley—

and the monstrous demon staggered back half a step.

But its fury intensified.

Its four eyes blazed with murderous crimson light, rage surging like a tidal wave.

Yara panted, nearly gasping.

"Go!" she shouted. "If you don't leave now, it'll be too late!"

Mo Han scoffed, but before any words could fully escape him, the Primordial Void Demon suddenly split into dozens of demonic blades that hurtled through the air straight toward Yara's brow.

He snarled,

"Spare me the nonsense. I'm not leaving unless I'm dead."

At that sentence, Yara's heart clenched violently—an emotion that felt unfamiliar, sharp, and almost painful.

Mo Han said nothing else.

Instead, he took a single step forward.

"Enough stalling," he said coldly.

"We live through this together—or we're not living at all."

Before his voice fully faded—

The ancient demon roared.

A monstrous sword of demonic energy shot from its maw, wavering between illusion and reality, tunnelling directly toward Yara's forehead.

Time shattered.

For Yun Yara, the world reduced itself to a single, violent stroke of action—a streak of profound crimson light that blazed past her peripheral vision and instantly became an impenetrable blur.

Before the reflex could compel her to raise the polished steel of her sword, before breath could fully re-inflate her lungs and command motion—Mo Han had violently hurled his body directly before her, transforming instantly into a human shield.

At that critical, impossible instant, the very **essence** of his being erupted in a blazing, all-consuming crimson radiance.

His long hair flew around him like strands of burning silk, his sleeves ignited like crimson fire. A glowing sigil pulsed at the centre of his chest—an ancient seal unravelling itself.

The demonic sword struck the crimson barrier, and with a tearing screech, the impact shattered the valley's stone walls, sending rubble raining across the abyss.

And the once-frenzied Primordial Void Demon—suddenly froze.

Crimson afterglow drifted around them like a shower of burning fireflies, cocooning Yara in their soft luminescence.

She stared at Mo Han's back, an unfamiliar heaviness swelling in her chest.

Her rejection, her wariness of him—

all dissolved in the face of this single, wordless act of defiance against death.

In the span of a heartbeat, Mo Han seized her and shoved her behind him, taking the next demonic strike entirely upon himself.

"Mo Han!"

But the sound of flesh being pierced never came.

Instead—a blinding burst of blood-light erupted.

Crimson power exploded from Mo Han's body.

Demonic markings crawled from the side of his neck, slithering upward like living serpents until they etched themselves into a wicked scar at the corner of his eye.

His pupils elongated into vertical crimson-gold slits.

His aura surged outward—violent and overwhelming, like mountains collapsing and seas roaring—crushing the entire abyss beneath its weight.

The demonic blade shattered the instant it touched him.

The ancient demon froze entirely.

"…My Sovereign…?"

Its voice trembled, metallic and broken, ghostfire in its four eyes flickering violently—

as though witnessing something it feared beyond reason.

The next moment—

The Primordial Void Demon crashed to its knees.

Its massive skeletal frame quivered as it bowed, prostrated fully before Mo Han.

Demonic qi scattered like terrified smoke dissolving into the wind.

Yara stood frozen.

In the lingering glow of blood-red light, Mo Han's silhouette towered— unshakable, immovable, a force more ancient than the abyss itself.

She had never seen him like this.

The demon bowed.

The spirits fell silent.

It was as though he had always been the true ruler of this hell.

"You…" Yara whispered, voice hoarse.

"How can you be… like this…?"

Mo Han offered no answer.

He lifted his hand.

With a single curl of his fingers, an invisible force crushed the ancient demon's skull—

shattering bone into drifting dust.

Only when the blood-light faded did he finally turn his head toward her, crimson-gold eyes gleaming with eerie brilliance.

A familiar mocking curve ghosted across his lips.

"Now you're afraid?"

Yara's breath shook. She gripped her sword tightly.

She wasn't afraid.

But she had never seen anyone look so dangerously beautiful, so monstrously enthralling—

so impossible to look away from.

The abyss fell silent.

* * * * *

Lili was carefully wiping her Spirit Egg with a clean piece of cloth, her voice soft and mumbling as she muttered to herself,

"Exactly *when* is this Spirit Egg going to hatch? And what in the heavens is it even going to hatch into?"

After polishing the egg for what felt like half a day, she ended up squatting beside the spirit fields again, staring wide-eyed at a tiny green plant demon as it stared back at her with its equally round, equally baffled eyes.

Just then, from the small pavilion in the rom the rear mountain pavilion, there came a loud burst of "cluck-cluck-cluck" laughter—so delighted and exaggerated it sounded like some overjoyed mother hen had just laid a golden egg.

Following the sound, she looked over.

There was Moony, holding something in her hands, pointing and tapping at it with her head lowered, smiling so broadly that she looked as if she had just won a hundred-thousand-spirit-stone jackpot.

Lili narrowed her eyes suspiciously and padded over like a nosy tabby cat poking its head around a corner.

"What are you holding in your hands? And why are you smiling like that—like… like a complete idiot?"

The moment Moony saw her, she smiled even more happily and patted the ground beside her.

"Come sit, miss! It's the **Celestial Mirror** ! Didn't you see one last time? Everyone in the entire cultivation realm is using it now! And the spell-duelling livestream today is *insanely* exciting!"

Obediently—and driven entirely by boundless curiosity—Lili sat down beside her.

"Let me see…"

Moony tilted the Celestial Mirror toward her and pointed excitedly at the glowing surface.

"Look at that male cultivator—hahaha!

He's late-stage Golden Core, and he's getting beaten all over the ground by a newly-built Foundation Establishment girl using a *fifth-grade frying spatula*! Isn't that satisfying?"

The moment Lili heard that, her eyes glued themselves to the mirror.

The image inside was chaotic and glorious: magic tools flying everywhere, fireballs exploding across the battlefield, the poor man screaming while scrambling headfirst into a pile of spirit beasts.

Bold subtitles flashed in the background:

"Today's Best Rolling Technique Award!"

"This thing is amazing!" Lili sat up so straight she practically bounced, her eyes sparkling.

"Can this mirror… see other things too? Like sword cultivators sparring? Or alchemists accidentally blowing up their furnaces?"

Moony nodded vigorously.

"It has everything! You can even add friends, post comments, and send spirit-fruit rewards!"

Lili, suddenly fired up with heroic enthusiasm, leaned forward eagerly.

"I want one too!"

Moony replied cheerfully,

"A standard model is just twenty high-grade spirit stones. The high-definition version starts at fifty. And the supreme version—with celestial-tone beauty filters—is one thousand spirit stones."

Upon hearing that number, Lili felt her heart tighten as if gripped by a cold claw.

"So… the difference in wealth is displayed this openly and this mercilessly, huh?"

She patted her shrivelled little pouch and opened it.

Inside lay exactly three mid-grade spirit stones and one half-flattened, previously bitten caramel coating fruits.

A breeze blew through her money pouch—she could almost hear the wind whistling through its hollowness—and her eyes nearly filled with tears.

"I only have three mid-grade stones left… at this rate, I can't even afford the *frame* of the mirror."

She slumped to the ground dramatically, sighing from the depths of her soul.

"This poverty… this is a tribulation sent to destroy my Dao heart."

Moony tried her best to comfort her.

"Miss, you can rent one first! Only three low-grade stones per day. Since you have three mid-grade stones… um… you can rent one for… two days."

…Two days?

Lili's lips drooped like wilting petals.

"Being broke is truly a fatal weakness…"

It turned out that cultivating immortality required money everywhere—spirit talismans needed spirit stones, weapons needed spirit stones, elixirs needed spirit stones…

"Miss, you really only have three mid-grade stones?" Moony's mouth twitched as she looked at Lili, who was so poor she could barely afford feed for immortal cranes. With the tone of someone accepting her tragic fate, she said,

"Then… you really need to think of a way to earn some."

What kind of misfortune was this?

Why did she end up following a young lady who was poor enough to make their entire sect lose face?

Lili hugged her three flying chickens and nodded pitifully, like a noblewoman who had fallen upon the hardest times.

Moony quickly raised her fingers, counting and offering ideas.

"I think… Miss, you can take sect quests! The Mission Hall has simple tasks every day—patrolling for spirit beasts, gathering spirit flowers, delivering flying-sword messages…"

Lili shook her head rapidly.

"No, no! I can't ride a sword. I have to walk everywhere. Look—last time I walked halfway up the mountain I was panting like an old ox! And then a talking spirit grass almost tricked me into giving it my shoes!"

Moony tried very hard not to laugh.

"Then… exorcising demons? With your cultivation, catching a small demon should be easy."

Lili shook her head even harder.

"Absolutely not. I can't fight! What if something scratches my face? Besides, some demons *talk*. That's terrifying."

Moony choked and continued trying.

"Then… how about opening a spirit field? You can plant a few spirit vegetables. Sell them for pocket money."

Lili gasped as if offended.

"Working under the sun would tan me!"

Moony's mental defences cracked.

"…What about working in the alchemy room? They need helpers—cleaning the cauldrons, sorting herbs. They even provide three meals and a dorm."

Lili wrinkled her nose so deeply it could crush a mosquito.

"That place is full of alchemists who explode their furnaces daily. Last time I walked past the door and smelled something burnt. I would rather starve."

Moony stared blankly.

"…Then… then how about sparring partner? Just standing there and letting people practice sword strikes on you. You don't even have to hit back."

Lili rolled her eyes toward the sky, her tone painfully sincere:

"That's even worse. I'd rather let my chickens kick me than let sword cultivators chop me all day long."

Moony finally gave up entirely and collapsed onto the grass with a long, despairing sigh.

"Then what *do* you want to do?"

With a serene, mysterious look, Lili lifted her head toward the golden clouds above and said slowly,

"I can sell things."

After all, back in Green Radish Village, she used to sell spirit herbs for a living.

Her three flying chickens flapped around her feet, and one even stole the half-eaten spirit pastry she had just picked up from the ground.

Moony looked at her dancing with her chickens and fell into wordless silence.

This young lady…

Not only was she poor, but she was also incapable of hardship…

Good thing her salary came from Lingxiao Sect directly, not from Lili herself—or she truly would have switched employers by now.

After a moment of shared silence, watching the three chickens flop around, Moony suddenly brightened.

"Oh! Or—Miss, you could *sell goods* on livestream! I just saw someone on the Celestial Mirror selling talismans the other day. A single third-grade Demon-Breaking Talisman sold for eighty spirit stones!"

The moment Lili heard that, she sat bolt upright—her eyes shining like two lanterns.

"Real? Truly real?"

Moony nodded solemnly.

"Really real. Why would I lie?"

Lili immediately sparked with renewed life.

"That's perfect! Selling things is what I'm good at! And I still have my three flying chickens—tonight we'll livestream delivering eggs! Hmph! Once I earn enough spirit stones, I'm going to buy the most expensive supreme Celestial Mirror! And I'll buy a mirror frame engraved with my name—golden, glittering, majestic—mortals stay back!"

Moony stared at her.

"…Miss, please earn at least twenty mid-grade stones before you start dreaming."

Chapter 17: The Mission to Earn Spirit Stones

With not a single Spirit Stone to her name, the notion of purchasing a Heaven-Illuminating Mirror was nothing more than the wildest of pipe dreams for Yun Lili.

Watching Moony happily swiping through the Spirit Net every single day, giggling at the screen, was dealing a stimulating and devastating blow to her fragile, impoverished young psyche.

In her heart, ten thousand celestial mud-grass horses galloped past in a stampede of frustration.

Finally, she made a firm resolution: at the very least, she had to scrounge up enough funds to get herself a Heaven-Illuminating Mirror first.

Early the next morning, as the dawn broke, she rounded up her three flying chickens and arrived at the Sect Mission Pavilion, brimming with high spirits and determination.

The massive mission board, stretching long across the wall, shimmered with the golden light of celestial metal in the morning sun.

Behind every listed mission, the reward amount in Spirit Stones was clearly inscribed, ticking the heartstrings with unbearable desire.

She started reading from the very top, her expression serious:

[Exterminate the Black Flame Spider Mother in the Northern Caves. Reward: 100 High-Grade Spirit Stones]

Lili's face stiffened instantly. "Absolutely not. I am terrified of spiders, especially ones that are mothers."

[Venture Deep into Soul-Breaking Valley to Retrieve Thunder-Fire Crystals. Reward: 80 High-Grade Spirit Stones]

She gritted her teeth and shook her head vigorously. "This will not work either. I do not know how to fly on a sword. Relying on these two legs of mine, how many years and months would it take to walk there? Furthermore, the name 'Soul-Breaking Valley' sounds exceedingly inauspicious. I value my soul."

[Assist the Pill King in Refining the Seven-Turn Soul-Returning Pill. Reward: 50 Medium-Grade Spirit Stones]

She hesitated, chewing her lip. "Hmm... this one... I have a fear of explosions. If the furnace blows, my face is ruined."

[Spar with a Nascent Soul Sword Cultivator for Thirty Rounds. Reward: 40 Medium-Grade Spirit Stones]

She fell into a profound silence. "This is even more out of the question... I am afraid of pain. Thirty rounds? I wouldn't last three breaths."

Reading all the way down the dazzling list, her gaze finally arrested at the very last line of text at the bottom:

[Accompany Training Partner for Breath Regulation and Meditation (Half-Day). Reward: 20 Medium-Grade Spirit Stones]

There was even a small line of text below it, a helpful footnote:

No combat required. Only companionship, cooperative guidance for calming the mind, and emotional support needed.

Her eyes lit up with the brilliance of a thousand suns. "This one works! I am most skilled at sitting!"

Her life motto had always been precisely this: *If I can lie down, I will absolutely not sit; if I can sit, I will absolutely not stand!*

Thus, she made a prompt, decisive choice. She pressed her hand against the sound-transmission jade token, accepting the mission. Her heart was filled with hope as she imagined those twenty shiny Medium-Grade Spirit Stones waving at her, calling her name.

The result—

She never in her wildest dreams expected that the person she had to accompany in training wasn't some solitary, aloof cultivator, nor an eccentric, elderly Daoist Lord.

Instead, she was faced with a glass-hearted male cultivator who had just been dumped, scolded by his master, and was stuck at the bottleneck of the Foundation Establishment stage.

His name was Xiao Ziyan.

Scarcely had she sat down on the meditation mat when Xiao Ziyan first let out a heavy, tragic sigh that seemed to drain the air from the room. Then, the floodgates opened:

"I cultivated for three hundred years just to reach Foundation Establishment! Three hundred years! And the moment I broke through, they called me trash with Heavenly Spirit Roots... Is the world blind?"

"She said she would ascend with me! We swore oaths under the moon! But the result? She is now dual-cultivating with a Nascent Soul Sword Cultivator! She abandoned me for a sword!"

"Tell me, Fairy... is my fate just naturally bad?"

"Do you think I still have hope in this life?"

"Am I unworthy of cultivating immortality? Should I just jump off the cliff?"

"*Woo...*"

On the surface, Lili nodded and smiled with the grace of a bodhisattva, but internally, she was screaming madly, her soul flipping tables:

"Can't you just calm your mind and regulate your breath?! We are here to breathe in spiritual qi, but you've been exhaling nothing but resentment this whole time! Hey!"

She tried to persuade him to enter a meditative state. "Fellow Daoist Xiao, perhaps we should focus on the *Qi*..."

But the other party suddenly looked at her with teary, shimmering eyes. "Fairy, you are the first female cultivator who hasn't walked away while listening to me speak. You are truly kind... You understand me!"

Then, he flung himself forward and hugged her arm like a drowning man clutching a piece of driftwood.

Lili: "......"

She really, really wanted to hit someone. What should she do?

Urgent. Waiting online for a solution.

Lili thought more than once about drawing her sword to terminate the mission right then and there.

But thinking of those twenty Spirit Stones, thinking of the Heaven-Illuminating Mirror, she gritted her teeth and endured it. She struggled to squeeze out a benevolent, amiable smile befitting a fairy:

"Come, let us take another deep breath. Imagine... imagine you are a little lotus flower... A lotus that has been struck by lightning, trampled by mud, but still wants to bloom... okay?"

Her very soul was trembling with the effort.

"These Spirit Stones... are truly earned with my life blood..."

Woo...

Three agonizing hours later.

She dragged her body back to her residence, feeling as if her primordial spirit had been drained empty and her energy hollowed out.

The three chickens were all sunbathing happily in the yard, carefree and joyous, while she collapsed beside the chicken coop, muttering to the heavens: "I almost lost my little life..."

The moment Moony saw her return, she rushed up to support her, her eyes shining with adoration.

"Miss! You are amazing! It's only been one day, and you've already earned twenty Medium-Grade Spirit Stones! You truly are a person of destiny; you even have such talent for earning Spirit Stones! To think you succeeded so quickly!"

Lili, who had originally felt like a rabbit about to freeze to death in the snow, felt her heart warmed by these cries of pure worship. She straightened her back instantly, the exhaustion melting away under the praise.

"Hehe, this is... nothing much, really."

She pretended to be breezy and nonchalant, adopting the air of an expert, though the corners of her mouth twitched upwards uncontrollably.

"Just accompanying a male cultivator for a chat, practising breathing techniques, hehe... nothing difficult. He was actually quite obedient to my words..."

Moony's face was practically plastered with the words 'Prostrate in Admiration'. She tugged Lili outwards with frantic energy. "Miss, go, go, go! We must not delay. We must go and buy a Heaven-Illuminating Mirror immediately. We cannot let your heroic bearing go to waste; it must be recorded and archived for posterity!"

The two of them rushed with fire-like speed to the sect's famous **"Pavilion of Ten Thousand Treasures and Myriad Phenomena."**

The moment they stepped across the threshold, they were greeted by a hall filled with flowing celestial light. The air itself was permeated with the faint, expensive scent of spiritual Ganoderma.

Right at the entrance stood a massive, glittering price list carved from spirit stone.

Rows of Heaven-Illuminating Mirrors dazzled the eyes with their brilliance, a feast of gems and jade. There were even small, intelligent spirit cranes flying around, demonstrating the refresh speed and image quality of various models. It felt less like a sect armory and more like a flagship store of the Celestial Realm.

All manner of mirrors were displayed upon shelves of spirit jade.

Several psychic cranes circled the displays, chirping melodiously: "The latest model Heaven-Illuminating Mirror! Today's special offer, only nine hundred and eighty Spirit Stones! To buy is to earn!"

Lili's gaze was captivated at the very first glance by a model on the topmost shelf. She walked towards it unconsciously, her eyes fixed unblinkingly on a mirror that shimmered with golden brilliance.

The body of the mirror was pale gold throughout, its edges inlaid with complex runes and floating cloud spirit jade.

Immortal *qi* coiled around it like a lover's embrace. The moment she approached, the mirror lit up automatically, accompanied by a spirit-consciousness guide with a voice as warm as jade—

*"Greetings, noble Immortal Friend. This is the **Luminous Glory Model 9: Mystic Spirit Filter Edition**. It possesses forty-nine varieties of celestial filters. One-click rejuvenation. Jade bones and ice skin are no longer a dream. Selfies lead to ascension; live-streaming makes you an immortal. Selling for only... nine hundred and eighty High-Grade Spirit Stones."*

Hearing this, Lili's hands pressed against the glass display case involuntarily, her face a picture of infatuation. "So beautiful..."

Moony peeled her fingers away from the case with a look of heartache. "Miss, you possess only twenty *Medium*-Grade Spirit Stones.

This one cost nine hundred and eighty *High*-Grade Spirit Stones. Please cease your fantasies of ascension. Come down; I will take you to browse the next section."

Thus, they made their way down from the astronomical price zone.

Next was a mirror with a jasper-coloured shell, the **Spirit-Speech Model 4**, which boasted voice control functions. *"Built-in three hundred immortal terminologies, automatic subtitle generation, and automatic removal of awkward stammers during recording. Price: Five hundred and twenty High-Grade Spirit Stones."*

Lili was tempted for exactly three seconds. Upon seeing the price, her soul departed her body once more. "Ah? Five hundred and twenty Spirit Stones?"

Further down was the **Phantom Mist Model 5**, possessing a white porcelain body that changed its theme background according to the weather. It could automatically transform your livestream background into celestial sceneries like "Coiling Immortal Mist," "Hovering Spirit Cranes," or "Purple Mansion Rosy Clouds."

"It costs only two hundred and fifty High-Grade Spirit Stones," Moony introduced.

Lili looked at another mirror with a pale pink border inlaid with spiritual runes.

The surface was clear enough to reflect the soul, and it automatically beautified her face, eliminating the dark circles of exhaustion under her eyes.

Her heart skipped a beat. "This is good. I want this one."

The shop attendant smiled. "This is the **Pink Cloud Model 3: Light and Shadow Spirit Rune Edition**. It sells for merely—fifty Medium-Grade Spirit Stones."

Lili looked at the "twenty-three Medium-Grade Spirit Stones" in her hand (the original twenty plus a few she had scrounged up). She calculated three times.

"......That is not a price that can be described with the word 'merely'..."

Finally, they arrived at the grid on the very bottom layer.

Moony hurriedly helped her flip through the tags, searching all the way to the lowest shelf.

Here, there was an inconspicuous little cabinet containing a few pitifully small mirrors.

One of them had a dusty grey body, and the paint was chipping off the corners, but it looked as though it could barely manage to start up.

Functions: *"Capable of viewing Heaven-Illuminating recordings and receiving spiritual missives. No filters, no beautification, no warranty. Interface subject to potential stagnation. Requires manual spirit-cranking to operate."*

Price: Eighteen Medium-Grade Spirit Stones.

Yun Lili stared at it in silence. She looked at it for a long, long time before finally letting out a long sigh. "Heh... am I only worthy of purchasing *this*?"

Moony smiled encouragingly. "Miss, this is already the most spiritual mirror we can encounter within our budget."

"Miss, this model costs only eighteen Medium-Grade Spirit Stones. Although it is a model from the previous sixty-year cycle and the spiritual light is somewhat unstable... it *is* viewable."

Lili gritted her teeth. She looked at the eighteen-stone model, then at the fifty-stone model, and then...

"Then... let us try it."

Moony followed at her side, her face full of comfort. "Miss, this model is actually quite decent... It saves energy, saves worry, and it even comes with a complimentary manual spirit-cranking cord! Other mirrors don't offer that!"

Lili: "I don't want to talk. Let me be quiet."

She looked as though she had just been struck by lightning—no, as if she had been struck three consecutive times by the Nine-Nine Heavenly Tribulation.

She walked while shaking the spirit-cranking cord.

With every crank, her sanity seemed to drop a few points.

The scene was the living image of a lonely, wild ghost shaking a bell in a desperate attempt to summon a spirit—

"Start up, start up... hurry up and start for me..."

The mirror finally flashed once, and a line of text emerged tremblingly: *Insufficient spiritual energy. Startup failed. Please continue cranking.*

Lili: "......"

She looked up at the sky and recited to herself: "Spirit Stones are precious indeed, and the price of dignity is higher still; yet for the sake of the Heaven-Illuminating Mirror, both can be cast aside."

Moony looked deeply moved. "Miss is truly risking her life for her dream! I must record this journey of your struggle!"

Hearing this, Lili let out a cold laugh, hugging the mirror protectively. "No, do not record this under any circumstances. Have a heart; let us pretend this dark chapter of history... never occurred."

Moony was brimming with enthusiasm. "But Miss, today you completed the miraculous mission of earning your first bucket of Spirit Stones in life! Would you consider accepting another one?"

In contrast to Moony's passionate positivity, Lili fell silent for a moment before turning away silently, her figure looking wind-blown and chaotic.

In the end, the two of them walked out empty-handed.

"I originally came to reward myself, so why does it feel as though my soul has been illuminated and found wanting..." Lili lamented in a low voice.

—A poor soul.

Moony comforted her. "Then Miss, why not go and accompany a training partner once more?"

Lili immediately shrieked, "Do not mention that bar... oh, no, that endlessly crying male cultivator again!!"

Her tone shifted, and she wilted once more, looking up to sigh at the heavens. "I still have to... continue earning Spirit Stones!"

"Let us just make do for now. We can buy a better one after we earn more Spirit Stones?" Moony suggested sincerely.

"......" Helpless against the jingling sound of poverty, Lili could only agree with resignation.

The two of them, holding onto a final shred of expectation, went to the counter to pay, only to be told: "Apologies, this item is sold out. You must wait for the next batch of spiritual merchants to restock."

Ah?

No way? No way? No way?

Even this cheap goods was sold out?

At this moment, three flying chickens descended from the heavens, landing on her shoulders with loud *cluck-clucks*, as if asking: *"Are we shipping out today or not?"*

Yun Lili felt as though she had been struck by lightning.

She walked out of the "Pavilion of Ten Thousand Treasures and Myriad Phenomena" with Moony, empty-handed, with three chickens standing on her head and shoulders.

She hadn't expected it, but her mood was already depressed enough. Yet, unexpectedly, at the doorway.

She encountered a livestreaming cultivator equipped with top-tier gear and a full set of beautification filters, shouting loudly:

"Thank you, Immortal Friend, for sending me one thousand Spirit Stones! See you at the next Immortal Grass Unboxing session..."

Her expression twisted. Inside, she roared a single thought:

"You people of the Immortal Realm are truly sick!"

Alas... she could only go and accept more bizarre missions!

Chapter 18: The Special Cultivation Method

Yun Lili had originally intended to head straight for the Mission Pavilion to continue accepting jobs and earning Spirit Stones.

However, the moment she stepped across the threshold of her courtyard gate, she ran headlong into Yu Sord.

His expression was cold and indifferent, his brows as pale and distant as the morning frost settling upon the pines.

"Today is the second lesson. You must not be late."

She froze in her tracks. "What lesson?"

"Mental Method Guidance Class. Follow me."

Yu Sord's tone was indifferent, devoid of any warmth.

He did not pause for even a second, turning and walking away with a sweep of his robes, as if whether she followed him or not was of absolutely no concern to him.

The "beautiful experience" of the previous lesson was still fresh in her mind, so this time, Lili was much calmer, no longer making a fuss over nothing.

However, when she actually followed him deep into the flower forest and stepped into the small pavilion, her gaze swept over the garden full of breathtaking scenery, and her brow still twitched involuntarily in surprise.

Within the pavilion, vermilion curtains hung lightly, swaying in the breeze.

Immortal cranes danced gracefully, their white feathers pure as snow, moving in formation over the small lake that lay ahead.

In the air, music sounded faintly, drifting down from the heavens as if someone atop a high mountain were playing a harmonious duet of the phoenix flute and the *guqin*.

The table in the centre of the pavilion was spread with a cloth of cloud-embroidered gauze, filled with crystal-clear, jade-like small pastries and fragrant tea, along with a plate of candied peach blossom crisps that emitted a faint, inviting spiritual glow.

Lili looked around a full circle, unable to resist asking,

"What school of cultivation class is... *this*?"

Wow, seriously? Is this environment not a little too beautiful?!

Yu Sord answered with a face full of seriousness, his voice steady: "Nurturing the heart is the foundation of cultivating the Dao. Immortal cranes are spiritual birds of heaven and earth; observing their rhythm and regulating one's breath and spirit can nurture the primordial spirit. Celestial music is the sound of the Dao; listening can lead to quiet enlightenment. As for the pastries, they are to replenish spiritual power and boost the soul consciousness..."

He spoke with such logic and reason, sounding utterly authoritative, yet Lili was half-believing and half-doubting. She lifted a cup of spirit tea, taking a skeptical sip. "Real or fake? Can doing *this* truly improve one's cultivation base?"

Yu Sord poured two cups of tea, handing one to her. His tone was unhurried, flowing like water. "The dance of immortal cranes can calm the *qi* and condense the spirit; celestial music entering the ears can suppress the soul and stabilise the heart. If you can quiet down and regulate your breath with the music, you can smooth your meridians and clear your mind. Cultivation is not limited to the single path of bitter asceticism."

Lili listened until she was dazed, understanding yet not fully understanding.

However, seeing his serious expression, she dared not act rashly. She could only sit down obediently, attempting to learn to regulate her breath with the rhythm as he did.

But having sat for only a few breaths, she was inevitably attracted by the spirit cakes on the table.

Unable to resist the temptation, she picked up a piece with her chopsticks and sent it into her mouth.

"This crisp seems to have jade Ganoderma powder added?" she asked vaguely around the food.

Yu Sord gave a low laugh but did not respond directly.

He merely raised his eyes to look at her, his voice warm yet brooking no argument: "If you can cultivate with a calm heart daily, within three months, the mid-stage of Foundation Establishment will be stable."

Lili's eyes lit up instantly, and she nodded immediately. "That would truly be wonderful!"

She looked down at the spirit cakes on the table again, then glanced at the immortal cranes dancing on the lake, and finally looked at the Sword Sovereign beside her who radiated an aura of pure immortality. Suddenly, an illusion born of a dream arose within her.

"Senior Brother... ah, no, Immortal Sovereign." She asked in a small voice, "Will such a cultivation method truly not result in the Sect Master punishing us to copy scriptures?"

Yu Sord wore a smile that was not quite a smile, his tone as steady as ever: "If you can calm your heart, you will naturally sense the Great Dao. If you cannot be calm, copying scriptures would do no harm."

Lili: ...*This is definitely a threat!*

She couldn't help but straighten her spine, sitting as steady as a great bell, hands clasped properly on her knees. In her heart, there were only four words:

Quiet! Must not be chaotic!

Sitting down to eat pastries, admire beautiful scenery, and having a handsome Immortal Sovereign as a companion could lead to Foundation Establishment? She couldn't help but exclaim in her heart:

This path of cultivation is simply too suitable for a little fairy like me.

Yu Sord smiled faintly, lowering his eyes to sip his tea, his tone remaining gentle: "If the heart is quiet, there will naturally be gains."

Lili only regarded him as a serious, good master, completely unaware that she had long since been guided step by step by him into a certain extremely gentle, yet deeply implied "special cultivation method."

She admired the scenery while biting into the dim sum, her gaze unconsciously falling upon the immortal cranes dancing amidst the water mist.

Suddenly, a flash in her peripheral vision caught Yu Sord's side profile reflecting the soft morning light.

The bridge of his nose was high, his brows and eyes picturesque, his aura leisurely; the whole of him was like an immortal of painting who had walked straight out of a scroll.

Her heart gave a sudden jump, as if plucked gently by an invisible string.

She jerked her head down, warning herself again: "What are you looking at, what are you looking at... Cultivate! I am here to cultivate!"

But that trace of strange emotion that had quietly bred was already unknowingly taking root and sprouting at the very bottom of her heart.

She glanced at the peach blossom crisps on the table, admonishing herself mentally that "at least it's free spirit food."

Just as she was about to pick up a piece, she suddenly sensed Yu Sord's gaze falling on her hand. That look contained a smile that was almost imperceptible.

Only then did she abruptly realise that the heartbeat in her chest had long since lost its rhythm.

This master... was truly possessed of a handsomeness not seen in the mortal realm.

Her cheeks flushed slightly. Forcing herself to be calm, she asked with feigned relaxation, "Dare I ask the Immortal Sovereign... how many more lessons like this are there?"

—Heh, it would be best if there were one every day.

Yu Sord's tone was as calm as usual, yet he left room for manoeuvre without leaving a trace: "It depends on how you cultivate. If results are seen... a class can be opened every seven days."

Lili took a bite of the peach blossom crisp. The fragrant crispiness filled her mouth, sweetness entering her heart, and the corners of her mouth unconsciously turned up.

* * * * *

When Yun Lili sat within the pavilion, leisurely admiring the dance of the immortal cranes, she never in her wildest dreams anticipated that the picturesque scene unfolding before her eyes was being livestreamed in real-time to the entire world.

But there was no helping it.

Who asked her to be seated beside the dignified Immortal Lord Silentstar, the number one sword cultivator of the Immortal Realm—Yu Sord? His every move and gesture had historically been the focal point of the masses' attention.

And now, he had made a rare appearance at Crane Lake, sitting in "silent cultivation" with the female cultivator who was currently the hottest topic of discussion. How could this fail to trigger a sensation?

On Crane Lake, clouds and mist coiled in ribbons, and the distant mountains resembled the painted brows of a beauty. In the mid-lake pavilion, immortal cranes spread their wings, dancing lightly upon the water mist.

Their long necks stretched high, wings like fans of snow, spiralling and crossing in time with the celestial music flowing from the heavens—a scene like a dream, like an illusion.

Yu Sord sat with composed elegance, his sleeves spreading lightly.

Between his brows lay an air of immortality that seemed untouched by the smoke and fire of the mortal world. His side profile, illuminated by the faint light of the thin mist, resembled an immortal painting descended to earth, causing countless viewers to lose their souls for a second.

And this entire scene was being recorded with crystal clarity by a **"Patrol Shadow Bead"** hanging on the horizon.

This Patrol Shadow Bead was no ordinary artifact; it was a high-tier "Imaging Spirit Treasure" of the Immortal Sects, usually reserved for monitoring anomalies and recording major events. For some unknown reason, at this very moment, it had automatically activated its "Omni-Sync Function."

The footage was being projected directly onto the recommendation slot of the homepage of the Immortal Realm's largest public platform—the **Heaven-Illuminating Mirror**.

It even thoughtfully added a headline and trending keywords:

—[**SHOCK! Immortal Lord Silentstar silently cultivates in the Lake Pavilion with a Mystery Female Cultivator. The visual is aesthetic, the atmosphere ambiguous. Has a romance been exposed?**]

—[**Come learn the "Crane Calming Method"! Calm the qi and condense the spirit; stabilize the mid-stage of Foundation Establishment in three months. Includes original voice guidance by the Immortal Lord!**]

The moment it aired, the view count instantly broke one million.

Countless cultivators' hands trembled. Alchemy furnaces exploded, magical artifacts misfired, and spirit beasts ran amok as everyone rushed to flood into the livestream room—either to cultivate or, more likely, to... spectate the drama.

The comment section was instantly submerged:

"This method of Foundation Establishment is too showy! I soaked in a freezing pond for half a month, and you're telling me I could have ascended just by sitting and drinking tea?"

"That fourth crane on the left just did a spin. It's dancing 'Arrogant Spirit Cloud', isn't it?!"

"Who has an immortal crane?! Urgently needed! Buying live ones for 300 Spirit Stones! Dancing ability preferred!"

"Is this cultivation, or a romance documentary? Begging for a compilation clip of Immortal Lord Yu's eyes!"

There were also sharp-eyed cultivators who immediately recognised Yun Lili's silhouette, and the gossip began to screen-wipe the feed like flying swords:

"Immortal Lord Ji-Ming poured tea for that female cultivator! And he spoke softly! If this isn't called a date, then what was I doing cultivating with my junior sister before?"

"The commenter above speaks the truth. Let's benchmark it again— pavilion, water scenery, cranes, tea fragrance, Immortal Lord Yu's gaze... I declare this the scene with the strongest Immortal Romance atmosphere of the year."

"Wait a moment, I saw that female cultivator smile! She even took a bite of osmanthus cake! Ahhh! Why is it so sweet!"

"I bet one hundred years of cultivation on this! The sour stench of love!"

And this trend spread rapidly throughout the Immortal Realm—

Within three days, the **"Crane Calming Method"** became the newly promoted hot cultivation method. Major sects scrambled to launch "Crane Silent Cultivation Experience Classes." Advertisements flew everywhere, business in the Spirit Beast Workshops exploded, and even the market towns set up "Silent Cultivation Photo Check-in Points."

The **Danxia Gate** hung up a banner: *"Crane Silent Cultivation Method, effective in three days! Comes with a complimentary portion of the original spirit cake!"*

The **Wuxiang Sect** simply launched a "Couple's Crane Silent Cultivation Ticket," brazenly displaying the slogan: *"Limited to couples. Cultivate the path and cultivate love simultaneously. Immortals cranes as witnesses, affection flowing like water."*

Even the historically hidebound **Lichen Valley** released a new product: *"Crane Array Projection Talisman. Stick it on to see phantom cranes. The top choice for home cultivation!"*

Small Spirit Beast Workshops transformed overnight into "Crane-Themed Breeding Bases." The price of an immortal crane skyrocketed from ten Spirit Stones to a hundred, yet supply still could not meet demand. Purchase limits followed; one had to take a number for a crane that could nod, and draw lots for one that could dance.

Meanwhile, Yun Lili, who was regarded as one of the instigators of this chaos—

She was still sitting in the pavilion, holding her teacup. She nibbled meticulously on a spirit cake while gazing at the dancing cranes on the lake surface, her expression tranquil and content.

This was already her third "Silent Cultivation Lesson."

She let out a long, leisurely sigh. "Mm... this method of cultivation truly suits my constitution. The pastries are excellent, and the scenery is beautiful."

Yu Sord raised his eyes to look at her.

The corner of his lips hooked up slightly, his eyes holding a smile, his voice sounding like the music of a spring flowing beneath the moon. "It is good that you like it. In the days to come, if there is time, we can hold a few more sessions."

Yun Lili's eyes lit up, her heart filled with joy. "Really? Then we must schedule quite a few more. I am someone who fears tedious cultivation above all else; this is just right."

She was completely unaware that she had already been consecrated by the entire Immortal Realm as the "New Star with the Most Cultivation Potential." Furthermore, introductory courses in various Immortal Sects had already incorporated the recording of her and Yu Sord admiring cranes side-by-side as exemplary teaching material for "Quiet Heart Cultivation."

It was not until she returned to her residence that the reality crashed down upon her.

Moony, her face flushed red with excitement, ran over cradling the Heaven-Illuminating Mirror, shouting incoherently:

"Miss! You're on fire! The entire Immortal Realm is imitating your cultivation method! You have already been at the top of the hot search list for three days!"

Yun Lili froze. She took the Heaven-Illuminating Mirror and looked, only to see herself in the screen taking small bites of osmanthus cake, her cuff even stained with a few crumbs. Her immortal aura was completely lost; the artistic style collapsed in a single second.

She covered her face and shrieked, "This can become popular too?! It's so humiliating! Find a way to delete it for me!"

Moony hesitated. "Um... deleting footage requires special permission. I heard... it costs at least ten thousand High-Grade Spirit Stones."

Lili: "......"

In the end, it was still poverty!

She lowered her head to look at the remaining half of the spirit cake in her hand, sorrow rising from within. *Indeed, poverty is the original sin, and moreover, the greatest obstacle on the path of immortal cultivation.*

But in the next second, she quietly raised her head to look at the colour of the sky.

However... if I can continue cultivating like this, it seems not too bad?

Who cares?

After all, her Foundation Establishment was stable, the spirit cakes were sweet, and she had the Immortal Lord for company—

She involuntarily curved the corners of her lips, her smile deepening.

Who said cultivating immortality must be tedious and bitter? Her path, it seemed, had cultivated a different world entirely.

What she saw was the cranes dancing on the lake and the sweet tea and pastries; while what he saw was the way the mountains and rivers remained unharmed and peaceful when she sat safely within the pavilion.

Chapter 19: I want to breathe with you?

Driven by the need to earn spirit stones, Lili found herself standing once more before the Mission Hall, looking up at the rows upon rows of dazzling mission notices on the board.

Her eyes were filled with struggle and resentment.

She muttered under her breath, "They're just spirit stones... Can I, Lili, really not earn them?"

With that, she gritted her teeth fiercely, as if marching to her execution, and pulled down a few notices that appeared "safe and non-violent." She was convinced that among them, there must be one that would allow her to sit comfortably and collect her reward. Yet... it was another series of disasters.

First Mission: Spirit Pet Translator.

The description was straightforward: "Sit beside the spirit pet and be responsible for translating its utterances to its owner."

When Lili saw this, she nearly wept with joy. Visions danced in her head: herself sitting leisurely, a docile spirit pet nuzzling her leg, translating a few phrases, and effortlessly walking away with the spirit stones.

The result? The moment she sat down, a seemingly fluffy, harmless-looking Fire Phoenix fledgling suddenly bristled. It slammed its wings against the ground and let out a deafening roar:

"Gugu gagagaga—!!!"

Lili looked bewildered, forcing a smile: "Is it... saying it's hungry?"

The spirit pet owner's face instantly darkened to the color of a pot bottom: "Fire Phoenixes are fire-attribute avian demons. They don't need to eat."

"Then..." Before Lili could finish, the Fire Phoenix flapped its wings and lunged at her, tearing her sleeve with a claw, then followed up with a rapid-fire series of ten consecutive roars.

In less time than it takes an incense stick to burn, she was personally escorted off the premises by her "translation subject," without even catching a glimpse of the spirit stones.

* * * * *

Second Mission: Spirit Field Chicken Supervisor.

This time, she was much more careful, choosing a task that involved dealing with "poultry." Thinking back to her experience raising a few domestic chickens in the mortal realm, she felt familiar with the territory and believed nothing could go wrong again.

The task involved tending a spirit field and a few spirit fowl for a female cultivator in seclusion.

"Watching chickens," she repeated to herself easily. "They're just chickens, not like guarding a Thunder Beast."

As it turned out, these were not chickens at all.

One was entirely crimson with fire blazing in its eyes, breathing flames at its companions the moment it saw them, as if picking a fight; another was black tinged with purple, capable of spewing poisonous gas; and yet another actually possessed the ability to earth dive, tunnelling through the spirit field, churning the earth as if it had just survived a chaotic magical array battle.

Lili chased the fire-breathing chicken all over the field, waving a spirit shield full of holes and yelling, "Are you even chickens?! You're just failed battle pets, aren't you?!"

By the time the flock finally settled down somewhat, she was left gasping for breath as she sat down. The entire spirit field, however, was already in utter disarray, with not a single plant left standing.

In the end, she barely managed to complete the task but only received half the promised reward—still not enough to afford even a low-tier Celestial Mirror .

When she returned to her residence clutching the meagre remaining spirit stones, she sighed mournfully: "Wah, my own chickens are so much better behaved."

* * * * *

Third Mission: Accompany in Na Tu Xi (In & Out) Breathing Technique

Issued by: Ziyan

Duration: Half a day

Reward: 20 medium-grade spirit stones

Lili had ten thousand reasons to refuse in her heart, but to buy the Celestial Mirror she yearned for, she endured it.

"Just half a day... two spirit stones per incense stick's time. Endure it, and it'll be over..." She seemed to be hypnotizing herself.

One incense stick's time later, in the quiet room.

Lili sat in the familiar spot. Across from her, Ziyan was still clad in his ink-black robes, his aura like a thousand-year frozen pond that had never thawed, his gaze lowered, his presence faint as dust and mist.

The moment he opened his mouth, it was the familiar, deep tone: "...Lately, I suspect my spirit root is deteriorating."

Lili's hand jerked, nearly dropping her teacup. She forced a smile: "Then... then aren't you still able to practice the Na Tu Xi breathing technique?"

Ziyan lowered his eyes without speaking. After a long while, he said softly, "While practicing the breathing... I started doubting life itself."

"......"

"This spiritual energy I inhale... it cannot fill the emptiness within my heart."

Lili took a deep breath, silently chanting "spirit stones, spirit stones, spirit stones" in her heart. She mentally flipped through the memory of that wordless celestial tome titled ***Helping Melancholy Cultivators Regain Confidence,*** striving to make her smile appear natural and gentle: "Then tell me, what exactly is troubling you?"

Ziyan sighed, his gaze lost: "Tell me... the chicken lays the egg, the egg hatches the chicken. Ultimately, which came first, the chicken or the egg?"

"......" Lili was silent for several breaths, a storm raging inside:

You're here to practice breathing, not to take a Daoist philosophy exam!

Ziyan continued murmuring: "I suspect that after practicing the Na Tu Xi breathing technique with you that day, my fortune began to decline... Is it that my destiny is unsuited for closeness with others, which is why she left me?"

"......"

Lili's face twitched. She nearly said, "Are you overthinking things?" But seeing the shimmering moisture in his eyes, she knew she couldn't provoke him. Instead, she softened her voice: "You're overthinking it. The path of cultivation naturally has its ups and downs. If your spirit root seems dim today, perhaps you'll break through a bottleneck tomorrow."

Ziyan lowered his head in contemplation, then suddenly asked, "Saying that... are you concerned about me?"

Lili nearly choked on her spiritual energy, but still managed to squeeze out a smile: "Yes, on the path of cultivation, we should support each other."

His eyes brightened for a moment, then dimmed again: "It's a pity... you don't truly mean it."

"How do you know I don't mean it?" Her tone finally carried a slight upward inflection.

His tone was indifferent: "...Because I paid twenty medium-grade spirit stones for you to be willing to talk to me."

"......"

Lili's smile stiffened. Internally, she was in turmoil, wanting only to shout aloud: "Since you know, why do you keep posting this mission every time!!"

While gritting her teeth and maintaining a companionable smile, she silently counted how much time remained, chanting to herself: "Spirit stones... oh, spirit stones... you must stay strong."

Finally, half a day later.

Lili dragged her nearly exhausted body back to her residence. The moment she pushed the door open, Moony greeted her, her face full of anticipation: "Miss, you finished the mission? That Ziyan didn't cry again today, did he?"

Lili sat down with a vacant expression, her voice hoarse: "He didn't cry."

Moony breathed a sigh of relief, her eyes lighting up: "That's great, finally—"

"He didn't cry today," Lili continued, her tone as calm as if stating the weather. "But he evolved."

"Evolved?"

"Today, he started discussing philosophy."

"......"

Moony looked horrified as she gazed at her Miss, as if she could see four illusory characters floating above her head: *Spirit Stones Are Hard-Earned.*

At this moment, she felt immensely grateful that her monthly stipend was uniformly issued by the Lingxiao Sect. Otherwise, following such an impoverished master, her own financial future would be truly worrisome.

* * * * *

Lili had originally thought that after completing the Na Tu Xi (Breath In & Out) breathing mission that day, they would part ways for good. She'd have her spirit stones, and neither would owe the other anything.

Who could have guessed that just a few days later, as she stepped out of her residence, she would find a pot—well, an excessively bizarre, bright red love flower—placed prominently at her door, complete with a placard: "May your cultivation path be smooth, your immortal grace everlasting—From Ziyan."

Lili: "......"

Not daring to look a second time, she turned away, intending to take the pot to the spirit beast garden to feed the chickens, only to discover that the flower could actually coo and was making heart gestures at her.

"Does this cultivator have nothing better to do?!" Lili was so angry she rolled her eyes.

But things escalated in the following days.

When she attended the public Spirit Vessel class, someone had saved a good seat for her.

When she went to the Mission Hall, someone pressed a box of pastries into her hands (and it was the flavour Ziyan had been crying about wanting last time).

She even queued overnight to snag a discounted Celestial Mirror , only for someone at the very front of the line to offer their spot: "Fairy, right this way. Your friend Ziyan mentioned you liked this model and queued up for you in advance."

Ziyan?!

Hearing this, she abandoned the queue altogether, decisively giving up.

Wah... what a pity. The long-awaited special offer, gone just like that.

Moony's eyes shone: "Miss, when did you learn to charm people like this? These methods are practically the textbook example of an immortal realm heartbreaker!"

Lili: "Moony! I'm innocent! At most, I said 'we should support each other on the cultivation path.' How did that get upgraded into a marriage proposal hint?"

The matter soon reached the ears of the Solitary Clarity Immortal Lord, Yu Sord.

That day, he had just returned from seclusion at the Spirit Spring Mountain and was thinking of finding Lili to continue their "lessons" when an attendant respectfully reported:

"Reporting to the Immortal Lord, Cultivator Ziyan has been frequently visiting Lili's cottage lately. He even boldly declared in the Celestial Mirror comment section, 'Cultivation partner undecided, waiting only for one person'... ahem... seemingly referring to Fairy Lili."

Yu Sord had originally been meditating, but upon hearing this, his eyes snapped open, and he shot a sharp glance towards the informant.

His expression impassive, he asked faintly, "Which sect does he belong to?"

"Replying to the Immortal Lord, he is an inner disciple of Falling Star Pavilion. His cultivation is at mid-Foundation Establishment. Recently, due to emotional fluctuations, his cultivation has been unstable, so he has posted several missions at the Mission Hall seeking practice companions... uh... to accompany him in the Na Tu Xi breathing technique... ahem... all of which were accepted by Fairy Lili..."

Yu Sord slowly took a deep breath, his tone calm and composed: "Prepare a visitor's card for Falling Star Pavilion for me. This lord intends to lecture on the topic of 'Emotional Interference with Cultivation' in the near future."

The attendant shivered inwardly, thinking: *That Ziyan probably won't live much longer.*

That evening, the top trending item on the Celestial Mirror was... *Why Did Immortal Lord Yu Sord Visit Falling Star Pavilion at Night?*

While the masses were shocked, the highest-rated hot comment was... *For the first time in a century, the Immortal Lord raises a hot topic: On the Importance of Emotional Interference in Cultivation!*

The second trending search was... *Ziyan Voluntarily Enters Seclusion for a Hundred Years to Cultivate His Mental State.*

From then on, Ziyan vanished from the mortal realm, and Lili finally gained a few days of peace.

Just as Lili was preparing to go to the Mission Hall to take on another easy Na Tu Xi breathing companion mission, the moment she stepped out, Yu Sord blocked her path.

His snow-white robes glowed softly in the morning light, his handsome yet aloof face betraying no emotion. Only his tone was composed as he said:

"I heard you've recently been assisting others in practicing the 'Na Tu Xi breathing technique'?"

Lili felt somewhat guilty and nodded: "...Yes. After all, spirit stones are hard to come by."

He frowned almost imperceptibly.

Clad in his moon-white robes, Yu Sord stood cold and clear under the moonlight, but his tone was rather unnatural as he continued, "...From now on, take fewer of those nonsensical companion missions."

Lili looked utterly confused: "Why?"

He, a dignified Immortal Lord, naturally couldn't comprehend the sorrows of her poverty-stricken state.

Yu Sord lowered his gaze without speaking. After a long moment, he said quietly, "As it happens, this Immortal Lord also needs to practice the 'Na Tu Xi breathing technique.'"

"You, Immortal Lord?" Lili was shocked. "The esteemed Solitary Clarity Immortal Lord still needs such a low-level Qi-nourishing technique?"

Yu Sord's expression remained completely unchanged, his tone utterly natural:

"Recently, while contemplating the opportunities of the Great Dao, I discovered that the circulation of my own energy channels is too balanced."

Being too balanced is also a problem?

If I didn't know he's been in prolonged seclusion, I'd think he was just bored with too much time on his hands!

Yu Sord nodded, continuing with a solemn expression: "Cultivation emphasizes the flow of Yin and Yang, the harmony of the five energies. However, my primordial energy is overly abundant, and my spirit channels cannot release it in a timely manner. If this continues, I fear it may lead to the opposite extreme—breaking through too violently during Divine Transformation, harming the soul."

Lili looked puzzled: "Uh... that sounds like... you're just too powerful?"

Yu Sord inclined his head, calmly responding: "Therefore, I need to rely on the Na Tu Xi breathing technique to guide the energy into breath, smoothly circulate the heart and spirit, thereby suppressing the excessive power."

He paused, then added a very measured statement: "And your aura is clear, harmonious, and natural, making it highly suitable for complementing mine."

Lili: "......"

Hearing this, she was utterly bewildered. Why did such a serious statement sound like a powerful expert was subtly saying—*I want to breathe with you?*

She narrowed her eyes suspiciously: "Might I ask, Immortal Lord, which ancient text is this method from?"

Yu Sord smiled slightly and actually countered: "The one you accompanied last time... Ziyan, which ancient text did he base his on?"

"...I don't know either. He just wanted someone to breathe with him," she muttered.

"Then it's the same." Yu Sord nodded, his tone gentle and appropriate. "Let us begin immediately."

Lili: "......???"

She silently lowered her head to look at her own withered spirit stone pouch, then raised her head to look at the transcendent, deeply articulate master before her. Only one sentence remained in her mind:

—These days, even Immortal Lords are stepping in to compete for Na Tu Xi breathing companion jobs?!

She felt the future of her spirit stone-earning path had become even more bleak.

Lili was inexplicably dragged by him to the pavilion to practice the "Na Tu Xi breathing technique." Throughout the entire session, he was calm and composed, while she was in complete disarray.

It was just the two of them sitting cross-legged in the pavilion, silent, facing each other... and then... you look at me, I look at you.

And in the live stream, the entire immortal realm was holding its breath, watching... the Immortal Lord and the female disciple, Fairy Lili, practicing "Dual Cultivation Na Tu Xi Breathing Technique"!

The top comment with the most likes was: "The Solitary Clarity Immortal Lord is so powerful, yet he still needs the Na Tu Xi breathing technique? No way? No way..."

"The Solitary Clarity Immortal Lord is truly a model for our generation, diligently studying even elementary techniques."

"Wait... isn't this actually the Breath of Love?!!!"

"Ah, no, I just want to ask, how is this Na Tu Xi breathing technique different from the one we practice?"

"I want the Immortal Lord's same breathing guidance! I want to sign up!"

"These damned pink bubbles... I'm going to smash my Celestial Mirror ..."

Meanwhile, Lili was completely unaware of everything happening. In her own view, she hadn't really done anything. She was merely living according to her own heart, striving for the things she wanted, step by step, relying on her own abilities to fight for them.

Chapter 20: The Ancient Demon Cushion

Deep within Fallen Mist Valley, clouds and mist were woven together like a tapestry.

The Ancient Demon of Absolute Void lay prostrate upon the ground, its body completely limp.

Its massive, furry demonic form had transformed into a sitting couch as soft as a cloud—plush, warm, and as obedient as a cat that had been thoroughly beaten into submission.

Yun Yara leaned against that demonic frame, sleeping heavily.

Her entire body seemed almost to sink into the softness of the "couch," revealing only a small section of her white wrist and her quiet, peaceful face.

She was exhausted to the extreme.

The journey here had drained her body and mind, and once she fell asleep, she slumbered for three days and three nights without waking.

Mo Han sat not far from her, guarding her in silence.

Aside from the wind passing through the treetops and the occasional swaying of the demonic vines, there was not a single disturbance in their surroundings.

The black robes with crimson patterns that he wore were somewhat tattered and damaged, adding a sense of broken fragility to his appearance, yet without a shred of dishevelment or awkwardness.

In his hand, he held a dilapidated ancient book—its origin unknown— which he had turned through countless times. Yet, for the vast majority of the time, his gaze remained fixed upon her.

She slept with absolute stability. Even in her dreams, her brows were knitted ever so slightly, as if she might frown in a way that incited pity at any moment. His gaze fell upon the corner of her mouth, which was turned up slightly, and he could not help but curve his own lips in response.

This was a rare moment of tranquillity for him. There was no need to deal with deception or mutual suspicion, no need to calculate the human heart. He needed only to sit quietly and look at her, and the passage of time felt gentle and affectionate.

Finally, Yun Yara woke leisurely.

The first thing she saw upon opening her eyes was Mo Han.

He was half-leaning on a seat woven from demon vines, the book resting on his knees, looking like an Immortal Lord who had walked straight out of a painting—motionless, watching her.

"...Why are *we* still here?" She rubbed her eyes, somewhat surprised.

We?

Hearing this, Mo Han inadvertently raised the corner of his mouth in a sexy arc. He liked this word.

Mo Han's expression remained unchanged as he spoke faintly: "I... my magical power is severely depleted. I cannot leave this valley for the moment. We have no choice but to rest here for a few days."

He spoke lightly, as if it were a matter of course, carried by the wind and clouds.

Not far away, the entire Ancient Demon—currently serving as a cushion-cum-heater—suddenly twitched its ears. It revealed an expression that clearly said, *"I can send you out, you know,"* and just as it opened its mouth to speak...

Mo Han swept a single glance over it. His eyes carried no killing intent, yet they were as cold as a ten-thousand-year-old ice lake.

The Ancient Demon: "......"

Its mouth twitched. It immediately shrank its head back and shut its mouth, continuing its role as a well-behaved, fluffy baby.

Yun Yara did not raise any suspicions, believing him eighty per cent. She tilted her head to look at him. "Then, for these past few days, you have been guarding here the whole time?"

Mo Han closed the book, his tone calm. "Where else could I go?"

Yara lowered her head, a fine thread of tenderness flashing through her eyes. She stretched her back, reaching out to stroke the soft demon fur beneath her, and sighed: "This couch... is actually quite comfortable."

The Ancient Demon of Absolute Void raised its tail, tears streaming in its heart: *This Demon, the majestic Supreme Being of the Nether Realm, has actually been reduced to a seat cushion. Woo... I don't want to live anymore.*

The smile in Mo Han's eyes deepened. Suddenly, he whispered, "If you like... I can catch a few more for you."

"Ah?" Yun Yara froze, then laughed out loud. "Catch demon beasts to use as sitting couches?"

Isn't there only one Ancient Demon? Are there actually several?

Mo Han looked at her rare, smiling face, his heart surging with excitement, but on the surface, he remained serious as he said: "For you, there are as many as you require."

These words were spoken too naturally, the tone too steady. For a moment, Yun Yara actually blushed.

She turned her head away. "What nonsense are you spouting."

Mo Han chuckled low. He said no more, but the space between his brows was filled with unconcealable tenderness and satisfaction.

The Ancient Demon: "......"

At this moment, it felt that its existence was entirely superfluous.

Woo... I am unworthy of living in this space where the sweetness levels exceed the target limit!

Yun Yara slept for another three days and nights.

When she finally woke, although her spirit was still somewhat weary, the deep slumber of the past few days had finally allowed her complexion to improve.

The moment she opened her eyes, she saw Mo Han lying lazily beside her.

He held a stalk of dry grass between his teeth, both hands pillowed behind his head, legs crossed and tilted upwards, looking the very picture of leisurely contentment.

That appearance resembled nothing so much as a wild cat basking in the sun—and not just any cat, but the kind with a vast territory that no one dared provoke.

And the "bed" beneath the two of them was none other than the Ancient Demon of Absolute Void itself.

It had transformed on the spot into a giant, fluffy living sitting couch, daring not to move a muscle, resigned to quietly serving as a living spirit-mattress.

Yun Yara looked at this tableau and felt that something was decidedly amiss.

She cast a sidelong glance at him, asking tentatively, "Didn't you say your magical power was exhausted and we couldn't leave?"

Mo Han turned his head lazily to look at her. Just as he was about to speak, he suddenly let out a low, muffled groan—*"Urgh..."*—and clapped a hand over his chest, frowning in feigned pain. "Alas... indeed, I have not yet recovered. It hurts the moment I exert my *qi*."

Yara raised an eyebrow. "Where does it hurt?"

Mo Han replied with a face full of seriousness, "The injury is internal; it cannot be seen on the surface. Without my cultivation techniques, I am merely a mortal frame."

His tone was so solemn it sounded as if he had truly lost all his spiritual power and martial arts.

Beneath them, the Ancient Demon of Absolute Void, serving as the bed, rolled its eyes so hard it nearly saw its own brain.

Does the Liege Lord truly take this tens-of-thousands-of-years-old demon for an ignorant cub with this hair-raisingly clumsy acting?

The Ancient Demon muttered internally:

The Liege Lord has lied six times today, abducted a person once, and lost control of his facial management twice... The way I see it, the Liege Lord's unrequited love... is a lost cause.

"I clearly remember drifting between sleep and wakefulness a few times," Yara said suspiciously. "It seemed I saw you over there yesterday teasing a rabbit, kicking stones, drinking spirit water..."

Before she could finish her sentence, Mo Han suddenly pulled her over.

She threw herself to his side, nearly crashing headlong into his embrace.

"What are you doing!" Yara's eyes widened.

Mo Han turned his head to look at her, his tone extremely innocent as he said, "No such thing occurred. I fear you must have been dreaming."

With that, his handsome brows knitted together fiercely, as if he were in extreme agony. "Ah, right now I have no magic whatsoever, and my body is ice-cold. You cultivate Yang spiritual energy... come closer and give me some warmth. That isn't too much to ask, is it?"

He then added a supplementary sentence: "Consider it lying on me to rest, and incidentally... helping me heal my injuries."

Yun Yara's face heated up slightly. Just as she wanted to struggle free, she saw him looking at her with an expression that said *"If you don't help me, you are leaving me to die,"* yet his tone was gentle without leaving a trace of pressure.

Yun Yara: "......"

The Ancient Demon could bear it no longer and muttered in a small voice, "I've never heard of Yang spiritual energy being used as a stove..."

Mo Han raised an eyelid without changing his expression, his tone faint. "Hmm?"

The Ancient Demon of Absolute Void shut its mouth immediately, shrinking itself into an even softer shape, striving to create the illusion of a competent seat cushion.

The corner of Yun Yara's mouth twitched, but in the end, she did not break free. She silently lay down beside him, her face turned outward.

Her heartbeat, however, began to beat subtly out of control.

She dared not ask in detail, for she was certain this fellow was spouting nonsense.

But for some reason... she actually felt that this... wasn't bad.

Mo Han watched the way the tips of her ears turned completely red. The corner of his lips hooked up lightly, and he smiled without a sound.

This "healing session" in Fallen Mist Valley was even sweeter... than he had anticipated.

* * * * *

The Ancient Demon of Absolute Void retracted its demonic aura, transforming its massive form into a body as soft as cloud-fleece.

Yun Yara and Mo Han lay quietly upon this fluffy expanse.

In the depths of the valley, mist curled in gentle spirals, and sunlight filtered through the valley mouth, casting dappled shadows upon the ground. The atmosphere was as tender as a dream.

Mo Han's heart was blooming with uncontainable joy. He was just about to lower his head and draw closer, his hand brushing against her fingertips, intending to bridge the final distance.

The corner of his lips had just hooked up into a roguish grin when suddenly...

"Your Highness!"

A call like a clap of thunder exploded within the valley.

Before he could react, countless demonic auras surged in from all directions.

The spiritual mist within Fallen Mist Valley was shaken until it scattered; the light of the sky changed abruptly as black clouds pressed down upon the borders.

Two Demon Generals and over a dozen demon soldiers arrived riding the wind. Leading them was Zhu Wue, the Left Commander of the Demon Realm. His face was filled with shock, rage, and disbelief.

At a single glance, he saw his own Crown Prince lying in an embrace with a female cultivator of the Immortal Realm.

Although their clothes were intact, their breaths were intertwined, and the atmosphere was ambiguous to the point of being... unbearable to behold!

The demon soldiers stared, dumbfounded. Only two words floated into their brains:

"Dual Cultivation?"

"Cough, cough... the situation is like this..." As the sole witness to the entire process, the Ancient Demon of Absolute Void was just about to offer a few words of explanation when it was pressed back down by a single look from Mo Han.

Mo Han, who a moment ago had looked like a leisurely wild cat, instantly retracted all his languor and smiles. He sat up straight, questioning coldly, "Who permitted you to trespass into the valley bottom?"

Zhu Wue clasped his hands, his expression difficult. "Reporting to Your Highness.

The Demon King learned that you fell into Fallen Mist Valley closely following this fairy and lost contact for several days.

He was furious, suspecting the Immortal Realm had laid a trap, and ordered us to bring troops for search and rescue... We did not expect..."

He cast a glance at Yun Yara, his tone carrying an unconcealable complexity and suspicion.

Yun Yara also sat up. Although she felt humiliated and annoyed inside, she gritted her teeth to maintain her dignity. She understood that this "misunderstanding" was already difficult to explain.

"Return to the Demon Palace. Your Royal Father awaits your report."

Mo Han gave a low "Mm," turning his head sideways to look at Yun Yara. Finally, a trace of reluctance surfaced in his eyes. "You too..." *Come back with me.*

"I will not go." She shook her head, cutting off his unfinished sentence. Her tone was calm but resolute.

Mo Han froze. In the next instant, he rose and took a step closer to her, his voice lowering. "Fallen Mist Valley does not suit you. Return with me to the Demon Palace. With me there, you need not hide in the east and conceal yourself in the west."

Yun Yara raised her head to gaze into the depths of his eyes, her tone colder than his. "Who said I wanted to hide? I am returning to the Lingxiao Sect."

"That place treats you so, yet you still wish to return?" Mo Han could not stop the chill spreading in his heart. She wanted to leave so freely and easily; did the days and nights they had spent together mean absolutely nothing to her?

"What do you mean?" Yun Yara shed her previous docile appearance, her beautiful face turning icy. "How has the Lingxiao Sect treated me? Do you also believe that with my current status, I am unworthy of returning to the Lingxiao Sect?"

"That is not what I meant..."

Before he could finish, she interrupted him, clasping her hands respectfully in a formal bow. "There is no need to explain. My entry into the Demon Realm was a moment of impulse during the incident that day. I hope Crown Prince Mo Han will let bygones be bygones."

The atmosphere of confrontation between the two silenced the surrounding demon soldiers. The Ancient Demon of Absolute Void shrank into a ball, attempting to blend into the background.

Mo Han lowered his eyes. After a moment of silence, he finally turned and instructed Zhu Wue: "Escort her out of the valley."

He intended to personally send her off for a stretch of the journey, but he was blocked by another elder—a personal attendant from the Demon King's seat, his expression stern and authoritative.

"The Demon King has issued a decree: The Crown Prince must not leave without permission. Please forgive our presumption."

Mo Han's brows locked tight. He turned back to look at her one last time.

Yun Yara said nothing. She merely nodded lightly, turned, and departed with the demon soldiers, her skirt fluttering in the wind.

He stood in place, letting the wind mess his hair, his gaze sinking inch by inch into the shadows.

The tenderness of moments ago seemed to be merely a dream. Now that the dream had awakened, he could only watch the view of her back as she left.

Mo Han stood rooted to the spot, watching Yun Yara's retreating figure in silence, uttering not a single word.

She walked with resolution, her steps steady, without even a peripheral glance back.

A cold wind brushed through the valley bottom, lifting the corners of his loose ink-black robes and disturbing the emotions he had suppressed at the bottom of his heart for so long.

His hand hung at his side; his knuckles trembled slightly, yet in the end, he did not reach out, nor did he take even a single step forward.

For days, they had travelled shoulder to shoulder through the mountains and rivers of the Demon Realm, sleeping in desolate forests at night, sharing a single mount.

He had thought—at the very least—she would have a moment of hesitation, that she would look back at him just once.

But there was nothing.

She truly left just like that. Following the demon soldiers guiding her way, her slender silhouette gradually vanished from his sight.

His face was expressionless, his gaze calm to the point of heartlessness. Only the fine crack appearing on the spirit jade clutched tightly in his palm silently betrayed his emotions.

Heh. He let out a lost laugh.

It turns out that even after I accompanied you across a thousand mountains and ten thousand rivers, through your lowest tides and darkest valleys, I am not worth a single backward glance from you... not even one.

His voice was extremely low, almost swallowed by the sound of the wind. But he heard it clearly himself.

Xie Wuchen
謝無塵

Chapter 21: Fairy 'Playing Solitude'

When Yun Lili stepped once more across the threshold of the Mission Pavilion, she distinctly felt the gazes of numerous cultivators sweeping over her—strange, probing, and laden with meaning.

There were those hiding behind their sleeves to snigger, those engaging in whispered colloquies, and those who brazenly whipped out their Heaven-Illuminating Mirrors to snap secret photos on the spot.

She couldn't be bothered to pay them any mind.

In any case, the skin of her face had long since been cultivated to the maximum level; she was here solely for Spirit Stones, regardless of the cost to her dignity.

She flipped through a few pages of the mission board.

The first few entries were relatively normal: seeking spirit herbs, driving away demon beasts, escorting noble personages... but the remuneration was heinously low, enough to make one's hair stand on end in indignation.

Gritting her teeth, her fingertip paused, then tapped open the mission that looked the most inexplicable of them all.

[Participate in the Immortal Realm Talent Show Livestream — Remuneration: 80 Medium-Grade Spirit Stones]

She had originally assumed this was a prank listed by some cultivator so bored they were growing mould. She never expected that in the very next instant, a system notification sound would chime in her ear:

"Mission accepted successfully. Teleportation initiating immediately."

A flash of brilliance blinded her.

By the time she recovered her wits, she was already standing upon a high stage ablaze with brilliant lights.

Before her lay a floating screen of light, where hundreds of thousands of cultivators were gathering to spectate.

Not far away, several cultivators with fluttering sleeves and faces brimming with smiles were taking turns showcasing their talents.

Some wielded swords in a dance, some played celestial music, and one was even appraising spirit wine against spirit pills...

The Performing Immortal Terrace was paved today with ten miles of a "Galaxy Carpet." Only when Lili stepped onto it did she realise it was made of solidified rosy clouds; with every step, ripples of seven-coloured light would spread out beneath her feet.

The Host Cultivator's voice pierced through the Thirty-Six Heavens:

"Let us welcome the phenomenal contestant, from the Inner Sect of the Lingxiao Sect—Fairy 'Playing Solitude'!"

With the host's passionate and exuberant shout, she was pushed forward by staff members, looking utterly bewildered, while a high-grade spirit zither (*qin*) was forcibly stuffed into her hands.

"What kind of ghostly title is this?!" Lili nearly crushed the jade flute—no, the zither—given by the sponsor.

Suddenly, a voice transmission rang out in her sea of consciousness:

"There is no helping it. In response to the sponsor's request, we had to use this name."

Yun Lili closed her eyes in despair. "......"

The voice in her head continued:

"It doesn't matter. Just play whatever you like. Remember the Three Key Secrets: Close your eyes, knit your brows, and finally, you must let out a light, profound sigh—remember this!"

She subconsciously wanted to say,

"I don't know how to play," but the voice in her head continued to remind her: *"Just strum a few times randomly. The temperament and atmosphere are paramount—remember, it must be that drifting, ethereal immortal vibe!"*

She took a deep breath, telling herself secretly that for the sake of the Spirit Stones, she would risk it all today.

The sound of the zither rang out, utterly devoid of method or law. There were even a few broken notes and stuck strings. Yet, unexpectedly, it combined with her slightly dazed and blank expression to cultivate an aura of "The profoundly melancholic me, and the you who cannot climb high enough to reach me."

The audience below exploded instantly.

"Wow, what an ethereal feeling!"

"This is my first time hearing such Abstract School Immortal Sound; my eardrums have been vibrated into enlightenment!"

"Her temperament is absolute perfection. I suspect she is not human, but the reincarnation of some ancient almighty being who has been in seclusion for a thousand years!"

"Great Sound is Silent! *This* is the realm of returning to one's original simplicity!" On the judges' panel, a Millennium Crane Spirit was so excited his feathers faded in colour. "Did you all hear the rhythm of the Forty-Nine Heavenly Tribulations hidden within those zither notes?"

"Vote for her! Quickly, vote for her! I want to see what earth-shattering work she can play in the next round!"

Thunderous applause erupted from the spectator seats. A sword cultivator achieved sudden enlightenment on the spot, the anomaly of "Three Flowers Gathering at the Summit" appearing above his head. There was even a flock of colourful birds—origin unknown—circling endlessly above her head.

Lili stole a glance at the real-time voting on the light screen—the numbers behind her name were soaring at a terrifying speed. In the blink of an eye.

She had suppressed the "Nine-Tailed Sky Fox Dancer" who had held the championship for three consecutive terms.

Turning her head, she caught a glimpse of that Nine-Tailed Sky Fox Dancer, whose nose was crooked with anger, fur bristling all over, with actual smoke rising from her head.

Yun Lili retreated from the high stage with a stiff smile frozen on her face. Her mind was still a void, but the notification sound of Spirit Stones chimed *ding-ding* incessantly.

Eighty Medium-Grade Spirit Stones were deposited into her spirit stone pouch, without a single cent missing.

She suspected this world had gone stark raving mad.

When she returned to her residence, Moony was already waiting at the doorway, her face radiant with excitement.

She held the Heaven-Illuminating Mirror in her hands, her eyes practically glowing. "Miss! You were truly too amazing today! That aura, that zither sound, that face... you actually shot straight into the Top Three of the Immortal Realm's Hot List!"

"...Ah?"

Yun Lili pinched the bridge of her nose. "What did you say?"

"Third place on the Immortal Realm Hot List! The net is full of people guessing which hidden hermit sect you, the Great Immortal, emerged from. Some say the Zither Dao Sect secretly sent you to crash the venue, while others say you must be a descendant of the Phoenix Clan, born with the natural cry of the phoenix."

"Let me see that!" She snatched the Heaven-Illuminating Mirror from Moony's hands and began swiping through it herself.

If she hadn't looked, she would have been fine; looking at it caused a rush of blood to her brain.

—*"Sister's frown has such a sense of broken fragility."*

—*"Begging for a class on how to play broken notes with the imposing momentum of a heavenly tribulation."*

—*"So in love with Sister's melancholic eyes."*

Lili: "......"

She really, truly wanted to curse someone.

She didn't even own a decent Heaven-Illuminating Mirror yet, but she had somehow exploded into an Immortal Net celebrity.

"Detestable!" She gritted her teeth and cursed in a low voice. "For such a highlight moment of my life, I actually have to mooch off *your* mirror just to watch the replay?"

As she spoke, she rolled her eyes towards the heavens.

She tossed the spirit zither—the very instrument upon which she had randomly strummed a miracle—to the side, huffing with a look of unwillingness. "For the sake of Spirit Stones, this Young Miss has already abandoned her face to the extreme."

Moony immediately leaned in close, her eyes sparkling like stars. "So, will Miss go again tomorrow?"

A raging fire of determination ignited in the depths of Lili's eyes.

"Go! Of course I will go! I will not stop until I buy that Heaven-Illuminating Mirror that comes with its own celestial *qi* filter and makes the skin glow!"

Her goal was crystal clear—Spirit Stones, Filters, Beautification. Of this holy trinity, not a single one could be missing!

* * * * *

Yun Lili sat upon a stone beside the spiritual fields, her gaze hollow and vacant as she watched the spirit chickens brawling not far away, patiently awaiting her next opportunity to take the stage.

She let out a sigh, fishing her purse from her sleeve and giving it a shake.

Mm, there is a bit of a sound. She felt a flicker of happiness.

Fortunately, she had earned a full eighty Spirit Stones today. *Heh,* last time, she had only earned thirty Low-Grade Spirit Stones translating for a spirit pet that enjoyed weeping in the night. Before the stones were even warm in her hand, half had been spent buying snake-repelling talismans.

"This won't do... if this continues, not only will I be unable to afford to replenish my pills, I won't even be able to afford the teleportation talisman to return to the sect." She clutched her head and wailed, "Not knowing how to ride a sword is like having no legs; I am forced to buy teleportation talismans!"

Just then, a familiar voice rang out leisurely.

"Yun Little Li?"

Lili turned her head to look. Xie Wuchen stood behind her, holding a fragrant pear in his hand. He ate and smiled simultaneously, wearing an expression that said, *"I have long since seen through everything."*

"...What are you doing here?" she asked grumpily.

"Naturally, I am here to bring you a new opportunity to earn Spirit Stones." Xie Wuchen blinked his eyes. "I watched your livestream yesterday, you know."

"What?" Lili raised her guard.

He extracted a glittering golden slip of paper from his sleeve, waving it mysteriously before her face.

"The Immortal Realm Talent Selection. How about it? Any interest?"

"...Hah?"

"The largest selection competition for genius rising stars in the entire Immortal Domain, jointly hosted by the Four Great Immortal Sects, exclusively broadcast by the Sky Mysterious Terrace, and livestreamed the entire way. *Tsk tsk,* with your looks and recent traffic volume, it would be a pity not to go."

The corner of Lili's mouth twitched; she suspected she was being treated as some sort of "Traffic-Driving Spirit Cultivator."

"Are you trying to tell me to become an opera actor?"

"They aren't called actors anymore; they are called 'New Stars', do you understand?" Xie Wuchen smiled harmlessly. "Furthermore, there are Spirit Stone rewards, magical artifact sponsorships, and investor funding. You could even be selected for the Immortal Sect's key cultivation list. Promotions, salary increases, and riding on cloud boats will no longer be a dream."

"......"

Lili was silent for three seconds, then asked, "So, do I just have to stand there and strike a random pose like before, or casually pluck the zither twice?"

"No, this is different from the format you participated in these past few days. This time, it is a competition of talent. You must sing, dance, fight monsters, have heart-to-heart talks, and... hmm... display your unique, exclusive skills."

"Mm, that sounds a bit difficult." She intended to beat a retreat.

"NO, NO, NO~" Xie Wuchen patted her shoulder with a face full of benevolence. "Everyone—oh, no, every immortal and cultivator—excels in at least one area. Think carefully; what are your strengths?"

"I... I can cook soup..." she said weakly after thinking for a long time.

Back in Cloud Village, after picking herbs, she would sell most to the apothecary, but she would also cook a portion into medicinal soups to sell for a little extra money.

Xie Wuchen slapped a heavy palm onto her shoulder, nearly causing her to lose her balance and fall forward. "Perfect! The Immortal Realm has been lacking 'Health and Wellness' stream fairies in recent years! I have already signed you up."

Yun Lili shook violently. "Uh? When did you...?"

"Just now, while you were counting your Spirit Stones. Don't worry, I even chose a stage name for you. It is called... Little Fairy Li."

Lili petrified on the spot.

Little Fairy Li? That counts as a stage name?!

It was barely different from her original name.

She truly doubted whether Xie Wuchen's literary attainments were learned from his physical education instructor.

But she had to admit, at least it was much stronger than that unreliable "Fairy 'Playing Solitude'" from yesterday.

Just as she wanted to protest, Xie Wuchen had already turned and strutted away, speaking as he walked: "Don't forget, the preliminary selection is tomorrow. Do not be late. I fought hard to get you a face-revealing shot; no need to thank me~"

"......"

Watching his retreating figure, Lili felt her scalp go numb.

Why did she feel that she had ceased to be a female cultivator... and instead become an artist under Xie Wuchen's management?

Oh, no. An *Artiste*!

* * * * *

Within the Black Hall of the Demon Palace, towering ten thousand fathoms high, demonic flames burned with ferocious intensity.

The atmosphere was heavy, pressing down like the weight of a thousand mountains.

Mo Han knelt on one knee at the foot of the dais. Behind him stood dozens of high-ranking ministers of the Demon Realm, standing in silent rows. No one dared to utter a sound; they heard only a low, heavy harrumph resounding from the high throne above.

"As the Crown Prince, you actually hid in Fallen Mist Valley for days for the sake of a petty immortal from the Celestial Realm?!"

The one who spoke was the Lord of the Demon Realm, the ruler of the Nine Nethers—Demon Lord Sha Yan.

This man had controlled the Demon Realm for a thousand years.

His cultivation base was unfathomable, his appearance handsome and sharp as a sword, but his eyes were a terrifying red-gold, like blood mixed with metal.

His joy and anger were indistinguishable, and those who offended his majesty were invariably reduced to flying ash and smoke.

Mo Han raised his head, his gaze calm. "Father, please quell your anger. Your son merely experienced a momentary fluctuation in cultivation and needed to enter the valley to regulate his breath."

Demon Lord Sha Yan slammed his hand upon the armrest of the throne, his voice booming like thunder: "Who do you think you are fooling?!

The entire Demon Realm knows you went missing alongside that woman from the Celestial Realm for several days. Rumours are rife outside that you and she have already engaged in 'Dual Cultivation'! Preposterous!"

A low murmur of noise rippled through the great hall. Some demon generals could not suppress their sniggers, but a single glare from Demon Lord Sha Yan silenced them instantly, making them as quiet as stone discs.

"Mo Han!" Demon Lord Sha Yan laughed in extreme anger. "I do not care whom you play with or whom you tease, but you are the Crown Prince of my Demon Realm! Playing is permitted; catching feelings is absolutely forbidden!"

"What you carry on your shoulders is the fate of a million demon soldiers and a foundation of a thousand years, not some trivial romantic entanglement!"

Mo Han was silent for a moment before looking up and speaking faintly, "Father, quell your anger. Your son was merely using her for some amusement."

"Oh?" Demon Lord Sha Yan's voice turned abruptly cold. "Then does You Luo count?"

As his voice fell, a figure walked out gracefully from the rear of the hall. Her waist swayed like a willow, her eyes were like peach blossoms, and her red robes were like fire. With a gait that swayed three times with every step, she arrived before Mo Han.

She was the First Demoness of the Demon Palace, You Luo.

This woman hailed from a branch of the Fox Clan; her maternal clan governed the arts of enchantment and mind control. She possessed a natural, devastating beauty and an innate seductiveness.

A single pair of fox eyes could hook the soul and seize the spirit; all who had seen her were left haunted by dreams of her.

She laughed softly, turning her delicate body sideways. "Your Highness, the Demon Lord says that as long as you are willing, I am your Crown Princess."

The atmosphere in the hall changed abruptly. The eyes of many demon generals flashed with envy and approval.

To have such a stunner as You Luo for a companion—would that not be the height of pleasure?

Yet Mo Han's complexion showed not a single ripple of fluctuation.

He merely averted his gaze indifferently, his voice as cold as a frozen sword edge. "Father, this son has never held romantic feelings for You Luo."

The smile on You Luo's face did not diminish, but her gaze grew a little deeper. "Your Highness, but I have intentions towards *you*."

Demon Lord Sha Yan laughed as well, smiling with a permeating killing intent. He leaned forward from his throne, looking down at his son. "Women are tools to assist you in stabilizing power and seizing dominance, not for discussing sentiment!"

"What use is 'like' or 'dislike'?"

"Can that little fairy help you seize power? Can she control the demons on your behalf?"

Mo Han's fists clenched tightly within his sleeves, his knuckles turning white. It was a long time before he spoke slowly: "She does not need to."

Demon Lord Sha Yan's smile deepened. "Planning to speak the truth now?" He looked as though he had seen through his son completely. "Your mouth is still hard. You still won't admit you intend to make her your Crown Princess?"

"Father need not worry. Regarding the position of Crown Princess, your son will deliberate on his own."

A deathly silence fell over the hall.

This sentence was like a heavy nail, landing with a muffled thud in the heart of every demon general. The demonic artifacts lining the hall began to vibrate and buzz, resonating with the sudden shift in atmospheric pressure.

Only the Crown Prince dared to be so impudent, speaking out to contradict and defy the Demon Lord.

Demon Lord Sha Yan retracted some of his anger. He stared at his son with sunken eyes, silent for a long while, his gaze seeming to want to pierce right through him.

"Since it is so..." he said coldly, "then you choose for yourself."

"If she truly has the qualifications to become your Crown Princess, then let her survive my test."

"I will be waiting to see if she is worth you are betraying the entire Demon Realm for her sake."

With those words, he turned and departed, his figure vanishing into the depths of the demonic flames, leaving the sound of a cold wind whistling through the full hall.

You Luo looked at Mo Han, her eyes turning, her seductive smile undimmed. "That sister from the Celestial Realm is truly intriguing... exactly how much skill does she possess to teach our cold-hearted Crown Prince the meaning of infatuation?"

Mo Han did not answer, though he was somewhat surprised by his Royal Father's final words.

You Luo's pair of soft hands were just about to climb up Mo Han's straight, tall back, but he flashed sideways, dodging her touch.

"Your Highness, why not give You Luo a chance..."

Mo Han simply turned away, gazing quietly into the distance, thinking...

He did not know if Yun Yara could walk into this Demon Palace, but perhaps, he could leave this Demon Palace for her.

She leaves the Lingxiao Sect, and he leaves the Nether Palace.

Is that not... just right?

Chapter 22: The Carbon Copy and the Crushing Arrival

The selection **pageant** was being held at the **Vast Immortal Terrace**, a designated site beneath the main Heavenly Esplanade. Cloud vapour wreathed the area, and a multitude of cultivators gathered.

The Four Great Immortal Sects had erected viewing platforms for dignitaries. Though Celestial Lord Jì Míng himself was absent, he had dispatched a **Transmission Mirror** to monitor the proceedings.

Furthermore, he had, inexplicably, commissioned several "Celebrity Commentators of the Immortal Realm" to provide live commentary and analysis.

The Heavenly Esplanade was experiencing an unprecedented turnout.

What was originally intended as a conventional youth pageant—a simple process for young disciples to garner acclaim and catch the eye of major sects—had somehow become entwined with Celestial Lord Jì Míng's surveillance mirror, causing the overall viewership to skyrocket.

The entire spectacle resembled the celestial equivalent of a reality television show entitled *The Immortals Have Talent*.

Yun Lili was hiding desperately behind the crowd, clutching the chicken in her arms, shivering visibly.

She had specifically chosen the most photogenic rooster of the three to accompany her onto the stage, believing that its proud, vigorous demeanour would surely earn her favourable reviews.

But now…

Well, she felt profoundly discouraged.

"Is this truly mandatory? I merely intended to earn some spiritual stones… why does it feel precisely as though I am about to be escorted onto the execution scaffold?"

Xie Wuchen, standing nearby, smiled with a knowing, almost malevolent amusement: "Heh heh, are you not acutely lacking in spiritual stones? To be selected within the top ten nets you one thousand superior-grade spiritual stones. Top three yields two thousand superior-grade stones, and if you secure first place… heh heh, that award includes three thousand superior-grade stones, plus one thousand medium-grade stones, and a formal letter of recommendation for major sect entry."

Truth be told, upon hearing the sheer quantity and quality of the spiritual stones on offer, Yun Lili was shamefully, irrevocably tempted.

Xie Wuchen continued his helpful counsel: "You must carefully assess your current level of cultivation. Relying on piecemeal labour and odd jobs will never allow you to save enough spiritual stones to purchase even one single, high-quality **Celestial Mirror**."

Yun Lili: "……" *To her immense chagrin, she could not offer a single counter-argument.*

Her lack of powerful techniques meant she constantly relied on purchasing supplementary talismans, such as simple sound-transmission spells.

Reluctantly, Yun Lili was forced to stand near the stage, watching the endless parade of contestants performing their talents.

"Next! We welcome Junior Sister Yu Qing of the Scarlet Lingxiao Sect, who brings us… the **Nine Heavens Phoenix Cry Sword Dance**!"

"Wow…" The assembled audience gasped in collective admiration.

Junior Sister Yu Qing leaped gracefully into the air, her long sword transforming into the illusionary image of a phoenix.

Landing with a smooth pivot, her figure was enchanting, and the phantom sword light even managed to cleanly cleave a spiritual peach tree at the edge of the stage, drawing searing glances from every male cultivator present.

Yun Lili: "…What kind of extreme, competitive Immortal beauty pageant is this?"

The next contestant: "The Spiritual Beast PK segment! Welcome Jing Yang, a disciple from the Mount Yuheng Sect! Please present your Spiritual Beast!"

Jing Yang flicked his sleeve, releasing a **Three-Eyed Golden-Feathered Mink**. The creature appeared, performed a seamless backflip, then stood on one paw, spitting fire and water in quick succession, drawing thunderous applause from the crowd.

Yun Lili silently looked at the chicken that currently occupied her spiritual beast pouch.

"…What can you possibly do besides roll around and steal my sugar spheres?"

The rooster: "*Cluck, cluck.*"

Following him, a maiden in white robes took the stage, playing a seven-stringed zither that had been subtly transformed from a flying sword.

The flowing music summoned colourful clouds from the sky, causing countless male cultivators in the audience to clutch their hearts in rapture.

The next contestant was a male cultivator in red robes. He roared loudly, releasing spiritual fire that materialised into a **'Golden-Flame Sky Fox'** in midair, then commanded it to perform a sequence of continuous side-flips and ball-spinning tricks.

The host praised him enthusiastically: "Magnificent! This contestant's combination of fire magic and spiritual beast talent is exceptionally creative!"

Meanwhile, her little rooster was quietly hiding by her feet, attempting to consume a dropped sugar sphere.

Yun Lili silently reviewed the entry in her own talent application form:

"Life-Nourishing Medicinal Spiritual Stew."

"…Seriously, what can you actually do?" she asked the chicken, clinging to a thread of hope.

The little rooster looked up: *"Cluck, cluck."*

"You can't even manage a simple roll-around out there?"

"Cluck, cluck!" (It then performed a quick roll, followed by an audible burp.)

"You also think they are being utterly excessive, don't you?" Yun Lili sighed heavily.

"Cluck, cluck."

"Oh, it truly leaves a person no room to survive." Yun Lili sighed again, even more heavily.

"Cluck, cluck."

She was silent for three seconds: "Fine, we shall simply adopt the 'heartwarming parent-child' culinary path, then."

The host: "Next, we welcome Fairy Lili of the Lingxiao Sect, who brings us… er, a cooking demonstration?"

Finally, it was Yun Lili's turn. She took a deep breath. The audience stirred with palpable curiosity.

Yun Lili walked onto the stage with forced fortitude. She summoned a special, hand-crafted **Immortal Soup Pot** intended for nurturing elemental *qi*, and began a live demonstration of how to brew a "Heart-Cleansing Essence-Stabilising Broth" using five different spiritual herbs.

Midway through the brewing process, the pot lid flew off with a loud *Pah!* Steam aggressively billowed out, causing the audience to break into a coughing fit.

"Cough…"

"Is that meant to be Heart-Cleansing Essence-Stabilising Broth? It smells rather strongly of an **Asura Illusion-Mist**."

"Has she come to compete, host an Immortal medicinal food lecture, or merely set up a spiritual barrier for obscuration?"

A bead of cold sweat trickled down Yun Lili's forehead. She stared at the thoroughly burnt broth in her pot with profound disbelief; all the meticulous lines of stage dialogue she had prepared instantly vanished from her memory.

The host attempted to smooth over the awkwardness with a forced, rigid laugh: "Heh heh, Fairy Lili's broth… well, the steam is certainly curling beautifully, and it looks undeniably unique, doesn't it?"

Yun Lili managed a cold, strained smile, while internally she was sweating profusely: "Heh heh, my sincere apologies. Since the broth demonstration has proved somewhat unsuccessful, I shall make a simple, immediate switch to brewing tea. My sincerest apologies."

Immediately, she summoned a spiritual brazier and a spiritual spring kettle, and began to brew a **'Heart-Calming Clear Tea'**. She was just about to launch into an introduction regarding the three types of floral spiritual herbs infused within the tea—claiming they could regulate the *qi*, soothe the liver, and stabilise one's cultivation—

Yun Lili steadied herself, preparing to aggressively inject some emotional appeal into her "wellness philosophy," when suddenly—

BOOM—!

A clap of thunder echoed through the sky, and rays of colourful light descended. A magnificent cloud-boat, shining brilliantly, dropped from the heavens!

"It's… the Lingxiao Sect's exclusive ceremonial cloud-boat!"

The crowd instantly erupted into pandemonium!

"Look quickly! Is that not Fairy Yun Yara! She has returned!"

Yun Lili froze by her pot, staring at Yun Yara, who was slowly stepping out of the cloud-boat. Her robes fluttered majestically, her countenance was as pristine as snow, and her elegant demeanour was tinged with an inexplicable, subtle languor. Though she was merely walking, her movements seemed to generate their own slow-motion effect and accompanying celestial music.

She was suddenly struck by an intense, painful feeling of inadequacy. The Immortal Maiden, the one who had been mistakenly swapped with her at birth, looked profoundly more like a true Immortal Sect heiress than she ever could.

"Did Fairy Yun Yara not leave the Lingxiao Sect the day her true background was revealed?"

"How is it possible that she is here now?!"

"Could she, by chance, also be entering this very selection pageant?"

The host, eyes wide with opportunity, immediately abandoned Yun Lili and sprinted towards the viewing platform. The live cameras instantly swivelled, and even Celestial Lord Jì Míng's remote viewing mirror cut directly to Yun Yara's image.

Yun Lili: "……?"

Where is my tea?

I haven't even had the chance to demonstrate my prized chicken yet?

And I was on the verge of passionately reciting the five-element theory behind spiritual herb decoction!

She stood stranded on the stage, still holding a small wooden ladle, her face a mask of utter bewilderment.

At that moment, a disciple discretely handed her a slip of paper: "Fairy Lili, you may now gracefully concede and retire. The moment Fairy Yun Yara appeared, the entirety of the trending topic has been forcibly redirected to her."

Yun Lili: "……Right."

She silently gathered her pot and kettle and made a slow, quiet exit. Her small rooster followed quickly, *clucking* softly as it munched on a stray sugar sphere.

It simply wasn't fair… the angle from which Yun Yara had flown away after her spiritual assessment was so impossibly elegant and tragically beautiful... why could I not manage to replicate that style? If only I could now sweep my failed soup pot aside and make a dramatic exit, at least I wouldn't lose face quite so profoundly.

* * * * *

Yun Lili was just about to turn and exit the stage, one foot already stepping across the boundary, when an ice-cold voice, sharp as a blade, sliced through the clouds:

"Halt."

The voice was not loud, but it instantly suppressed the entire auditorium's clamour.

Yun Lili stiffened, turning her head slowly. She saw the woman in the snow-white robes on the high platform slowly rising.

A pair of eyes, cold as a deep pool in midwinter, were fixed immovably upon her.

The audience's chat-screens instantly exploded with a fresh barrage of comments:

It truly is Fairy Yun Yara...

Wow, Fairy Yun Yara has actually returned.

Aaaah! It is Fairy Yun Yara!! She just spoke out loud!

That formidable aura... too cold, too elegant, I cannot cope!

A confrontation of twin Immortals! Is this a battle between goddesses or a destined showdown?!

Yun Lili's heart leaped sharply. She instinctively clutched her sleeve, muttering quietly: "Heh heh, the timing of this intervention… it could not possibly be more inconvenient…"

Yun Yara stepped forward, her tone still completely devoid of discernible emotion: "You claim that tea to be a spiritual brew, yet you only stated its common name. Since you dare to present it on a selection stage, do you truly intend to depart without detailing its actual efficacy?"

The question landed like a bucket of cold water. The audience quieted for two tense breaths, before a wave of nervous whispers began to spread.

Yun Lili's mouth twitched, her smile fixed and strained. She attempted to placate the situation with falsely charming eyes: "This **'Heart-Calming Clear Tea'**, you see… er, it possesses nothing terribly special… it is simply, as the name suggests, calming, stabilising the mind and spirit, supplementing spiritual energy, and allowing the drinker to, well, feel a little better?"

Yun Yara's expression remained utterly unreadable. She spoke a single, uncompromising word: "**Taste.**"

Yun Lili stiffened her spine and, with immense inner reluctance, poured a fresh cup of the recently brewed tea, offering it to Yun Yara. In her mind, however, she was already rapidly calculating the fastest possible escape route should this moment turn into public humiliation, ensuring she could bolt without having her face caught on camera.

Yun Yara accepted the tea, lifted the cup with deliberate grace, and drank the entire contents in a single, fluid, elegant motion. After a slight, agonising pause that stretched the tension of the hall to its breaking point, she finally delivered her verdict:

".........Not bad."

Just two simple, understated words: *Not bad.*

But pronounced by Yun Yara, the words resonated as though they were the highest possible form of celestial commendation, carrying more weight than a thousand stanzas of praise.

BOOM!

The entire venue instantly erupted into fresh chaos, the silence utterly shattered.

"She offered praise! Fairy Yun Yara actually offered praise to a participant!"

"I put it to you, this tea must surely be the very legendary brew that Celestial Lord Yu was once seen partaking of, must it not..."

"The gentleman in the gallery is quite correct; I distinctly recall seeing the live stream before—Fairy Lili and Celestial Lord Yu were seen preparing tea and engaging in deep, meaningful conversation!"

"Wait a moment, my dear fellow, are you absolutely certain that was 'heartfelt conversation'?"

"Ehh, I recall hearing that it was merely a 'private lesson' regarding the basics of *qi* flow?"

"Aaaah! Please start selling it immediately! My spiritual stones are practically burning holes in my hand!"

Yun Lili was stunned into immobility for a second, then realised she was still stranded in the centre of the stage, being regarded by thousands of cultivators with intensely fervent, hungry eyes. She instantly felt her legs turn rather weak.

She managed a timid, awkward smile towards Yun Yara: "……My deepest thanks?"

Yun Yara, however, had already turned to leave. Her long sleeves fluttered once, her **aura** utterly transcendent, leaving behind a profound vacuum of silence and the lingering echo of her assessment.

* * * * *

Yun Zhou leaned lazily upon a jade throne, his fingertips lightly drumming against the armrest, his gaze fixed upon the projected light screen hovering in mid-air.

The image showed Yun Lili, coping awkwardly but determinedly with the host's challenging questions, managing to maintain a resolute façade of composure despite her obvious nervousness.

Xiao Yan stood beside him, arms crossed, his eyebrows slightly raised, his tone deeply layered with subtle meaning: "Your younger sister possesses considerable **nerve**… to dare participate in the Immortal Realm's selection pageant with a cooking pot."

The subtext was clear, echoing the earlier jibe: She has the hide of a rhinoceros, which explains why she dared pick up that random man's fallen trousers.

Yun Zhou merely snorted in disdain, his gaze shifting to another light screen which reflected Yun Yara's cold, aloof figure.

Cultivators respectfully stepped aside as she passed, bowing deferentially as she ascended the main platform.

"Yun Yara still carries the most formidable weight," he stated coolly. "A single, silent appearance is enough to effortlessly command and silence the entire venue."

Xiao Yan heard this, and glanced at him with a noncommittal, half-smile: "Heh, it seems both of your younger sisters are rather extraordinary individuals. Yun Yara, with her innate, cold pride and austere distance, is certainly… rather distinct from both you and the Sect Master Yun."

*—The clear implication being: Given the vast difference in **demeanour**, surely she cannot be your natural sibling?*

Yun Zhou narrowed his eyes dangerously: "Different in what precise manner, dare I ask?"

Xiao Yan's mouth twitched slightly, hesitating, avoiding eye contact.

—Doesn't the obvious truth already reside deep within your own conscience? You and your father adopt a righteous, solemn façade in public, only to immediately reveal your true, frivolous, and sarcastic selves the moment you open your mouths. You are, quite frankly, the Immortal Realm's equivalent of a notorious, wisecracking Hip-Hop Duo.

"Do elaborate further, I demand it." Yun Zhou demanded impatiently, rapping his finger on the table.

"Ahem…" Xiao Yan cleared his throat for purely tactical reasons, then chose his words with meticulous caution: "I was merely suggesting… do you not perceive that young Lili, your sister, actually resembles the two of you far more closely?" Seeing Yun Zhou's eyebrow twitch sharply, he swiftly added, "For instance, right now—her entire bearing of 'Fear no celestial authority, only ensure the spiritual stones are accounted for' is an absolute replica of your own past attitude."

Yun Zhou fell silent, his gaze returning to Yun Lili. The maiden was discreetly attempting to pocket the spiritual fruits offered by a sponsor, her movements so practised it was almost endearing.

After a long pause, he murmured: "She resembles me?… She certainly never worked as diligently as I did in my youth, I assure you."

"You worked diligently?" Xiao Yan sneered openly. "A sheltered second-generation Immortal relying entirely on his father's backing—do you honestly expect anyone to believe that statement yourself?"

Yun Zhou's face instantly darkened. He snatched up the spiritual melon seeds at hand and hurled them fiercely at Xiao Yan.

Xiao Yan deftly dodged the missile, not forgetting to add fuel to the fire with a pointed remark: "Are you agitated? It appears I have accurately hit upon the truth—"

Before the sentence was fully finished, the entire hall suddenly trembled violently. The constellation map on the vaulted ceiling violently illuminated.

Both men turned their heads simultaneously, focusing on the palace entrance—

A figure in pristine white robes, Yu Sord, stepped across the threshold, visibly shattering the protective seals. His sword was still sheathed, yet the **pressure** emanating from his being caused cracks to spider across the floor tiles.

He lifted his gaze, his eyes like razor blades fixed intently upon Yun Zhou:

"I heard your younger sister is severely lacking in spiritual stones?"

"Uh…?" Both men looked at the newcomer, their expressions a confused mixture of shock and utter bewilderment.

Yun Zhou recovered first, his handsome brows furrowed in suspicion and defensive annoyance: "No, I just asked, what business is it of yours if my sister lacks spiritual stones?"

Xiao Yan: "……"

Chapter 23: The Androgynous Madman and the Trembling Rabbit

The night was deep, the wind biting, and all creation had returned to silence.

Yet, the plum blossom forest behind Lingxiao Mountain remained fragrant.

Every tree and every branch was dusted with pale snow, the clear scent drifting to the farthest distance.

Yun Zhou strolled forth alone. In his left hand, he held a pot of plum brew; in his right, he clasped a raw, unpruned plum branch.

He leaned lazily against a stone platform within the forest, tilting his head back to down a mouthful of wine.

His mood was depressed, his brow slightly furrowed as he murmured, "That madman living atop Mount Alioth is simply baffling. Asking such a foolish question? Is my Lingxiao Sect lacking in Spirit Stones?"

With a flutter of movement, he flew upwards, leaning obliquely against a treetop branch. Behind him, a half-moon hung in the sky, silhouetting his profile and making him appear even more ethereal and immortal.

"Why doesn't he die of showing off? Is he, surnamed Yu, the only one with money?"

His posture was dissolute and roguish, hovering between righteous and wicked.

His long fingers flicked idly against the blue-and-white porcelain wine bottle.

"Tsk... this plum wine is inferior to the spirit tea brewed by my sister."

Scarcely had his voice faded when chaotic footsteps sounded from within the forest.

Several male cultivators, dressed in the robes of a different sect, stumbled drunkenly into the plum forest.

The leader caught a glimpse of Zhou and his eyes went straight. He excitedly patted the shoulder of the person beside him.

"Oi, oi, look over there... *Hss*, where did such a... fairy come from in this plum forest?"

"Truly a beauty with cold bones..."

"Tsk, the temperament is truly cold. Is she perhaps some hidden sect's... Come, let's go over and strike up a conversation."

Zhou had his back to them. His robes were as white as the moon, his long hair half-bound, his silver crown tilted slightly askew.

He shook his head slightly in his drunkenness, revealing a red mole on one side of his neck. He was beautiful to the point of unreality.

The male cultivators exchanged glances, emboldened themselves, and walked forward.

"Fairy, this humble one is Li Chengfeng of the Taiyuan Sect. Meeting you today is truly fate. I wonder if I might—"

Before he could finish his sentence, that "fairy" who had been leaning back and drinking turned his face sideways.

A pair of phoenix eyes glanced over, holding three parts drunkenness and seven parts killing intent.

Even with his face full of murderous intent, the male immortals still stared, dumbstruck.

"Fairy..."

"...Who said I am a fairy?"

In the next breath, the sword named *'Liu Hua'* (Flowing Brilliance) flew from his sleeve. A cold glint swept instantly before the crowd.

Bang—!

Plum branches shattered and fell. The sword *qi* swept horizontally through the air, instantly carving several inch-deep sword marks into the ground.

The men were so frightened their legs went soft, and they fell to their knees.

"Y-Y-Y-You are a man?!"

"Cut the crap." Zhou brushed his hair back, his tone deadly faint. "If you ask that again right now, this Immortal Lord will immediately turn *you* into a woman."

With that, he waved his hand. The group scrambled and rolled out of the plum forest, their voices cracking with terror in the wind.

"Still not scrambling?!"

"That is Yun Zhou—that androgynous madman of the Lingxiao Sect!!"

"Let's go, quickly!"

Zhou paid them no further heed. He merely raised his head to drink the last mouthful of wine, cursing in a low voice. "Trash!"

He shook the wine bottle and found that the plum wine inside had all spilled. Anger rose from nowhere, and he casually tossed the wine bottle to the side.

Suddenly, a *thud* sound, accompanied by a tiny rustle, rang out from nearby—as if something had been startled and shrunk into the grass.

Zhou tilted his head slightly. He saw a snow-white little rabbit squatting beneath a cluster of fallen plum blossoms, shivering and trembling, its ears standing straight up.

He froze, staring at it for a moment.

After a few breaths, he stood up, walked over, and half-squatted down.

"...Were you scared by me as well?"

The little rabbit trembled, its twin red eyes staring at him, daring not move a muscle.

He suddenly let out a soft chuckle. Extending his long fingers, he lifted the white rabbit by the scruff of its neck, bringing it level with his own line of sight.

"Actually... rather cute."

The little white rabbit kicked its hind legs futilely, its red eyes glaring accusingly at the mischief-maker before it.

After regarding it for a moment, he set the little white rabbit down. He then untied a dry cloth from the edge of his sleeve, folded it, and placed it before the rabbit. "I startled you today. It is a pity the plum wine is finished, but in the days to come, I shall gift you a bottle by way of apology."

Then he turned to depart, the view of his back proud and aloof, yet carrying a subtle trace of desolation.

Yet he halted his steps once more. Turning back to glance at the little rabbit, he suddenly bent down and gently planted that unpruned plum branch into the earth beside the cloth.

"This sprig of plum blossoms... I leave it for you."

He murmured in a low voice, "When the flowers bloom next year, if you still remember me—"

The sentence remained unfinished. He had already turned and walked away. Snow fell upon his shoulders, melting into the corners of his robes.

As for that rabbit, it was a long time before it hopped two steps forward. It hid itself between the dry cloth and the plum branch he had left behind, curling itself into a tight ball.

The plum blossom swayed gently, shaking loose a single petal of snow.

Its red eyes stared blankly at that retreating figure, motionless, as if it were carving the scent of wine, the colour of the moonlight, and the brow and eyes of that man from this night, all together into its very bones.

* * * * *

Ever since that livestream of the Immortal Realm Talent Selection, the four words **"Calming Spirit Clear Tea"** had become the hottest vocabulary within the entire Lingxiao Sect, and indeed, beyond.

Originally a trivial entry item that no one had cared to ask about, it had now transformed into a scorching hot spiritual commodity within the cultivation world.

It was rumoured that several Nascent Soul Patriarchs had specifically dispatched disciples to queue up and purchase it before entering seclusion.

There were even a few elders from the Heavenly Sword Sect who, in their scramble for the final packet, nearly drew swords and crossbows at the door, escalating the matter until the Law Enforcement Hall had to intervene to mediate.

In the final reckoning of the Immortal Sect Talent Selection, the first place had gone to Junior Sister Yu Qing, who had performed the sword dance. As for Lili, she hadn't even scraped into the top ten.

However, seeing that this tea had unexpectedly exploded in popularity, she was already grateful to the point of shedding tears of gratitude.

Meanwhile, in a remote, small spirit tea workshop within the Lingxiao Sect, Moony was already busy to the point of seeing stars spinning before her eyes.

"Right away, right away! One portion of three catties to the Xuandu Sect; two portions of one catty to Purple Cloud Peak... This Great Virtuous One wants ten catties?! Please trouble yourself to affix the sect seal! Eh? Who stuffed Spirit Stones into my sleeve?! We value integrity and honest trading here!!"

The table was piled high with paper talisman orders and bags of Spirit Stones.

Moony scribbled furiously, recording orders with a flying brush, while occasionally roaring to stop the three spirit chickens from flying wildly around the room.

"Ah Hong! Ah Qing! Ah Jin! Hurry up and fly this batch to Clear Sound Valley! If you steal a bite again, I'll pluck your tail feathers!"

The three spirit chickens—oh, it should be noted that these were originally three utterly ordinary roosters.

However, due to stealing and eating an excess of spirit herbs and spirit berries, their chicken lives had been irrevocably altered, transforming them into spirit chickens capable of flying into the heavens and burrowing into the earth.

One red, one cyan, one gold. Each carried a small bundle larger than its own body on its back. Clucking loudly, they flew out of the window, tracing three beautiful arcs through the air before vanishing instantly into the clouds and mist.

Yun Lili sat to the side brewing tea.

Her expression was no longer as flustered as it had been in the past; her movements in brewing tea now possessed a measure of calm composure.

Although there was still a trace of hollow surprise on her face, her eyes clearly hid a hint of smug satisfaction.

"Who could have imagined it..." she mused. "Just one sentence from Sister Yun Yara, and this tea has become a sought-after treasure."

Moony ran over, panting for breath, and slapped a stack of orders onto the table with a *pah!*

"Didn't you say it had no special efficacy?! The result? That gang of Sword Cultivators claims that after drinking this tea, their speed of concentration doubled, and their energy for training multiplied! Now everyone wants a sip!"

Lili's focus, as always, was delightfully different from the norm.

She giggled foolishly, celebrating her foresight in bringing the three chickens. "If not for relying on Ah Qing, Ah Jin, and Ah Hong, I wouldn't even have a delivery service right now."

"Miss... is the issue right now *who* is delivering?" Moony was simply speechless.

"I... I truly didn't expect the effects to be so obvious back then. Wasn't time tight at that moment..." The corner of Lili's mouth twitched. "I pulled those spirit herbs randomly from the back mountain."

"Randomly pulled?!" Moony sucked in a breath of cold air. "Then hurry up and write down *where* you pulled them from! Tomorrow, the spirit chickens and I will go and sweep that entire area clean!"

Just then, another sound transmission talisman drifted in through the crack in the window. With a *snap*, it self-ignited, projecting a notification.

Moony read two lines, and her entire person went dumb.

"Li... Li-Li-Li-Li-Li Fairy!!"

"What is it?!" Lili jumped, nearly dropping the teapot.

Moony stuffed the notification directly onto her face. "The Immortal Goods Ranking has updated!! Your Calming Spirit Clear Tea has squeezed directly into the third spot on the 'Market Spirit Goods List'! It is second only to the Origin Union Pill and the Capital Glory Jade Liquid!!"

"Hah?"

"Furthermore, it has been officially labelled as... er... the 'Dark Horse Spirit Product of the Year,' receiving full marks in the triple categories of utility, taste, and appearance!"

Yun Lili remained in a dazed stupor for three full breaths before murmuring to herself, "...How is this possible?"

This world was truly too fantastic and bizarre.

Moony covered her face and collapsed onto the table laughing. "We truly must give thanks to 'Sister Fairy Yara'."

In an instant, her form of address for Yun Yara had become even more intimate and fervent. Just a moment ago it was "Sister Yun Yara," and in the next breath, it had transformed into "Sister Fairy Yara."

Lili: "......"

She looked at Moony with a face full of disdain; that sycophantic, fawning appearance was simply too unbearable to look at directly.

As they spoke, the three spirit chickens flew back from outside, invoices clamped in their beaks.

One even held a bag of Spirit Stones, another had its tail feathers knotted, and the third... actually brought back a **pink** spiritual message paper with small gold foil characters on it:

"Seeking a single meeting with Fairy Yun Lili. Willing to exchange three hundred High-Grade Spirit Stones for a pot of tea brewed by her own hand."

Lili stared at that piece of paper, sitting blankly for a long while, before sighing in a low voice:

"Three hundred High-Grade Spirit Stones... Is this tea... truly my greatest skill on the path of immortality?"

Thinking back to when she accepted missions before, toiling like a beast of burden for an entire day just to earn twenty or fifty Spirit Stones... and now, just brewing a pot of tea by hand could earn a net profit of three hundred High-Grade Spirit Stones?

Moony laughed *hei-hei*. "Who cares! As long as the Spirit Stones are in hand, the Celestial Mirror will be in hand immediately!"

"You speak the truth." Yun Lili nodded ferociously.

* * * * *

Scarcely had Yun Yara stepped down from the Spiritual Platform, before the tips of her embroidered shoes could even graze the dust of the earth, when numerous streaks of flowing light sped towards her from all directions like meteors chasing the moon.

Several immortal officials, clad in golden robes heavily embroidered with cloud patterns, surrounded her without a word of explanation.

Their expressions were grave, unyielding, and surrounded her so tightly that not even the wind could pass through.

The leader of the group was the Left Patrol Censor of the Decree Execution Bureau.

He held a jade tablet reverently in his hands, his voice not loud, yet every syllable was enunciated with a crystal clarity that cut through the noise of the crowd:

"Fairy Yara has received a summons. Please proceed immediately to the Tianxuan Hall for questioning."

Upon hearing the three words **"Tianxuan Hall,"** the complexions of the bystanders changed universally.

That was no ordinary administrative office.

It was the central hub governing the discipline and laws of the Heavenly Dao within the Immortal Realm; unless one was a high-ranking Immortal Sovereign or involved in a matter of grave, earth-shattering import, one would never be summoned there.

Furthermore, the phrase *"please proceed immediately"* was no polite invitation. To the ears of those who knew the ways of the court, it meant simply...

Please come right now. Instantly. Without delay. Do not even think of refusing.

Yun Yara's brow knitted ever so slightly. Her face remained a mask of cold, clear indifference, yet a minute, almost imperceptible tremor in the fabric of her sleeve betrayed a ripple of spiritual fluctuation within. She understood clearly: this was no routine official business.

She spoke softly, her voice cool, "I have only just returned to the pavilion, and already I am to be seen? I wonder which Immortal Sovereign is so impatient?"

The Left Patrol Censor's expression did not shift in the slightest, rigid as stone. He replied, "The Immortal Lords are all waiting respectfully within the hall. We hope Fairy Yara will offer her cooperation."

Watching this scene from a distance, Yun Lili's heart gave a violent *thump—ge-deng—*and her face drained of colour by half. She understood that this was no ordinary summons.

Once the Tianxuan Hall issued a call, everyone in the Immortal Realm knew what it signified—it meant the judging gaze of the Heavenly Dao had fallen upon a specific individual.

Moony cried out in panic, clutching Lili's sleeve, "Miss, what shall we do?"

Yun Lili gulped down a mouthful of saliva with difficulty, her throat dry. "Not necessarily... perhaps... perhaps they are merely inviting her for a cup of tea?"

Moony looked utterly despairing, her voice rising in disbelief. "Who invites someone for tea at the Tianxuan Hall?! Unless that cup of tea can investigate the karma of three lifetimes!"

Under the attentive, heavy gaze of the multitude, Yun Yara showed no fear. With composed steps, she followed the immortal officials onto the Floating Cloud Flying Boat.

Her snow-white long robes lifted slightly in the rosy light of the setting sun, resembling a silent, unspeaking ice lotus drifting towards an unknown fate.

Chapter 24: Interrogation of the Ice Lotus

Inside the Tianxuan Hall, celestial light shimmered with blinding brilliance.

From all four directions, Immortal Lords sat solemnly upon mats of cloud, their divine consciousnesses interwoven like a dense, invisible net that pressed down until the very air vibrated with tension.

Yun Yara was guided to the centre of the hall, standing beneath the jade steps carved with lotus patterns.

She was clad in robes of snow, her brows and eyes as cold as an icy spring.

Her expression remained unaltered, appearing not as though she stood beneath the judgment of the Heavenly Dao, but rather within her own tea pavilion, without a shred of fear or panic.

Immortal Lord Bai Heng was the first to speak. His tone was gentle, yet every syllable concealed a needle: "Fairy Yara, not long ago you departed from the Immortal Realm. Signs indicate that you had contact with the Crown Prince of the Demon Realm, Mo Han. Can you detail the beginning and end of this journey?"

Yara raised her eyes, her gaze clear and unclouded. "I fell into Fallen Mist Valley to investigate the cause of the disappearance of our predecessors. I encountered the Demon Crown Prince, Mo Han, by chance. He was injured; whether by reason or emotion, I could not sit idly by and watch him die."

Within the Tianxuan Hall, the glazed roof suspended starlight, and several Immortal Lords sat high in the hall, the atmosphere grim and frosty.

Yara stood in the hall, a figure of white like snow, her sleeves moving without wind, her appearance cold, severe, and clear. She looked up at the lords above, her gaze calm as a lake, without a trace of fear.

The next to speak was Immortal Lord Xuan Yin. His voice was as clear and bright as a copper bell, yet every word carried a blade: "Fairy Yun Yara, it is said that within Fallen Mist Valley, you and the Demon Prince Mo Han stayed in the same place for a duration of seven days?"

"More than seven days," she replied, her voice calm, her brows unmoving. "It was difficult to move even an inch within the valley. He and I each took what we needed; it was a temporary alliance."

"Each took what you needed?" To the right, Fairy Yao Hua laughed lightly, her tone dripping with sarcasm. "Then are you aware of the 'Dual Cultivation' arts of the Demon Realm? They allow one to borrow spiritual power from another to coexist, a method especially suitable for maintaining one's cultivation base in dire straits. During your seven days together, did you engage in... such conduct?"

As soon as these words were spoken, a low hum of noise erupted from the surroundings. Many immortal attendants and disciples held their breath in anticipation, their gazes sharp as knives.

The faces of several Immortal Lords changed slightly, and Fairy Yao Hua's expression stiffened, as if she had been slapped.

"In other words," another Immortal Lord continued, his tone carrying the momentum of an interrogation, "during this time, was your body ever invaded by demonic *qi*?"

"We coexisted for several days in mutual peace. As for demonic *qi*..." Yara paused, slightly lifting her pale wrist. "If the Immortal Lords suspect me, you are welcome to investigate."

Yara raised her eyes, sweeping a cold glance across the hall, her voice unhurried.

"Furthermore, if we had truly engaged in Dual Cultivation, would the Immortal Lords still be able to speak with me here? If I had truly been tainted by demonic *qi*, I would have transformed into the Dao and perished on the spot. Why would I bother standing here to endure your interrogation?"

"That statement is too heavy," Immortal Lord Zi Heng, seated on the left, frowned. "Will you permit me to use the *Qi* Probing Art to view your spiritual veins?"

"Permitted." Yara extended her arm generously, her spiritual energy restrained and cold as ice, showing no fear whatsoever.

Zi Heng circulated his *qi* to investigate. After a long while, his brow slowly relaxed. "Indeed, there are no traces of demonic *qi*..."

Just at this moment, another beam of celestial light fell into the hall. It was the real-time observation result obtained from the external barrier:

"Reporting to the Lords. There is no demonic qi upon Fairy Yara's person. Her divine consciousness is clear; there are no signs of demonic possession."

Double verification confirmed the same result: Yun Yara was completely free of demonic energy.

"Then how do you explain the demon robes she is wearing?" another Immortal Lord asked coldly.

Yara's tone was faint, yet it cut like a knife through ice and stone. "In the valley, I was left with only bloodied rags. I changed into these clothes for self-preservation. If the Lords dislike them, you may burn them, but do not judge a person by their garments."

Her voice was bone-chillingly cold, yet her sharpness was fully revealed; not a single word allowed for insult.

To the side of the hall, several fairies who were usually jealous of her wore ugly expressions. One of them could not resist a cold sneer: "I wonder why the Demon Prince looked upon you with such favour. Could it be that you offered some special..."

"Enough." Before she could speak, the spiritual attendant standing behind her shouted abruptly.

Yara turned her head to glance at him. Her eyes were waveless as she spoke faintly, "There is no need. Let them speak; it does no harm. Idle gossip cannot obstruct my heart."

Scarcely had her voice faded when numerous Spirit-Probing Talismans fluttered towards her like a swarm of moths.

They landed around her, instantly encasing her within a dazzling array of spiritual light.

The light swept over her, searching every inch, yet it revealed nothing unusual—not even a wisp of residual demonic *qi* was detected.

To the side, a fairy named Jiang Yanran covered her lips with a delicate hand, letting out a soft titter. "Nowadays, the methods of the Demon Realm are profoundly brilliant; perhaps it is merely hidden a little deeper? Fairy Yara possesses the appearance of jade and ice; it is hardly surprising that the Demon Lord might be moved to emotion. perhaps there is some unknown... romantic entanglement?"

On the surface, these words were teasing; in reality, they were brimming with malice.

Hearing this, Yun Yara merely cast a sidelong glance at her, the corner of her lips hooking up slightly. "If I were truly romantically entangled with him, I fear I would have long since been welcomed into the Demon

Palace by the Demon Lord as the Crown Princess. Would I still be standing here, allowing you to speak such sarcastic, windy words?"

"You!"

Jiang Yanran choked on her words, her expression shifting continually. Those nearby could not help but chuckle in low voices.

Immortal Lord Qi Zhao spoke in a deep, sinking voice, his brow carrying an unquestionable majesty. "Immortals and Demons follow different paths. Fairy Yara, as a member of the Immortal Realm, you should not have such intimate dealings with those of the Demon Realm. Are you aware that the Demon King is already greatly angered by this matter? The situation is perilous."

Yun Yara raised her head with indifference. Her gaze was calm as water, her tone peaceful yet firm. "I know full well the severity of this matter, and my heart is open and unashamed. If the Demon King is angry, it is because his son was bored to the extreme and treated me as a plaything to relieve his tedium. Why, then, should I be implicated? This is not a matter I can control."

The Immortal Lord frowned, his tone becoming even more severe. "Your words, I fear, appear somewhat arrogant. The rules of the Immortal Realm are strict. If you are careless, I fear you will damage your own reputation and that of the Immortal Realm."

Yun Yara smiled faintly, her gaze torch-like as she looked directly at the gathered Immortal Lords. "I am not arrogant; I simply see things clearly. I saved a person in distress. If I am to be condemned for this, who in the Immortal Realm will dare to extend a hand to help in the future? Could it be that simply because the other party hails from the Demon Realm, I should allow his soul to dissipate and his spirit to scatter, denying justice its due? If so, what meaning does such an Immortal Realm possess?"

The moment these words were spoken, the gathered Immortal Lords fell into immediate silence. No one dared to easily offer a rebuttal.

Everyone knew that if she had truly not extended a helping hand, and if the Crown Prince of the Demon Realm had suffered any mishap because of it, the Immortal Realm would likely be facing endless retaliatory attacks from the Demon Realm.

She stood alone, surrounded by the interrogation of the immortals. Her brows and eyes were indifferent, her posture straight and upright. Her words were neither humble nor overbearing, composed as a solitary pine atop a wind-swept, snowy peak.

She did not need to raise her voice, yet she drew the gaze of all; clearly the loneliest person present, she appeared to be the steadiest existence in the entire hall.

She looked once more at the Immortal Lords in the hall, her voice as calm as ever. "If the censure ends here, may I leave?"

Her gaze met the eyes of the Immortal Lords directly, without a shred of fear—cold, severe, and clear, just like the Frost-Flying Jade Ridge under the light of dawn: isolated and noble.

It was at this precise moment—the instant before the Master of the Hall of Tianxuan Hall, Yun Wuntang, broke through the void to arrive.

Just as the crowd prepared to question her further, a streak of spiritual crane signal-light sped in from beyond the heavens. Yu Sord had transmitted a brief, concise evaluation:

"Breath pure, reasoning clear. She does not resemble one whose heart has been bewitched. I ask the Immortal Lords to investigate clearly."

Beside him, Xie Wuchen read it and offered a simple sentence:

"If we are discussing punishment and responsibility, before it is your turn to speak, shouldn't you ask the people of the Lingxiao Sect first?"

Meanwhile, in another location, Yun Zhou was rubbing his chin as he watched the livestream in the Spirit Light Pavilion, murmuring, "Yara's tongue... how is it even sharper than Father's? I must be careful in the future."

Xiao Yan looked shaken to the core. "This little fairy... neither humble nor arrogant, every word hitting the mark. Impressive!"

In the lens, Yun Yara gently brushed her sleeve. Her snowy robes moved slightly; a single sentence had become the wind.

Outside the Tianxuan Hall, clouds surged violently. In an instant, anomalies rose on all sides. Several bolts of lightning cleaved straight down from the cloud layer, shaking the entire palace until it trembled.

"Who dares to tamper with the array?!" An Immortal Lord rose abruptly, the blue vein between his brows twitching.

An immortal attendant from outside the hall rushed in, panic in his voice: "It is the Venerable One of the Hall of Tianxuan Hall of the Lingxiao Sect! He has descended!"

"Why has he come?"

"Indeed, was it not specifically arranged not to notify the Lingxiao Sect, to avoid conflicts of interest?"

"Heh, and yet here he is, is he not?" Xie Wuchen watched the drama with the grin of one who feared no chaos, a roguish smile on his face. "I told you to ask the people of the Lingxiao Sect."

Scarcely had the voice faded when the hall doors burst open with a thunderous *boom*.

A figure trod upon the void to enter. His cloak flapped wildly like a blazing fire, his brows and eyes were grim as a dense forest, and the fury radiating from his entire being seemed powerful enough to overturn the very roof tiles of the palace.

Yun Tim.

He was the Hall Master of the **Hall of Tianxuan Hall** of the Lingxiao Sect, and the cousin of Sect Master Yun Wuntang. In stark contrast to Yun Wuntang's gentle temperament, Yun Tim was renowned for his explosive conduct.

He held the power of punishment and established the disciplines, his rank honoured above the Four Pavilions.

He had always acted without leaving any face for others, earning him the moniker **"Mad Blade Venerable."** The moment he appeared, even the several Immortal Lords seated above instinctively straightened their spines.

"Who dares interrogate a junior of my Yun family?!"

His voice shook the hall like a clap of thunder and his gaze swept like lightning across the hall of immortals, finally landing on Yun Yara. Seeing that she was unharmed, his fury abated by merely half a degree.

"Hall Master, this is merely routine questioning..." Immortal Lord Bai Heng began to speak, only to be cut off ruthlessly by Yun Tim.

"Questioning? My lass Yara returned from the bottom of Fallen Mist Valley in the Demon Realm, a journey of nine deaths and one life. Before she could rest for a single day, you locked her up in the Tianxuan Hall for investigation? Asking her if she was moved to romance, asking if she was possessed by demons... are such vulgar questions the style of an Immortal Lord?"

He took a single half-step forward.

Boom!

The celestial light of the entire great hall trembled violently. A current of rosy clouds surged backwards in a reverse tide, and the complexions of the several Immortal Lords changed universally.

Yun Yara's brow twitched. She advised in a small voice, "Martial Uncle... please do not strike..."

Yun Tim huffed, waving his hand. "You withdraw first; I will handle this."

The moment she retreated to the side of the hall, Yun Tim pointed an angry finger at the gathered immortals. "Gentlemen, ask yourselves: if the one who fell into the Demon Realm today was not Yun Yara, but your own disciple, your nephew, your apprentice—would you still speak with such righteous strictness? You have investigated for demonic *qi* two rounds over, yet you still do not release her. Do you intend to question her until she is forced to admit fault?"

Every word struck like a tolling bell; every sentence vibrated until it made one's chest feel stifled.

Silence fell over the hall. Some immortals coughed in low voices; others looked embarrassed.

"Since Yun Yara has been proven innocent, the entirety of the Lingxiao Sect shall protect her. If any of you dare to chatter one more word today... Hmph!" Yun Tim's gaze turned cold, his smile radiating chilling air. "I shall debate the sword with you on the spot, and see whose logic is harder."

Bai Heng gave a light cough. "Since Venerable Yun has arrived, this matter ends here..."

"You had best remember the words you have spoken today." Yun Tim huffed coldly. He turned to look at Yun Yara, his tone instantly shifting to one of warmth: "Let us go. Return to the Lingxiao Sect. Your father is waiting for you; it was he who asked me to bring you back. Once we return, I will have someone brew you some Black Ganoderma Soup to calm your nerves."

The Crowd: "......"

She nodded, her heart filled with emotion, and departed alongside him.

Once the view of their backs had faded into the distance, the hall remained silent and soundless.

Suddenly, someone sighed in a low voice: "Yun Tim's temper... truly ten years like a single day. It has never changed."

Another Immortal Lord shook his head. "Back then, he dared to contradict even the Grandmaster. I see he hasn't restrained himself by even a fraction now."

"Hmph. In this old man's view, although no demonic *qi* was detected today, things are not so simple," another reminded coldly.

The hall fell into silence once more, the air seemingly permeated with an invisible pressure.

Yet at this moment, no matter what anyone thought in their hearts, they had to admit: in today's confrontation, Yun Yara had won beautifully. And Yun Tim's intervention had ensured that the entire Immortal Realm remembered who her backer was today.

It was not Yun Wuntang, nor was it Yu Sord.

It was the **Mad Blade Yun Tim**, the man capable of cursing the Council of Immortal Lords into overturning on the spot.

Chapter 25: The Reunion at Cloud-Embracing Cottage

Yun Yara stood before the gate of Mist-Gathering Cottage for a long time—longer than she cared to admit.

Her fingers rested lightly against the chilled wooden doorframe, the lingering morning fog curling around her sleeves. She was not someone easily shaken, yet today her steps refused to move forward.

She understood all too well: if she wished to stand firmly within Lingxiao Sect, Lili was a hurdle she could not avoid. Better to face the girl now than stumble into an awkward confrontation later.

She inhaled deeply, steadying her pulse. At last, she crossed the threshold. Her skirt brushed softly over the stone steps, barely stirring the silence—at least, the silence she *expected*.

But the moment she entered—

Noise.

Chaos.

Life.

All of it slammed into her like an unexpected wave.

Where she anticipated serenity, she found absolute pandemonium.

Spirit chickens darted across the courtyard like feathery comets, wings flapping madly. One nearly collided with her boot, squawking in outrage as if *she* had wronged *it*.

A young temple boy sprinted through the yard holding a tray piled high with spirit fruits—only to be chased by a silver-furred immortal hound who looked seconds away from stealing the entire tray.

Around a stone table, three young attendants sat locked in a heated debate, faces flushed and hands waving dramatically.

"I'm telling you, the Jade-dew water should only be added three parts! Lili Fairy was crystal clear last time!"

"You must have misheard! She said five parts—five! The flavour blooms properly only then!"

"Three parts!"

"Five!"

The argument had the passion of an immortal court debate, and none of them noticed the dignified Yara standing bewildered at the entrance.

Yara froze.

Was this… truly a Lingxiao Sect residence?

Why did it feel more like a rowdy tea stall in a mortal marketplace?

Before she could regain her composure, a bright, crisp voice chimed near her elbow:

"Fairy, are you here for a tea tasting? Our Heart-Calming Spirit Brew is sold out today, but you can reserve your portion! Once the next batch finishes refining, we'll deliver it right to your sect gate!"

Yara turned toward the voice.

A girl of fifteen or sixteen stood there with an eager smile, hair tied into two high loops, cheeks flushed from running between tasks. She carried a tiny tea-pot as though it were a priceless relic.

"Ah… I'm not here to buy tea," Yara responded, momentarily overwhelmed.

She half-considered leaving and returning another day—perhaps one where spirit chickens weren't staging a rebellion—when Moony burst out from the inner hall.

The girl skidded to a halt, nearly stepping on a fleeing chicken, and stared wide-eyed.

"Yara Fairy?!" Moony yelped.

In an instant, she rushed forward and grasped Yara's arm, her face full of apology and excitement.

"You should've sent word! We're honoured you came today—truly!"

"…What exactly is happening here?" Yara asked, her brows drawing together as she glanced at the lively chaos.

Moony sighed with both pride and exhaustion.

"It's all thanks to you helping us spread the word that day! Our Heart-Calming Brew has exploded across the sects. Orders are piling up faster than we can refine the leaves—higher than a whole mountain of spirit fruit!"

As she spoke, she guided Yara toward the inner room, weaving gently between spirit chickens and frantic attendants.

Behind them, someone shouted:

"NO—NOT SIX PARTS! I SWEAR SHE SAID THREE!"

Another responded instantly:

"FIVE! I'LL BET MY SPIRIT STONE POUCH ON IT!"

Yara paused mid-step, stunned once more.

This… was Lili's domain?

Where was the rumoured quiet, cultivated serenity?

Instead, Mist-Gathering Cottage was overflowing with warmth, energy, noise, laughter—

and life.

And somehow, impossibly…

it suited Lili perfectly.

The room inside was entirely different from the chaos outside.

Neat. Quiet. Almost austere.

A single pot of orchid sat on the low table, its fragrance faint and clean.

Bamboo shadows swayed beyond the window lattice, casting ripples of jade-green light across the floor—finally, something that resembled the tranquil air of a proper immortal sect.

Yara took a seat.

Yet the strange turmoil in her chest refused to settle.

She had come today believing she needed to draw a line to settle the past, to establish clear distance between herself and Lili.

Moony poured tea carefully, her voice tentative.

"You… are here to see our fairy, right?"

Yara blinked, surprised for a moment, then nodded.

"Yes. Is she… available?"

She lifted the cup to her lips, letting the soft steam brush her face.

But before she could speak again, a flurry of footsteps and grumbling rose from outside.

"This batch of leaves needs sun-drying *before* the spirit refinement— then we have to use the spirit-chicken flame, but those blasted birds either go on strike or deliver to the wrong address! And when I scolded them, they burned a hole in the tea shed—"

The complaint was cut short.

Lili stepped into the room with a thump, one boot still dusted with bits of roasted tea leaves, her sleeve half-crumpled as if she'd fought through seven small disasters just to get here.

The moment her gaze fell upon the pale-clad figure in the room, she froze mid-step.

"…Yara?"

For a heartbeat, she merely stared.

Then her eyes lit up—

and she launched forward like an excited spirit fox, throwing her arms around Yara in a sudden, tight embrace.

"Yara! You finally came back!"

Her joy practically lifted her off the floor.

"I'm so happy you're safe! After the selection you were taken away so suddenly, not a single message—I was *worried sick*! "

She reluctantly released Yara to look her over from head to toe.

Seeing her unharmed, she exhaled in relief, her smile blooming like sunlight through spring clouds.

"And really—thank you! If you hadn't given me those two precious words that day—'Not bad'—I'd probably still be embarrassing myself on that stage! And now look—instant fame!"

Yara couldn't help a faint, helpless smile.

"The tea was indeed… not bad."

Lili planted her fists on her hips with triumphant pride.

"I knew it! My tea was only missing its moment! Now thanks to you, the tea house has lines stretching all the way to the outer courtyard—we're practically measuring spirit stones by the bucket!"

Behind her, Moony popped her head out, nodding furiously, her whole face glowing with delight.

Lili grabbed Yara's arm again.

"I told you—ten percent of the profits is yours! Spirit stones, spirit fruits, whatever you want, take as much as you like!"

Yara laughed softly and patted her hand away.

"That won't be necessary. I merely spoke on impulse—nothing worth rewarding."

But then she paused, brows drawing together ever so slightly.

"…But why are you working this hard? You look like you haven't rested in days."

Moony answered before Lili could even inhale.

"It's for the premium model of the Heaven-Reflecting Mirror!"

"Yes! Exactly!" Lili chimed in instantly, eyes sparkling like twin stars.

"That mirror is a divine-grade artifact! It has built-in beauty spells, starlight illumination, automatic aura-softening array—one glance and your face looks smoother than jade dust! Even Sword Immortal Yu Sord said I looked more celestial than a spirit crane that day!"

"…?"

Yara gave her a long, measuring look. The silence stretched so thin it almost hummed.

Then at last, she asked the question that struck directly at the heart—

"…Then where is your *private treasury*?"

Lili froze.

Moony's smile froze with her.

And then—

The most terrifying thing in the world happened.

Silence.

Sudden, total, cosmic silence.

The immortal attendants outside—who had been arguing passionately about whether the tea needed three parts of Jade Dew Water or five—

fell quiet at the exact same moment.

The spirit chickens stopped running.

The tea dog rolled over and played dead.

The bamboo grove stilled mid-sway.

Even the fragile vine that had been hanging off the corner wall seemed to decide this was not the time to move, and clung motionlessly to the stone.

The entire Cloud-Gathering Residence became so quiet

that Lili's very audible swallow echoed like thunder.

"…Private treasury?"

She finally spoke, voice stiff, as if she were encountering those two words for the first time in her life.

Yara's tone remained calm—too calm.

But every word landed like a heavenly lightning strike.

"The standard private treasury of the Yun clan's direct line—

I remember it quite clearly.

Ten thousand high-grade spirit stones.

Five thousand medium-grade stones.

Three storage rings.

Two escape talismans.

Three defensive formation plates.

Anything lower than medium-grade stone is not even qualified to be placed inside."

Another earthquake of silence.

Lili and Moony turned toward each other, their faces simultaneously displaying the same expression:

Heavens strike me down—why did no one tell us this?!

In the corner, the spirit chicken gnawing on tea scraps made a tiny "puk" sound and spat out its tea leaf in shock, as if its beak had gone numb.

The air congealed for three heartbeats.

Not even the wind dared to breathe.

Lili slowly, painfully turned her head, her voice trembling from pure disbelief.

"Moony… h-h-have you ever, in your entire life, heard of us having… h-having a *private treasury*?"

Moony's eyes darted around like a guilty rabbit.

"N-no… never heard of it… not even once…"

Damn it all!

If she had known—

If she had known they were supposed to have a treasury with **ten thousand high-grade spirit stones,**

why in the nine heavenly layers had she done all those ridiculous missions?!

She had chased chickens, swept spirit fields, babysat spirit beasts,

and even performed emotional counseling for mentally collapsing sword cultivators!

All for twenty or thirty stones a day?!

The more she thought about it, the more Lili felt the urge to look up at the sky and scream until the clouds broke.

Then—

"…Moony."

Lili suddenly turned, expression solemn as a prophet receiving divine revelation.

"Didn't we have something we still haven't done?"

Their master-servant unity was terrifying.

One glance—

and Moony immediately understood exactly what she meant.

"Yes! Spirit-root soup!" Moony immediately echoed, looking as though she had just received a military command.

Lili grabbed her by the wrist and headed straight out with decisive steps. "Yara, sit for a bit. I'll go stew a tonic soup for you right now!"

Find the private treasury. Now. At once. Immediately.

Who still had time to think about the tea house or that heavenly photo mirror? The treasury came first. Above all else.

No one noticed—not even Lili herself—that her way of addressing Yara had already shifted unconsciously from the formal "Yara Fairy" to the intimate "Yara."

Yara watched the two disappear through the doorway in a streak of motion, their sleeves trailing behind like afterimage shadows. A quiet suspicion rose in her mind.

Were this master and servant… truly unaware that the private treasury even existed?

Lili stood at the entrance of Zhou's study, pacing back and forth three times before finally taking a deep breath on the fourth. She leaned her head in cautiously.

"Zhou?" she called tentatively.

Inside, Zhou sat by the window, reading beneath the soft light. His long fingers turned a page with unhurried grace, his expression cool and distant as always. He didn't even look up when he heard her voice—only a faint chill drifted in the air.

"What is it?" he asked, eyelids lowered, tone lazy. "And what's with that overly familiar way of addressing me?"

Lili clung to the doorframe with a sheepish grin, squeezing herself into the room. "I just… came to check if you've eaten yet?"

Zhou's hand paused. He lifted his eyes and gave her a single indifferent glance. "Thanks. I am in fasting cultivation."

Oh. Right. She always forgot he didn't eat.

"Then… thirsty? Want me to brew you some tea? It's new tea! I roasted the leaves myself at Cloud-Gathering Residence! It even won—uh, that part doesn't matter. Anyway, I make really good tea!"

"No. Not thirsty."

Lili gave two awkward little laughs. Seeing him lower his head again to read, she muttered, "Then… how's your cultivation lately? Any bottleneck? I heard Qingming Pavilion came out with some new technique. Want me to go check it out for you?"

"No need. But thank you for the concern."

"Then…" Lili desperately scrambled for another topic.

Zhou's movements stilled once more. Finally—

With a sharp snap, he closed his book and lifted his gaze, cool and cutting.

"Lili," he asked, eyes narrowing, "what exactly are you trying to do?"

His stare was like frost wrapped in deeper snow. Lili shivered on the spot. Seeing she could no longer dodge the question, she shrank her neck, crept closer with the guilty look of a thief, and whispered, "I… I just heard something, you know. That Yun clan children… all seem to have a… um… private treasury somewhere."

"Oh?" Zhou raised a brow, his voice slow and layered with meaning.

Being stared at made Lili's scalp prickle. She forced out a laugh. "J-just that thing, you know… the so-called standard package… one thousand superior-grade spirit stones, five thousand medium-grade, plus some magic tools and storage rings and… whatever… Why have I never seen mine? Do you have yours?"

"Who told you this?"

"Uh… Yara."

Zhou narrowed his eyes at her, studying every inch of her expression. After a long moment, he let out a short, humourless breath—half sneer, half laugh. "And here I thought you came out of concern for my cultivation bottleneck. But no. Turns out you came for the private treasury. And the spirit stones inside."

Lili's face flushed red. She immediately switched to boot-licking mode, laughing weakly. "Hehe, I'm not after the spirit stones! I just… I just think it's terribly unfair, you know? I, Lili, am also a dignified direct descendant. I deserve a share too, right? Don't you think so?"

"Isn't that tea of yours selling extremely well?" Zhou gave her a sideways glance, unfiltered. "It shows up in advertisements on the Immortal Net every day."

"…What?!" Lili's eyes widened—she genuinely had no idea.

Zhou snorted softly. "And you still claim to be short on spirit stones?"

Lili's mind spun quickly, and she immediately argued, "I'm short on spirit stones not because I'm poor, but because my business is just about to take off! I need turnover! It's a cash-flow issue!"

Zhou gave her a look that clearly said he could see through all her excuses. Then he spoke two crisp words: "Don't. Have."

Her whole body deflated. She dropped into the seat opposite him like a defeated fledgling bird, shoulders sagging in utter despair.

The private treasury—of course it had a thousand superior-grade stones, five thousand medium-grade stones, and a full standard set of magical equipment.

She wanted to cry.

Lili sniffed twice, beginning a full-scale tragic monologue. "I… I once tried a new fasting pill for fifty low-grade spirit stones… ended up with diarrhea for three straight days…"

She began to ramble, her mind flashing back to one miserable scene after another.

"And also! That bizarre mission from the Artifact-Refinement Sect! They made me pretend to be an iron sprite and talk to the refining furnace— said the furnace was feeling lonely and needed emotional resonance through spirit energy. I stood there like an idiot, performing a 'spirit dance' in front of that broken furnace for two hours… And then those people had the nerve to laugh and say I wasn't dancing at all, I was doing physical exercise…"

Just remembering it made her scalp go numb, her voice nearly piercing the sky.

"And that… that ridiculous spirit-chicken delivery mission! They clearly said it was escorting a Fire-Feather Spirit Chicken, but what arrived was a basket of ordinary field chickens! Then they accused me of switching chickens on purpose, demanded compensation, and even almost dragged me to the Discipline Hall! I nearly fell to my knees crying injustice!"

"And… and I even went to that poetry symposium, pretending to be a scholar cultivator! Then they forced us to draw lots on the spot and compose a poem! How would *I* know how to do that? I could only run away…"

Lili looked utterly miserable as she continued, "And that guy, Xiao Yan… said he was practicing the 'Breath-Cycle Meditation Method,' but ended up clinging to me and dumping three full hours of emotional garbage onto my head…"

She suddenly grabbed her own hair, eyes round with exploding grievance. "And there I was—drinking bitter spirit tea while fake-smiling through it, trying my best to earn a few spirit stones—only to find out I HAD A PRIVATE TREASURY THE WHOLE TIME!!! AND! IT! HAS! TEN! THOUSAND! SUPERIOR-GRADE! SPIRIT STONES!!!"

Zhou: "…"

He'd known she was taking odd jobs, but he had assumed she was simply bored. He certainly hadn't known her missions were this insane.

She raised her head sharply, her gaze slicing toward him like frost-forged steel. "You knew all along, didn't you? You did this on purpose, didn't you? You were waiting to watch me make a fool of myself, right?!"

Sitting behind the desk, Zhou paused in the middle of turning a page. He lifted his eyes toward her and finally softened a little, speaking quietly. "All the private-treasury inventory lists, the spirit-stone ledgers, the transfer documents—I had them sent to you… three times. You said they 'looked troublesome' and you'd 'deal with them later.'"

"…" Lili's pupils trembled violently. "I thought that was your reading list for me!!!"

Zhou: "…"

He added dryly, "Your treasury is in your storage ring. It was previously tied to the clan's ancestral seal, and it generates spirit-interest every month, so… yes, you should have about thirteen thousand now."

Lili experienced a level of social death she had never known in her entire life.

Her eyes went blank as she stared at the ceiling, muttering,

"So I was… I was… a rich young lady crying while carrying sacks of rice… living like a pauper while having spirit fruit growing out of my pockets…"

Just then, Moony poked her head into the room from the doorway and whispered, "Miss, the spirit crane just sent word— the latest Celestial Mirror s have arrived. Whenever you're free, you can go choose one!"

Lili: "…"

She rose silently from the floor, patted down her robe, inhaled slowly, and assumed the demeanour of a cold, aristocratic immortal.

"Moony, starting today, I only buy— the PRE-MI-UM EDI-TION!!"

Chapter 26: The Eye of Heaven and the Demon's Grip

The Eye of Heaven and the Demon's Grip

The light of the heavens was pure and cleansing. Atop the Spirit Terrace, clouds and mist churned and roiled, as if the rumble of thunder were about to break.

The Spirit Net was still fervently discussing the interrogation of Yun Yara at the Tianxuan Hall. Thousands upon thousands of comments scrolled by at flying speed.

Hashtags such as #YunYaraSoberSpeech and #TheDemonPrinceAndTheGoddess:ATrivialAffair... temporarily stormed to the top of the trending charts.

When she walked out of the Tianxuan Hall clad in white robes, her posture was so upright and unyielding that it caused the hearts of countless observers to tremble.

Some praised her courage and insight; others cursed her for lacking reverence and awe. Yet no one could deny that after this storm, there was no one left in the Immortal Realm who did not know the name Yun Yara.

Upon returning to the Lingxiao Sect, she spoke not a word.

Her expression was cold and clear, yet the depths of her eyes harboured an unconcealable weariness.

Yun Tim stood before the hall, watching her approach. Finally, he spoke in a deep, sinking voice: "They owe you an apology."

She shook her head, her voice faint. "It matters not. Such is the nature of the Immortal Realm. It is not the first time, nor will it be the last."

A spiritual breeze brushed lightly over her white robes.

Yun Yara lowered her head, looking at the residual talisman mark remaining on her palm—the lingering force left behind by Immortal Lord Zi Heng when he probed her *qi* moments ago.

She had been marked by name by the Tianxuan Hall. From this moment forth, her every move and action would be placed under the scrutiny of the Eye of Heaven.

New trials, new storms, were quietly raising the curtain.

Meanwhile, far away in the Demon Realm.

Mo Han sat upon a chair of frosted stone, idly turning an ancient token in his hand.

His face was cold and indifferent, yet hidden within the depths of his eyes were turbulent undercurrents.

"Is she... unharmed?" he asked faintly.

The attendant lowered his head. "Fairy Yun Yara was questioned at the Tianxuan Hall. She departed safely this morning and has returned to the Lingxiao Sect."

Mo Han fell silent for a fleeting instant. Then, his hand tightened violently around the sceptre in his grip.

* * * * *

Outside the Pavilion of Ten Thousand Treasures and Myriad Phenomena, the stream of people flowed in an endless tide.

A mistress and her servant strode out of the pavilion with spirits soaring ten thousand *zhang* high, their steps so buoyant they seemed on the verge of treading upon clouds.

Yun Lili cradled that glittering **Luminous Glory Model 9: Mystic Spirit Filter Edition** Heaven-Illuminating Mirror in her hands, looking for all the world as if she had just received the sole divine weapon of the Three Realms directly from the hands of the Heavenly Emperor.

The smile on her face could not be stopped; it flew upwards, nearly blossoming into a flower, stretching from the corner of her mouth to the root of her ear, refusing to come down for a long time.

She held the mirror with the utmost caution, even lightening her breathing by a few degrees, as if a single mishap would cause this divine artifact to transform into a streak of flowing light and fly away to immortality.

First, she brushed the body of the mirror with her sleeve, then pinched a velvet cloth from the cloud-hem of her robe and rubbed it furiously, polishing the surface until it was as bright as a lake, clear enough to reflect the soul. Then she switched hands to test several angles.

Under the sunlight, the mirror surface suddenly revealed circles of exquisite spiritual runes, shimmering with ripples of light, looking as though they could seal a fairy's countenance within a glazed palace of the Ninth Heaven.

"Ahhhhhhh—!!!" Lili was so excited she nearly performed three consecutive somersaults in mid-air. "This light sensitivity, these details, this colour temperature, this fill-light array, these soft-focus spirit runes—it is simply stunned-senseless beautiful!!"

She turned her head to stare at Moony. "Do you know! This filter is real! It is alive! It automatically calibrates skin tone based on spiritual pressure! Even if I stayed up all night refining pills and broke out in acne, or failed a tribulation and scorched half my face, it can still produce the feeling of an immortal with clear muscles and jade skin!"

"Real or fake?!" Moony also got high on the excitement.

Lili nodded vigorously. "Of course! Once this mirror is turned on, it can even photograph a thousand-year-old female corpse looking like an eighteen-year-old fairy!"

"Moony, look!" Lili had already begun hugging the mirror to practise selfie poses—now propping her chin in deep thought, now twirling a flower with a light smile, her angles as precise as a general arranging troops. "This angle! This lighting! This highlight on the brow and eyes even fine-tunes itself automatically! Ahhh, it is too beautiful!"

Moony nodded fiercely at the side, her eyes radiating light. "In the future, I must save my monthly stipend to buy one too! With this mirror in hand, I hold the winds and clouds of the Immortal Realm!"

Lili laughed until her shoulders shook. She turned back to flash Moony a look that said, *"Rest assured, Big Sister has money,"* and patted her chest proudly. "Rest assured! One day, Big Sister will buy one for you!"

Her tea-selling business was earning gold by the bushel daily; her little Moony also had to have a Supreme Edition Heaven-Illuminating Mirror!

Heh heh, she was just such a generous and beautiful little mistress!

"Thank you, Miss! Miss is the best!" Moony jumped up on the spot in joy.

The two of them instantly burst into loud laughter, laughing until passersby looked sideways. Even an immortal official passing by paused in his steps, whispering to his companion, "Did they just return from surviving a heavenly tribulation? Why are they laughing so wantonly?"

Lili completely disregarded the gazes of others. She spun a circle while holding the mirror, took a deep breath, and spoke with a face full of piety:

"Ah-Yara was right. Of the ten thousand matters in the world, apart from one's life, everything can be discarded. If you ask what is a destiny ordained by fate... then it is I and this Heaven-Illuminating Mirror!"

Moony, meanwhile, was fully cooperative, her hands carrying seven or eight bags of colourful accessories, striving to maintain her professional smile as the Number One Working Immortal Servant.

"Miss, did you not just add a purchase of a...?" Moony was rummaging through the accessories in the bags.

"Yes, yes, yes! It is the **P-I-N-K F-U-R-R-Y C-A-S-E**!" Lili also began to rummage. "It is the plush style! With two ears! And it even emits little stars on its own!"

As she spoke, Lili fished that unreasonably dreamy protective case out of her storage bag. Holding the mirror in one hand, she clumsily installed it with the other, occasionally checking the instruction manual to carefully tighten the Black Iron buckles.

"This is a Limited Edition! Only one hundred sets were released in the entire Immortal Realm! You must know, this thing has been speculated up to three thousand Spirit Stones on the net auction platforms. I only spent two thousand seven hundred, and it even came with a Mirror Surface Spirit-Protection Talisman! Massive profit!"

Moony: "...Heh heh, Fairy, you have earned a fortune."

Maxing out the emotional value for the boss is the basic cultivation of a working immortal.

Lili was currently like a child who had gotten her wish. She spun in a circle holding the mirror, then proceeded to open other functions and modes, playing with endless delight, mumbling all the while:

"This filter! It is simply a divine miracle! Even the mole at the corner of my eye comes with its own halo effect! Worthy of being the designated collaboration model of the Spirit Shadow Pavilion!"

Moony chuckled along happily. "Miss, take a picture of me too..."

Lili put on a serious face. "I haven't finished taking pictures of myself yet."

Having said that, she held the mirror and murmured with deep affection: "Mystic Spirit Baby, you have finally arrived in my hands... From now on, you follow me. Eat with me every day, sleep with me every day, understood?"

The mirror naturally did not answer, but it glowed faintly with a soft light, as if silently emitting a resonance of spiritual consciousness.

Just as the mistress and servant were beside themselves with excitement, a Sound Transmission Talisman drifted down from the sky.

"Yun Lili. Today's lesson. Do not forget. Do not be late."

* * * * *

Upon receiving Yu Sord's notification for class once again, Yun Lili did not feel the mountain-crushing pressure she had in the past. On the contrary, she accepted the summons with bubbling joy, unable to wait to show off her new treasure to him.

When Yun Lili stepped into Yu Sord's Cloud-Light Pavilion, the delight hiding in the corners of her eyes and brows could not be concealed.

Unlike her previous arrivals for lessons, which always carried the air of a martyr struggling towards death, today her steps were as light as one admiring flower during a lake excursion; even the corners of her robes fluttered with an extra degree of grace.

Yu Sord sensed this change clearly and could not help but look sideways. "You are in such high spirits today; has there been a joyous occasion?"

Hearing this, Lili instantly revealed a smile that was equal parts smug and shy, like a child impatient to share a secret but slightly afraid of being mocked.

She reached into her bosom with the utmost care and extracted an object. "Heh heh, it is this..."

With a *voilà*, an exquisitely magnificent Heaven-Illuminating Mirror appeared abruptly in her palm.

The body of the mirror scintillated with light, carved with gold and inlaid with jade. Yet, the most eye-catching feature was the layer of **pink, fluffy protective casing** wrapped around its exterior. It even had two small ears sewn onto the top, and a small, glowing spirit bead hanging from the tail.

Yu Sord: "......"

Lili hugged the mirror as if embracing a supreme spirit treasure, her face radiating light as she spoke with brimming enthusiasm: "The Supreme Edition Heaven-Illuminating Mirror! Did you know, Immortal Lord? It comes with built-in celestial light filters and beautification illusion functions! Even when I wake up with a swollen face in the morning, one look in this mirror can instantly transform me into a fairy descending to earth! It also has automatic night-light adjustment, voice recording, image capture... it is simply omnipotent!"

He knew, but he did not say.

"And this protective case is a Limited Edition! It is made from the fur shed by the Jade Rabbits of the Moon Palace. The touch is like a cloud! I nearly didn't manage to snatch one!"

She spoke with dancing brows and radiant eyes, shining with a pure joy and passion, as if this tiny object were the source of her entire happiness.

Yu Sord fell silent for a moment. Turning his body slightly, he quietly tightened his grip on an object hidden within his sleeve.

It was a Heaven-Illuminating Mirror of extremely similar style—only the colour was a pale purple, and the frame was engraved with a clear pattern of bamboo shadows.

 He had personally won it at an auction in the Heavenly Market Tower just last night. His original intention was... if she succeeded in her coursework, he would give it to her as a reward.

At this moment, watching her cradling that tender pink, plush version with a heart full of joy, he suddenly felt he had purchased the wrong model.

He tucked the mirror in his sleeve a little deeper inside, letting out a soundless, lost laugh.

When, exactly, had he too been moved to thoughts of ingratiating himself for the sake of a woman's smile?

"Today's lesson is... Freehand Landscape Painting," Yu Sord gave a light cough, pulling the topic back to the proper track.

"Ah, painting?" Yun Lili's smile instantly retracted as she muttered in a low voice, "I don't know how."

"No matter. I will teach you."

Yu Sord walked to stand behind her. Leaning down, he reached out to cover the hand holding the brush.

He was consistently cold and restrained, yet his movements were surprisingly gentle. His fingertips merely corrected her slightly askew wrist bone, guiding her stroke by stroke to outline the lines of distant mountains.

"The wrist must be steady, the force hidden in the pads of the fingers, the tip of the brush slightly retracted."

When he spoke, his voice was low and slightly husky, his breath brushing past the side of her neck.

The roots of Yun Lili's ears instantly turned a patch of red. She felt only a warmth transmitting from his palm, seeping through her wrist all the way into the bottom of her heart. Even the Heaven-Illuminating Mirror seemed to lose its spiritual power in this moment, sliding silently to the corner of the desk.

"Immortal Lord, you... you paint truly well..." Her voice was weak, and her heart skipped a beat.

Yu Sord smiled faintly, lowering his brow to look at her. "Once you are skilled, I will no longer need to support you like this."

Lili hurriedly said, "No, I feel my painting skills require another three to five years of practice..."

Due to the intimate proximity, Lili could not stop her heart from accelerating. In her heart, she secretly cried out: *The Immortal Sovereign is truly so handsome!*

From a distance, up close, looking up, looking down, looking left, looking right... no matter from which angle one looked, it was a calamitous face capable of charming people to death.

The two exchanged a glance. Yun Lili was the first to be unable to resist, laughing shyly in embarrassment, and Yu Sord also curved the corner of his lips.

Upon the painting paper, a gentle, distant mountain had already taken shape, just like the throbbing in her heart that she had not yet detected, quietly climbing to the peak of her soul.

* * * * *

Yu Sord sat in solitary silence within the small pavilion of the side courtyard. The slanting sun was soft and gentle, casting dappled light and shadow through the eaves of the pavilion to land by his side.

He leaned quietly against a small wooden table, his expression showing a rare trace of frozen contemplation.

Upon the table lay a Heaven-Illuminating Mirror of exquisite aesthetic. The body of the mirror was edged with high-quality purple bamboo and inlaid with crystals that sparkled like a multitude of stars. The surface was as light and thin as a feather, faintly circulating with spiritual light.

It was none other than the latest high-end **"Supreme Edition for Female Cultivators,"** boasting beautification filters and aura skin-protection functions; even the sealing rune patterns were shaped like little peach hearts.

He propped one hand against the edge of the table, the other resting against his forehead. A faint look of helplessness surfaced on his handsome face, accompanied by a smile that was not quite a smile.

"...How could it... have come to this stage?"

Having spoken, he actually laughed at himself, a low laugh filled with restraint and self-mockery.

Suddenly, the air shifted minutely. A phantom image turned lightly, and a human figure had already fluttered down to sit opposite him at the wooden table.

"So, even the renowned Immortal Lord Silentstar, Yu Sord, whose name shakes the Cultivation World... is capable of such sentimental distress over a female immortal?"

Xie Wuchen was clad in long robes of profound azure embroidered with cloud patterns, his temperament leisurely and elegant.

His long, slender fingers propped up his chin as his gaze swept back and forth over the mirror on the table, the corner of his mouth hooked up in an ambiguous arc.

Yu Sord did not so much as lift an eyelid. He spoke coldly: "Speak if you have words; do not be eccentric."

Xie Wuchen pointed at the mirror with feigned innocence. "I merely wish to ask: what is this object?"

Yu Sord finally cast a sidelong glance at him, his gaze filled with a cold look that said *'Stop playing the fool'*: "You do not recognise it?"

Xie Wuchen laughed lightly, the corner of his eye holding a glint of teasing light. "I naturally recognise this object. It is merely that... *heh*, I fear there is someone whose heart has moved without him realising it, or perhaps... he simply dares not admit it."

Hearing this, Yu Sord raised a brow. Suddenly, the corner of his lips hooked up lightly, a thin, cool smile rippling like water.

"Is that so?"

His tone was extremely faint, yet every word was clear. "I wonder who exactly is the one lacking self-awareness." He pretended to think carefully for a moment. "Oh, at this moment, I recall a past event from thirty years ago. I heard that someone chased all the way to the entrance of the **'Lu Yue Cave'**. Kneeling, begging, praying... Yet Fairy Lu Ling said not a single word, turned around, and entered seclusion—a seclusion from which she has not emerged for thirty years to this day. That person... if not you, Xie Wuchen, then who else could it be?"

The originally lazy, leaning figure of Xie Wuchen stiffened instantly. The smile on his face froze for a moment before retracting completely.

"...You are too lacking in virtue." He gritted his teeth. "You even bring up matters from thirty years ago?!"

Yu Sord continued to sit as upright as a pine, his gaze still as water, but the smile at the corner of his lips could not be suppressed no matter what.

"Naturally, the memory is fresh. After all... back then, you had even drafted the Eight Characters of Birth for the two of you; the only thing missing was carving them onto the Stone of Three Lives."

"YU! SORD!"

The blue veins on Xie Wuchen's forehead throbbed slightly. He glared at the other man for a long time before finally turning his face away in stifled anger, muttering a sullen sentence: "...Do not mention that matter, or we shall fall out."

"Acceptable." Yu Sord chuckled low, speaking faintly. "I shall not mention it."

Outside the pavilion, the wind passed, and the bamboo shadows danced. The two remained silent for a moment before Yu Sord suddenly asked:

"Tell me... if she knew that *I* was the one who bought this Heaven-Illuminating Mirror, what would happen?"

Xie Wuchen rolled his eyes at him, huffing coldly. "What? So you are simply admitting it now?"

Yu Sord gave no comment, but that leisurely appearance was a tacit admission in Xie Wuchen's eyes. Xie Wuchen could not resist a sarcastic remark: "If she knew, *heh*, I fear she would laugh at you from beginning to end."

"...That is fine, too." Yu Sord murmured in a low voice. His lowered gaze carried a slight smile, yet within that smile lay a silence and solitude that others would find difficult to perceive.

Xie Wuchen looked at him, then suddenly tilted his head and smiled.

"Brother Yu, I suddenly look forward very much to the day when you, too, go and kneel outside her door to beg for a chance."

Yu Sord did not speak. He merely pushed the mirror a little further away. His smile deepened, yet he did not deny it.

Chapter 27: The Closing of the Tea Stall

The morning light spilled across the earth like liquid gold. As was her custom, Yun Lili set up her tea stall along the small path at the foot of the mountain.

Today the weather was clear and bright, and the fragrance of tea permeated the air in all directions. Moony bustled about at the side, helping to arrange the tables and chairs.

Before half a stick of incense could burn down, several male cultivators had already followed the scent to arrive.

One of them held a jade bottle in both hands, offering it with a solicitous smile. "Junior Sister Yun, I refined a furnace of Skin-Protecting Jade Frost yesterday. Applying it to your fingertips can prevent burns from spiritual *qi*. With this, you need not fear your hands turning red from selling tea."

Another man, smiling beamingly, presented a carved spirit fan. "This fan can dispel heat and cool the temper. When brewing tea, it ensures one does not easily get overheated."

Lili laughed as she accepted the items, not even having time to open them to look. Unbeknownst to her, amidst the clouds and mist of a certain celestial mountain behind her, a wisp of formless divine consciousness hovered quietly, condensed but undissipated.

It was none other than Yu Sord.

He sat upon the jade terrace before the Lingxiao Hall and his expression appeared as normal as ever, yet in reality, his line of sight was condensed upon the space between her brows and eyes.

Here comes another delivering spirit fans. Here comes another delivering jade frost.

His divine consciousness shifted, watching the little fairy smile until her eyebrows curved, even joking with one of them: *"Really? Is this Jade Frost truly so effective?"*

...A fire of unknown origin rose secretly in his heart.

Such lively clamour and noise—what benefit does this yield for cultivation?

Half an hour later.

Moony rubbed her wrist, speaking wearily, "Fairy, there are so many people today. My legs are sore."

Yun Lili poured a cup of tea that she didn't even have the strength to drink herself. As she lifted her hand, she bumped her index finger, causing a sharp pain. She frowned. "It's all red..."

She pouted, looking at that reddened finger, and suddenly recalled her small treasury.

That's right. The Spirit Stones for the Heaven-Illuminating Mirror have long since been gathered, haven't they?

Furthermore, a few days ago, the Lingxiao Sect had sent her a "Spirit Stone Subsidy," stating it was a *"Reward for Fairy Yun's pure-hearted cultivation and dual cultivation of virtue and conduct."*

Why did she still need to work this hard, risking life and limb?

"Moony, Little Moon, shall we... perhaps stop selling?"

To be honest, she was a little tired!

Hearing this, Moony nodded immediately. "Not selling, not selling! This business is exhausting to the point of death, and it damages the skin. Fairy, you are someone who relies on your face to cultivate!"

Just at this moment, another handsome male cultivator walked up, smiling brilliantly. "Junior Sister Yun, give me two pots of today's Spirit Honey Heart-Clearing Tea, plus a smile from you."

Lili rolled her eyes towards the heavens. She stood up, patted the tea dust from her apron, and gave a sweet, saccharine smile.

"Not selling anymore. The tea stall is closed. Going home to sleep~"

The male cultivator looked astonished. "Eh? But I walked across three mountains—"

"Go back~" Lili waved her hand dismissively. "There are many mountains, but few girls. Go drink water instead."

With that, she packed up her stall and left without turning her head back.

That wisp of divine consciousness trembled lightly in the air, appearing to stretch and relax amidst the clouds.

Lingxiao Sect.

Yu Sord opened his eyes. He took a sip of clear tea, and the corner of his lips hooked up in a rare, gentle arc.

Clean and quiet; the noise has ceased.

Now, this looks like a little fairy cultivating immortality.

* * * * *

High atop the Lingxiao Sect, Yu Sord sat in meditative silence upon the Jade Terrace, reading a book. He appeared composed and idle, his plain robes as white as snow.

However, his divine consciousness had long since condensed into a silent, invisible presence, hovering before Yun Lili's tea stall for a considerable time.

He watched as that male cultivator—the one who had refined the finger-protecting balm—turned red in the face and thick in the neck, shamelessly presenting flower fans, jade bottles, and jade frosts. And he watched as she, smiling all the while, actually tucked that jade bottle into her sleeve.

...Is this what she calls "cautious and prudent, cultivating the heart in silence"?

Yu Sord's gaze did not waver. The phantom scent of tea drifted across the sea of his heart, yet it served only to draw his brows into a tight, disapproving knot.

These people... they all claimed to be cultivating the heart and the Dao, yet day after day, they circled her tea stall without ceasing. Where was the cultivation? This was clearly a boisterous marketplace!

With a subtle shift of his divine consciousness, he pinched his fingers together to perform a quick divination, obtaining the omen: **"Too much movement, too little stillness; prone to damaging the foundation."**

Thus, with a casual wave of his hand, he inscribed a note:

"Tea affairs bring much disturbance; they labor the form and consume the spirit. It is suggested that Fairy Yun temporarily cease secular duties and focus on cultivating her nature."

This jade slip bore no signature. It was marked only with the official seal of: **"Suggestion for Internal Cultivation Prescription of the Immortal Sect."**

One stick of incense later, Yun Lili duly received this jade slip.

She read it twice, curling her lip in dissatisfaction. "Where did this suggestion come from? Why suddenly say that selling tea consumes the spirit?"

Moony rubbed her sore and aching arm, whispering, "I feel... it is not without reason. There were so many people today; you brewed tea until your fingertips turned red."

Lili held up her hand. Indeed, she discovered a layer of faint redness floating on her index finger; it felt sore and numb, and there was even a tiny patch of peeling skin.

"...Brewing this spirit tea is truly too hard. It is not as if I rely on this to survive." She pouted. "In any case, the money for the Heaven-Illuminating Mirror has been gathered. Furthermore, I now have—"

She lowered her voice, rolling up her sleeve to reveal a small spiritual talisman pouch. "My little treasury has gained a great many more Spirit Stones!"

It turned out that half a month ago, the Lingxiao Sect had suddenly issued a reward under the nominal title of **"Reward for Success in Silent Cultivation."** The amount was neither more nor less—exactly equivalent to the price of a Supreme Edition Heaven-Illuminating Mirror.

At the time, she had only felt pleasant surprise and hadn't thought much of it. Only now did she chew over the details: "Eh... where exactly did I succeed in silent cultivation during this period?"

Moony looked blank. "Were you not selling tea the whole time?"

Lili touched the pouch, casting a slightly suspicious glance in the direction of the Lingxiao Hall, then shook her head. "Whatever! The money is earned. I am closing the stall today!"

With that, she stood up, shook out her apron, and beckoned Moony to pack up the tea set.

Just at this moment, another male cultivator arrived carrying spirit fruit tea cakes, his face brimming with smiles. "Fairy Yun, how about two pots of today's Heart-Clearing Tea?"

Lili didn't even look at him. She smiled and waved her hand.

"Not selling! Closing the mountain today, resting tomorrow... as for the day after, we shall see~"

* * * * *

High above the heavens, amidst the swirling clouds and mist.

The wisp of divine consciousness slowly, gradually withdrew.

Yu Sord raised his eyes to gaze beyond the hall. The drifting clouds were faint and pale. He took a gentle sip of his tea.

The fragrance of the tea had not altered, yet his state of mind had suddenly become significantly more tranquil and clear.

He had always disliked external affairs and possessed a disposition that was far from approachable. Yet at this precise moment, the corner of his lips curved up soundlessly into an extremely slight, almost imperceptible arc.

It is good that she closed the stall. It saves her hands from turning red.

And it saves him... from heartache.

* * * * *

Finally!

For half a month of continuous sunny days without a cloud in the sky, Yun Lili's spirit tea stall had become practically the hottest sensation along the entire path before Flying Cloud Peak.

The spirit spring water bubbled and boiled day in and day out, the heat releasing a fragrance that permeated the entire stall, attracting wave after wave of cultivators to stop in their tracks.

Handful after handful of tea leaves were brewed. Moony's technique was skilled; she could practically flip the pot with one hand while greeting guests with the other. Yun Lili, meanwhile, handled the visitors with a beaming smile.

Even the three spirit chickens were not idle. One was responsible for *clucking* to welcome guests, one jumped to the tea table to help carry water, and the third shuttled back and forth holding a small tray to serve tea.

Their chicken lives had reached an unprecedented peak.

However, in all things, too much is as bad as too little. This business, bursting at the seam's day after day, had finally caused the three chickens of the small stall to collapse from exhaustion.

On the afternoon of this day, the sun was fine and the wind not dry. Yun Lili finally sent away the "last male cultivator who loved tea as much as his life." She flopped back onto the straw mat like a cat flattened out, gasping for breath with her mouth wide open.

"I am exhausted to death... Is this still a body cultivating immortality? It is simply inferior to even a mortal! I feel my spiritual power has been squeezed dry!"

Moony collapsed beside her, pounding her own shoulder as she whispered mournfully, "Miss, that Golden Core male cultivator today... he drank nine pots of tea in one breath and still said it wasn't enough, insisting you pour it personally. That look in his eyes... clearly harboured unruly intentions!"

Lili clicked her tongue. "I don't care what he harbours, as long as he pays... However—"

As she spoke, she rolled up her sleeves, opening the small spirit talisman coin pouch tied at her waist. Inside, strings of Spirit Stones were stacked neatly, still emitting a faint glow.

"Moony, Little Moon, look! Our Spirit Stones are overflowing, the Heaven-Illuminating Mirror has been bought, and the small treasury has been nurtured... I think perhaps we shouldn't continue selling this tea?"

The three spirit chickens collapsed at her feet in unison, like three cloth chickens that had lost their souls. One even rested its wing on the other's head, too lazy to let out even a single *cluck*.

"Aiya, you three feel tired too? I know, I know. Wait until I see the situation tomorrow... perhaps... we shall rest?"

Moony's eyes lit up immediately. "Really? That is wonderful! My fingers are blistered from the heat; even the Spirit Spring can't save my shoulders... Miss, I am still young; I don't want to go bald at an early age!"

Lili laughed. "Heh heh, where exactly are you young? You are several hundred years older than me!"

Moony thought about it. *It was actually true!*

"Heh heh, so I am still 'Fairy Yun,' but I see that you have been tortured by this tea-selling business into becoming 'Auntie Moon'."

"Miss has changed! You never used to mock me before!"

Lili began to dismantle the spirit tea canister while muttering unhappily, "The male cultivators coming to drink tea these past few days... truly, each one is more abnormal than the last."

Moony nodded fiercely, curling her lip. "Yes, yes. The eyes of those few who came to drink tea were practically glued to your face. Even when the tea was getting cold, they couldn't bear to look away."

Lili rolled her eyes towards the sky. "There was one who even said— *'Fairy Yun, every night in my dreams there is the beautiful silhouette of you brewing tea.'* Ahhh... is that not disgusting? If you can add water and brew tea in a dream, why don't you just ascend to immortality in your dream?"

Moony nodded as she wiped a cup. "I even heard that male cultivator at the early stage of Foundation Establishment say: *'Fairy, your fingers are truly beautiful.'* He wasn't here to drink tea at all; he was here to look at hands!"

Yun Lili huffed, lifting her fingertips to examine them critically. "The result is that my hands have now developed calluses. If he comes again, I shall close the doors. I am not selling anymore."

The three spirit chickens sat to the side, listening to the gossip with keen interest. One of them even let out an untimely *cluck*.

Lili immediately turned on them. "If you lot pass tea to those strange male cultivators again in the future, I will deduct your rations."

The three spirit chickens: "......"

Amidst their banter, the two suddenly spotted several male cultivators approaching from a distance. They fell silent abruptly.

A moment later, Moony was the first to break the silence. "What do we do? What do we do? Those few have actually come. Is it too late to hide now?"

"Not good!" Lili's face changed. She sprang up instantly, her reaction as fast as if she had been struck by lightning. "Moony, pack up the stall, quick! Hide! Pretend we are closed, pretend! Hurry up, **San Bao**, **Er He**, let's retreat!"

In the heat of the moment, the group—plus three chickens and two cranes—was in a chaotic flurry. Lili muttered complaints as she worked: "Do these people think I am holding a matchmaking session? And that one who gifts jade, coming three days in a row... yesterday he even asked me—*'Fairy Yun, what colour of hairpin do you prefer?'*"

Scarcely had her voice faded when, sure enough—a familiar figure in the distance strode quickly towards their tea stall. It was none other than that persistent "Jade Ring Male Cultivator," who brought his own teacup every day and quoted poetry like a flowing stream!

The three spirit chickens, seemingly veterans of a hundred battles, kicked their legs into action. One jumped into the tea crate, one drilled under the tablecloth, and the last one simply sat its bottom down on the spirit tea canister and played dead, perfectly displaying the full range of chicken acting skills.

Lili pulled the curtain of the tea shed shut with a smooth motion. Turning around, she displayed a **"Closed Today, Do Not Disturb"** spirit talisman. She didn't forget to quickly pat her face, squeezing out an expression of extreme exhaustion and overwork.

She turned her head, asking in a whisper, "Have they gone?"

"Not yet. He is looking at the straw mat you were sitting on just now..."

Lili: "???"

Moony: "He is now... squatting down... he is... *sniffing*... Miss, don't hit me, *woo*... I am only relaying the scene!"

"Wahhh!" Lili's spiritual power exploded on the spot. "How is this person more terrifying than a ghost?! I want to move house!"

And at this very moment, a thousand miles away at the summit of the Lingxiao Sect, Yu Sord sat in meditation with closed eyes. Yet, his divine consciousness had long since fallen far away, hovering before Flying Cloud Peak.

He saw that male cultivator squat down to look at the straw mat, and he saw Lili packing up her stall and fleeing with a face full of horror. The corner of his lips hooked up; within his coldness lay a few hints of hidden... indescribable amusement.

Chapter 28: The Painting of the Chicken and the Teapot

As the first light of dawn broke the next day, Yun Lili, carrying her painting tools on her back, walked lazily towards the Lingxiao Lecture Hall.

She nibbled on a spirit peach as she muttered to herself, "Painting again today... my fingers hurt so much... Even in my dreams, I was shaking pots and brewing tea, while the spirit chickens were crowing to beat the rhythm. How is cultivating immortality more exhausting than life in the marketplace?"

Her whole body ached—back sore, waist painful—and her hands, in particular, felt as though they no longer belonged to her.

The moment she entered the lecture hall, Yu Sord was already standing upon the high platform. His white robes surpassed snow, his ink-black hair bound in a cloud crown, his demeanour as cold and waveless as ever. Only his gaze swept imperceptibly across the hall doors, coming to rest upon her.

He watched as she walked in slowly, settled into her seat, and fished out her brush holder—as expected, she had hidden a few candied fruits inside. When she sat down, she twisted her waist, looking as though her bones had gone soft from the exhaustion of the previous day.

"In today's lesson, painting a mountain is not about the form, and painting water is not about the flow. It lies in the birth of artistic conception, which aids in cultivation."

Yu Sord's voice was like wind brushing through ancient pines—clear, distant, and long-lasting. He swept his sleeve, and a scroll of ink-wash landscape painting appeared suspended in the air, devoid of brush marks. Mist and haze were hazy, layers of peaks stacked upon one another, and amidst the shimmering waves of light, a world of its own was formed.

"You shall copy this image, then paint what you see and what you feel."

She frowned, brush in hand, staring blankly at the paper for a long time. When she finally put brush to paper, she actually painted a fat chicken squatting on the mountain peak, with a spirit teapot circling the mountainside, billowing thick smoke.

Yu Sord descended from the platform to inspect. He stood silently by her side, lowering his eyes to look at her half-finished painting. His voice was faint, yet it carried a trace of unconcealable astonishment: "Is this truly the appearance of the mountains and rivers you see in your eyes?"

Lili did not lift her head, pouting her lips. "It isn't that I want to... The moment I close my eyes, it's spirit tea, spirit chickens, spirit guests."

"Not Spirit Stones?" He pricked her bubble mercilessly with a single sentence.

She laughed awkwardly, shaking her hand with a face full of weariness. "Heh heh, it's this tea-selling business. Every day brewing tea, passing water, and having to smile... Immortal Lord, tell me, I clearly came here to cultivate immortality; how did I cultivate into a waiter at a spirit tea house?"

She spread her palms and brought them close to his eyes for him to see. Her slender ten fingertips were all red and peeling, clearly the result of being soaked in water for long periods.

"Look, look. Alas, earning Spirit Stones is truly a matter that tires the heart."

Yu Sord's brow twitched slightly, his voice remaining calm. "So, you no longer like selling tea?"

"It isn't that I dislike it... Er, it was quite interesting at the start. But you know, the thing about fun is that it can be ground down to nothing by a queue lasting three sticks of incense."

She shook her head, then pouted and added a sentence: "Besides, my Spirit Stones are sufficient now. I bought the Heaven-Illuminating Mirror, and even my small treasury is stuffed full... The stipend stones given by the Lingxiao Sect are so high... If I continue to set up the stall, wouldn't that be a bit foolish?"

Yu Sord's gaze darkened. He tapped his finger lightly on the corner of her paper, causing the painted spirit chicken to tremble as if its soul had been shaken.

"Then do you still plan to continue setting up the tea stall?" He asked calmly, seemingly casual.

Lili shook her head immediately, speaking decisively: "Not setting it up anymore! Tired, vulgar, and I have to deal with those male cultivators... I might as well concentrate on painting, planting spirit flowers, and reasoning with the spirit chickens. How leisurely and comfortable that would be~"

Being a happy little fairy should mean not partaking in the smoke and fire of the mortal world. Heh.

She muttered a supplementary sentence: "Besides, earning here and there, the Lingxiao Sect still pays out the fastest..."

Yu Sord uttered not a word. He turned and returned to the lectern. His sleeves moved like the wind, his white robes dragging on the ground as the tip of his brush fell lightly.

He painted a mountain. The shadows of the mountain were heavy, yet amidst the flowing clouds and mist, there was an added warmth.

On the mountainside in the painting, there was a small pavilion. Within the pavilion, faintly visible, a figure seemed to stand by the water, brewing tea—or perhaps no longer brewing tea, but sitting idly to admire the mountain.

Lili stole a glance at him, sighing inwardly once again at the Immortal Lord's peerless beauty, which was, as always, handsome enough to make both gods and men indignant.

Looking again at the painting under his hand—small pavilion, small chicken, small mountain, small fairy... she felt that the mountain in the Immortal Lord's painting today seemed exceptionally... lively and happy?

She did not notice—the Immortal Lord, usually cold as frost and snow, had actually curved the corner of his lips extremely lightly, extremely faintly, when she inadvertently said, *"Not selling tea anymore."*

It was as if that single sentence, *"I am not setting up the stall anymore,"* was the most satisfactory stroke of his brush today, beyond painting mountains and writing water.

* * * * *

After the lesson concluded, Yun Lili finally completed her masterpiece— a mountain populated by spirit chickens, a pot of scalding hot spirit tea, and a tiny figure sprawled out dozing on the mountainside, with a piece of candied fruit still clamped between their teeth.

As Yu Sord passed by, he swept a low glance over it. His tone was faint, yet he uttered four words that were rare and precious coming from him:

"The conception is precious."

Having spoken, he departed with hands clasped behind his back, his retreating figure resembling clouds rising and rosy mist scattering.

Yun Lili tilted her head, pondering for a long while, before finally scratching her nose.

"The Immortal Lord... he was praising me, right?"

And in the distance, the spirit chickens within her painting were mimicking her, dozing off as well.

* * * * *

Yun Lili cradled today's artwork in her arms. Scarcely had she stepped across the threshold of the Cloud-Embracing Cottage when she shouted with a beaming smile:

"Moony, Little Moon—come quickly! Help me hang this up! Hang it right in the centre of the main hall, in the most conspicuous position!"

Moony poked her head out from the kitchen, still holding half a piece of spirit cake in her hand, her speech muffled as she chewed. "What is it? What is this painting?"

Lili puffed out her chest with immense pride. "This is the *magnum opus* of your Young Miss today!"

She spun in a circle hugging the painting, then deliberately cleared her throat, mimicking Yu Sord's calm, emotionless tone: "He actually said— *The conception is precious!*"

Moony, who had been in the middle of biting her spirit cake, paused mid-chew, the corner of her eye twitching slightly.

The conception is precious?

Wasn't that obviously a roundabout way of saying the Miss's painting skills were terrible? It was likely the Immortal Lord couldn't even bring himself to say it was bad directly, so he took a detour to praise the "idea." It was truly... extreme mercy.

Yet, her family's Eldest Miss Yun wore a face full of spring-breeze satisfaction, treating it as the highest of accolades and savouring the aftertaste repeatedly. Moony gritted her teeth, forcefully swallowing the honest words roiling in her belly. She could only stiffen her face and squeeze out a smile. "Yes, yes... this painting... overflows with spiritual *qi*; it is vivid and lifelike."

Lili actually took this as genuine agreement, her spirits soaring even higher. "Tell me, is my composition not a world of its own? That mountain is transformed from a spirit chicken; that spring is the spirit water for brewing tea; and that mist is the morning celestial fog!"

Moony looked at the mountain on the paper that resembled a chicken's backside, and the lake that looked like a bubbling soup pot. The corner of her mouth twitched. "Mm... it does possess a certain... Spirit Tea Hell sensibility."

Lili failed to hear the mystery within the words. Instead, she nodded like a pestle pounding garlic. "I like those words! Spirit Tea Hell indeed! This is the peak work I painted with my eyes closed!"

Moony: "......"

Fine, let it be the peak, as long as you are happy.

She lowered her eyelashes, silently telling herself: *Moony, you must be calm. It is not the first day you have witnessed your Miss's brain. She has merely misunderstood the underlying meaning of the Immortal Lord's words. In any case, that Immortal Lord didn't correct her, so let's just pretend no one heard it... Fake smile. Give me a fierce fake smile.*

Moony let out a *pfft* of laughter. "Like that clump of a mountain that resembles a spirit chicken? And that bubbling spirit teapot? Miss, you are truly capable; you have painted an entire Spirit Tea Hell."

Lili huffed, just about to retort, when suddenly—

Crack—

A subtle yet crisp sound of an eggshell fracturing rang out from the corner.

Mistress and servant froze in unison. Turning their heads to look, they saw that upon the surface of the Spirit Egg, which had been warming in the spirit nest for so long, a fissure had actually appeared.

Before Lili could even shout, the three spirit chickens had already lunged forward with a fierce dive. They were so excited they *clucked* wildly, circling the Spirit Egg in a frenzy, occasionally extending their claws in an attempt to help pry the shell open.

"Hey, hey, hey! Careful! Don't peck it broken!"

Lili hurriedly threw herself forward, joining Moony to block the spirit chickens and shove them aside, squatting down anxiously before the Spirit Egg.

Within the confines of the shell, a pair of large, spirited eyes first rolled about with lively intelligence. Then, following a series of crisp *crack-crack-crack* sounds, the entire eggshell slowly split open.

A tiny silhouette, radiant with hues of golden-yellow and tipped with crimson, poked its head out. It possessed extremely long tail feathers that shimmered with a halo of light, swaying gently in the air like a living flame.

It stretched its neck and let out a long *Cheeep—!*, the sound immature yet full of spirit.

"What is... this?" Moony's eyes widened as she frantically flipped through the *Compendium of Spirit Birds*.

While flipping through the book, Moony cast a suspicious glance at the painting Yun Lili had just hung up. Suddenly, she froze. "Wait a moment... Miss, upon the mountain peak in your painting, is there not a bird standing there that looks exactly like this?"

Yun Lili paused, hurriedly looking over. Indeed, there was a golden-red feathered shadow in the painting that was virtually identical to the little creature in her arms.

"Eh, it really is."

Lili cupped the small bird with both hands, lifting it up. The bird was not afraid of strangers; it drilled headfirst into her embrace, its tail winding around her wrist, its small claws clutching her lapel, refusing to let go.

"Aiya, these feathers... look, how beautiful!" Lili's eyes lit up. "Does this not resemble the Spirit Feather Finch deep within the volcanoes in the Immortal Lord's scroll?"

"It does not. Spirit Feather Finches are not this clingy," Moony frowned, reading the book. "However, there is a **'Red Flame-Tailed Bird'** mentioned in ancient texts, said to be a rare spirit bird bred from Fire Spirits, but it has been extinct for many years..."

"Then this one... is that extinct little cutie?" Lili's face was full of joy. "Ai, ai, we must give it a name—let's call it **'Little Flame'**!"

"Cheeep!" Little Flame cried out fiercely, its tail flashing with brilliant gold as if in response, rubbing its head against Lili's chin.

The three spirit chickens stared dumbfounded at this new companion, their faces full of suspicion: *"Cluck, cluck, cluck?"*

This isn't a chicken! If you aren't a chicken, don't snatch the Master's embrace!

Little Flame seemed to sense something. It abruptly leaped to the ground, spreading its tail feathers at the spirit chickens in a posture that clearly asked, *"Who is the new boss?"* It even deliberately paced a circle around them.

"Miss, I fear this bird is a little *too* confident..." Moony didn't know whether to laugh or cry. "However, you must think clearly. If we raise this, how many spirit fruits and spirit tea leaves will it eat when it grows up?"

Lili held Little Flame up. "I have plenty of spirit tea. Besides, it is so cute! What if it can help me fly to the heavens when it grows up?"

"You want to ride it out the door *now*? It hasn't even grown to the size of a palm..." Moony rolled her eyes.

"Cluck, cluck, cluck—!" The spirit chickens cried out angrily, as if filing a complaint: *We haven't even ridden on your shoulder to fly yet!*

Lili's face was brimming with smiles as she hung the scroll high up, with Little Flame perched nearby.

"Come on, this is now our family's Guardian Spirit Painting: Spirit Chicken Mountain, Spirit Teapot, myself, plus Little Flame! How about it, Moony? In the future, it will surely be selected as one of the **Top Ten Funniest Images of the Cultivation World**!"

"No, it will be the **Top Ten Supernatural Phenomena of the Cultivation World**..." Moony murmured.

And just outside this noisy Cloud-Embracing Cottage, far away above the cloud layer, someone gazed for a moment.

Watching that shining little bird and the painting, the corner of his lips hooked up unconsciously.

—Yu Sord.

He whispered softly: "Not brewing tea anymore? Then... just raise a bird."

Chapter 29: The Prince's Embroidered Ball

Ever since she was startled into the realisation that she was, in fact, an invisible little rich girl, Yun Lili's aura had become inexplicably different.

Sipping the Peach Clear Tea she had newly blended herself, while counting the profits of this month on her fingers, she felt that life was truly full of hope. With the clear tea business unfolding like a raging fire and orders streaming in from all directions without end, she finally possessed that grounded sense of security that comes from having *"so many Spirit Stones one could sleep hugging them."*

Thus, early this morning, seized by a sudden whim, Lili summoned Yun Yara and Moony, speaking with an air of mystery:

"Today, we do not cultivate, nor do we refine tea. We are taking a trip to the mortal bustling market!"

This was new intelligence she had inadvertently gleaned yesterday. Today, there was a fair in Liang City in the mortal realm, and quite a few cultivators and immortals were discussing making a trip there to join the liveliness and incidentally restock their supplies.

Liang City was a small city situated closest to the intersection of the Mortal and Immortal Realms; it was a place where humans, immortals, and even demons and spirits mingled together.

Moony blinked her large eyes, her face filled with excitement. "Really? Can we eat candied hawthorns and watch lion dances?"

Yara, however, frowned. "Too many people, too many mixed tongues; it is improper."

Lili patted her shoulder, speaking with grave earnestness: "Ah-Yara, you are simply too well-behaved, which is why you haven't experienced how fragrant the smoke and fire of the mortal world can be. Rest assured, I've got you covered."

Consequently, the three changed into the attire of ordinary commoners and quietly descended to the mortal realm.

Lili shopped and ate her way through the streets, walking with the energy of someone injected with chicken blood. Sugar cakes, nougat, flower lanterns, fondant figurines... anything and everything could elicit her gasps of admiration and a generous opening of her purse.

It was Moony's first time seeing such a lively scene; her eyes simply weren't enough to take it all in. She looked left and right, her mouth stuffed with two sticks of candied hawthorns, her face the picture of satisfaction.

Yara, meanwhile, remained cold and aloof throughout. She allowed the crowd to jostle, yet she generated her own aura, following behind with a dignified indifference that commanded respect without anger.

In the bustling market of Liang City, the sun was just slanting towards the west. Lanterns were just being lit on both sides of the long street, and red curtains and yellow flags swayed in the wind. The roar of the lively crowd came in wave after wave.

The cries of street vendors rose and fell:

"Candied hawthorns here! Osmanthus flavour, and Rock Sugar Purple Perilla too!"

"Butter shortbread fresh from the pot! So fragrant even immortals would descend to snatch a bite!"

"Thousand-Layer Cake! No two layers represent the same sample; today we even added peach blossom powder!"

In the centre of the long street, a troupe of acrobats had set up a bamboo stage for a performance. One man was tossing and spinning a large vat on his head, while another danced with fire torches that moved like flying dragons and slithering snakes, attracting countless children to applaud and cheer.

To the side, an opera troupe was performing *The Legend of the White Snake.* Xu Xian and Bai Suzhen, fully made up in costume, gazed at each other with deep affection, singing in melodious, lingering tones that caused the young girls in the audience to clutch their hearts and sigh.

The air was a mix of the sweetness of popcorn, the fragrance of fried cakes, and the smoky scent of grilled meat skewers by the roadside. Steam rose from bamboo steamers, sugar powder flew in the air, and stalls beneath red cloths sold all manner of wood-carved scented sachets and hand-embroidered purses.

Even the ring-toss stall was surrounded by a circle of people; the children were all incredibly excited, with cheers of *I got it!* ringing out from time to time.

Moony's eyes didn't know where to look, and her small mouth was never idle—tasting red date cake one moment, then eyeing the sugar paintings the next.

Lili, on the other hand, acted like an experienced regular, picking and choosing left and right—saying this shop's candied fruits weren't as sweet as that one's, or commenting that the *huqin* artist was playing out of tune, inferior to the one in her previous Cloud Village...

Yara stood amidst the crowd. Her expression was faint as always, yet she could not help but look back a few extra times at the children chasing butterflies and the wind-chime carts circling the streets.

That lively prosperity of the mortal dust, compared with the cold, water-like Heavenly Palace of the Immortal Realm, seemed like a dream of two different worlds, making it momentarily difficult to distinguish reality from illusion.

Just as they were strolling with enthusiasm, the crowd suddenly grew tumultuous.

A high platform draped in red silk had been erected in the heart of the street, with several bailiffs maintaining order. Upon the high platform, a man dressed in brocade held a red ball in his hand. He was looking east and west from the edge of the stage, seemingly...

"Eh?" Lili blinked. "Throwing an embroidered ball to recruit a spouse?"

"Why is it a man?" Moony couldn't help but exclaim.

They heard the surrounding discussions, mortals gossiping without restraint:

"Is that not... Prince Xuan, Du Shao?!" said Passerby A.

"Haha, the forest is big, so all kinds of birds exist. To think that in this lifetime, I would see a dignified Prince throwing an embroidered ball to recruit a spouse," said Passerby B.

"This Prince Xuan is truly too out of favour... He is a Prince, after all, yet he has to throw the embroidered ball himself. It is truly losing face all the way home!" said Passerby C.

"Brother, you don't understand. I heard the Emperor loves cultivation. Some days ago, Prince Xuan found a high expert to tell his fortune. That expert bluntly criticized him, saying Prince Xuan was destined to have an 'Immortal Connection', and he must throw an embroidered ball to meet them... Isn't this Prince Xuan actually trying it out?" said Passerby D.

"Heh, can the words of such a warlock... be trusted?" said Passerby E.

Amidst the uproar of the crowd, Du Shao stood upon the high platform, his expression surprisingly calm. He was born with a handsome, unworldly air; though clad in the royal robes of the mortal realm, his brows and eyes carried a detachment that seemed out of place, as if he harboured no concern whatsoever for this farce. He merely raised the embroidered ball in his hand slowly.

Just then, Moony suddenly tugged nervously at Lili's sleeve. "Miss, Miss! He... seems to be looking in our direction!"

Lili froze. Just as she was about to say "Impossible," the embroidered ball was flung with a violent motion...

A crimson shadow sliced through the air, trailing a tail of red silk behind it. Resembling a bright red swimming dragon in the sky, it flew abruptly towards the section of the crowd where they stood.

The crowd shrieked and scattered. It was hurtling straight towards Yun Lili's direction!

"Ai, ai, ai?!" Lili had no time to dodge. She could only watch helplessly as the embroidered ball traced a bizarre trajectory in the air, flying straight at her face.

Just as the entire audience fixed their unblinking gazes on the falling embroidered ball, it suddenly seemed to be struck by some unknown force in mid-air, causing it to shift its angle slightly.

With a soft *thud*, it landed steadily in someone's arms.

The surroundings fell instantly silent; one could have heard a pin drop.

Moony stared, dumbfounded, at the embroidered ball in her own hands.

Yun Yara cradled her forehead. If she hadn't secretly flicked her finger just moments ago, that embroidered ball would likely have landed in Yun Lili's embrace.

Yun Lili lowered her head to look at the ball in Moony's arms, then raised her head to meet Du Shao's smile that was not quite a smile. Her entire face went pale.

"Woo... wah!" Only then did Moony seem to wake from a dream. She let out a shriek, her hands trembling, and actually hurled the embroidered ball from her arms violently to the side.

The ball smashed precisely into the arms of a matron clad in bright red embroidered wedding robes. A copper gong and red silks hung at her waist, and rouge was piled upon her face like three layers of peach blossoms. The moment she caught the ball, her eyes lit up, and she immediately let out an excited shout: "An auspicious omen!!"

With a single gesture from her, several sturdy family servants who had been prepared behind her stepped forward immediately. They surrounded Moony tightly, as if guarding a future Princess Consort, their movements astonishingly agile.

"Come, come, come! Everyone make way! Today a fairy descends from the heavens to tie the knot with my Lord Prince. This is a marriage bestowed by Heaven!"

The matron spun in a circle herself, her smile so exaggerated it nearly split her face. "This humble one is **He Yingchun**, the Gold Medal Matchmaker of Liang City, second to none, specializing in the weddings of high officials and nobles! Do not look askance at my red attire; this is the standard equipment of the trade, *heh heh*, born specifically for good matches!"

He Yingchun's face was piled high with smiles. "The one throwing the ball today is the current Prince Xuan, Du Shao. Little Lady, you were chosen by the heavens to catch the ball; this is the will of Heaven and Fate. The marriage destiny cannot be defied!"

"Ah?" Seeing this battle array, Moony's face had already turned white with fright.

He Yingchun, face brimming with smiles, held the embroidered ball and stared straight at Moony's face, getting more excited the more she looked. "Little girl, this appearance of yours is simply flower-faced and moon-like, sinking fish and falling geese, eclipsing the moon and shaming the flowers, a jade appearance of celestial posture!"

She paused for a moment, her eyes cheerfully scanning the girl before her from top to bottom, sighing with every phrase: "Look, look! Miss, your brows are like distant mountains, eyes like autumn water, skin like congealed fat, lips like dotted vermilion... *Ah, pah!* I have spoken auspicious words for so many years, but seeing your fairy-like pretty appearance today, I truly feel my vocabulary is exhausted!"

Moony was praised until the roots of her ears burned hot. She waved her hands repeatedly. "No, no, no, you have mistaken the person..."

He Yingchun paid no heed to her words whatsoever. Instead, she waved the embroidered ball on her own accord, turning to shout to the gathered crowd:

"Fellow townsfolk and elders, today's ball-throwing recruitment can be counted as having no precedent in history and no equal in the future! Prince Xuan is extraordinarily handsome, his belly filled with poetry and literature, radiating an innate elegance; and this young lady is fresh and

273

refined, free from vulgarity, a fairy descended to earth! *Heh*, if you ask me... this pair is a match made by Heaven and an alliance arranged by Earth. It is simply a marriage register that even the Queen Mother of the West would nod in approval of!"

The crowd erupted in roaring laughter and cheers. Someone even clapped their hands and shouted: "The little lady has fortune! Marrying a Prince—ascending to the heavens in a single step!"

He Yingchun grew even more spirited upon hearing this, patting her chest to guarantee: "If I, He Yingchun, speak a single wrong word, I shall write the character for 'Happiness' upside down! Come, come, bring the new bride to drink the joyful tea first."

Immediately following, a man dressed as a chief steward stepped forward with a beaming smile, holding a red lacquered wooden box in his hands. "Distributing joyful candy! Distributing joyful candy! Everyone come and taste the sweetness."

With a single gesture from He Yingchun, a swarm of people dressed as "family servants" surged forth from who knows where with a *whoosh*. Each held red ropes, brocade umbrellas, and wedding flowers, swiftly surrounding Moony in a tight circle.

Before Moony could recover her wits, she felt like a lost deer being driven into a pen. She looked in panic and confusion towards the direction of Yun Lili and Yun Yara: "Miss! Save me!"

As she shouted, she was jostled and dragged by the crowd towards the edge of the high platform. Surrounded by the masses, with the sound of joyful music rising on all sides, it felt as though the grand wedding were to be held this very instant.

"Moony, Little Moon!" Lili was greatly startled. She wanted to squeeze in, but no matter how she tried, she could not push through that "wedding reception team" whose enthusiasm was like fire. She could only watch as Moony's figure grew further and further away.

Yun Yara's brow locked tight, her gaze turning cold. She raised a hand, intending to cast the **Shadow Escape Art** to snatch the person back. Her fingers moved slightly, and spiritual light faintly rippled in the air...

But in a split second, her expression changed. She abruptly retracted her hand, grabbing Lili and pulling her back towards the rear of the crowd.

"What are you doing? Moony is about to be abducted!" Lili jumped in anxiety.

"We cannot strike," Yara whispered through gritted teeth. "This is the Mortal Realm, and there are many people here. If the Realm Patrol Envoys discover us casting spells here, we will be banned from descending to the lower realms for at least one hundred years. In severe cases, it will be reported to the Celestial Hearing..."

Lili was stunned. "Then... what do we do?"

One hundred years banned from the lower realms... so serious?

Yara stared tightly at the tide of red people crowding further away, her voice pressed extremely low, yet her gaze condensed like glacial ice:

"We must not startle the snake in the grass for now. We will memorize their appearances and origins, then think of a way to rescue her once we return. She is not a mortal; if someone truly wishes to marry her, they must first pass her test."

"...Alright." Lili nodded heavily, forcibly suppressing the unease in her heart.

At this moment, Moony, having been ushered onto the high platform, had eyes swimming with tears. She turned her head to look towards the distant Yun Lili, helpless and flustered. She heard He Yingchun's matchmaker voice ring out, high and bright:

"The Prince and the Fairy, a match made by Heaven, a good union of gold and jade! Come, come, change the Fairy's clothes and comb her hair! Protocol Officer, prepare the rites!"

"I don't want to... *Mmph*..." Moony's small mouth, crying for help, was suddenly covered by a square of wedding cloth, leaving her able only to make muffled sounds.

Yun Lili clenched her fists tightly. "I swear... Moony, Little Moon... rest assured... Your Miss will definitely find a way to come back and save you!"

She swore, she had only descended to the mortal realm this time to join in the fun. How could it be that with just one careless slip... *Woo...* before the campaign even started, Moony was abducted first!

Yun Zhou
雲昭

Chapter 30: The Barrier of the Mortal Prince

The night was as black as ink, the starlight faint and feeble. The streets and alleys of Liang City had long since sunk into tranquility.

With a flicker of their silhouettes, Yun Lili and Yun Yara leaped onto the outer wall of Prince Xuan, Du Shao's auxiliary residence.

The lanterns hanging high at the manor gates had long been extinguished, leaving only a wooden plaque inscribed with the two characters "Du Manor". The calligraphy was ancient and unadorned, utterly lacking the imposing grandeur befitting a Prince.

Lili stared blankly for a moment, whispering, "This is a Prince's manor? Isn't it a bit too shabby?"

Yara frowned, correcting her: "This is an auxiliary residence. His true Princely Manor is in the capital. This is merely a place of temporary lodging."

Lili nodded. In a flurry of clumsy movements, she fished a stack of talisman papers from her sleeve. "I brought Array-Breaking Talismans, Shadow-Hiding Talismans, Breath-Silencing Talismans... which one do you think we should use?"

Yara glanced at her, speaking helplessly: "Are *you* the Heavenly Spirit Root, or am *I*?"

Lili: "......"

I feel insulted.

She wore an awkward expression, turning her head to look inside the walls. Just as she was about to vault over, Yara grabbed her arm. "You don't know a single spell, your talismans are only good for bluffing mortals, and yet you want to break into a Prince's manor in the dark?"

Lili stuck out her tongue, retracting her hand. She looked at Yara with admiration. "I don't know how, but I have you!"

Yara sighed helplessly. With a wave of her sleeve and a point of her finger, a crystal-clear Night-Luminescent Pearl suspended itself in mid-air, its soft light illuminating the path ahead.

Lili exclaimed, "How are you so amazing!"

Alas, she truly doubted whether she really possessed Heavenly Spirit Roots? Compared to Yara, she felt like the real piece of trash.

Yara gave a light huff, ignoring her exaggerated flattery, and was the first to leap down from the wall.

The two flew to the top of another inner courtyard wall. Just as they were about to land lightly inside, Yara's spiritual consciousness extended outwards, instantly touching an invisible barrier.

Only a soft *hum* was heard—like wind, like water, as if invisible ripples were spreading out. Immediately following, a tyrannical counter-shock force rebounded violently!

"Careful!"

Yara immediately erected a spiritual shield to protect Lili. The two were blasted backwards, flying out to land heavily on the grass several *zhang* away from the wall. Lili let out a muffled groan, falling on her back with limbs splayed.

"Ouch! That hurts me to death!" Lili grimaced in pain.

Scarcely had they landed when an invisible fluctuation suddenly surfaced before them, rippling like the surface of water. It was actually a barrier, heavily guarding the residence!

With a soft *pop*, the spiritual power at Yara's fingertip touched it and was instantly repelled.

Lili also saw that something was not quite right. "W-What is wrong?"

Yara's expression changed slightly. She lowered her voice, speaking gravely: "Someone has actually set up a barrier... This is not a capability an ordinary Prince could possess."

This barrier was not difficult to break, but once broken, the one who set it would likely be notified immediately. Not knowing the background of this person was the most troublesome aspect.

"Ah, my butt... it hurts so much!" Lili rubbed her waist, the rims of her eyes turning red.

Yara's face changed drastically. The spiritual power in her hands turned rapidly, attempting to sense the aura of the barrier just now. A moment later, she whispered in shock:

"This is not the array of a mortal mage... This barrier is Immortal Sect Grade."

Lili was stunned. "Immortal Sect Grade? Wasn't it said that Prince Xuan is merely a mortal Prince? Where would he get such a high-level barrier?"

Yara fell into a heavy silence. Her gaze was dark as she looked towards that quiet, waveless manor wall, as if seeing the conspiracies and calculations hidden behind it.

Lili's face instantly filled with anxiety. "Then what about Moony? She is an immortal; if she is forced into marriage..."

"We cannot barge in; it will alert the person laying the array inside. Someone helped him set this barrier, and it is no ordinary person... There is a big problem here."

Lili stopped joking around, looking at her nervously. "Then... can we still enter?"

Yara looked at the faintly glowing patterns of the barrier, her expression solemn. She shook her head. "No. If a barrier of this level is forcibly broken, it will certainly alert the caster. Moony has no worry for her life for the time being; we cannot advance rashly at this moment."

At least, we must first probe to find out who set the barrier.

"But..."

"Return to the Immortal Realm first." Yara interrupted her coldly. "If it truly is a barrier set by an immortal, we cannot act blindly. We need to return to the Heavenly Domain to ask the elders for instructions, or investigate who is intervening in the mortal realm."

Lili stamped her foot in anxiety. "Then what do we do?"

Yara grabbed her, her tone calm yet firm. "Return to the Immortal Realm to discuss first. This manor is not a simple place. If it truly involves a high expert of the Immortal Realm, we must be even less reckless in our actions."

Yara cast a sidelong glance at her, saying no more. The two reactivated their talismans, borrowing the spiritual light to hide themselves in the curtain of night, quietly disappearing amidst the grass and trees.

Meanwhile, in the inner hall of the Du Manor.

Yue Liuchuan held a tea cup. Suddenly, he gave a light chuckle, seeming to sense something. "Came fast, retreated fast as well."

He raised a finger slightly, drawing a light line in the air. The array rippled like water, returning once more to silence.

"The little things from the Immortal Realm... they came in the end..."

* * * * *

The Princely Auxiliary Manor was utterly silent and still. Only the dim glow of the lamps lit the interior, a wisp of clear smoke rising from an incense burner.

Du Shao, clad in informal attire, stood on the stone steps beneath the porch. His bearing was extraordinary, his countenance cold, his gaze sharp as fire.

He performed a salute before speaking:

"Esteemed expert seeks audience at this late hour of night; may this one enquire as to the matter?"

By the stone table, Yue Liuchuan, clad in a single azure robe, remained seated. His long fingers lightly grasped a single chess piece, letting it fall onto the board with a soft click.

He wore a smile that was not quite a smile, his tone leisurely:

"Congratulations, Your Highness. Your immortal destiny has arrived. The Princess Consort is settled. Having secured this beauty among mortals, you now possess three more parts in your favour on the path to succession."

Du Shao's expression remained unchanged. He said faintly:

"The esteemed expert and this Prince both know that the embroidered ball ceremony was an act of sheer farce. The so-called 'Princess Consort' is merely a measure of expediency, meant to conceal the truth from His Majesty." The corner of his lip hooked up in a sneer. "One can deceive everyone in the world, save for oneself."

Yue Liuchuan heard this and laughed instead of growing angry. He raised his eyes to look at the Prince, his gaze concealing the depth of a thousand-year-old pool.

"Whether it is expediency or mere scheme, the piece that is destined to fall, must ultimately fall. The fairy has entered the manor. Everything is now upon the chessboard."

Du Shao fell silent for a moment. He finally spoke, his gaze scrutinising:

"Even at this stage of affairs, is the esteemed expert unwilling to disclose his origins?"

"That matters not. Your Highness only needs to remember that this one holds a grudge against the Immortal Realm."

Yue Liuchuan merely lifted his tea cup slowly, taking a gentle sip, and chuckled low. "Should Your Highness successfully seize the succession and become Emperor, this one's humble vengeance may find hope of being repaid."

Just at this moment, even as they spoke, Yue Liuchuan's brow twitched minutely. He looked toward a corner of the void and whispered, "Interesting... someone actually dared to disturb my barrier."

He turned his fingertip, and fine, invisible ripples spread around the barrier, akin to the faint trembling of a spiderweb, yet they vanished instantly into nothingness.

"Your Highness's manor is truly becoming lively too early."

Du Shao's gaze darkened slightly, yet he did not ask who had come to probe. He knew his cooperation with this expert would inevitably attract disruption. However, he maintained his cold voice:

"As long as it does not obstruct this Prince's affairs, the esteemed expert is free to dispose of the comings and goings of idle persons as he sees fit."

A dark light flashed in Yue Liuchuan's eyes. "Fear not, the intruder could not breach it."

Du Shao turned, preparing to depart. His voice was cold and resolute:

"What this Prince requires is more than just opportunity. This Prince not only demands the downfall of the Crown Prince, but also the vindication of his birth mother, and that the entire capital watches the day of this Prince's coronation."

Yue Liuchuan watched his retreating figure, murmuring softly:

"Your Highness possesses great ambition—to ascend the throne and become a Dragon. And this one intends to burn the heavens for vengeance... Heh heh, let this one wish Your Highness success in your heart's desire."

* * * * *

Low-hanging brocade bed-curtains, woven with threads of gold, enclosed the space. The subtle scent of incense smoke coiled lazily within the air.

Moony stirred from a deep sleep, instantly aware of the oppressive weight of the robes upon her body and a persistent ache throbbing at her brow.

She raised a trembling hand to touch her head; the icy weight of the **Phoenix Crown** felt as though it might crush her skull. The overwhelming vision of the cinnabar red draperies surrounding her seemed to ensnare her within a vivid, elaborate dream that was profoundly not hers.

She felt a sharp pain above her eyes. Her eyelashes fluttered, and she slowly opened her eyes. What met her gaze was a strange, ostentatiously furnished sleeping chamber.

The bed-curtains, woven with gold brocade, appeared less like a canopy and more like the elegant bars of a gilded cage. She looked down in terror and discovered herself clad in the full ceremonial **Phoenix Crown and Robes of Rank** (*Feng Guan Xia Pei*). The phoenix hairpins swayed gently, and the bridal robes flared like living fire—a sight that terrified her soul, causing her to abruptly throw off the quilt and rise.

"Where is this place?"

She rose suddenly, the ceremonial robes of rank sliding down her body and the heavy brocade quilt tumbling to the floor. The light from the palace lamp slanted in from an angle, drawing a long, solitary silhouette across the chamber.

A man sat quietly on a chair not far away, watching her. He wore a silver coronet and robes of crimson, his countenance like cold jade. His eyes were like a frozen pool in the night, still and waveless, as if he had been waiting in silence for a long time.

"This... what is the meaning of this?!"

Her voice echoed in the sleeping chamber, carrying an unmistakable blend of trembling fear and apprehension.

Moony spun her head around abruptly, startled by the sight of the man sitting near the head of the bed. He, too, was clad in robes of red. With his sword-like brows and star-bright eyes, his bearing was one of profound composure and cold elegance.

Those eyes, deep as a glacial pool, watched her silently, as though he had been anticipating her awakening for hours.

"You are awake." A voice, calm and steady, like the sound of jade striking ice, sounded from his direction.

Moony instinctively retreated towards the foot of the bed, demanding warily, "Who are you? Why am I dressed in such attire?"

Moony suddenly recalled the scene in the bustling market—the moment she had unexpectedly caught the embroidered ball, followed by the surrounding clamour. Then, somehow, she had lost consciousness, and the subsequent memory was a blank void.

Du Shao rose indifferently, performing a slight, formal salute. His voice was steady and cold as jade striking ice:

"This one is Du Shao, courtesy name Zichuan, the title Prince Xuan. Pray do not panic, young lady. You have not been disgraced, nor have you truly been married. All of this... is merely an expedient measure."

"Expedient?" Moony frowned, tightly clutching the fabric of her sleeves. "Release me and let me return immediately!"

Du Shao's expression remained placid. His tone was calm, yet permeated with apology. "The events of yesterday involved many unintended offences. I hope the young lady will be broad-minded and forgive them."

Moony's heart clenched violently. She recognized him instantly as the Prince she had seen throwing the ball in the market. She suppressed her terror, questioning him with a sudden coldness, "Where exactly is this place? What exactly do you intend to do with me?"

Du Shao did not answer immediately. He stood up, taking two steps closer. The hem of his robe brushed against the green bricks of the floor, and his voice was unhurried.

"This is an auxiliary residence under my name; no one will disturb you here. Regarding the events of last night... this Prince knows that the young lady harbors resentment in her heart, and thus, I must offer my sincere apologies."

Moony gave a cold sneer, her fingers tightening on the bedsheets. "The ball-throwing by He Yingchun, my selection... all arranged by Your Highness, is that not so?"

Du Shao nodded slightly, not denying it, yet his words carried an excuse of mitigating circumstance:

"The young lady is wise. Your Highness knows that in a chaotic mortal world, everyone wishes to seize opportunity. If I had not acted with such immediacy, I fear... others would have been even less courteous."

The reigning Emperor is deeply immersed in the pursuit of eternal life, commissioning people to search widely for immortal elixirs and secret methods. Consequently, the Daoist sects of the mortal world, secluded cultivators, and various unconventional figures of the martial world are all stirring restlessly in this new climate.

Everyone knows that the Emperor's will is absolute. If one can present a miraculous method or a sign of the supernatural and find favour before the Heavenly Visage, one can rise rapidly in the world, ascending to the heavens in a single step.

This intense competition has incited forces from all walks of life to scramble to seek immortal traces and plot schemes, causing the boundary between the mundane and the cultivation world to become increasingly blurred and dangerous.

"So you used this marriage charade to confine me here?" Moony ground her teeth, a flash of anger igniting in her eyes.

He was silent for a moment, his gaze lowered, as if suppressing some profound emotion.

"I genuinely wished otherwise. But as affairs stand, I can only ensure your safety."

Moony's heart was thrown into deeper turmoil. She spoke anxiously, "I don't need that! I just want His Highness to release me and let me return!"

Woo, she desperately needed to find her Miss.

Du Shao looked at her, speaking slowly and deliberately:

"Only when my goals are accomplished, when the opportunity presents itself, will I personally escort the young lady away."

These words carried such sincerity that Moony was momentarily rendered speechless. She could not see through his gaze, yet she felt that those eyes concealed an endless, heavy mist.

"Will you really let me go?" After a long moment of silence, she finally spoke the words, sobbing lightly.

Woo... Miss, Moony misses you so much.

Du Shao spoke in a low voice: "The young lady appeared on the street, holding the embroidered ball; that too is the will of Heaven. I will surely repay the kindness of today in the days to come."

Moony lowered her eyes, her heart still surging with unresolved emotions.

She had merely been indulging in a moment of playful levity, yet she was mistaken for the chosen Princess Consort of the embroidered ball, turning it into a full farce. Now, she was even clad in these robes of rank, and a Prince spoke repeatedly of "repaying a debt."

Everything that had happened was simply too absurd to believe.

"But... why should I place my trust in you?" Moony remained wary, showing no intention of easily believing anything he said.

Du Shao watched her silence, his gaze unwavering. The corner of his mouth hooked up into a smile of ambiguous meaning: "The young lady need not trust me. You only need to remember that this place is, for the time being, the safest place for you."

With that, he turned and walked away, his steps steady and measured, leaving her alone in the Phoenix Crown and Robes of Rank.

Moony finally let out a sigh of relief, unsure whether she should be angry or simply relieved. She gazed at this man—calm, reserved, perfectly courteous, yet felt like ice in a cage, difficult to approach.

The following passage is a continuation of the conversation between Moony and Prince Xuan. It has been translated in the requested unabridged, publishing-grade narrative style.

* * * * *

Moony's heart was thrown into deeper turmoil. She spoke anxiously:

"I don't need that! I just want His Highness to release me and let me return!"

Woo, she desperately needed to find her Miss.

Du Shao looked at her, speaking slowly and deliberately, emphasising every word:

"Only when my goals are accomplished, when the opportunity presents itself, will I personally escort the young lady away."

This promise, delivered with such profound sincerity, rendered Moony momentarily speechless. She could not see through his gaze, yet she felt that those eyes concealed an endless, heavy mist.

"Will you really let me go?" After a long moment of silence, she finally spoke the words, sobbing lightly.

Woo... Miss, Moony misses you so much.

Du Shao spoke in a low voice: "The young lady appeared on the street, holding the embroidered ball; that too is the will of Heaven. I will surely repay the kindness of today in the days to come."

Moony lowered her eyes, her heart still surging with unresolved emotions.

She had merely been indulging in a moment of playful levity, yet she was mistaken for the chosen Princess Consort of the embroidered ball, turning it into a full farce. Now, she was even clad in these robes of rank, and a Prince spoke repeatedly of "repaying a debt."

Everything that had happened was simply too absurd to believe.

"But... why should I place my trust in you?" Moony remained wary, showing no intention of easily believing anything he said.

Du Shao watched her silence, his gaze unwavering. The corner of his mouth hooked up into a smile of ambiguous meaning: "The young lady need not trust me. You only need to remember that this place is, for the time being, the safest place for you."

With that, he turned and walked away, his steps steady and measured, leaving her alone in the Phoenix Crown and Robes of Rank.

Moony finally let out a sigh of relief, unsure whether she should be angry or simply relieved. She gazed at this man—calm, reserved, perfectly courteous, yet felt like ice in a cage, difficult to approach.

Chapter 31: The Temple of Heavenly Pivot

Yun Lili was clutching a corner of the embroidered skirt left behind by Moony in the mortal realm, her eyes an alarming shade of crimson, looking for all the world like some poor, much-put-upon little bunny.

"She was only a tiny sprite, how on earth could *so* many people be after her, you simply *must* tell me why, why, why—"

Yun Yara, beside her, maintained her signature glacial composure, a mere flick of her sleeves having already traced the Heavenly Road back to the Immortal Realm.

"Come along now. It's not too late for further histrionics once we've reached the Temple of Heavenly Pivot."

Yun Lili nodded whilst frantically dabbing at her tears, and with a single joint upward thrust, the two transformed into streaks of shimmering light, hurtling straight into the heavens and stepping into the Immortal Realm.

In the Cloud Gate's Floating Crossing of the Immortal Realm, amidst a vista of white clouds and golden pavilions, two sudden escape-lights appeared—one azure, one white—coalescing into two female Immortals who sped onward with urgent haste.

"Faster, faster, faster, do stop floating about!" Yun Lili was practically muttering a litany as she flew, tears still threatening to spill over, her hands clamped tightly around Yun Yara's sleeve. "A-Yara, Moony really is going to be in dire straits! That so-called Prince looks colder than an ice-house, and what if he's a... a *pervert*, what do we do, oh heavens, what do we do!"

Yun Yara, whose face remained as placid as still water, interrupted her with a chillingly level tone: "If you continue to shriek like that, and Moony genuinely comes to grief, it may have nothing to do with the Prince. She might simply have been shouted to death by you."

"...I call this *concern*!" Yun Lili retorted with a wounded little bounce, her eyes welling up again. "We were merely out for a bit of a jolly spectacle, how on earth did a Mortal Prince manage to capture her! That whole 'tossing the embroidered ball' thing was clearly a nefarious *trap*! I shall rip out every single hair of that He Yingchun's head, I tell you—"

"Less prattle. Stay sharp. Stay close."

Yun Yara clapped a Divine Seal; a flash of white tore through the clouds as the two shot into the Temple of Heavenly Pivot.

* * * * *

Inside the Temple of Heavenly Pivot, a host of Immortals were gathered, currently debating the anomalies in the mortal realm's celestial phenomena.

Yun Yara was the first to make a low, steady bow, her voice clear and her steps composed.

She cupped her hands and presented her case: "The Immortal of Luminous Moon, Yun Yara, submits an urgent report—the mortal city of Liangcheng recently had a powerful barrier erected, involving a surge of celestial energy. We suspect it is the result of deliberate manipulation and humbly request an investigation."

The assembled Celestial Lords exchanged glances, their expressions betraying no significant emotion.

She continued: "This matter clearly involved the intervention of a highly skilled master. Yun Lili and I personally experienced it and were nearly injured by the backlash. This is a matter of serious import, and I implore the High Lords to deliberate. Furthermore, the Immortal scion Moony has been implicated and remains imprisoned." Her delivery was precise, unhurried, and her demeanour remained perfectly collected.

"It is merely a minor Immortal trapped, with no damage to any established Immortals. Why such a fuss?"

"The Heavenly Edicts prohibit reckless meddling between the mortal and immortal realms. Without concrete proof, a rash intrusion into the mortal court risks inviting calamity."

"Furthermore... you claim this female is entangled in the mortal Prince's struggle for succession? That seems quite a coincidence."

Yun Lili was so incensed her hands were trembling, and a vein throbbed visibly on her forehead.

She suddenly raised her voice: "She is my friend! She is our little Immortal sprite from the Celestial Realm! I don't care if she strayed into the mortal world; she is now being held captive, yet we are sitting here, holding a meeting, drinking tea, and listening to the breeze! What sort of Immortal Realm is this?!"

The Temple of Heavenly Pivot fell into a sudden, shocked silence.

In stark contrast to the quiet, Yun Lili looked desperate enough to fly across and physically tug at a Celestial Lord's sleeve: "She is truly innocent! She's just a little fairy! The mortal Prince has imprisoned her in his back chambers and is forcing her to wear some sort of... what was it... a phoenix coronet and robes of office! That clearly signifies marriage! Why on earth are none of you dispatching someone to investigate?!"

The assembly of Immortals looked at each other, but not a single one offered a reply.

After a long silence, the Heavenly Balance Immortal Lord, who had the visage of a middle-aged man, slowly spoke: "While this sounds unusual, there is no conclusive evidence. The barrier may not necessarily have been set by an Immortal, and since the mortal and immortal realms are inherently separate, a hasty intervention could interfere with the mortal realm's karma."

Another Immortal Lord chimed in agreement: "Though Moony is an Immortal scion, her cultivation is incomplete, and she has yet to be formally registered as a Primary Deity on the Celestial Roster. Her current identity is that of a mortal being, and she will not be listed for immediate rescue."

"What if I say she's my sister, then!?" Yun Lili's eyes were blazing red with fury. "If I go down to the mortal realm and tear down that barrier, anyone who tries to stop me, I'll... I'll... I'll *bite* them!"

Oh, that came out far less majestic than I'd intended. Biting? Really, Lili?

The moment the words left her mouth, Yun Yara gave a faint cough. "...Silence."

Yun Lili huffily clamped her mouth shut, her nose tingling, and her body trembled ever so slightly.

Silence settled over the chamber.

The Celestial Lords were about to resume their debate when they suddenly noticed a tumultuous surge of spiritual energy around Yun Lili. Faint, blue-azure light patterns began to manifest, and the spiritual energy at her fingertips was in restless agitation, causing even the floating lamps within the Temple of Heavenly Pivot to tremble slightly.

The expressions of the assembled Immortals shifted.

—Her spiritual root is stirring.

Inside the Temple of Heavenly Pivot, a host of Immortals were gathered, their pure white divine robes fluttering. Each held a jade tablet, their demeanours solemn.

Yun Lili and Yun Yara stood in the centre of the hall, facing the Celestial Lords, the atmosphere having been deadlocked for a considerable time.

"If aid is not immediately dispatched, Moony will likely be in mortal peril!" Yun Lili cried urgently, her tone laced with an un-cleansed, mortal-like impatience and anxiety. "She is my sister! Be she mortal or possessor of immortal bones, how can that mortal Prince be allowed to confine her? Have you no human decency left?!"

The Immortals exchanged glances, and finally, one Celestial Lord shook his head and spoke: "Mortal realm affairs operate by their own causality. Should the Immortal Realm interfere recklessly, it risks damaging the balance of the Heavenly Dao."

Another Celestial Lord added: "Furthermore, this matter has not been thoroughly investigated. Whether Moony is there of her own volition is unknown. Immortal Yun Lili, why this display of temper?"

"Temper? You call this *temper*?" Yun Lili immediately placed her hands on her hips, pointing furiously at the assembly. "You ancient deities sit on the clouds sipping dewdrop water, completely unmoved by the plight of trapped mortals! If I were a mortal, I wouldn't worship any of you!"

"You claim Moony is unregistered on the Celestial Roster and therefore unworthy of rescue. What then is the purpose of rank and title in the Immortal Realm?" Yun Lili's voice trembled slightly, her eyes completely red-rimmed. "If the one trapped today were a personal disciple of one of your own seats, you would surely have mobilised the entire realm, wouldn't you?"

Her voice grew frantic, bordering on a sob, "Moony did nothing wrong! She merely wished to shield me from a ridiculous mortal farce, and now she is suffering humiliation and imprisonment, yet not a single one of you will lift a finger?"

She lifted her head, fighting back her tears, and practically roared: "If you refuse to rescue her, I shall descend to the mortal realm alone—even if it means defying the Celestial Edicts, I will bring her back!"

"Forgive her trespass!" Yun Yara pulled her back, whispering urgently, "Lower your voice, this is the Temple of Heavenly Pivot..."

"How else can you hear the fire raging in my heart if I'm not loud enough!" Yun Lili was flushed crimson with anger. She flicked her sleeve, and the jade bell on her cuff jingled sharply. A peculiar spiritual wave vibrated outwards, and threads of azure light actually began to shimmer in the hall.

Xie Wuchen, standing on the steps below, frowned deeply. He murmured, "This is not good... Her spiritual root is beginning to awaken."

The Immortals, sensing the anomaly, changed colour collectively.

"How can her body contain..." Before one Celestial Lord could finish his sentence, Yun Lili's eyes began to glow. Blue light surged from within her body, like a tempestuous wind or a waterfall, instantaneously sweeping across the entire Temple of Heavenly Pivot.

BOOM!

The jade tables shook, the wall carvings flickered with light, and the glazed cups on the seats shattered with a *clatter*. Someone gasped, "It's the Supreme Spiritual Root!"

"This is impossible! She isn't..."

"It's a Variant Spiritual Root!" Yun Zhou abruptly rose from his high seat, his eyes wide with shock. "This kind of spiritual wave, I've only read about it in the ancient scrolls... How can she possibly possess it..." *Good heavens, a descendant of the Primal Spirits? It says so in the second volume of The Three Scrolls of Celestial Spirits...*

Yun Lili was entirely oblivious, continuing to jump up and down in rage: "Since you claim to uphold the fairness of the Heavenly Dao, then investigate! Right now, immediately, this instant! Moony is drinking cold water every day in the mortal realm while you hold this endless meeting without a result!"

The azure light intensified, and even the 'Serenity Barrier' above the hall began to tremble faintly.

It was precisely then that a soft yet resolute voice gently drifted in: "Her spiritual meridian is unstable. Forcing its operation will damage her foundation. Allow me."

The aura arrived before the person.

The spiritual light around Yun Lili was surging like a torrent, on the verge of breaking the barrier and causing the faces of the Immortals in the Temple of Heavenly Pivot to pale.

Yun Zhou suddenly stood up from his high seat, a wash of azure light coalescing in his palm, clearly preparing to use an art to stabilise her.

But before he could act, a clear, water-like thread of sword energy ripped through the air from the back hall, swift as a streak of light, yet gentle as a spring breeze.

It was Yu Sord.

The silken thread of sword energy instantaneously encircled the surge, gingerly lifting and gently containing the runaway blue spiritual power, one careful inch after the next.

Yun Zhou paused, his hand gesture retracting, and he cast a side glance, his expression darkening slightly.

Ah, I see. The perpetually icy one has decided to actually do something rather than merely brood.

Yu Sord's brow was furrowed almost imperceptibly as his gaze settled upon Yun Lili's unconscious face. He appeared as remote and aloof as ever, yet concealed within his sleeve, he quickly sealed her spiritual meridian with a Spirit Sealing Seal, thus mitigating any further threat of an explosive spiritual relapse.

The assembly of Celestial Lords, upon witnessing this turn of events, exhibited a spectrum of differing expressions.

Yun Yara inquired with a low, weighted voice, "Her spiritual root is..."

"The Celestial Root."

Yu Sord's soft utterance was nevertheless as chillingly precise and definite as falling ice and snow.

"She herself is entirely unaware of this. The recent eruption was merely the initial, turbulent sign of the Celestial Root's manifestation. It is currently highly unstable, and should anyone attempt to capitalise on this fragility, it risks fatally damaging her foundation. Given that you, Lords, are the dutiful custodians of the Immortal Realm's laws, dare you stand idly by and permit a Celestial Root to be annihilated in the mortal realm?"

At this pronouncement, the countenances of the Immortals within the Temple of Heavenly Pivot underwent a noticeable shift. *Well said, Yu Sord. Nothing quite moves a bureaucrat like the threat of damage to a rare celestial asset.*

Yun Yara shot a glance towards Yu Sord, a flash of an unreadable, subtle meaning passing through the depths of her eyes.

He instantly flashed to Yun Lili's side, a golden seal materialising in his palm, which he pressed without the slightest hesitation onto the nape of her neck.

"Yu Sord, what in the celestial names are you doing! Are you attempting to silence me! I haven't finished my—"

Before the sentence could be completed, her entire body went utterly limp, and he caught her securely within the protective cradle of his arms.

Her spiritual light, having been carefully placated by the delicate sword energy, gradually subsided and grew quiescent and her vision became progressively blurred, and amidst the chaos of her irregular breathing, she drifted heavily into a profound slumber.

In this precise moment, no one present could fail to observe that beneath Yu Sord's renowned cold exterior lay a fierce depth of devotion that none others would dare to presume or measure.

Honestly, for a man so dedicated to emotionless posturing, he does put on a rather good show of panicked tenderness. Very effective.

Amidst the stunned silence of the Immortals, the cold-faced youth gazed down at the now-sleeping maiden held fast in his embrace, and his voice, though lacking any marked inflection, was remarkably tender: "Should you persist in this manner, your spiritual meridian will utterly rupture."

He carefully helped her to a seated position, his fingertips swiftly moving to seal her vital energy points. He murmured quietly, almost to himself: "You are permitted to be angry, you are permitted to make a scene, but you are not permitted to harm yourself... If something were truly to befall you..."

Before the sentence was finished, he suddenly broke off, his gaze sweeping over the assembled Immortals. A nascent thread of frigid intent instantly solidified between his brows.

"What she said is undeniably correct," Yu Sord finally spoke, his voice raising and sounding distinctly cold. "If the Immortal Realm is genuinely content to sit here and disregard this, then it would be better to simply abolish all its governing laws, shut its celestial gates, and offer a collective apology to the heavens."

The Immortals were left completely speechless, and notably, Yun Zhou's expression was one of absolute astonishment.

Suddenly, a distinct, clear cough echoed from the jade steps on the left side of the hall.

The Immortals turned their heads, only to see an elderly figure with lengthy, pale eyebrows and robes of dark indigo slowly emerging.

It was the long-serving senior Celestial Lord of the Tribunal Department, **Celestial Lord Su Yuan**.

He leaned on his whisk, his voice raspy yet imbued with an unmistakable, commanding authority: "The Celestial Laws, established in those ancient years, were originally intended to safeguard all living souls and affirm the Heavenly Dao."

His gaze was weighty and profound as he swept it across the assembled audience: "If this case is not meticulously investigated, my Tribunal Department shall serve as the spearhead. Regardless of whom this matter involves, all shall be judged according to the full measure of the law."

Having spoken, he tossed his jade tablet. It landed precisely upon the central light platform with a sharp, resonant sound.

Celestial energy surged, the formation patterns reignited with vigour, and the entire Temple of Heavenly Pivot shifted faintly with a play of light and shadow, as if an ancient, solemn decree had been quietly activated. Even the four monumental Divine Steles in the corners of the hall began to subtly hum and vibrate in response.

In that single, tense moment, the expressions of all the Immortals changed drastically.

Although Yun Lili remained deeply asleep, she seemed to have perceived something of the event, for her brow twitched ever so slightly.

Yu Sord's eyes narrowed perceptibly. He whispered softly, "…At last, there is one who remembers the initial purpose."

Chapter 32: I Don't Trust Him

Yun Lili had already fallen unconscious, held securely in Yu Sord's arms. His blue robes were tinged with her faintly rolling spiritual aura, seeming to imbue his usually cold and aloof presence with a sense of urgency.

"This Immortal Lord is taking her back to the Inquiry Sword Pavilion," he stated flatly. His voice wasn't loud, but it brooked no argument.

Yun Zhou stared at him coldly, spiritual light subtly circulating within his sleeve. "Stop. Lili is my direct younger sister. She should naturally return to Lingxiao Palace. Yu Sord, this decision is not yours to make."

Their gazes clashed. An invisible wave of energy exploded within the Heavenly Mystery Hall, causing the hanging scrolls on the walls to tremble slightly.

A young immortal attendant nearby staggered back three steps, his face pale.

Yu Sord didn't respond. He merely lowered his head slightly to carefully adjust Lili's collar, his movements as gentle as an ordinary person tucking in a loved one.

But when he looked up again, his stance was that of a drawn sword, forcefully cleaving through Zhou's obstructive posture.

"You—" Zhou's eyes turned icy cold. He struck out with a palm, transforming the swirling light into an array that shot rapidly towards Yu Sord.

Holding Lili, Yu Sord sidestepped to evade. His long sleeve swept up a cold gleam, summoning sword energy to meet the attack head-on.

The two immortal powers intertwined mid-air, wind and thunder roared, and the spiritual light of the entire Heavenly Mystery Hall shook, alarming the immortals in the upper hall.

"Enough!"

Yun Yara flashed between the two men, her purple robes fluttering. With hands forming a seal, she forcefully intercepted the two colliding streams of spiritual energy. Her expression stern, she said sharply, "Do you want Lili to suffer another impact?"

Both men halted their movements simultaneously, their auras still not fully restrained.

After a moment of silence, Yu Sord remained standing, holding Lili. Zhou's face was full of anger, yet he had no choice but to take a step back.

"Where she goes is not for you to decide," Zhou said through gritted teeth.

"This Immortal Lord's will..." Yu Sord glanced at him briefly, his voice low and faint, yet carrying an inexplicable firmness, "...is reason enough."

These three words defied immortal logic, were utterly unreasonable, yet were spoken with absolute resolve. He needed no proper justification. Simply because it was *her*.

Yara shook her head with a soft sigh and finally made the decision: "The Inquiry Sword Pavilion is remote from worldly affairs and has Spirit-Sealing Arrays for protection. She shouldn't be disturbed by too much noise right now... Let Yu Sord take her."

Zhou ultimately said nothing more. Only as Yu Sord passed by him did he utter a cold, low warning: "If she suffers even the slightest harm, don't blame me for disregarding our past ties. I will ensure she receives justice."

Yu Sord's steps didn't pause. He merely replied faintly, "You can try."

* * * * *

Outside the Heavenly Mystery Hall, the clouds hung low, and a spiritual wind began to stir quietly.

Zhou stood upon the high steps, his red robes flapping sharply in the wind, his gold-and-silver eyes cold as frost and snow.

His originally handsome, aloof features were now shadowed as if a thundercloud in the deep night.

The spiritual aura around him was chaotic, with swirling light and cold gleams intertwining faintly at his fingertips.

A young immortal attendant glimpsed him from afar and felt his mind and spirit tremble. He immediately knelt and prostrated, not daring to look for long.

Yara had just landed below the steps and hadn't yet spoken when his furious roar shook the ground beneath her feet: "You truly have some skill—"

Before his voice faded, the energy field of the entire Heavenly Mystery Hall trembled slightly. A crimson thunder rolled from the cloud layers, as if the heavens themselves echoed his wrath.

"Lili is severely injured and hasn't awakened! You didn't protect her, instead letting her fall into Yu Sord's hands! That man is deep and scheming, obsessed to the bone, and you actually trust him? Are you and he now singing a duet, and for whose benefit?"

Yara frowned slightly, about to offer an explanation, when she saw Zhou take a step forward, his aura suddenly shifting—

Icy and fiery spiritual auras tangled behind him, coiling like dragons and serpents. The power of his dual spirit roots surged forth violently at this moment, causing even the Celestial Mechanism Stone Platform to show cracks.

He turned towards the assembled immortals, all traces of laughter gone from his gaze, replaced by sharpened blades. Yet his voice was extremely soft: "You all saw it, yet remained silent. Do you think her leaving is the best outcome? Are you also eager for her to leave Lingxiao Palace sooner, to better maintain your elegant and benevolent facades?"

An elder immortal tried to speak, to advise him, but was silenced by a cold glance that sent a chill straight to his heart.

When he turned back to Yara, his tone abruptly tightened, killing intent flashing out. The very air congealed with interwoven currents of ice and fire:

"Yara, you and I weren't born of the same lineage, but we grew up together since childhood. I've never trusted people, only you. Now that you're siding with an outsider like this, does her departure put your mind at ease? If she vanishes from this Lingxiao Palace, will you have your wish?"

These words pierced as if ten thousand blades, striking directly at the spiritual platform.

Yara's expression finally shifted slightly, yet she still responded in a low voice: "I only acted for her own good."

"For her own good?" Zhou let out a light, cold laugh. "Her tribulations are hers to bear. Her life is hers to choose. You didn't even ask her once, yet you decided for her. Are you trying to save her, or destroy her?"

Thunder rumbled again. A wave of energy swept past the rocks before the steps, and a green pine at the cliff's edge was snapped in half.

A demonic aura began to appear in Zhou's eyes, gold and silver intertwining. He stepped closer to the immortals, his whisper like a curse: "She pleaded with every word, just to save her personal maid, Moony. Yet you, several Immortal Lords, sit high upon the clouds, but can't even save one little fairy. If this gets out, wouldn't it make the world laugh their heads off?"

As his words fell, swirling light erupted from his sleeve, transforming into silver blades that shot through the air, aiming straight for the sky.

It wasn't until Yara shouted sharply and formed a seal, suppressing his spiritual energy, that he coldly withdrew his power.

He turned and stepped into the wind, his red robes like blood, his back both demonic and immortal, impossible to look upon directly.

Before the echoes of one heavy thunderclap had faded, a silver streak split the sky above the Heavenly Mystery Hall. Within the lingering, unsettled spiritual energy, a middle-aged man clad in purple-gold ceremonial robes suddenly materialized.

His brow and eyes carried a solemn authority, his aura as deep and cold as great mountains and sinking peaks.

"Zhou, you've certainly grown bold, daring to cause trouble even in the Heavenly Mystery Hall!"

The newcomer was none other than the Enforcement Elder of Lingxiao Palace, the Yun clan's uncle—Yun Tim.

Zhou glanced sideways, his cold smile not yet faded, the gold and silver light in his eyes still shimmering. "Has Uncle come to hold me accountable?"

"If I were any later, would I have witnessed you tearing down the entire Lingxiao Palace?"

Yun Tim's cold voice held fury, its sound as if the clashing of metal and iron. "Your words know no restraint, your actions are unruly. You even berated your own sister so harshly. Do you still consider yourself a member of an immortal sect? Do you still think this is a place where you can act recklessly?"

Zhou's gaze was indifferent, not a trace of fear. Instead, he sneered, "I'd like to ask: by readily handing Lili over, where does that leave the face of our Lingxiao Palace?"

"Enough!" Yun Tim's shout was as if thunder. Spiritual power, wrapped in overwhelming pressure, instantly shook the spiritual veins across the entire pavilion roof.

Dozens of restriction arrays trembled faintly, and the young immortal attendants nearby fell to their knees, unable to rise.

He continued, "Immortal Lord Yu is upright, his sword heart clear and bright. Moreover, he has a master-disciple bond with Lili. Right now, her mind is unstable, her spiritual power running wild. Taking her back to the Inquiry Sword Pavilion to recuperate in peace is the right path, both emotionally and logically. Should we instead keep her here, in this place of churning immortal energy and thicket of disputes, to delay her recovery?"

"If Lili is a member of the Yun family, then there is absolutely no reason to let Yu Sord take her away."

It makes it seem like our Yun family has no one.

"I want to ask you, what is your reason for blocking Yu Sord? He is upright by nature, his cultivation firm and steady, and he has always had a master-disciple connection with Lili. Right now, she is unconscious. Him protecting her safety is right and proper. Do you truly intend to push someone to their death just to vent your anger? If you act arrogantly for even one more moment, don't blame me, your elder, for disregarding past affections!"

A sharp glint flashed in Zhou's eyes. Swirling light rose again within his sleeve as a spirit sword adorned with crimson patterns materialized in his palm. The sword tip pointed at the ground, but his voice was like an icy spring in the deep night, its cold piercing to the bone: "Then disregard them."

In the next instant, both men released their spiritual power simultaneously. Flames and golden lightning collided, the explosive roar deafening.

The inner walls of the Heavenly Mystery Hall shuddered violently.

Flames roared upward, spearing toward the vaulted ceiling, and within the blast of erupting spiritual force, the ancient jade lamp-dragons lining the chamber shattered into glittering shards.

Yara immediately formed a seal, placing herself between the two. Gritting her teeth, she rebuked, "Enough! If this continues, will it still be proper?"

But neither man yielded, their auras clashing forcefully. Zhou was enveloped in crimson light like blood, icy and fiery breaths coiling around his sword's edge, resembling a demon god descended to the world. Yun Tim's body was wreathed in rolling purple-gold energy, steady as Mount Tai.

The pressure between them intensified, actually causing the surrounding air to vibrate faintly. All the immortal attendants and youths retreated to a safe distance, cold sweat beading on their foreheads.

Yun Tim roared in anger, "Do you think relying on your dual spirit roots allows you to act without restraint? If you continue like this, forget Lili, even you yourself won't be able to escape unscathed!"

"Then Uncle Yun might as well try." Zhou's voice was low and cold, carrying a hint of madness, yet a trace of pain was hidden deep within his eyes.

He knew full well drawing his sword was unreasonable, yet he stood firm with blade in hand, for one reason alone—she was his only blood sibling.

Spiritual light radiated in all directions, sword energy overflowed, and a dragon's roar resonated through the air, as if heaven and earth itself tensed in response.

* * * * *

The Inquiry Sword Pavilion was situated atop a secluded Cliff, far removed from the other peaks, shrouded in perpetual clouds and mist.

There were no morning bells or evening drums here, no palace rules or disciplinary teachings—only the soft rustling of wind through green bamboo, like whispers or sighs.

Yu Sord, holding Lili in his arms, stepped into the quiet room without pause. A long couch had long been prepared, the spirit array faintly activated. Bamboo shadows swayed, flowing like shifting light.

He lowered his head and gently laid her upon the couch. Her complexion was pale, her breath uneven, the faint red mark between her brows flickering intermittently.

Yu Sord's gaze fell upon that golden seal. His fingertips twitched slightly, wanting to erase it, yet he stopped.

He was always calm and decisive, but at this moment, he hesitated—a rare occurrence.

A moment later, he flicked his sleeve and unfurled a crystal-clear black jade mirror, summoning the protective array's spirit light to seal the entire Inquiry Sword Pavilion within the formation, ensuring no one else could disturb them.

He retrieved a light purple pill bottle. With a tremor of his fingertip, a warm, moist medicinal aura dispersed, its lingering fragrance brushing against their faces. He murmured softly, as if speaking to himself, and also to her—

"You're always... so troublesome."

As the medicine drops entered her lips, Lili's brow furrowed slightly, a soft hum escaping her throat. Yu Sord's knuckles paused.

Slowly, he drew her closer, lightly touching her icy forehead, channelling spiritual power, attempting to stabilize her frantic spiritual consciousness.

Within the quiet room, only the sound of wind through the bamboo grove could be heard, along with the faint whisper of their intertwined spiritual auras.

After a while, a soft murmur came from Lili's lips, so faint it was almost imperceptible—

"...Yu Sord...?"

Yu Sord, who had his eyes closed, jolted, his eyelashes fluttering.

He opened his eyes to look at her, his voice low and hoarse:

"I'm here."

But Lili sank back into unconsciousness, as if it were merely a name uttered softly in a dream, with no further response.

For a long time, he gazed at her face, his eyes reflecting her unresolvable weakness and the faintly pulsing red glow at her brow.

"When... will you finally remember?"

He murmured, his tone devoid of anger or resentment, yet concealing immense endurance.

Suddenly, the distant array stirred slightly. A paper crane broke through the wind, landing on the windowsill. It unfolded to reveal faintly visible handwriting:

—*Zhou: Before the end of the decade, Lili must be sent back to the sect. Do not make unauthorized decisions again.*

Yu Sord stared at the letter for a long time. Finally, with a flick of his finger, it turned to ash in a flash of fire.

He looked down at the person on the couch, his voice as heavy as a broken sword striking stone:

"If you don't wish to return, no one will take you away."

Yu Sord sat quietly by her bedside, his knees drawn together, his robes pooling on the floor.

The candle flame flickered slightly, illuminating her serene sleeping face. Her brows were slightly furrowed, her lips unconsciously pressed together, as if still trapped in a chaotic nightmare.

Although the golden seal on her brow had somewhat receded, it still resembled a wound that could not be sealed, pulling him back to a past he was unwilling to mention.

He lifted his gaze to look at her, a rare fluctuation of emotion rising in his eyes.

Flashing through his mind were memories of his previous life, and hers.

Chapter 33: Heartbroken at Myriad Tribulation Cliff

Previous Life

Heavenly Firmament Immortal Realm, Cloud Terrace Peak.

Yu Sord sat quietly within the hall, his fingertips moving slightly as he placed a piece upon the Go board.

Spiritual mist lingered; the game was unfinished, yet a killing intent had long been laid. His brows and eyes were slightly lowered, his aura as tranquil as mountains and rivers stretching ten thousand miles, yet a trace of obscure shadow flickered in the depths of his eyes.

He had already performed thirty-three divinations—Lili's thunder tribulation would descend within three days.

She was exceptionally gifted, possessing Phoenix bloodline, but due to her unstable temperament, her innate spirit platform was difficult to consolidate. This thunder tribulation had nine layers. Without external help to pass the fifth, her soul and spirit would be utterly destroyed.

He could not permit such a future.

This wasn't her first time facing a tribulation.

He remembered her first tribulation at one hundred years old, crying as she fled the thunder array; it was he who used sword energy as a shield, step by step blocking the lightning for her.

Later, when she suffered a Qi Deviation and her Dantian-the inner energy core collapsed, it was he who personally pulled her back from the brink of death.

The first time, she had just turned one hundred, still unaware of what a "tribulation" was. At the first stir of heavenly thunder, she panicked and fled.

He used sword energy as a barrier, guiding her step by step through the sea of lightning, her eyes filled with tears yet still looking back at him.

The second time, she had some cultivation, but fell into Qi Deviation within the tribulation array. Without hesitation, he sacrificed a part of his own primordial spirit, propping open a clear space to stabilize her amidst the chaos.

The third time, the nine-heaven thunder pillars fell, and she was unconscious for three days. He kept vigil by her bed for three nights, constantly using Cold Ice Jade to repair her Dantian.

The fourth time, she voluntarily entered the tribulation, claiming she was prepared, yet was severely injured and spat blood at the first thunder strike, her soul nearly shattering.

When he rushed to her, covered in wounds himself, he only said faintly, "Next time... let me face it with you."

After that, he never again set foot on the **Myriad Tribulation Cliff**. He only watched from afar, refining artifacts, setting up arrays, calculating her tribulations for her—he had never truly left.

These days, he had scarcely left Cloud Terrace Peak. Using Ten-Thousand-Year Cold Jade as the core and Nine-Purity Golden Lotus as the veins, he personally forged the soul-protecting artifact "Primordial Soul Wheel," capable of preserving a thread of vitality when the soul was on the verge of shattering. But he knew it was still not enough.

Her fifth tribulation required someone to share the burden.

He found mention of an object in an ancient text at the Myriad Phenomena Pavilion—the "Heavenly Firmament Tribulation-Transforming Pearl," which could draw lightning into oneself and bear another's tribulation.

But the pearl's refiner had perished, and the object itself had long been lost. Until yesterday, a letter arrived from Chu Qing, daughter of the Director of the Bureau of Destiny, stating she had obtained this treasure and wished to deliver it in person.

She arrived today.

* * * * *

Chu Qing, clad in purple robes, her demeanour graceful and elegant, presented the pearl before the desk. Her warm smile held a hidden sharpness.

"This pearl is extraordinary; its refiner has already entered the endless abyss. It is the only one of its kind in the world." She offered the pearl, her voice soft. "For you, Immortal Lord, to strive for Fairy Lili to this extent, expending so much spirit and effort... If not for deep affection and profound loyalty, who else would dare act thus?"

Her gaze shifted, falling upon the talisman array diagram on the desk. She said quietly, "Lili's destiny is noble, yet it seems she has never... done anything for you, Immortal Lord. If she could channel such devotion into her cultivation, why would you need to personally labor over every matter for her?"

Yu Sord's fingertips lightly touched the pearl's surface, his spiritual consciousness probing inward. The thunderous aura within surged violently; it was indeed genuine. He remained silent, merely flicking his sleeve to store it away and covering the scroll on the desk.

Seeing his silence, Chu Qing smiled again and said, "For you to treat her with such deep affection and loyalty, Immortal Lord... is it truly worth it?"

He finally lifted his eyes, his voice so faint it was almost without ripple: "Her fate holds a thunder tribulation. If I can block even a small part of it for her, I will."

Chu Qing's expression froze for a moment, then she covered her lips with a light laugh, turned, and took her leave, leaving only a soft remark carried by the wind: "Immortal Lord, you truly... are no different from those bound by mortal sentiments."

Outside the cloud steps, Lili stood holding a stack of talisman manuals. She had originally come to deliver today's assignment annotations for him.

Before she could speak, she happened to overhear this conversation, and her footsteps halted involuntarily.

She stood there in a daze, her gaze fixed on the slightly ajar hall door. Her fingers tightened around the talisman manuals, the paper creasing under her grip.

She wasn't someone prone to overthinking. But how could she not understand the meaning behind those words?

"If she would just cultivate a few more days..."

"You are the Mysterious Origin Immortal Lord..."

"You were originally free from the tribulations of love."

Each sentence fell like fine, dense needles upon her heart.

She remembered Chu Qing's appearance, remembered that day in the immortal forest secret realm when she stood shoulder-to-shoulder with Yu Sord. Chu Qing, while laughing and saying she was "mischievous and didn't understand the Immortal Lord's thoughts," had personally straightened the spirit patterns on his sleeve.

Even then, she had felt a slight sting in her heart. Now, hearing these words again, she felt that sting gradually sinking into her bones.

And him... did he truly wish to block the thunder for her?

It wasn't that she hadn't heard—once the Heavenly Firmament Tribulation-Transforming Pearl was activated, if the person casting the array lacked a firm Dao Heart and heavenly-grade primordial energy, they could lose all their cultivation and have their soul shattered.

If he went to such lengths for her, what if...

Her eyes grew warm, but she forcefully suppressed it.

She was unwilling. And she was unworthy.

Even if she was a descendant of the Phoenix Clan, with pure spirit blood, and had received the reverence of thousands over the years, if she couldn't even protect herself, what right did she have to demand his protection to such an extent?

She was born atop the Nine-Layered Heavens, a descendant of the Phoenix Clan, raised in the immortal realm by Lingxiao Palace since childhood. Her immortal destiny was innate, peerless in nobility.

But the Heavenly Dao seeks balance; those with overly potent destinies often suffer for it. Since childhood, her fate had been fraught with numerous tribulations. Trials came one after another, several times nearly scattering her soul to the winds.

The denizens of the immortal realm either revered or feared her, some flocked to her, others were jealous.

Some hailed her as heaven's chosen, others secretly plotted, seeking to seize her phoenix bones and golden blood. But beneath the myriad whispers, only one person consistently stood by her side.

He was the Solitary Clarity Immortal Lord of Lingxiao Palace's Inquiry Sword Pavilion, bearing the immortal name Yu Sord. Cold-hearted and taciturn, aloof and unfeeling, yet for her, he traversed stars and moons, silently guarding her for over a decade.

He was also her betrothed.

And her? She believed she had already cultivated with all her might, no longer indulging in mischief or folly. Yet, when the thunder tribulation approached, it was still him who procured rare treasures, refined artifacts, set up arrays, even willing to impair his own cultivation, all to ensure her safety.

She was unwilling.

She also wanted to cleave through the sea of lightning with a single sword, to transcend relying on her own strength and radiance, independent of others.

If this was her fate, then she should bear it alone.

This time, she would not let him block it for her again. That night, Lili did not appear.

* * * * *

The next day at dawn, Myriad Tribulation Cliff.

This was the place in the Heavenly Firmament Immortal Realm closest to the heavenly dome's thunder eye. Not a single blade of grass grew for miles around, only scorched black rock bones and countless piles of rubble.

Thunderclouds never dispersed year-round, the spiritual energy was chaotic and restless, like a forsaken extremity abandoned by the Heavenly Dao.

Thunderclouds rolled, heaven and earth hung suspended.

Under the clear skies stretching ten thousand miles, thin mist surrounded the area like smoke and fog. Lili stood alone in the centre of the tribulation array, clad in white robes, without a single protective magical treasure.

Within the Cloud Light Pavilion, Yu Sord was just about to deliver the array diagrams and the Heavenly Firmament Pearl when a violent tremor shook his heart.

With a sweep of his sleeve, he divined that the thunder tribulation had already begun. With a shock, he realized—she had gone to the Myriad Tribulation Cliff ahead of time!

His figure transformed into light, piercing through the sky.

That day, all living beings in the immortal realm witnessed—

At the summit of the Tribulation Platform, heavenly might pressed down, ten thousand thunders galloped. That young girl stood alone in the floating void, her figure frail, yet she did not retreat half a step.

The moment the thunder light fell, Lili lifted her head with a smile, a trace of playful resolve actually appearing between her brows.

Her voice wasn't loud, and it was soft and gentle, yet it seemed to penetrate the thunder and spread across the mountains and rivers for ten thousand miles—

"Immortal Lord, you needn't come... This time, I want to face it myself."

She knew he would come, just like before.

But she didn't want that anymore. This time, she didn't want to remain the one who was always protected, always saved.

—She didn't want to spend her whole life standing behind him, being called the fairy protected by Yu Sord, merely basking in the glow of a marriage contract for half her life.

She was a descendant of the Phoenix Clan, the Heaven-Destined Maiden, the Body of Myriad Tribulations.

She ought to shoulder this fate herself, not have him break his soul and shatter his spirit for her, time and time again.

Her smile was gentle, yet carried a resolute determination.

This tribulation was hers.

Even if her body was crushed and her bones shattered, she only wanted to walk this step upright and honourably.

The next moment, the fifth thunder strike fell.

Lili's figure shattered under the thunder's final blow.

She stood so straight, yet like a prophecy, turned to flying dust within the tribulation light.

A phoenix shadow suddenly spread its wings across the sky, like a fiercely burning karma fire, consuming everything, until it finally extinguished, without even leaving behind a sigh.

The way she smiled with closed eyes resembled a beautiful goddess willingly offering herself as a sacrifice, transforming into a dazzling silhouette within the thunder and flames, not even a lingering fragrance remaining.

And he finally arrived.

Yu Sord stood at the edge of the Tribulation Platform, his blue robes flapping sharply in the wind, his gaze fixed upon that empty space at the heart of the sky.

Between heaven and earth, silence suddenly fell.

The wind stopped, the thunder ceased, even the floating clouds halted their flow.

In his hand, he tightly clutched that phoenix-shaped jade hairpin— crafted by his own hand, Once pinned within her dark hair—now only cold remnants remain.

He walked step by step up the Myriad Tribulation Cliff, his pace firm, yet each step deep.

It wasn't an ordinary ascent of a cliff, but more likely walking into a predestined burial ground.

"...Lili."

He called her name, his voice so low it was almost inaudible, yet it pierced his chest like an icy blade.

He had been one step too late.

* * * * *

Within the dusty light, a wisp of soul aura lingered, like the final, nearly extinguished spark amidst the motes.

He bent down and caught that faint white soul light. His fingertips trembled slightly, his movements so gentle he hardly dared touch it.

That soul light was as still as thin smoke, settling in his palm, light as if it weren't there, yet it struck his heart, churning his flesh and blood.

He had always been aloof in expression, measured in speech, his joys and angers never showing.

But now, the corner of his lips moved, yet he couldn't speak. His chest felt as if torn into a thousand pieces.

Cracks bloomed in the depths of his eyes.

It was the kind of shattering even an immortal soul couldn't repair.

Spiritual power surged within him. He wanted to seal that soul aura into a jade box, but just as his spiritual energy was about to cover it, he suddenly paused.

He was afraid. Afraid that this minuscule breath, along with his last shred of hope, would be destroyed by his own hand.

He didn't utter a word, only murmured lowly: "...Lili Lili."

That voice was so broken it didn't sound like an immortal's, but like a mortal who had lost their beloved in the dusty world.

He could have protected her—

He had calculated the heavenly numbers, prepared all the magical tools, breached forbidden grounds, sought celestial secrets.

Only one step away—

A single step's distance, yet it brutally severed her present life from his.

He closed his eyes, raised his palm, and pressed the phoenix-shaped jade hairpin against his heart, reciting a chant in a deep voice.

A strand of pure white primordial soul rose from his fingertip, hovering above the heart of the sky where the thunderclouds hadn't yet dispersed.

At the peak of the Myriad Tribulation Cliff, the thunder's breath still rumbled dully.

He pressed the jade hairpin against his brow. Three hundred years of cultivation ignited within his spirit platform.

Using the method of burning the soul with the primordial spirit, he sought the nine-turn cycle of reincarnation, abandoning his immortal form, all to mend a single soul of hers.

This art was called 'Solitary Lament,' originating from the ancient scrolls of the Heavenly Ruins, recorded in the Sword Venerable's secret manual, passed to only one person, never taught to outsiders.

It could be performed only once in a lifetime, requiring one's own primordial spirit as sacrifice to forcibly reverse heavenly fate and mend a soul.

If the art succeeded, the soul would scatter without anchor, the Dao foundation severed forever.

—A solitary life lamented, in exchange for one person's return.

He was willing to try.

"Lili Lili..." His voice trembled. No longer was there coldness in his eyes, only utterly collapsed tenderness.

"If this life is destined to be without you, then I will burn all I have... to send you back."

The phoenix hairpin slowly rose in his palm. A thread of blood-red light pierced through from his heart, infusing that wisp of remnant soul.

Snow atop the cliff flowed backwards, thunderclouds gathered once more, the spiritual breath of all things was in chaos yet silent.

In the next instant, the phoenix jade shattered into ten thousand points of golden light, falling into the mortal world like meteors.

She would forget him, forget the immortal realm, forget that moment of despair on the Myriad Tribulation Cliff.

And he would forever remember this tribulation—

Forever remember the way she smiled as she left.

The vast, azure heavens stretched above, but he was utterly disheartened, all hope gone.

He stood in place, his indigo robes tattered, immortal energy swirling around him like thin mist.

His gaze fell upon the scorched marks on the Tribulation Platform, where a girl he loved had once smiled and said, "This thunder... I'm not afraid of it."

And he had believed her, yet failed to protect her.

He said softly, "I will find you again, no matter... how many cycles of reincarnation."

The next morning, envoys from the Heavenly Mystery Hall arrived as ordered. The area above the Myriad Tribulation Cliff was empty.

Only a sword remained, thrust among the rocks at the cliff's peak, its blade broken, the vermilion on it not yet dry.

Yu Sord's figure never appeared again.

That night, he had used his immortal form to forcibly sever the cycle of reincarnation, sealing a soul within the dust.

She would be reborn in the mortal realm, and he, from then on, would not question heavenly fate, but only seek one person.

—His tribulation had only just begun.

Chapter 34: The Bamboo Grove

In the deep recesses of the Demonic Domain palace, the jet-black lamps flickered, and the surface of the Scrying Mirror rippled with rings of faint luminescence.

Mo Han was leaning languidly upon a crescent-shaped jade couch, a slender jade branch held between his fingers.

The mirrored surface reflected a secluded, utterly abandoned bamboo pathway within the Celestial Realm. There, Yun Yara was strolling by herself, her countenance pallid and understated, yet failing miserably to conceal the stubbornly suppressed grief etched into her brow and eyes.

She was visibly isolated and alone, yet refused to utter even a single plea for assistance.

Occasionally, she would halt her steps, her fingers clenching tightly into a fist, only to slowly relax it again, as if she were meticulously crushing and swallowing every last vestige of her vulnerability.

Mo Han watched her, and suddenly let out a sardonic snort: "The unvarying celestial light of the Immortal Realm, even at its softest, cannot possibly illuminate that temperament of hers, determined as she is to hold on until she breaks."

His tone was detached, yet his gaze remained fixed on the mirror, not shifting an inch.

"She could very well be the Prince Consort of the Demonic Domain and enjoy every imaginable honour, but no, she insists on scurrying back to the Celestial Realm only to endure such cold, indifferent glances… Truly, a tiresome level of foolishness."

But that tiny fragment of frigidity at the tail end of his sentence made it unclear whether the irritation was directed at her, or rather, at himself.

One does find a resolute refusal to be rescued quite vexing, particularly when the rescuer happens to be oneself.

Just at that moment, the curtain hangings swayed gently, and Youluo entered the hall.

A sudden, sharp fragrance wafted from behind the drapery. Youluo stepped out barefoot, her crimson sheer veil resembling a fine mist, with several strands of silver-vine flowers dangling from her temples, swaying softly near her earlobes.

Her waist was exquisitely slender, and her footsteps seemed to conjure a soft breeze. The smile on her lips was captivatingly sultry, yet her eyes bore a deliberately enhanced, lustrous quality.

"His Highness is observing that little Immortal once again. *Heh,* what utter devotion, I must say."

Her voice was sweet and cloying, tinged with a soft laugh. As she spoke, she moved slowly closer, propping one hand beside the armrest of Mo Han's couch, leaning her body down halfway, allowing her trailing hair to fall upon his shoulder.

Her fingertips brushed lightly and suggestively across his palm, then hooked a corner of his sleeve—an action of the utmost intimacy.

"Does His Highness not wish to… choose a different person to distract you and ease your worries?"

Her fingertip traced the decorative pattern across his chest with a feather-light touch, pressing her body even nearer, an air of feigned innocence mixed with sultry ambiguity in her eyes. "If she is the source of your gloom, then perhaps… allow me the opportunity to attempt to bring you some pleasure."

Having spoken, she slightly tightened the pressure of her fingertip, giving a small, provocative scratch like a cat, the move being incredibly alluring.

Her breathing was deliberately lowered, and her soft, fragrant presence was immediately within his reach.

However, Mo Han merely lifted his gaze to look at her, his eyes utterly unruffled, as though observing a common gnat.

"That paltry trick of yours—" His tone was so level it bordered on callousness. He let out a low, soft chuckle. "And you dare offer it up as a treasure?"

The lack of imagination in the Demonic Realm's courtship rituals is frankly disappointing.

He reached out and flicked his hand, sending her fingertip away, without even allowing his robe to crease. He then rose to his feet, coolly withdrawing his entire commanding aura from her immediate vicinity.

Mo Han's expression remained unchanged as he lazily shifted his gaze to her. Those deep purple eyes were like an abyss, sending a chill directly down one's spine.

"Hmm… truly dull."

He slowly stood up, brushing away the delicate hand Youluo had pressed onto him. The action was supremely gentle, yet permeated with chilling indifference.

"That meagre repertoire of yours," he lowered his eyes and smiled, his tone bone-chillingly cold, "What distinguishes it from a common courtesan in a mortal brothel?"

Youluo's face stiffened slightly. She tried to speak again, but saw that Mo Han had already turned his back and walked away, his robes fluttering like a shadow swept by the night wind.

He left behind only a single, cold, lingering remark: "If you wish to truly please this Lord—at the very least, you must learn how to genuinely move someone's heart."

His retreating figure was composed and utterly magnificent, each step generating an aura of frost, though no one else knew that the Scrying Mirror had already shattered into a carpet of fine cracks on the floor.

Youluo stood frozen on the spot, a stifling pain clenching her chest.

She had always prided herself on knowing exactly how to satisfy a man, and had never truly deferred to anyone, yet this Prince of the Demonic Domain was as cold as a bottomless abyss, refusing to spare her even the slightest flicker of emotion.

She bit down hard on her lip, a mix of humiliation and jealousy silently spreading in her eyes. She stared fixedly at the shattered fragments of the Scrying Mirror on the ground, the silver light flickering like shards of ice, as if the image of that little Immortal from the Celestial Realm had yet to truly dissipate.

"What exactly is so *good* about her..." she murmured softly, unable to suppress the acid ache in her voice.

Meanwhile, on the stone steps outside the palace, Mo Han walked all the way to the front of the hall, lifting his head to gaze at the dim, oppressive Demonic Moon. His eyes were calm and unperturbed, yet he reached up and gently took down a small, ice-blue jade pendant that rested on his chest—it was the one Yun Yara had left behind when she was last in the Demonic Domain.

He rubbed the surface of the pendant with his thumb. After a long silence, he uttered a single, low sentence: "Truly... so very tiresome." Of course, he never once considered simply discarding it. That would be far too straightforward.

With that, he carefully tucked the jade pendant back into his sleeve. He paused for a brief moment, but never once looked back.

* * * * *

In the deep recesses of the bamboo grove, the mist hung heavy and pervasive.

The forest floor, slick and moist after the recent fine rain, was subtly slippery, and the sound of the wind sweeping through the timber carried an echoing murmur, making each verdant bamboo stalk rustle as if it were uttering low secrets.

Yun Yara, clad in her plain, moon-white robes, walked alone along this solitary, seldom-trod path. Her feet were splashing mud onto her robes, yet she seemed completely oblivious to the resulting stains.

She proceeded with her gaze lowered, her complexion as placid and composed as still water, yet utterly incapable of masking the tempestuous surge of emotion churning in the depths of her eyes.

Just moments ago, Yun Zhou had publicly and furiously rebuked her, accusing her of 'bending her arm outwards' (a Chinese idiom for favouring outsiders over one's own people) and being 'happy that Yun Lili had left'.

Each word had been like a razor blade, carving wounds into her heart.

She had simply bitten her lip, refusing to offer a single retort.

It was not that the pain was absent; rather, it was simply her ingrained way.

She was stubbornly taciturn, crushing all emotion deep within her breast, allowing anyone and everyone to judge and misunderstand her as they pleased.

One would think, after all these centuries, they might have grasped the concept of 'understatement', but no, drama always wins in the celestial courts.

Suddenly, a rustling sound echoed through the woods. Yun Yara stiffened, whipping her head around, just as a dark shadow bolted towards her like a streak of lightning.

She instinctively readied her spiritual energy, yet in the instant the shadow collided into her embrace, she froze utterly.

"…Little Star?"

It was a small, entirely black spiritual cat, its fur glossy and deeply lustrous, like pure ink. Its eyes, however, were carved from shimmering amber, emitting a glittering radiance that was as dazzling as a constellation of stars.

The little spiritual cat rubbed against her robe with familiarity, sniffing her scent, and letting out a low, rumbling purr, as if trying to communicate: *I am back now, do not be sad any longer.*

Yun Yara was momentarily startled, and a sudden, thick mist quickly welled up in her eyes. She bent down and scooped Little Star up into her arms.

"It is you, after all..." Her voice was slightly hoarse as she raised her hand to gently stroke the furry head.

"What others think of me, I truly do not care... But you understand me, do you not?"

Little Star gave a faint *meow*, which sounded both like an answer and a comforting affirmation. Yun Yara curled the corners of her lips, her smile exceedingly faint and soft, yet undeniably genuine.

Holding Little Star, she settled herself upon a patch of grey-blue stone amidst the bamboo.

She looked up at the pale light filtering through the dense canopy of the grove. The wind brushed the stray hairs across her forehead, and simultaneously seemed to sweep across the littered disarray within her heart.

The Celestial Realm, in this very moment, feels impossibly cold and utterly cruel to me. Yet, with you here beside me, perhaps the journey ahead will not be quite so difficult.

She lowered her head and whispered softly, "I know that I am neither quick-witted nor do I possess a particularly endearing nature, but all I truly desire is to... to do what is right."

Little Star let out another gentle *meow* and rubbed its head against her palm.

She smiled, her nose slightly pink.

"Even if it proves to be the wrong path, it is still the one I have chosen for myself."

She held Little Star tighter, the resolve in her eyes hardening perceptibly. "For her sake, I shall go and save... Moony."

* * * * *

In the secluded, annexed courtyard, the shadow of a willow tree slanted across the scarlet window.

A gust of wind lifted the corner of the curtain, and a single, ancient plum tree in the yard extended its new green shoots.

Moony was sitting quietly by the window, her figure draped in plain white, her posture poised.

She was meditating cross-legged, adjusting her breath and her fingertips moved subtly, and her aura, like mist or smoke, was ethereal and indistinct.

Footsteps approached outside the door, and Du Sord strode in, his eyes cool and detached, yet his tone was not as sharply incisive as usual.

"This Prince has received word that the maiden has not consumed any food or drink for three days."

Moony opened her eyes, casting him a cursory glance. Her eyes were like icy springs, and her voice was as level as still water: "I do not require sustenance, you see."

Du Sord froze for a moment, a trace of bewilderment flickering across his brow and had initially supposed she was being consumed by sorrow and falling ill.

Only now did he realise—he had simply been overthinking the matter.

"…This Prince, rather regrettably, forgot that the maiden is not a person of the ordinary mortal world."

"May I now be permitted to leave?"

Du Sord paused slightly, a hint of hesitation passing through his eyes. He was notoriously ill-equipped to deal with the subtleties of women, let alone someone from the Immortal Sect such as she. Her utterly tranquil tone, conversely, left him momentarily at a loss for a suitable reply.

"…Since the embroidered ball landed in your hand, you are, by all accounts, already this Prince's property." He curved his lip into a faint smile, his tone bearing a measure of self-mockery. "To put it so plainly, it does sound rather like forcing someone's hand."

Moony tilted her head, watching him, her tone still light and airy: "So you intentionally detained me here?"

"I wouldn't call it 'intentional'," Du Sord shifted his gaze to the ancient plum tree outside the window. Its branch shadows swayed, mirroring the disquiet in his own heart. "This Prince was merely borrowing the guise of a matrimonial contest to mislead the court and distract His Majesty and the Crown Prince. I certainly never anticipated—that the embroidered ball would actually fall into your hands."

Reaching this point, he actually let out a small laugh, his voice tinged with both vexation and resignation: "That embroidered ball possesses its own spiritual power; for it to fly straight into the maiden's embrace is surely a predetermined thread of fate."

Moony lowered her gaze and remained silent, before speaking after a moment: "Regardless of the circumstances, keeping me here is pointless. I am incapable of doing anything."

Du Sord let out a soft, low laugh: "What this Prince seeks is power and vengeance; forcibly detaining an Immortal serves no real purpose. If you are willing to assist me, then it becomes a mutually agreeable arrangement. This Prince merely requires the Immortal Maiden to make a visit to the Imperial Palace in the capital. It would take, at most, a few months of your time."

It was only then that Moony paid him a more concentrated look, a tiny ripple of light appearing in her eyes, yet she still asked softly: "You vastly overestimate me. I am only a minor Immortal attendant; I can do nothing of consequence."

"It matters not," Du Sord's voice was placid. "Since we have met by fate, this Prince dares not ask for more. I only hope that… the Immortal Maiden will consider the fact that I have caused you no physical harm, and lend me a hand."

"Help you seize the throne?" she inquired.

"Help me exact my vengeance," his voice was deep, concealing a deep-seated hatred and obsession that had lingered for years: "My maternal consort died unjustly, the Crown Prince is insidious and cruel, and His Majesty is muddled and weak. If I do not ascend to the highest position, my death would be utterly meaningless."

Moony listened quietly, then said softly: "The transient glory and wealth of the mortal realm mean very little to us. However, if you are so profoundly determined… then perhaps this royal seat is genuinely more difficult to obtain than eternal life."

Du Sord let out a self-deprecating chuckle. "Perhaps so."

Moony suddenly spoke: "Do not all mortals desire to cultivate to Immortality? How about I bestow upon you a wisp of spiritual energy and help you step onto the Immortal path?"

Du Sord's expression flickered, then he shook his head and smiled: "I thank the Immortal Maiden for her kind intentions… but it is not necessary."

"You genuinely do not wish to cultivate?" she blinked, asking with genuine curiosity. "That is quite odd; I have never heard of anyone who did not want to become an Immortal."

"What use is endless longevity?" His gaze was tranquil. "With loved ones dying young and enemies holding sway, eternal life merely serves to prolong loneliness indefinitely."

This time, Moony was silent for a moment. Then, she suddenly broke into a light laugh, her voice clear and slightly playful, like snow falling upon bamboo shoots—soft, yet resonant.

"…That is actually quite an interesting perspective. It is the first time I have ever heard it."

Having said this, she smiled more openly, laughing spontaneously, her voice clear and charming like jade beads dropping onto a plate.

She cocked her head, looking at Du Sord, her eyes filled with vivacious interest.

"Will you then become the sort of Emperor who sits on a golden throne all day long, reviewing memorials and having one hundred dishes placed on the dinner table?"

Du Sord was slightly taken aback: "…One hundred dishes?"

"Yes, indeed," she said with utterly serious composure. "I heard from other Immortals that Emperors are served over a hundred dishes at every meal, and having to eat all of them must be terribly hard work."

Du Sord could not help but laugh. "There are indeed one hundred, but one is not obliged to consume them all. One merely samples a few mouthfuls of each."

Moony looked puzzled: "Isn't that rather wasteful?"

She pondered this, still not quite grasping the concept. "We consume elixirs; at most, one bite, and there is no waste whatsoever."

As Moony spoke, she simply hugged her knees tighter, sitting in an even more rounded posture. "Since you refuse to cultivate, then you should engage in activities that bring joy. For instance… gardening?"

Du Sord lowered his gaze: "Gardening cannot bring vengeance."

"But it can make people smile," Moony blinked, her expression utterly matter-of-fact, even carrying a hint of small pride. "I am just a little flower sprite, you see. The Celestial Lord planted a row of Immortal Sunflowers behind his house, and I am one of those small Immortal Sunflowers."

She looked up at him, her smile crescent-shaped: "The way you look right now, with your brow furrowed, you look exactly like the spirit beast belonging to my Lady, who constantly worries someone is going to steal its fruit."

Upon hearing this, Du Sord finally let out a soft, low, and brief laugh that was, nevertheless, completely genuine.

Chapter 35: The Quiet Mountain

The night was deep and utterly silent. Mist was gently rising and swirling over Mount Yuheng, and all the sounds of creation were hushed.

Yu Sord formed a seal within his sleeve, then raised his palm to cover her brow.

A faint, secluded luminescence filtered through his fingers, and his spiritual breath spread out slowly, like water ripples—clear and moist, yet never aggressive—as if a pool of moonlight were sinking directly into her soul.

He consciously withdrew some of his force, his fingertip resting upon her forehead, yet not moving away and called out to her in a low voice: "Lili."

The sound was low and protracted, as though he feared disturbing some fragile dream.

Yun Lili's breathing hitched momentarily, and her eyelashes fluttered involuntarily.

She remained sunken in deep slumber, her consciousness seemingly enveloped by a layer of impenetrable fog, unable to locate an exit.

Yet, that spiritual breath was profoundly familiar, like a single thread of morning light lodged deep within her memory; even across the gulf of lifetimes, it remained warmly reassuring.

She frowned instinctively, her lips moving slightly, as if murmuring something indistinct.

Yu Sord's gaze intensified, yet he dared not accelerate the process too fiercely. He understood that her soul had not yet fully re-anchored.

A rash action would be akin to tearing apart the threads of a silkworm cocoon, fundamentally damaging her very essence.

He silently recited his core mantra, allowing his own spiritual power to flow incessantly into her *dantian*, then separating a few additional strands to gently guide them along her meridians.

The force he exerted was exceedingly gentle; even the passing wind felt heavy by comparison.

A faint warmth radiated from his palm, and the spiritual breath wove itself thread by delicate thread into her sea of *qi*, aligning her channels, calming her spirit, and firmly stabilising her soul.

This particular technique was one that demanded extreme concentration and depletion of the mind, yet his eyes betrayed no sign of exhaustion.

He remained utterly focused upon her brow, his ice-jade eyes reflecting only her single image.

This, perhaps, is what the Immortals call commitment, even if I must look like an utter fool performing this delicate ritual.

Yun Lili suddenly let out a low, indistinct murmur, though it carried a distinct thread of unease. Her fingers curled slightly, and her brows furrowed momentarily.

Yu Sord's movements paused. He leaned slightly closer, whispering softly into her ear: "Fear not. I am here."

Yun Lili's fingertips trembled lightly, as if she were calling out to him within some forgotten dream.

She mumbled a single phrase: "…Do not leave…"

The sound was scarcely audible, yet it felt as if a thousand needles had pricked his heart.

Yu Sord's throat worked, and he answered her in a low voice: "I shall not leave. Not in this lifetime shall I leave you."

His tone was so gentle it was almost like the wind passing through the pine forest, sounding like the most common of promises, yet freighted with an immense and tender weight of emotion.

He had spoken these very words once before, and he had subsequently broken that vow.

This time, he desired only to quietly remain, to keep his silent watch.

She had no need to remember who he was, and no need to ever look back towards him again.

So long as she awoke safely, so long as her eyes were clear and bright, his heart would find its peace.

The night deepened further. Moonlight slanted through the window, falling upon her forehead and reflecting a thin sheen of light.

Her breathing gradually steadied, her aura as fragrant as an orchid, and deep within her consciousness, a faint light seemed to be quietly gathering.

And he, still maintaining his steadfast watch without any change in expression, kept his fingertips resting over her heart, allowing his spiritual power to continuously pour into her like a flowing spring.

He was in no hurry. All that mattered was that she woke up, gently, in her own good time.

* * * * *

The peaks of Mount Yuheng were wreathed in spiralling vapours, with the glow of the clouds illuminating the vast sky.

A streak of sword-light sliced through the void and descended just outside the mountain gate, where members of the Yun family were already standing upon the cloud platform.

The delegation was headed by the Yun family's Grand Elder, **Yun Wuntang**, accompanied by the venerable **Old Matriarch Yun**.

Though technically guests, their presence carried an immensely overbearing momentum, causing even the spiritual birds in the mountains to take cover and fall silent.

A classic power play, bringing the intimidating matriarch to enforce maximum pressure.

A disciple of Yuheng Mountain was tasked with receiving them, murmuring in a low voice: "Would the two esteemed Immortals please wait briefly? Our Honoured Lord is currently in closed-door cultivation and is expected to emerge shortly."

The Old Matriarch Yun swept him with a frigid look, the staff in her hand giving a minute tap.

Her voice was sharp and cold: "Yun Lili is the legitimate daughter of my Yun clan. While her being taken into Mount Yuheng for recuperation may be fate, as her grandmother, I cannot possibly refrain from enquiring after her well-being. If your Honoured Lord is truly in retreat, then this old woman shall simply remain right here and wait for his emergence."

No sooner had the words been uttered than a figure drifted effortlessly from amidst the pines of the cloud ridge. His **demeanour** was like a cypress standing firm in the frost—his features were mild and composed, yet concealing an immovable, boundless *qi*.

Yu Sord gave a slight cup of his hands in salute: "I offer my respects to the Old Matriarch Yun and the Clan Master Yun. You have travelled a great distance; forgive my failure to receive you sooner."

The Old Matriarch snorted disdainfully, yet was nonetheless obliged to return the courtesy: "Celestial Lord Yu has finally condescended to appear. Is Lili with you? This old woman insists on seeing her with her own eyes."

"She is," Yu Sord replied, his tone courteous but meticulously measured, securing every step of his argument. "Her consciousness has been unstable recently. I am currently using a Soul Art to stabilise her spirit and supplement her *qi*. She has yet to fully awaken."

"If that is the case, then allow this Clan Master to escort her back to the Yun family for quiet convalescence," Yun Wuntang stated, his face grave and cold. "The Yun family possesses its own miraculous healing methods, and there is no need to trouble your esteemed sect to intervene."

Upon hearing this, Yu Sord paused in quiet contemplation, a flicker of snowy light crossing his eyes. "Yun Lili's current state stems from the shock delivered to her Dao Heart over the matter of Moony, compounded by an unresolved past-life soul **tribulation**. She requires this sect's **'Soul-Crossing Method'** as a guide, and must recuperate upon the **'Clear Spirit Platform'** for precisely forty-nine days. This technique is an ancient secret of my Yuheng Mountain; no external party can sustain it. To forcibly interrupt the process would risk the terrifying prospect of her soul dissipating entirely."

Though his tone was light, every word was like a needle, firmly piercing the hearer's heart. Hearing this, Yun Wuntang was momentarily unable to formulate a rebuttal. *One cannot argue with a technicality, especially when the threat of 'soul dissipation' is attached. Utterly brutal.*

Yu Sord's voice remained perfectly calm. What he neglected to mention was that this particular karmic debt was entirely his own to repay.

Yun Wuntang cupped his hands, his tone stable but carrying an implicit, crushing pressure: "Honoured Lord Yu, Lili's body is weak; to remain long upon this mountain is hardly a sustainable long-term plan. Furthermore… your Honoured Lord has long had an engagement with my Yara, and this action appears rather unsuitable."

The Old Matriarch Yun at his side nodded slightly: "The betrothal agreed upon between the two families long ago was personally affirmed by the Clan Master. Now, with widespread rumours circulating, should people mistakenly believe that the Honoured Lord harbours feelings for Lili, it would be detrimental to both your **honour** and to **good faith**."

Yu Sord listened to their points, standing silently beneath the shadow of the pine. The wind ruffled his robes, making his azure garment sway like the boughs of the pine itself.

After a long silence, he finally lifted his gaze. His eyes were as clear and moist as jade spring water, yet held an unquestionable, serene **composure**: "The betrothal that the Yun family established with Mount Yuheng in those years, while secured by a token, never explicitly named a person. At that time, this one also dispatched a reply, only—" He paused briefly, offering a gentle smile. "—a written response has yet to be received to this day."

Yun Wuntang's face paled slightly, and the Old Matriarch's brow sank: "Does the Honoured Lord, by this statement… intend to **repudiate** the betrothal?"

"By no means," Yu Sord replied gently. "This one does not repudiate it, but rather wishes to uphold this auspicious union with the Yun family. However, now that it is known that Maiden Lili is the legitimate, direct descendant of the Yun family, possesses a pure Celestial Root, and exhibits a gentle, refined nature, should we discuss the marriage in earnest—"

His voice broke off, and he turned his attention towards the direction of the alchemy chambers on the mountainside, his voice becoming low but undeniably resolute: "—The person this one desires is **Yun Lili**."

The mountain wind swept by, and for a single instant, all sound ceased.

A declaration so quiet, so devastating, and so perfectly delivered at the most inconvenient time. The man is a master tactician, even in love.

The Old Matriarch Yun's face turned slightly ashen. Yun Wuntang stammered for a moment, then finally asked in a solemn voice: "But you and Yara…"

"There are no private feelings between us," Yu Sord stated, conceding not an inch. "I respect her and protect her merely because she is a daughter of the Yun family. It has no bearing on her as an individual."

His tone was unhurried, yet it was like a cutting blade, severing the connection with sharp finality: "Should this matter still cause your esteemed clan doubt, this one is willing to prepare a written affidavit as proof, to rectify the record."

The Yun family delegation exchanged glances, utterly at a loss as to how to respond.

This fiercely anticipated confrontation, which had arrived with such an overwhelming momentum, had been subtly and elegantly dissolved by his mere few words.

He had even managed to express his admiration for Yun Lili with an air of sophisticated detachment that was utterly unimpeachable.

The Old Matriarch frowned: "Even so, you have no right to conceal her so strictly. My granddaughter is a member of the Yun clan, not a mere puppet in your Yuheng Sword Array."

Yu Sord offered a gentle smile, neither hurried nor impatient: "Before she awakens, any external force could potentially agitate her Sea of Consciousness and cause her soul to break. As I have vowed to protect her, I dare not act recklessly."

Yun Wuntang asked with a cold voice: "Then how long must we wait?"

"At the soonest, forty-nine days. At the latest, one hundred days. Once she verbally expresses her wish to return to the Yun family, I will naturally not obstruct her." Yu Sord's words were mild, yet like a pine tree encased in ice, he refused to retreat a single step. "If she does not wish to… I am likewise in no position to force her departure."

This statement both secured Yun Lili's right to self-determination and served as a clear, final rejection of guests by Mount Yuheng.

The Matriarch's face was deeply unpleasant, yet she could find no grounds for refutation. She could only sweep her sleeve sharply: "See that you do not fail her!"

Yu Sord bowed his head with a slight smile: "Should she remain un-awakened for a single day, I shall not depart from within three *zhang* of her person for that day."

* * * * *

The night was deep and utterly still over Liangzhou. The wind had risen, and the courtyard was quiet and the scarlet windows of the side chamber were dark, the lamps extinguished, and the old plum tree in the yard swayed gently in the night breeze.

Moony stood silently in the corner by the courtyard wall, her gaze cast outwards into the pitch-black night. She was dressed in her pale, moon-white gown, her hair simply tied back at the nape of her neck.

This was her third attempt to flee this princely estate.

For reasons unknown to her, her spiritual power was completely drained, and all her magical arts were rendered utterly unusable.

She was forced to resort to the most clumsy method imaginable: sneaking out.

Whilst that particular Imperial Prince had treated her with courteous warmth and observed all due propriety, she still questioned why on earth she should feel obliged to assist him in his grand schemes.

One should never feel compelled to participate in a mortal man's mid-life crisis, regardless of how polite he is about it.

Taking advantage of the night's solitude, she launched herself over the courtyard wall.

Her robes fluttered upwards, and she landed with barely a whisper of sound amd her movement was light and graceful; her toe barely kissed the blue flagstone as she darted swiftly along the covered walkway.

However, the moment her foot crossed the outermost perimeter of the princely estate's wall—

"CRACK!"

An invisible barrier abruptly detonated, and a wave of silver light, like a turbulent surge, slammed into her, forcibly throwing her back!

Moony groaned softly, stumbling and collapsing onto the ground, her *qi* and blood surging violently in her chest. She raised her palm to examine it, only to find her skin red and scorched, and her sleeve blackened by the shock.

"…A **Celestial Sect Barrier**?"

She froze on the spot.

This was emphatically not the sort of thing mere mortals were capable of erecting.

She tried circulating her inner *qi* once more to probe the area, sensing only a silent, invisible layer of force encompassing everything—from the main gate to the side gardens, from the roof tiles to the shadows of the trees—like an omnipresent, confining net.

She retreated back into the courtyard, settling beneath the old plum tree. She gently massaged her faintly throbbing shoulder, her eyes gradually turning cold.

"Within this estate… is there, besides her, another… **Immortal**?"

She gazed mutely at the faint glow of the clouds on the horizon, silent, either lost in deep thought or perhaps simply too utterly weary to contemplate the matter further.

Just as she was thus immersed in her contemplation, a faint but extraordinarily pure thread of spiritual breath suddenly drifted from some direction deep within the courtyard walls.

That spiritual breath was like snow falling into a cold pond: quiet, unhurried, and sweeping past her ear. It was remarkably cold, perhaps even giving one a momentary shiver of apprehension.

Moony was slightly startled. She instantly straightened up, cocking her head to listen intently.

Being a flower spirit by nature, she was extremely sensitive to spiritual *qi*, and though this wisp of breath was exceptionally well-concealed, it carried a familiarity that she simply could not ignore.

—This was not Du Sord's aura, nor was it the breath of any mortal within the estate.

She murmured aloud, her voice unconsciously lowered, gazing distractedly in the direction where the aura had dissipated. Her heart was subtly yet undeniably stirred.

"It seems there is another Immortal present here?"

Had the barrier been erected by a mortal, she could have managed an escape; but this barrier, and this spiritual breath, clearly originated from the Celestial Sect, and what was more… it carried an energetic signature that she had once seen recorded in the forbidden texts of the Immortal Realm.

She slowly rose to her feet, shaking the scattered plum blossoms from her robes.

The lingering sense of frustration and loneliness she had felt from being trapped had, in that instant, quietly transmuted into a trace of profound suspicion and lingering dread.

This was simply impossible. How could an Immortal be so audacious as to set up a fully unveiled Celestial Sect barrier without any disguise?

She stared blankly towards the direction where the spiritual aura had vanished, whispering to herself: "How can this be… that person was long ago…" *Surely not. The audacity would be quite spectacular, but the implications are far too messy for a mere mortal kingdom.*

After pondering for a short while, she turned and headed back towards her room and her eyes were bright and clear, yet her state of mind was already vastly different from when she had first arrived.

The corner of her mouth lifted slightly, and she spoke to herself, the tone reflecting a blend of deep thought and explorative interest. "This residence, it turns out, holds far more than meets the eye."

On this night, the plum blossoms did not fall, and the wind and the moon remained silent. As for her, she had already formulated a completely different plan in her heart.

Little Fira
小焰

Chapter 36: The Mirror of Awakening

In the ethereal Celestial Hall, wreathed in spiralling mists, an absolute silence reigned supreme.

This was the Spirit Platform, an expanse of jade flagstones suspended high above the Ninth Heaven.

A screen of mirrored water shimmered at its perimeter, and though there was no discernible breeze, spiritual breath perpetually flowed and diffused through the space.

In the centre, an ancient mirror hovered in mid-air and the surface of the speculum was turbulent, throwing off wave after wave of faint yet piercing golden-red markings, like the nascent signs of a Phoenix plume stirring to life.

Suddenly, the heart of the mirror began to violently vibrate.

A single, slender thread of light blossomed from the depths of the glass, inching its way towards the mirror's edge. In the very next moment, the thread of light instantaneously projected itself from the mirror's face directly onto Yun Lili's brow.

Her breathing was erratic, her long hair was plastered to her skin, and cold sweat beaded on her forehead. She abruptly cried out in a shout that tore through her sleep.

"Mo... Moony!"

She snapped her eyes open. Her pupils reflected the lingering light of unspent thunder and fire, as well as the faint glint of a barrier. The very first word to leave her lips was that beloved name.

Yu Sord, who was seated below the mirror, raised his eyes slightly and then a single crimson feather drifted from between his fingers, instantly dissolving into smoke and spiritual dust. He moved to stand before her, his voice still that clear, cool, and detached sound, yet it lacked his usual profound indifference, seeming instead to carry a hint of extremely well-concealed worry.

"You are awake at last."

The cold sweat on Yun Lili's forehead had not yet dried. She struggled to rise, but his palm gently pressed against her shoulder, keeping her confined.

"Your emotions were far too volatile previously; your spiritual energy surged too violently within your body, damaging your fundamental *qi*. You must not move recklessly just now."

"But Moony…" she whispered, her voice husky and rough. "I feel as though I saw her in my dream, trapped inside a barrier. That was not something mere mortals could erect… that aura, it was the breath of an Immortal…"

Yu Sord did not speak immediately, merely observing her for several breaths, before slowly nodding his head. His tone was as outwardly calm as usual, yet it carried an unusually heavy sense of authority: "I am aware."

Yun Lili's eyelashes fluttered: "You…?"

"She is detained within the Princely Estate of Liangzhou, sealed inside a restrictive barrier. That barrier is not the handiwork of the mortal Prince Du Sord; it belongs to someone else." His voice was cool and devoid of explicit emotion. "Before your awakening, I had already clarified this matter. Now, you must focus on your recovery. As for this affair, I shall determine the proper course of action."

"No, I cannot…" Yun Lili gritted her teeth, stubbornly forcing herself to sit upright. "Moony accompanied me to the mortal realm because of me… she is my friend… how can I simply stand idly by and ignore her plight?"

Yu Sord remained silent for a moment, then abruptly leaned forward, gently wiping the sweat from her brow. His voice dropped to a lower pitch: "Yun Lili, if you destroy your fundamental spiritual essence, even should ten thousand spirits beg for intervention, I would be unable to save you again."

Though his words were cold, they were his chosen manner of protecting her. *The girl has the audacity of a thousand storms, but absolutely no concept of self-preservation. One must use fear, apparently, when affection fails.*

Yun Lili froze.

After a moment, she nodded faintly, but her eyes retained their stubborn insistence: "Then you must promise me you will investigate her safety for me… and bring her back quickly."

Yu Sord gazed intently at her, and finally nodded: "I grant you this."

—His tone was exceedingly soft, yet it was like a frosty blade sliding into its sheath; there was no possibility of falsehood.

The ancient mirror on the Spirit Platform subtly rotated. Upon its surface, the network of *qi* threads had already begun automatically seeking its target in the mortal dust.

Yun Lili finally settled back down slowly beneath Yu Sord's careful guidance. As she closed her eyes, her lips still held a trace of a lingering whisper.

"She must be… terribly frightened now."

Yu Sord lowered his gaze, his fingertips lightly brushing the faint, flickering phoenix pattern between her collarbones. His expression remained unruffled.

"She will not be…" he murmured softly. "Nor do you need to be afraid."

This single promise, faint as the wind, nevertheless echoed throughout the hall for a considerable duration, refusing to dissipate.

* * * * *

In a stone pavilion nestled in the side court, Yue Liuchuan and Du Sord sat facing each other. A cold wind whistled through the bamboo window lattice, and the tea on the table had grown slightly cool.

"The situation in the Capital has shifted significantly," Yue Liuchuan stated, cutting straight to the point, his gaze sharp as a sword. "The Third Prince has been summoning his old subordinates with increasing frequency of late, and the Crown Prince's faction is showing signs of instability. If the Prince does not return to the Capital soon, I fear the consequences may be dire."

Du Sord tapped the tabletop lightly with his finger, his voice utterly placid: "So, the reason for the Celestial Lord's great haste is to propel this Prince back into that ignoble struggle for power?"

Yue Liuchuan responded: "Naturally. Since the Prince, being of Imperial blood, has already secured the aid of an Immortal, it is only proper that you should return to the Capital without delay. Mortal affairs may permit procrastination, but the intersection of the Immortal and Mortal Realms allows not a sliver of hesitation."

A glint of sharp insight flashed in Du Sord's eyes, and his tone became chilling: "I suspect that the Celestial Lord's urgent journey was not solely for this Prince's benefit, but rather for the position of the Imperial Preceptor, was it not?"

Yue Liuchuan met his gaze without evasion, stating coolly: "It is both. If we can successfully deliver the Immortal to the Capital, the Prince's merit will be clearly known to the Heavens. Although you may lack the immediate power to topple the Crown Prince, it will be sufficient to stand against him. Should there be any failure en route, however, then the court will afford the Prince no ground upon which to stand."

A brief, tense silence settled over the pavilion.

Du Sord picked up the cold tea and drained the cup entirely. When he set it down, his voice was like ice: "If that is the case, then let us depart as soon as possible."

Yue Liuchuan, standing by the side of the pavilion in his long grey robe, maintained his stern **demeanour**.

From his palm, a silver chain talisman suddenly emerged, spiritual energy flowing to form a coiled, serpent-like shape, which crystallised into a set of ethereal shackles.

Du Sord's brow furrowed slightly, his gaze piercing: "What is the purpose of this object?"

"This is the **'Soul-Capturing Lock'**. It causes no harm to the mortal body, but it can utterly lock the subject's spiritual meridian and magical power, thereby preventing the Immortal Maiden's escape en route," Yue Liuchuan explained, his voice as unforgiving as cold iron, without the slightest hint of apology.

Du Sord was silent for a prolonged moment, then suddenly gave a sharp, cold laugh: "Does Celestial Lord Yue truly feel the stability of this realm, and the fate of this entire dominion, must be secured by shackling a young girl who is utterly without the power to fight?"

Yue Liuchuan's expression tightened slightly, and he was unable to speak immediately.

Du Sord shook his sleeve violently. A powerful surge of internal force struck the object, and the **'Soul-Capturing Lock'** was instantly flung into the adjacent lotus pond.

"If that were genuinely the case, would this dominion not be a shameful prize to seize?"

In earlier years, his own ambitious father, the Emperor, had built his path to the throne upon a foundation of bloodshed and countless marriage contracts.

To curry favour with the great families and gather the powerful elite, he had constantly engaged in political matrimony with the legitimate daughters of various houses.

The deep inner palace was, therefore, nothing more than a series of meticulously planned political chessboards.

His own mother, though of humble birth, had once enjoyed Imperial favour, only to be manipulated and framed with the baseless crime of 'private illicit relations with a guard'.

Under the horrified gaze of the assembled court, she had been tragically presented with a cup of poisoned wine, thereafter, sleeping eternally upon a cold stone slab in the abandoned wing of the palace.

From that day forward, he had harboured a deep and corrosive aversion to the entanglement of power and marriage—disdaining any path to the throne that relied upon the kindness of a woman's skirt.

He had originally presumed the embroidered ball courtship to be a mere farce, embarking upon it with a tentative, speculative mindset, believing the theatrics would simply run their course.

Who could have foreseen that this staged performance would actually ensnare an Immortal of unfathomable origin?

Given the situation, he would naturally not treat her with carelessness.

Since fate had ordained they should travel together, he deemed it essential to treat her with the utmost courtesy.

He could employ schemes and power plays, and he could navigate the treacherous court politics, but he would absolutely refuse to imprison her as a mere bargaining chip, treating her as a caged, pitiful beast.

Yue Liuchuan's eyes were coldly gleaming, yet his voice remained detached: "The Prince exhibits such effeminate clemency. Should she fall into the hands of others, this Lord fears the Prince will find himself utterly incapable of seeing the light of day."

Du Sord's gaze was like a knife. He turned, pulled back the curtain of his carriage, and looked at the sleeping Moony within.

His voice was cold, yet profoundly resolute: "She currently possesses no spiritual power whatsoever, making her vulnerable to mistreatment by anyone. If this Prince cannot fully guarantee her safety, what right have I to claim to be a man of honour?"

Yue Liuchuan was silent for a moment. He eventually withdrew his spiritual command token, and said in a low voice: "Should any mishap befall her on the journey, not only will your claim to the succession be hopeless, but the Prince's own expedition… will likely prove impossible to conclude unscathed."

Du Sord replied coolly: "There is no need to discuss this further. The Immortal seeks her own Celestial path; this Prince seeks Imperial power. She remains, for the moment, this Prince's consort, and must be treated with appropriate respect. Should anyone dare to insult her… they can abandon all hope of securing the position of Imperial Preceptor."

Yue Liuchuan stood motionless, his knuckles slightly tightened beneath his sleeve. After a long pause, he spoke with a wry, half-smile: "The Prince's benevolence is noted. Very well, we shall depart tomorrow. This Lord shall take the main route, and the Prince shall take the side path with her. A spiritual passage has already been prepared for the Prince, one that will evade all spies and eavesdroppers."

Du Sord asked calmly: "And the Immortal?"

"This Lord has his own path to tread," Yue Liuchuan replied, turning to leave, his voice chillingly dark. "But let the Prince remember this: the mortal realm is not as forgiving as the Immortal Sect. Along this journey… if the Prince fails to protect her, then do not blame this Lord for taking matters into his own hands and seizing the girl."

Du Sord did not respond. It was only when Yue Liuchuan's retreating figure was about to vanish into the forest that he murmured softly: "Then you had best ensure you never have the opportunity to intervene."

* * * * *

The following morning, the cloud-mists had yet to fully dissipate.

Du Sord stood outside the side-courtyard gate, clad in his deep, ink-black robes, his expression composed and severely **austere**. Behind him was a compact company of simply-equipped retainers; the carriage had long been made ready, awaiting only the signal for immediate departure.

Moony stood by the courtyard entrance, her simple, moon-white gown unchanged, wearing only a thin veil of silk draped over her shoulders. She was looking downwards, rubbing her fingertips together, appearing to be simultaneously in deep deliberation and wrestling with some profound uncertainty.

She suddenly lifted her head, casting her gaze upon the modest carriage—the one covered with a grey canvas hood and sporting mud-splattered wheels—her brow subtly furrowed.

"Travelling by carriage, then?" Her tone betrayed no hint of disdain; rather, it was one of pure, unadulterated curiosity.

Du Sord nodded: "Indeed."

"And how long must one sit in this carriage?"

"At the quickest, ten days; at the slowest, a fortnight."

"Oh?" Moony's eyes widened significantly. "Half a month?!"

Du Sord glanced at the plain conveyance, his voice carrying a slight apology: "I fear I have shown the Immortal Maiden a lack of proper consideration. This is but a remote, rural area; resources are limited, and the carriage is crude. I sincerely hope the Maiden will not take offence."

Moony blinked her eyes slowly. "The crudeness is well enough, I suppose, only… we normally just fly, you see."

Du Sord became silent.

Confronted with the stark realities of celestial mobility, all apologies regarding the quality of mortal transport become rather redundant.

Moony raised her hands, spreading her arms wide. With a graceful flick of her sleeves, her wide cuffs fluttered, making her look precisely like a butterfly just spreading its wings.

She demonstrated with utter seriousness: "Just like this, you know, a couple of little movements, and one is airborne."

Du Sord remained silent for an even longer duration.

Moony's brow was slightly furrowed now, indicating a measure of displeasure: "It is a great pity that I have absolutely no spiritual power right now. Otherwise, I could simply fly and avoid being jolted about in this carriage for half a month… my bottom shall surely be flattened entirely."

Du Sord finally let out a low, muffled laugh, his voice slightly husky: "…Should the Immortal Maiden wish to leave at any point during this journey, no one will be able to detain you. But if you are willing to accompany us, this Prince assures you I shall exert my utmost effort to protect you completely."

Moony did not respond directly. She simply tucked her hands back into her sleeves, and said softly: "I am not doing this to assist you… As for me… I merely wish to see, with my own eyes, exactly what the Imperial Palace of the mortal realm looks like."

Du Sord paused for a fleeting moment, then his gentle laughter returned, his voice deep and magnetic: "Then this Prince shall escort the Immortal Maiden to behold it—the most magnificent, yet the most firmly secured, cage in this entire mortal world."

* * * * *

The travelling party, having endured a full day of arduous jolting and rattling, finally arrived at a coaching inn as night descended.

Within the inn, hot soup was bubbling merrily, and a few simple dishes were laid out upon the wooden tables.

Several of the retainers were huddled in a corner, consuming their meal in hushed tones, taking great care not to disturb the atmosphere at the central table.

Du Sord held his chopsticks, consuming his meal slowly and methodically, his movements unhurried and precise.

However, his gaze occasionally, and quite involuntarily, drifted towards the young maiden seated opposite him.

Moony, for her part, was resting her chin upon her hands, her eyes fixed brightly upon him, not blinking for a moment, as if she were meticulously observing some exceedingly rare specimen of fauna.

One must forgive her; the social mores of an ambitious mortal Prince are, after all, arguably more peculiar than those of a thousand-year-old toad-spirit.

Finally, he gave a slight cough, setting down his chopsticks. He spoke, a hint of awkwardness in his manner: "Immortal Maiden… do you truly subsist entirely without the smoke and fire of the mortal world?"

Moony blinked slowly, shaking her head. "It is not that I cannot eat, you see, I am simply… not hungry."

She paused to consider, then added: "We are perfectly capable of eating, you know. My Lady, for example, absolutely adores the mortals' osmanthus cakes. She is constantly commissioning Immortals assigned to the lower realms to smuggle several boxes back for her."

Du Sord raised a delicate eyebrow: "And what of the Maiden herself?"

"Oh, I have sampled them a few times myself," she tilted her head in recollection. "The taste is acceptable, I suppose, only… they are not as sweet as Immortal peaches, nor do they possess quite the same fragrance."

Du Sord offered a faint, sardonic smile: "The Immortal Maiden possesses such broad experience; this Du is duly ashamed of his own limitations."

Moony rolled her eyes, then replied earnestly: "But I speak the absolute truth!" Her tone carried the stubborn insistence of a petulant child. "However… your mortal foodstuffs do possess one solitary advantage, which is—they are piping hot, and therefore comforting to eat."

As she spoke, her gaze fell upon the soup tureen on the table, a flicker of novelty and confusion crossing her eyes. "Where we are, there is generally no food… and if there *is* food, it is always perfectly tempered, neither too hot nor too cold. But… it simply never appears like this—"

She reached out and made a gesture as if catching a wisp of smoke: "—the feeling of the steam rising, just looking at it makes one feel… somewhat warm, doesn't it?"

Du Sord was momentarily taken aback, he lowered his gaze to the bowl of soup, which was still emitting delicate plumes of white vapour.

He suddenly felt that these mundane, mortal provisions possessed a little extra measure of preciousness worthy of being cherished. An involuntary, small arc curved the corner of his lips.

Chapter 37: Embarrassed Dream

Dawn mist drifted gently as light spilled from the mountaintop, scattering across the water in countless glimmering shards.

Yun Lili stood frozen in place, unsure whether she was breathing.

Beneath her feet lay a path of warm, jade-smooth stone steps; from somewhere unseen, the soft murmur of a spirit spring threaded through the air, carrying with it a faint cool vapor and a fragrance too light to name. Even the wind passed delicately, brushing her temples with a trace of chill.

She felt as though she had stepped into a dream—

a dream impossibly long, impossibly distant.

Her heart fluttered in disquiet, yet beneath that unease pulsed an inexplicable sense of familiarity.

Almost without thinking, she turned her gaze around her.

For reasons she could not grasp, a tremor of unease rippled through her chest—as though she did not belong here… and yet, every blade of grass, every drifting shadow felt intimately known to her.

In the distance stretched a grove of pale-violet bamboo; when the breeze stirred, the shadows swayed in soft, tranquil waves, serenity folding upon serenity.

And then, in the next heartbeat, her gaze caught the two figures seated on the stone platform ahead.

She stopped breathing.

There was Yu Sord.

That face she knew better than her own reflection, that cool, moonlit composure—he sat cross-legged upon the stone dais, aura restrained, white robes luminous as snow.

A wisp of spiritual light hovered between his fingertips as he guided it with quiet, measured concentration.

But what sent her heartbeat stumbling was the girl sitting opposite him.

The girl wore a blue blouse and white skirt Lili knew all too well. Her hair was tied in a high knot, and at the corner of her lips clung a faint, glistening sheen of fruit juice—

Lili lowered her gaze.

In her own hands rested the very same spirit fruit.

The same size.

The same bite mark.

The same faint glow along the rind.

And that girl…

looked exactly like her.

Her steps halted as though invisible hands had pressed upon her shoulders.

Not suspicion—

but shock.

A deep, bone-striking shock.

Who was that "her"?

At that moment, she heard Yu Sord speak, voice calm as winter water:

"Steady your mind."

"Her" agreed readily enough—but still sneaked bites of the fruit, her eyes darting toward Yu Sord when she thought he wasn't looking.

Lili stared, breath slowly leaving her chest.

It felt like watching a play, a play in which she was both spectator and protagonist.

Then—

"Lili."

Yu Sord's phoenix-shaped eyes opened.

A cool, cutting glance swept across the air, and landed squarely upon her.

What?!

Her entire spirit shuddered.

That voice had unmistakably called her.

Her name.

Not the girl opposite him—

her.

Only then did the truth crash into her like a wave.

The woman seated with Yu Sord, the one stealing fruit bites and pretending to meditate—

that girl was her.

Herself.

What…was happening?

She even felt her own spine tighten, not because she was being called, but because the *other* "her" within this dream had been summoned.

She heard the girl answer, lazy and drawling,

"…I'm listening…"

Then came the tone Lili wished she had never heard in her life—

that overly familiar lilt, the shameless whining, the wayward attempts to dodge responsibility,

and a voice so mortifying she felt an urgent desire to disappear into the nearest crack in the earth.

"I don't want to cultivate… it's boring…"

Lili stared in disbelief.

The dream-version of herself was… she could scarcely admit it, absolutely insufferable.

But Yu Sord…did not reprimand her.

The girl—

the one who looked exactly like her, down to the way her lashes curved—

murmured an obedient "yes,"

yet kept her hands perfectly idle, nibbling on the spirit fruit and stealing sidelong glances at him whenever she thought he wasn't paying attention.

"All right, all right," the girl said eventually, her gaze wandering as she slipped the fruit into her sleeve and straightened herself with theatrical earnestness.

Yu Sord's voice remained infuriatingly calm.

"I asked you to draw in spiritual energy for three breaths. You were eating.

I told you to still your mind. You were daydreaming and staring at me.

Then I instructed you to regulate your breathing and enter a meditative state. You fell asleep. Three times."

Lili watched the girl widen her eyes in an outrageous imitation of innocence.

"I did not fall asleep three times… at most two and a half."

His eyebrow twitched—minutely, but enough to betray a crack in that icy façade.

"All right, all right, I said I was wrong,"

the girl chirped, leaning toward him in a swift, practiced motion, looping her arm through his as though it were her natural habitat.

Her voice melted into something sweet enough to rot fruit on the branch. "Yu—my love teaches so well, so patiently… Lili is trying very, very hard....rally, she is. It's just... that's all she is…. she's tired…"

Yu—*my love*?

Lili nearly choked on air.

She—the actual, conscious *she*—would never, in any sane waking moment, address Yu Sord—her austere, untouchable master—as *"my beloved Yu."*

The shame was so intense her scalp prickled.

But Yu Sord merely lowered his gaze toward "her," expression unreadable, an almost amused glint hidden beneath the calm.

"Tired?"

"Yes," the girl replied with devastating sincerity.

"You were teaching me night meditation yesterday. I sat until midnight. My legs went numb. Of course I'm tired today."

Yu Sord was silent for three breaths—just three, but they stretched like an eternity.

Then, in a tone light enough to feel like a sigh against her skin, he asked,

"That was meditation?"

"…Was it not?"

A faint shiver moved through his throat, the closest thing Yu Sord had ever shown to laughter, and his lips curved, subtle as moonlight rippling across water.

"If you used even a fraction of this effort for cultivation," he murmured,

"you would have ascended long ago."

The dream-version of Lili drooped instantly, eyes large and pitiful.

"But once I become an immortal, I want to sleep every day… eat fruit… and go out to play with you…"

He allowed the faintest, barely perceptible curve to touch his lips, though his voice remained calm and without ripples.

"If you continue to make trouble, I'll have you copy the Heart Sutra three hundred times."

"Go ahead, punish me, punish me," the girl said breezily, waving it off as though such a task could not faze her in the least.

"Before that—let me lean on you for a while."

She blinked up at him, and without the slightest hesitation slipped into his arms, rubbing her cheek lightly against his chest. Her tone dripped with honey, so sweet it seemed almost impossible that it came from a human throat.

"Yu Sord's arms are the most comfortable place in the world."

This time, he did not push her away.

Instead, he lifted a hand and brushed aside the fine strands of hair that had fallen over her brow. His tone was helpless, yet unbearably gentle— so soft it seemed almost afraid to disturb the air.

"…I truly have no way to deal with you."

She let out a sleepy little laugh, utterly unashamed, settling against him as if she had every right to make his arm her pillow. Within a few breaths, she had begun to doze, curled loosely against his chest.

Though his voice remained mild, his eyes held warmth—quiet, unmistakable warmth—

and an indulgence so deep it reached all the way into the bone.

Watching this—watching *herself* behave with such careless affection while Yu Sord accepted it with such natural, unthinking tenderness—

Lili stood frozen.

It wasn't the stirring of a bystander's heart.

It felt like something within her was being gently unlocked—

a soft knock against a half-forgotten door,

a blurred memory rising like mist from the depths.

It was her.

It was him.

And together, they moved with the ease of two people who had long lived inside one another's orbit—

too natural, too familiar, too intimate to be illusion.

The dream began to dissolve like water cupped in trembling hands.

Her fingertips turned cold.

The sweetness of the spirit fruit faded from her lips.

Even the wind in the bamboo forest retreated slowly, thinning into silence.

Before she could piece any thought together—

she jolted awake.

Her eyes flew open. Her chest rose and fell in small, startled breaths, and her fingers curled as if still holding that half-bitten fruit.

The sound of the spirit spring was gone.

The purple bamboo forest vanished as though it had never existed.

Only the quiet of her room remained.

She lifted her hand instinctively and brushed her fingertips across the corner of her lips, as if checking whether the sweetness still lingered.

But her lips…

were curved.

Slightly, softly—as though she had carried a trace of that dream's warmth back with her.

* * * * *

Lili opened her eyes again—slowly, cautiously, and the first thing she saw was light.

A soft, pale glow washed over the room.

The ceiling soared high above her, its silken canopy quietly drifting like morning mist.

Near the window, spiritual fog curled and unfurled with a life of its own, carrying a faint, cleansing fragrance that seeped gently into her breath.

She stared blankly at a corner of the roof for a long moment before her wandering thoughts began to settle.

This was not the Lingxiao Sect.

Nor was it her own little dwelling.

Her hand lifted instinctively toward her forehead.

The moment her fingertips brushed her skin, a faint chill clung to them—as though remnants of thunder and fire from her dream had not yet fully faded.

She drew in a breath, pushed aside the thin quilt, and rose to sit upright.

Her gaze swept the room.

The chamber was sparse, almost ascetic in arrangement; nothing excessive, nothing gaudy.

On the table rested several scrolls of scripture, neatly stacked, and beside them a cup of tea whose steam had only just begun to cool. The scent drifting from it was unfamiliar—yet for some inexplicable reason… she felt she had breathed it before.

As though she had smelled it in a dream.

Or perhaps… she had once sat with someone here, sharing the same quiet fragrance.

Barefoot, she stepped down onto the carpet.

The moment her toes touched its surface—soft, warm, and exquisitely woven—she froze.

The pattern was unmistakable.

Stylized phoenix feathers in flowing arcs, and at the edges, two threads of gold, sewn so finely the ends were gathered in a perfectly clipped flourish.

She knew that stroke.

That craftsmanship.

That habit of tightening the final knot with almost obsessive precision.

Her breath stilled.

She turned toward the desk.

The scrolls were arranged with absolute symmetry; the brush stand held an agate-red paperweight placed at a precise angle—neither stiff nor careless, but in a way that felt… aligned with her own preferences.

So aligned it unsettled her.

A strange heaviness stirred inside her chest, just as if something had been locked away in a tightly cupped hand, and now, at last, a sliver of light had begun to break through the fingers.

She walked toward the window.

Her fingertips brushed the carved wooden lattice.

The raised grain beneath her touch traced the silhouette of a phoenix mid-flight, wings extended in a sweeping arc.

She had never seen such a window design in any other residence—

yet she remembered, with startling clarity, resting her elbows on a window just like this one silent afternoon…

folding paper cranes…

and sneaking an entire dish of spirit fruits before being caught by someone whose shadow fell across her.

Her heart faltered.

This was not her home.

And yet every corner, every nuance, every soft edge felt so achingly familiar that something deep within her trembled.

Until her gaze lifted—and she saw the plaque hanging on the far wall.

Ink strokes fluid and cold, carrying the faint echo of sword intent, and written across its surface were two elegant words:

Phoenix Hall.

Her chest tightened.

A memory—no, a thousand fragments—seemed to stir beneath the surface of her mind, rising like petals through water.

Footsteps whispered at the door.

She turned.

And there, clad in pale blue robes that moved like quiet wind, stood Yu Sord—

his steps silent, his presence as calm as the first thaw of snow,

his eyes clear and cool as the world after rain.

Yu Sord.

Lili blinked, stunned for a heartbeat, and the words slipped out before she could stop them.

"Why… why is the Immortal Lord here?"

Yu Sord's gaze did not so much as flicker. His voice was calm, level, carrying the faint chill of high-altitude snow.

"This is Yuheng Mountain."

"Yuheng… Mountain?"

Her voice wavered slightly, and she tried—very unsuccessfully—to sit straighter, as though steadiness could be forced into existence.

"Yes. Yuheng Mountain."

He paused for half a breath, then added with that same composed tone:

"The Sword Inquiry Pavilion… and this place is called Phoenix Hall."

Phoenix Hall.

The moment those three syllables fell, something in her memory—buried deep, pressed under a thousand layers of dust—shifted.

Moved.

Opened.

Her heart lurched.

"Huh?"

She remembered that name.

One of the outer peaks of the Lingxiao Palace, on the southern Cliff of the Cloud Range.

Perpetually veiled in spirit mist.

A place she had never visited, and yet—somehow—could picture with alarming clarity.

She had come to Yuheng Mountain a few times in the past, but this… this should have been her first time stepping into the Sword Divinity Gate.

And more importantly—

Right before she fainted, she had clearly still been inside the Tianxuan Astral Council Chamber.

"How… how did I end up here?"

Yu Sord's tone was steady, without a ripple, as though delivering the most ordinary explanation in the world.

"Your spiritual meridians were in disarray. Your consciousness unstable.

After your rather forceful debate that day, you collapsed before the crowd. Seeing you unwell, I brought you here to stabilize your condition."

"…Huh?"

She blinked hard.

"That is… I mean… why not return me to the Lingxiao Sect?"

"They believed that the cultivation methods here would better restrain your spiritual turbulence. So you were left here to recuperate."

"Oh… I see."

She paused, uncertain.

The explanation sounded perfectly reasonable—too reasonable, perhaps.

His voice flowed so smoothly it brushed past her doubts before she could grasp them.

Yet somewhere inside her chest, a quiet intuition whispered:

This was all too natural.

As though planned in advance.

But she couldn't put a finger on what felt wrong.

She lowered her gaze, cheeks warming slightly.

"I… I see. Then… I shouldn't keep troubling you. I should head back."

Yu Sord arched a brow very lightly, expression unreadable.

"Your soul has not yet recovered. Your meridians remain unstable. If you move recklessly, you may damage your foundation. Better to remain here a few days until your breath and spirit settle."

"Oh… well… that…"

She faltered.

And then—

Just like a tide sweeping quietly back into the shore, her dream resurfaced in her mind.

His voice in the dream and his hand resting over hers.

Her own shameless behaviour—

the clinging, the leaning, the calling him…

Yu, sweet heart…

Her face nearly caught fire again.

She still had no idea how to explain it, so her head simply nodded on its own.

Yu Sord, seeing her dazed expression, dipped his chin slightly.

"Since you will be recuperating here, treat this place as if it were the Lingxiao Sect. Move about as you wish."

Then, with no more than a whisper of cloth, he turned and walked toward the entrance.

The hall doors closed behind him with a soft thud.

Lili continued sitting on the bed, still stunned—like someone whose soul had been delayed on the road back to her body.

It was only several breaths later that her mind finally caught up with itself.

And her cheeks—already warm—began to glow a deeper shade of red.

She lifted both hands and covered her face.

"…What a strange dream. Why would I dream something so embarrassingly ridiculous…"

The memory of her dream played again—her leaning against him, her clingy voice, the way she clearly had no shame at all.

Mortifying.

Utterly mortifying.

She flopped back onto the bed and pulled the blanket over her head.

She didn't want to face herself.

Or him.

Or reality.

Yuheng Mountain… unstable meridians… recuperation…

She felt like she believed it, and at the same time, she absolutely did not.

But Yu Sord had said it with such impeccable seriousness, such calm certainty, that she simply had no grounds—or courage—to question him.

All she could do was lie there, heart full of little ripples she couldn't name, couldn't smooth, couldn't ignore.

As if a breeze had passed over a still lake, leaving behind trembling rings of water long after the wind had gone.

Chapter 38: Relax. I'm Not That Reckless

Night draped itself over the mortal realm in a vast, ashen sweep.

A waning crescent clung to the horizon—thin, silvered, and sharp as an overturned hook.

Yara stood alone in the courtyard, her robes stirring faintly in the cold breeze.

Her brows knit by a fraction, and her gaze—keen as a drawn blade— swept across every corner of the compound.

She released her spiritual sense in a quiet ripple.

Nothing.

No lingering trace of immortal aura, no echo of spiritual force, not even the faintest remnant of a boundary spell.

Moony was unquestionably long gone.

Her lips pressed into a fine, hard line.

With a subtle flick of her fingers, something slipped from her sleeve—a slim shuttle-shaped artifact, drifting upward as though weightless.

Silver from end to end, it looked forged from the moon itself: delicate yet impossibly refined, threaded within with dense transmission sigils and a gentle, master-grade protective barrier. One glance would tell even a novice that it was no ordinary tool.

She was just about to pour spiritual power into it—to chase after any thread of a lead—when—

A cold aura surged behind her without warning.

It came like a tide at midnight, heavy and merciless, slamming toward her back with enough force to crush bone.

Her eyes sharpened instantly.

Her body turned with the speed of a hunting crane, sleeves curling through the air.

Wind roared; her spiritual energy surged into her palm, coiling with a crackle of lightning. Frost rimed her fingertips.

But in the split second before her strike could land—

Swish—

A hand—large, icy, unyielding—closed around her wrist.

Five fingers, rigid as iron clamps.

A steady spiritual pressure locked her strike in place, choking her power before it could fully surface.

And then—

Her body hit the wall behind her with a force she could not counter.

Thud.

Her head clipped the wooden panelling; dust shook loose from the beams.

The wall was unforgiving beneath her palms—rough, cold, grounding.

And inches away from her—

A face.

A devastatingly handsome one.

One arm braced the wall beside her ear, caging her in with an intimacy so sudden it felt like a blow.

Mo Han.

His ink-black hair hung loose and untamed, shadows sliding over the sharp lines of his jaw.

His dark eyes narrowed, carrying a glint that hovered between amusement and danger—an expression that could be either a smirk or a threat.

He was close. Far too close.

Close enough that she could feel his breath brushing her cheek, warm against the chill of the night—like a spark in dry tinder, unsettling in ways she refused to acknowledge.

"Don't move."

His voice was low, almost a murmur, but edged with command… and a trace of something like laughter.

Yara's chest heaved with restrained fury. Her gaze was as cold as a tempered blade.

"Release me."

Her voice was firm, razor-steep, not yielding an inch.

"Mm." His gaze darkened, a deep and unreadable shade, his voice lazy yet heavy with pressure. "Not a bad reaction. If I were truly an enemy… you would be dead already."

"Why is it you?" Yara gritted out, her tone cutting cold.

"Who else did you want it to be?" He lifted a brow, as if genuinely curious, watching her every twitch of expression with a kind of idle amusement.

"Ridiculous," she snapped, attempting to raise her hand and pull away—but to her shock, he stepped in instead of back.

He came closer.

Close enough that she could see the faint red shimmer flickering deep within his pupils; close enough that the subtle heat of his breath skimmed her cheek; close enough that even his steady heartbeat seemed to echo faintly between them—an intimacy so abrupt it bordered on unbearable.

Yara's lips tightened, but her heart gave an involuntary tremor. This distance—this outrageous, calculated proximity—made her feel as though she had walked straight into a trap.

Her eyes were sharp as frost, yet her heartbeat betrayed her, skipping once before she forcibly dragged her gaze away from his unflinching stare.

"Move," she ordered, her voice icy. Lingering power surged at her fingertips, coiling with the threat of breaking through by force.

"I saved you." Mo Han's tone was even colder, like winter settling over frozen stone—calm to the point of indifference.

"I do not need your help." She bit down on each word, a spark of dangerous light flashing in her eyes.

The air between them tightened—drawn tense like a bowstring stretched to the brink, vibrating with unspoken challenge.

Yara suddenly twisted her wrist, a burst of spiritual light exploding between her fingers as she struck toward his shoulder.

Mo Han's eyes sharpened; he released her and shifted back half a step, allowing her to leap free in a single swift motion.

Moonlight unfurled again, pouring over them—two figures in black and white, standing apart across the courtyard, sharp-edged and strangely haunting beneath the night.

They faced each other in wordless tension.

Yara's sleeves fluttered in the night wind, her breath slightly uneven, the cold gleam in her eyes still intact. Yet she did not strike again.

This was Mo Han.

Not an enemy.

And never… someone easily dismissed.

Inwardly, she ground her teeth. This infuriating man.

Someone who should never come close—yet again and again, he intruded into her rhythm without permission, without restraint, without the slightest sense of distance.

Moonlight skimmed over Mo Han's tall form. His red-tinged eyes glimmered, deep and unreadable, settling upon the silver-white message shuttle in her hand.

"What are you doing with something like that?"

"It has nothing to do with you."

Mo Han's lips curved faintly, his black eyes gleaming like a still pond beneath moonlit night—quiet, reflective, yet holding a glint far too deliberate to be innocent.

"Of course it's none of my business," he mused lightly. "However… I recall there's a little rule in the Celestial Code. Something about not carrying personal artifacts down to the mortal realm without permission… hm? Are you familiar with that one?"

"…"

Yara's jaw tightened, her fingers curling slowly into a fist. If he weren't standing this outrageously close, she would have long since planted a fist across that irritatingly handsome face.

He was doing it on purpose.

This man was absolutely doing it on purpose.

Mo Han scratched his head in mock casualness.

"Unauthorized transport of a magic artifact to the mortal world—fairly serious, you know. Unless…" His tone dipped lower, a thread of amused darkness hidden within. "This little thing… is it meant for that girl called Moony?"

Yara shot back coldly, "If not her, should I give it to you?"

Mo Han actually laughed—soft, low, and entirely too self-assured.

He no longer pressed in, yet his next words were tossed out with maddening composure:

"She doesn't need that.

Right now… the only thing she needs is me."

"You?" Yara finally lifted her gaze fully, eyes slicing toward him with a razor-thin arc of disbelief. A cold, mocking laugh slipped from her lips. "She needs you?"

"Don't believe me?"

He said it with a tilt of his head, as if the matter bored him, and turned as though to leave.

But just as he passed her—

he leaned ever so slightly closer, voice dipping into a low murmur meant only for her ears:

"If you truly don't believe it…

then don't follow."

He kept walking, posture relaxed, steps unhurried.

Yet as he reached the shadow at the courtyard's edge, he glanced back over his shoulder—a single look, paired with a smile sharp enough to hook beneath the ribs.

"…But I'm guessing you will."

Yara: ",,,..."

This insufferable man.

* * * * *

Outside the post station, the night wind sighed through the trees, a cold current brushing across the earth.

Mo Han walked ahead without slowing, one hand carried idly behind his back, his presence faint and elusive—like he existed only when he wished to be perceived.

Behind him, Yara followed with an expression carved from frost. Her divine sense had long spread outward, combing through every corner of the distance, yet she still could not sense anything.

"Ah—!"

She crashed straight into his back.

Her eyes snapped up—and met his dark, gleaming pupils, quietly amused, as if he had been waiting for that exact moment.

"…Why did you stop all of a sudden?"

"Come here."

He did not bother with an explanation. His hand swept back, catching her right arm.

A flick of his fingers and their figures vanished, reappearing in the inner courtyard of the post station.

The moment they landed, Yara's gaze sharpened like a blade.

Moony sat at the table.

Calm.

Intact.

Smiling.

Her eyes curved like crescent moons, a soft, luminous joy resting on her face.

In her hands was a small plate piled neatly with osmanthus cakes, from which she was nibbling with unabashed delight.

Across from her sat Du Shao.

He spoke to her in a warm, measured voice, refined in both bearing and tone. As he spoke, he lifted the teapot and poured her a cup of tea with the ease of someone accustomed to doing so.

The atmosphere between them was gentle, quietly harmonious—so natural that if not for the muted spiritual pressure blanketing the courtyard, Yara would have thought she had stumbled upon a mortal bride chatting leisurely with her newlywed husband.

Yara halted mid-step.

Her expression stiffened.

Then twisted.

Then stiffened again.

For one absurd moment, she wondered if her spiritual eyes were malfunctioning.

Or if the heavens were toying with her sanity.

She had expected Moony to be restrained.

Or weakened.

Or perhaps frightened into tears.

Instead—

Moony sat upright with bright eyes, full of spring warmth.

A tiny dusting of sugar clung to the corner of her lips, glittering faintly in the lantern glow—of which she was completely unaware.

Du Shao said something in a low voice.

Moony coughed twice, then turned aside to glare at him with mock indignation—cheeks lightly flushed, but unmistakably smiling.

He chuckled softly, reached for a silk handkerchief, and leaned forward.

His fingers brushed her cheek with deliberate gentleness as he wiped the sugar dust from the corner of her lips—an action so smooth, so practiced, it was as if he had done it countless times.

Moony didn't pull away.

She simply pressed her lips together, tilting her head slightly toward him, and her eyes softened to a watery shimmer.

"...Is that really true?" she asked, voice delicate as falling petals.

Du Shao paused mid-pour.

Then his smile deepened—warm lantern light reflecting in his eyes, merging with the image of her face.

He murmured something in reply.

Moony laughed again—soft, breathy, sweet.

Yara, hidden in the shadows, stared blankly.

"...What in the world is this."

This was not a rescue scene.

This was—

A scene requiring chaperones.

She suddenly recalled her dramatic descent from the heavens—her urgency, her worry, her righteous determination.

Had she... overreacted?

She turned sharply toward Mo Han, her voice ice-cold as she pointed at Moony.

"You said earlier that she… 'needed you'?"

Mo Han did not answer at first.

He only smiled—slow, lazy, infuriatingly confident.

Then he lifted one finger.

A small strand of spiritual energy drifted from his fingertip toward Moony.

And in the next breath—

There was a sudden *boom*—

an invisible wave of force rebounded from the courtyard and snapped the strand of spiritual energy back toward him. The aftershock shuddered across the tiles, making the floor quake beneath their feet.

Mo Han lifted a brow.

He shifted his stance by a fraction, stabilizing his footing with effortless grace.

Yara's expression sharpened.

Her sleeves stirred as spiritual power surged from within; in the blink of an eye, three defensive talismans flared into existence around her.

"What did you do?"

Mo Han flicked his wrist once, as if brushing off dust.

His lips curled in a lazy arc.

"This isn't an ordinary post station," he said, almost conversationally. "There's a Nine-Turn Spirit-Locking Formation woven into this courtyard. Deeply embedded. Even you didn't sense it earlier."

He spoke like someone commenting on the evening breeze.

"A formation like this—" he continued, "—even those old fossils in the upper realm might fail to break it. As for her, with her spiritual power emptied? She can't escape, even if she tries."

His gaze slid back to Yara.

A low chuckle rumbled from him—warm in tone, but threaded with provocation.

"So that's why," he murmured, eyes glinting faintly red at the corners, "I said… right now—she only needs me."

Yara stared at him for a long moment before speaking flatly:

"You didn't do anything."

Mo Han blinked once.

Then glanced away, as if pondering a matter of grave importance.

"I discovered the Nine-Turn Spirit-Locking Formation for you, didn't I?" he said, tone perfectly earnest.

Yara: " ..."

That counts?

This man, this situation, this Moony—none of it was normal.

But could she really turn away?

* * * * *

Yara's brows drew tightly together as she stared at the Nine-Turn Spirit-Locking Formation—

an invisible veil to the naked eye, yet dense and intricate as woven steel.

The moment her spirit sense brushed against it, a sharp recoil snapped back, numbing the tips of her fingers.

With a barrier like this before them, Moony could not possibly escape on her own.

Which meant that Yara could only—

She lifted her hand, reclaiming the silver flying-shuttle artifact. Her figure blurred as she prepared to leap away.

"Going somewhere?"

A long, defined hand barred her path.

Mo Han's voice sounded beside her, low and even, without a ripple of emotion.

"Planning to run back to the Celestial Realm and file a report?"

Yara turned back, face cold as frost.

"Now that we've confirmed the existence of the barrier, naturally this matter must be reported to the Tianxuan Astral Council Chamber and decided by the elders. It is not something I can determine alone."

"Oh?"

Mo Han looked at her with a faint, crooked smile, tilting his head ever so slightly.

"The Celestial Realm's methods and their… reactions. Have you forgotten?"

Just one sentence.

But her body froze mid-step.

After a long, tense silence, her spiritual force slowly dissipated from her fingertips.

How could she forget?

"Less prattle. Stay close." Yun Yara struck a Divine Seal, and a sweep of white light carried them upward—piercing the clouds in an instant before depositing them within the Temple of Heavenly Pivot.

Of course she hadn't forgotten.

"So what then?" she asked quietly, exhaustion threading through her tone. It was subtle—yet impossible to miss.

Mo Han lowered his gaze to her, voice turning rougher, darker—an intoxicating blend of wicked and wild.

"I can save her," he murmured, "but it comes with a price."

"A price?" Yara arched a brow.

"Mhm."

Mo Han raised a hand—as though he meant to brush his fingers across his lips—but the instant her gaze sharpened, he shifted the motion into a careless laugh instead.

"Just teasing."

His tone dropped into something deeper.

"If I truly wanted something from you, would I be standing here wasting breath?"

Yara let out a cold, derisive scoff and turned away, clearly unwilling to remain tangled with him.

"Hey—"

Mo Han caught up in a single stride, tugging lightly at her sleeve with a lazy hand.

"I said I was joking. Must you be so stingy?"

Yara shot him a sideways glare.

She didn't pull away, but she didn't indulge him either.

He sighed—soft, almost imperceptible—and his voice finally calmed.

"I can make a move and saving her is easy. But the Celestial Realm has already sent people to investigate this matter."

He paused, eyes dimming faintly.

"If I intervene now, someone will inevitably accuse you of colluding with the demon race."

The words were spoken lightly, as though it were nothing.

But something in his gaze shadowed.

Yara's expression shifted—just a flicker, but a real one.

Before she could speak, he curved his lips again, dismissive and irreverent.

"Relax. I'm not that reckless. For now, we do this step by step—play along with whoever set this formation and see what medicine they've hidden in their little gourd."

As he finished speaking, he let her sleeve slip from his fingers, as if nothing had ever happened.

Yara looked at him in silence for a long breath and in the end, she did not turn to leave.

Chapter:39: The Betrayal of the Candied Peach Cake

Mount Yuheng was thoroughly swathed in drifting silver mist, the protective barrier on its mountainside gently pulsing like a quiet lake illuminated by the moonlight.

Threads of potent spiritual force moved silently beneath its surface, carrying the severe, disciplined air of a well-established Immortal sect's restricted grounds.

The very moment Yun Yara received word that Yun Lili had finally awakened, she came rushing over with an unusual haste—not, one must note, to offer her exhausted sister any form of comfort or succour, but rather for a full, unexpurgated briefing: the details of Operation Moony–Mortal Realm Rescue, complete with the indisputable weight of first-hand visual evidence.

The Echo Mirror was placed squarely before Yun Lili before she even had the chance to settle properly into her seat.

Yun Lili stared blankly at the scene reflected within the shimmering surface.

She remained silent for several long breaths.

Then she blinked slowly and repeated her question, adopting the careful tone of someone trying desperately to cling to the very last, fragile threads of sanity available in the cosmos:

"...Are you absolutely, unequivocally sure the mirror isn't malfunctioning, or perhaps experiencing a momentary celestial hiccup?"

"It is functioning perfectly, in accordance with established celestial standards," Yun Yara replied with infuriating, glacial calm.

"Then… maybe I haven't fully woken up yet? Perhaps this is merely an elaborate, post-traumatic dream sequence?"

Yun Lili proceeded to tap her forehead repeatedly, like a meticulous mechanic suspecting a loose screw or a catastrophic misfiring of her inner circuits.

"You woke up yesterday, fully and lucidly," Yun Yara delivered the reply, merciless as the drop of a falling guillotine.

"…Then maybe my eyes are blurry, or perhaps they've sustained some form of residual scorch damage from the barrier explosion?"

She rubbed them so hard with both hands that one might have expected sparks to fly.

"Your eyes are fine," Yun Yara stated flatly, without a hint of warmth.

",,,…"

Three immensely heavy seconds passed in oppressive silence.

Then, Yun Lili completely exploded.

She shot up from her chair like a frightened, airborne carp, the sheer force of her movement nearly knocking the table over with a deafening crash.

"This simply cannot be real! This—this—this is not the scene of someone being tragically captured by mortal authorities! This is—this is—this is practically a disgustingly saccharine honeymoon!"

Inside the Echo Mirror, Moony sat at a small, elegantly appointed table, smiling so widely and sweetly that her sheer happiness practically illuminated the entire room.

She was holding a slice of candied peach cake delicately between two fingers, taking a tiny, reserved bite, then leaning forward and offering the remaining, perfectly shaped half of the piece towards the handsome man seated across from her.

"My lord, you should try this too, please~"

Du Sord's normally frigid eyes softened to the consistency of warm butter.

He reached out with a gesture of elegant restraint and gently brushed aside a single loose wisp of hair that had strayed near her ear.

"The taste is good," he murmured. "The kitchen made a fresh batch precisely for you this morning."

Yun Lili's eyelid twitched so violently she genuinely feared she might have sprained the delicate muscle.

The mirror image shifted—

Moony was now completely submerged up to her shoulders in warm water, enjoying a luxurious hot spring bath laced with fragrant rose petals.

Two young maidservants were attending her every need: one kneading her shoulders with practised ease, the other tapping gently along the length of her spine, ostensibly performing some form of mortal wellness routine.

Moony looked utterly serene, practically glowing with beatific bliss, exhibiting the genuine expression of someone who was emphatically not imprisoned, not distressed, but rather on the precipice of ascending directly into paradise.

Then another swift shift—

Moony was standing in a sunny courtyard, happily holding a skewer of sugared hawthorn berries.

Du Sord said something—too soft for the mirror's audio pickup to transmit.

Whatever the content, Moony burst into peeling laughter, doubling over with genuine mirth, the hawthorn berries nearly tumbling from her hand.

The Prince watched her with an expression so devastatingly tender it seemed capable of single-handedly drowning the entire mortal world in saccharine sentiment, as though he desperately wanted to fold her entire existence into his arms and keep her there, cherished, forever.

Yun Lili jabbed a trembling, accusatory finger directly at the mirror.

"I nearly got myself utterly obliterated! The entire upper hall was screaming and on high alert! Even the Immortal Sovereign deigned to show up! I risked my celestial life attempting to initiate her rescue—and she's down there consuming so well she's visibly getting chubby, soaking in extravagant wellness baths, performing tedious mortal health routines—with red dates for nourishment, no less?!"

"Are you completely kidding me?!"

"I honestly thought she'd been hit with some ancient, irreversible binding curse," Lili sputtered, her voice rising octave by painful octave, "suffering untold miseries in the mortal realm, trapped, genuinely tormented—"

"THIS is torment? This is a hot spring bath with snacks on the side, served in a silver tray!!"

Yun Yara delivered yet another merciless, crushing blow.

"She even voluntarily agreed to return to the capital city with that mortal prince. It was her own choice."

"What?" Yun Lili's jaw nearly dislocated itself in sheer shock.

"I nearly detonated my spiritual core and died on the spot for her—"

"And she—she seriously believes this entire ordeal is a scheduled vacation tour of the mortal realm?!"

She was incandescent, furious enough to combust spontaneously into fine spiritual dust.

"This isn't merely slapping my face—"

"This is violently ripping out my entire three souls and seven spirits and slapping each one individually for good measure!!"

Yun Yara rubbed her temples, her voice crisp, cool, and utterly steady.

"Calm yourself. That prince may be a mortal, but the power operating behind him is clearly not simple. If you charge down now, in this state, you might very well spark an immortal–mortal diplomatic disaster of unprecedented scale."

"I absolutely do not care!" Lili roared, now physically trembling with rage.

"If she dares to smile at that mortal prince ONE more time, I swear upon the celestial tablets that I shall rush down there, grab her by the collar in front of all his subordinates, drag her straight back to the Lock-Spirit Cliff, and force her into shut-in cultivation for ten entire years! We shall see how she manages to smile THEN!!"

Just at that peak of her tirade, the Echo Mirror flickered again, delivering the final, catastrophic insult.

Moony materialised—now nestled against Du Sord's shoulder, her eyes sparkling with happiness, her voice soft and sweet as aged wine. "Good thing that silk-ball fell on me~ Otherwise I'd never have known how immensely fun the mortal world is!"

Lili: ",,,..."

She inhaled a sharp, ragged breath.

"Smash the mirror!!!"

* * * * *

Yun Lili was so profoundly furious her entire face flushed a deep, alarming crimson.

With a dramatic, furious sweep of her sleeve, she truly looked ready to storm down the mountain, cut directly across the celestial realms, and descend upon the mortal world herself—just for the sole purpose of tearing those two utterly shameless creatures apart:

one to be hurled forthwith into the Northern Ice Sea, the other to be permanently banished to the desolate Southern Wastes, just to ensure maximum separation.

Yun Yara, displaying genuine horror at the potential collateral damage, slapped a restraining hand onto her shoulder.

"Control yourself, sister. At least exercise restraint and do not smash the mirror. Think of the paperwork."

"I will NOT calm down!" Lili snarled, struggling against the restraint.

"Why, in the name of all that is holy, should I?!"

"If you break the mirror, you will need to spend an alarming quantity of spirit-stones to purchase a functional replacement," Yara added, her voice drier than desert sand.

Yara's observation struck straight at her sister's most acutely vulnerable point: her celestial savings.

Lili instantly froze.

",,,…"

"…If you act impulsively, something costly will invariably go wrong," Yara added, with clinical accuracy.

Lili's eyes still burned like twin, flickering blades.

"If something disastrous happens to me, then so be it! But I utterly refuse to allow her to continue drinking sweet soup like she's on a frivolous holiday!"

Yun Yara lowered her voice, her tone turning sober and grave, hinting at the true depth of the situation.

"And that barrier… have you already forgotten your own suspicions?"

Lili blinked, the fury momentarily checked.

"You were suspicious from the very beginning, weren't you?" Yara continued, pressing the point home. "That residence was excessively strange. The boundary around it felt delicate, yet intricate—far beyond what any mortal artisan or sorcerer could arrange. And when Moony initially vanished, that ripple of aura you sensed… it truly did not feel like she moved of her own accord, but rather was moved."

Lili's mouth dropped slightly ajar.

The fire surging up her spine was suddenly and violently doused, as though someone had emptied an entire basin of icy cold water directly over her head and shoulders.

Seeing that the logic had finally landed, Yara's tone softened by a fraction.

"The Echo Mirror only reveals the visual surface. Whatever obscure power lies behind that illusion… may not be what we think. Perhaps Moony is genuinely trapped inside something she cannot perceive or comprehend herself."

Lili stared intently at the mirror once again.

Moony was laughing, a soft curve to her mouth, her eyes shimmering with pleasure as Du Sord tenderly fed her another piece of pastry.

She looked utterly content.

Safe.

Far too safe, in fact.

"…You are right," Lili murmured, the fight draining from her posture.

The raw fury in her eyes slowly dimmed, shifting instead into a potent sense of unease—a subtle, sharp, and deeply analytical alertness.

"Moony never even liked the Immortal Pools back home. How could she suddenly love mortal hot springs so much she's giggling like a small dumpling floating serenely in broth?"

She turned sharply and began pacing back and forth across the expanse of the room.

Her expression grew notably darker with every single step she took.

"And she's only known him for a few short days. A *few days*! How could she already look that… happy? That simply is not in character for her."

She spun back toward the mirror, her gaze narrowing dangerously as she stared at that infuriatingly smiling face once more.

Her teeth gritted audibly.

"…I knew it all along. There's no way this is genuine. That sweet-toothed, easily-distracted troublemaker…"

She drew a hard, furious breath.

"…The one who loves eating and playing is supposed to be ME!"

Yara blinked slowly, then deliberately lifted a brow, her lips curving into a faint, highly amused smile.

"Oh?"

Lili instantly froze, her face caught mid-rage.

The crushing realization of what she had just accidentally admitted hit her like a bolt of divine thunder.

She cleared her throat violently, waving both hands in frantic, utterly unconvincing denial.

"Oh what? I—I meant—"

"The one who genuinely enjoys experiencing life… is me. That is what I meant to convey."

"Mm-hmm," Yara affirmed.

"Stop that humming! I am being entirely serious here!!"

"Let us depart. We are marching down right now to settle this entire affair with Moony—"

"I need to see exactly what in the heavens is going on down there!"

With a stomp that echoed loudly like distant thunder, Lili charged forcefully toward the door.

She managed exactly one—and only one—step.

Then she abruptly froze.

Absolutely, monumentally froze.

As if she had been struck straight through the skull by an actual bolt of divine lightning, rendering her instantaneously immobile.

She whipped around, slapped her own forehead in panic, and yelped out a horrified cry:

"WAIT WAIT WAIT—absolutely not! Abort!"

"I need to run back to Moonview Cottage first—"

"I forgot ALL my talismans!!"

Yara: ",,,..."

Before that eloquent silence could even finish forming its shape, Lili spun around and bolted back into the room with frantic urgency.

Her skirt whipped behind her in a frantic arc, flaring like the plumage of an enraged peacock.

She muttered nonstop as she dashed inside, her voice a stream of panicked inventory:

"Three teleportation talismans—three! Those things always manage to explode for absolutely NO discernible reason, so I need sufficient backups. Earth-burrow talismans too—one cannot go anywhere near mortal formations without being suitably equipped with those. And that fire-signal charm… the triple-threat one that self-ignites, writes complex messages in the air, AND explodes violently—yes, yes, the triple-threat lifesaver… I am definitely bringing that."

As she muttered her inventory, she tore the bedding apart, ripped open cabinets, and upended boxes with ruthless abandon—Moonview Cottage instantly devolved into a chaotic battlefield of flying charms, rattling jars, rolling jade bottles, and a vast collection of clattering magical junk.

"Talisman of Concealment, Talisman of Silence, Anti-Swollen-Face charm… this one—uh—is the anti-wardrobe-malfunction talisman… Fine! I'll bring it too, just in case!!"

Within moments, she was literally hugging an entire mountain of paper talismans and bottles, stacked so perilously high they nearly swallowed her small form whole.

She looked precisely like a wandering warehouse supported by two frantic legs, yet still managed to rally her spirit between hurried breaths:

"Finding Moony is a matter of both personal dignity AND celestial truth. This time, I, Yun Lili, absolutely refuse to go in unprepared! Full gear is mandatory! If some insolent, spare-wheel-man dares to show up on the other side, I'll slap him with a talisman stack thick enough to send him straight into another reincarnation cycle!!"

At the doorway, Yun Yara watched the utter chaos unfold—scrolls flying, jars tumbling, talismans showering down like sudden, unexpected snow—her expression a perfect, crystallised blend of disbelief and helpless, utter resignation.

"…Do you really, genuinely need that many talismans?" she asked at long last.

"Of course I do!" Lili declared righteously, puffing up her chest.

She patted the bulging folds of her robe—now stuffed until she resembled an oddly lumpy spirit-gourd—and spoke with the absolute sincerity of someone whose entire cultivation system consisted of one single, sacred word: external tools.

"I move exclusively through the medium of these things! I do not possess innate spiritual power—I rely entirely on teleportation talismans, sound-transmission charms… and fasting pills to keep me alive until I can find some sustenance!"

Yun Yara fell silent for a long, eloquently protracted beat.

"…Right." *Fine. She really should have known better than to ask.*

Lili, meanwhile, wore the painfully sincere expression of someone introducing their priceless heirlooms to a philistine.

"You simply do not understand—these talismans cost a fortune in spirit stones. Look—this teleportation talisman alone costs ten mid-grade spirit stones. And this sound-transmission one? Eight mid-grade spirit stones. Eight! For a single sheet of paper that might disintegrate upon activation!"

Just as she was growing heated, listing price tags like a meticulous celestial accountant on the verge of tears, a soft chirp cut through her frenzied lecture.

Chiu.

Little Fira, the spirit bird, hopped neatly and delicately onto her shoulder.

Instantly, Lili melted—completely, utterly melted.

She scooped the tiny creature up and rubbed her cheek against its fiery feathers, her voice turning syrupy-soft, as though gently coaxing a toddler to sleep.

"Yan-baby… it is you… Do you want to come down to the mortal realm with me to play—"

"No—no, not play."

She quickly cleared her throat and straightened her face, adopting the stern look of a career criminal pretending absolute innocence.

"This trip is a righteous mission. A justice operation. We are going to investigate suspicious activity, dismantle questionable relationships, and rescue Moony from deep mortal suffering. You—yes you—are my strongest—"

She didn't finish the sentence.

Because Little Fira suddenly let out a clear, ringing, high-pitched cry— and erupted.

One moment it was a fluffy, palm-sized spirit bird.

The very next—

Light blazed outwards like a strike of divine thunder. Moonview Cottage instantly glowed bright as midday. The roof tiles rattled loudly, sounding as though they were attempting to flee the scene entirely. A whole patch of spirit grass at the doorway spontaneously combusted on the spot.

Lili's fingers spasmodically contracted. Half a teleportation talisman slipped tragically from her grasp before she could even bend to retrieve it—

And then—

WHOOSH.

Little Fira expanded in a mighty burst of crimson flame, stretching, elongating, igniting the air until a scarlet streak—at least ten fathoms long—split cleanly through the sky. Fira filled the entire courtyard, its wings vast enough to blot out half the celestial light.

Its tail feathers burned so fiercely the earth beneath them cracked and smoked, as though an actual god-beast had descended straight from the highest heavens.

"W–W–W–WHAT ARE YOU DOING—?!"

Lili had just enough time to scream before the massive bird dipped its enormous head, grabbed her by the back of her collar with surgical, terrifying precision, and tossed her onto its back like one would throw a load of damp laundry onto a line.

The moment her feet left the ground, she thrashed wildly and desperately.

"AAAAAAAH!!! I DIDN'T ACTIVATE MY TELEPORT TALISMAN YET—"

"I SAID I TRAVEL BY TALISMANS, NOT BY LIVING CREATURES—"

"I DON'T WANT TO RIDE ANYTHING WITH A HEARTBEAT—!!!"

Little Fira did not so much as twitch an eyelid in response.

The great spirit bird simply beat its immense wings harder, slicing through the clouds with the unstoppable, divine momentum of a god-beast on ceremonial patrol.

The firelight rolling off its feathers scorched the nearby clouds a sickly yellow; in the distance, even the Celestial Sky Patrol Envoys paused abruptly mid-flight, convinced that an unprecedented omen or heavenly anomaly had just violently awakened.

"I can't—I can't—I'm going to die—!!!"

"I must have owed spirit beasts grievous debts in my past life—WHY do birds always bully me—"

"WAIT—MY TALISMANS—!!"

A fresh gust of wind whipped up violently from the bird's wings, flipping her sleeves completely inside out.

Her talisman pouch burst open with a tragic, muffled *PAP!*

Sheets of teleportation talismans, concealment charms, anti-mosquito talismans, and even a highly expensive "Seek-Person Talisman"—all meticulously prepared specifically for the purpose of chasing down Moony—now scattered across the sky like fragile dandelion fluff.

She watched them drift away in pure horror, utterly powerless to stop the calamity.

Before she could even manage to reach out to grab one, a collision-prevention talisman activated on its own with a crisp snap.

It slapped itself directly onto her forehead.

A faint *pop* sounded.

A translucent green barrier inflated instantly around her head, exactly like an oversized bubble helmet, shimmering faintly with protective runes… and, worst of all, glowing text floated cheerfully across the surface:

"Protective Dome Activated — Safety First."

"I'm SAFE, yes!! BUT I LOOK RIDICULOUS—!!"

Her voice echoed from inside the bubble with humiliating, distorted, watery sound.

And the bubble—was green.

Green.

GREEN.

Little Fira suddenly dove sharply.

Lili somersaulted forward, head-down, feet-up, flailing wildly like a sausage hung precariously over a boiling pot.

"AAAAH—MY SPIRIT STONES—!!!"

Two spirit stones rolled out of her sleeves.

One tumbled away into the endless, nebulous sea of clouds.

The other dropped straight onto her forehead, slid down her nose, bounced off her lips—and she nearly swallowed it whole in a fit of absolute rage.

"You just wait—you just WAIT till we land down below—I'm going to roast you—ROAST YOU—I'll make braised spirit bird tail out of that flaming backside of yours—!"

Little Fira flicked its blazing tail feathers, looking entirely delighted, as though it were being actively encouraged by her threats.

It gave two extra, entirely unnecessary whips of its tail.

A powerful jolt of raw spiritual heat went straight through her spine.

She yelped like a strangled cat.

"LITTLE FIRAAAAA—STOP!! STOOOOP—!!"

Meanwhile, Yun Yara drifted gracefully behind at a steady, elegant pace, riding a serene silver spirit cloud as though on a leisurely afternoon stroll through a municipal park.

She even took a composed sip of tea.

Ahead of her, flames streaked across the sky, talismans fluttered away like frightened cranes, and Lili rolled end over end on the back of a giant, terrifying phoenix-like beast.

Yara pressed her fingers to her brow.

She withdrew a communication talisman that Lili had conveniently dropped earlier, tapped it lightly, and the charm immediately activated.

A shriek blasted from the other end—loud enough to rattle mountains:

"YARA HELP MEEEE!! I—I THINK I ACCIDENTALLY SAT ON SOME KIND OF SKY-SHATTERING, ULTRA-SPEED RUNETRACE TALISMAN—I'M FLYING LIKE I'M BEING STRUCK BY LIGHTNING—!!! I DON'T WANT TO RIDE THIS THING ANYMORE!!! IT'S NOT A SPIRIT BEAST—IT'S AN AIR DISASTER—IT'S—IT'S A SENTIENT EXPLOSION—AAAAAH I CAN SEE THE BORDER OF THE SPIRIT REALM ALREADY—!!!"

The communication talisman trembled violently, as though permanently traumatized by her sheer volume, then promptly auto-muted itself for self-preservation.

Yara stared at the fiery streak rapidly disappearing into the horizon, then at the talisman still quivering in her palm.

At last, she exhaled in a thin whisper of profound resignation:

"…She really does survive solely on those teleportation talismans."

Chapter 40: The Extra-Curricular Revenue Stream

The great fiery beast, Little Fira, finally seemed to grow weary of its relentless flight just as Yun Lili felt utterly certain she was about to be violently flung completely out of the Spirit Realm's atmosphere.

With a sudden, jarring halt, it sharply retracted its massive wings and let out a single, piercing **Chiu**.

She was tossed out like a broken sack of cotton, plummeting headlong into the dense veil of clouds. Her shriek ripped through the sky with such devastating volume that even the spiritual tea in Yun Yara's hand, descending far below, rippled perceptibly.

—THWUMP!—

She landed with colossal, unexpected force directly inside a stark-white **funeral canopy**.

Then the coffin, with a horrible, strained **groan**, abruptly rattled open. The person inside—no, the corpse—no, the person who was merely *almost* a corpse and was now shocked back to consciousness—bolted instantly upright.

The entire funeral procession let out a unified, terrified **chorus of disbelief**.

"An Immortal Maiden has fallen from the sky! And she's smashed open the coffin!"

The coffin lid had utterly exploded outwards, the white burial canopy billowed high above them, and the offerings of paper money were scattered everywhere, swirling like a chaotic snowstorm caught in the sudden, celestial downdraft.

The funeral musicians, who moments before had been dutifully playing their mournful laments and weeping loudly for effect, instantly fell silent, frozen like silent, carved wooden statues.

"Save us all!!!"

Yun Lili, frantically clutching her severely ringing head, was sitting bolt upright inside the funeral palanquin, her hair standing on end like a mad electrical current, her face a mask of utter bewilderment: "...Did I just die, or did I simply scare someone else to death with my arrival?"

Yun Yara, in the meantime, had descended slowly and with effortless elegance. She surveyed the scene before her—the entire assembly weeping and crying out to the Heavens, the overturned coffin, and the explosion-haired Immortal Maiden poking her head out of the funerary vessel—and was once again plunged into a moment of profound, dry contemplation.

She delivered a single, measured commentary: "…With an entrance ceremony like that, you have practically **inaugurated your own Sect**."

Yun Yara had absolutely no idea at that moment that her casual remark would, years later, become a devastating, literal prophecy.

"Stop with the entirely irrelevant nonsense! We must flee this place immediately!" Yun Lili grabbed Yun Yara by the wrist. She climbed out of the palanquin with a deeply **in**elegant scramble, hiking up her skirt, ready to bolt. Unexpectedly, a group of mourners moved even faster, instantly blocking their desperate escape route.

"Immortal Priestess, save us, please!" The entire group cried out in unison, immediately falling to their knees and bowing low before the two 'Immortal Priestesses.'

The old man leading the mourners wept profusely, wiping away tears with his sleeve as he explained: "Our young master died prematurely in the prime of his life! Only twenty years old! We beg the Immortal Priestess to grant us mercy and save his life! Ooh…"

Yun Lili felt a violent, throbbing headache blooming behind her eyes. Instinctively, she cast a frantic glance towards Yun Yara, only to be met with a perfect, dismissive **eye-roll**, which clearly communicated:

See what catastrophic mess your antics have created?

Yun Lili stiffened her spine, rapidly dusted down her utterly dishevelled robes, and managed to squeeze out a forced, trembling air of Immortality: "Ahem… I was merely passing through the lower realms, I am not here to undergo reincarnation or to collect souls."

"Immortal Priestess, we implore you to save our young master! He was frail and sickly since childhood, and before he could even be properly wed, he… he…" The old man couldn't finish his sentence, his sleeve already irrevocably smeared with snot and tears.

Yun Yara's expression shifted slightly. She transmitted a low, clinical whisper to her sister: "The young master's soul has not yet fully dissipated. There is indeed a faint thread of vitality remaining. If we employ the **'Soul-Reversal Decree'** technique, he might yet be saved."

"The Soul-Reversal Decree?" Yun Lili frowned. "Isn't that the legendary method that requires one to forcibly *yank* on the Scroll of Life and Death using one's own spiritual power?"

"Precisely. If you succeed within the space of one incense stick's burning time, he will live. If you fail to secure his return, a full **seven-tenths** of your spiritual power will be utterly depleted."

"…Is there no other, perhaps less self-destructive, alternative?"

"None. Furthermore, that Soul-Reversal Decree technique costs… ten thousand high-grade spirit stones, I should think?"

Yun Lili was startled: "Are you suggesting… we buy his life, using spiritual currency?"

"Yes."

She stared for an even longer moment: "Wait a moment. Would… would the King of Hell himself even agree to this unseemly transaction?"

"It would, I believe, be conveniently classified as… part of his **Extra-Curricular Revenue** stream."

"Damnation!"

The surge of anger hit Yun Lili, and she couldn't help but roll her eyes dramatically. Yet, upon observing the old man, whose tears and snot were now flowing freely and mingling disastrously, and then looking at the young master, who was as pale and lifeless as a paper cutout, her heart inevitably softened.

Just as she was about to surrender to the inevitable fate of self-sacrifice, a flash of inspiration—or sheer desperation—struck her.

"…Wait a moment! I believe I still possess a certain little treasure here!"

Saying this, she immediately squatted down, opening her accompanying satchel with frantic urgency. She muttered to herself as she rummaged through the contents: "Let me just see… it's all Little Fira's fault, flying about recklessly; several of my crucial spiritual talismans have been irrevocably lost."

Yun Yara: ",,,…." *The audacity of blaming the aerial catastrophe on the creature that just saved her life.*

"This is… the Pure Spirit Talisman for when one cannot bathe, the Cleansing Charm for when one encounters a filthy aura, the Calamity-Averting Pill from that time I mistakenly consumed poisonous mushrooms, and this Exploding Talisman…"

"And what precisely are you carrying an Exploding Talisman for?"

"In case one needs to make a hasty escape during a brawl, naturally! And this one… hmm, does this appear to have a speck of rice stuck to it?"

She shook the rice grain off her hand with palpable disgust: "Ugh, well, the 'Soul-Reversing and Luck-Shifting' Talisman. It should still function, shouldn't it? Rice is, after all, supposed to be spiritually fortifying..."

Yun Yara finally leaned her head sideways, her tone laced with genuine bewilderment: "…What precisely do you spend your immortal income on, typically?"

Yun Lili replied with irrefutable justification: "I purchase anything and everything, simply for eventual necessity. I live by only one simple motto—when travelling, never fear carrying too many clothes, only fear not bringing enough supplies."

She continued her frantic search, and finally unearthed a strangely colourful talisman marked with a shining orb of light: "Found it! This **'Soul-Reversal and Luck-Shifting'** Talisman. This should prove useful… **I think**?"

Yun Yara frowned deeply: "…'Soul-Reversal and Luck-Shifting' Talisman?"

"Yes! Reversal of Fate and Shifting of Luck, they only differ by one little syllable! The efficacy should be almost identical, surely?"

"…I am currently experiencing a compelling urge to simply **incinerate** that sheet of paper."

Yun Lili cautiously smoothed out the talisman paper, gazing at the large, glittering golden characters emblazoned on it, which read: "**Destiny Self-Turns, Fortune Strong-Armoured**." She mused aloud: "This looks decidedly more like a good-luck charm, doesn't it? But then again, perhaps not! Perhaps with such an immense influx of fortune, the person will simply spring back to life all by himself?"

Yun Yara had already begun pinching the bridge of her nose in silent agony: ",,,..."

"This talisman cost me a whopping **ten high-grade spirit stones**; it was terribly expensive," Yun Lili remarked, patting the paper in her hands with an air of immense reluctance and treating it like the most treasured object in existence.

Yun Yara could no longer bear the delay and spoke with a low, severe voice: "If you fail to reach a decision immediately, the young man's soul will have irrevocably dispersed."

At this, Yun Lili immediately leapt to her feet: "Fine, fine, fine! I shall proceed at once! Wait, where is the incense? Does anyone possess a match? This is the mortal realm; I cannot use Celestial Fire…"

Yun Yara had already silently produced a stick of incense, lit it, and thrust it into her hand.

"Gratitude! Praise be!" Yun Lili immediately hiked up her sleeves and knelt down, adopting a deliberately theatrical, half-finished Immortal posture: "The Heavens have eyes, the Jade Rabbit offers its protection, the Spirit is upon the Heavens and the Earth! I shall now reverse the cosmos and retrieve this soul for salvation—!"

A gust of wind blew, sending the ash from the incense flying directly into her face, coating her nose with grey dust.

"Cough, cough, cough! …Ooh, dear! Ash in my eye! Is this talisman a complete forgery—"

Just as she was caught between the disastrous choice of blindness and spiritual self-mutilation, she suddenly saw a streak of sword-light cleave the sky in the distance. It approached with a chilling, resolute intent, causing the clouds to churn and every bird in its path to scatter in frightened flight.

Yun Yara lifted her gaze to the approaching light. She spoke softly, a certain finality in her tone: "He has arrived."

* * * * *

Yun Lili's scalp instantly prickled with acute discomfort. Before she could even process the sudden change in air pressure, the streak of sword-light landed directly before her eyes.

Yu Sord stood there, holding his longsword, his robes billowing dramatically. He raised his hand and lightly waved it towards the assembly.

A flash of spiritual light instantly washed over them, and the mortal mourners collectively lost consciousness, yet remained frozen in their exact poses, as if instantaneously caught in a celestial photograph.

That wretched little creature, Little Fira, had immediately shrunk back to its tiny, harmless size, now fluttering obediently beside Yu Sord.

Yu Sord smoothly sheathed his sword. He cast a single, severe glance at Little Fira, his tone remaining utterly unruffled: "…Did you harm her?"

Little Fira's tiny neck visibly retracted, and with a flurry of *Chiu-Chiu-Chiu*s, it instantly bolted away into the distance.

The cowardice of certain majestic spirit beasts is truly quite staggering.

Yun Lili, who was still frantically wiping the tears and nose-ash from her eyes with her sleeve, exclaimed in utter disarray: "Hmph, well, why has it simply flown off?"

She gave a nervous, slightly idiotic giggle, looking thoroughly discomfited.

Yun Yara paused, gathering her thoughts after a momentary lapse into speechless bewilderment, and explained the situation: "Yun Lili was preparing to perform the Soul-Reversal Decree, armed with a questionable talisman from an unknown source, and was just about to light the incense and open the sacrificial altar."

"Unknown source?" Yu Sord's cold eyes flickered towards Yun Lili.

"Uh… a reincarnated divine fortune-teller gave it to me at a market!" Yun Lili suddenly produced the gaudy, flowery talisman, which bore a line of glittering golden script: "**Strong Luck Reversal, Meet Danger Become Chicken.**"

Yu Sord: "…Become **Chicken**?"

"No! Become **Auspicious**! A typo, a typo!" Yun Lili tried frantically to hide the talisman, but a gust of wind caught the sheet of paper. It fluttered gracefully away, only to be snatched mid-air and swallowed whole by a nearby spiritual chicken.

The spiritual chicken let out a confused little burp, and then promptly passed out cold.

Everyone: ",,,,..."

Yu Sord raised his hand to massage the bridge of his nose, taking a profound, slow breath, as if he were forcibly suppressing an emotion that had been brewing for a thousand years.

"So, you were just now intending to use that… 'Spiritual Luck Reversal' Talisman, to forcibly pull a soul back and save a life?"

",,,,..." Yun Lili lowered her head, her face a mask of earnest sincerity, and maintained silence for two full seconds.

"I apologise; I was mistaken."

",,,..."

Yu Sord offered no further verbal reply. He merely raised his hand and lightly tapped the forehead of the young man in the coffin. A clear, gentle light flashed from his palm.

"One incense stick's time. Life and death can be reversed. If you genuinely intend to save him, cease wasting any more time."

Yun Lili's mouth dropped open in astonishment: "You—you are going to help me save him?"

He lowered his gaze to meet hers: "Since you are the one who smashed his coffin, you should shoulder the responsibility."

"...Responsible? Why does that sound precisely like the dialogue one hears from a complete scoundrel of a man?"

Yu Sord raised a sharp, questioning eyebrow: "What precisely did you just murmur?"

"Nothing at all!!!" Yun Lili instantly sprang to attention, lighting the incense and forming the spiritual seal with furious haste: "Then let us save him, let us save him! Who can blame me, blessed as I am with such innate kindness and a soft heart—"

Half an incense stick later, the young man's eyelashes fluttered. He slowly, uncertainly, opened his eyes.

Yun Lili was just about to conclude the spell, but in the next instant, that beautiful, sickly face lifted, and his eyes fixed directly upon her.

His gaze was that of someone who had just encountered his pure, white moonlight from three past lives and three future **reincarnations**; his voice was weak but profoundly affectionate: "You... who are you?"

Yun Lili cleared her throat twice, adopting an air of manufactured profoundness. "You were meant to be dead, but I have restored you. No need for thanks."

The young man finally seemed to regain his senses, looking at the funereal setting around him. The trappings of his own funeral immediately clarified the situation.

"Immortal Priestess... it was you who condescended to save me... Might I enquire after the Priestess's Celestial Title?"

"...Heh heh, Priestess is too high an **honour** for me. And truly, I said no thanks are necessary." Yun Lili adopted a deliberately aloof yet modestly virtuous **demeanour**, appearing as one who performs great deeds but leaves no name.

The young man, overcome with emotion, attempted to prop himself up on the edge of the coffin to offer a kowtow, but lacked the necessary strength to sustain himself. With a loud "*Thump*", he promptly tumbled back inside.

"Though this disciple is foolish and dull, I vow to follow the Immortal Priestess in cultivation for the rest of my days, seeking only to repay this gift of life renewed!..." He lay flat on his back, shouting his proclamation, his tone so profoundly devout that it sounded as if he might **ascend** to Immortality in the very next moment.

"Heh heh, truly, no need for thanks; it was merely a small favour…" Yun Lili's face was a mixture of smug pride and shy embarrassment as she scratched her head awkwardly.

Upon hearing this, Yun Yara's eyes were rolling so hard they were on the verge of disappearing into her **cerebral cortex**. *Whose* small favour, exactly?

"This disciple, having received the Immortal Priestess's divine compassion, and being restored from death to life, has been blessed by an immense favour from the Heavens. From this day forward, I vow to burn incense and sever all mortal desires, dedicating my life to the path of the Dao, serving at your side for the remainder of my existence. I wish only to repay this recreation of my being! Even should it entail traversing a thousand mountains and ten thousand rivers, enduring the knife-like winds and the sword-like frost, my initial resolve shall never waver!"

"…Heh heh, if you absolutely **must** bow to someone, perhaps you should worship the one behind me whose hair is even silkier than yours!"

Yun Yara gave a chilling side-glance: "Do not look at me. It was not I."

"Then…" The young man struggled to look at the third figure present, "This Celestial Elder…"

Yu Sord lifted an eyelid, his gaze cold and sharp: "You have already encountered an immense karmic opportunity; you are fortunate across three lifetimes. Do not attempt to covet more than is due."

Yun Lili immediately tugged desperately on Yun Yara's sleeve: "We really must run now."

Yun Yara replied with masterful understatement: "Indeed. It is quite time to withdraw."

Yu Sord: ",,,..."

And so, in the very next instant, one person hiked her skirt and bolted in a frenzy, one person drifted away on a serene silver cloud, and one person followed closely behind with his hands clasped behind his back. The three figures successfully broke away from the scene amidst the flurry of paper money.

Only then did the assembly of mourners, who had been momentarily petrified, suddenly regain their ability to move, as though an invisible acupressure lock had been suddenly released.

"What in the Heavens just happened?"

"Eh?"

"Did we forget something important?"

Once they had finally shaken off their pursuers, Yun Lili was still complaining breathlessly: "I truly came within an inch of having a temple erected and a golden statue cast in my likeness, just now! What sort of nonsense was that…"

Yu Sord remained utterly expressionless: "If you were willing to cultivate properly, all of this could have been avoided entirely."

"Can you not offer a single word of praise? I was prepared to risk my life to save him, you know."

"You were precisely one movement away from being entombed along with him."

",,,…"

"Furthermore, the person who actually performed the rescue… was me."

"It amounts to the same thing! It was a joint effort by **us**."

Us…

Upon hearing the word, a faint, subtle arc curved the corner of Yu Sord's lips.

Yun Yara calmly delivered the final summary: "We must infiltrate the city quickly. Did you not state that you intended to confront Moony?"

Yun Lili gritted her teeth: "Precisely! That is the very reason I came down here!"

Yu Sord interjected coolly: "Not to rescue someone, then?"

Yun Lili: "Rescue whom? I came to **break up!** Yes! To break up! A pair of scoundrelly lovers!!"

Yu Sord turned his head to look at her, his gaze so profound it seemed capable of penetrating all her thoughts across the Three Realms and Six Paths: "…As expected, this was not for a serious, righteous matter."

"You are not the serious matter!" Yun Lili subconsciously retorted. The words were out before she realised her mistake, and she instantly corrected herself: "I meant you are not the important matter that I need to attend to!"

",,,…"

Yu Sord finally fell silent for a moment, then spoke with a slightly knowing, enigmatic smile: "Very well. Then I shall accompany you to attend to your 'serious matter'."

Yun Lili's face flushed crimson. She turned her head away, refusing to look at him, yet her heart gave a sudden, sharp tug. "Who asked for your company…"

As the words left her mouth, she subconsciously took a step back, positioning herself behind him, like a small, stubborn hamster whose mouth is bolder than its heart, her eyes flitting everywhere but at his face.

Yun Yara silently turned her head, gazing at the drifting clouds on the distant horizon, and uttered a cold, resigned sigh: "Fools arriving in pairs. Truly, a defiance of natural order."

The wind rose, the paper money drifted down like snow, and the three figures proceeded towards the city. One person walked with a light step and a guilty conscience, one person maintained a serene, frigid expression, and one person… had eyes that concealed an undeniable thread of humour, like moonlight quietly blossoming in the gathering dusk.

Chapter 41: Ironic & Punchy

The following morning.

Outside the Hall of Imperial Governance, the winter wind cut as if a blade.

Fresh snow glazed the eaves in a pale sheen, and beneath that cold brilliance, the gathered officials stood in solemn rows, breath misting, robes stilling.

A hush rolled across the court, as Du Shao approached.

Clad in a black court robe embroidered with gold, a mantle of silver fox fur sweeping behind him, he walked with unhurried steps—steady, composed, utterly without fear.

For a heartbeat, even the wind itself seemed to still, as though pausing in respect or warning.

The moment he crossed the threshold of the great hall, every minister turned toward him.

Some startled.

Some suspicious.

Some wary.

A hundred thoughts simmered behind lowered lashes.

Someone whispered under his breath, unable to hide his shock:

"He truly returned?"

Another murmured darkly, "And not empty-handed… The rumour of an immortal might not be a lie after all."

On the imperial throne, the Emperor's gaze lowered. His tone appeared mild—gentle, even—yet carried an unmistakable note of probing curiosity.

"Shao…" he said, "We had assumed you would remain some days longer in the south. We did not expect your return to be as swift as storm and lightning."

Du Shao bowed deeply, voice firm and resonant, as if stone striking bronze.

"Your Majesty, this son was executing the southern inspection as commanded. Upon reaching the foothills of Cloud-Peak Cliff in Liang

Prefecture, an anomaly split the heavens. A celestial sign descended—and from the clouds fell an immortal, wrapped in a silk-embroidered ball.

Your son dared not neglect such a portent, and thus brought the immortal to the capital for Your Majesty's judgment."

The hall erupted at once.

"There truly was such a person?"

"It wasn't a marketplace rumour?"

"If the one he found is a true immortal—could this not be a heaven-sent omen? A sign of great fortune for the dynasty?"

Beneath the imperial dais, the Crown Prince, Du Jing, stiffened.

The memorial he held between his fingers had been creased nearly to shreds.

That very memorial was the one he had submitted days earlier, a carefully worded thesis arguing that the princes held excessive power, that their territories must be reduced, their military rights curtailed.

Its intended target…no one needed to spell out.

At that moment, the Crown Prince felt a chill sharpen beneath his ribs.

Du Shao had not only returned unscathed—but returned with an "otherworldly being."

It was as if Heaven itself had tipped the scales in his favour.

"Father Emperor—"

The Crown Prince stepped forward, voice respectful yet edged with steel.

"The realms of immortals and mortals must remain distinct. Should such a rumour prove false, it may unsettle the court and mislead the common folk."

The Emperor did not reply.

He lifted a single finger.

From the shadowed entrance of the hall, a figure stepped forth.

Clad in half-ink robes embroidered with gold, hair dusted with frost, a whisk in hand—cool, austere, untouched by mortal air.

The newly appointed National Preceptor: Yue Liuchuan.

"Preceptor," the Emperor spoke with rare warmth.

"You entered the palace last night. What is your assessment?"

Yue Liuchuan bowed, voice clear as a mountain spring:

"This minister beheld the individual with my own eyes. Their breath is restrained, their consciousness deep, attuned to myriad spirits yet unstained by worldly qi.

If not of immortal lineage, then they stand upon the threshold of ascension—far beyond what any mortal body could achieve."

The great hall fell silent.

Then erupted with a deeper, wilder tremor of voices.

The Crown Prince's expression did not shift—but his gaze darkened.

Yue Liuchuan, once a recluse, had only returned to court by imperial command.

The Emperor already trusted him.

And now, for him to speak in support of Du Shao…

It was nothing short of placing a heavy game piece squarely onto Du Shao's side of the board.

The Crown Prince spoke, voice low and sharpened:

"May I ask the Preceptor, if such a figure refuses our dynasty and is instead coveted by foreign states… how shall our court safeguard itself?"

Du Shao's lips curved faintly, a smile without warmth.

"Immortals are solitary and pure of heart. They do not meddle in mortal disputes.

Their arrival in the capital is guided solely by Heaven's will, not by any desire for rank or gain.

If Your Highness doubts, you may confirm it with your own eyes."

The tension in the hall tightened like drawn bowstring.

The Emperor deliberated for a long moment, then finally spoke:

"Very well.

By our decree—tomorrow at midday, a banquet shall be set in the Purple Dawn Hall.

Let all ministers gather to witness the 'immortal' for themselves."

His gaze swept once—subtle, unreadable—between the Crown Prince and Du Shao.

Then he flicked his sleeve, signalling the end of court.

When the officials began to disperse, the Crown Prince remained motionless.

Only his trusted aide leaned close and whispered:

"Your Highness… Du Shao returned far too swiftly.

This situation… someone must have aided him from the shadows."

The Crown Prince's answer was ice-cold:

"Yue Liuchuan."

The aide instantly fell silent.

After a long pause, the Crown Prince turned, voice low and ominous:

"Du Shao… if you intend to use an immortal to overturn the game—

we shall see whether you can bear the karma that comes with commanding a god."

* * * * *

Winter had already sunk deep into the capital.

The wind grew colder by the day; frost bloomed pale across the flagstones each morning, and the parasol trees along the palace walls had shed all their leaves overnight, leaving only bare, slanting branches against the sky.

Du Shao stepped out from a side hall of his princely residence, silver fox cloak draped over his shoulders. As he crossed past a carved screen wall, he caught sight of Moony standing alone in the courtyard.

She was still dressed in nothing but a thin gauze robe, its sleeves embroidered with drifting white clouds, its front traced with scattered pearls that caught the light and gleamed faintly. In the cutting winter air, that lightness of cloth made her look almost unreal, as if a wisp of mist hanging in the wind.

His brows drew together. He turned to the attendant at his side.

"Has the household not prepared any proper clothing for her?"

"Your Highness, the old madams would never dare neglect her," the attendant replied quickly. "The winter cloaks were laid out at dawn. It is only that…"

Du Shao's frown deepened, as if he were asking himself rather than the servant.

"She goes around dressed like this. Does she not feel the cold at all?"

"The immortal envoy said..." The attendant lowered his voice. "That immortals are untouched by heat or frost."

Du Shao let the matter drop without further comment.

He only reached out and took a purple sandalwood umbrella from the stand by the steps.

The sky was dim and low. The wind came slicing down like it had rolled straight from the mountaintops, worrying the shadows of the trees so they shivered and swayed.

Then, all at once, a weight of moisture descended from above—at first as if a thin veil of fog, and in the space of a breath, it turned into a fine, dense winter rain.

Du Shao's brows knit. He lengthened his stride, lifting the umbrella, intending to step out and shield her from the rain.

Yet in the instant he turned toward her, his feet stopped dead.

Moony was standing in the middle of the rain, and yet it was as if a thin layer of mist separated her from the rest of the world.

Her robe was white as snow, her wide sleeves flowing. Not a single drop of water clung to the fabric.

Bare feet touched the stone, but her posture was so light and unburdened she looked as though she might drift away at the slightest breeze.

When the cold rain fell, every droplet curved away of its own accord— skirting the ends of her hair, missing her fingertips, sliding around the line of her shoulders. Around her body it gathered into a faint sheen, a halo like a soft ring of light upon a lake under the moon.

Then, she moved.

There was no music.

No flute. No singing voice to guide her.

Even so, she began to dance in the middle of the wind and rain.

With one smooth turn, her skirt flared as if a ribbon of colour through ink.

Her long sleeves swept out in arcs of pale cloud. Her hair followed the motion of her body, dark strands lifted and spun by the air, weaving together with the falling rain until the whole courtyard seemed transformed into a living scroll—a wash of storm-grey sky, silver rain, and an immortal figure dancing between them.

For a moment, Du Shao's grip on the umbrella slackened.

The carved handle slipped in his palm, and the umbrella slowly lowered, its canopy folding in on itself.

He stayed beneath the eaves and simply watched her.

It felt as though he were looking at a scene far beyond his reach, something that existed on the other side of a river he could not cross. In that fleeting span of time, the winter chill, the rain, the city, the dust of the mortal world—all of it receded, becoming distant, unimportant.

Only when Moony gradually stilled her movements did the spell begin to loosen. She came to a gentle halt, smoothed back a few strands of hair that were not truly wet, even after all that rain, and turned back toward him with a wide, bright grin.

"Was it beautiful?"

His Adam's apple moved. It took a moment before he could make a sound, and when he did, his voice came out lower and rougher than usual.

"…Very."

"How beautiful?" Moony pressed, smiling so hard her eyes curved, delight and mischief shining in them as if she had never once doubted the answer.

"It was… like a dream."

Moony tilted her head. "What kind of dream?"

He looked at her—looked at the way she seemed untouched by the mortal world, as if cold and rain simply did not apply to her—and answered softly, "A dream that doesn't belong to the human realm."

She blinked, then laughed lightly. "Hehe, the Immortal Realm doesn't have rain. This is the first time I've ever been rained on."

"Mm."

Du Shao lowered his gaze, trying—and failing—to steady the sudden, heavy thrum in his chest.

After speaking, Moony paused again, as though replaying the sensation of raindrops brushing past her skin. She lifted one hand, letting the rain slip through her fingers. Her brows arched in quiet delight.

"…It tickles," she murmured with a soft laugh. "But it's interesting."

Du Shao watched her in silence.

Watched the innocence on her face, the light at her fingertips, the way she stood in the rain as though she belonged to a different sky.

Two people.

Two worlds.

Yet somehow, he was beginning to crave this fragile, impossible closeness—as if a single smile from her could erase every boundary the heavens had written between them.

"Come," he said at last, voice lower than before. "We should go."

"Go where?" Moony asked.

"The palace has summoned us. We're expected before the Emperor."

His gaze swept over her gauze sleeves and bare feet, expression unreadable. "If you go dressed as if that, you may startle more than a few people."

"Why?" she blinked. "Is something wrong with it?"

"…Aren't you cold?"

"No." Her eyes were wide, sincere. "I've dressed like this for a hundred years."

A hundred years.

Du Shao's breath caught. His throat tightened. When he spoke, the steadiness in his tone seemed carved by force.

Her offhanded words—*the Immortal Realm doesn't have rain, a hundred years*—poured over him like cold water. They pulled him abruptly out of the illusion he'd been lost in while she danced.

He reminded himself again and again, silently, fiercely—

Be calm.

Be rational.

Remember what she is.

He was a mortal. A man with a lifespan that could be counted.

She… was something the world could not measure. A being who could dance in rain without being touched, who could live through centuries without leaving a wrinkle in time.

She could smile at him as if this today—

—and he, foolishly, could feel his heart fall apart piece by piece.

But she would still look the same after he was long gone.

He lowered his lashes. When he finally spoke, his voice was barely more than a breath.

"Will you… remember this rain?"

Moony turned to him, blinking, and smiled as brightly as ever.

"Hm? What did you say?"

He shook his head lightly, smoothing away the moment as though it was nothing at all.

"Nothing. Let's go. We shouldn't keep my father waiting."

She nodded, her skirt sweeping softly as she stepped forward onto the damp stone path. Du Shao looked at her for a long, quiet second, then finally folded the umbrella he had never raised, and followed in her wake.

Moony hesitated only briefly before smiling again; raindrops fell along her lashes, sliding off her like dew rolling from a flower petal—never touching her skin.

"All right," she said cheerfully. "I've always wanted to see a mortal palace."

He let out a quiet breath—almost a laugh—and extended a hand toward her.

His voice was soft, nearly swallowed by the wind.

"Then you'll have to hold on to me."

He paused, lowered his gaze, and gently hooked a finger around her palm, the words barely audible as they left him:

"Otherwise… I might wake from the dream."

* * * * *

The wind had not yet settled; spirit-money drifted through the air as if were pale snow as the three of them stepped into the city. Lili was already brimming with fury.

She strode at the front, steps sharp and swift, skirts whipping behind her as though she were about to storm into someone's bedchamber to drag adulterers out by the ears.

"Slow down," Yara asked from behind, her tone unhurried and almost lazy. "Do you even know where Moony is?"

"The prince's manor! I'm going to find that— that Moony and settle this with her!"

She charged through the alleys of the capital, muttering under her breath, indignation practically sparking off her hair: "And here I was thinking she was suffering, terrified, in danger— and what is she doing? Honeymooning her way across the mortal realm! Making me worry for nothing— absolutely nothing!"

Yara arched a brow, the corner of her eyes tilting with deliberate languor. "So you're here to rescue her? Or to catch her?"

"I'm here to drag her back!" Lili's cheeks burned red, voice rising another octave. "I want to see with my own eyes whether Moony was— was—"

"Was what?" Yara lifted an eyebrow. "Which 'was' do you mean?"

"You know what I mean!" Lili stomped once, as if giving herself a dignified exit, then added with fierce bravado, "I'm going to make her face her karmic consequences!"

Yu Sord followed behind them in silence, head slightly lowered, brushing a fingertip across the edge of his sleeve—almost as though hiding a smile.

Suddenly Lili halted. She yanked her pack from her back and dug through it violently.

"Right! The mirror! I have that— that Celestial Mirror that shows where people are! Hurry, give it here! I'm going to check where Moony is right now!"

"There's no need," Yu Sord said, his voice breaking the moment like a blade of cool air.

He lifted his hand lightly. A subtle turn of his fingers, and the wind curled inwards; a thread of sword-qi carved a bright silver arc through the air. It stretched, shimmered, then condensed into a suspended screen of light—

And an image bloomed.

The rear garden of the prince's manor.

Warm incense drifting.

A spring-green canopy of silks falling as if mist.

A young maiden in white reclined on a low couch, smiling so brightly she looked moments away from melting into laughter. She held an osmanthus cake delicately in one hand, her other hand propping her chin as she listened to someone speaking.

Across from her sat Du Shao—his dark ceremonial robes impeccably arranged, his demeanour soft as warm honey—as he poured her tea with eyes full enough to drown in.

The image froze.

Lili's eyes widened to the size of full moons.

"…What— what is this?! This— this can't be real! I thought she was suffering!"

Even though she had mentally prepared herself, she still couldn't accept the sight of Moony living so luxuriously—so indecently happily—in the mortal world.

"Hm. She seems well," Yu Sord said calmly, as if commenting on the weather.

"She— she's even eating pastries…" Lili's teeth clenched hard. "This wicked girl is doing this on purpose!"

Yara's voice slid in, cool as a needle dipped in frost. "She does look rather pleased."

"If I don't drag her back right now, she'll forget which way the heavens even are!"

Shaking with fury, Lili grabbed Yara's sleeve. "Hurry! Fly me over— we're breaking in right now!"

Yu Sord and Yara exchanged a look—one sighed quietly, the other lifted her hands in helpless resignation.

"No need for such trouble," Yu Sord murmured again.

He lifted his hand a second time, tracing a fine streak of silver through the air. Sword-qi unfurled like silk threads, and in an instant, a translucent barrier enclosed the three of them.

Heaven and earth pinched inward, spiritual energy spiralled, and the scenery around them twisted, folded, and vanished.

The prince's manor materialized ahead, impossibly near.

"Hey! Didn't you say celestial techniques shouldn't be used lightly in the mortal realm?!" Lili shouted, staring at the rapidly shrinking distance as if the world had been yanked backward.

"You immortals are absolutely— absolutely double-standard—!"

Yu Sord regarded her, expression utterly placid. "Yes."

He nodded once. Calm. Unapologetic.

Lili: "…"

She kicked him.

Or— tried to.

Her foot hit nothing but air; the recoil snapped back through her ankle and left her hopping in place, foot numb.

Wind rushed past them as the manor loomed ever closer.

Chapter 42: It is just a show

This so-called "rescue mission," launched with such murderous momentum and powered by a certain someone's skyrocketing blood pressure, was now barrelling toward—

the most ridiculous "lover-breaking scene" imaginable.

Inside the manor, flower shadows swayed against lacquered pillars.

Silk canopies hung low, stirring when a breath of spring wind drifted through, carrying a touch of sandalwood that curled lazily into the gauze-draped windows.

Moony sat cross-legged on a cushioned couch, turning a small square of osmanthus cake between her fingers.

The confection was delicate, soft in colour, with tiny golden petals resting on its surface. Its fragrance floated up, warm and gentle.

She took a small bite.

Her brows curved as if crescent moons, and she let out a soft sigh.

"The mortal realm… can even make the scent of flowers taste tender."

On the table beside her lay several other small treats; she had only sampled a little of each, savouring the flavours rather than seeking fullness.

"The immortal realm has countless blossoms, yes," she murmured as she gazed toward the window, where fragments of light and shadow danced among the branches. "But none of them have this warmth of smoke and fire. Mortal blossoms grow closer to the earth. Their fragrance has heat to it—like something that's alive."

She set the cake aside and brushed a few crumbs from her lap. With a flick of her fingers, the osmanthus petals atop the confection lifted into the air, trembling delicately before gathering at her fingertip.

They twirled once, then dissolved into a thin trail of scent.

"Can't just eat," she reminded herself gently. "I need to write this down."

She unfurled a sheet of paper, her brush moving with calm precision:

Dried osmanthus folded into the dough; use fragrance lightly, lingering on the tongue for three breaths—best.

When she finished, she tilted her head, thinking for a moment before smiling faintly.

"When we go back to the immortal realm, the cooks at Hundred Blossom Palace must try this. I'm certain Miss will love it."

The bead curtain swayed in the breeze.

Moony set down her brush, reached for another small cake, and chewed with tranquil delight. Seated on the couch, she looked like a slightly tipsy blossom—blooming in the mortal spring with unguarded, blissful ease.

Then, utterly content, she grabbed another piece of cake and popped it into her mouth, her eyes sparkling with simple, unfiltered happiness.

She hadn't yet swallowed when—

BOOM!

The door slammed open.

"Moony——!!"

Lili burst in like a volcanic eruption, radiating an aura that practically crackled across the room.

Across her face were three unmistakable words:

UTTERLY!

FURIOUS!

EXPLODING!

Moony jumped in fright, blinked once—

And then her eyes lit up completely.

"Waaah! Miss, you came to see me!" she cried, throwing herself forward and hugging Lili with both arms.

Before she could even set down the piece of cake, Lili had grabbed her by the collar and hauled her upright.

"So this is your miserable struggle—your tragic kidnapping into the prince's manor?!" Lili demanded, voice breaking with indignation. "You're eating better than I am!"

"Mmmff— w-wait— look, look— I wrote down the recipe... I was thinking— I'd make it for you in the immortal realm..."

"Don't be so rash..." Yara attempted, reaching out to restrain her.

"Be quiet," Lili snapped, her voice trembling with anger. "I'll deal with her first."

Moony's lips wobbled, her expression a portrait of wounded innocence.

"W-wait, I didn't stay here because I wanted to…"

Lili stared.

Moony, thinking fast, stuffed the very last piece of cake into her mouth. She mumbled around it, voice small and pitiful:

"B-but don't hit me… I saved you a piece."

Lili opened her mouth to scold her—

and instead let out a short, furious laugh. She yanked Moony against her chest with one arm.

"At this rate," she growled, "you're going to end up selling yourself one day and *helping them count the silver while you're at it!*"

But Moony didn't sputter or whine as she usually did.

Instead, she grew quiet.

She lifted her gaze, meeting Lili's eyes with a rare seriousness.

"Miss… I stayed because I truly had something to investigate."

Lili froze.

Moony lowered her head slightly. Her voice turned steady—gentle, but threaded with alertness and unease.

"The moment I arrived at this manor, I sensed something wrong. That night I was brought in, I walked through the gates and ran into an invisible… barrier."

She paused, brows knitting, and continued in a low voice:

"It wasn't one of those crude household wards. It was—something that responds to spiritual currents, something designed to mask qi signatures. And it wasn't a single layer. It was intricate, deeply concealed. If I hadn't trained in the Immortal Realm's concealment arts, I would never have even brushed against it."

She raised her eyes again. The usual brightness was gone—replaced by a sharp, crystalline glint.

"A person who can weave such barriers… cannot be mortal."

Lili's face changed at once.

"And that's not all," Moony went on, quieter still. "Inside this manor, I found traces of spiritual energy on the herbs, the incense mixes, even on certain teaware. Someone has deliberately suppressed the fluctuations so they wouldn't be noticed. It feels like… someone is trying to hide from being discovered."

Her voice tapered off, but every word felt heavy.

"If it were just some mortal tricks, such secrecy wouldn't be necessary. But if Prince Du Shao has a cultivator by his side—or ties to a cultivation faction—then using me as a pretext… is far more than a little 'sham mysticism.'"

Lili's voice dropped.

"So, you stayed on purpose. To learn the truth."

Moony nodded firmly, the determination in her eyes startlingly at odds with the girl who had been devouring pastries moments ago.

"If I ran away without finding out, and they actually did something that crossed the line—drawing the Immortal Realm into mortal politics… how would I face the Immortal Sovereign?"

Only then did Lili realize—

ever since Yu Sord had used his power to send them directly into the manor garden, he had not appeared again.

A faint tremor rippled through her chest.

She looked around instinctively.

Only drifting osmanthus blossoms.

Only dew-touched grass, quietly glinting.

Only a courtyard too still, too empty.

There was no trace of that moonlit-white figure—

no cool, ethereal presence lingering at the edge of her senses.

"He… didn't follow us?" she whispered.

A faint crease formed between Lili's brows, a subtle shadow of unease touching her lips—so light it might have been imagined.

Moony, meanwhile, was still talking at full speed.

With a dramatic sweep of her tiny hand, she straightened her back and declared with righteous fervour:

"I wasn't eating—I was infiltrating! This is undercover investigation! I'm doing this for the safety of the Immortal Realm, for the honour of our Lingxiao Sect, and for—"

Her speech cut cleanly in half as Lili slapped a hand over her face and pushed her back onto the couch.

"Can you swallow the pastry before you start delivering patriotic speeches?"

"Mmff— but it really smells so good…" Moony protested weakly from behind the hand, crumbs and dignity equally crushed.

Beyond their bickering, the air itself seemed to tighten—

for the storm on the imperial court had already begun to gather, silently, invisibly, like thunder building behind distant clouds.

And behind Lili, Yara turned her head slightly, brows narrowing by the smallest degree.

Her gaze drifted toward a faraway point—beyond the courtyard, beyond the manor walls.

Toward the direction of the Purple Dawn Hall.

Where the ceremonial drums would soon strike,

and the banquet would begin.

* * * * *

Night had deepened over the capital, settling as though a heavy mantle.

The cold thickened in the air, sharp enough to bite through layers of brocade.

Above the city, the moon hung as if a curved blade—bright, remote, its light diffused by a veil of mist that draped itself over rooftops, courtyards, and stone-paved streets as if a diaphanous shroud.

Du Shao walked with her hand in his.

Her palm was small—soft and warm in a way that felt achingly fragile.

His, in contrast, was cold to the point of trembling, and when it closed around her fingers, even his pulse stuttered beneath the skin, tripping over itself in uneven beats.

Moonlight unfurled over the ground, turning their intertwined shadows long and still, stretching across the quiet road like brushstrokes of ink.

He said nothing.

She asked nothing.

Together, they walked—step by deliberate step—across stone bricks glazed with frost, past crimson walls and dark roof tiles, through a night so vast and silent it seemed to amplify every heartbeat lodged in his chest.

Yet the farther they walked, the heavier his heart grew.

The shadow wall of the prince's manor loomed before them, only a few paces away. Around them, the world lay hushed—no cicadas, no distant chatter, only the soft whisper of the night wind brushing at the hem of her robe.

And the quieter the world became, the louder the storm inside him roared—so loud it felt capable of splitting bone, of shattering him from within.

He thought of the eyes waiting for him in the palace—calculating, scrutinizing, hungry.

He thought of the questions he would be forced to endure, the ambitions that prowled beneath every polite bow.

He thought of her, moments ago, dancing barefoot beneath the rain, ethereal and luminous, like a dream strayed into the mortal realm—something too pure, too alive to be touched by filth or used as leverage by anyone.

Not even by him.

A carriage awaited them at the gate, lanterns lit, wheels slick with dew.

Du Shao took a single step toward it—

And stopped.

He released her hand.

Without a word, he shrugged off the silver-furred cloak around his shoulders.

The fabric shimmered faintly in the moonlight as he drew it forward, wrapping it around her small frame, folding it carefully over her collarbones and arms.

She was lighter than he remembered.

Thinner.

The silk beneath his fingers didn't warm her—if anything, her skin felt cold as the night itself.

"The palace," he murmured at last, voice low, gentler than she had ever heard from him, "will wait for another day."

"We're not going today."

Moony blinked up at him, startled.

"Huh? Why not?"

He let out a quiet laugh—a breath of frost and moonlight.

In his eyes, the silver of the night pooled and deepened, as though a thin layer of winter frost had glazed the surface.

"Because the battle waiting there," he said softly, "is a battlefield of the mortal world. And you… shouldn't step into it for my sake."

To anyone watching, he seemed calm collected, even serene.

But inside him, everything was chaos: hooves thundering, banners snapping, a war he had been fighting his whole life threatening to break lose all at once.

That night, beneath the clear and merciless moon, with winds stirring the city like a prelude to something vast—

Du Shao made his decision.

He paused.

His fingers lifted, drifting through her hair with an unfamiliar tenderness, as though memorizing its softness, its warmth.

Then, almost in a whisper, he added:

"Wait for me."

* * * * *

Purple Dawn Hall was steeped in ceremonial splendour: pale incense spiralled toward the lacquered beams, golden goblets shimmered in the lantern glow, and musicians, flutes poised in feather-light fingers, wove a delicate prelude into the air.

It was meant to be a banquet celebrating the descent of an immortal.

Yet the hall was heavy with unease.

Across the ranks of ministers, expressions shifted—anticipation in some, suspicion in others, but all waiting for the same thing:

the appearance of the so-called celestial being.

She did not appear.

Not until the third quarter past midday did a solitary figure step through the great doors of the hall.

Du Shao entered dressed in deep black court robes, a golden coronet binding his dark hair.

A thin aura of cold seemed to follow him, as if night clung to his shoulders even beneath the blazing palace lamps.

He brought no attendants.

And—most strikingly—he brought no trace of the immortal girl the rumours had promised.

The entire hall stirred.

Soft murmurs broke out between ranks like ripples across a still pond.

From the Dragon Throne, the Emperor's gaze darkened.

"Shao…my son…," he said, his voice low with displeasure, "where is the immortal?"

Du Shao walked to the centre of the hall, bowed with impeccable form, and spoke in a voice clear, resonant, yet impossibly steady.

"Your Majesty—

the immortal does not exist."

Those six words crashed into the court as through a stone hurled into a lake of glass.

The hall erupted.

"What does the prince mean by this?! His statements earlier—"

"But even the Grand Preceptor confirmed her presence—does His Highness imply that the Grand Preceptor—"

"Silence!"

The Emperor's jade ruyi slammed against the throne with a thunderclap.

"Du Shao, do you understand the weight of what you say?!"

Du Shao's expression did not waver. His eyes were the stillness of deep water.

"She exists, yes—but she is merely a mortal woman, without divine power.

The tale of an immortal was fabricated. Entirely.

It has no bearing on the truth."

His words carried through the hall, calm yet devastating.

"It was a ruse Your Son devised together with the Grand Preceptor, Yue Liuchuan.

A fabrication born of necessity—

and unrelated to state affairs beyond its intended purpose."

The Emperor shot to his feet, fury gathering like a storm.

"You say *what*?!"

Du Shao continued, unflinching.

"Our intent was never more than to agitate the court and upend the succession, provoking the Crown Prince to act before he was ready. For this offense, I am guilty and submit to your will."

A hush fell.

Not a single minister dared exhale too loudly.

The Grand Preceptor had not yet arrived.

The whole court waited, taut with dread.

Suddenly, Crown Prince Du Jing rose to his feet, voice sharp as a drawn blade.

"Outrageous! To seize the throne, you dare invent divine omens, deceive the Emperor, and tarnish the Grand Preceptor's name—

you dare?!"

The Emperor's glare was winter incarnate.

"Guards—seize Du Shao at once. Summon Yue Liuchuan!"

Spearmen rushed forward, armour clattering.

Du Shao did not step aside.

Instead—

he laughed.

A soft, crystalline laugh, cold as falling snow.

"Father," he said, "from the day you ordered me to the frontier of LiangZhou, I understood this ending.

If we succeeded, good.

If not—death awaited.

Knowing there was no retreat, why would Your Son regret anything?"

A chill swept through the officials like a ghost slipping past their ranks.

Some officials bowed with their heads lowered, their breaths unsteady as though afraid the air itself might shatter. Others kept their eyes wide open, watching the shifting currents of power with a calculating stillness. A few retreated by half a step, their trailing robes brushing quietly across the stone floor, the soft scrape sounding far too loud within the suffocating hush of the hall.

Amid that vast and heavy silence, Du Shao remained kneeling before the throne. His court robes fanned across the polished tiles as he lifted his head to meet the gaze of the ruler seated high above.

When he spoke, his voice was quiet, yet it carried clearly to even the farthest pillars of the Golden Hall.

"Since Father places faith in immortals… does Father also believe in reincarnation?"

The Emperor's brows drew together.

"What riddles are these?"

Du Shao's expression remained impassive, carved from stone.

"If reincarnation exists…then Your Son must ask—in the next life, or in the true Heavenly Realm, when Mother looks down from above…"

His voice softened, turning heavy—darker.

"With what face will Father meet her?"

A silence so deep it felt like the world stopped rotating swallowed the hall.

The musicians had long ceased.

The ministers dared not breathe.

Even the incense smoke seemed to freeze mid-air.

Du Shao's final words dropped as if a blade:

"Will Father meet her as the Son of Heaven—or as the man who wronged her for a lifetime?"

He bowed deeply, forehead touching the cold stone.

"Your Son has committed sins. But answer me this, Father—was Mother guilty of anything?"

His question cleaved through the palace like lightning through an old, unspoken wound, splitting open years of silence, years of truth buried under imperial edicts and the weight of a throne.

For one suspended moment, Du Shao stood alone in that vast hall—a single man daring to confront both empire and destiny.

Chapter 43: If My Life Is The Price

Du Shao's expression was solemn, almost desolate, and when he spoke, his voice struck the air like polished jade—clear, ringing, and merciless in its accusations.

"Twenty years ago," he began, "the Noble Consort was framed—accused of conspiring with traitors and condemned to die in disgrace. She took her own life beneath that weight of slander. In truth, it was nothing but a convenient purge. Someone used the chaos to eliminate rivals and destroy the loyal."

A breathless stir rippled through the ministers.

"The dying words of an old eunuch," Du Shao continued, "revealed where the truth was hidden. Evidence lies within the sealed chamber of the Cold Palace. Your Son was too weak to overturn the injustice. All I could do was stake my life, set this plan in motion, and drag the truth into the light."

A faint twitch pulled at the corner of the Emperor's eye.

Beneath his sleeve, his fingers dug into the carved armrest with a tension impossible to hide—yet his face remained ironed flat, emotionless as cast metal.

"I knelt three times and kowtowed nine," Du Shao said, voice rising with a raw and terrible strength. "I begged for a retrial. I pleaded for justice. But Father rebuked me—saying the honour of the imperial house must not be stained."

He laughed then—quiet, hoarse, almost broken.

"Honor?" He lifted his gaze. "If honour demands silence, then I would gladly carve today's truth in blood: *The Noble Consort was innocent. Your Son has no regrets.*"

He said no more.

But the question he had already posed—sharp, merciless, unyielding—had frozen the entire court into a palace of ice.

As his eyes lowered, another world surged into his mind.

A snow-choked night, more than a decade ago.

He was only seven.

Dragged out of the warm chambers, forced to kneel on the jade steps as frost climbed up his tiny legs.

Just one door away—his mother's breath was fading.

The hall doors slammed shut.

The eunuchs barred him.

He could only press his cheek against the narrow gap and listen to her final sigh seep into the cold.

Since that night, the same dream had returned to him again and again:

His mother sitting beneath the flickering oil lamp in the Cold Palace, her once-elegant robes in tatters, her fingers trembling as they closed around his small hand.

"My son, Shao, do not weep... One day you will grow. One day, you must clear Mother's name..."

He always woke with his face wet.

Now—

he no longer woke from that dream.

Because there was nothing left in him to wake.

If this gilded palace was built on sins and blood,

he would gladly become the blade that shattered its foundations, so the world could finally see whose crimes were buried beneath its stones.

Shock rippled across the court.

The Crown Prince went rigid, his face draining of colour then flushing a violent shade.

The Emperor's expression solidified into iron.

Du Shao's next words rang like struck metal:

"My heart is not set on the throne. I seek only justice for my mother. If my life is the price, Your Son does not hesitate."

Silence engulfed the hall, thick as frost descending a thousand fathoms.

A banquet meant to welcome an immortal had become a tribunal.

And the man standing at the foot of the golden steps, unbowed, unafraid, was a lone wolf advancing through a blizzard, leaving footprints of defiance in the snow.

As Du Shao's final words faded, even the lantern flames seemed to falter, strangled by the cold.

The Emperor's knuckles whitened as he pressed down on the jade ruyi, the tension causing a faint crackling sound to whisper through the hall.

For a single heartbeat, a flicker of pain crossed his gaze—

but it was swiftly crushed beneath the crushing weight of imperial dignity.

To the Emperor's left, the Crown Prince grew stiff as stone.

His complexion shifted from pale to a sickly blue-green.

The crease between his brows tightened sharply.

Veins stood out along the back of his hand.

The folding fan hidden in his sleeve began to splinter under the force of his grip.

* * * * *

When Yue Liuchuan entered the Purple Dawn Hall, the air inside was already so cold it felt as though frost might crystallize in midair.

His steps were unhurried—measured, graceful, almost disdainfully calm. Snow flecked the edges of his blue robes, melting slowly into darkened threads as he crossed the threshold.

His gaze swept over the hall, grazing briefly across the young man kneeling alone at the foot of the golden steps.

His lips moved by a fraction.

"Fool."

Only he heard it.

A murmur too soft for any mortal ear, carrying with it the weary scorn of someone evaluating a chess piece he had painstakingly raised for years— only to watch it make an unsanctioned move that unravelled the entire game.

Or perhaps it was irritation, sharp and sour, at a grand design collapsing before its final checkmate and he should have been above this.

He—the Grand Preceptor whom all realms, mortal and celestial, whispered about with awe.

The man whose strategies spanned worlds, whose mind could weave destinies.

Yet at this moment, all he felt was a breath lodged in his chest, a suffocating heaviness with no outlet.

His spiritual sense swept across the entirety of Purple Dawn Hall in a single breath.

Not a single heartbeat escaped his notice. He felt the faltering breaths of the ministers, the simmering fury coiling beneath the Emperor's stillness, and the Crown Prince's sharpened intent that hovered like a drawn blade.

Even the long-buried stench of that Cold Palace scandal—sealed away for decades—seemed to rise again, loosened by the mere shape of Du Shao's question.

None of this was part of the plan.

Du Shao should never have spoken those words.

He should not have torn open the board.

He should not have laid bare the entire design.

A flicker of impatience—and contempt—passed through Yue Liuchuan's eyes.

He advanced, each step measured, indifferent to the horrified gazes of the ministers.

When he finally stopped, he bowed in flawless court etiquette.

"Your servant greets Your Majesty."

The Emperor let out a humourless laugh, one edged with ice and rage.

"Yue Qing, how impressive! You dare conspire with a prince of my bloodline—setting schemes under my very nose. Do you even comprehend the crime of deceiving the Son of Heaven?!"

Yue Liuchuan did not answer.

Instead, his gaze slid back toward Du Shao.

The young man still knelt where he had been—back straight as a pine, eyes fixed forward, utterly unshaken. As if he neither feared blame nor betrayal. As if he had severed all paths of retreat long before stepping into this hall.

"For a woman," Yue Liuchuan murmured, so soft that only the nearest few might have sensed the movement of his lips, "you destroyed my entire layout… and severed your escape."

His mouth curved—not in amusement but in a razor-thin, mocking line.

"Du Shao, Du Shao… you truly disappoint me."

His gaze chilled, depths turning glacial.

"I intended to use your princely status to pry open the world's power balance. To force the Immortal Realm to reveal itself openly. And now? You've overturned the entire board."

But before he could continue—

A pressure surged.

Sudden.

Silent.

Devastating.

Like a bolt of lightning dropping into the hall without thunder, a spiritual force of impossible purity and sharpness.

Yue Liuchuan's pupils contracted.

His fingers twitched inside his sleeve, quickly forming three consecutive seals, erecting triple-layered spiritual barriers in rapid succession. Only then did he manage—barely—to blunt the impact aimed straight for his core.

He lifted his head sharply, staring toward the entrance of the hall.

And for the first time that night, his heart lurched, a violent, unmistakable jolt.

A spiritual aura descended from the heavens—cold, searing, merciless, as though the blade of a sword forged in the highest sky, plummeting through clouds and atmosphere to spear itself into the mortal palace.

The very air within Purple Dawn Hall constricted.

Incense smoke froze mid-spiral.

Lantern flames bent low, as if bowing.

That was not the aura of a minor immortal.

Not even close.

It was—

Yue Liuchuan's head snapped toward the side, his eyes darkening to the color of deep, starless water. A warning bell shrieked through his mind.

Impossible.

How could it be him?!

That aura settled over the hall like a frost meant to pierce bone. It was cold, immeasurably vast, a presence that seemed to span heaven and earth until even the pillars themselves felt compelled to bow. And it matched—down to its chilling precision—the memory Yue Liuchuan had spent years burying: the silhouette of a man standing upon the ninety-nine steps of the Ninth Heaven, his sword raised against ten thousand demons, his sheer presence enough to split the firmament.

Outside the Purple Dawn Hall, wind and thunder collided as black clouds churned violently across the sky. From within that roiling tempest, a single white-clad figure descended.

His face had not yet come into view, yet his sword-intent struck first—a piercing, immaculate tide of cold that crashed into the spirit like a thousand mountains falling at once.

Yu Sord had arrived.

The instant his aura crossed the threshold, the ministers' complexions drained to white.

Even those who did not know his name felt their bodies react on instinct—knees giving way, foreheads lowering toward the floor, hearts quailing before something far beyond mortal comprehension.

Terror was carved into the soul long before thought could form.

Yue Liuchuan stood at the lower steps, and whatever composure he carried earlier had already shattered.

His gaze fixed on the entrance where that white silhouette gathered into clarity. His throat tightened.

Within his sleeve, his fingers shaped the beginnings of a seal—only for him to realize, with a jolt of horror, that his spiritual energy had been suppressed. Locked. Frozen. Caged.

He had sealed the heavens themselves.

The realization barely had time to settle before Yue Liuchuan's eyes hardened.

With a sharp flick of his sleeve, something flew forth—a bead no larger than a thumb joint, milky white and translucent, its core threaded with wavering strands of gold.

The moment it left his hand, the air warped violently, as though space itself recoiled.

Thunder cracked.

Space distorted as if a jagged tear had ripped across it.

A blinding white radiance surged out, coiling into a storm that flung waves of spiritual wind outward.

"Not good!"

The old eunuch before the Emperor shouted, rushing forward to shield the sovereign—

only for his vision to warp and shatter as water under a thrown stone.

In that instant, all within the hall saw nothing but flashing white.

A blink later—

Yue Liuchuan's body blurred.

No—dissolved.

His form thinned into a fading wisp, a drifting afterimage falling soundlessly to the polished floor.

Yu Sord had not moved.

He merely lifted an eyebrow.

"…A Phantom-Escape Pearl."

His tone was placid, without surprise—almost bored.

As though he had expected Yue Liuchuan to flee from the moment he appeared.

Wind halted.

The storm of spiritual mist peeled away.

Light returned, sharp and crystalline—

And space shifted.

In the span of a heartbeat, the two men—pursuer and fugitive—were no longer in the palace,

but standing upon the jagged summit of a remote mountain range.

Fog roiled beneath them in endless tides.

A stone platform jutted out from the peak—ancient, cracked, its surface coiled with dried, withered vines.

It resembled an altar suspended above the void.

Yue Liuchuan's form materialized there, stumbling a half-step.

His complexion had turned ghostly pale.

A metallic taste surged up his throat; he swallowed the spiritual blood back down with effort so violent it twisted his features.

He spun toward the emptiness behind him—

toward the presence he could feel, sharp as a blade pressed to the spine.

His voice was hoarse, laced with rage and the remnants of fear.

"You were waiting for me."

The moment the words left Yue Liuchuan's lips, a current of wind swept across the mountaintop—thin, sharp, carrying the delicate sting of drifting snow.

From the folds of cloud and mist, a figure in white emerged.

He did not brandish his sword; he did not need to.

His sword-intent arrived first—pure frost, absolute and solitary, pressing upon the world like the weight of a thousand ancient peaks.

Yu Sord stepped into full view, standing ten paces before him.

His expression was cold—cold in the manner of the moment frost first blooms upon stone.

"You knew," he said, voice as quiet as distant thunder, "that the moment you touched an immortal… your retreat was gone."

Yue Liuchuan let out a short, derisive laugh.

"How amusing. I was unaware the illustrious *Jieming Immortal Lord* had taken it upon himself to manage such trivial affairs."

A faint shift flickered across Yu Sord's eyes, not anger, not surprise.

Merely a shadow passing beneath still water.

He did not answer.

He simply lifted his hand.

In his palm materialized a long sword—plain, unadorned, no engravings or jewels,

yet it radiated an ancient, glacial force as if it were forged from the deepest strata of primordial ice.

The instant the **Flowlight Sword** appeared, the air trembled.

Sword-qi rippled outward, silver radiance spilling as liquid light.

Yue Liuchuan scoffed and swept his arm back.

A black iron mirror snapped into existence behind him—its surface webbed with fractures, gleaming faintly with the pale shimmer of a dying moon.

Within its cracked reflection, a thousand distorted soul-shadows writhed in silence.

A muscle twitched between Yu Sord's brows, yet his voice remained tranquil—ice atop a frozen lake.

"Speak. What is your purpose?"

Yue Liuchuan's stance did not waver.

He lifted his chin slightly—no longer wearing the courtly pretence he donned in the mortal palace,

but revealing a raw, unfiltered madness.

He laughed once—low, soft, curling through the mist like a strand of ghostly incense.

"You've already guessed it, haven't you?"

He stepped forward, shadows of the clouds rippling beneath his feet.

"I orchestrated everything.

I used the mortal prince, Du Shao—nudged him into the turbulence of succession, groomed him to ascend the throne.

And then—"

He paused.

His voice dropped into something sharp enough to cut flesh.

"—then I would raze the Dao itself.

Crush the Buddhas.

Kill the heavens…

and slay the gods."

Yu Sord's composure cracked—barely, yet visibly.

Energy stirred around him, restless, dangerous.

Destroy the Dao?

Exterminate the heavens?

To even speak such words was blasphemy across realms.

Yue Liuchuan's gaze gleamed with dark satisfaction, and he continued in a tone so soft it chilled:

"I was once a disciple of the Heavenly Way. Robe of hemp, heart like the moon, reciting the scriptures. I believed myself righteous." A thin smile carved across his lips.

"And what did it come to?"

He advanced another step.

"My venerable master, high and pure upon his lotus dais,

accused me of stealing a sacred relic—

to protect his useless son.

A single decree cast me out, stripped me of everything."

His voice twisted, spiraling into a cracked mockery of a laugh.

"Tell me—do these immortals possess even a shred of justice?"

He lifted his arms slightly, as if addressing the heavens.

"I knelt beneath the lotus platform for three days and three nights and my blood stained the floor. He did not spare me even a glance."His fingers curled, trembling.

"That was when I understood 'Dao' and 'Divinity' are nothing but shackles to tame the obedient." Yu Sord lowered his gaze. When he spoke, his voice was like water dripping from a glacial cliff—slow, cold, inexorable.

"And for this… you would drag the immortal realm and mortal world into blood and ruin?"

"What of it?" Yue Liuchuan hissed.

Each word froze the air further.

"If the heavens are heartless, then this world has no need for heavens."

"I want Du Shao to take the throne—not for power, not out of gratitude,

but so he can wield imperial authority to destroy the Dao itself.

To burn temples, shatter scriptures,

seal the mountains and sever the spirit veins."

He smiled—wide, unhinged.

"When that day comes, your Lingxiao Sect—and every sect under heaven—will become a laughingstock for mortals, that will be justice." Yu Sord's eyes lowered, and the tip of his sword brushed the earth.

Grass beneath it froze instantly, fracturing into brittle shards.

"You are mistaken," he said softly.

"You cannot destroy the Dao.

You will only destroy yourself."

Yue Liuchuan's laughter rose—wild, jagged, echoing off the cliffs.

"Then try me, Yu Sord. You can guard the mortal world. But you cannot guard the hearts of men." Yu Sord lifted his head, the motion gentle as snow falling into still water.

Though his sword remained unmoving, his voice carried a piercing clarity like moonlight on a frozen lake.

"The Dao does not rest upon golden statues or lotus thrones. It lives in the heart. When the heart is upright, the Dao endures." He paused.

The air around him stilled.

"You may burn the temples and tear the scriptures. But you cannot extinguish the light born in the hearts of living beings."

Another breath.

Then his eyes met Yue Liuchuan's directly, and his tone deepened, weighted by something solemn… and heartbreakingly gentle.

"You say I cannot guard the hearts of men." His voice dropped low and soft, but resonant as a sword drawn from its sheath.

"Yet even if only one heart remains faithful to the true path…then for that one heart, I will guard both heart and Dao."

Those three words—"that one heart"—were barely louder than a whisper,

yet they fell into the space between them

like a blade touching a trembling string.

For an instant, the entire mountaintop froze.

The Flowlight Sword hummed faintly, resonating with the chill in the air.

Even the heavens seemed to hold their breath for this inevitable, inescapable reckoning between two fates intertwined by betrayal, ideals, and the remnants of a shattered past.

Chapter 44: The Demonic Intervention

"Enough," Yu Sord said, his voice quiet yet carrying the immense, crushing weight of midwinter.

"Submit yourself. Come with me back to Celestial Xuandome Hall… and stand trial."

His tone did not rise a single note. His blade did not tremble. The very tip of the Flowlight Sword touched the fractured stone beneath them with a crystalline chime, and a tide of absolute cold swept outwards like severe frost reclaiming the desolate land.

Yue Liuchuan's face was utterly ashen, a thin trail of blood tracing from the corner of his mouth—yet he began to laugh.

He laughed, hollow and fractured, akin to the despairing sound of a man standing precariously at the very edge of the abyss with absolutely nothing consequential left to lose.

"Impossible. Kill me, Yu Sord."

He staggered backward another step, his robes snagging and ripping against the jagged stone, his voice hoarse yet unyielding in its final defiance.

"I would rather have my soul torn apart and scattered to the four winds… than return to that filthy, polluted place."

The final word had barely fallen when he suddenly surged forward with a desperate lunge.

With a roar that tore viciously through the heavy mist, Yue Liuchuan drew his own blade. A cloud of murky, crimson sword-*qi* violently exploded outwards, instantly shattering the surrounding spiritual currents. Though grievously wounded, his strike carried the sheer, frantic ferocity of a doomed comet, desperate in its final trajectory to drag Yu Sord into a state of mutual ruin.

Yu Sord did not so much as flinch.

His expression remained unchanged by the threat.

He simply lifted his hand—a light, seemingly effortless gesture—and the Flowlight Sword slid horizontally across his body, a single silent, crystalline movement that neatly cleaved Yue Liuchuan's lethal killing intent cleanly in half.

Steel savagely collided with steel.

The impact detonated a massive wave of force that surged through the sky.

The wind shrieked like a banshee as sword-light tore through the very fabric of the air. The two figures crossed paths again and again, each collision sending powerful, systemic shockwaves rippling across the precarious mountaintop.

Yue Liuchuan's movements were frantic, utterly unhinged, and soaked in cold bloodlust—the sputtering final defiance of a dying torch against the encroaching night.

Yu Sord, by contrast, stood in the unshakeable, perfectly calm centre of every storm. His swordsmanship flowed like inexorable water, unhurried yet absolute, guiding Yue Liuchuan step by calculated step… toward a final, inevitable defeat.

At last, Yu Sord delivered a direct, calculated blow—a concentrated burst of spiritual force that struck squarely against Yue Liuchuan's already ravaged meridians.

A sharp, audible crack rang out.

Blood sprayed through the air like a sudden scarlet rain.

Yue Liuchuan was flung backward, his body smashing hard into the shattered remains of an ancient Buddha statue.

Stone splintered loudly. Dust erupted everywhere.

He collapsed heavily to his knees amidst the rubble, gasping like a dying beast, his eyes bloodshot yet still—still refusing to bow his head.

Yu Sord approached him with slow, deliberate steps.

The Flowlight Sword remained drawn, its cold, silent light gathering like the profound breath of midwinter nights.

"This ends here, Yue Liuchuan."

He raised his blade—each step deliberate, precise, unhurried, and heavy with the absolute certainty of finality.

And then—

Heaven and earth shuddered.

The air around them trembled violently.

The mist convulsed abruptly as a strange, devouring force erupted from the void; a tear in space split open like a fresh, hideous wound.

From within surged a thick, ominous wave of demonic energy, crackling fiercely with crimson lightning.

A voice cut through the ensuing chaos.

"—Stop."

The sound arrived seconds after the figure.

A streak of rich red plunged down in the manner of a blazing meteor. Crimson robes flared dramatically. Black demonic flames curled possessively around a tall silhouette.

The moment his boots touched the ground, the very weight of the battlefield shifted—the ambient pressure dropped, violently, as if someone had pressed a colossal hand against the very sky itself.

Mo Han had arrived.

With a casual, almost bored motion of his fingers, he summoned a blade—a blood-forged arc that materialised in midair, halting Yu Sord's descending sword with a thunderous clash that echoed across the peaks.

Demonic *qi* surged upward, twisting like a living storm, instantly shielding Yue Liuchuan behind his back.

The collision of their forces sent tearing ripples through the mountain mist.

Yu Sord's advance halted abruptly.

His sword hovered in the air, mere inches from crossing into the destructive radius of Mo Han's devouring aura.

He lifted his gaze, his brows knitting together for the very first time.

"What are you doing here?"

Mo Han cast Yu Sord a single, glacial glance—a look sharp enough to slice cleanly through the mist still trembling in the air.

"Saving him," he said.

Just two words, low and steady, as if they inherently weighed more than a thousand arguments.

He offered no further explanation. With a sweeping motion of his crimson sleeve, demonic winds coiled outward like living flame, lifting Yue Liuchuan's half-kneeling form cleanly off the ground.

The disgraced immortal tried to speak—tried to protest the interference—but Mo Han's hand pressed firmly onto his shoulder, silencing him completely without the need for a single word.

Yu Sord's gaze darkened, frost tightening in the profound depths of his eyes.

He moved in a single flash—a streak of white lightning cutting downward as the Flowlight Sword met air, aimed straight toward Mo Han's heart.

"If this immortal recalls correctly," Yu Sord said, his voice like a blade sheathed in ice, "this man is not a subject of your demon realm."

"And more importantly—he has deliberately orchestrated chaos in the mortal world. His crimes are beyond any hope of forgiveness."

Mo Han raised a mocking, lazy, and dangerously elegant brow.

"And what of it?"

His tone was light, almost offensively bored.

"This prince wishes to save him. That alone is reason enough. I require no other justification."

Demonic power roared to life around him, a surging darkness thick as midnight, rolling in turbulent waves behind his back.

The blood-forged blade in his hand whipped horizontally, meeting the Flowlight Sword head-on.

The collision detonated like thunder splitting a mountain in half.

Gale winds tore the clouds apart.

Two unmatched forces — the righteous heavens' sword and the demon crown prince's infernal might — collided without restraint.

For a moment, neither yielded ground. Silver light clashed with seething crimson flame, weaving through the air as though two opposing comets were locked in violent, fatal orbit.

The sky visibly dimmed. The mountain trembled. The world itself seemed to pull back in utter dread as their opposing wills tore at existence.

Strike after strike, the two exchanged blows—each impact carving new, permanent scars into the stone underfoot, shredding the wind, splitting the clouds, and warping the very air around them.

Then, finally—they broke abruptly apart.

Both combatants were forced several paces back.

Yu Sord's boots touched the ground in a whisper of frost. He steadied instantly, sword angled downward, his robes settling around him like falling snow. Not a single breath betrayed any hint of exhaustion.

Mo Han slid half a step back, positioning himself squarely in front of Yue Liuchuan. He wiped a smear of blood from his lip with the back of his hand and let out a short, derisive laugh.

"What's wrong?" he taunted, his voice low. "Already tired?"

Yu Sord said nothing, but the look he cast Mo Han was sharper than honed steel—containing no discernible rage, only the coldest and most unyielding resolve.

"The demon crown prince," he murmured, his voice sounding like a blade meeting stone, "truly, your reputation is not exaggerated."

Mo Han returned the remark without blinking.

"Likewise. The Immortal Realm's First Sword—Secluded Bright Immortal—lives up to his rather impressive name."

Behind him, Yue Liuchuan let out a breathless, broken laugh—half-mad, half-exultant. Cornered on all sides yet still impossibly alive, he spat his scorn toward the heavens.

"You righteous cultivators love to preach," he rasped. "Always talking of virtue, compassion, and the inherent suffering of mortals… Tell me— which of you has ever truly remembered the hardships of the people below?"

Yu Sord was silent for a prolonged moment.

Then—slowly—he lowered his blade, but his eyes remained immovably fixed on Mo Han.

"Leave him," he said quietly. "Otherwise… I will no longer hold back any power."

Mo Han's answer was a cold, unwavering snarl:

"Impossible. Which means this prince has no choice but to accompany you—to the very end."

The mountain suddenly stilled. The wind stopped. Even the clouds above seemed suspended in a breathless, terrified wait.

It was the kind of silence that sat precariously on a blade's edge—one wrong motion would inevitably spill blood across the sky.

Then—

A ripple of divine will tore through the clouds high above.

A golden talisman streaked across the heavens like a falling star, descending straight into Yu Sord's sleeve.

He glanced down at it, and for the first time since Mo Han's arrival… his expression shifted.

A profound shadow flickered across his eyes.

He sheathed his sword.

Without another word, without so much as a backward look, he turned and strode away—his voice echoing through the fractured air such as the crack of splitting winter ice:

"See to your own consequences."

White light surged, red light instantly recoiled.

Two figures—one demonic flame, one celestial frost—parted ways through the storm of drifting mist.

And thus, upon the desolate mountain peak, a confrontation meant to shake the realms fell abruptly silent, leaving only the soundless echo of wind sweeping over the shattered stone.

* * * * *

Moonlight hung precariously at the tips of the forest canopy, a pale, shivering arc suspended over the brittle branches.

The pungent scent of heavy demonic energy had not yet faded from the air.

A streak of deep crimson sliced through the woods like a gust of severed wind.

Mo Han's figure descended upon the desolate northern grove—the Broken Forest of Yanbei—where dead, skeletal trees leaned akin to fractured ribs against the cold night.

The fallen leaves rustled with palpable unease.

Behind a curtain of withered vines lay a half-collapsed stone grotto built around an ancient, forgotten well. Firelight flickered weakly within, revealing the cracked, moss-rimmed mouth of the old stone structure.

Mo Han tossed Yue Liuchuan harshly against the stone wall beside the well; the impact was dull and heavy.

Turning his sleeve, he summoned a spark. A ghostly red flame burst into life, spreading across the cavern like living embers and illuminating the darkness in pulses of blood-coloured light.

Yue Liuchuan slumped against the wall, breathing raggedly. His face was white as bone, yet when he wiped the blood from his lips, a crooked, mocking smile lifted the edge of his mouth.

"Why save me, exactly?"

Mo Han set the demonic fire in place. His crimson robes clung to him, soaked through with Yue Liuchuan's own blood; droplets hit the ground and hissed faintly where they met his turbulent aura.

In the wavering glow, his features were hewn sharp and cold as if carved from obsidian.

"What this crown prince chooses to do," he said flatly, "requires no commentary from you."

Yue Liuchuan let out a low, broken, hoarse, and probing laugh.

"The world moves only for profit. Even the demon crown prince would not soil his own hands for nothing. I refuse to believe that you—"

He didn't finish the thought.

The entire stone chamber froze instantaneously.

A suffocating, intense killing intent sealed the air shut. Silence thickened like ice forming rapidly on a pond.

Only the crackle of the demonic flame broke the stillness.

Mo Han lifted his gaze.

A glint of scarlet ignited in his eyes—razor sharp, piercing straight into the very soul.

"You speak far too much," he said, his voice dripping with frost.

"I may have saved you—but I can change my mind at any given moment… and kill you where you sit."

A bolt of agony shot through Yue Liuchuan's chest; fresh blood split from his barely-mended wounds. Under that chilling gaze, his remaining words died soundlessly in his throat.

Without another glance, Mo Han flicked his sleeve.

Something clattered onto the stone floor between them. A black jade vial lay there, etched with dormant demonic sigils that slithered faintly beneath the surface.

"Three days," Mo Han said. "With this, you will recover. I require you to remain—temporarily—alive."

Yue Liuchuan picked up the vial, his eyes cold and bitter as winter water.

"So that's it?" he sneered softly. "Your puppet now?"

Mo Han's expression didn't shift a fraction. His voice was akin to night wind rushing through sand—quiet, but sharp enough to cut.

"If you wish to die, you may. Anytime."

A brief pause.

"But not before you've served the purpose I have specifically for you."

He turned to leave.

Behind him, Yue Liuchuan's voice rasped through clenched teeth—injured, but still edged with defiance.

"So, the mighty crown prince of the Demon Realm… truly needs someone as low as me?"

Mo Han's steps halted—barely perceptibly.

His back remained to him, his shadow long against the stone. His voice drifted out, soft as a blade slipping between ribs:

"One more word, and I will end you now."

No hesitation. No warmth.

He vanished into the consuming night without another backward look. Crimson robes swept through the darkness, his demonic aura folding seamlessly into the vast, turbulent night.

Yue Liuchuan stared after that departing silhouette, his lips curling into a thin, humourless smirk.

* * * * *

The Celestial Mirror, rimmed in cherry-pink tassels, shimmered faintly. Gold-white light rippled across its surface like the breath of a waking star, revealing a scene deep within the imperial palace.

Three small heads were currently pressed together in front of the mirror—so close their noses were nearly touching the surface.

All three stared unblinking, solemn as little sages… and looking absolutely ridiculous clustered together like a knot of highly agitated gossips.

"Aiya! Would you look at that!" Moony suddenly yelped, her voice hopping as if she had stepped on a stray branch.

"No wonder that silly prince said he wanted to take me on a palace tour yesterday! And what happened, hmm? Instead of sightseeing, he went in to hand-deliver his own execution!"

Within the mirror's rippling glow—

Du Shao was kneeling on one knee in the Golden Throne Hall, speaking in open court. The hall was tense as a bowstring. The emperor on the dragon throne was red with rage, ministers stiff and pale, and Du Shao—calm and resolute—was openly denouncing the old injustice of the imperial harem.

All three girls froze.

Silence.

Slow blinking.

Very slow inhaling.

"You mean… he's just—" Lili widened her eyes, lifted a hand, and slashed it across her own neck in a very unsubtle, theatrical gesture.

"Mhm!" Moony nodded vigorously and proceeded to spill every detail Du Shao had told her—his plans, his request for her help, every single detail—all delivered with dramatic hand gestures and sparkling eyes as if she were narrating the most thrilling opera of the century.

"So this mortal prince begged you—you, a supposed immortal—to help him win the succession, all to avenge his mother…" Yara concluded softly, her voice flat but her brows faintly knit. "…yet now he has abandoned the plan entirely and exposed himself?"

Moony nodded harder.

Yun Yara continued staring at the mirror, her voice perfectly level.

"Weren't we just trying to see where he was, so we could scout out that so-called 'other cultivator'? What is the point of watching now? He's already marching himself straight into a trap inside the imperial palace!"

Her tone remained calm, but there was no mistaking the sheer gravity beneath.

"Not everyone can simply walk into the Golden Throne Hall and denounce the Emperor. This action is… extremely unusual."

Lili's heart clenched with alarm. She blurted, "If only Yu Sord were still here… why did he suddenly disappear?"

Moony shrugged helplessly, palms up.

"Even if he were here, it's not like he could save Du Shao. The palace is far from here. By the time we rush over—well, the flowers on his grave would already be wilted."

"…That's true," Lili nodded rapidly, grave and defeated in equal measure.

Moony pouted, folding her arms, still fuming about Du Shao's "voluntary execution."

Lili, however, slowly turned her head toward her—eyes narrowing with a look so strange that Moony instantly felt the back of her neck prickle.

"Miss… why are you looking at me such as that…?"

Moony edged half a step back, spooked by the intensity of her stare.

Lili leaned in, her voice dripping with meaning, her tone rising knowingly: "Moony… you and that mortal prince… is there something going on between you two? Don't lie to me."

"What—what?!" Moony almost choked on her own spit. "There's nothing going on! Don't you talk such nonsense!"

"Oh really?" Lili folded her arms, indignant as if she were the one being cheated on. "We all saw it in the Celestial Mirror! The way you two walked together—honestly, it looked exactly like you were on a honeymoon. You were smiling like spring peach blossoms!"

Yara turned her head slightly, her voice utterly calm as she delivered the fatal, understated blow:

"And the hand-holding."

"That—that was because he said there were bad people around! And that if there were too many people, I might get lost—he dragged me, okay?! Dragged!" Moony flailed both hands in protest, her eyes going red at the corners from sheer indignation. "I was obviously working for the immortal realm—investigating that mysterious cultivator beside him! I swear on my celestial title—absolutely no personal feelings involved!"

Lili narrowed her eyes, clearly not convinced in the slightest.

"Oh? And what about the tea drinking? The hot springs? The cozy blanket? The candied hawthorns?"

"That was strategy, okay? Strategy! Stop looking at me like that!" Moony covered her face with both hands, as if she wished she could burrow straight into the ground and disappear.

"I've taken note of everything," Lili declared with a prim little huff—though the mischievous smile leaking from her eyes betrayed her teasing intent.

Watching this absurd display, Yara spoke quietly:

"If you truly felt nothing, why are you panicking this much over his fate?"

"I—I'm just angry he rushed off on his own! His brain is so simple it rattles, that's all. It has nothing to do with me…" Moony's voice grew smaller and smaller, until the last syllables practically hid inside her sleeves.

Finally satisfied, Lili patted her shoulder with the air of an elder fairy dispensing life wisdom. "All right, fine—we'll believe you this time. But honestly, that prince is in deep, deep trouble now. We'd better move quickly."

Suddenly, a spark lit in her eyes—as if a heavenly secret had just struck her brain. She slapped her own sleeve so abruptly that Moony nearly jumped out of her skin.

"I've got it!"

"What?" the other two chorused.

Lili flicked each of them a sharp thump on the forehead.

"What are you imagining? Obviously, I mean I have an idea."

"Miss came up with a plan that fast?" Moony blinked up at her in awe, admiration bursting out of her like miniature fireworks. "My lady is truly brilliant!"

Lili grinned, smug as a fox, and proudly pulled a silver-edged charm slip from her robes—its red sigils gleaming faintly beneath the lamplight.

"The Immortal Realm forbade the use of immortal arts—but they never said anything about talismans."

Her eyes curved into crescents, the smile of a little fox who had successfully found a colossal loophole and was now ready to cause maximum chaos.

Moony clicked her tongue.

"Your brain really does add special effects to the Celestial Mirror."

Yara remained serenely calm, yet for the first time a genuine glimmer of interest stirred in her eyes.

"Talismans aren't restricted… It's possible to bypass the Edicts with that logic."

Moony nodded repeatedly.

"The mortal world has plenty of street magicians selling charms. There's no celestial law against purchasing those!"

"Then let's go." Lili unfurled the talisman, her gaze lifting toward the still-glimmering palace scene within the mirror.

Her expression cooled, sharpening with renewed purpose.

"We're going to bring Moony's little silly prince… back alive."

Chapter 45: Truth-Speaking Incantation activated

The gold-white glow emanating from the Celestial Mirror had not fully receded when the intricate sigils on Yun Lili's talisman detonated in a decisive burst of light.

A sharp, momentary flash—the usual accompanying sound of wind was violently cut out entirely—and in the very next immediate heartbeat, the three girls materialised deep within the expansive palace grounds, standing precisely beside a winding corridor delineated by tall vermilion walls and meticulously neat rows of blue-brick paving stones.

Moony barely had sufficient time to gasp out a delighted, whispered observation of, "Wow, the palace tiles are so astonishingly clean, even in the shadows—"

When several cold, hard, unmistakable flashes of polished steel sliced toward them from all conceivable directions.

"Who goes there—!"

"Stand where you are this instant, do not move!"

"Unauthorised intruders—seize them immediately!"

More than ten blades instantly snapped into position, their honed edges pressed aggressively and menacingly against the girls' respective necks.

This was emphatically not the subtle, heroic entrance they had envisioned; in fact, it proved to be considerably more disastrous than anyone's worst possible expectation.

Yun Lili blinked twice, her face frozen mid-expression. Moony wore an expression that screamed: *I t*

old you the flowers on his grave would be wilted by now, and now we shall be joining him in a thoroughly undignified fashion.

Yun Yara merely drew her brows together, and though she hadn't yet uttered a single syllable, her sheer, formidable presence alone subtly quieted the entire stone path by a perceptible half-breath.

"Sigh… not a single blessed moment of peaceful infiltration, ever, huh?" Lili muttered under her breath, a note of resignation creeping into her tone.

Then, with an air of grim, reckless determination, she reached deeply into her sleeve.

"All right—Tickle Talisman, rise and shine and perform your duties with excessive diligence."

Snap.

A lopsided talisman, its sigils drawn in a distinctly chaotic, almost amateur manner, violently slapped into the air.

Silver sparks exploded outwards immediately, showering the area.

Instantly—

"Wh—why—itch—?! Aaaah!! Merciful Heavens!"

"Not under the arms—NO—NO—help—my back! My waist! What cruel and unusual sorcery is THIS—?!"

"Throw the sword! Throw it THROW IT—okay I was wrong I WAS WRONG—!!"

The palace guards collapsed into a chaotic, flailing, shrieking tangle of limbs. They rolled, writhed, and clawed desperately at every inch of themselves as though a million tiny, fuzzy caterpillars had launched a coordinated, utterly ruthless assault on their collective spines.

Three official belts flew off entirely, adding to the general confusion. Someone lost a boot.

"Go, go, go!" Lili bolted forward, urging them on. "Before they finish being delightfully itchy!"

Yara drew her own sword without a sound, the motion a sleek whisper of steel.

Moony clutched her head and wailed, "Miss! Exactly how many peculiar types of talismans did we bring, specifically?! And why did you choose this deeply humiliating one NOW?!"

"Doesn't matter—speed is absolutely everything right now!" Lili laughed, already whipping out the Celestial Mirror and pouring spiritual energy into it with desperate urgency.

"Du Shao, reveal your exact location to this immortal, immediately and without delay."

The mirror shuddered violently, gold light rippling fast across its surface. Scenes shifted at a dizzying speed until finally—

There he was. Du Shao in the very centre of the Golden Throne Hall, kneeling on one knee, his eyes unflinching, locked in a fierce, public argument.

Above him, the Emperor sat rigid on the dragon throne, his face a veritable thundercloud ready to erupt into full Imperial fury.

"Quick—this way!" Lili barked, sprinting forward while following the shifting light within the Celestial Mirror.

She darted left, cut sharply right, and unleashed talisman after talisman along the route, their explosive ripples systematically shattering layers of palace wards and hidden restrictions with loud, cracking bursts of light.

At last, just as the three reached the final flight of polished marble steps before the grand hall, a cold, imperious command echoed from within— deep, authoritative, and utterly merciless:

"Guards—drag Du Shao away. Throw him into the Heavenly Dungeon— "

"—STOP RIGHT THERE!"

A bellow, far too coarse and spirited for such a sacred, dignified space, tore through the hall's oppressive air.

Moony burst through the entrance, breathless, her skirts flying behind her like a bright, pink banner of absolute chaos.

Lili and Yara froze mid-step, looking utterly aghast.

Oh no. Oh no no no.

Who taught her that line? Who allowed her to shout that line in such a place?! This is worse than the tickle talisman!

Every gaze in the hall snapped violently toward the doorway.

The guards—those who hadn't been utterly incapacitated earlier—had regrouped and now surged forward, blades drawn once again, surrounding them with a crackling tension that could snap at any moment.

"Let me—let me just see what kind of talismans we have left—" Moony wheezed as she frantically grabbed Lili's embroidered shoulder bag and plunged her hand inside like a desperate gambler searching for his last coin. "Didn't you say pulling out a talisman would stabilize the situation!?"

"I said that—yes—but I also don't know what specific talismans I actually brought!!" Lili wailed, her voice on the verge of outright tears.

But Moony, for all her panic, did not stop rummaging. One sharp yank—

Snap.

A thin talisman edged in pale gold sprang from her hand.

The instant it appeared, its script ignited in midair.

A serene, omnipresent voice—rich, echoing, and profoundly otherworldly—resounded throughout the entire throne hall:

"Truth-Speaking Incantation activated."

"Please voice your most honest, unfiltered inner thoughts."

The voice hung in the air as if the solemn decree of a celestial judge. It even had a holy echo.

The three girls: ",,,..."

The Emperor: "…?"

Du Shao: "…Moony? What on earth are you doing here?"

Lili: "We're doomed."

Yara: "Excellent. I look forward immensely to everyone's absolute honesty."

Moony: "…I would truly like to die now."

Everyone in the hall froze.

Then—

"…In truth," the Emperor announced gravely, with the solemnity of discussing crucial national policy, "this dragon crown is giving me a truly terrible headache."

The entire court: ",,,..."

The content, however, made several key ministers immediately reconsider whether the Son of Heaven had perhaps completely lost his sanity in the last half-hour.

Du Shao's voice followed, soft and raw, slipping out before he could possibly stop the confession:

"…Right now, all I truly want is to hold her."

His eyes—dark, conflicted, and painfully earnest—were fixed immovably upon Moony. That whisper of a confession echoed threefold across the vaulted ceiling, repeating his heart's deepest truth for every single soul in the hall to hear.

"I don't believe he actually has any concrete evidence!"

A senior minister suddenly shrieked—his voice cracking like a terrified rooster at dawn.

The moment the words left his mouth, he froze, staring into the void as if his own soul had physically slapped him across the face.

"I… I cheated in the imperial examinations ten years ago—my father-in-law explicitly leaked me the test answers—aaahhh forgive me, ancestors…"

Another minister's legs buckled entirely. He collapsed to his knees and began sobbing loud, ugly tears.

"I… I like Consort Rong…"

Someone else blurted in a strangled roar of humiliation—then instantly turned beet-red, covered his face with both hands, and sprinted straight out of the throne hall, dignity utterly forgotten.

For a moment——

The entire Golden Throne Hall descended into pure, uncontrollable chaos.

Truths spilled out like tragically overturned water basins, unstoppable and utterly catastrophic.

No one could control their own mouth. Every man looked terrified, their hands flying to their lips in futile attempts to stop the flood—but every syllable kept bursting out as if a confession extracted under severe celestial torture.

"…I didn't want to say I deeply enjoy wearing women's clothing—Heavens help me—I'm finished! I'm finished!!" A certain general hopped in place like a panicked rabbit, his eyes brimming with tears.

"—ENOUGH! All of you—shut your mouths!!" The Emperor roared, but his command had barely touched the air—

Lili had already folded over against Yara's shoulder, laughing so hysterically she nearly lost her balance entirely.

"I—I think I'm about to become a historic criminal—HAHAHAHA—this is glorious—!"

Yara remained outwardly tranquil, but her eyes glimmered with frosty amusement.

"A once-in-a-lifetime court assembly of absolute, unfiltered honesty."

Meanwhile, Moony's face had turned the alarming colour of a fully ripened tomato. One hand clutched Du Shao's sleeve in despair, the other tried desperately—hopelessly—to clamp her own mouth shut.

But the incantation spared no one, not even the perpetrators.

"I did NOT want him to hold my hand! I did NOT get flustered!!" she screamed involuntarily.

As soon as she finished, she looked like she wanted to combust into a firework on the spot and rain down glittery regret across the whole hall. *Damnation. Even they were caught in the Truth-Spell backlash!*

Du Shao blinked, the shock in his eyes softening into something warmer—deeper. A slow, unmistakable smile curved across his mouth.

"…I see," he murmured, his voice low and steady.

"What do you see!? What exactly do you think you 'see'!?" Moony shrieked, half feral, half mortified, wishing she could smash her head straight into the Celestial Mirror and die gloriously.

The throne hall was devolving into a spiritual disaster of catastrophic proportions—a soul-leaking, reputation-obliterating frenzy triggered by a single, poorly chosen talisman.

At that moment, standing near the ceremonial steps, the Crown Prince went pale—then green—then a violent shade of purple as he felt an undeniable truth rising in his throat like a volcanic eruption he could not stop.

"…The truth is—I've never wanted to listen to those tedious old men from the Ministry of Rites," he blurted stiffly. "And—I don't even like the Grand Tutor's daughter…"

The words echoed once—twice—thrice. He looked as if divine lightning had just struck him where he stood. Eyes wide, hands snapping up to cover his mouth, he staggered backward half a step, his mind screaming internally: *I'm dead. I'm dead. I'm dead. I'm absolutely dead—!*

Beside him, the Grand Tutor: ",,,..."

"I— I RESIGN!!" The Grand Tutor spun around, ready to bolt out of the hall. He made it exactly two steps before the spell yanked another confession from his throat:

"To be honest—I've always wanted to marry my daughter to the Third Prince anyway! At least that boy is better-looking than the Crown Prince—if not for the fact His Highness was the future heir—!"

Inside the Golden Throne Hall, the entire imperial court stood collectively petrified. Every minister's expression rippled like an overturned pond—yet each one forced their face stiff, as if holding back critical internal injuries.

One minister muttered under his breath, his voice full of profound grief: "Damn this Truth Spell…"

Another man looked just as if his soul had fled halfway to the underworld. "Did I… did I really just admit I hid silver in Lake Gusu?"

"…Heavens above, please take me now." The seventy-year-old Minister of Revenue dropped straight to his knees and began slapping himself. "Your Majesty, this old minister should not have said you were an incompetent ruler!!"

Du Shao's expression twisted into pure mortification. He opened his mouth, trying desperately to stop himself—but the spell punched another confession straight out of him.

"I don't actually want the throne… I only fear my mother will grieve for me even in the afterlife if I fail to avenge her."

The moment his words fell, the entire hall froze for three full breaths.

Then—

Behind a dragon pillar, Lili had already collapsed in half from uncontrollable laughter. "This—this is like watching the most unhinged, brutally honest palace drama ever filmed— I'm laughing myself to tears—!"

Yara, still propping her sword against the floor, added in a cool, surgical tone: "Outwardly noble, inwardly rotten. Every last one of them."

And in the next instant——

Dozens of officials, princes, royal guards, eunuchs—all reacted with identical panic.

Hands flew to mouths.

Faces went corpse-white.

Every single man wished he could slap himself unconscious with his own boot. The movement was so synchronised it looked rehearsed.

Silence slammed into the hall such as a falling mountain. Only the booming thud of terrified heartbeats echoed under the vaulted ceiling.

"…Surely that session just now doesn't count as legally binding testimony?" The Crown Prince forced a smile so stiff it was nearly a grimace. His molars creaked. "Royal Father, your son was merely bewitched—rambling nonsense under the influence."

The Emperor's face was as black as a scorched iron cauldron. He growled: "If anyone dares mention what happened just now again, I will personally sentence him—to execution of nine generations!"

Just as the absurd disaster of a court assembly spiralled toward full mental breakdown—

Lili sensed danger and slammed her palm onto the Celestial Mirror. "Celestial Mirror—mute the sound! Now!"

The mirror's surface flickered, dimmed, and at last the effects of the Truth Spell gradually dissipated.

Officials slumped over, clutching their chests like survivors of a shipwreck, eyes unfocused, their very spirits forcibly ejected from their bodies. Only the Emperor stood swaying with rage, glaring around the hall.

"You—you lot… what kind of useless creatures has the Son of Heaven raised…?"

"—Protect His Majesty! Guards! GUARDS!!" A eunuch finally snapped back to reality and screeched for reinforcement.

Lili shouted: "RUN!"

Yara had already drawn her sword.

Lili grabbed Moony by the wrist. The three of them spun around and bolted toward the exit. Lili frantically dug through her sleeve pouch for a teleportation talisman—

When Moony suddenly yelped: "Wait!!"

Lili had barely raised the teleportation talisman when Moony suddenly seized Du Shao's sleeve, her fingers tight, her eyes clear yet trembling with urgency.

"Are you coming with me?"

Du Shao paused. His gaze dropped to where her fingertips clutched the edge of his sleeve—a single fragile point of contact between two worlds.

For one breath, he simply looked. Then he exhaled a quiet laugh—soft, warm… yet carrying a gentleness born from absolute resolve.

Moony met that look—and instantly understood. Her voice cracked.

"You… you don't want to leave this?"

"Moony," he murmured, curling his hand around hers in return, "just hearing you say that is enough for me."

There was serenity in his eyes—serenity, and finality.

"But you could cultivate!" Moony pressed, desperation sharpening her tone. "I could guide you. I can pass you spiritual energy—"

Du Shao shook his head. His voice was gentle, but firm as iron beneath velvet.

"My path is not the path of personal ascension. My path is the great road—the road of all under heaven. This land… these suffering common folk…"

He never finished. A deafening shatter exploded from the imperial throne.

The Emperor, in a fury, hurled his wine cup. Porcelain burst like rain against the marble tiles, shards skittering in every direction.

"Cultivate immortality?" he roared. "I'll take it! I want it!"

His glare speared straight toward Du Shao, thunder in his voice. "Shao, my son, since you can ascend the immortal way—why not offer it to Us? I'll trade you this entire throne for it!"

The Crown Prince nearly choked. "Father!"

The Third Prince snorted with poisonous amusement.

"Out. You have no place here," the Emperor snapped at the Crown Prince without even sparing him a look. Then he turned back to Du Shao, and his tone flipped—honey-smooth and coaxing: "Shao, my son… you know about your mother's case… your father regrets it, truly. This cultivation opportunity—why not give it to Father, hmm?"

Du Shao straightened his spine, righteous fire in every syllable.

"If Father truly seeks lasting peace, then first purge the palace of its inner turmoil; ease the people's poverty; strengthen the army and protect the land. Only then… may immortality be discussed."

"You—! Insolent child!" The Emperor's beard bristled with fury; his face went crimson.

But Du Shao didn't yield. He bowed deeply; his voice still filled with solemn respect:

"To pursue immortality while neglecting the state is to crave longevity only to cling to power—it is neither the Great Way, nor the path of a true ruler."

Silence crashed over the hall. No minister dared breathe.

Behind a dragon pillar, Lili whispered under her breath, eyes shining: "…Okay, that's actually kind of handsome."

Yara shifted her sword, her cold gaze sweeping the guards closing in. "He speaks cleanly enough," she remarked, almost approvingly.

Moony's heart was a knot of panic and emotion—then she heard Du Shao speak again, in a tone so soft it reached only her ears.

"I know your heart. That is enough for me. When the storm settles—if fate allows—I will come find you."

Moony's ears flushed scarlet. She swallowed hard… and loosened her grip on his sleeve.

"Your Majesty—" Lili suddenly stepped out from behind the pillar, raising the teleportation talisman with a crisp flick of her wrist. "Since that is settled, this humble girl will take her two companions and withdraw—lest we further disturb Your Majesty's august composure. If the world truly changes one day… perhaps we shall meet again."

Light burst forth from the talisman. Wind spiralled around them. Lili grabbed Moony; Yara lifted her sword to carve open the formation.

Before the imperial guards could react, their three figures blurred into streaks of luminous motion—and vanished.

The guards lunged forward, only to grasp at empty air—then froze, too terrified to give chase.

Inside the Golden Throne Hall, wine still steamed in shattered porcelain. The fragrance of liquor clung to the air like a ghost.

Du Shao bowed low, unwavering. His voice rang through the hall:

"May Your Majesty quell your anger—for your son is willing to offer his life in pursuit of the Great Way for all under heaven!"

And beyond the great doors, the wind lifted three silhouettes high above the crimson roofs and golden Cliffs of the imperial city. The sparkles of the teleportation talisman scattered through the night like falling fireflies.

The absurd palace debacle had ended, yet within the palace walls, and within countless hearts, the ripples it left behind would be long… and deep.

Mo Han
墨寒

Chapter 46: The Phoenix Origin Core

A streak of argent light tore through the heavens, a single arc of spiritual brilliance flashing across the firmament like a falling star,

piercing straight into the summit of Mount Yuheng, descending into the celestial heart of the **Hall of Tiansuan**.

Yu Sord strode into the hall in a sweep of azure robes, sword-sheath still unreturned to his back.

He had barely taken one step past the threshold when several blades of divine consciousness slashed toward him—keen as sword-light, cold as winter steel.

The killing intent woven through the hall was so dense it seemed to hang in the air like thick, suffocating smoke.

Within the Hall of Tiansuan were gathered the most powerful authorities of the Immortal Realm.

At the head of the assembly sat Supreme Lord Yu Sord, master of Tiansuan Hall.

His expression was tranquil as a still lake, his silver-white sleeves drifting like mist, his aura vast and complete—profound enough to swallow heavens yet calm as untouched snow.

To his right sat Lord Yun and Xiao Yan, one stern, one solemn, both clouded with worry.

Before them hovered a vast projection of starlight—

a living astrolabe, galaxies flowing across its surface as they discussed and deduced in grave tones.

On the side stood Sang Lee and Yun Tim, the former holding a celestial divination disk, the latter recording runes and deductions with relentless focus.

Neither spoke a word.

Yet the silence of their pens and the tension in their shoulders made the atmosphere nearly unbearable.

"Supreme Lord," Yu Sord said at last, his voice steady yet cutting through space like a blade traveling through ten thousand li of wind and frost, "your clash with the Demon Realm's Crown Prince in the mortal world—we are already informed.

But this summons concerns matters of even greater urgency."

Yu Sord bowed deeply.

"Your orders."

Lord Yun flicked his fingers.

A surge of radiant energy bloomed midair, unfurling into a grand map of the Four Realms.

"In recent months," he replied, "the Demon Realm and the Beast Realm have forged covert alliances.

They have yet to deploy armies openly, but their probing along the borders grows increasingly bold.

The Beast King claims neutrality, yet his stance leans unmistakably toward the demons.

The Demonic Clan intends to exploit the Beast Army as their vanguard, delaying our forces."

Xiao Yan let out a cold, humourless snort.

"Beast folk are greedy and fickle—unworthy of real fear.

The true threat lies in the Demon Realm's ambition for the **Array Core** of the *Seven-Star Heavenly Formation*."

He pointed toward the centre of the star map.

There, a pattern of crimson-gold runes glimmered—

an immense formation shaped like the Big Dipper, anchored at the junction of all Four Realms.

"This array has remained sealed since the Great Chaos ten thousand years ago," Xiao Yan continued.

"If it is breached, the barriers dividing the Four Realms will falter.

The Immortal Realm and Mortal Realm will bear the brunt of the collapse."

"Which is why," Sang Lee added, tone taut as drawn bowstring, "the demons plan to let the Beast Army ravage the eastern boundary stones— while they slip in to destroy the formation's heart."

"Destroying the Array Core," murmured another elder, "would shatter the equilibrium of the Four Realms.

Such boldness reveals the Demon Realm's true ambition—expansion is merely the beginning."

A white-bearded elder gave a grim, mirthless laugh.

"Mark old me on this: Flamebane Demon Lord does not merely seek land.

He seeks to raise an army large enough to crown himself **sovereign of all Four Realms**."

Silence rippled through the chamber.

"Thus," Yun Tim muttered quietly, "the priority is to *restore* the Seven-Star Heavenly Formation.

But its Array Core can only be rebuilt using the **Phoenix Origin Core**— a divine core that forms naturally within the purest bloodline of the Phoenix Clan."

Sang Lee nodded.

"Yes. The Phoenix Clan has always crowned its queens from among their 'Phoenix Maidens.'

Only the reigning Phoenix Sovereign carries a true Phoenix Origin Core in her body.

There is only one such pill in existence at any given time."

"And thus," Yun Tim proclaimed, his voice soft yet absolute, "whoever bears the Phoenix bloodline capable of forming the Pill… is by right the next Phoenix Queen."

A silence fell across the hall—so profound it seemed to press against the very ribs of heaven itself.

Every gaze turned, almost in unison, toward **Lord Yun Wuntang of the Cloud Hall**.

Every immortal present remembered with stark clarity the vision from Lili's spiritual-root assessment—the radiant phoenix silhouette blooming across the Mirror of Spirit-Luminescence, a phenomenon that had shaken half the Immortal Realm.

And Lili was, after all, the long-lost daughter whom the Sect Master had only recently reclaimed.

Supreme Lord Yu Sord remained composed, expression placid as always, his voice gentle yet carrying unfathomable weight.

"This matter is but a deduction for now," he muttered. "We must prepare contingencies.

No one here seeks to force that child into peril—

but should calamity reach its brink, a decree must exist.

Lord Yun Wuntang, you know as well as I… there is only *one* person remaining in this world who bears any possible connection to the Phoenix Origin Core."

Yun Wuntang was silent for a long moment.

His lashes lowered slightly, and his voice came soft and low—like a man forcing himself through thorns:

"If the day truly comes that Lili's Phoenix Origin must be used as the formation's core—"

He got no further.

For a voice, sharp as struck jade, cut across the hall in an instant.

"I, Yu Sord—will NEVER consent to this!"

The declaration crashed through the chamber like thunder.

Several immortals stiffened.

Some wore solemn resignation; others showed outright shock.

For Yu Sord—so famed for restraint, calm, and cold clarity—now stood with a storm behind his eyes.

His aura, normally serene as silent frost, surged violently; silver-white mist rippled behind him like unsheathed moon-blades.

"She may carry a trace of phoenix lineage," he said, every word hammered in steel,

"but the girl has yet to even form a proper foundation.

Where, then, would a Phoenix Origin Core come from?

You base your entire deduction on a faint remnant of phoenix essence in her body—and with that, you presume she can serve as the heart of a world-defending array?"

His gaze swept across the hall.

A faint glint—cold, lethal—flashed in his eyes.

"If such logic stands, who comes next?

A lone dragon-blooded child?

A stray Kirin descendent?

During the Great War ten millennia prior, the Phoenix Clan were the vanguard.

They bled first, and they burned first—until their race was nearly extinguished."

His voice sharpened—

"Now only my son Zhou and my daughter Lili remain.

And you would have her pay the price *again*?"

At those words, Yun Wuntang's lips pressed tight.

Though his face stayed tranquil, his spirit churned violently beneath the surface.

Even Yun Tim paused mid-stroke, glancing sideways.

Yu Sord had never—*never*—spoken out of turn in an assembly like this.

Not once had he ever raised his voice.

Yu Sord drew a breath—not of calm, but of brimming fury barely held in check.

"She grew up in the mortal world," he muttered quietly,

"without guidance, without cultivation, without even the stability of a formed immortal bone.

All she ever wanted was safety and obscurity."

His hands tightened at his sleeves.

"Who was it," he continued, voice roughening,

"who summoned her back?

Who now intends to thrust her onto the altar of calamity *again*?"

He stepped forward—a single stride that resounded like a crack tearing through the hall's solemn stillness.

"If blood must strengthen the formation—why should it be hers?"

His voice dropped low, each word like a seal struck into stone.

"If the world must reach its darkest hour…

then it should be **us**—the ones with higher cultivation, with broader shoulders—who lay down our lives to guard the realms."

"Not her."

The hall froze.

Even the drifting celestial lights dimmed for a beat.

For one breath—two—three—

even Supreme Lord Yu Sord said nothing.

At last, he lifted a hand, stilling the rising tide of divine auras.

His voice softened fractionally.

"Immortal Lord, your sentiments are noted.

This matter is not decree—it is only contingency.

No decisions have been made.

Rest assured, no private feelings are at play."

At that moment, the one who had remained silent the longest finally stepped forward.

Cloud Lord Yun Wuntang moved with unhurried grace, clad in plain white robes, his presence steady as an ancient mountain.

He lifted his gaze toward the suspended light-screen, and when he spoke, his voice was calm—so calm it seemed nothing in the world could stir it.

"Lili's mother," he began quietly, "was indeed of the true Phoenix line.

Years ago, during my exploration of the Southern Spirit Ruins, I chanced upon her, the last survivor fleeing from her clan's annihilation."

The hall grew utterly still.

"When the Phoenix Clan fell, she went into hiding alone.

I formed a life-bond with her, and in the years that followed, she bore Zhou'er and Li'er.

To preserve the children's bloodline stability, she sealed her remaining shred of phoenix essence into the womb…"

His voice softened, almost imperceptibly.

"…and soon after, her spirit scattered."

Though he spoke without tremor, each word landed with the weight of stone.

"That was the very last life she chose to protect," Yun Wuntang murmured.

"Lili is my beloved daughter. No father would ever be willing to offer her as the core of a formation."

He lowered his eyes, a shadow of grief passing over his calm expression.

"Her kin… her mother… the entire Phoenix Clan has already died for the stability of the Four Realms.

Lili wandered all her childhood, uprooted and alone.

Only recently has she been reunited with her family."

His voice thinned to a near-whisper.

"To place the burden of the realms upon her shoulders again—this should not be her fate."

Silence descended once more.

Not a single immortal raised a rebuttal.

For in the depths of every mind present, the truth was clear: the Phoenix Clan had already paid their debt in blood.

Supreme Lord Yu Sord looked upon Yun Wuntang for a long, contemplative moment, before he finally let out a faint, almost imperceptible sigh.

"This matter shall be entered into the Celestial Record," he explained.

"We shall continue to observe.

If the Demon Realm truly moves upon the array's heart… we may deliberate again.

There is still time."

Only then did the oppressive silver aura behind Yu Sord slowly dissipate.

He slid his sword back into its sheath with a soft, final click, lowered his gaze, and said nothing more.

Though the hall appeared serene on the surface,

beneath its calm ripples surged—

an undercurrent of dread, of unspoken tension, of futures uncharted.

For all in that place knew:

This debate was only the beginning.

The storm to come…

would be far greater than any of them had yet named.

* * * * *

Behind the main hall of Mount Yuheng, the wind lay still as a sheet of glass.

Sang Lee closed the celestial divination disk in his hands.

With a flick of his sleeves, the lingering lights folded in on themselves, the ripples of spiritual force settling like water falling back into a deep well.

He did not leave at once.

Instead, he turned sideways and cast a thoughtful glance toward Yun Tim.

"What do you make," Sang Lee asked quietly,

"of what he said today?"

Yun Tim stood beneath the eaves, one hand clasped behind him, the other idly brushing the phoenix-carved jade ring at his waist.

His eyes were cool—almost indifferent—but the calm carried a razor-edge beneath it.

"If he hadn't said it," Yun Tim replied,

"he would not be Yu Sord."

Sang Lee's eyebrow lifted ever so slightly.

"But the Phoenix Origin Core… truly is the only stabilizing core for the array."

"And what of it?" Yun Tim countered, raising his gaze.

His voice held a light, mocking chill.

"All I know is that the child in question carries the blood of our Yun family."

Sang Lee was silent for a long breath.

Then, quietly:

"If the formation collapses, the Four Realms will crack.

The Demon Realm will march.

Countless beings will perish.

When that happens—what then?"

Yun Tim stepped forward, the faintest scoff escaping him.

"A little girl," he said, "bearing the fate of four realms?

If that's not a cosmic joke, I don't know what is."

He paused, and when he spoke again, his voice sharpened like a blade pulled from frost.

"A hundred thousand years ago, the Celestial Realm begged the Phoenix Clan to hold the line—three days, they said. Three days to guard the array."

He laughed, low and cold.

"And what happened?

Three days became three months.

One by one, the phoenixes died until the clan was ash.

The Celestial elders today—have they all conveniently forgotten their own betrayal?"

Sang Lee's lashes trembled, but he said nothing.

Yun Tim looked toward the distant halls, shrouded in drifting clouds.

A faint, sardonic curl touched his lips, though his eyes dimmed with something darker.

"Regardless," he murmured,

"she carries Yun blood.

As her uncle—at the very least—I will not let her walk the same ruinous road her mother did."

Sang Lee exhaled softly.

"You know well… her mother chose it willingly."

"Willing?" Yun Tim huffed, a cold sound.

"No one is willing.

They were cornered—every last one of them."

He flicked his sleeves, already turning away, his steps sharp with restrained fury.

"If she truly is a phoenix," he stated, voice echoing low and final behind him,

"then she will have her own tribulation."

A pause.

"But that tribulation," Yun Tim finished,

"Should be hers to choose—

not something decreed by anyone else."

He strode into the drifting mist, leaving the rear hall steeped in a deeper silence than before.

"This calamity is hers to face, hers to name; it shall not be chosen on her behalf."

* * * * *

The night wind drifted through the bamboo grove outside the Yuheng Hall, brushing the leaves until they whispered like distant rain.

Yu Sord stood beneath the open corridor, the long sword in his hand still sheathed in neither scabbard nor serenity.

The blade gleamed faintly—cold white light reflecting the anger he had not yet dispelled.

He had lived and cultivated for a thousand years.

He had walked through blood and thunder, observed the rise and fall of sects, witnessed hundreds of mortal dynasties flicker like sparks in the wind.

And never—not once—had he lost his composure before a council of immortals.

Not until today.

To shield her is my selfishness;

to refuse to shield her would be my sin.

He murmured the words under his breath, jaw tightening, the tendons in his hand tightening around the hilt until the knuckles blanched.

His gaze drifted toward a distant cluster of buildings veiled in drifting cloud—the small pavilion whose lantern glowed faintly through the mist.

* * * * *

Fenghua Pavilion.

The place where she lived.

Where the girl who had once stepped alone into a thunder tribulation just to prove she was more than fate allowed—breathed and slept and laughed.

Her past life, he had failed her.

Her present life—he would not lose her again.

He simply would not.

If the day truly came when they demanded her life to mend the array…

He would defy fate itself.

He would cut his way out of the heavens if he must.

* * * * *

Inside the great hall, the immortals had dispersed.

Outside the Tianxuan Astral Council Chamber, no one remained—save a single dying lantern, trembling atop the stone steps.

Two shadows lengthened beside it.

"You did not speak just now," an old man rasped as he stepped from the darkness.

His voice scraped like wind through dead branches, carrying a faint curl of mockery.

"You let that Yu Sord brandish his sword and glare down an entire council. Had this old man not known better, I would have thought you frightened."

Across from him stood a figure in silver-threaded black robes—calm, tranquil, stern as winter frost.

The one known as Palace Master Suyuan.

He lowered his gaze slightly.

His voice was quiet, light as drifting smoke.

"Those who speak too heavily," Suyuan stated, "are remembered too deeply."

The old man's laugh was cold.

"He can guard her for a moment. Can he guard her for a lifetime? If the day truly comes when the Phoenix Origin Core is needed… will you truly be willing to give her up?"

Suyuan did not answer.

He merely lifted a hand and gestured toward the place where the star-lit projection had vanished hours before.

His tone was soft, but as merciless as falling frost.

"The fate pattern is unsettled. Everything may yet change. A proper divination," he murmured, "Always prepares three paths."

The old man's eyelids flickered.

"And if the girl refuses to surrender the pill?"

"Then someone," Suyuan replied,

"will ensure she consents."

His voice was so gentle it chilled the bones.

"The Phoenix Origin is sealed in the core of the dantian-an inner energy core. If she cannot activate it herself, it is not impossible to extract it by array."

A shadow crossed the elder's face.

"…You planned this already?"

Suyuan did not deny it.

"When she was first brought into our realm," he whispered slowly, "I placed a mark upon her—a boundary seal belonging to this world. Should an emergency arise, the seal can bind her spirit and lock her divine core."

His expression did not change.

His voice did not waver.

"As long as her name remains on the celestial register, **she will never escape** Tianxuan's jurisdiction."

A beat of silence.

Then the old man exhaled a thin, humourless laugh.

"Of all of us," he murmured behind his sleeve,

"you… are the cruellest."

Suyuan said nothing.

He only turned, his sleeves brushing the stone like drifting snow, and walked soundlessly into the darkness.

The wavering lantern flame cast one last flicker against the stone steps, a cage of light wrapped around a single spark, quiet, suffocating, sharp as a concealed blade.

Chapter 47: The Allure of the Mortal Market

The palace gates had already closed slowly and definitively behind them, the golden tiles and crimson walls reflecting long, stark silhouettes in the evening light.

The streets were bustling with noise, the marketplace as lively and vociferous as usual, as if the extraordinary celestial anomaly witnessed earlier that day was nothing more than a fleeting, distant dream.

Yun Lili, however, could not resist turning her head for one final, uncertain look.

She stood at the street corner, her gaze fixed intently upon the high wall. Her expression was slightly frozen; she had the distinct, unsettling feeling that something vital had gone missing.

She pulled out her bronze mirror, her thumb lightly tracing the cool surface, her voice suppressed to a mere whisper: "**Celestial Mirror**, assist me… where precisely has Yu Sord gone?"

The surface of the bronze mirror flickered with a faint light, then was immediately enveloped in a thin layer of mist. Within the swirling vapours, the area where a figure or spiritual aura should have been reflected was utterly blank; not even the ambient sky-light seemed able to penetrate the void.

She frowned slightly, and called out his name once more: "Yu Sord?"

The bronze mirror remained utterly silent, the mist growing heavier and denser, finally settling into a thick, dark cloud that pressed down upon the entire mirror's surface, as though a powerful, sophisticated barrier had completely masked the person's spiritual essence.

"Moony," Yun Lili suddenly called out in a low voice.

"Eh?" Moony, eating a candied hawthorn skewer, leaned in closer, her cheeks sticky. "What is it? Are you searching for Celestial Lord Yu?"

"…I can't see him," Yun Lili said, her expression peculiar as she tucked the mirror away. "He was with us just moments ago; how did he depart so suddenly, and why is the mirror displaying nothing?"

Moony paused, startled: "Odd? Yes, how can the mirror possibly see nothing at all?"

Yun Lili did not respond, her expression hardening with several degrees of gravity. The Celestial Mirror, while certainly not omnipotent, was capable of reflecting atmospheric spiritual signatures and locating souls; even a soul deep in slumber would leave some observable trace… yet this time, there was only utter blankness.

"Do stop worrying, Miss," Moony said, cheerfully shaking her hawthorn skewer. "He is so immensely capable; he has simply returned to the Immortal Realm to file an immediate incident report, perhaps."

"He might have had the decency to bid us farewell before leaving," Yun Lili muttered, rolling her eyes, yet unable to conceal a thread of profound unease in her tone. "I just feel an odd disquiet in my heart…"

"Oh, do stop fretting, Miss! Truly!" Moony tugged at her sleeve enthusiastically. "We are still in the mortal realm! This is a rare, excellent, and unrepeatable opportunity; don't you think we should seize the chance to thoroughly enjoy ourselves?"

"Enjoy?" Yun Lili was momentarily taken aback. "Now?"

Moony widened her eyes, her face a picture of utterly righteous conviction: "No enjoyment now means wasted opportunity! If you don't seize the moment, next time you crave candied hawthorn, you'll have to humbly petition the Celestial Court for a **mandate**!"

"Oh…"

Suddenly, Moony's eyes narrowed suspiciously as she scrutinised Yun Lili, making her mistress feel completely uneasy.

"What exactly is that look supposed to mean?"

"Your personality seems to have undergone a strange alteration, Miss? You aren't immediately thinking about food and play just now?"

Yun Yara, standing nearby, suddenly spoke: "…A spot of enjoyment would do no harm."

Yun Lili turned to stare at her.

Yun Yara's expression was perfectly blank, yet her gaze was fixed upon the distant activity of the marketplace. Her eyes reflected the fleeting lights of the stalls, seeming both distracted and entirely indifferent. Having delivered her approval, she said nothing further, merely turning slightly and stepping resolutely into the bustling market.

"Who says I don't want to play?" Yun Lili deliberately arched her eyebrows, giving Moony a sharp, playful slap on the back. "Come along! We are going to consume some delectable steamed dumplings, sugar pastries, and a massive braised pork knuckle!"

"…She actually agreed to it, then?" Moony exclaimed in surprise. "Quickly, quickly, let us proceed!"

Yun Lili, unable to maintain her own internal disquiet in the face of such enthusiasm, had no choice but to push the worry aside and follow.

The trio strolled along, browsing the colourful lamp stalls, buying shortbread, and playing ring toss. Even Moony managed to capture a paper carp lantern, which she clutched happily to her chest. Yun Lili, initially preoccupied, slowly began to relax amidst the fragrances of sugar and the cheerful cacophony of human voices.

As evening approached, the sky gradually darkened, and the market stalls began the process of packing up.

"Look! Over there is a stall selling spirit lamps! I think they offer wish-drawing slips!" Moony spotted a stall with sharp eyes.

"That's just cheap nonsense designed to fleece simple children; I've seen plenty of that sort of **palaver** in villages before…" Yun Lili muttered, her tone one of professional, lofty disdain.

Moony ignored her mistress's incessant muttering, enthusiastically pulling the other two around the street corner and into a small alley hung with numerous red lanterns.

The alley was long, narrow, and deeply shadowed; the stone paving was slightly damp. The red lanterns lining the walls swayed gently in the breeze, emitting a soft, faint, creaking sound.

Most strangely, although the sky had not yet fully darkened, the alley was dim and profoundly murky, as if it existed in its own self-contained realm. With every step deeper inside, it felt as though they were crossing the threshold into another world entirely.

"This place feels rather peculiar," Yun Lili muttered, immediately feeling a subtle, unnatural drag on her feet the moment she stepped onto the stone.

Moony, skipping excitedly ahead, called back: "Look quickly! It's right here!"

At the end of the alley stood a small stall draped with vividly coloured floral cloth. Upon it were displayed a variety of bizarre, ancient-looking pots—fat pots, slender pots, pots with twisted spouts, and even one item shaped rather unmistakably like a toad.

"These pots have very strange aesthetics," Yun Lili remarked suspiciously, picking up one item that resembled a teapot, grey with dust and missing half its lid.

The stall owner, a heavily hunched old man, stroked his sparse beard and let out a soft, knowing chuckle: "The young lady need only rub the body of the pot with her hand, and a delightful surprise shall surely be revealed."

Moony's eyes immediately sparkled with excitement: "Rub it quickly, rub it quickly, Miss!"

Yun Lili, operating under the profound suspicion that she was actively contributing to the decline of her own dignity, tentatively gave the pot a cautious rub. Suddenly, a plume of intense purple smoke *Poof* violently outwards!

A small genie with tightly coiled hair and a high, piercing voice instantly popped into existence.

He introduced himself as Gus, the thirty-ninth **Wishing Pot Guardian**, and launched into an aggressive sales pitch for his bespoke 'wish packages,' even boasting that he had personally brewed tea for the Dragon King of the East Sea.

Before the trio could fully recover from the sheer absurdity of the first genie's arrival, Moony had already pounced upon the next item—a bronze pot shaped like a fierce beast's head: "I want this one!"

She gave it a vigorous rub. A deep *Thump* sounded, and a massive, heavily bearded genie clad in rough animal hides exploded forth from the pot's spout.

He spoke with a rough, booming voice: "I am the **Ferocious Tiger** Wish-Forging Master! No payment is required if the wish is unsatisfactory! I am the premier choice for all wishes pertaining to strength and raw power!"

"……" Moony observed him with intense seriousness. "He looks distinctly like the Howling Celestial Dog belonging to the Lord Erlang, doesn't he?"

Yun Lili suppressed a laugh, and with a weary sigh, simply snatched up a small, exquisitely made pink porcelain pot and gave it a quick rub.

Following a clear, sharp chime, a tiny fairy with dual glowing wings popped out, complete with self-generated sparkling background effects: "I am **Wish Sparkle Number Seven**! Your wishes can be completely DIY! Maidenly themes, romance, transformation into beauty, weight loss, increased intelligence—if you dare to conceive it, I dare to act it out for you!"

"Which Celestial Department authorised your collective entry into the mortal realm?" Yun Lili finally demanded, unable to restrain her curiosity any longer.

The three Wish Genies immediately lined up in a neat row, declaring in perfect, synchronous unison: "We possess legal registration! Our file number is 807 of the **Bureau of Wishes**!"

They even enthusiastically pressed business cards upon the girls, complete with perfume and glitter, along with a small printed booklet detailing wish categories.

Yun Yara watched the antics of these hyperactive, utterly undignified genies and felt a distinct, throbbing headache brewing.

She turned to make an immediate, strategic retreat, but Moony grabbed her: "Wait, don't leave! I still want to rub the fourth one—"

Yun Lili, displaying impressive presence of mind and commendable quickness, swiftly intervened by laying a firm hand upon yet another of the curious vessels.

In the very next instant, a powerful torrent of dense, indigo vapour erupted from the spout with an audible *whoosh* and substantial force!

Following a sound rather akin to a prolonged, loud exhalation, a small purple genie, wearing a bizarre ritual robe and hair coiled like a fluffy sheep, was forcefully ejected. He collided with the side of the stall with a loud *Ouch*, before crouching down, clutching his head in pain.

"Who dares—which audacious, ill-mannered scoundrel dared to smoke me out of the pot like that!"

Yun Lili: "……Er?"

Yun Yara lifted her hand to her forehead, sighing silently, and expressionlessly took a strategic step backward.

Moony clutched her stomach, convulsing with laughter: "Hahahaha! That was utterly brilliant!"

The small genie rubbed his forehead, looked up, and upon seeing Yun Lili, his eyes narrowed with profound disdain: "Well, well, well, a novice Immortal Embryo? Or perhaps one just promoted from the absolute **Cabbage Patch** tier?"

Yun Lili: "And who might *you* be, exactly?"

"Who am I?" The little genie placed his tiny hands aggressively on his hips. "**This one** is the thirty-ninth **Wishing Pot Guardian—Merlin Fatty Potts**! I have served three thousand diverse wish-makers, and let me tell you, even the Dragon King of the East Sea has used me to brew his tea!"

"It was *you* who was brewed in the teapot, surely," Yun Lili could not help but mutter in retort.

"Hey, little maiden, do you desire a wish? Only three simple conditions apply: one, you must not ask me why; two, you must not say you regret the wish once granted; and three, you must not wish for anything as dreadfully commonplace as making someone fall in love with you."

Yun Lili: "I wonder if I could wish for you to simply shut up?"

Moony: "May I wish for it to produce more smoke? The visual effect is utterly sensational and dramatic!"

Just as Moony was excitedly preparing to rub the next pot, the old stall owner suddenly let out a low, profound cough.

"Esteemed Immortals," he said. He slowly lifted his head, his gaze coming from behind the floral cloth. His eyes, though cloudy, held a thread of strange, unsettling intensity. "A wish, you see, always comes with a price."

Yun Lili raised an eyebrow: "Did you not just promise us a surprise upon rubbing the pot?"

"A surprise there is, indeed, but… sometimes, the surprise holds a **thread of fate** within it," the old man said, stroking his beard, his voice low and eerie. "Wish too often, and the pot itself will grow resentful. All things in the world possess a spiritual essence; even these pots choose their patrons with care."

"Whichever pot holds a profound grievance, a deep-seated lingering thought, or an unbreakable obsession—the person who rubs it must inevitably accompany it on its journey to resolution," the old man continued, his voice low and eerily drawn out. "Do not say I failed to issue a clear warning: this particular alleyway… when the night fully descends, the boundary between pot and person, between the real and the spectral, becomes utterly and dangerously blurred."

Moony listened, utterly stunned into silence. She was about to ask another question, but she looked up and realised that the old stall owner had completely and inexplicably vanished.

The floral cloth still lay neatly spread on the ground, the bizarre pots were still lined up precisely, and the lanterns swayed gently. The alley was profoundly empty and silent; even the distinct sound of the wind was gone.

"…He was sitting right here just a moment ago, wasn't he?" Yun Lili whispered, her voice barely audible, confirming the impossible.

"He was, and I was convinced he was going to demand payment," Moony replied, recovering slightly and scratching her head. "And now the person himself is completely gone?"

Yun Lili offered no further comment, but the old man's unsettling words felt like sharp needles, quietly and menacingly pricking her back.

In the next moment, she instinctively glanced towards the singular purple-patterned pot in the darkest corner—the very one she had last rubbed.

This prolonged episode of chaotic absurdity had sent the three girls into gales of laughter, yet no sooner had the mood passed than the lanterns at the end of the alley suddenly extinguished themselves all at once. The brief red light vanished like ink dissolving into water, and a thick, oppressive vapour abruptly arose—

Mist, rising chillingly from their feet.

Deep in the alley, it was as if some immense, unseen entity had opened its eyes within the shifting fog.

The ground grew abruptly cold beneath the stone. Wisps of thin mist began to stream from the cracks in the paving stones, and in a short few breaths, the fog had risen past their ankles, thickening into a dense, silent sea of vapour.

"Why is this fog so immensely, unnaturally thick?" Moony looked around frantically. "Wasn't the sky completely clear just moments ago?"

Yun Lili instinctively reached out and took out the **Celestial Mirror**. The surface lit up, reflecting the figures of the three girls… and then the mist. There was only the mist in the reflection, and only their three figures were visible in the glass; the surrounding area seemed to have been entirely consumed by some form of spiritual vacuum.

"Yun Yara?" she suddenly asked in a low voice, a clear thread of fear tightening her throat.

No one answered.

"Moony, did you see her?" Yun Lili spun around, her voice suddenly spiking in pitch.

Moony also turned to look around, her pupils contracting sharply: "Where is she?"

They had been standing together just moments before, yet in the blink of an eye… Yun Yara had completely disappeared into the dense mist, without a sound, without even the echo of a footstep.

Yun Lili rushed towards the fog, but found that the mist behaved like a sentient, living entity; beyond a single step, she could no longer distinguish the shape of her companion.

"Yun Yara!" she shouted loudly, but her voice felt stifled, as though plugged with thick cotton. The sound only travelled a few steps before it was swallowed, leaving no echo.

Moony tightly grasped her sleeve, asking with a visible tremor in her voice: "Did you… did you hear any sound just now?"

"No," Yun Lili's palms were ice-cold. She suddenly looked down—on the stone ground, there was an extremely faint, reddish trace, like smoke or fine silk, winding along the cracks in the paving stones, gradually dissolving into the mist.

She crouched down, her fingertips lightly touching the fading red mark, and a sudden, profound coldness shot straight up her spine. She instinctively reached out to pull Yun Yara back, but only grasped a handful of cold, empty mist. A strange, elusive fragrance still lingered in the air, a scent so deeply familiar it was utterly unnerving.

"…How could even A-Yara suddenly vanish like that, without a whisper?" she whispered, her voice laced with dread.

The fog had not dissipated, and the distant streetlights felt impossibly far away. The alley was terrifyingly silent; the very air felt heavy, as though pressed down by some immense, unseen weight.

Yun Lili tightened her grip on the bronze mirror. The surface, just as before, reflected nothing but blankness.

Only that lingering, faint reddish trace remained, not yet fully gone.

Chapter 48: The Pot Spirits?

The fog did not lift.

The back of the alley was silent—too silent, as though sound itself had been swallowed whole.

Moony pressed herself against Lili's side, her fingers curled death-tight around Lili's sleeve.

Her voice trembled. "Miss… did we… did we just run into a ghost?"

Lili tightened her grip on the Celestial Mirror , her tone low and steady.

"This fog isn't ghostly qi. It's… a restriction. A barrier. Someone doesn't want us to leave."

"Someone?" Moony's face blanched. "Who in the realms would be bored enough to trap *us* of all people?!"

Lili didn't answer.

Her gaze returned to the faint red trace on the ground—

a thin, wavering line, almost illusion-like, threading through the cracks between bricks and leading deeper into the alley.

She thought for a moment, then spoke softly:

"Follow it. Quickly."

"F-follow it? Miss, are you *sure* this isn't a road leading us straight to death? Because suddenly I really miss the safety of the Celestial Realm…"

"If we don't follow it, we'll stay trapped here."

Lili's voice was unexpectedly calm as she glanced at Moony.

"But you can stay behind if you want. I'm going to find Yara."

Moony bit her lip hard.

"…Then I'm coming. If you die, I'm dying with you."

"…That is *not* a healthy sense of loyalty."

Lili rolled her eyes—yet the corner of her lips lifted.

They followed the red mark, Lili pressing the Celestial Mirror to her palm as she moved.

The mist coiled around their steps, shifting like sentient water, stirring with each footfall but refusing to disperse.

Suddenly, Moony gasped. "Miss—there!"

The red mark ended abruptly at a section of cracked brick wall.

Between the broken bricks was a narrow, impossibly thin gap.

Lili frowned, crouched, and peered into the slit.

Fog still poured out from within, curling like breath exhaled from another world.

But then the Celestial Mirror shivered in her hand, its surface flickering, and a faint silhouette appeared in the reflection.

Yara.

"She's inside!" Lili sprang to her feet. "We have to go in!"

Moony stared at the tiny gap. "But the slit is so small! How do you expect us to fit? You can't honestly think—"

"I'm serious." Lili planted her hands on her hips.

"I've trained for this. When I lived in the village, I could squeeze into water tanks and even steal eggs out of chicken coops—"

Before Moony could answer, Lili pressed the mirror directly against the wall.

A ripple spread across the bricks like water disturbed by wind.

"We'll manage. No need for chicken coops today."

Her voice softened, and she seized Moony's wrist.

And the two of them fell, tumbling into a world of darkness, of silence, and of something ancient waiting beyond the shattered veil.

The bricks and lanterns tore apart like paper, collapsing into spirals of fragmented light.

* * * * *

Mist.

Mist everywhere.

There was no sky, no ground—no sense of up or down. Only an endless, suffocating white void, as if they had fallen into the bottomless throat of a cloud well.

Moony murmured under her breath, voice barely holding steady:

"Miss… d-do you think the Celestial Mirror dragged us into its mirror-world?"

Lili did not answer.

The mirror in her palm flickered faintly—

and suddenly she saw another her reflected on its surface.

Another Lili stood within the fog.

Silent. Expressionless.

And in that reflection… Moony was nowhere to be found.

Her chest tightened.

She snapped her head to the side—

Moony was gone.

"…Another one," Lili muttered, her expression growing grim.

This wasn't an ordinary barrier.

It was a formation crafted with intent, a Soul-Splitting Mist Realm designed precisely for them.

Separate the group.

Trap each within an isolated illusion.

Let each person believe they were still in reality…

while, in truth, every one of them had been scattered into their own solitary world.

She lifted the mirror again.

Inside it, the reflected "Lili" took a step toward her—quiet, empty-eyed, lips parting slightly as if attempting to speak.

"Who are you?" Lili asked, voice cold.

The reflection paused—then smiled.

Her voice was *exactly* Lili's own.

"I am what you hide."

"…Hide what, exactly?"

"What you dare not say.

What you've lost.

What you fear you'll never reach in time."

Lili narrowed her eyes. "Cut the riddles. What kind of illusion are you? And—where is Moony? What did you do with her?!"

The phantom did not answer.

Instead, she slowly lifted her hand.

A ribbon of mist swirled in her palm, condensing into a crystalline **memory jade slip**.

Her voice turned lilting, eerie—almost coaxing:

"Take a guess… what do you think this is?"

Lili frowned, lips pursed, refusing to humour it.

Her gaze darted through the fog, assessing escape routes—

The illusion ignored her distraction and continued sweetly:

"It's Yu Sord's memory~"

"…Yu Sord's… memory?"

Lili froze for a breath.

Her heartbeat stumbled—an involuntary misstep.

The phantom leaned closer, tone soft and beguiling:

"Do you want to see it?

Want to know where he went… after he left you?"

Her smile widened, cold as a blade.

"And the things he said to you…

Which words were real?

Which were lies?"

Lili took one abrupt step forward—

Then halted.

She inhaled slowly, lifting her chin.

Her gaze sharpened with wary clarity as she studied the illusion that wore her own face.

"Are you kidding me? Why would I need his memories?"

Her whole posture bristled with suspicion.

The reflection's smile faded, turning thin… and chilling.

"You truly don't want the truth?"

"What truth?"

The phantom Lili let out a tinkling laugh, airy and almost cruel.

"Your past life with him, of course. You really don't know?"

"…Huh? Past life?"

Lili blinked, genuinely caught off guard.

"With whom? Yu Sord?"

"That's right."

The reflection tilted her head, voice slippery as fog.

"With that ever-so-elegant yet frostbitten Yu Sord—Secluded-Might Immortal of the Silent Radiance."

Her expression grew exaggeratedly mysterious.

"You and he had a past life with a very, *very* tragic ending~"

The surface of the Celestial Mirror shivered.

A web of silver cracks rippled across it—

and then an image surfaced, pale and distant, like a memory dredged from a forgotten dream.

* * * * *

A peach grove in early spring.

Petals drifted in the wind like blushing snow.

A young man in pale cyan robes stood beneath the blooming canopy, hands folded behind his back.

His hair was ink-dark, cascading down like a waterfall of night.

He carried a calm aloofness, the ends of his eyes lowered, gaze resting quietly upon the young woman before him.

The woman wore soft apricot silk, the fabric fluttering with every breath of wind.

Her eyes curved delicately, her smile warm and gentle.

She offered him a small, embroidered pouch—silk patterned with gold-thread clouds, faint spiritual light leaking from within.

He accepted it.

A barely perceptible nod.

There was no sound in the memory,

but Lili *saw* it—

the small, subtle curve of Yu Sord's lips.

Not his usual distant, polite, cultivated smile.

A true one.

Soft.

Intimate.

Something inside her chest tightened, a sharp, inexplicable twist.

She could not tell if it was anger…or a strange, vulnerable ache she wished she didn't feel.

* * * * *

The scene dissolved.

A blizzard howling across the Abyssfall Cliff.

Endless white—wind shrieking like a wounded beast.

A lone figure trudged through the snow.

White robes whipped violently in the gale, hair tangled, steps unsteady yet unyielding.

Her eyes were hollow, unfocused; her spiritual veins were in disarray, the surrounding qi distorted into a mournful tremor.

She was alone.

No one walked beside her.

No one followed.

No one came.

Lili stared at the image of herself in white, standing against the blizzard.

Her reflected self lifted her chin—expression impassive—

and yet tears slid silently down her frozen cheeks.

Then she turned.

Without hesitation and without a single backward glance, she continued her climb, ascending higher and higher until she reached a strange altar at the cliff's peak, a structure warped by age and fractured by ancient storms.

The winds screamed.

The sky trembled.

And suddenly, a bolt of heavenly lightning tore the world open. The altar burst into blinding light.

The mirror snapped dark.

The illusion shattered, and the fog realm snapped back into place.

Silence rushed in, thick as frost.

Lili stared blankly at the mirror in her hand.

Her lips had gone pale, her chest tight, breath lodged somewhere between her ribs.

For a long moment, no sound left her throat.

Only after several heartbeats did she slowly peel herself away from the afterimage in the mirror.

And then—a thought struck her like a falling star.

A memory surfaced.

Her entry questionnaire from the day she first joined the Immortal Sect.

That ridiculous sheet she had filled in while half-eating a pastry.

Her eyes twitched violently as she recalled the next question:

"Have you ever dreamed of your past life?"

☐ *I dreamed I was a surviving orphan of some ancient immortal clan*

☐ *I dreamed I met a tragic end with the Sword Sovereign*

☐ *I dreamed I was struck by lightning and turned into a chicken*

☐ *I dreamed I ascended while filling a form*

Back then, she had lazily ticked one of the boxes with a sesame-oily finger,

mocking the absurdity of the options for half an afternoon.

But now…

Given the results of the spiritual test that day—

combined with the vision she had just witnessed—

She was a surviving descendant of the Phoenix Clan.

She had indeed been struck by heavenly lightning upon the Abyssfall Cliff.

And she and Yu Sord…

had met a tragic end in their previous life.

And as for "ascending while filling a form"?

Well, after completing that questionnaire… she did get admitted into Lingxiao Sect.

Which was, in a way… a kind of ascension.

Her pupils constricted.

Goosebumps exploded across her arms, a cold prickle climbing up her spine.

Sweat gathered in her palms as an unspeakable realization dawned on her.

"I… got all of them… right?"

Every box.

Every absurd option.

She had mocked them, but she had matched them all.

"Bah! Nonsense—utter nonsense!"

Lili shook her head violently as if to fling the thought out of her skull.

"This is all that stupid illusion's fault! Bad omen! Bad fantasy! Bad everything!"

She tried to wave her discomfort away, but the chill at the nape of her neck refused to leave.

A shiver ran down her back.

She flipped the mirror sharply toward the phantom reflection, preparing to scold it—

but the moment her fingers brushed the rim, the mirror suddenly pulsed with violent light.

A burst of spiritual force.

A crack like thunder.

And then, the mirror shattered!!

"Eh—?"

Lili froze.

"A-ah—my mirror!!"

The broken fragments trembled in her palms, scattering like bits of fallen starlight.

And her heart—

her poor heart—

felt split cleanly in two.

No… No no no, that was my favourite mirror…

How am I supposed to do my hair now? Who am I without it?!

But the silver shards dispersed into drifting motes, and where the mirror had shattered, a path opened: a silver-lit rift that cleaved the fog realm in two, forming a luminous passage.

In her panic, her foot tapped lightly against the ground—

and suddenly, her body rose.

She floated.

"Huh?

I… I can fly?"

Astonishment blossomed on her face.

For an instant she forgot the grief of her broken mirror.

Forgot the phantom.

Forgot the lingering dread.

She pushed off again—

Her figure lifted like a streak of silver moonlight, cutting across the entire fog-bound world.

Mirror shattered, fog split, reflection turned into a path.

"Fine! If you're going to trap me—

I'll just fly my way out!"

With a determined breath, Lili shot toward the pale cliff of mist that had formed ahead, a gleaming arc threading through the endless white. Mirror-light spilled around her, guiding her path as fog curled away in spirals, recoiling like startled spirits.

The air grew colder and heavier, each heartbeat echoing sharply in her ears as if the realm itself were listening.

Still, she did not slow. She would tear through this illusion, rip open any barrier that stood in her path, and shatter this maze of shifting mist to break free.

* * * * *

A sudden convulsion tore through the mist—the world reeled, vision collapsing into pitch-black.

And then—

A colossal vision slammed into Lili's mind with the force of a falling star.

Blood and fire fused across the heavens.

Flames surged like a tidal wave, staining the sky a furious crimson.

Countless figures—neither wholly human nor wholly bird—filled the firmament, their wings blazing with dazzling gold and searing scarlet.

Phoenix feathers rained from the heavens—each one burning brilliantly as it fell—

yet the moment it touched the desolate earth, it melted away like a single flake of snow, vanishing before it ever cooled.

The sky split apart.

Rivers of demonic energy, black as coiling dragons, plunged downward.

Their roars shattered mountains.

The ground quaked violently; great formations buckled and burst.

Blood and fire churned together, forming an endless, hellish tide.

At the centre of this inferno stood a single woman.

She was clad in once-white garments now entirely drenched in blood.

Two vast wings unfurled behind her like a burning sunset.

A delicate crown—intricate, ancient, exquisite—rested atop her head.

Her robes were torn and tattered, but that crown alone still shone with blazing gold, refusing to dim.

Wind, snow, and flames twisted violently around her lone figure.

Her silhouette, solitary and unyielding, stretched across heaven and earth like a rainbow piercing the sun.

She threw back her head and released a cry—clear, fierce, heart-rending.

As she screamed, a blinding crimson sphere of light was forcibly torn from her chest.

A phoenix's lament answered her, ringing through all nine skies.

That sphere—

Lili had no name for it.

Yet instinct surged up from deep within her bloodline, forcing three words into her consciousness:

Phoenix Origin Core.

In the same instant, a faint glow ignited within Lili's chest.

A small orb of golden-orange light burst from her own lips—

and the two spheres, hers and the woman's, twisted toward one another, spiraling, rising, intertwining—

until they slowly merged into one, releasing a radiance so bright it swallowed the world.

Fire roared outward.

The flames surged like a collapsing sun, striking the demonic army with unstoppable force,

driving them back, tearing apart darkness within ten thousand miles.

Lili forgot to breathe.

The woman's face was hidden, erased deliberately by the mist realm, leaving only the haunting silhouette, the wings, the crown, the blood.

But at the exact moment that light was carved from the woman's chest—

Lili felt her own heart ripped open.

A hot, knifing pain shot through her ribs, deep enough to carve into bone.

From the depths of her blood, a cry erupted, a phoenix's scream, wild and mournful, resonating violently with her soul and shaking her so hard her knees buckled. She nearly collapsed. Her eyes stung, and tears spilled without warning.

"Who… is she?"

Her voice trembled, thin as ash.

No one answered. Only the sound of phoenix wings burning to nothing, and the wrathful howls of the demon horde, collided endlessly across the vast battlefield, narrating a war long buried beneath ages of dust. And then, before she could swallow the ache in her throat, a single word slipped uncontrollably from her lips.

Soft.

Hoarse.

Almost a sob.

"Mother..."

* * * * *

The inferno dimmed—

and as the flames withdrew, the mist thickened again, knitting itself into yet another world.

Before Lili's eyes, a small attic room took shape, lit by a single warm, flickering lamp.

On a low couch sat a woman dressed in plain white robes.

Her features were blurred by the mist, yet her presence radiated a gentleness so deep it pressed against the ribs.

Cradled in her arms was a swaddled infant.

The woman cradled her tenderly, allowing a low, melodious lullaby to escape her lips.

It was a melody of prodigious antiquity, profoundly older than the stolid, enduring mountains themselves—the veritable whisper of a **Phoenix folk-song**, transmitted purely through the subtle currents of successive generations.

The baby cooed, tiny fists waving in soft, chaotic joy.

The woman lowered her head, brushing her fingertip across the infant's palm.

Her voice flowed like a warm breeze:

"Do not fear... Mother is here."

A violent tremor tore through Lili.

She had never seen this woman—

and yet, the moment the voice touched the air, something inside her soul cracked open, raw and aching.

"Mother…?"

The word broke from her throat, fragile, trembling.

Tears spilled freely, streaking down her face.

The woman did not lift her head.

Instead, she smiled softly and pressed a kiss to the child's brow—tender, slow, heartbreaking.

"My child… wherever you walk, whatever the world may call you… you and Zhou will always be my children. But you—little one—you were born a girl. Born the next Phoenix Queen. My heart aches for you… Yet phoenixes enter this world with destiny already woven into their wings.

This path… you must face it in the end."

Her voice grew thinner—

fading, like a lantern flame sinking beneath water.

The attic dissolved at the edges, colors bleeding away as if soaked in ink.

Shadows peeled from the walls and drifted into darkness.

The woman raised her gaze for the last time, turning toward some unseen horizon.

Her final whisper was a plea wrapped in love:

"Live… my child."

The moment the words fell, her form shattered into a myriad of golden lights—

each one resonating with the Phoenix Source glow in Lili's chest.

Lili's hands shook violently as she reached forward—

grasping at the vanishing light—

catching nothing.

"Don't go—!

Mother!!"

But the world answered only with silence.

The glow faded.

The warmth dissolved.

And only the echo of that voice lingered, carved into her heart like an old wound reopened.

Lili collapsed to her knees in the swirling mist.

Her vision blurred with tears.

Her chest clenched so tightly she could barely breathe.

In that moment, she finally understood. That missing piece of her childhood, the blank, aching void she had never been able to name, had been here all along.

Buried in fire.

Buried in song.

Buried in a mother's final farewell.

Chapter 49: The Return of the Missing Heart

The moment the illusionary mist collapsed, the very fabric of heaven and earth felt as though it were being ripped violently asunder.

Yun Lili felt an immense, staggering force explode outwards from all her limbs and meridians.

Her entire body was flung away. Her vision immediately went black, followed by an aggressive, blinding flash of white light that fractured like a thunderclap.

She landed heavily upon cold stone steps, her throat tasting sickly sweet and she barely managed to suppress the urge to vomit blood.

The silence surrounding her was terrifyingly absolute; only a deep, persistent —*HUUUM*— roared in her ears, shaking her spirit to its core.

Just as she felt she was about to completely lose consciousness, a familiar, powerful aura sliced through the air and arrived with blinding speed.

Silver light, like frost and snow, neatly cleaved the thick fog. A figure in azure robes sped urgently towards her.

His longsword had not yet been returned to its sheath; his pure sword intent raged, forcibly breaking the mist-lock and suppressing all residual traces of the illusion. His body visibly trembled from the exertion, and his lips were faintly white.

"…Yu Sord!"

Yun Lili's tears burst forth like a sudden floodgate, utterly out of her control. She abandoned all decorum and threw herself violently into his arms, clinging to him desperately.

"Wuwuwu… I was so terribly frightened…" Her sobs shook her entire frame. "They have all vanished… Moony… A-Yara… they are all gone! I—I cannot find them anywhere…"

Yu Sord's entire body stiffened in shock. He looked down at the young girl in his arms, her face smeared with tears and dust. His heart felt as though it had been viciously cleaved open by a sharp blade.

He immediately wrapped one arm around her in a protective embrace, his palm pressing firmly and steadily against her trembling back. His voice was exceedingly low, yet utterly firm:

"Lili, do not be afraid. I am here with you."

Yun Lili drew in ragged, gasping sobs, clinging tightly to his sleeve like a lost soul who could not find her way home.

"But… but I am truly so scared…"

She was weeping incoherently, her fingers clenched painfully tight. "And… and I also saw a very beautiful woman… er… I think she was my mother…"

Yu Sord's fingertips stilled momentarily on her back.

The Phoenix Empress?

"Mhm, yes." Yun Lili, her face streaked with tears, nodded vigorously. "I think so, yes. She had such beautiful wings; they were completely golden."

He instinctively held her tighter, the habitual coldness in his eyes completely replaced by an intense, visible anguish.

"But, why is she gone? It seems as though she died in battle… wuwu…"

"Yes, I know," he murmured softly. "Whatever you have seen, be it real or be it mere illusion… you must remember this one thing: in this life, you are absolutely not alone."

Yun Lili's heart gave a wrenching squeeze at the sound of his voice, and her tears flowed uncontrollably.

"…But I am truly, terribly afraid."

Yu Sord lifted his hand, his fingertips gently wiping away the tears at the corner of her eyes. His tone was softer than it had ever been, yet carried an undeniable, resolute conviction:

"Be afraid, or weep bitterly, you may indulge in either—**I am here**."

The moment the words fell, he swept his sleeve, his longsword vibrating sharply. His sword intent transformed into a surge of silver light that sliced through the lingering fog, shielding the two of them at the centre.

The world abruptly shifted.

When Yun Lili regained her senses, she had been brought back to the Hall of Heavenly Sword on Mount Yuheng.

The spiritual resonance of his **Realm Transfer** technique had not yet faded, and its lingering echo resonated outside the hall.

Inside the coldly solemn Sword Hall, an absolute silence reigned, broken only by her own sporadic, muffled sobs.

Yu Sord lowered his gaze to her in his arms, his eyes complex and unfathomably deep. He asked himself why, after a thousand years of cultivation, his heart should be as still as stagnant water, yet in this very moment, her crying rendered his heart soft and painfully undone.

"Lili," his voice was extremely low, bordering on a deep sigh, carrying a rare warmth. "Even if you are afraid, you must remember this one fact—you are not walking this path in solitude."

* * * * *

Inside a vast, ornate hall, the air was thick with fragrant incense, and grand palace lanterns hung high.

Moony's body was ice-cold. She clutched the edge of her skirt tightly, her eyes wide with tension, afraid to move a muscle.

The table before her was laden with steaming, exquisite delicacies, and gold-splashed vessels were filled to the brim with potent wine.

Several palace maids slowly approached her, their skirts moving without a breeze, their smiles bright yet chillingly unnerving.

"Little maiden, this is your rightful home now."

"Since you accepted the embroidered ball, you are the rightful and proper Princess Consort. You should now sit upon your throne obediently."

Moony vehemently shook her head, retreating until her back hit a massive pillar, her voice trembling: "No, no, I certainly won't! My Lady would never consent to be a consort! I... I don't want to either!"

As she spoke, her heart felt a sudden ache. It wasn't that she hadn't longed for a stable life, good food, fine clothing, or even a tiny amount of recognition.

But through her stumbling journey with Yun Lili, she had long realised one thing—separated from her Lady, she couldn't even manage to look after herself.

"I want to go back!" she screamed, her voice amplified and sharpened by the echoing walls of the palace.

The smiles of the palace maids suddenly froze, slowly distorting, their eyes becoming vacant and hollow. They chanted in unison: "Go back where? This place **is** your home."

"No—!" Moony shivered uncontrollably in terror, tears welling up in her eyes, her voice raw but desperately fighting to be heard: "My Lady is waiting for me! Let me go!"

She charged forward, wildly waving her hands, attempting to push aside the terrifying phantoms before her.

In an instant, the lavish feast on the table transformed into countless blood-red flower petals, scattering everywhere, the cold fragrance sharp and choking, as if attempting to violently consume her entirely.

"Aah—!" She let out a piercing scream. The light before her shattered, and the world abruptly collapsed.

Her entire body felt as though it were being violently dragged into a whirlpool; her ears were filled with a deafening roar, and her heart felt as though it were about to rupture.

After an unknown period, she slammed heavily onto a hard surface, the cold penetrating deep into her bones.

Moony tentatively raised her head, her vision slowly clearing—she was, astonishingly, back in the Grand Hall of the Imperial Palace, with its carved dragons and painted phoenixes, the palace lanterns still glowing, everything as it should be.

She stared, her chest heaving violently. After a long, painful moment, she gave a shaky little laugh: "Hoo… thank goodness… thank goodness I managed to return…"

Her strained nerves finally released their tension entirely. Her legs felt weak, and large, fat tears began to roll down her cheeks.

Like a child who had finally found her way home, her heart was filled only with the immense relief of surviving a great tribulation.

"Lady… I am back…" she murmured softly, her voice as thin as the passing wind.

The next moment, her eyelids grew impossibly heavy. Having completely exhausted her last remaining strength, her body slumped sideways, falling heavily onto the cold stone floor of the hall. She struggled desperately to keep her eyes open, but could only perceive the surroundings as a hazy blur.

The night wind blew through, stirring the bronze rings on the palace doors, which emitted a low, resonant *—HUM—*.

The vast Imperial Palace held only her small, isolated form, deeply asleep, like a tiny child who had finally escaped a profound nightmare, still anxious and afraid.

Just then, the seam between illusion and reality seemed to tear open, and hurried footsteps sounded from outside the hall doors.

A tall figure walked in against the light of the palace lanterns, his robes moving slightly. His features were obscured by the interplay of light and shadow, yet he carried an undeniable aura of reality that suppressed the final aftershocks of the illusion.

Du Shao.

Moony's tears immediately began to flow again, yet she suddenly felt a profound sense of stability in her heart. The illusion had not fully receded, but this was undeniably the real him.

The man seemed to look towards her, his gaze gentle, and he even offered a faint smile beneath the lamplight.

Moony stared blankly, murmuring faintly: "...It is you."

The tightly strung cord in her heart finally, completely gave way.

In the next instant, her legs gave out entirely, and her body fell heavily.

In the moment before losing consciousness, the last things she saw were that gently smiling, comforting figure, and his low, anxious cry:

"Immortal Maiden Moony!"

The palace lanterns flickered, casting her small figure onto the cold floor of the great hall, where she quietly sank into the darkness.

* * * * *

The mist was thick and deep, the atmosphere profoundly **chaotic**, like a single, colossal prison forged in the void.

Yun Yara stood entirely alone in the boundless white vapour, the silence around her terrifyingly absolute and suffocating.

Beneath her feet, a faint, almost non-existent stone pathway stretched out towards an invisible, utterly unknowable horizon.

Her heart pounded violently and frantically in her chest.

She attempted to call out for Moony and Yun Lili, but her voice felt completely stifled, as though blocked by thick, smothering cotton; it merely echoed briefly within the fog, receiving no reply whatsoever from the silent expanse.

"Is anyone truly there?" she tried desperately to suppress the acute trembling in her voice, yet the profound anxiety still managed to pierce the quiet air.

Suddenly, a figure coalesced and emerged before her with shocking clarity.

It was… **herself**.

The apparition was wearing a magnificent, heavily embroidered Imperial robe, her features cool and profoundly arrogant, seated serenely upon a cloud-couch adorned with the fierce, complex pattern of the Phoenix.

Countless Immortals stood perpetually bowed before her, cupping their hands and calling out in unison: "**Phoenix Empress**."

Yun Yara's pupils contracted violently, and her breathing grew sharp and shallow, seizing in her throat.

That was unmistakably her own face, yet it was imbued with a chilling dignity far greater than she had ever witnessed; even the deep expression in her eyes reflected the innate, cold, and unyielding authority of a born ruler.

"No… that is not me," she murmured faintly, a powerful, wrenching fear surging up from the very depths of her heart and consciousness.

The illusory version of herself slowly turned its gaze, looking down upon her with supreme, chilling condescension, its voice as cold as severe frost and cutting snow:

"You, you are merely the **substitute**. The true Phoenix Empress was never, in any sense of the word, you."

The statement was like a sharp knife, brutally plunged into her very core and twisted cruelly.

Yun Yara's entire body swayed precariously. Her fingers dug fiercely and painfully into her palm, yet she still felt an overwhelming, bone-deep coldness spread instantly through her hands and feet.

The mist churned violently, and countless voices rose and fell around her, like the insidious, mocking whispers of vengeful spirits:

"Yun Lili possesses the true bloodline…"

"You are nothing more than the mistakenly adopted child…"

"Should she return to the fold, you will become utterly meaningless and obsolete…"

The voices roared like incessant thunder, painfully assaulting her ear drums.

"No! I am the daughter of the Yun family! I am—" Yun Yara tried desperately to argue forcefully, to shout down the accusation, but her voice was so thin it was almost instantly swallowed by the swirling fog.

The illusory version of herself suddenly rose, walking towards her step by deliberate, stately step.

Her robes billowed majestically, the Phoenix pattern radiating a blinding, aggressive light. With every step the apparition took closer, Yun Yara felt the stone pathway beneath her feet violently cracking and crumbling, the entire world pressing down upon her, negating and repudiating her existence.

"You are unworthy," the phantom looked down at her coldly, its voice chillingly cruel and absolute.

"You are unworthy of everything you possess."

Yun Yara's chest constricted violently, and her throat felt sickly sweet. She involuntarily spat out a mouthful of warm blood.

She stumbled and fell hard to the ground, her eyes hot and wet, her vision instantly blurred and distorted by the rush of tears.

Suddenly, a violent gale swept through the space, and the illusion shattered with a deafening, echoing crash, dissolving into countless scattered points of brilliant light.

The white mist receded like a powerful tide, and the world abruptly tilted sideways, violently. Her entire body was flung mercilessly into a seemingly bottomless abyss.

"Aah—!" Yun Yara screamed, her voice immediately swallowed by the raging, consuming wind.

After an unknown duration, a tremendous, bone-jarring impact caused her to fall heavily onto solid ground.

She slowly lifted her head, her vision gradually clarifying—the surroundings were sheer, towering mountain cliffs, with ethereal wisps of cloud and smoke floating aimlessly.

The area was profoundly silent and utterly desolate, with only the rustling sound of dead leaves scattering across the valley floor.

The **Smoke-Falling Valley**.

She stared blankly, her chest still heaving violently, as if she had just miraculously clawed her way back from the absolute edge of death.

Just then, a faint sound of robes fluttering reached her ears from ahead.

She fiercely lifted her gaze—

Within the lingering mist, a tall, slender silhouette stood with his hands clasped firmly behind his back. Black robes snapped lightly in the cold wind, his long hair flowed loosely, and his aura was as cold and isolated as a lone, remote mountain peak.

Mo Han.

He stood sideways at the valley entrance, his expression completely concealed in the profound shadows.

Only his silhouette remained utterly desolate, conveying an inexplicable, deep-seated sense of loneliness and coldness.

Heaven and earth were still, save for his figure, which stood like a single, solitary sword plunged into the heart of the silent, barren valley.

Yun Yara's entire body trembled. Her heart was overcome by an intense, inexplicable, and profound sorrow, yet she found herself completely unable to utter a single word of greeting or surprise.

She knew she had finally escaped the clutches of the illusion, yet the raw, isolated scene before her felt even more profoundly unsettling than any phantom image.

In the Smoke-Falling Valley, the wind howled mournfully. Between her and him, there remained only a vast, yawning, unbridgeable distance.

And that solitary figure, seemingly destined for eternal solitude, was beyond the true reach of any emotional companionship.

The sound of the wind was like a sharp blade, sweeping up the scattered leaves and spinning them violently in the air before allowing them to slowly descend to the valley floor.

Mo Han slowly turned, his dark hair flying behind him in the wind. The depths of his black eyes held a thread of gloomy, searching light, and the corner of his lips curved into an ambiguous, half-mocking smile.

Mo Han spoke in a low voice: "Do you finally see the truth now? The Celestial Realm has never genuinely treated you as a true daughter. In their eyes, there is only bloodline, only the mission. Only I possess the power to liberate you from these suffocating, existential shackles."

Yun Yara's face immediately turned frigid. Her fingers clenched tightly into her sleeves, her voice suppressed yet utterly resolute: "Silence! I am a daughter of the Yun family! Whether my blood is true or false, I belong to the Immortal Realm. How dare I align myself with the demonic fiends of your realm?!"

Mo Han advanced a single step, his gaze locking onto her, his voice a low, seductive whisper that promised ruinous comfort: "Align? That is merely an excuse fabricated by the common world. You know in your heart that you are not of the Yun bloodline—if one day the Celestial Realm casts you aside and exposes your truth, who will stand up to defend you? They will only pressure you and ruthlessly utilise you until your spiritual essence is utterly drained. Only I will offer you genuine, unconditional freedom."

Yun Yara abruptly retreated a step, her eyes glistening with unshed tears, yet her resolve became even fiercer: "Be quiet! The freedom you speak of is purchased through mass slaughter and chaos! I would rather willingly die than associate myself with your kind!"

Mo Han leaned slightly closer, his dark shadow enveloping her entirely. His voice was husky, slow, and devastatingly intimate: "Yun Yara, do you truly dare to say that? Did your heart… truly not waver for a single, fleeting moment when I offered you refuge?"

"Waver?" She let out a cold, short laugh, and the tears finally burst forth and streamed down her cheeks, yet she met his gaze without flinching: "Yes! I did waver! But precisely because I wavered, because I felt that moment of temptation, I understand even more clearly that I and your Demonic Clan—we are sworn enemies for all eternity!"

The valley wind suddenly howled, a sudden, powerful blast that whipped her hair around her face, and simultaneously scattered the very last thread of possible warmth between the two of them.

Mo Han's smile instantly vanished, his gaze turning profound, depthless, and utterly inscrutable. He stared at her silently. After a long, heavy pause, his voice became as cold as an ice-forged sword edge:

"Very well… then remember the words you have spoken today. Should you ever regret them in the future, know that there will be absolutely no path for you to return to my side."

With those final words, his robes fluttered, his silhouette utterly desolate, and he turned to vanish into the thick mist at the bottom of the valley.

Yun Yara was left standing alone in the Smoke-Falling Valley, her hands trembling, her chest heaving uncontrollably.

Her fierce answer had sliced through all vague boundaries like a honed blade, but it had also firmly placed her on the absolute opposite side of the cosmic divide from him forever.

The whirlwind slowly began to rise again, sweeping up bursts of fallen leaves that spun and flew violently in the air.

As the wind grew steadily stronger, Yun Yara instinctively raised her hands to shield her eyes. In a sudden rush of extreme disorientation, her body was also caught in the vortex, lifted off the ground, spinning rapidly and wildly… until she finally lost all consciousness.

Chapter 50: Come And Find Me

The wind howled with a feral edge, tearing through the depths of Fallen Mist Valley. The heavy fog there churned and boiled, like the laments of ten thousand tormented spirits.

Yue Liuchuan hung bound by iron chains, his spine stubbornly straight even as blood seeped through the torn fabric at his shoulders from struggling. His jaw clenched, voice hoarse with fury as he spat out each word:

"Mo Han! What in the world are you trying to do?! If you want to kill me, then kill me now! Why imprison me in this cursed place?!"

The chains clattered sharply, each metallic ring mingling with his roar.

Mo Han lounged casually against the stone wall, arms crossed, posture almost lazy. His black hair drifted in the wind, and his lips curled into an indolent arc—yet the glint in his eyes was sharp, cruel, and entirely unmasked.

"Kill you?"

His tone lengthened with mockery, almost playful.

"Yue Liuchuan, you truly underestimate yourself. Killing you—what good would that do? It would merely remove one more discarded disciple from the Immortal Realm."

Yue Liuchuan barked a cold laugh.

"If I am a discarded disciple, then what does that make you? A demon prince too cowardly to face the Immortal Realm in open battle—only capable of skulking in the shadows—"

Before the sentence could finish, Mo Han flicked his fingers.

A streak of black light shot forth, slamming against the iron chains with a violent crack.

The impact reverberated directly through Yue Liuchuan's chest, cutting off the rest of his words with a suffocating jolt.

Mo Han's gaze darkened, and he stepped forward slowly, voice dropping to a soft, chilling register:

"As long as you remain in the mortal realm—and remain in my hands— the Immortal Realm will not sit idle. In time, someone is bound to come looking."

He paused.

A flicker of something wild, obsessive, almost deranged lit his eyes.

A thought curled within him like a secret flame:

Perhaps Yara… she will come find me herself.

Then—

The wind changed.

A violent, twisting gust ripped through the valley, as though some unseen forces were tearing the heavens apart. Above them, the clouds churned violently, and a vortex spiralled open, splitting the sky into a gaping, shadowed rift.

Mo Han's head snapped upward, pupils tightening sharply.

From that dark fissure, a single figure drifted down—white-robed, unconscious, like a fallen feather carried gently by invisible hands. She descended slowly, her black hair in disarray, eyes closed tight, her breath faint and fragile.

—Yara.

Time froze.

Mo Han's hand moved instinctively—yet also as if he had been waiting for this moment all along. The white-clad girl fell neatly into his arms, so light she felt weightless.

The wind around them stilled in an instant.

He lowered his gaze, staring at the girl in his hold. Under the pale moonlight she looked almost ethereal, the delicate pallor of her features stirring something inside him—an unfamiliar tightness, a painful tug, as though his heart had been seized in a clenched fist.

Yue Liuchuan glared at the scene, shock and fury twisting violently across his face. He thrashed against the chains and bellowed:

"Mo Han! Put me down this instant!"

But Mo Han did not spare him a single glance.

His lips curved into a cold, unreadable smile, voice dropping to a soft murmur—half to her, half to himself—yet unable to hide the faint tremor of exhilaration:

"…Why is it you?"

* * * * *

Night pressed heavily upon the valley, the wind outside the Falling-Smoke ravine howling like a living thing.

Inside the small wooden hut, the lamp burned low.

Firelight flickered against the walls, casting long, wavering shadows that swayed with every breath of wind.

Yara's eyelashes trembled before she slowly opened her eyes.

The first thing she saw was a face—unfamiliar, yet painfully familiar.

Mo Han.

He sat not far from her, posture relaxed, expression composed. In one hand he idly played with a pitch-black jade slip, letting it roll between his fingers.

When his gaze shifted to her, something in his lips curved upward, a faint smile cutting across his cool features.

"You're awake."

Yara jolted upright on instinct—but the moment she moved, a sharp pain shot through her arms.

Her breath caught. Her meridians felt constrained, tightly bound; her wrists were reddened as though something had pressed against them.

A chill spread down her spine.

Her voice, though hoarse, remained stubborn and steady.

"What… is this place? And why—why are *you* here?"

Mo Han did not answer her question. Instead, he set the jade slip down with a soft tap, his voice gentler than she had ever heard it—gentle to the point it felt utterly wrong on him.

"I'm not sure why," he replied with a low murmur, "but you… fell straight from the heavens. Directly into my arms."

"That's impossible."

He paused. A flicker of emotion crossed his eyes—something she could not decipher, a shadow of something dark and unspoken. When he spoke again, his voice dipped lower.

"Is this… not your will?"

"Absurd!" Yara snapped, fury flushing her pale cheeks. And yet—her heart dropped violently in her chest.

Because she remembered.

In that wretched wish-spirit's illusion, in a single fleeting moment, she had wondered—

What is he doing right now?

It had been nothing—nothing but a flash of curiosity, a stray thought she had crushed the instant it appeared. She had denied it, shoved it down, rejected it with all her will.

And yet—

That infuriating, untrustworthy spirit had taken it as a real wish?

Her jaw clenched. Her voice trembled, sharp and ragged:

"Whatever happened, I'm leaving. Now."

Mo Han regarded her quietly, as though seeing straight through her.

There was laughter in his eyes—cold, needle-fine, and merciless.

"You wish to return to Lingxiao Sect?"

His tone deepened, laced with that dangerous, hypnotic pull of his.

"Since fate has already brought you here… why not stay with me for a few days?"

A shiver ran down Yara's spine. She opened her mouth to retort, but—

A metallic rattle broke the silence.

From the shadows in the corner, chains clinked softly.

Her head snapped toward the sound.

Yue Liuchuan stood bound hand and foot in heavy shackles, cold iron biting into his skin. His gaze was sharp as a blade, locked onto her and Mo Han with unmistakable warning.

His voice was hoarse yet forceful:

"Yara—don't listen to a word he says! You belong to the Immortal Realm. How could you ever stand beside a demon prince?!"

Yara's throat tightened. Her eyes stung, tears threatening to spill.

She wanted to speak. She wanted to tell Yue Liuchuan she knew, she understood, she—she hadn't chosen this.

But the thought of the wish-spirit's eerie warning flashed across her mind—

Every wish comes with a price.

And her "price"

—was this.

This suffocating guilt, this crushing sense of *betrayal*, as though she had turned her back on her sect… even though she hadn't chosen anything at all.

It was a burden she now had to carry simply because of a single, fleeting thought.

A price extracted without mercy.

Even if she had done nothing—

even if all she had was a single, fleeting thought of him at the worst possible moment—

just that one slip, that brief image flashing across her mind, had been enough for the spirit in the pot to seize upon and hurl her here.

Because of that, she could no longer face herself without shame.

Her whole body trembled. She forced herself upright, teeth clenched so tightly her jaw ached, and lifted her head to glare at Mo Han with all the fury she could muster.

"Get away from me! You and I… are impossible!"

Mo Han merely let out a low, quiet laugh.

A shadow stirred in his eyes—dark, dangerous, unreadable.

"Yara, you may hate me. You may reject me."

His voice dropped to a murmur, soft but cutting.

"But you cannot deny it—this time, you came to me on your own."

He didn't wait for her rebuttal.

He turned, one smooth motion pushing the wooden door open.

A chill night wind rushed inside, scattering the strands of hair across her forehead.

His silhouette was solitary, stark against the swirling fog of Fallen Mist Valley.

With each step, his figure dissolved into the mist, swallowed bit by bit until nothing remained.

And Yara was left alone in the dim hut, hands trembling uncontrollably, breath shuddering in her chest.

A heavy weight surged through her—a pressure so suffocating it felt as though it might crush her ribcage from within.

She finally understood.

Tonight, she was truly trapped.

No matter how fiercely she denied it, no matter how she struggled—

there was no escaping the price she had already paid.

* * * * *

The hall gleamed with lavish splendour—gilded beams, jade pillars carved with coiling dragons, incense drifting like pale mist. Luminous night-pearls cast a soft brilliance, turning the entire chamber as bright as day.

Moony slowly opened her eyes, momentarily stunned by the overwhelming magnificence. She lay on a gold-threaded couch embroidered with phoenix patterns; the brocade beneath her felt impossibly soft, unreal, like clouds woven into fabric.

Silken tassels draped around her, swaying gently, while crystal beads shimmered coldly under the light.

"The little immortal has awakened!"

Two palace maids hurried forward, kneeling beside the couch. Their eyes brimmed with reverence as they called out in unison:

"Immortal maiden!"

There was such earnest respect in their voices—so much care in their movements—that even their breathing felt restrained, as if they feared disturbing her.

Moony panicked at once. She fumbled to sit up, but her body was too weak, nearly collapsing back onto the cushions.

"W-Where... where am I?" she stammered.

One maid smiled reassuringly.

"You are in the royal palace. His Highness learned that the immortal maiden had fallen unconscious and personally ordered you brought to the inner hall. He instructed us to attend to you with utmost care."

"His... His Highness?"

Moony's heart lurched violently.

Who? Why?

She had barely formed the question when the great doors suddenly swung open.

With a deep creak, the heavy gates parted—and a tall, familiar silhouette entered against the warm glow of palace lamps.

Wide sleeves. Clear, refined features.

The face she had secretly imagined countless times in her dreams—

Du Shao.

His steps halted. For an instant, something trembled in his eyes. He quickly schooled his expression back into calm, yet the faint lift of joy at the corners of his lips could not be hidden.

"Moony," he murmured softly.

"You're awake."

She lurched toward him on unsteady legs, nearly falling—

but Du Shao moved immediately, catching her with firm, steady hands.

Moony looked up at him, and tears rolled down her cheeks in quick, uncontrollable drops.

"I… I only wanted… just to see you… and then… and now… truly…"

Her words tangled, breath hitching.

Du Shao froze for a beat, startled. Then his lips curved in a gentle arc as he lifted a hand to wipe her tears away, his tone softer than she had ever heard:

"Silly girl. Since you've seen me now… all is well. I… am greatly pleased."

A bittersweet tide rose in her chest—pain and sweetness mixing until she didn't know whether to cry or smile.

Then suddenly, she went rigid.

Something felt wrong.

Her body felt empty.

Completely, terrifyingly empty.

Moony lifted her hand abruptly, trying to summon even the faintest glimmer of spiritual light—

but nothing, not even the weakest spark, answered her call.

Her breath caught.

"N… No…"

Her entire body shook, colour draining from her face.

"My… my spiritual power… it's gone."

Du Shao's brows furrowed at once. He sensed the shift immediately.

"What is it?"

Moony clutched her chest, voice cracking.

"My cultivation… it's gone. All of it."

The realization destroyed her composure. Her cultivation had never been high, but it had been hers—it was the only thing she had relied on since childhood. And now, in one stroke, it had vanished completely.

It meant she might never step onto the cultivation path again.

Her breathing turned ragged. Panic washed over her until her slender frame trembled uncontrollably, her small face turning ashen.

Du Shao remained silent for a long, steady moment, simply watching her.

Then he reached out, drawing her gently but firmly back into his embrace.

"Don't be afraid," he murmured quietly.

"I will protect you."

His calm certainty struck her like a warm flame.

Moony stared up at him, stunned, before tears surged anew—not from fear this time, but from a soft, aching sweetness she could not contain.

She let out a tiny, tremulous laugh, eyes reddened.

"To be able to see you again… it's enough."

Du Shao's expression shifted faintly—complicated, pained, tender all at once. At last, he held her even tighter.

—And somewhere deep within the palace, the unseen pot spirit let out a faint, echoing laugh.

"Wish fulfilled," it murmured.

"And the price… has begun."

Gongs resonated in the distance. Dawn light spilled over the golden tiles, freezing this fragile, extravagant moment in time.

Moony closed her eyes, burying her face into Du Shao's chest, whispering to herself:

"This pot spirit… really is effective."

Chapter 51: The Reunion in the Mist

The Scared Kitten

The sound of the wind outside the Grand Hall had only just ceased when Yun Lili's entire body barrelled straight into the unsuspecting arms of Yun Duntang.

"Father, oh, Father—!" The moment she opened her mouth, her tears began to pour down like snapped pearls, falling uncontrollably. She wept incoherently, utterly beside herself, "I remember everything now… My mother, did she, did she truly sacrifice herself?! Wuwuwu…"

Yun Duntang was momentarily stunned into immobility, his hands still half-raised in the air. He awkwardly received this daughter, whose face was a sudden, complete mess of snot and tears. The solemn, imposing Clan Master of the Lingxiao Sect, in that instant, looked precisely like a man utterly bewildered by a small, frantic kitten that had been violently flung at him.

"Lili… my child… speak slowly now, do not weep with such profound distress—"

"What shall I do! I am so terribly afraid!" she hiccupped wildly, her fingers clutching desperately onto his sleeve, like a child who fears the dark and cannot be placated. "Moony has vanished, and A-Yara has vanished, too… wuwuwu… even my most beloved mirror is irrevocably shattered!"

Yun Zane, standing nearby, could not resist giving a light cough, discreetly concealing the smile in his eyes. He muttered under his breath: "She can still vividly recall that broken bronze mirror of hers; she must possess some lingering thread of conscience, at least."

"What broken bronze mirror!" Yun Lili immediately whipped her head around, tears still clinging to her face, yet managing to glare fiercely at him. "That is my treasure! My very life! Wuwu… and now it's all shattered…"

The assembled elders exchanged bewildered glances, unsure whether the protocol dictated they should offer stern counsel or simply succumb to laughter.

Yun Duntang finally managed to regain his composure. He gently patted her back, his voice adopting a rare, soothing softness: "Silly child, do not fear. There will surely be news of both Moony and Yara soon enough. As for your mother..." Here, his voice faltered slightly, finally dissolving into a deep, heavy sigh.

Yun Lili wept even more uncontrollably: "Father, I do not want any grand, terrifying mission; I simply wish for everyone to be well and safe... wuwu..."

She was crying so intensely the entire world seemed to swirl around her, her voice thick with nasal congestion, making her words almost unintelligible. Yun Zane suppressed his mirth for a long, torturous moment, then finally let out a low chuckle: "In this state, she resembles nothing so much as a runaway little maid, certainly not a descendant of the formidable Phoenix Clan."

Yun Lili lifted her head, her eyes red and swollen, glaring at him petulantly: "I am a little maid, and what of it! Little maids are allowed to cry, too, you know!"

The entire hall fell silent for a moment, before several elders unexpectedly burst into soft laughter. The oppressive, heavy atmosphere, which had been thick with anxiety, was thus unexpectedly diluted by her fit of weeping and chaotic fuss.

Yun Duntang gazed down helplessly at the daughter clinging to him, crying and making a profound scene, yet a subtle warmth slowly spread through his eyes. *Perhaps... precisely because she could still act so spoiled and weep so shamelessly, he truly felt, deep down, that his daughter had actually returned to him, completely whole.*

* * * * *

Night was deep and heavy. Mist shrouded the main hall of the Lingxiao Sect. In the flickering, agitated light of the lamps, Yun Duntang stood with his hands clasped behind his back, his expression profound and deeply contemplative.

Yun Zhou pushed the door open and strode in. His face was dark and overcast, yet his eyes held an unconcealable, raw urgency.

"Father!" he spoke in a low, voice, tightly controlled, yet laced with desperation. "If that devastating day truly arrives, allow me to go and mend the array core!"

Yun Duntang's body stiffened abruptly. He turned, his expression revealing a faint, profound bitterness: "Zhou... do you fully comprehend the immense magnitude of what you are suggesting?"

Yun Zhou bit down hard on his jaw, his hands clenched into fists of white bone: "Why is it forbidden? I, too, possess the Phoenix bloodline!

Since this is the dreadful task, why can I not be the one to endure the suffering and the sacrifice?!"

Yun Duntang let out a deep, heavy sigh, his gaze burdened. His tone carried a thread of resigned, bitter mockery: "Alas, the rules of the Phoenix Clan are impossibly strict; the Clan Master has only ever been passed down through the female line since antiquity. The Phoenix Origin Core only crystallises within the spiritual body of the Phoenix Sovereign. Zhou, no matter how much you might resemble a female, no matter how profoundly effeminate your energy may be, you are not of the female gender… within your physical form, the Phoenix Core Pellet will never, ever form."

The statement was like a razor blade, ruthlessly slicing through Yun Zhou's heart. His eyes instantly darkened, yet they were still filled with a profound struggle and deep, searing resentment.

"But Lili…" he growled in a low, pained voice, his eyes shimmering faintly with unshed tears. "She is so innocent and such a coward; how can she possibly bear the weight of such an immense, fatal responsibility?! By what divine decree should she be chosen to face certain death?!"

A flash of intense pain crossed Yun Duntang's eyes. He slowly closed them, his voice low and heavy as rolling thunder: "Zhou, do you truly believe your father desires this outcome? The Phoenix Core Pellet is merely the most simplified, expedient method… it is, in fact, not the only one available. But should we seek an alternative solution, it would require the combined, unified strength of many more Celestial Sovereigns, and the resulting casualties would be far greater and more devastating."

"If that is truly the case!" Yun Zhou violently cut him off, his voice charged with fierce, righteous emotion, his eyes completely bloodshot. "Why will the assembled Immortals not unite their efforts and cooperate?! Why must the entire dreadful plan pivot upon a single, frightened young girl?! What kind of Celestial Realm is this that permits such cowardice?!"

His words vibrated so forcefully the lamps in the hall trembled slightly.

Yun Duntang remained silent for a long, heavy duration, his eyes filled with immense, crushing sorrow. Finally, he spoke slowly: "Because this way… the overall casualties are minimised, and the outcome is statistically the most secure."

Yun Zhou froze on the spot, his chest heaving like a drum. He finally ground his teeth together, let out a cold, bitter laugh, and spun around abruptly.

"Zhou!" Yun Duntang commanded, his voice deep and sharp as a thunderclap. "Where precisely do you intend to go?"

Yun Zhou's footsteps halted, yet he did not turn back. His shoulders were tense and rigid, and his voice was hoarse yet utterly resolute: "I am going to find Yun Yara."

With that, he did not pause again. His robes flew out behind him, his silhouette one of pure, desperate finality, and he vanished into the night mist.

Yun Duntang watched the direction of his departure, his expression complex and riddled with pain, then his fingers gripped his walking stick so tightly that the wood emitted a faint, sharp, cracking sound.

After a long silence, he murmured softly: "Zhou, my son… be it you or be it Lili, your father wishes he could bear this terrible burden for both of you right now."

* * * * *

Deep within the garden, the late evening breeze blew softly. Yun Lili's hand was tightly clutching a stalk of phoenix-tail grass, her expression growing increasingly frayed, restless, and deeply irritable.

Three persistent chickens were clucking loudly, circling perpetually and annoyingly around her feet.

One was determinedly pecking at the grass; another insisted on hopping onto a nearby stone to squawk aimlessly at the sky. The combined, relentless racket was giving her a truly monumental headache.

"Be quiet, all of you!" Yun Lili couldn't help but stomp her foot hard, yelling angrily. "Why must you *cluck, cluck, cluck* all day long, without cease? Can you not simply remain quiet and cease your dreadful commotion for one single, solitary moment? My ears are about to be permanently deafened by your collective noise!"

The three chickens collectively paused, tilting their small heads in unison. Their clucking, however, only grew louder, sounding distinctly like a unified, aggrieved protest against the injustice of her sudden command.

Yun Lili rolled her eyes in exasperation, then glanced up, only to see Little Fira silently perched on a high branch. Its golden feathers gleamed coldly in the setting sun, and its eyes were fixed immovably, disconcertingly, upon her.

Her heart leaped violently in alarm. She instantly sprang up, shouting: "Why are you standing there so silently?! Why are you lurking?! Are you intentionally trying to give someone a fatal fright!"

She froze then, realising the utter absurdity of her outburst and feeling a sudden wave of unreasoning guilt wash over her.

Lili looked down at the three chickens, then back up at Little Fira, finally speaking in a quiet, chastened whisper: "…Fine, fine, I was completely out of line just now. You are neither loud enough nor quiet enough for my current sensibilities, it seems… Oh, I am simply dreadfully preoccupied and my nerves are shattered. Please, do not hold my ridiculous outburst against me, alright?"

The three chickens seemed, somehow, to fully understand.

They slowly shuffled towards her feet, their clucking softening into a low, profoundly comforting murmur. Little Fira, however, suddenly ruffled its plumage, and its wings abruptly expanded, growing several times larger in an instant.

Its enormous pinions kicked up a sharp gust of wind, scattering the surrounding leaves in a noisy, sudden shower.

"Aah—!" Yun Lili's face went white with abject terror. The phoenix-tail grass *clattered* onto the ground, and she immediately turned and bolted away.

"Do not seize me with your beak! I do not wish to fly again, I tell you!" she shouted frantically as she ran, her voice thick with residual, overwhelming panic. The traumatic memory of Little Fira's last aerial rampage, which had nearly flung her from the heavens to her demise, was still devastatingly fresh in her mind.

Little Fira, however, lowered its flight path, flying close to the ground, seemingly deliberately teasing her. One moment it swept just over the crown of her head, the next it swooped down low, threatening to snatch her hair.

The three chickens, meanwhile, added to the confusion with panicked squawking, scattering everywhere.

"Little Fira! I apologise! I promise never to complain about your silence again! Just do not seize me with your beak!" Yun Lili was half-crying, half-laughing in sheer hysteria. Her foot slipped, and she nearly stumbled, clinging desperately to a nearby tree, panting for breath.

Little Fira landed on her shoulder, shrinking back instantly to its small, innocuous size. It tilted its head, adopting a perfectly innocent expression.

Yun Lili, drenched in cold sweat, patted her chest and gasped for air, her teeth grinding in frustrated fury: "You utterly wretched bird! You are going to scare me to death one of these days, mark my words…"

But by the end of the sentence, her voice involuntarily softened. She reached up and gently scratched Little Fira's chin, sighing: "Oh, well. It's fine. None of you are truly malicious… it is simply my own mind that is in such profound disarray."

The three chickens clucked softly again, nudging close to her feet, burying their heads near her ankles. Little Fira rested quietly, its feathers radiating a subtle, comforting warmth.

Yun Lili looked at these bizarre, faithful companions who had followed her through so many trials. The turmoil in her heart suddenly lessened, replaced instead by a familiar, stinging sensation in her nose.

* * * * *

Yun Lili's feet had only just been held steady by a streak of azure light, and her entire being was still reeling from the shock. She descended tremulously onto the stone steps, her legs instantly giving way beneath her, nearly sending her crashing to her knees.

"Phew… I was almost killed in that fall…"

She gasped for breath, then looked up, roaring at the sky: "You wicked Little Fira! You merciless, faithless bird! You nearly killed me with a fall last time, and now again—waaah, my ears are still ringing with the noise!"

The three chickens clucked loudly, scrambling quickly towards her, hopping and fluttering as they circled her in a frantic display of concern.

Yun Lili instinctively scooped up one of them, hugging it fiercely, scolding it with a blend of tears and laughter: "Only you three know how to show me any compassion! That wretched bird is clearly attempting to commit **host-murder**!"

Just as she was speaking, the mist around them suddenly stirred. A profound **sword intent**, cold as a tidal wave, surged towards them.

Yun Lili froze, spinning around sharply. She saw a figure in azure robes emerge slowly from the mist. His longsword was sheathed behind his back, his robes snapped lightly in the wind, and the cold light reflecting off his subtle armour almost stung her eyes.

"…Yu Sord."

Yun Lili was momentarily stunned. Then, her nose suddenly stung, and her tears burst forth in a torrential, undeniable flood. She let out a desperate, muffled cry, "*Waaah!*", and lunged, clinging tightly to his waist.

"Wuwuwu! I was so terrified!" she cried, breathless and incoherent, burying her entire face into his chest. Her voice was fractured and ragged: "Moony has vanished, A-Yara has vanished, I was terrified to death all alone in the illusion… and my mirror is completely shattered, too… wuwuwu…"

She wept hysterically, her fingers digging fiercely into his sleeve, as if afraid he, too, would vanish without a trace.

Yu Sord's entire body stiffened sharply. He lowered his gaze to the young girl in his arms, her face wet with tears. His heart felt as though it had been fiercely struck by something immense.

He immediately wrapped one arm around her, his palm pressing steadily onto her back, his fingertips trembling slightly. His voice, however, was extremely low and utterly steady: "Lili, do not be afraid. **I am here** with you."

"But it was truly… so utterly horrible and terrifying…" Yun Lili cried, her face streaked with tears, lifting her head. Her eyes were unfocused and utterly helpless. "I thought I would never be able to see you again in this life…"

Yu Sord's gaze was deep and profound, as though he were rigorously suppressing some powerful, volatile emotion, yet his embrace only tightened further in response.

"Silly girl," he murmured, his voice softening. His fingertips gently wiped away the traces of tears from the corner of her eyes, his expression holding a rare, profound warmth. "If you could not find me, then I would simply come to find you. No matter where you were, I would have found you."

Yun Lili hiccupped, staring at him. She suddenly burst into even louder sobs: "But my mirror is shattered! My most favourite mirror in the entire world!"

The more she thought of it, the more profoundly wronged she felt, her voice thick with genuine, wounded pathos: "You do not understand, you see! That mirror has been with me for such an immensely long time; it accompanied me to check my face, to check the chickens, and it even accompanied me to check for terrifying ghosts…"

Yu Sord froze momentarily and he was unexpectedly and thoroughly charmed by her utterly absurd reason for "checking for ghosts," and his features instantly softened.

He could not resist gently patting the top of her head, his tone one of weary resignation mixed with utter, complete devotion: "The mirror is broken; it can be replaced. But if you were broken… where, precisely, would I go to find you again?"

Yun Lili gasped, her tears still clinging stubbornly to her face, but she couldn't help but offer a small, tearful smile.

"You… you saying things like that only makes me want to cry even more, you see…"

She burrowed her head back into his embrace, her sobs now laced with undeniable traces of laughter, smearing tears and snot all over his pristine azure robes.

Yu Sord showed no sign of revulsion. He simply held her tightly, his long lashes lowered, his expression finally shedding the long-held, icy façade of rigidity.

Chapter 52: The Replacement Mirror

Within the Celestial Sword Pavilion, a profound silence reigned.

Only Yun Lili's soft, lingering sobs and the low, steady rhythm of Yu Sord's heartbeat intertwined in the cold mountain air.

Yun Lili's hands were still tightly clutching the three persistently clucking chickens. Feathers clung to her in disarray, her hair was a mess, and her eye sockets were vividly red, showing the clear evidence of her prolonged crying fit.

She covertly lifted her gaze to peer at Yu Sord, seeing him standing quietly, his sword-brow like a distant, immutable mountain, his gaze deep and profound, his expression completely unmoved. A sudden flutter of panic seized her heart, like a child caught out in a foolish transgression.

She forced out two awkward, dry laughs and frantically tried to smooth down her messy hair. Her voice was small and laced with acute guilt: "That… I really don't know why, but Little Fira suddenly… suddenly just dragged me over here…"

As she spoke, she felt her cheeks growing hot with embarrassment. She finally gave up, lowering her head to kick at a small stone by her feet, her voice dropping to a low, barely audible hum like a buzzing mosquito: "Actually… actually, I was trying to buy a new mirror. My old one, when I was in the mirror-world… I don't know how, but it just shattered."

When she uttered the word "shattered," her mouth pursed high with profound grievance, her eyes filled with unconcealed unwillingness, as if a most cherished treasure had been brutally snatched from her grasp.

Suddenly, she lifted her head, her eyes flashing with a sudden, bright thought, and her tone shifted instantly: "Did you know? I was incredibly powerful inside that mirror-world, truly! I could even fly!" She spread her arms wide, gesticulating wildly, her expression radiating proud, triumphant excitement. "But the moment I came out, I couldn't do it anymore! Oh, isn't that just the worst luck? I finally gained some abilities, and in the blink of an eye, they were gone again!"

Yu Sord's gaze subtly shifted. His finger turned over. Azure light, like gentle, spreading water ripples, emanated from his palm. In a moment, a mirror of crystal clarity hovered in his hand. The mirror body was smooth and purple like fine jade, its frame delicately etched with intricate patterns of purple bamboo. Its spiritual light was contained and unassuming, yet it carried an air of clean, elegant refinement, like a clear stream flowing through a mountain gorge—refined and deeply resonant.

He held the mirror out flatly, his voice faint, yet carrying a barely perceptible thread of tenderness: "If you do not find it lacking… this item, you may accept it as a gift from me."

Yun Lili's eyes instantly widened and shone. Her gasp of surprise nearly sent the three chickens flying off her arms: "Wow—it's so beautiful!" She immediately dropped the chickens with a *thump* onto the stone floor, receiving the mirror with both hands. Her eyes were sparkling brightly; she looked ready to fuse with the object itself.

"Yes, yes, thank you so much!" She smiled until her eyes curved into crescents, instantly clutching the mirror tightly to her chest in an attitude that loudly declared, "No one is getting their hands on this!" She treasured it immensely.

Yu Sord watched her, and a warm sensation spread through his heart. The young girl before him, holding the mirror carefully yet radiantly delighted, seemed to be bathed completely in the light of spring sunshine. The corner of his lips could not help but curl up in a subtle, genuine smile, and the cold sword-light that usually resided in his eyes quietly melted away.

"…I am glad you like it."

Finally, he thought, he had found an opportunity to present this mirror to her.

Yun Lili lowered her head, her fingertips tracing the intricate patterns on the mirror's surface, her eyes bright with fascination. But the brightness quickly faded, and her expression suddenly grew serious.

"With this mirror… I can finally start searching for Moony and A-Yara." She bit her lower lip, her voice hushed, as if speaking to herself, yet simultaneously forcing herself to make a solemn vow. "They are still missing, and I am genuinely worried sick about them…"

She looked up, the red traces of her tears still visible around her eyes, yet now imbued with an unexpected, fierce determination.

"I must, absolutely must find them."

Yu Sord observed her resolute appearance. His heart stirred sharply, and his sword-brow furrowed slightly, as if a thousand words were struggling to escape. But in the end, he simply stretched out his hand, resting it firmly and steadily on her shoulder, his voice low yet as solid and certain as a mountain:

"Do not worry. No matter where they are, **I will help you search for them.**"

* * * * *

Inside the Heavenly Pivot Hall, Yu Sord's sword intent descended with the chilling force of a sudden downpour, instantly shattering the light of the great celestial astrolabe. The entire chamber was rendered frigid and austere by the reflection of the azure-white sword-light.

After a moment of profound, frozen silence, an Elder with white eyebrows shouted harshly:

"Yu Sord! Your actions are intolerably **presumptuous**! This matter concerns the crucial security of the Four Realms; how dare you recklessly obstruct proceedings merely for the sake of a singular, personal affection?"

Another Celestial Lord offered a cold, sharp snort of agreement: "Precisely! Since you are an Immortal Sovereign, your priority must be the well-being of the common people. To protect the Four Realms, what consequence is there in sacrificing one solitary life?"

Their voices reverberated through the hall like iron striking stone.

Yu Sord's eyes flashed with cold intent. He pointed his longsword directly at the void, and the blade sang with a furious hum like roaring thunder: "If any of you dare to project that sentiment onto her again—you shall address my sword first!"

Such aggressively domineering words caused the faces of many assembled Sovereigns to pale significantly with shock.

One minister frowned, murmuring quietly: "He is truly emotionally involved now..."

Others remained silent, their gazes complex and uneasy.

Yun Zane suddenly let out a faint, brittle chuckle, a sound that seemed casual, yet effectively suppressed the rising aggression in the chamber: "Why must we be so relentlessly aggressive? Today's deliberation is still at the stage of deduction and review, not final consensus. Furthermore—"

He swept his gaze across the hall, his voice faint yet laced with sharp, corrosive sarcasm, "If we truly intend to resort to sacrificing a single bloodline, which of you seated in this Heavenly Pivot Hall can offer an absolute guarantee that the sacrifice will not, eventually, fall upon your own descendants?"

At this statement, the voices of those who had previously agreed to the sacrifice instantly choked into silence.

Some pondered the dark implication, their complexions shifting noticeably. Others darted their eyes shiftily, choosing not to speak again.

Sang Li slowly stepped forward. He raised his hand, gathering the scattered light from the broken astrolabe, his tone composed yet laced with chilling candour: "It is undeniable that the Phoenix Core Pellet is the most reliable strategy. But I insist it is by no means the only option. It is simply that—the alternative methods carry a far greater and more unpredictable cost, and the resulting casualties are impossible to measure."

"Then all the more reason to discuss alternatives, rather than simply insisting on one single, desperate course!" another younger Celestial Official couldn't help but interject, his face etched with profound struggle. "The Phoenix Clan has already exhausted their lineage for the sake of the Four Realms. Now, only a single orphan remains. If we continue to press this issue… should news of this blatant coercion spread, how will the Immortal Realm continue to claim moral impartiality?"

This statement caused the already precarious atmosphere in the hall to shake once more.

Yu Sord watched the entire assembly with cold, unwavering eyes, his voice low and firm as iron: "I shall state this again—as long as this Yu remains in this plane for one single day, none of you shall presume to harm her."

As he finished, his longsword hummed loudly, and the azure light shot straight towards the roof of the hall, shaking the very roof tiles of the Heavenly Pivot Palace as if they were about to catastrophically collapse.

Celestial Lord Su Yuan finally raised his hand, his silver sleeve waving. He suppressed the aggressive sword-qi, his voice clear and cold as frost and snow: **"Enough."**

He swept his gaze over everyone present, his voice steady yet carrying an irresistible, profound authority: "The proposal concerning the Phoenix Core Pellet is hereby temporarily shelved. The Demonic Army has not yet moved, and the Four Realms remain stable. We shall seek alternative methods; we will reconvene when a definitive solution has been found. It is not too late for further discussion."

The Immortals fell into a strained silence, no one daring to speak another word.

Yu Sord sheathed his sword, but did not speak again. His silhouette remained cold and rigid, like an isolated, formidable mountain peak, standing firm and unmoving regardless of the ensuing chaos.

* * * * *

Inside the **Phoenix Glory Pavilion**, the afternoon sunlight streamed in obliquely, catching the soft, slow sway of the curtains. The light fell in broken, dancing patches, as mottled and restless as water reflections.

Yun Lili was cross-legged on the couch, tightly hugging the new purple-bamboo-etched mirror. Her fingertips traced the edges repeatedly, and she mumbled softly under her breath:

"Moony, Moony, please come out now…"

The mirror's surface suddenly flashed. Her heart clenched, and she held her breath, gazing intently at the glass.

The light and shadow instantly coalesced, forming a scroll-like image of the imperial palace: golden tiles and cinnabar beams, fragrant mist rising thickly.

Within the scene, Moony was nestled happily beside a low table, her eyes curved into crescents of pure delight. Facing her sat Du Shao, who was, astonishingly, personally pouring her tea. His expression was gentle, and his demeanour was stripped of its usual frostiness, revealing a delicate, barely perceptible tenderness.

Their movements and interactions showed an exceptional, natural harmony.

Yun Lili stared for a moment, unable to suppress a faint, sweet smile that lifted the corners of her lips. Yet she whispered to herself: "That girl… she is truly **favoured by fate**, isn't she?"

Despite the words, a thread of obscure sourness involuntarily surfaced in her eyes. She quickly hid it, simply giving the mirror a light tap, and continued her quiet summoning.

However, no matter how desperately she called out, the mirror's surface remained stubbornly blank. Spiritual light churned beneath the glass, but it refused to coalesce into Yun Yara's image.

Yun Lili stared until her expression grew heavy with anxiety, and a low sigh escaped her lips: "A-Yara… where on earth have you gone…"

Just at that moment, the door to the hall was pushed open. A wisp of clear, chilling sword intent drifted in with the breeze, instantly dispersing the gloom that clung to her.

Yu Sord entered in his azure robes, his steps steady, his eyes as calmly composed as frost and snow.

He saw her tightly clutching the mirror, her face etched with profound worry. His footsteps paused slightly, but his voice remained level: "Do not rush. She will, eventually, show herself."

Yun Lili's heart fluttered. She offered a soft "Mhm," but still could not contain her sigh of distress. She hugged the mirror even tighter, then suddenly looked up, her voice so light it seemed afraid of being blown away by the wind: "Actually… I think I've remembered a few things."

Yu Sord's pupils contracted sharply, yet he managed to maintain a façade of calm, asking only in a seemingly casual manner: "What did you recall?"

Yun Lili lowered her head, tracing the border of the mirror with her fingertips. Her voice was fractured and intermittent: "Just this place… the **Phoenix Glory Pavilion**… and… the **Myriad Tribulations Cliff**."

As the three words "**Wan Jie Ya**" left her mouth, Yu Sord's spirit was violently shaken. His fingertips trembled, and his chest felt as if it had been cruelly slashed by a sharp blade. Finally, he could no longer suppress the overwhelming surge of emotion. He reached out abruptly and pulled her into a fierce, tight embrace, his voice low and trembling. The word that escaped his lips was laced with utter finality and desperate longing—

"Lili!"

Yun Lili's heart hammered wildly against her ribs from the sudden, unexpected force of his embrace. Her cheeks flushed intensely. She hastily pushed against him, yet still attempted to maintain her composure, muttering: "Oh, well… that's all in the past now… it's not like I feel anything about it, you know."

As she finished, she turned her face away, secretly musing in her mind:

—

It's actually quite embarrassing. To think she had a romantic entanglement with such a distinguished, handsome Immortal Lord in her past life… Heh heh, she had definitely hit the jackpot, hadn't she?

Yu Sord was completely unaware of the absurd, fantastical musings in her mind. He simply held her tighter, all the coldness in his eyes and brow completely melting away. Inside the Phoenix Glory Pavilion, only the sound of her frantic heartbeat and his suppressed, yet burning, breathing intertwined in the quiet afternoon air.

Chapter 53: Love in the Four Seasons

"Your Majesty," Moony spoke softly, her voice delicately threaded with both hesitation and a palpable unease. "After all these intervening years… are you truly never going to take another consort to share your burdens?"

Du Shao lifted his gaze towards her. His expression was gentle, profound, and utterly unchanged—just like the earnest, resolute boy he had been when they first met.

"I have formally drafted the decree," he whispered calmly, though his tone carried the gravity of a profound and unshakable resolve. "I intend to name my twelfth brother as Crown Heir to the Dragon Throne."

He continued, his voice steady and measured, never once adopting the lofty hauteur of an emperor before her. "He was but five years of age when our father passed away. He has now grown—a courteous, steady young man, inherently worthy of this vast realm. I… can finally allow myself to feel at ease."

Moony's throat tightened painfully, and the corners of her eyes prickled with intense heat. She understood the deeper meaning—his so-called "ease" was simultaneously a public explanation to the entire empire, and a quiet, devastatingly final promise whispered only to her.

"But…" she began, her protest already forming, only to have him raise a hand, gently halting her unfinished words.

Du Shao's eyes never left her face for a moment. In them, there was only the clear reflection of her perpetual form.

"Moony," he whispered, the name itself a profound declaration, "One mortal lifetime, spent wholly with you, is abundantly enough."

Moony lowered her head, her fingers curling tight and white around the fabric of her sleeve.

But inside, she knew the cruel arithmetic of the cosmos only too well—

This, then, was the bitter cost of the Vessel Spirit's wish. Her youth would remain untouched by the years. Her face would never show the faintest trace of age.

But him? A man of fragile mortal flesh—even one shielded by the formidable dragon aura—could not, by any grace, withstand the inevitable, crushing erosion of time.

These past years, she had learned to draw faint silver streaks at her temples, to soften the brightness of her eyes with subtle shadows, to deliberately paint her features with a touch of age, just enough to make it seem as though she grew older alongside him.

Yet every time she wiped away the makeup, the copper mirror revealed the same young face as before, clear eyes, smooth skin, lips unmarked by years.

Worse still—

her spiritual power was gone.

The day the Vessel Spirit fulfilled her wish, her cultivation ebbed away like a receding tide.

Now, she couldn't muster even the simplest gathering technique.

She had become, in every sense of the word, an ordinary mortal.

Night fell deep over Phoenix Palace.

The inner chambers were silent, the lamp's glow swaying faintly with the wind.

Moony sat alone before her bronze mirror,

her fingertips slowly brushing across her youthful cheeks.

Suddenly, a wave of longing—sharp and tearing—surged through her chest.

— *Miss... in this lifetime, will I ever see you again?*

The thought rose unbidden.

She remembered the days in Lingxiao Sect, remembered Lili's half-joking scolding and mock anger, remembered the three noisy chickens clucking around the courtyard.

Tears pricked at the corners of her eyes, yet she forced them back.

She was an empress—she could not show weakness, could not let anyone witness her solitude.

Only in the deepest chamber of her heart, she releases a faint sigh:

"Miss… I miss you so much."

Night deepened.

Moony eventually fell asleep, her breathing soft and steady,

her face peaceful.

"Even divested of the splendid phoenix robes, her essence remained consistent with that younger, occasionally stumbling figure witnessed years prior in Lingxiao, her facial structure retaining a disconcerting, absolute resistance to the inevitable erosion of time.

Du Shao remained seated quietly at the edge of the sleeping couch, his gaze fixed upon her resting state. His fingertips lifted slightly in a minimal gesture toward her forehead, yet he halted the movement—as though any physical disturbance might compromise the profound stillness of the room.

"Moony..." he articulated, the sound low, measured, and steady. " A full two decades had elapsed, yet her form entirely defied the relentless passage of years; her appearance remained immutable, reflecting precisely the visual consistency of the time before...."

A brief relaxation of expression was observed, swiftly replaced by a contemplative assessment.

He registered the situation acutely: this was demonstrably not a mere favourable condition bestowed by the natural order.

She exhibited no signs of aging, not in the slightest detail.

Simultaneously, his own existence was marked by the slow infiltration of white strands through his hair and the increasing physical mass of his imperial body with each passing year.

The observed disparity reinforced his comprehension of the exact cost associated with her sustained physiological stasis.

For the sake of rekindling a bond long severed, she had trapped herself in a destiny with no way back.

He knew all of this, yet he never asked. He never pressed, never uncovered the truth she carried alone.

Here is the smoothed and lightly expanded version:

"Moony… if this is fate, then let me grow old by myself. You remain forever in springtime, with no need to share my snow-white hair."

"All I ask is that you dance once more, the way you danced in the rain that year, untouched by a single drop. It was the most beautiful sight I ever saw, and at the end you turned back and asked me, 'Was it beautiful?' "

He tucked the quilt gently around her, his fingertips trembling with a tenderness he could no longer hide. Under the wavering lamplight, his silhouette seemed lonelier than ever, like an old tree standing stubbornly through wind and rain, weathered yet unbowed.

Sleep gradually claimed her. Moony shifted closer into his arms, slipping into dreams with a small, comforted sigh. In that dream, she seemed to hear something; her brows drew together lightly as if reacting to a distant call, and she murmured softly:

"…Miss…"

Du Shao stilled.

His expression darkened.

After a long moment, he let out a soft, bitter laugh, a sound sharp with quiet pain. "Silly girl… in this whole lifetime, your heart was never mine alone."

* * * * *

The newly planted bamboo in the courtyard had yet to take root; its leaf tips were tinged with yellow.

Yun Yara stood beneath the eaves, turning her palm gently, attempting to gather even the faintest wisp of spiritual light.

Her fingertips remained cold—

nothing formed.

She tried again.

And again.

Each attempt made her chest tighten further, as though an unseen hand was slowly tightening around her ribs.

— *The price.*

Those two words dropped through her heart like cold stone.

"Don't hurt your hand."

A quiet voice drifted from beneath the roof.

She spun around.

Mo Han stood among the shadows of the bamboo, his green robe plain and simple, his expression calm—as though none of this surprised him in the least.

Yara bit her lip.

"I… I can't seem to use anything anymore."

Mo Han fell silent for a moment.

He lowered his gaze to her, his voice still mild:

"You suffered a shock inside that rift. And the barrier in this mortal region is peculiar—spell work is easily suppressed."

As he spoke, he lifted his hand, as though intending to test a technique.

But his fingertips halted—barely noticeable—within his sleeve, as though something tugged against him.

In the end, he simply pressed his palms together and withdrew the motion.

"I'm the same," he added quietly.

"For now, I can't move my qi either."

He murmured it slow and steady, almost serene.

But Yara felt bitterness rise to her throat.

She *knew* it wasn't the barrier.

She had thrown her spiritual power into a place she could never retrieve—

when the pot-spirit granted her wish, it had taken her cultivation along with it.

The price.

She did not dare speak it aloud.

She barely dared think it.

"I have to go back," she whispered.

"The sect… A-Li… and Moony."

Mo Han glanced at the sky, as if calculating something unseen.

"The rift hasn't closed. Moving against it will draw thunder. Even if my spells were intact, I wouldn't dare force a path now."

He paused, voice gentle yet leaving no room for argument:

"Stay here first. I'll find a way."

Yara lowered her eyes, her knuckles turning pale from how tightly she clenched her hands.

She wanted to argue—wanted to deny everything choking her from within—

but in the end, she only managed a single, fragile word:

"…Alright."

The moment the word *"alright"* left her lips, it felt as though her heart had been gently returned to her chest—

yet at the same time, firmly nailed into this unfamiliar place of blue tiles and white walls.

Mo Han turned away, stepping toward the corner of the courtyard to pick up a fallen twig.

He tidied the bundle of firewood beside the stove with calm, deliberate movements.

The wind brushed past the eaves, lifting his sleeve.

A fleeting curve of amusement flickered in his eyes—so slight it vanished beneath the shifting bamboo shadows.

"The mortal realm isn't so bad," he whispered quietly.

"There are four seasons, and warm meals, and roads to walk. Warm your hands first."

Yara murmured a soft *"mm."*

Her voice was barely audible.

She drew her empty palms closer to her chest, holding them as though they were her last remaining pocket of warmth.

The weight of those two words—*the price*—still ached heavily inside her, but she no longer dared let them slip past her lips.

Outside the courtyard, the wind stirred the bell.

Ding—

One clear, lingering chime.

At the moment the sound faded, someone among the bamboo shadows released a breath they had been holding—a breath only he knew existed.

That day, autumn deepened in the mortal realm.

The maple leaves across the mountains glowed like fire.

Yara carried a bamboo basket filled with freshly gathered chestnuts, a few wild mushrooms, and mountain yam.

She walked along the stone path with her sleeves rolled up, the mountain wind brushing past her hair and bringing with it a crisp, cool fragrance.

"Careful. The path is slick."

A warm hand suddenly reached out, steadying her arm.

She turned her head.

Mo Han walked beside her, dressed in a simple robe of dark green, his expression as calm as ever.

In the slanting light he looked even more refined, more quietly handsome.

He carried a pot of spring water in one hand, while the other hovered unobtrusively near her—guarding her as naturally as breathing.

"I'm not a child," Yara murmured, feigning a tiny pout.

Mo Han only answered with a soft hum, offering no argument.

Side by side, they made their way back to the small courtyard at the foot of the mountain.

The place was not large: white walls, blue tiles, a few bamboo stalks swaying gently in the wind.

A wind chime hung from the eaves, and each breeze sent it ringing— clear, cool, like running water.

—This was where they had taken temporary shelter in the mortal world.

Yara set the basket down and bent over to light the stove.

Though she had grown up as a cultivator, now she had to learn the mortal way of doing things—

one slow, humble step at a time.

When the matches failed to strike, she tried again and again.

When the pot darkened with soot, she scrubbed it patiently.

Mo Han watched for a long moment before stepping forward and taking the fire striker from her hands.

"I'll do it," he replied.

With a slight turn of his hand, a spark leapt forth—

shh—

a clean flame bloomed, catching on the thin kindling.

Yara froze for a moment, then muttered softly,

"You're not even good at this. Still pretending to look calm."

Mo Han lifted his eyelids a fraction, answering in his usual faint, unreadable tone:

"Learning it will do."

The firelight reflected across his brows and lashes, softening him with a touch of earthly warmth.

Yara stared at him—

her heart tightened, just a little.

She used to believe he was cold as a solitary mountain peak, unreachable and untouched by human warmth.

But now, watching his eyes redden ever so slightly in the glow of the flame,

she suddenly felt—

he, too, was someone who could be warmed by a small fire.

* * * * *

A few days later, they descended the mountain together for the village fair.

The town at the foot of the mountain was lively.

Vendors shouted from both sides of the street; a little boy ran past with a pole of candied hawthorns, the bells tied to it jingling *ding-ding-dang-dang* as he weaved through the crowd.

Yara had rarely seen such scenes.

Her eyes sparkled with unhidden curiosity.

"Mo Han, I want this one," she said, pointing eagerly at a fresh, glossy string of candied hawthorns.

Mo Han's brow shifted slightly.

He touched the small pouch hidden in his sleeve—there were only a few lonely copper coins inside.

Even so, he paid for a skewer and handed it to her.

Yara's smile blossomed like light itself.

She took a bite; sweet and sour flavors burst across her tongue.

"You're not eating?" she asked.

"I'm not hungry."

She thought for a moment—then broke off a single hawthorn and pushed it stubbornly against his lips.

Mo Han paused, clearly taken aback.

He seemed ready to refuse,

but seeing her bright, hopeful eyes,

he lowered his head and bit into it.

The sweetness melted on his tongue.

His expression did not change—

but the tips of his ears flushed a quiet shade of red.

Warmth spread through Yara's chest.

She whispered, almost to herself,

"Days like this… are really nice."

* * * * *

Night deepened, and the courtyard grew quiet.

Moonlight lay across the stone tiles, soft and silver, while the bamboo cast wavering shadows.

Yara sat on the steps with a qin cradled in her arms.

Her fingertips plucked at the strings, producing a simple tune—nothing skillful, but gentle and peaceful.

Mo Han stood beside her, listening without interruption.

When a breeze drifted by, he spoke quietly:

"If you like playing it, then keep playing."

Yara chuckled.

"I'm so clumsy at it. And you can still listen?"

"It's not the song."

He hesitated, voice dropping slightly, rougher than usual.

"It's the person."

Yara paused, lifting her gaze.

In Mo Han's quiet eyes, moonlight shimmered faintly, and reflected within that pale light

was her own shadow.

Her heart tightened, as though something had struck it softly from within.

In that moment, she understood, life in the mortal world was not only calm and steady.

It was a time when two hearts, without noticing, drew closer.

* * * * *

Autumn rain came in sheets.

Yara was caught in a downpour while outside; by the time she returned, she was burning with fever.

She curled up on the bed, her forehead hot to the touch, her breaths shallow and quick.

Mo Han sat at her bedside, a bowl of ginger soup warming his hands.

Yet he didn't wake her.

He simply kept vigil, unmoving, expression unreadable.

Only when she knit her brows in sleep and murmured,

"A-Li… don't go…"

did something inside him jolt violently.

In that instant, he thought, if possible, he would rather she remain an ordinary girl all her life,

never again burdened by anything beyond her small world.

He reached out, gently pulling the blanket higher around her shoulders.

Quietly, he whispered.

"I'm here. I won't leave."

His voice was soft as drifting wind—

yet in the depth of the night, the words fell heavily.

* * * * *

Winter arrived.

Snow piled high across the courtyard, a thick, white expanse.

Yara was happily building a snowman, hands reddened from the cold but entirely unconcerned.

Mo Han walked over and pulled her sleeves down over her wrists.

His tone remained mild, though laced with helplessness.

"Your hands are freezing."

She lifted her face, still smiling.

"But it's almost done!"

The snowman leaned slightly to the side, clumsy and crooked.

Yara stuck two dried twigs into its sides, patting her hands proudly.

"There! Finished!"

Mo Han studied it for a moment, then picked up a small bamboo-eaved hat left by the doorway and gently set it atop the snowman's head.

"Now it looks proper."

Yara looked at the snowman, then at the man beside her, and all at once, she felt this winter day was warmer than any celestial sanctuary she had ever known.

* * * * *

Spring arrived.

New bamboo shoots pushed from the soil, and the wind rustled through the leaves with a soft, steady whisper.

In the courtyard, firewood was stacked mountain-high.

Yue Liuchuan worked with an axe, sweat running down his temples, each strike sending splinters flying.

Yara approached with a bamboo basket in her arms.

She tilted her head, puzzled.

"Why isn't he talking today? He used to chat quite a bit before, didn't he?"

Mo Han cast Yue Liuchuan a single, casual glance.

His expression remained as calm as still water, and his tone carried the same unperturbed softness.

"Perhaps the mortal world doesn't suit him."

Yara let out an "oh," half understanding, half puzzled.

But she didn't press further.

She turned and headed into the kitchen.

The moment her figure disappeared past the doorway, the calm in Mo Han's eyes faded—

icy cold sliding into place like a blade leaving its sheath.

His fingers moved the slightest bit.

A thin thread of spiritual light slipped from his sleeve, swift and invisible.

Yue Liuchuan happened to look up at that exact moment.

He met those indifferent eyes—eyes that held a killing intent sharp enough to freeze bone.

A chill shot through his spine.

"Chop the wood."

Mo Han's voice was quiet—so quiet only Yue Liuchuan could hear it—

"Do your work. And keep your thoughts clean.

If you dare meddle again…

one strike is enough to end you here."

Yue Liuchuan's breath hitched.

The axe nearly fell from his hands.

He hurriedly lowered his gaze and forced his numb fingers to keep chopping, faster and faster.

Woodchips flew.

Sweat stung his eyes.

But he didn't dare utter a single word.

Not far away, Yara's laughter drifted from the kitchen—bright, clear, untouched by shadow.

Mo Han turned back toward the sound.

His brows softened; his expression returned to gentle serenity, as though nothing had ever happened, as though the moment of cold blood had been nothing but a passing breeze.

Yara was standing at the kitchen doorway now, gazing out at the distant mountain Cliffs.

After a moment, she spoke softly:

"Mo Han… if life stayed like this forever, wouldn't it be… kind of wonderful?"

Mo Han was silent for a beat.

Then he turned his head toward her, the quiet depths of his eyes holding a stillness like moonlit water.

"Yes."

Just one word—lightly spoken.

Yet it carried the weight of mountains, the steadiness of flowing rivers, and something deeper still.

Yara smiled, her eyes warm, her entire face brightening.

She knew this peaceful life in the mortal world could not last forever.

But right now, in this small courtyard under the shifting seasons, they truly, wholly had each other.

Chapter 54: The Gambit of the Soul-Binding Mirror

Within the lofty confines of the Main Hall of the Soaring Heavens, the Lingxiao Sect, the lamps cast a tremulous, wavering light. A palpable, oppressive spiritual mist clung low, lending the atmosphere a funereal weight.

Seated throughout the vast chamber were the assembled Immortal Sovereigns and venerable Elders, their postures rigid and ceremonial. Above them, celestial astrolabes, the *xīngpán*, pulsed with a scattered, cold illumination, suspended mid-air.

The play of light and shadow reflected the immense, gaping fissure beneath the **Abyssfall Cliff**. Within that colossal rupture, an oily, noxious dark miasma churned and writhed, resembling nothing so much as the massive, predatory fangs of the Demonic Host, poised to tear the divine barrier, the *Jie*, to absolute shreds at any moment.

Yun Lili stood precisely at the chamber's centre, still cradling that distinctive mirror, etched with the intricate pattern of purple bamboo. Her eyes were visibly swollen and reddish, her nose stung faintly with residual tears, yet a weighty, dreadful presentiment had settled heavily upon her heart.

"—The core of the formation has fractured; it is a breach curable solely by the **Phoenix Core Pellet**."

Immortal Sovereign Sang Li's voice was disconcertingly calm, yet it acted like a blade of ice, slicing through and utterly extinguishing all extraneous noise within the hall.

At this devastating pronouncement, the entire assembly was seized by an intense, collective tremor.

The White-Browed Elder immediately slammed his hand upon his seat and rose to his feet, angrily tossing his long sleeve. "What unspeakable meaning does this hold? The **Phoenix Origin Core** is a rarity unseen for ten millennia; the Phoenix Clan has long been utterly extinguished, leaving only this unfortunate orphan... Are you suggesting, then, that she must sacrifice her own life to refine this elixir?!"

A deep, reverberating voice amongst the Immortals sombrely concurred: "If this truly is the case, are we to trade the life of one small girl for the collective well-being of the Four Realms' populace?"

Another voice, however, let out a chilling, detached laugh: "If the salvation of all under heaven is assured, the life of a single person, however poignant, is surely negligible."

The atmosphere within the hall instantaneously became intensely charged and confrontational, the tension thick enough to cut with a dull knife.

Oh, the dreadful, pragmatic calculus of these high-minded individuals! They always find a way to make the necessary sacrifice someone else's child.

Yun Lili felt a sharp, restrictive clench deep in her chest. Her fingers involuntarily tightened their desperate grip upon the mirror's frame. She bit her lip, yet her voice was brittle and shaking: "The **Phoenix Origin Core** ... what precisely is it?"

Sang Li's gaze settled heavily upon her, a blend of profound burden and deep, unsettling pity. Finally, he spoke, slowly and with measured weight: "In the Phoenix bloodline, the female lineage, whenever a Great Catastrophe approaches, a Phoenix Origin Core will gestate within their being. This elixir demands life itself as its oblation; it is capable of repairing the celestial rift and securing the barrier."

Yun Lili froze entirely, a deafening internal roar filling her ears. She subconsciously retreated a step, her body unsteady, nearly tumbling to the stone floor.

"No..."

The word escaped her as a desperate, choked murmur, and the tears instantly surged, blurring her vision.

At that very instant, a burst of bright cyan light and the violent clang of a sword suddenly resounded, the cry of the blade like a peal of thunder.

Yu Sord entered swiftly from the main doorway, his long sword now slung across his back, his expression severe and unforgiving. His voice, however, descended like a sudden, violent squall: "Whosoever dares suggest sending her to her doom again shall first answer to my sword!"

The entire hall was shaken to its foundation.

The White-Browed Elder angrily struck his armrest and yelled: "Yu Sord! As one of the Immortal Sovereigns, how can you display such a shocking disregard for the greater scheme of things!"

Yu Sord gave a cold, contemptuous laugh, pointing the tip of his sword directly towards the hall's centre. "What is this 'greater scheme'? In my sight, she is the **only** thing that matters! Should this dreadful edict be finalised, I shall declare myself irreconcilably opposed to the Immortal Realm!"

Every single word, sharply articulated, caused the hearts and minds of the gathered immortals to shudder.

Yun Lili stared at him, utterly dumbfounded, feeling as though her very heart were being squeezed tightly by an invisible hand. Her tears blurred her vision, yet she could not help but whisper, low and choked: "Yu Sord..."

Suddenly, Yun Zhou stepped out from the side of the hall, his voice constrained by profound emotion yet scalding with urgency: "If the formation indeed requires a sacrifice, then I ought to be the one! Even if I do not possess the **Phoenix Origin Core**, I am still wholly willing to fight the Demonic Realm to the very last breath!"

The entire company was taken aback.

Yun Wuntang's expression instantly turned to one of profound alarm: "Zhou'er, hold your tongue!"

But Yun Zhou fixed his gaze unswervingly upon the Immortals, gritting his teeth as he insisted: "I also possess the Phoenix Clan bloodline! There is but one Phoenix Core Pellet, yet the demonic armies are countless. If this is the terrible choice, then I, Yun, am equally prepared to offer my own person as sacrifice."

Sang Li slowly shook his head, his gaze heavy with unconcealed sorrow. "The Phoenix Core Pellet gestates only within the female form, within the core lineage of the Phoenix Lord. My Lord Yun Zhou, you may possess the bloodline, but you shall never be able to produce the Pellet."

This declaration struck Yun Zhou like a precisely aimed blade, sinking directly into his heart. His face instantly drained of colour, his eyes filling with a raw, bitter mixture of indignation and utter powerlessness.

Yun Lili was fiercely jolted by the words, a cold sweat breaking out on her palms, her vision swimming with tears. She wished desperately to speak, but only managed a single, trembling articulation: "I..."

The remainder of the sentence lodged painfully in her throat, as if restrained by ten thousand crushing weights, refusing to pass her lips. Her mind became a chaotic tangle, her chest rising and falling in rapid, shallow spasms; she was perilously close to collapsing entirely.

Yu Sord, however, had already closed the distance in a swift stride, pulling her securely into his embrace. His formidable sword aura surged around them, and his voice was so cold it seemed ready to splinter: "You dare not contemplate it! While I stand here, no one shall lay a hand on you!"

Yun Lili's body trembled violently within the shelter of his arms, yet she still managed a small, sobbing whisper: "But... this is my duty, surely... If I am the only one capable of this, I cannot simply stand by and watch everyone perish..."

A profound silence descended upon the hall, broken only by her disjointed, wrenching sobs.

After a protracted interval, Sang Li sighed, a low and weary sound: "This matter... there *is* another path. However, the price would be far heavier, and the resulting casualties far greater."

The White-Browed Elder's voice was sharp and unforgiving: "For the sake of the populace, merely adopt the first viable solution. What need is there for further discussion?"

Yun Tim suddenly let out a small, quiet laugh, his expression inscrutable and knowing: "If that truly is your ethos, I wonder, would you utter such frigid sentiments on the day that one of your own progeny was required to mend the formation core?"

At this potent remark, the entire hall once again succumbed to a profound and uneasy silence.

Yu Sord held Yun Lili tightly, his eyes glacial and ruthless like rime and snow, yet he lowered his voice, murmuring fiercely into her ear: "Remember this: no matter what they decree, I shall never permit you to die."

In the previous lifetime, he had already lost her once upon the Abyssfall Cliff. He would not, could not, allow her to be annihilated before his very eyes again.

Yun Lili's eyes were swimming, her voice thick with tears and a faint, trembling hope: "But..."

Yu Sord bowed his head closer, his voice intensely low yet utterly resolute: "There are no 'buts'."

Outside the hall, the wind suddenly intensified, and the distant, plaintive call of a Phoenix was faintly heard.

The terrible choice between the decree of fate and the fierce devotion of love thus hung suspended over the heart of every soul present. Yu Sord remained absolute in his protective defiance.

The clamorous argument within the hall had not truly subsided; the Cranes of Destiny pattern continued to vibrate restlessly upon the spiritual mirror. In the flickering play of light and shadow, it seemed ready to shatter the entire Lingxiao Sect itself.

His voice, cold as frost and snow, dropped like a hammer blow, making even the lamp flames appear to tremble.

The White-Browed Elder's face immediately darkened; he angrily swept his sleeve and pounded the armrest: "Yu Sord! As an Immortal Sovereign, you are utterly disgracing yourself for the sake of a mere mortal girl! Does the life of the entire populace not weigh more heavily than her solitary existence?"

"It does not!" Yu Sord countered, syllable by syllable, his voice cold as tempered iron, yet a barely suppressed fire was blazing in his eyes. "The lives of the populace have others to protect them. If she is gone, then whom shall I protect?"

As this final, devastating question was delivered, the hall was plunged into a deathly stillness.

Yun Lili stared up at him, her heart giving a sudden, violent lurch. She wanted to weep openly, yet she suppressed the urge; the tears spun in her eye sockets, but ultimately, she lowered her head, afraid to meet his gaze any longer.

To think, she could hear such words escape his lips—a sudden, unexpected warmth blooming sweetly in her heart amidst all this ruin.

* * * * *

The council was finally dispersed. Night had fallen heavily, and an icy wind scoured through the long corridors.

Yun Lili was all but half-dragged out of the Main Hall by Yu Sord, her steps unsteady, her hand still desperately clutching the mirror.

"Yu Sord..." she began in a small, quavering voice. "What if this is truly my fate? What if... what if only I can mend the formation core?"

Yu Sord stopped abruptly, looking directly down at her. The moonlight caught the severe, rigid lines of his face, which were nonetheless strained by a fiercely repressed emotion.

"I told you: there are no 'what ifs'."

He reached out and gripped her shoulders firmly, his voice low but shaking with intensity. "Lili, listen carefully. Even if this were divine destiny, I would still tear it apart."

A sharp pang of sorrow seized Yun Lili's heart, and her nose instantly prickled with heat. She bit her lip, finally allowing a small, strangled sob to escape. "But I am truly terrified... terrified that you will all perish, that everyone will suffer because of me..."

Before she could finish the dreadful sentence, she was suddenly and completely swept into a tight embrace.

Yu Sord held her pressed firmly against his chest, one large palm resting against her back. His voice was extremely low and utterly steady: "With me here, you have no reason to be afraid."

He spoke with such absolute conviction, a conviction as solid as a defensive rampart, blocking all the trembling confusion within her.

Yun Lili's tears finally broke free, streaming down her face.

* * * * *

The following morning dawned, casting a pale light upon the mountain peaks.

Yun Zhou stood alone upon the summit, the fierce wind whipping his robes around him. He kept his eyes closed, his mind still echoing with the terrible resonance of Sang Li's words from the previous night: "The Phoenix Core Pellet gestates only within the female form."

That single sentence was like a razor-sharp cut, leaving his chest feeling raw and bloodied. *The injustice of the celestial mechanism is truly breathtaking in its sheer cruelty. To possess the heart of a protector and the impotence of a spectator—it is an ignoble fate.*

"Brother."

The soft voice of Yun Lili drifted to him from behind.

He turned, observing her approach. She was carrying a small basket of green plums, her breath still slightly unsettled from the climb, and her eyes were noticeably rimmed with red.

"Last night... I heard you arguing, desperate to take my place," her voice was low, carrying the hoarse timbre of recent weeping. "But it is futile, is it not? Brother, why must you put yourself through this?"

Yun Zhou's gaze was deep and weighted with suppressed emotion. He finally spoke: "When you were a child, you were most terrified of the thunder, and you would always insist that I hold you whilst you slept."

Yun Lili paused, caught off guard by the memory.

"Even then, I determined that no matter what tempest or calamity befell us, I would stand in front of it for you."

His eyes burned with a fierce intensity, yet they were shadowed by a powerless, bitter misery. "And now... must I simply stand here and watch you walk towards this final, mortal catastrophe?"

Yun Lili's nose instantly stung with overwhelming emotion, and the basket in her hands nearly slipped. She rushed forward, throwing her arms around his waist, her voice cracking with sobs: "Brother, please do not speak like that... I truly fear you will sacrifice yourself for my sake. If only one of us must be offered up, then let it be me."

Yun Zhou's entire body shuddered at her plea. His hands trembled, but eventually, they lifted and settled upon her shoulders, drawing her into a tight, desperate embrace.

"Foolish girl..." His throat tightened painfully, his voice dropping to a low, husky rasp. "If that dreadful day truly arrives, I will not allow you to go alone."

* * * * *

The afternoon unfolded quietly within the Phoenix Splendour Pavilion, the *Fèng Huá Xuān*.

Yun Wuntang had, for a rare moment, relinquished the burdensome dignity of the Sect Leader, trading his formal robes for simple linen garments. He sat at a low table, watching Yun Lili approach with a steaming bowl of *Húntun* (wontons).

"Please, do try some. I made them myself," **Yun Lili** offered, a nervous smile stretching her lips, though her eyes held a fragile, desperate hope.

Yun Wuntang paused, then used his chopsticks to select one of the wontons. He ate it slowly. The flavour was simple and unpretentious, yet undeniably warming to the stomach. He placed his chopsticks down, his eyes softening and taking on a faint, internal glow.

"Lili..." he murmured, his voice laced with a restrained tremor. "If your mother were still here, she would be immensely proud of you."

Yun Lili felt her tears threaten to surface again, but she fought hard to keep them back. She simply lowered her gaze and whispered: "Father, I do not crave any grand mission... I only wish for our family to be safe and whole."

Yun Wuntang reached out, his rough, calloused palm settling gently upon the crown of her hair. He remained silent for a long moment before finally speaking: "Silly child. There are many affairs in this world that are simply not ours to choose."

* * * * *

As the night began to descend, a deep, ominous rumbling suddenly erupted from the direction of the **Abyssfall Cliff**. The barrier was violently vibrating, and the black, noxious *miasma* was already beginning to spill outwards like a rising tide.

The celestial astrolabe spontaneously materialised in the centre of the main hall, its light rapidly flickering and jumping, signalling that the core of the formation was perilously close to collapse.

"This is disastrous!" an Immortal official cried out in alarm. "The Demonic Host has commenced a full-scale assault! The formation core could shatter at any moment!"

All eyes in the hall snapped simultaneously to Yun Lili.

Her entire body was racked by a violent tremor. The mirror in her hand pulsed with a weak, desperate light, and her heart was a chaotic, tangled mess of fear and uncertainty.

But within that terrible confusion, she suddenly heard the echo of Yu Sord's voice, low yet absolutely unwavering—*With me here, you have no reason to be afraid.*

A fierce, poignant warmth surged up to her nasal passage. She lifted her head, looking towards that familiar silhouette in the cyan robe.

—*Regardless of the ensuing disaster, she understood now that in this final, terrifying conflict, she was no longer utterly alone.*

Chapter 55: The Phoenix Stitch

Before the **Myriad Tribulations Cliff**, the sky was steeped in ink, utterly dark and menacing.

The vast mountain range was visibly split into deep, terrifying fissures.

A powerful, toxic black wind poured relentlessly out of the cracks, sucking in crashed stone and dead branches, roaring and churning like a thousand gaping, predatory beasts baring their jaws.

The glowing circle at the core of the great array was dimming rapidly, and the layers of spiritual barrier were being gnawed away, inch by inch, by invisible, relentless teeth.

The great astrolabe hovered precariously in the air, its points of light scattering in complete chaos, emitting an extremely low, resonant hum of profound distress.

"Demonic Essence overflow is at precisely thirty percent," Sang Li declared, sweeping a thread of starlight from his sleeve onto the astrolabe's centre. His expression was cold and severe, devoid of any weakness. "Any further delay, even a single, crucial moment, and the array core will inevitably collapse entirely."

The White-Browed Elder gave a heavy, stern shout: "Send her forth! Celestial Profound Layer Four, synchronize and increase power—**now!**"

The surrounding Immortals instantly answered in unison. Seals of arcane power descended like a meteor shower, layers of spiritual light crashing heavily into the deep canyon.

The black wind was momentarily suppressed, then violently surged back, recoiling three hundred *zhang* (approx. 1km), tearing the falling radiance into fragmented ruin.

Yun Lili stood precariously near the stone ledge, clutching the purple-bamboo-etched mirror tightly. Her knees were visibly trembling.

Little Fira perched on her shoulder, its golden feathers ruffled into fine lines by the yin wind. The three chickens huddled together, shrinking close to the edge of her skirt, their distressed *clucking* strained and almost squeaking.

She swallowed with difficulty, mumbling softly: "Mother protect me, Ancestors protect me, all the Immortals I know and do not know, please, please preserve me…"

A warm, steady hand enclosed her chilled fingers.

Yu Sord stood beside her, his azure robes whipping fiercely. His sword hummed deeply against his back, like a living mountain waiting for release.

"If you are afraid, hold fast to me," he said in a low voice, his tone so utterly certain it seemed to nail her firmly to the ground. "**I am here with you**."

Yun Lili sniffed hard, nodding forcefully, but she still couldn't stop her panicked stream of consciousness: "I… I don't necessarily *have* to go up, right? What if the moment I step onto the array, I just—"

"You will not 'just'," Yu Sord's eyes were colder than the storming wind. "I have forbidden it."

—Forbidden her to die, forbidden her to be harmed, forbidden her to step even one inch away from his protective grace.

Yun Zhou led a squad of sword cultivators towards the cliff's core. He glanced back at her, his gaze heavy, like both a knife and a shield: "Little sister, if the situation turns critical, **I will take your place**."

Yun Duntang stood upon the high platform. He flung out his long sleeve, his Sect Master's command sounding as profound as a great bell: "Activate all arrays! Shield the Young Mistress as she proceeds!—Sang Li, **activate the Astrolabe!**"

The Astrolabe rang out with a mighty boom. Silver-white engraved lines lit up from the four corners of the Myriad Tribulations Cliff, snaking like countless dormant serpents within the rock layers.

The wind tunnel instantly collapsed inward, the black essence erupting in a towering wave that violently slammed against the silver array barrier.

Yun Lili was lifted by a sheet of azure light, suddenly suspended in mid-air. She shrieked in terror—

She gripped the mirror desperately, her toes kicking wildly at the empty air: "No, no, no— I can't— my legs are weak! They are genuinely, physically weak!"

The three chickens were dragged upwards by Little Fira, who gripped their tail feathers. Their *clucking* turned into a chorus of panicked cries.

Little Fira looked completely impassive (could a bird look impassive?). It gave its wing a shake, gripping one chicken in its beak, appearing to be carrying three small, agitated **furry balls**.

The moment she landed on the array platform, the black wind swarmed towards her like hungry wolves catching the scent of fresh blood.

"Waaah, don't crowd me!" Yun Lili instinctively raised the mirror.

The purple-bamboo-etched mirror surface suddenly flared, and a circle of pale purple flowing light expanded, **scalding** the nearest wisp of demonic essence, which hissed *zzzt* and dissipated into a plume of grey-white steam.

The Elders seated on the four platforms all gasped in shock. Sang Li murmured: "The mirror spirit can draw upon the Phoenix Blood."

Yun Lili herself was stunned. She mumbled: "See? My little mirror has a spirit… If only it hadn't broken…"

Her voice suddenly caught, her throat feeling constricted, and her eyes welled up with painful redness.

She took a sharp breath, forcibly swallowing the raw emotion: "Don't cry, Yun Lili, don't you dare cry now!"

Yu Sord's voice reached her from a distance: "Watch my hand-seal."

He held his two fingers together, and a point of azure light on his sword illuminated the array core, signalling to her: "**Follow me.**"

She mimicked his stance, lightly tapping the back of the mirror with her index and middle fingers. The mirror surface responded as if awakened, an extremely fine Phoenix design surfacing upon it.

The Phoenix pattern was faint, like a thread pulled from the deepest part of her heart, causing a painful tightness in her chest and a tremor in her breath.

"It hurts," she whispered.

"I know," Yu Sord replied with two simple words, but his sword intent had already flown into the array core, shielding her from the first wave of backlash.

The black wind howled in fury.

The Myriad Tribulations Cliff seemed to come alive, the entire cliff body roaring, and the faint sound of fracturing bones could be heard from deep beneath the ground.

The Astrolabe *clanged* downwards. Sang Li's expression tightened: "Array core collapse—twenty percent."

The White-Browed Elder slammed his hand onto his desk: "Sacrifice the Phoenix Core Pellet **immediately**!"

His gaze stabbed directly towards the small figure on the array platform.

Yu Sord's sword light suddenly flared upright in the air, forming a solid, impenetrable wall, ruthlessly cleaving that hateful glare from the Elder in two. His voice was not human, but possessed the cutting finality of ice: "**Who dares.**"

In the instant the aggressive tension froze, the array core plunged further downwards.

Yun Lili was shoved by a powerful blast of wind, staggering half a step, nearly falling to her knees. The three chickens scattered in terror. She scooped up the nearest one: "Don't run! You are my treasured **house-guarding chickens**!"

As she said it, she suddenly remembered something, her eyes flashing bright with desperate clarity: "Chickens—chickens can find light!"

She grabbed the mirror, quickly pressing the three chickens towards its surface, her words tumbling out like a rapid drumbeat: "Listen! Red, Gold, Green, don't ask why I'm naming you now—go, **go find the light! The light inside the mirror! Grab it all and pull it out!**"

The three chickens responded: "…Cluck?"

Little Fira tilted its head in utter, avian disdain.

Yun Lili stamped her foot in frantic urgency: "Hurry! Prize reward—**Roasted mealworms!**"

The three chickens exchanged a quick, meaningful glance. Then, they all simultaneously stretched their necks, let out a unified "**Cluck—**" and instantly buried their heads into the mirror's surface.

The mirror rippled as if three stones had struck water, and three extremely fine threads of light were suddenly *pulled* out of the mirror by the chickens—literally held fast in their beaks!

Yun Lili: "???"

The Elders: "???"

Sang Li's eyes snapped wide open in shock: "**Mirror Spirit Split-Guidance**—she is dismantling the phoenix meridian into multiple fine streams!"

White-Browed Elder paled, utterly horrified: "Nonsense! The Phoenix Origin, if divided, will scatter and dissipate!"

"Not entirely correct," Yun Zane snapped his folding fan shut, his voice slow and precise, cutting through the chaos. "The Phoenix Origin, if **directly flooded**, will explode. If **finely guided**, it may yet be woven for mending…"

It is akin to patching a piece of torn brocade; one does not slam a burning lump of material onto it. One must use silk threads, finer than hair, stitching the rupture one careful needle at a time.

Yun Lili comprehended none of this intricate, celestial metaphysics. She understood only one single, desperate truth: "I refuse to die, and I refuse to allow you all to die! I shall live and patch this hole myself!"

She pressed the mirror fiercely to her chest, her teeth grinding audibly: "Come now! I am terrified, but I can sew!"

The phoenix patterns on the mirror flared intensely, like pure fire. One thread, two threads, three threads… under the gentle guidance of the three chickens "tugging" the bright filaments, the light threads flowed out like three obedient streams, slowly seeping towards the collapsing edge of the array core.

Little Fira suddenly beat its wings, shaking its golden feathers, which transformed into tiny, razor-short feather-blades. They fell neatly along the broken rim—like carefully pressing pins into torn cloth before stitching.

As the Phoenix threads spread outwards, the **Star Vapour Sword** automatically sang, azure light intersecting with phoenix gold—two forces knitting the sky together like a pair of celestial needles.

Yu Sord instantly comprehended the extraordinary method.

He drew his longsword, and the tip split into nine threads of blue radiance. They laid themselves across the rupture's outer edge, weaving together with the three phoenix strands to form a small, delicate—yet incredibly stable—**patch**.

"Esteemed Immortals," Sang Li's voice dropped with the force of a stone into a deep pool. "Use thread, not hammer. Slow the pressure, thin the infusion, cycle your force. If anyone dares to 'smash' their power again, I will personally destroy their hand seals."

The surrounding Immortal Sovereigns exchanged uneasy glances. They finally, unanimously, shifted their violent outpouring of power into the finest, gentlest drizzle-like streams of spiritual energy.

The disastrous roaring of the Myriad Tribulations Cliff genuinely began to slow, if only by a fraction.

Yun Lili felt as though half her very soul had been entirely drained. Her legs trembled violently, fine sweat trickling from her temples. Yet, she continued her frantic monologue: "Little Fira, behave—do not play by plucking my hair! Ah-Hong, slow down, do not snap the thread—ow ow ow, my chest feels like it is being gripped—No, no, I am not afraid, I am not afraid..."

She felt the profound urge to weep again. But she did not. Her teeth bit hard against her lower lip, her eyes red like wind-chapped peaches, and she pressed the mirror even tighter to her chest: "Do not be afraid, all of you—I am even more afraid than you are. But afraid or not, I will sew one stitch, and you will secure the next... and then... we will all survive this."

Yu Sord heard her delirious stream of consciousness in the midst of the howling wind. His chest constricted sharply, yet his sword-force only grew steadier and more resolute.

He stood precisely half a step to her left for the entirety of the ordeal, deliberately pulling every violent counter-strike meant for her straight into his own protective sword domain, forcing the malicious black essence down to hair-thin threads before allowing any of it to merely graze the edge of her mirror.

White-Browed Elder watched the delicate manoeuvre, looked again, and finally bit down hard on his teeth, suppressing his pride. He lowered his voice: "I shall suppress the northern corner."

He was the very first elder to yield his authority and accept the method. Following him came the second, the third—"I shall brace the eastern edge." "I shall hold the southern waist."

The faction that had previously been the most aggressively rigid, the loudest voices advocating for "one life for ten thousand," now ceased their bellowing entirely.

Instead, they feared their own overwhelming power might accidentally tear apart the meticulous, one-thread-one-stitch effort unfolding in the small girl's hands.

The aggressive wind pressure pushed lower, inch by inch. The broken mouth of the array pulled inward, fraction by fraction.

The light of the Astrolabe moved from chaos to order. The jagged edges of the massive rupture were being slowly bound by the Phoenix threads—like a deep, mortal wound gradually **scabbing** over.

Suddenly, without warning, from the deepest heart of the rupture, a black column burst forth, far more vicious and potent than anything before—lancing straight toward the sky!

"Array-heart backlash!" Sang Li's face paled completely. "Everyone retreat half a step—"

It was too late. That pillar of darkness struck down like an inverted spear, aimed precisely at the centre of Yun Lili's chest.

The world slowed to a painful crawl. Yun Lili had time for only one thought: *I'm dead.*

Her shoulder was yanked back with brutal force—Yu Sord swept her entirely into his embrace, and a screen of pure azure light exploded violently from his back like an immense shield.

He took the entire, catastrophic blow across his back. The azure screen cracked in three long fissures. The fabric along his spine was sliced open by the storm winds, and blood quickly seeped through, dark and heavy.

"No!" Yun Lili's cry tore her throat raw.

She shoved the mirror upward with one hand and fiercely pushed against his chest with the other. "Retreat! You must retreat! Get back—Yu Sord, **MOVE!**"

Yu Sord acted as though he had not heard her desperate command. He merely whispered—so lightly she barely caught the sound: "Don't be afraid."

Yun Lili's eyes brimmed instantly with tears. Then something critical snapped within her—a hard, metallic taste of absolute resolve flooded her mouth. "I—I have a way!"

She lifted the mirror high above her head. With a sharp crack, a fine ring of deliberate fractures spread across the back of the mirror—she wasn't breaking the mirror; she was willfully **dismantling the mirror-spirit** on purpose, splitting it into dozens of sharp shards. Each shard carried a wisp of her phoenix breath.

Like tiny, frantically released sprites, the fragments vibrated, then shot outward toward the black pillar.

Every shard that touched the darkness gave off a crisp *ding*, **stripping** a layer of miasma away.

The three chickens, each still clutching a shard, flapped madly above her head, circling like three furious, tiny tailors, seizing every rotten thread they could find and shoving it back toward the needle-hole.

"By dispersing the edge..." Sang Li murmured, and for once his voice actually trembled. "She broke a direct strike into... thousands of solvable points..."

Yu Sord seized that precise opening and his azure sword split from nine threads into eighteen, each one fine as a shuttle, weaving violently between the mirror shards and phoenix strands, unravelling the black pillar inch by inch.

White-Browed Elder gave a cold snort, his sleeve flicking as he hurled out a spiral-pattern jade ring. "Hmph! This old man knows how to weave as well!" The jade ring spun, unfurling into a massive thread-hoop, catching the scattered pieces of black miasma and hauling them inward like tightening cord.

The wind roared one last, final time—then broke into a ragged, dying cough. The black pillar disintegrated into drifting shadow-dust, layer by layer hemmed in by mirror shards, sword threads, jade hoop, and golden pinfeathers.

Finally—as though poured into an invisible well—it obediently sank out of sight.

Silence fell, the kind that presses heavily on the chest only after a catastrophic storm finally yields.

The last of the dark column broke apart, reduced to pale fragments that Lili's mirror-light and Yu Sord's sword-silk pushed back into the fissure, inch by meticulous inch.

The cliff face rumbled, then abruptly stopped—leaving only fading echoes trembling between the stone walls.

Even the wind stilled. In the dim afterglow, every heart on the field loosened at once.

Lili clutched the mirror so tightly her fingers had gone numb. She tried to speak, her lips parting, but her voice dissolved on the breeze.

The lights in front of her blurred, the ground swayed—Her knees buckled forward.

Yun Lili's eyelashes fluttered. She made no response, only hugged the mirror fiercely to her chest as if it were her last anchor in the world.

Yu Sord's arms tightened around her in an instant. He gathered her firmly into his embrace, utterly ignoring the blood soaking down his back, murmuring her name again and again, low, steady, and desperate.

The posture looked exactly like the lovesick immortal lords featured in exaggerated mortal storytellers' books.

The three chickens surrounded them, tilting their heads. Their clucks fell in uncanny unison, like conspiring whispers:

"Mm. The immortal lord looks very handsome."

"Cluck— textbook courting technique."

"Master is cooperating very well."

Little Fira half-lowered his golden eyes, fluttered down onto Yu Sord's shoulder, and added—cold as ever—

"Tch. Obviously, this is the part where she's supposed to faint."

Chapter 56: I Am Still Me

The light points on the Star Disc returned smoothly to their proper orbit. Sang Li let out a long, profound sigh of relief: "The array heart—it is stable now."

The roaring motion of the Abyssfall Cliff subsided inch by arduous inch. Only a residual, cold wind still swept ceaselessly across the rock face.

In the far distance, the Demonic Army, having clearly sensed the decisive failure of their assault, the black tide retreated.

The residual black mist at the cliff bottom churned restlessly for a moment, then, finally, as if in utter, reluctant defeat, allowed itself to be compressed back into the dark fissure.

Yun Lili's entire being felt utterly drained, her legs giving way beneath her.

She sank unceremoniously onto the array platform, landing squarely on her posterior and she let out several deep, ragged gasps—*Phew*—and the very first thing she did, tilting her head to the side, was frantically search for her three avian collaborators.

"Ah-Hong—Ah-Qing—Ah-Jin—"

The three chickens sequentially emerged from the unexpected hiding places of her sleeves, her knees, and even her hair bun.

They were each still proudly clutching a tiny, glistening fragment of the small mirror, looking exactly like highly decorated veterans returning with the spoils of war, clucking with an air of immense, insufferable arrogance.

Little Fira landed upon her shoulder, its phoenix eyes half-closed. It stretched its mouth and gently pecked away a single, wind-blasted stray hair that had adhered to her forehead. Y

un Lili pulled a miserable face, then finally let out a genuine laugh—a laugh that quickly dissolved into a sudden, fresh flood of tears.

She cried and yelled simultaneously: "You terrified me! I thought I was about to—to be smashed into tiny little bits of celestial debris! Wuwu… and my mirror…"

She raised her hand to look at the mirror. The main mirror surface was intact, but its edge was visibly missing an entire ring of petals.

Those shattered fragments were still circling obediently in the air, like a well-behaved flock of small, shimmering fish, humming as they returned to the mirror body, diligently attempting to slot back into place—save for one tiny, rice-grain sized chip missing from the upper corner.

Yun Lili immediately covered that small, glaring gap with her finger, wiping away her tears as she solemnly announced: "It is not ugly! My mirror is still the most beautiful in the cosmos, wuwu..."

My heart aches with the sheer cost of this operation!

The Celestial Officials surrounding them: ",,,,..."

Even White-Brow Elder choked back a silent laugh, turning his back to discreetly clear his throat with unnecessary force.

Yu Sord stood with his sword retracted. The fabric across his chest was irreparably torn, marked with deep and shallow traces of blood.

He walked over, looking down at her. His eyes, finally soft in the cooling wind, resembled a folding knife slowly being sheathed and put to rest.

He knelt down, reaching out a steady hand to gently wipe the lingering tears from her cheek. His touch was firm and reassuring: "You have performed brilliantly."

Yun Lili sniffed: "I... I actually came perilously close to urinating myself, you know."

Yu Sord: ",,,,..."

Yun Zhou, standing nearby, covered his forehead, finally unable to suppress a loud, amused laugh.

Yun Lili realised she was being openly mocked and immediately exploded in indignation: "What are you laughing at! What is wrong with being afraid of death! I may fear death, but I still saved every single one of you useless lot!"

She grew more intensely aggrieved as she spoke, finally delivering a fierce, cutting retort: "And I was immensely heroic just now! I split the threads, I stitched the damage, I dismantled the pillar! My brain was operating at the speed of a thief!"

"Mm," Yu Sord nodded, his agreement almost unnervingly serious. "The speed of a thief, indeed."

He paused, lowering his gaze to fix upon her, his voice profoundly low: "In the future... you are only permitted to be that quick, never quick to seek your own demise."

Yun Lili froze for a breath, her ear tips slowly flushing scarlet. She wanted desperately to bury her face in her sleeves, yet she also wanted to puff out her chest and maintain her grand, heroic posture: "That, that is obvious! I cherish my life immensely!"

Saying this, she scooped up the three chickens: "Come! We are going back for roasted mealworms! And I shall make you all fortifying chicken soup!"

The three chickens collectively raised their heads and emitted a resonant "Goo—," as if responding: "A hero's meritorious reward is justly deserved!"

On the high platform, Yun Wuntang slowly lowered his sleeve, his gaze fixed upon the cliff core for a long time.

He finally closed his eyes and his eyelashes trembled once. He opened his eyes, looking at the little girl holding the chickens, her nose still red. The cold severity in his gaze was melted away, inch by inch, by a wash of spring water.

He nodded to her—not the formal affirmation of a Clan Master to a subordinate, but the profound pride and humble awe of a father for his daughter's undeniable courage.

Sang Li neatly packed up the Star Disc, turning to bow formally: "The method has succeeded. The array heart is temporarily stable."

He looked at Yun Lili, his voice shedding its usual coolness, even carrying a hint of genuine amusement: "The 'Fine-Thread Weaving and Mending' technique shall henceforth be recorded in the Ten Thousand Cliff Array Catalogue. This method was created by you, and shall be named the 'Lili Patch'."

"'Lili Patch'?" Yun Lili, tears still clinging to her face, looked up blankly. "That sounds… terribly like a piece of common cloth."

Yun Zhou let out a soft *Pfft* of laughter, snapping his fan shut: "Perfectly fitting. The heavens are torn like cloth; you were the needle and thread. Utterly marvelous."

Yun Lili wrinkled her nose petulantly, yet still managed to mutter: "Hmph, it sounds so completely un-immortal and terribly unglamorous…"

Yun Lili was now being half-supported, half-carried by Yu Sord down from the array platform. The moment her feet touched the ground, her legs still felt profoundly weak. She swayed slightly, looking up at him: "Your back…"

"Merely superficial cuts," he said.

She opened her mouth, intending to say, "*But my heart aches for you,*" but before the words could leave her lips, Yu Sord turned his face slightly, and placed the lightest, briefest of kisses upon her forehead.

"A reward," he murmured.

Yun Lili: "!"

Her mind instantly exploded into a cloud of pink, sugary confusion, like cotton candy. She nearly dropped the three chickens.

"You—you—how can you do that in broad daylight, with everyone watching…?"

Yu Sord replied placidly: "With everyone watching, who, precisely, dared to look?"

Yun Lili: ",,,…"

She viciously slammed her fist down on the metaphorical table in her mind: Good, good, good! This man is cold on the outside, and on the inside—inside he knows how to kiss!

Yun Zhou emerged from nowhere, tapping his fan playfully: "My lords, while Abyssfall Cliff is stable, this is hardly a wedding hall suitable for such displays."

Yun Lili immediately blushed crimson to her earlobes, shrinking back behind Yu Sord. Yu Sord, without changing his expression, pressed her further against his back and cast Yun Zhou a single, lethal glance: "Be gone."

Yun Zhou retreated with a smile, but secretly, beneath his sleeve, he sealed the jade slip recording the array data—he was determined to compile today's 'Fine-Thread Weaving' method into an official tome.

This whole ordeal had taught the entire Immortal Realm—and himself—one crucial lesson: Not every hole must be plugged with a life. Sometimes, one must use one's heart, one's fear, one's cunning ingenuity, and a few tears and laughs to keep life intact and mend the cosmos.

The sunset faded, and a string of protective lanterns was lit along the cliff edge.

In the distance, the horizon finally revealed a thin, pale thread of gold.

Yun Lili leaned against Yu Sord's shoulder for a brief nap. She woke when her nose tickled—Little Fira was gently nudging her with its feather tip.

She scooped it up, burying her face in its warm plumage: "Thank you…
and thank you, all of you." She looked down at the three chickens, whose
small eyes gleamed brightly.

"We go back for roasted mealworms," she announced.

The three chickens responded in unison: "Goo!"

At the foot of Abyssfall Cliff, the wind finally ceased to cut like a knife.

Yun Lili looked up at the mended 'wound' on the cliff face. She suddenly
whispered to it softly: "Do not dare to tear open again. I beg of you."

Like consoling a child.

She turned, showing Yu Sord her mirror: "Come on, let us go home. I
intend to sleep for eighty hours straight."

Yu Sord "Mm" softly. He looked at her reflection in the mirror—eyes
red, nose red, and bearing faint marks from the whipping wind.

He reached up and gently touched the rice-grain sized chip missing from
her temple: "It is nothing."

Yun Lili instantly shielded the mirror: "Don't you dare call it ugly!"

"I said it is nothing," he clarified, his tone profoundly warm. "It is
beautiful."

*—Only with a visible flaw does one remember the life-and-death effort
required to mend it.*

A wisp of wind rose again over the cliff, this time sounding like someone
gently sighing in contentment.

Yun Lili looked at the mirror with its small, missing corner, and suddenly
whispered internally: *—I am still me, a mere mortal who fears death and
lacks a spiritual root. But even a mortal can mend the heavens; that, I
suppose, is enough.*

Yun Lili: ",,,..."

*She viciously slammed her fist down on the metaphorical table in her
mind: Good, good, good! This man is cold on the outside, and on the
inside—inside he knows precisely how to kiss!*

Yun Zhou emerged from seemingly nowhere, tapping his fan playfully:
"My lords, while Abyssfall Cliff is successfully stabilised, this is hardly a
wedding hall suitable for such public displays of affection."

Yun Lili instantly blushed crimson right up to her earlobes, shrinking
back in mortification behind Yu Sord.

Yu Sord, without changing his expression, pressed her further against his back and cast Yun Zhou a single, lethal glance: "**Be gone**."

Yun Zhou retreated with a profound, knowing smile, but secretly, beneath his sleeve, he sealed the jade slip recording the crucial array data—he was determined to compile today's 'Fine-Thread Weaving' method into an official, definitive tome.

This entire chaotic ordeal had taught the entire Immortal Realm—and himself—one crucial, immutable lesson: Not every catastrophic hole must be plugged with a willing sacrifice.

Sometimes, one must use one's whole heart, one's profound fear, one's ingenious quick wit, and a few tears and laughs delivered with snot and grace, to keep one's life intact and successfully mend the very cosmos.

The sunset faded completely, and a string of protective lanterns was swiftly lit along the cliff edge.

In the distance, the horizon finally revealed a thin, pale thread of gold.

Yun Lili leaned heavily against Yu Sord's shoulder and drifted into a brief nap.

She woke when her nose tickled—Little Fira was gently nudging her with its feather tip.

She scooped it up, burying her face completely in its warm plumage: "Thank you… and thank you, all of you." She looked down at the three chickens, whose small eyes gleamed brightly.

"We go back for roasted mealworms," she announced firmly.

The three chickens responded in a collective, triumphant "Goo!"

At the foot of Abyssfall Cliff, the wind finally ceased to cut like a knife.

Yun Lili lifted her head, looking at the newly mended 'wound' on the cliff face. She suddenly whispered to it, very softly: "Do not dare to tear open again. I beg of you."

Like consoling a frightened child.

She turned, showing Yu Sord her mirror: "Come on, let us go home. I intend to sleep for eighty hours straight without interruption."

Yu Sord "Mm"ed softly. He looked at her reflection in the mirror—eyes red, nose red, and cheeks bearing faint scratch marks from the wild wind.

He reached up and gently touched the rice-grain sized chip missing from her temple: "It is nothing."

Yun Lili instantly shielded the mirror: "Don't you dare call it ugly!"

"I said it is nothing," he clarified, his tone profoundly warm. "It is beautiful."

—Only with a visible flaw does one remember the life-and-death effort required to mend it.

—And only with profound fear, is one truly called courageous.

A wisp of wind rose again over the cliff, this time sounding exactly like someone gently sighing in contentment.

Yun Lili looked at the mirror with its small, missing corner, and suddenly whispered internally: *—I am still me, a mere mortal who fears death and lacks a spiritual root. But even a mortal can mend the heavens; that, I suppose, is enough.*

* * * * *

The fierce winds over the Abyssfall Cliff finally died completely.

The black miasma, which had raged like a beast, had been successfully repressed back into the deep abyss, leaving only a profound, eerie silence.

Only the occasional chip of stone slid down the cliff face, the sound almost imperceptible.

Yun Lili sank onto the stone railing, gasping deeply.

The three chickens clustered anxiously around her, clucking incessantly like demanding creditors.

She held one in each hand, and one clamped between her knees, a look of exhaustion mixed with exasperation: "All right, all right, I know you are all great heroes! Stop the noise! I will give you all roasted mealworms when we return, alright?"

The three chickens instantly fell silent, neatly shaking their wings in unison, as if they fully understood the term "**extra repast**."

Yun Lili breathed a sigh of relief, but suddenly felt a chilling sensation in her chest. She looked down.

The phoenix pattern that had been faintly glowing in the mirror was now completely dim.

Her spiritual energy had receded like a tide, and no matter how she urged it, there was no reaction.

"Eh?" She blinked blankly. "Did it… did it just break again?"

She grew frantic, tears almost welling up once more: "No way! I just finished mending one massive hole; how can my own mirror break first!"

Yu Sord walked closer, his gaze falling upon her chest.

His expression tightened momentarily.

He reached out to cover her pulse point. A thread of spiritual energy probed her, and his features instantly relaxed: "It is fine. You are perfectly whole."

With that, Yu Sord couldn't help but let a small smile curve his lips, the profound peace that follows great alarm evident in his eyes.

Yun Lili stared blankly at him, her eyes wide: "Then… then my mirror…"

"I shall purchase you a brand new, latest model," Yu Sord finished for her, his voice profoundly low.

She paused for a long moment, then suddenly clapped her hands over her face and let out a loud, drawn-out cry of "Waaah!" "Truly?"

The assembled Immortals still thought she was overcome with grief. They were about to step forward to offer comfort, only to hear her call out in a choked sob: "I also want a pink fuzzy cover for it this time!"

The entire field went silent.

White-Brow Elder nearly choked on his own breath, suppressing his reaction for a long moment before letting out a cold "Hmph! Utter nonsense!" Yet, he turned his back, wiping his mouth discreetly with his sleeve.

Sang Li, however, let out a soft laugh, bowing formally towards Yun Lili: "Maiden, this is precisely a good thing. You have mended the array heart, and you have emerged completely unscathed; this is a true blessing from the heavens."

He paused, his gaze deepening. He said seriously: "The method of 'Fine-Thread Weaving and Mending' shall be recorded in the celestial canon starting today. This technique, created by you, shall be formally named the **'Lili Patch'**."

"'Lili Patch'?" Yun Lili, tears still clinging to her face, looked up blankly. "That sounds… terribly like a piece of common cloth."

Yun Zhou let out a soft *Pfft* of laughter, snapping his fan shut: "Perfectly fitting. The heavens are torn like cloth, and you are the needle and thread. Utterly marvelous."

Yun Lili wrinkled her nose petulantly, yet still managed to mutter: "What ever next? It sounds so completely **un-immortal** and terribly unglamorous…"

Chapter 57: All of It Will Be Yours

Night had deepened.

Before the main hall of Lingxiao Sect, lines of fire torches burned quietly, their light wavering in the wind and painting every face with the same weary glow.

The day's battle had drained even the sky—clouds pressed low, like they too were exhausted.

Yun Wuntang, for once, had laid aside all the majesty of a sect master.

He wore a plain robe, his back slightly curved as he sat on the front steps, looking nothing like the untouchable lord of a great sect—just an aging father who had nearly lost his child.

Yun Lili shuffled over, the soles of her shoes making small sounds against the stone.

She settled down cross-legged beside him, so close their sleeves almost brushed.

The mirror was still hugged tightly in her arms, as if it were a talisman that could keep everything from falling apart.

"Dad."

Her voice was barely louder than a whisper, soft and cautious, as though one wrong word might shatter the fragile calm between them.

"Does this mean... I'll never be able to fly again?"

Yun Wuntang stiffened for a moment, caught off guard.

The question was childish, almost ridiculous in the face of what had just happened—but perhaps it was precisely that childishness he had been afraid he'd never see again.

He slowly exhaled, the breath misting faintly in the cold air.

"Lili," he said at last, his tone low and tired, "being able to fly or not... is that truly so important?"

"Of course it is!" Lili shot back without thinking, panic flaring up. "I was terrified of heights to begin with! It took me ages to get used to flying. I only managed to fly properly a few times and now—now it's just gone!"

Her cheeks puffed up, eyes round with grievance.

She looked less like a saviour who had just helped mend a world-shaking rift and more like a little girl who'd had her favourite toy snatched away.

Yun Wuntang gazed at that familiar, sulking expression, and something in his chest twisted painfully.

Yet, in the midst of that ache, a low chuckle escaped him.

He reached out and mussed the top of her head, fingers rough but careful, his voice gentler than it had been in many, many years—so gentle it barely resembled the sect master of Lingxiao at all.

"You being alive," he whispered quietly, "is the real miracle."

Lili blinked, taken aback. The words slid into her heart, warm and heavy, and for a moment she didn't know whether she wanted to laugh or cry. Her throat tightened.

"…Mm," she murmured, head drooping, but the corners of her lips curved ever so slightly.

* * * * *

On the other side of the mountain Cliff, Zhou stood alone where the wind hit the hardest.

The world before him was dark—the rift at the base of Abyssfall Cliff now silent, yet in his mind it still roared.

His sleeves were whipped back by the night wind, but he didn't move, his gaze fixed on the shadowed abyss below, his brows drawn tight as if carved there.

Lili ran up the slope, panting a little, mirror bouncing against her chest. She grabbed hold of his sleeve with one hand, fingers still faintly trembling.

"Brother!"

"Aren't you supposed to be resting?" Zhou frowned, the reprimand automatic, yet his voice lacked its usual sharp edge.

"I wanted to find you," she said. She tipped her head back to look at him, eyes still rimmed red from all her crying. "Brother… from now on, please… don't try to die in my place anymore, okay?"

Zhou's chest gave a sharp, almost painful throb. For a long while, he said nothing.

The wind rushed between them, tugging at their clothes and hair.

Finally, he lifted his hand and laid it gently over her shoulder, fingers tightening as though he were afraid that if he didn't hold on, she'd vanish.

"Silly girl," he whispered softly. "If you can still laugh and stay alive… that is already victory."

Lili's nose stung again. Her eyes blurred, but she forced herself to blink the tears back and nodded, hard, like she was making a promise.

Zhou turned his face away, looking out over the dim outlines of mountains and shattered clouds.

The wind brushed past his temples, carrying with it the faint scent of smoke and blood that still lingered in the air.

After a moment, he spoke, his voice lower than before.

"I'll be going down the mountain."

"Where to?" Lili's heart lurched, panic rising all over again.

"The mortal realm."

Zhou's gaze sharpened for a heartbeat like a drawn blade—then, at last, something in it loosened.

The edge softened, replaced by a rare hint of release, as if an old knot had finally been untied.

"To walk. To see," he said. "To take a look at the world we've been trying so hard to protect."

He paused, then lowered his eyes to her again, looking as much like an older brother as a sword cultivator.

"You," he replied, "have to live well."

Lili stared up at him, her chest tight, breathing gone a little uneven.

She could feel the heaviness behind his words, all the things he wasn't saying. Before the tears could spill over, she suddenly flung up her hand, raising her voice as if to chase the gloom away.

"Then you'd better remember to come back!" she blurted. "I still have to make roasted chicken wings for you!"

Zhou blinked, startled—and then, slowly, the corner of his mouth lifted. He reached out and flicked her on the forehead with the ease of long habit.

"Alright," he murmured, the single word carrying a promise heavier than he let on.

* * * * *

For three full days after the battle, the entire Lingxiao Sect was consumed with repairs.

Talismans were replaced, broken formations were redrawn, and sword cultivators moved back and forth like a tide.

Even the air smelled faintly of burnt spiritual force.

And Lili—dragging three chickens in a line like a chaotic little procession—insisted on "checking the progress" every morning.

She never made it far.

Yu Sord caught her every time, one hand lifting her by the collar as easily as if she were one more feathery creature under his care, and marched her straight back to her room.

"What are you doing!" Lili protested, cheeks puffed up in outrage. "I'm a major hero, okay?!"

Yu Sord didn't even blink.

"Major heroes also rest."

"But I don't even *have* spiritual power anymore!"

"That is exactly why mortals need to rest even more."

Lili opened her mouth—

—then closed it again, completely blocked by logic she really, really didn't want to accept.

She glared at him with all the ferocity of a wet kitten.

Before she could think of a retort, Yu Sord suddenly reached out and pulled her into his arms.

Lili froze.

His breath brushed her ear when he spoke, low and steady, a warmth wrapped in steel:

"You've already done enough. From now on… it's my turn to protect you."

Lili's mind went utterly blank. Then her face turned red—slowly, painfully, from the collar all the way up to the tips of her ears. Her heart thumped so loudly she could hear it echoing inside her own skull.

It took her a very, very long time before she managed to whisper:

"…Th-Then you're not allowed to think I'm useless."

Yu Sord huffed a laugh, the sound soft yet amused.

He gently pinched the tips of her fingers.

"You're afraid of dying and you cry too easily," he stated, completely serious, "but no one is braver than you."

Lili blinked. Her eyes instantly filled with tears again.

Before he could react, she shoved her head into his chest, smearing tears and snot across his robe with tragic determination.

"Uuugh—don't say things like that, it makes me want to cry *more*!"

Yu Sord simply held her tighter.

All the sharpness in his expression—every inch of the icy, unreachable sword cultivator—melted away entirely.

Only the quiet warmth remained, steady as the mountain behind Lingxiao itself.

* * * * *

Three days later, beneath the Abyssfall Cliff, the final barrier-light shimmered into place—steady, whole, unbroken.

Sang Lee sealed the formation records himself, the sleeve of his robe sweeping over the glowing scripts before he turned and announced:

"The battle is concluded. The Four Realms… may rest, for now."

A long breath rippled through the gathered immortals. Relief softened rigid shoulders; even the air seemed lighter.

In the middle of the crowd, Lili hugged her mirror against her chest. She pursed her lips, hesitated—then muttered under her breath:

"…Then from now on, please don't call me to mend the heavens anymore. I—I'm terrified of dying. I'm really not suitable for that job."

For a heartbeat, there was silence.

Then someone snorted.

Another chuckled.

Laughter spread like ripples across a still pond, soft at first, then warming the entire cliffside. Even the usually stone-faced elders failed to suppress the upward twitch of their lips.

Yu Sord watched her—watched her fidget, watched her blush, watched her insist she was "not suitable" when she had just saved them all.

The corner of his mouth lifted.

But in his eyes, there was something deeper… a warmth so steady it seemed to wrap around her like a silent promise.

—The storm had finally passed.

—And the little girl he had vowed to protect… was still here.

* * * * *

Spring waters rose along the mountain path, and the rhododendrons bloomed in a riot of colour.

At the foot of Mount Lingxiao, the small town had opened its once-every-three-days market again: candied haw sellers, flower-pin stalls, dough-figurine artisans, monkey tamers—whole families spilled onto the street, bustling with a warmth that seemed to shake off the last shadow of winter.

Lili rolled up her sleeves, carrying a small bamboo basket in her hand. Inside, three chickens—Red, Blue, and Gold—poked their heads out proudly, each wearing the unmistakable expression of *"Ahem, we are war heroes."*

Little Fira lounged on her shoulder, golden feathers catching sunlight, looking as though it was suffering terribly from being dragged to a mortal marketplace.

"Three skewers," Lili declared to the vendor, holding up three fingers with righteous severity. "Pick the biggest one on the outside for me. The rest… give him."

She jerked her chin toward Yu Sord.

Yu Sord stood behind her, hands clasped behind his back, blue robes trailing in the breeze, sword silent at his side.

His expression had been calm—until his gaze rested on that tiny grain-sized chip on her mirror, and his features softened without him noticing.

Hearing her "distribution order," he only let out a quiet laugh.

"Understood."

Lili handed a skewer each to Red, Blue, and Gold, then took the fourth for herself, happily crunching into it, eyes curving like crescents.

"You're not eating?" she asked, pushing the reddest candied haw to his lips.

Yu Sord lowered his gaze and bit into it, the tips of his ears turning red ever so faintly.

"I thought those were for them."

"It's the same if it's for you," she waved generously. "You're also one of my chick—ah no, I meant you're my—"

Halfway through, she realized the crisis and slammed the brakes.

"You're my important… um… very important… person…"

Yu Sord gave a low laugh, brushing a thin thread of syrup from the corner of her lips.

"I know."

Her heart thumped like a drum. She ducked her head immediately, pretending to inspect the basket.

"One for Red, one for Blue, one for Gold… Listen to me—no choking!"

On the day Zhou left the mountain, the wind was perfect.

He carried only a sword and a simple cloth bundle—no time for farewells—before bowing deeply to Yun Wuntang and Lili.

"The mortal world is a long road," he stated. "Full of injustice, full of good wine. Let me walk it once… then I'll come back and listen to your nagging again."

Lili's nose burned hot; tears gathered at the rim of her lashes.

Trying to act fierce, she dragged her three chickens to block his path.

"You dare not come back," she warned, "I'll— I'll eat all your favourite grilled wings myself!"

Zhou broke into a helpless laugh.

"Then I have even more reason to return. Can't have you overeating and getting a stomachache."

He bent down and flicked her forehead lightly before turning away, stepping onto the path that stretched down the mountain.

His figure grew smaller, drawn into the wind like a sheathed sword seeking its rightful place in the world below.

Before he left, he slipped something into her hand—a wooden comb.

Its teeth had been polished smooth.

"Good peachwood," he explained. "It won't clash with that little chip on your mirror."

Lili clutched the comb, sniffing hard.

"Who says a chipped mirror is ugly! It's— it's battle-scar aesthetics!"

Yun Wuntang stood on the steps above, sleeves folded behind his back.

He watched in silence for a long time, and only when he turned away did he speak, voice low, almost gentle.

"All is well."

It sounded like a man finally setting his blade back onto the table—

willing, at last, to show his back to the kitchen fire and the smell of cooking rice.

* * * * *

Capital City, Phoenix Palace.

Spring thunder cracked across the sky, and willow catkins drifted beyond the palace walls like falling snow.

On the old huai tree in the courtyard, tender green buds had pushed out—bright and unreasonable in their vigour.

Moony walked along the covered corridor in a plain gauze cloak, her steps no longer as light as they had been in her youth.

Time had brushed a faint grey along her brows.

But when she turned her head, her eyes were still as clear and bright as before.

Du Shao sat by the stone chess table on the steps, wearing a simple cloak over his shoulders. A few silver strands now threaded through his hair.

He reached out to take the food box from her hands, smiling gently.

"You made ginger cakes again?"

"Mm."

Moony arranged the ginger cakes one by one, then carefully took out a small porcelain cup.

Inside were three tiny dried mealworms.

"For… offering, I suppose."

Du Shao couldn't help laughing.

"And who are we offering *these* to?"

"The young miss's three chickens."

Moony lowered her gaze. A faint ache flickered in her eyes before she hid it away.

"They achieved great merit. Even though they're far away in the mountains, they deserve a reward."

Du Shao covered her fingertips with his palm, warming them gently.

"Then we'll double it."

Moony gave a soft hum of agreement and tilted her head upward, as if looking at someplace impossibly far away.

In her heart, she spoke without sound:

Miss, I'm here. I'm living well. You must live well too.

That evening, a squad of traveling sword cultivators arrived in the capital, bringing news from Abyssfall Cliff.

The crisis resolved, the mirror-mending successful.

Later, Du Shao set aside his memorials for the night and told her quietly:

"My mind… is at ease now."

Moony lowered her eyes. Her fingers tightened subtly on the edge of his robe.

After a long moment, she whispered, "Good."

One by one, the palace lanterns lit up.

With every passing breeze, their flames rose and dipped—

like the whole palace breathing together.

Across mountains and seas, two threads of fate finally stopped tearing in opposite directions.

Instead, they lay back where they belonged—resting obediently upon the same vast weave.

In the small courtyard on the slopes of Lingxiao Mountain, the hearth fire rose.

Lili tightened her apron, presently locked in battle with a pot of bubbling broth.

The pot gurgled; the mealworms lay obediently in a basin at her side.

She stared left, stared right, then leaned toward Yu Sord, whispering like she was plotting treason:

"Can I give them two first? They're war heroes. Heroes need benefits."

Yu Sord sat on a stool at the doorway, long legs folded, the sharpness in his features worn softer by the passing days.

He blinked once, speechless.

"You already gave 'benefits.'"

"That was overtime pay," she explained, perfectly righteous.

Little Fira—napped lazily on the beam, its tail feathers hanging to brush the tips of Yu Sord's hair.

The three chickens lined up before the stove in a straight row, like seasoned generals awaiting rations, eyes glued to the pot as if afraid happiness might escape if they blinked.

"All right, all right."

Lili brought out bowls of chicken soup, giving each chicken a respectful portion before piling the largest pieces of meat into Yu Sord's bowl.

She kept half a bowl for herself, sat down, took a sip—

"*Hiss*—" She jerked her neck back, eyes watering. Then brightened. "It's good!"

Yu Sord looked at her for a moment.

"Too much salt."

She instantly shielded her bowl like someone threatening to draw a sword.

"I *like* a lot of salt! Salt extends life!"

"Who said that?"

"I said that."

She jutted her chin, arms akimbo—pure rascal.

Yu Sord couldn't help a quiet laugh. He used his chopsticks to lift the lighter broth from her bowl, transferring it to his own.

"Then I'll have the shorter life."

Lili froze. Her ears flared red like lanterns.

"No you won't!"

Back and forth they went. Outside, the wind swayed bamboo shadows across the courtyard.

It was a kind of day with no flying swords, no exploding star-charts—only the sheen of oil on the soup and the restless clucking of chickens.

* * * * *

After dinner, Lili took the peachwood comb and sat on the threshold, using her cracked mirror to comb her hair.

The tiny chipped corner rested quietly at the rim; she tapped it with a finger and muttered:

"You better behave. No more running off."

The mirror stayed as still as water, reflecting her back—bright eyes, a slightly upturned nose, a trace of mischief in her brows.

Yu Sord sat behind her, long legs stretching out, casually drawing her into his arm.

"I thought you were going to tell it—'pretty.'"

Lili leaned naturally into his chest and shook the mirror.

"That too."

She tilted her head toward her reflection and, slowly and very solemnly, stated:

"I'm pretty. You're even prettier. And together we're the prettiest."

Yu Sord: "...Mm."

He lowered his head and brushed a soft kiss onto the crown of her hair, his voice so low that the evening breeze nearly kept it for itself:

"All pretty."

* * * * *

Dusk deepened. From the town below came the slow thrum of the evening drum.

Warm lamplight filled the room, softening the beams and doorframes—and their shadows.

Lili suddenly murmured, "I had a dream."

"Tell me."

"In the dream, Abyssfall Cliff. cracked open again, and everyone yelled for me to patch it. I grabbed my mirror and ran—ran and cried—shouting 'I'm scared!' And then you grabbed me from behind."

Yu Sord hummed faintly.

"You said: 'If you're scared, hold on.'"

Lili tilted her face upward, her lashes casting tiny fan-shaped shadows in the lamplight.

"And then… I really wasn't scared anymore."

She paused, then added, very seriously:

"Well—half not scared. I saved the other half. Just in case."

Yu Sord actually chuckled.

"In case of what?"

"In case I forget I'm a mortal."

She pressed the mirror to her chest, her voice earnest.

"I treasure my life a lot."

He didn't laugh this time.

Instead, he was quiet for a breath before speaking:

"Good."

Fear—was what made courage real.

And that was the truth he had learned from her.

* * * * *

The next morning, mountain mist climbed out of the valley like a bolt of pale silk.

Lili was jolted awake by frantic clucking. She threw on an outer robe and rushed outside.

"Who dares make noise outside my window—oh. It's you three."

The three chickens lifted their heads in perfect unison.

"Goo."

Little Fira glided down from a branch, smoothing its feathers with dignified disdain.

Yu Sord was in the corner of the courtyard practicing his sword. His blade showed no sharp gleam—only the rhythm of breath and footwork, steady and even, like a heartbeat made of steel.

Lili stood there watching him for a moment before picking up the water bucket to water the vegetable patch.

The water pattered against the soil, soft and steady.

She tipped her head up toward the small patch of blue sky peeking through the mist.

"Hey—Abyssfall Clif. Don't crack again, okay?"

She glanced at her mirror, hugged it like a secret, and added:

"I still have to live a long time. I have marketplaces to visit, candied hawthorn to eat, overtime mealworms to give the chickens. And I still need to…"

Her voice softened, her ears flushed pink.

"…I still need to argue with him."

Yu Sord finished his form and walked toward her, taking the bucket from her hands.

His knuckles brushed her palm—just lightly, but enough to make her heart skip.

"Down the mountain today?" he asked.

"Down." Lili nodded vigorously.

"I'm buying ten sticks of candied hawthorn, five pounds of mealworms, three of the prettiest hairpins, and also that thing that will definitely make you blush—"

Halfway through, she snapped her mouth shut, coughed twice in the least convincing way possible.

"Ahem. Anyway—lots of things. *You* carry them."

Yu Sord simply said, "I'll carry all of it."

She tilted her face up, smiling so brightly it lit the whole morning mist—

In her eyes, spring had already arrived.

* * * * *

On their way back that evening, the mountain wind slipped upward through the forest, as if it were escorting them home.

The basket in Lili's hand was heavy with mealworms; half the candied hawthorn was already gone.

Two of the hairpins she'd bought now glimmered in her hair, and the third she kept tucked safely in her sleeve—

"For when my brother comes back," she said, as if this were an oath.

When they reached the bend in the path, Lili suddenly stopped.

She turned around and looked at everyone at Yu Sord, at the three chickens clustered around her feet, at Little Fira perched on her shoulder, and even at the mirror in her arms with its tiny chipped corner.

She took a deep breath, puffed out her cheeks for courage, and declared with utmost seriousness:

"I don't want to be any kind of Phoenix Lord."

"I want to stay alive."

"I want my mirror. I want my chickens. And—"

She looked at Yu Sord then, her voice shrinking into something soft and sweet:

"…and I want you."

Yu Sord froze for half a heartbeat.

A thin wash of light passed through his eyes—like the first piece of sky after a storm.

He drew her into his arms, touched his forehead lightly to hers, and whispered with a quiet laugh:

"Very well. All of it will be yours."

The three chickens clucked three solemn "goo!"s in approval.

Little Fira let out a tiny, disdainful hum—

the kind that meant: *I suppose I agree too.*

In the distance, the evening drum sounded from the town below,

and it felt as though the entire mountain nodded with it.

* * * * *

Many years later, an extra page quietly appeared in the records of Lingxiao:

"She who mends the Rift does not seal it with life, but stitches it with the heart. Not with heroic sacrifice, but with a clumsy, stubborn courage that weaves peace back into the human world."

When Lili eventually read that line, she was lazing on the bed, hugging her mirror, rolling over with a grumble.

"Hmph. Makes it sound like I only had strength to mend the rift because I'd eaten enough first."

Yu Sord glanced over.

"Then have another bowl."

"Okay!"

She sat upright at once, eyes lighting up like two tiny lamps.

"And add salt!"

"…Mn."

The lamp's glow softened; their voices mingled like warm breath in early spring.

Far away, the Abyssfall Cliff slept in silence.

Across the horizon stretched a faint, fine thread of gold—as though someone had drawn the final stitch across the fabric of the sky.

Extra chapter 1

Though the winds around the Abyssfall Cliff had at last fallen silent, far beneath the world—deep within the Abyssal Palace of the Demon Realm—another tide was beginning to rise.

From the black sea of the Nine Hells, a colossal palace of obsidian and gold surfaced slowly, as if dragged upward by a thousand unseen chains.

Nine lanterns—eternal night-lamps forged from demonic bone—hung from the vaulted ceiling. Their flames never dimmed; each burned with an ink-black fire that cast layer upon layer of shifting shadow across the massive hall.

Outside, a legion of spirits wailed. Their cries churned the undercurrents of the abyss, turning the waters violent.

Within the hall, **nine demon lords** sat in a long arc.

At the foremost seat stood the Palace Master—face veiled, robes black as a starless night, hands clasped behind his back. His gaze cut through the gloom like a blade.

Before him, a demon commander knelt, trembling.

"Master… reporting. The Abyssfall Cliff… has stabilized."

Silence crashed over the hall like a falling stone.

"Stabilized?"

The Palace Master's voice was like stone splitting open.

"For a thousand years, the celestial array has decayed, the heavenly anchors loosened. We have waited—burrowed, hidden, endured—all for that single breach. And now you stand before me… saying it is stable?"

The commander pressed his forehead to the floor, cold sweat pouring like rain.

"I saw it with my own eyes. The heart of the cliff was already shattered—yet a woman… used a mirror to draw phoenix blood… and stitched the breach shut."

"A woman?"

A deputy lord let out a thin, cold laugh.

"Even a high immortal cannot mend that rift. A mortal woman? Ridiculous."

The commander whispered even lower:

"She did not seem to be… an ordinary mortal. She carried an ancient mirror—etched with violet bamboo patterns. A phoenix crest emerged from the mirror itself, and the blood sealed the rupture. Such a method… has never been recorded."

A ripple of unease passed among the demon lords, though their expressions hardened into sharper malice.

"Phoenix blood…" one murmured.

"If she truly invoked it, she should have perished instantly. The fact she survives means… the mirror took the backlash."

"A mirror-spirit."

Another demon lord's voice dropped to an icy hiss.

"If it can draw phoenix blood, it can also steal phoenix blood. Seize the mirror. Seize the woman. The cliff will be ours again."

The Palace Master remained silent for a long, oppressive moment.

At last he spoke, voice hoarse like thunder smothered by smoke:

"Send the Shadow Disciples. Watch her. A flesh-body carrying phoenix blood must pay a price. When her life-essence falters, the Abyssfall Cliff will split anew."

Another demon kneeled forward.

"But the Demon Monarch's spirit suffered grievous harm during this battle. Without him, the throne may fall into chaos. We must summon the Crown Prince back immediately—if the Celestial Realm attacks while we are unprepared—"

"Then summon him," the Palace Master said.

"Dispatch all search battalions. Find the Crown Prince. Bring him back to the Demon Palace at once."

The nine night-lanterns trembled violently. Their black flames erupted upward, flooding the hall like a sea of shadow-fire.

Outside, countless silhouettes rose from the abyss—like a swarm of obsidian wings—and scattered toward the mortal world.

The Celestial Realm believed the storm had passed.

But in the eyes of the Demon Palace…the hunt had only just begun.

Meanwhile, unaware of the looming darkness, common folk had already built small shrines at the foot of the once-fractured cliff. They lit incense, whispered their earnest wishes:

"Phoenix Lady… please bless my family…"

"Keep our village safe…"

The incense smoke rose gently, star-like in the dusk.

None of them knew that because of their prayers—

that woman's name would begin to shift, to root itself into belief, into temple, into deity.

In the seam between shadow and light, the silhouette of the Phoenix Shrine fell softly upon the world for the first time.

Extra chapter 2

Not far from the capital, beside a clear river, stood a newly built shrine.

It was small—white walls, blue tiles, modest in height—yet smoke from incense rose day and night, never once dwindling.

Across the front beam hung three freshly carved characters:

Phoenix Lady Shrine.

The origin of this mortal legend could be traced back years earlier, to a funeral that had taken a very unexpected turn.

Inside, the statue of the goddess bore no serene face, no gentle smile like the deities mortals were accustomed to. Instead, the figure had an enormous puff of wild, frizzy hair—almost explosive—and in her arms she held a green round-headed creature, as if hugging some bizarre spirit-beast.

Yun Lili froze at the threshold of the shrine.

Her entire body stiffened.

"…Who… is that?" she asked, voice trembling as she pointed at the statue.

The shrine keeper, earnest and devout, replied at once.

"That is the Phoenix Lady, of course! Young miss may not know the story—years ago, our lord died young. The funeral was already prepared. But then—a host of immortals descended from the sky! One goddess fell straight onto the coffin, knocked the lid clean off, and then used divine arts to bring our lord back to life!"

Lili: "…"

And then she remembered.

She remembered far too well.

Back then, Moony had carried her into the air in a panic; in the frantic up-and-down chaos, she had accidentally fallen—straight onto someone's coffin.

It was Yu Sord who had stabilized the situation and saved the dying man.

A breath caught painfully in her chest. She twisted toward Yu Sord, glaring as though her soul were leaving her body.

"You brought me here on purpose! Just to show me… this?!"

Yu Sord looked perfectly calm. His azure robe fluttered slightly in the wind, the picture of dignity.

"I only knew the man became motivated afterwards, studied hard, and ranked first in the imperial exam. As for the shrine… I am learning of this today as well."

"How could that be? That statue looks exactly like me!" Lili nearly exploded. "And why is Moony carved at the bottom?!"

Sure enough, the pedestal showed a bold and proud red-gold bird, chest puffed out aggressively like a seasoned veteran claiming all credit.

The shrine keeper added helpfully,

"Indeed! It is said the Phoenix Lady descended riding a red-gold divine bird. So our lord had it carved there, to show gratitude."

Lili's entire face turned crimson.

She muttered through clenched teeth, "What riding down? I was dropped! Dropped!"

From her basket, the three chickens popped out their heads and clucked once in perfect agreement.

Only Moony gave a sideways glance and a sharp, offended chirp.

A small crowd of villagers had already gathered inside the shrine. They nodded earnestly.

"The Phoenix Lady is very effective! We all pray to her sincerely!"

Lili: "…"

She felt that even if she screamed her lungs out, not a single person would believe her.

As she fumed helplessly, her gaze snagged on a little boy kneeling before the incense table, palms pressed tightly together.

"Phoenix Lady… please let my mother get well…"

The incense flame leapt upward, as though caught by an unseen force.

Lili's heart jolted.

She instinctively touched the bamboo-patterned mirror inside her robe.

It had cracked once before, shattered even—but now, under those rising prayers, faint warm light shimmered across its surface, like something responding.

Yu Sord noticed as well.

His eyes deepened for a brief moment, though he said nothing.

With a small motion, he reached over and tucked an errant strand of her hair gently behind her ear.

"If you dislike this place," he said quietly, "we can pretend we were never here."

Lili pressed her lips together.

After a long silence, she muttered, "I don't want to be a god. Gods have to work every day."

And behind her, as if fate insisted on opposing her wishes, the statue bathed in the setting sun, glowing gold from head to toe—majestic, solemn, impossibly divine.

Far away in the Celestial Realm, an elder unrolled a jade slip, murmuring,

"Phoenix Lady Shrine…? Mortals forming a deity through wish-power?"

Deep within the Demon Palace, a shadow laughed quietly,

"Mortals creating a god of their own—will the Celestial Realm allow such insolence? That girl… she will fall into our hands eventually."

All this while, a little mortal girl—who feared death more than anything—had no idea she was being turned into a divine figure by accident.

Lili slapped a hand to her forehead, expression collapsing into utter despair.

"…It's over. I've become an overworked employee of heaven."

The three chickens and Moony all clucked in perfect unison, clearly agreeing.

After another long moment, she dropped her voice even lower, defeated.

"I don't want to be a god. Gods work overtime… and they don't even get paid."

Yu Sord's eyes curved ever so slightly.

He still wore that cool, aloof expression—

yet the corner of his mouth betrayed the faintest, helpless smile.

Extra chapter 3

Inside the Phoenix Palace, the night lamps flickered softly.

By the couch, the incense burner sent up light ribbons of smoke, the scent of herbs tangled with the faint sweetness of palace incense.

Du Shao leaned half-upright against a brocade pillow. His complexion was pale as frost; each cough came in a trembling wave, shaking his thin frame as though the sound rose straight from his bones.

"Your Majesty, please rest."

Moony set down a bowl of warm water, gently lifting him so he could wet his throat.

Only after several breaths did the coughing subside.

Du Shao lifted his gaze to her—his dimmed eyes reflecting the lamplight, softening into that familiar tenderness that had once belonged to a proud young man.

"Moony…"

His voice no longer carried a ruler's thunder; it was worn, quiet, but steady.

"Fifty years. And you are still here."

Moony's throat tightened. Her eyes stung—but her smile remained gentle as she smoothed his graying hair.

"Of course I'm here. You said you wanted me with you for your whole life."

Du Shao stared at her, gratitude simmering warm and deep. Slowly— painfully—he lifted a hand. His fingers were thin, the joints protruding, but he stubbornly tried to reach for hers.

"Moony… in this life, you are what made up for everything I lacked."

His voice was hoarse but every word was clear.

"You saved me. Without you, I would have long been strangled within these palace walls… lost in schemes and ambition."

Moony looked at him dazedly, something gripping tight at her chest.

Fifty years.

The boy he once was—now lined with age and white hair.

She, still youthful in face, unchanged, frozen in the appearance of the day she fell to the mortal world.

He, already at the end of his mortal span.

She lowered her gaze, wrapped his hand in hers, and whispered, "I've thought a lot, these fifty years."

Du Shao blinked, surprised.

"I may have lost my immortal arts. I don't know if I will ever return to the immortal realm again."

Her voice was soft, like speaking to herself.

"But watching you work each day… reading memorials, carrying the weight of the people… and finally bringing peace to the lands…"

She lifted her eyes—bright, clear, carrying a small, sincere smile.

"It made me happy. Truly."

Du Shao's throat trembled, moisture rising in his eyes.

Moony tugged the quilt higher around him. Her hands shook a little, but her smile remained.

"Everything has a price. Mine… was being separated from my lady, and staying in the mortal world for fifty years."

Her voice quieted.

"But I've never regretted it. Because my heart's wish… was simply to stay by your side, until the very end."

The room fell still—so still that only the small crackle of the lamp wick remained.

A tear finally slipped down Du Shao's cheek—yet he was smiling.

He tried to lift a hand to wipe her tears, but she caught his hand first.

"Silly."

Moony's eyes were red, but her tone tender.

"It wasn't only me accompanying you. You were also the one who kept me company."

He released a faint, trembling breath—

as if letting go of every burden he had ever carried.

"With you," he whispered,

"this life has already been… enough."

Moony leaned down until her forehead rested lightly against his.

Her voice was soft as a vow carved upon fate itself.

"Go without worry. I will wait for you.

Fifty years, a hundred years—however long it takes.

One day, we will meet again."

The last glimmer in Du Shao's eyes settled upon her face—

as though he wished to carve her into his very soul.

After a moment, he closed his eyes.

A faint smile lingered on his lips.

The lamp flames flickered gently.

Moony held him quietly.

Only then did her tears fall—slow, steady.

She did not wail.

She simply whispered:

"Your Majesty… no—Shao.

This was my choice.

And I am already fulfilled."

Outside, the night wind drifted in, carrying the faint fragrance of early spring blossoms beyond the palace walls.

Spring would come soon.

The world was at peace.

And in the Phoenix Palace, a youthful woman remained—unchanged by time—guarding fifty years of love and its quiet, complete ending.

Moony lifted her face toward the night sky, eyes shimmering through her tears.

Then she smiled softly.

"My lady… when I see you again, I'll bring his stories with me.

And our… happy ending."

Extra chapter 4

The late spring of Jiangnan draped itself in mist and rain.

By the stone cliff of the little riverside town, water murmured beneath the arch; willow branches swept the ground, and the bustle of street vendors blended with the beat of flower drums.

Zhou wore only a plain white robe.

No silver coronet.

Just a bamboo pin holding his hair, rain beading lightly on his shoulders.

One hand swung a wine flask; the other toyed idly with a bamboo dragonfly he'd bought from a street child. His expression was lazily amused.

"This mortal wine… tastes terrible," he muttered—though he still took another sip.

"But compared to the endless fighting in the cultivation realms, this noisy little place has its charms."

He walked toward a teahouse, intending to sit under its awning until the rain eased.

Then—he saw her.

A woman in plain robes sat by the window.

Slender frame, cool temperament… yet there was something quietly clumsy and adorable about her.

She bent over a tray of tea leaves with great seriousness.

After hesitating, she picked up a tender leaf, lifted it to her lips—

—and began chewing it.

Zhou's step faltered.

…She's eating the tea leaves?

A corner of his mouth curved, a memory rising—

a snowy night, a plum grove, a trembling little white rabbit he'd startled, glaring up at him with pitiful defiance.

He narrowed his eyes slightly and approached.

Rain tapped against the eaves; steam from the teahouse curled upward.

Sensing a presence, the woman looked up.

Her eyes—

clear, tinted with soft red, glowing like sparks in snow.

Spiritual aura.

A rabbit spirit.

A jolt passed through Zhou, followed by a laugh under his breath.

He slid into the seat opposite her.

The wine flask hit the table with a casual thud as he leaned back, tone lazy but carrying unmistakable dominance:

"Miss, eating raw leaves isn't exactly a mortal delicacy."

She froze for half a second—almost panicked—then lowered her gaze and replied coolly,

"To each their own."

Zhou drummed his long fingers on the table.

"Mm? That look... why does it seem familiar?"

She lowered her head further, as if shrinking into her sleeves. The leaf she'd chewed was quietly placed back into the tea bowl—like nothing had happened.

His smile deepened.

He leaned forward, eyes glinting.

"Have we met before?"

Her fingers trembled; a few drops of tea splashed out.

She said nothing.

Then Zhou reached out—gently hooking a strand of hair behind her ear.

The woman stiffened.

Her gaze fled.

But her ears—very clearly—turned red.

"Well, well..."

Zhou laughed softly.

"That reaction isn't what I'd call a first meeting."

At last, she raised her head.

Her red-tinted eyes met his.

There was panic—

there was struggle—

and a brief flicker of stubbornness that only rabbit spirits possessed.

After a long moment, she exhaled, resigned.

From her sleeve, she produced a preserved yet withered branch of plum blossom—

the very one he had left decades ago in that snowy grove.

"…Here. Take it back."

For a heartbeat, the market's noise seemed to fade into silence.

Zhou blinked, then his gaze darkened—

before a slow smile unfurled across his mouth.

"So it really is you."

His voice dipped, a shade rough, carrying an emotion he never let others hear.

Her fingers trembled, but she still set the branch on the table with cool defiance.

"Yes. This is the second time I've met you."

Zhou stared, smile widening—almost wicked.

"I remember now.

You're the little white rabbit who shook like a leaf… but still tried to glare at me."

She pressed her lips together, not knowing how to respond.

Then Zhou suddenly leaned close, their gazes crossing over the plum blossom, his voice low and dangerous:

"Little white rabbit, do you know who I am?"

She nodded, stiff but honest.

"…Zhou, eldest son of the Yun Clan. The Immortal Lord."

Zhou's grin sharpened.

"Good.

Now—what's your name?"

She hesitated.

"…Little White."

His laughter exploded.

"Hahaha—Little White the rabbit is actually named Little White?"

Her cheeks flushed pink.

",,,…"

Instinctively, she tried to bolt.

But Zhou moved like wind—one stride, long leg sweeping to block her path, trapping her between him and the door.

"The plum branch is still here," he drawled.

"So why is the rabbit trying to run?"

Her heartbeat lurched.

She tried to stand, but his hand closed around her wrist.

Not tight—just enough to keep her from slipping away.

She looked up.

Straight into his phoenix eyes.

Her thoughts scattered.

Zhou lowered his voice:

"Little rabbit… since this Immortal Lord intends to travel the mortal world, why don't you come with me?

Be my companion for the journey.

What do you say?"

"No—"

She panicked, yanking her hand, but his grip held firm.

Her strength was no match for his; her struggle only made her appear even more like a frightened rabbit.

"Come now," Zhou coaxed, leaning in, tone shameless.

"Traveling with me has benefits. Your cultivation will soar.

And I'm very generous—"

The sun dipped lower, casting long shadows across the street.

One tall figure, one small one—

their silhouettes stretching together down the stone road,

like the beginning of a story neither of them had expected.

The pale glow surrounding Mount Lu Yue finally dispersed.

After thirty years of seclusion, the last tides of spiritual energy ebbed away, and the barrier on the cave mouth let out a crisp, ringing note—

and dissolved.

The stone door opened with a slow, ancient groan.

Lu Ling stepped out clad in snowy white.

Sword-light still clung to her sleeves; the years had not touched her features, only carved a sharper calm in her eyes—a chill steadiness forged through countless silent nights.

She drew her first breath of open air—

—and immediately caught a strange scent.

She lowered her gaze.

Someone was squatting at the entrance.

Xie Wuchen—Sword Sovereign of the Nine Peaks—sat cross-legged on the stone steps, legs clearly numb out of their sanity.

In his arms was a chaotic bouquet of wildflowers, plucked who-knew-where, tied together with what looked like a torn strip of his own sleeve. Colours clashed, petals drooped, and the entire thing leaned pitifully to the side.

He held it solemnly, as if it were an imperial treasure.

But his eyelids kept drooping—he was at the edge of falling asleep.

Lu Ling's brow twitched.

"...Wuchen."

He jerked awake like someone struck by lightning.

When his eyes found her, they lit—bright as a blade just unsheathed.

"Ling!"

He bounded to his feet... and promptly stumbled, one leg giving out. Half the bouquet flew from his hands, scattering petals across the threshold like a chaotic offering to the mountain.

But he didn't seem to notice.

He grinned—boyishly, recklessly, stupidly delighted.

"You're out!"

Lu Ling stared at the battlefield of broken flowers at her feet.

Her voice was cool as frost:

"What is all this?"

"Flowers!"

Wuchen immediately gathered the remaining half and thrust it toward her, chest puffed, expression proud.

"I thought about it for thirty years. First thing I see you—there should be a gesture.

I can't arrange flowers, so… just pretend it looks fine?"

Lu Ling froze.

She stared at his face—

that shameless "look how thoughtful I am" expression—

and her temple throbbed.

"Thirty years," she said, voice dangerously even.

"You did nothing else?"

"I did plenty," he answered, utterly unfazed.

"I came here. Every day. When the flowers wilted, I picked new ones. Different seasons, different varieties.

Figure if you didn't come out, I'd at least keep you updated on the mountain flora."

He paused, then added with complete sincerity:

"Good thing I'm a sword cultivator. My legs held up. A mortal would've lost them ten years ago."

Lu Ling shot him a glacial look and turned on her heel.

Wuchen instantly followed, stride long, brushing her shoulder.

"Ling, you've been gone thirty years. I haven't complained once.

You walk out and start glaring? That's cold."

"Who told you to wait?" she snapped.

"Who told you to be worth waiting for?" he countered.

She inhaled sharply—

the retort stung somewhere she didn't want to acknowledge.

"…Presumptuous."

His eyes curved, amused.

He stepped ahead of her and blocked her path, lowering his voice:

"Ling. Thirty years ago, I knelt right here.

You didn't speak. I thought you refused me.

But now you've come out—so I'll take that as your answer."

"You—!"

Her hand closed around her sword hilt.

"Go on," he invited cheerfully.

"Cut me down. I won't even dodge. Worst case? I'll kneel another thirty years."

Lu Ling was livid—yet inexplicably speechless.

Before she could decide between slashing him or ignoring him, he shoved the mangled bouquet into her arms.

"Look. Ugly or not, I picked these myself.

Lu Ling of Mount Lu Yue—will you take them?"

She looked down.

The flowers were a mess—tilted stems, mismatched colors, petals that looked like they'd lost hope long ago.

She meant to throw them aside.

She really did.

But her fingers didn't move.

Her voice was cold as ever:

"These are hideous."

Wuchen laughed—openly, triumphantly, eyes bright like he'd just won a war.

"Great. Then tomorrow I'll learn flower arranging.

Thirty years waiting—what's thirty more days of lessons?"

Lu Ling: "…"

She spun away and strode downhill.

He followed behind without shame—half whispering, half teasing:

"Ling, what'd you think about all those years? Me, right? Couldn't sleep?

Dreamed of me? Missed me terribly—"

A sharp whistle of air—

her sword flashed, cleaving a pine branch above his head cleanly in half.

She turned, eyes icy.

"One more word, and I won't aim for the branch."

Wuchen didn't flinch.

In fact—his grin widened, wild and bright.

"Alright, alright, not another word.

But don't think you can get rid of me."

Lu Ling felt irritation rise—

yet beneath it, something warm curled quietly in her chest.

This man—

the one who knelt outside her cave thirty years ago—

was still here.

Still waiting.

Still smiling like a fool for her alone.

She could not avoid him.

Could not cut him out.

And perhaps…

didn't need to.

The mountain winds surged.

Flower petals scattered around them like drifting snow.

One cold, one warm—one step ahead, one step trailing—

a pair of sword cultivators descended the mountain side by side,

their paths, after thirty years apart,

finally merging into one.

Extra chapter 6

Deep in the ravine, mist pressed low over the treetops, heavy with moisture.

Beside a stone trough, Yue Liuchuan scrubbed bowls with his sleeves rolled up, cold water splashing over his knuckles. His jaw was tight, resentment simmering under his breath.

Behind him came Mo Han's cold, clipped voice—followed by a casual kick to his calf.

"Remember the corners. Wash them properly. Did you hear me?"

Yue Liuchuan gritted his teeth so hard his jaw clicked.

"Why in the world should I be washing dishes and vegetables for the crown prince of the Demon Realm—"

He never finished.

In a blink, Mo Han's hand was at his throat, a blade-sharp chop pressed just enough to warn—no further, no mercy.

"Keep talking," Mo Han said softly, "and I'll ship you straight back to the Heavenly Court for interrogation."

The threat was quiet.

And terrifyingly real.

Yue Liuchuan swallowed his pride and blood.

"...As you command."

At the wooden table, Yara sat silently sorting herbs. Her expression was always cool, her lashes lowered, indifferent to Yue Liuchuan's misery.

But when Mo Han spoke, she lifted her gaze for just an instant. The brief look was colder than the mist around them.

Mo Han leaned one hip against the table, posture relaxed and arrogant, lips curved in something like amusement.

"Come," he said lightly. "Let him finish the dishes. We're going to look at flowers."

He reached out to slide an arm around her shoulders—

—but Yara moved away before he even touched her.

She glared at him.

"Don't put your hands on me. I can walk myself."

The valley had been peaceful—until a sudden thunder of hooves shattered the quiet.

From beyond the ravine, a military horn blared.

The earth trembled.

Shadows gathered like a storm of black armor; killing intent rolled in waves like winter frost.

"Your Highness!"

The lead general dismounted and dropped to one knee, his voice booming through the valley.

"During the Soul-Suppressing Ritual, the Demon King suffered a backlash from the shattered array core. His primordial spirit has fractured—he has fallen into eternal slumber!

The armies of the realm unanimously call for Your Highness to return at once and ascend as our sovereign!"

The shout struck like thunder.

Yue Liuchuan flinched; the bowl in his hand slipped, shattering in the trough. Water splashed red where shards cut his fingers.

Yun Yara's brows drew together, a faint crease between them. She said nothing, but her gaze sharpened on the kneeling general.

The general's forehead nearly touched the dirt.

"Your High—no… Your Majesty. We pay respects to the new Demon King. Long live our king!"

Mo Han did not look at the army first.

He looked at Yara.

Instinctively—almost helplessly—his hand reached toward her.

"Yara…"

She stepped back.

"You should go," she said quietly.

"Yara." His voice was low, heavy, like a mountain on the verge of breaking.

"Come with me. Return to the palace."

Yara shook her head.

"That is your place. Not mine."

"I want you beside me."

Mo Han lifted his gaze—black eyes sharp, burning, unguarded.

"Come with me."

She laughed—a cold, brittle sound—but the faint tremor in her lashes betrayed her.

"The Demon Palace is a sea of blood. Once I enter, there is no turning back.

Why should I carry your burden?"

Mo Han was silent for a long moment.

Then—before anyone could react—

he turned and knelt before her.

The kneeling of a demon king.

The kneeling of ten thousand armies.

Gasps rippled through the ranks. Even the air seemed to stop.

"Get up," Yara hissed. "What are you doing?"

Mo Han's voice scraped raw—yet each word was painfully steady.

"Yara… do you know when I first loved you?"

Her fingers twitched—but her tone remained frost.

"Stop talking nonsense."

"Years ago," he said, eyes never leaving hers,

"when you and the immortals passed through the mortal realm, I was hunting a rogue beast. You were at the end of the procession. You looked back—once.

That one glance struck me like a blade.

From that moment on, I could not forget you.

You became my obsession."

He lowered his head further, pressing his forehead to the back of her hand.

"Yara. I bare my heart to you here and now.

If you will not come with me—then I will not return."

A hush fell over the valley.

Thousands of demon soldiers held their breath.

Only that rough confession echoed between mountain walls.

Yara's chest rose and fell rapidly.

Her voice was steady—but her eyes wavered.

"You know my heart still carries the Heavenly Realm.

If one day… I choose to return—?"

Mo Han rose slowly, meeting her gaze head-on, midnight eyes unwavering.

"Then you may return," he said softly. "I will not stop you.

But right now—I ask only that you stand at my side.

Come back with me."

Yue Liuchuan opened his mouth—

"…Don't get moved, you're from the Heavenly—"

Mo Han flicked a finger.

Yue Liuchuan choked and went silent instantly.

"Mm—!"

Yara's lips trembled.

Her fingers curled inward, tightening against her own palm.

"If I say no?"

Mo Han answered without hesitation:

"Then we will stay here.

One day.

Two people.

Three meals.

Four seasons.

Until you change your answer."

Yara closed her eyes for a long moment.

Then:

"…Help him up," she murmured.

"A new Demon King kneeling in the dirt—what does that look like?"

A spark lit in Mo Han's eyes—

quiet, fierce, overflowing—

He stood, slow and controlled, and reached for her hand.

* * * * *

The grand hall of the Demon Palace blazed with ten thousand lanterns, a sea of fire rolling across the vast chamber.

Mo Han sat upon the high throne, the black coronation crown draped over his shoulders like a mantle of night.

Below him, the gathered officials dropped to their knees in waves, their voices rising like a thunderous tide.

"WE GREET THE DEMON KING—

AND THE DEMON QUEEN!"

The cry crashed through the pillars, shaking the mountain to its bones.

At the side of the hall stood Yara, clothed in white, her silhouette like frost against the sweeping crimson of the palace banners. Her gaze remained fixed ahead—silent, unmoved, austere.

At the first roar of "Demon Queen," her heart tightened—just barely.

She lowered her lashes, letting the storm of kneeling figures blur into a dark ocean.

Her fingertips curled inward, hidden in her sleeves.

A thousand lanterns blazed.

A thousand voices bowed.

Far behind the ranks, Yue Liuchuan stood squeezed among lesser demons and servants, his face pale as chalk.

Great. Absolutely great.

He'd survived dish-washing in the valley only to be dragged into the coronation of a demon king.

He barely lifted his head before Mo Han's chilly voice cut through the hall:

"Keep an eye on him. Take him back."

Two demon generals seized Yue Liuchuan by the arms before he could even protest.

"H–hey—! I told you, I would rather DIE than—"

He didn't get to finish.

A filthy rag was shoved straight into his hands.

"The Demon Palace has many dishes," the general said flatly.

"We are short on manpower."

Yue Liuchuan stared at the rag.

… …

For a moment, he truly felt blood rising to the back of his throat.

Of all the possible fates—execution, torture, eternal imprisonment—

being forced into lifelong dishwashing was somehow the cruelest.

Maybe he *should* have let Mo Han send him back to the Heavenly Court.

Let the immortals interrogate him, rip out his soul, scatter his ashes—

anything was better than being the official dishwasher of the Demon Palace.

Above him, the crowd roared again, "DEMON QUEEN—LONG LIVE HER MAJESTY!"

Below, Yue Liuchuan saw his future flash before his eyes:

endless cauldrons, greasy pots, mountains of bowls, demonic leftovers, and a lifetime supply of rags.

His vision darkened.

So this was his fate.

While the new Demon Queen received the reverence of ten thousand—

he was about to begin his first shift.

The era of Yue Liuchuan,

Dish Laborer of the Demon Palace,

had officially begun.

Extra chapter 7

The night in the Demon Palace garden was unusually still.

Moonlight pooled like frost on the pavilion tiles, the lotus pond below smooth as polished jade.

Yara sat alone beneath the curved eaves, fingertips resting lightly on the stone table, her breath steady as she sorted the unsettled thoughts in her chest—

the coronation, the firelit hall, the kneeling masses, Mo Han's burning gaze.

Just as the silence settled into something almost peaceful—

plunk.

A ripple spread across the water's surface, as if someone had tossed a pebble straight into the centre.

Yara's brow tightened.

Her gaze lifted.

The pond brightened—

a shimmer, a flash—

and then the entire water surface turned flat and glossy, like a mirror polished by unseen hands.

And from that mirror came a voice.

"HELLO? HELLOOO? ANYONE THERE?!"

Yara: "…"

Before she could decide if this was an illusion, a spirit message, or some new kind of magical harassment, a face suddenly *exploded* out of the water.

A face so familiar she almost dropped her composure.

Lili—

hair a chaotic bird's nest, eyes shining like she'd just defeated a celestial beast, cheeks flushed with pure excitement.

"Yu Sord! Is this even working or not?!"

"Lili?"

Yara stood abruptly, the calm on her face finally cracking.

"Lili—? Is that you? Lili?!"

"AH! CONNECTION SUCCESSFUL!"

Lili slapped both palms on the water-mirror like she'd invented the thing, then turned and yelled at someone off-screen.

"Yu Sord! LOOK! It really connected!!!"

The image shook violently, and half of Yu Sord's shoulder came into view—his expression cold, elegant, and already mildly judgmental.

"…Why is the image distorted?"

"Wait, wait, I'm adjusting the filter!"

Lili smacked the water twice—*PAK PAK*—

The image warped.

Her entire head stretched into a melon-shaped blur.

"What—HEY—why is the picture GONE AGAIN?!"

She started screaming into the water,

"Yara? Yara?? Don't hang up! Don't hang up on me!"

Yara: "I didn't do anything."

Yu Sord cleared his throat, voice calm as always:

"Stop slapping the mirror."

"Oh. Right—okay—AH! IT'S BACK!"

Lili beamed, triumphant.

She was just about to launch into a full report when—

Ding.

The water surface chimed like a new call had connected.

The image split neatly into three panels.

In the new panel appeared Moony's face.

Moony froze for half a heartbeat—

then shrieked:

"M—MISS!!!"

She practically dove toward the mirror…

and slammed her forehead into it with a painful **BONK**.

"OW—!"

Lili burst into wild laughter.

"HAHAHAHA! This mirror is AMAZING!!"

Yara lifted a hand to her forehead.

"Moony… please be careful."

"Exactly!" Lili puffed up proudly.

"I upgraded the whole system! Now the celestial realm, mortal realm, and demon realm are all connected. A full three-way hotline! Anytime voice chat!"

Moony's eyes were still red, but she was smiling through them.

"Miss… now I can see you every day!"

Lili's eyes sparkled with mischief.

"From today on, this is our official three-realm chatroom. Instant replies only. If someone doesn't come online, then…"

Moony blinked, rubbing the forehead she'd just slammed into the mirror.

"Then what?"

Lili crossed her arms with dramatic authority.

"Then I'll personally come drag you online! Hahaha—"

Yara: "…"

Yu Sord murmured behind Lili, voice cool:

"…Who approved these rules?"

"My rules!" Lili announced, chin high.

"I'm the group leader!"

"I vote with both hands!" Moony raised both arms so fast she almost hit the mirror again.

On the water-surface, three faces filled three neat panels, one glowing with excitement, one teary and smiling, one cold as winter frost, and in the fourth corner, half of Yu Sord's impossibly handsome face leaning in.

A moment later, another shadow pushed its way into the frame—

Mo Han, appearing behind Yara with clear displeasure.

"Hurry up," he said coolly. "The coronation ceremony is about to begin."

The moment the words "coronation ceremony" left his mouth, the mirror erupted into shrieks.

"WAAAH—YARA, YOU'RE BECOMING A DEMON QUEEN? Turn around! Let me see! Is the queen's robe pretty? Show me! SHOW ME!"

Lili even grabbed Yu Sord by the wrist and dragged him closer to the mirror.

"You say! Tell me! Isn't Yara gorgeous in that outfit?"

Mo Han snorted.

"Anything she wears looks better than your celestial styles."

Yu Sord shot him an icy look.

"Nonsense. Lili is the daughter of the Phoenix. Red-gold plumage, divine radiance—she is the most resplendent."

Yara turned and glared at him.

"What are you two comparing for? Say one more thing, and I won't go."

"Exactly! What's there to compare?!"

Lili glared at Yu Sord in solidarity.

And then—a gentle, slightly aged voice drifted in from the mortal realm panel.

"Our Moony looks beautiful in anything."

It was Du Shao—his fingers sliding around Moony's hand with tender care.

He gazed at her as if the whole world had narrowed to one person.

"I'm sorry," he said softly.

"No matter how precious mortal treasures are, they can't compare to the celestial realm. But I would give you everything I have."

Moony's flushed face filled the panel again.

"Gongzi… w-what are you saying in front of everyone?!"

Yara felt her temple throb.

Lili squealed.

Yu Sord's expression darkened like a storm.

Mo Han stared, offended on instinct.

And the mirror—

blissfully—

kept them all connected.

Moony flushed, cheeks turning soft pink as she nestled shyly into Du Shao's arms.

"You are my everything," she murmured with a sweetness that could melt jade.

"HEY—wait, Moony, did you seriously become the Empress Dowager already?"

Lili's eyes sparkled like gossip lanterns. "That phoenix crown is huge—doesn't your neck hurt?!"

Moony giggled, embarrassed yet glowing.

"It's true. Shao has already abdicated. He's taking me traveling through the mortal realm for a few years."

Lili lit up instantly.

"That's amazing! Go have fun! And when Du Shao eventually reaches his… uh, mortal 'expiration date,' I'll have Yu Sord make another one of those—uh—what was it—'Soul-Rewind Fortune Sticks'?"

She snapped her fingers proudly. "Just like the sickly young master from last time—"

Yara pressed two fingers to her temple.

"It's *Reversal Soul Fate Talisman*. Not 'fortune stick.' I've corrected you a hundred times."

"Close enough!" Lili waved her hand, refusing to be corrected.

"With Sord around, nothing will happen to Du Shao. Moony, you can relax!"

She puffed up with confidence, then leaned sideways to confirm:

"Right? I'm right, aren't I?"

Yu Sord gave her a soft, indulgent smile—

the kind of smile that meant he would agree even if she rearranged the rules of heaven.

"You are always right."

Lili clapped happily.

"Perfect! From today on, across all three realms, the three of us will stay best friends forever. One life, one lifetime, always together, always loving each other—"

Her voice got louder and louder, more dramatic by the second—as though she were declaring a Three-Realms Eternal Alliance Treaty.

Moony laughed until her eyes curved into crescents, Du Shao drawing her closer with a gentle arm.

Yara looked away, lips unmoved, but her eyes softened—just slightly, quietly.

Far off, Mo Han gave a cold snort, but didn't actually object.

Yu Sord tapped the edge of the water-mirror with a long finger, as if silently approving this absurd vow.

Three faces—linked across a mirror, across realms—glowed together in the same rippling water-light.

Lantern fire reflected like a soft, fragile promise forming in the air.

Lili hugged the mirror frame, eyes shining like she might burst into fireworks.

"Forever and forever! If anyone dares disappear or stop showing up, I'll personally knock a bowl at your front door!"

Moony: ",,,...Haha, Miss is still the same."

Yara: ",,,...You dare knock a bowl at the gates of the Demon Realm?"

The other side of the water-mirror went quiet for two full seconds.

Lili cleared her throat.

"Well... depends on my mood."

Three realms connected—

noisy, chaotic, and unbelievably warm.

More eternal than any celestial spell.

Spring waters lapped softly against the embankment; willow branches let the wind knead them into silken threads.

The market noise rolled up the street in warm layers, and when the sugar sculptor's copper ladle hit the edge of the pot with a crisp *ding*, sweetness drifted out with the crowd.

Lili's hair was a wild mess blown up by the breeze.

She held a mirror in her left arm and a wicker basket in her right, while three chickens inside poked their heads out, curious as spies.

"One, Red. Two, Blue. Three, Gold. Anyone who strays more than three inches from this basket—will be punished with time-out!"

The three chickens clucked in perfect unison, as if replying, *"Understood."*

Lili lifted the mirror again, scrutinizing the tiny grain-sized chip at its edge.

She tapped the rim solemnly.

"Be good. You're not allowed to look ugly today."

She didn't need to talk to it—but saying it out loud steadied her heart.

It was a little trick she learned in the mortal realm, a charm more effective than any immortal incantation.

"Don't get swept away."

A hand reached over her shoulder and lifted the basket for her.

Yu Sord's voice was as calm as a still river—an unshakeable presence anchoring her to the spot.

He wore a plain azure robe; his shoulders in the sunlight were like a mountain that simply refused to move.

Lili made a face at him.

"You walk too fast. My legs are short!"

"I'll slow down."

"If you *really* slow down, I'll think you're injured," she muttered.

Her mouth was sharp, but her feet obediently kept up.

* * * * *

The crowd thickened near the busiest intersection where a storyteller slapped his wooden clapper awake.

He was narrating *The Peril on Abyssfall Cliff.*

As people surged forward, Lili plunged straight to the front.

Just as she elbowed her way into the best spot, the storyteller smacked the table and boomed:

"And the Phoenix Master stood holding the divine mirror!

Her three spirit-chickens clutched long silk threads in their beaks, stitching the sky—one needle, one line—mending the great rift of heaven—"

"WRONG!"

Lili practically exploded.

"There is *no such thing* as 'three chickens clutching silk thread'! I split the silk first! Then Little Fira presses the needle! You mortals don't understand anything—"

The storyteller nearly swallowed his clapper.

The crowd roared with excitement.

Yu Sord reached out and pulled her back, lowering his voice.

"If you correct him again, tomorrow he'll be spreading rumours that you can embroider by yourself without even using your hands."

"…That's not necessarily a bad rumour," she muttered—then her eyes lit up.

"Wait—look! That sugar-cake stall! Two—no, four! Buy four!"

She stuffed the cakes in her mouth, cheeks puffed like a little chipmunk.

When she saw Yu Sord hadn't touched his, she pressed the reddest piece to his lips.

"Here. Smile a little."

He had no choice but to bite.

The sugar brushed his ear like a whisper, tinting the tips the faintest shade of red.

"Your ears are red."

"…It's warm."

Lili narrowed her eyes suspiciously. Then suddenly grinned.

She waved the remaining pieces in front of her chickens.

"Special rations for our heroes!"

The chickens clucked excitedly—

only for her to yank the cakes back at the last second.

"—In your dreams! Too much sugar and you'll shed feathers!"

She was still scolding them when someone at the street corner yelled:

"THIEF—!!"

A dark figure shoved through the crowd, sprinting down a narrow lane.

Lili hugged her mirror tightly.

"Oh NO—my chickens!"

The figure brushed past—fingers reaching—

Lili jerked instinctively, spinning the mirror outward.

A flash of light flared across the thief's face like a divine slap.

The man's footing vanished beneath him—

He pitched backward like a toppled statue, hitting the ground face-first with a resounding *THUD*.

She startled herself too, heart pounding wildly, though her shoulders still shook with false bravado as she blurted,

"See that?! I may be scared of dying—but I've got a *mirror*!"

Yu Sord steadied her with one arm, tossed the unconscious thief toward the constables with the other, then turned back.

Her hand gripping the mirror was still trembling.

He clasped her fingers—firm, chastening, and yet unmistakably approving.

"Next time," he said quietly, "don't dive into the middle of a crowd."

"I really got a little scared just now…" Lili muttered as she leaned closer, voice small with grievance.

"You should reward me."

Yu Sord considered this. "Sugar cake?"

She shook her head immediately. "A kiss. Right here." She tapped her brow.

His ears reddened even deeper, but he still lowered his head, murmured a faint "Mm," and brushed a kiss onto her forehead.

Someone in the crowd whistled.

Lili clapped a hand over the spot and laughed so hard her eyes watered.

"Ahhh—okay, okay, okay, that's enough. Any more and I'll get addicted!"

She covered her mouth, still snickering, feeling as if a string of tiny lanterns had been lit inside her chest.

The city buzzed around them, willow shadows melted into the light, and the taste of sweetness lingered on her tongue.

For one clear moment, she felt she had properly seized her own life—

fearful or brave, flustered or fierce—

whatever she was, she wanted to live loudly, vividly, messily, joyfully.

* * * * *

Capital City, Phoenix Palace

Late spring draped the palace grounds in blooming crabapple blossoms—

petals pale-red as spilled sunset, falling on blue stone like softened sighs.

Inside the hall, the scent of medicine hung faint and bitter.

Du Shao leaned against embroidered pillows, coughing—his voice worn like jade that had endured too many hands.

His fingers, thin and rigid, still rested steadily atop Moony's hand.

"Moony," he murmured, "I've reviewed everything… Thirty thousand troops withdrawn from the frontier. Relief silver distributed. Civil granaries can sustain two seasons."

Moony smiled, though her eyes shimmered.

"You… even now, you're thinking about the world."

"Only because you're here," Du Shao whispered.

His gaze—still clear, still gentle like in his youth—held hers.

"My life was full of hardship. Having you… mended all the broken parts."

Moony smoothed the hair at his temple; her fingers paused behind his ear.

She still looked young, unchanged by time, but her brows carried a softness that had taken decades to form.

"I've made peace with it," she said quietly.

"I lost my immortal arts. Whether I return to the heavens… that no longer matters."

Her voice grew even softer—like leaves brushing water.

"For fifty years, I watched you rule—saw you steady the realm, protect the people. This is the path I chose. Everything has a cost. My cost was losing my powers… and being parted from my lady. But my wish—"

She swallowed. "—my wish was to walk one lifetime beside you. And that has already come true."

Tears pooled in Du Shao's eyes, finally falling as he smiled.

"Complete," he echoed, as though fastening the word onto his heart.

His eyes drifted closed, still holding her hand.

Moony leaned down, pressing her brow to his palm.

Her whisper trembled like a vow carried by wind:

"Go ahead. I'll wait for you.

I'll wait until the flowers bloom again… until the wind returns."

A breeze stirred the blossoms outside, and a soft rustling swept beneath the crabapple trees—

as though someone, somewhere, answered her with the gentlest *yes*.

* * * * *

Night spread across the Demon Realm's Endless Sea like a roll of silk slowly unfurling.

Lanterns drifted one by one over the dark water, swaying into a thin, trembling line of gold.

Yara guided the small boat into the reeds and, with a flick of her wrist, tossed a lantern over the water.

She did not rush to make a wish.

She simply watched it glide away—gentle, steady, as though a private thought had finally found the right pace.

At the stern, Mo Han lifted the oar.

His sleeves were damp with mist, catching the faintest shimmer of light.

"You're not talking again," Yara muttered, unable to stop herself.

"Heaven and earth are this quiet, and *you* have to be even quieter."

"What should I say?" His voice was unchanged—cool, calm, absolutely himself.

"For example…" She cleared her throat. "That you like me."

Mo Han froze for a beat.

Then—surprisingly earnest—he copied her tone with solemn obedience:

"I like you."

Yara laughed before she could stop herself, and the laughter left her nose stinging with unshed tears. She leaned her head against his shoulder—a soft cloud resting upon an unmoving mountain.

"You," she whispered, half in tease, "are learning far too fast."

Life bloomed and quieted in the smallest of moments. At dawn, he chopped wood; she cooked congee. She taught the village children to read; he honed his blade beneath the eaves.

She insisted she could carry the rice sacks herself, he took them from her with one hand and casually brushed the ends of her hair with the other.

When the first snow of winter fell, Yara attempted sweet potato cakes but ruined the heat.

She scowled and tried to throw them away.

Mo Han took one, ate it slowly, and finally said: "…Good."

Yara glared at him, but her heart melted helplessly into warm syrup.

She thought, absurdly:

If life stopped here, this moment would already be enough.

The river flowing, lanterns drifting, and someone by her side—

someone who spoke little, because knowing her was enough.

"Lili…"

That night, she sat before the bronze mirror and softly called her distant friend's name.

Only her own clear, steady eyes stared back at her.

Mo Han's arms slipped around her waist from behind, his brow coming to rest against her hairline. "You are enough," he murmured, his voice as low as a dark tide.

Yara smiled and nodded, her reflection trembling gently in the mirror's light.

"We're both enough," she whispered.

* * * * *

The sky over Mount Lu Yue was painfully bright, the kind of sharp, new-cleansed blue that made the world feel freshly forged.

The barrier around the cave had long since dissolved.

New vines crawled up the stone gate, and the mountain wind slid down pine needles, scattering their shadows like spilled ink.

Wuchen was crouched at the cave entrance, tying together a bouquet of wildflowers, crooked, uneven, clearly assembled with **confidence** and **absolutely no skill**.

Lu Ling stepped out, sword at her back.

One glance, and her verdict dropped like a blade:

"Ugly."

Wuchen nodded gravely.

"Ugly because I tied it myself."

Then, without shame, he shoved the flowers into her arms.

"Take it."

Lu Ling shot him a sidelong look and turned down the mountain path.

He followed immediately—like a very persistent, very enthusiastic shadow.

"Ling, now that you're finally out—any wishes?"

He walked backward in front of her, animated.

"Should I take you to see the sea? Or down the streets for that sticky candy that glues your teeth?"

"Noisy."

"Then—'sword.'"

His eyes lit up.

"We can go down the mountain and slay some monsters."

Lu Ling stopped. She stared at him a beat.

"Your sword faster than your mouth now?"

Wuchen nodded solemnly.

"My mouth will never outrun your sword."

For a heartbeat, the corner of her lips almost betrayed her—

almost.

She huffed instead.

"…Go."

* * * * *

At the foot of the mountain, beneath the shrine's ancient tree, a foul aura curled like smoke.

A fox demon was wearing a human skin, selling medicine at a roadside stall, preying on the town's children, stealing their dreams at night and selling "remedies" by day.

Wuchen stepped forward, hand on his sword.

The fox's eyes rolled white—it bolted.

He was about to give chase when his collar got yanked hard.

Lu Ling had grabbed him by the back of his robe, dragged him aside with effortless strength, and with a single flick of her blade—**the fox's tail hit the ground.**

Wuchen blinked.

"…I was letting it run three steps on purpose."

Lu Ling's tone was ice.

"I wasn't."

The fox demon yelped and tried to flee.

Wuchen's sword flashed upward, slicing clean through the beam above.

For a breath, the entire street fell silent—

as though the roar of the marketplace had been seized by the throat.

Pinned between two converging sword auras,

the fox's fur puffed into a terrified, perfect ring.

Lu Ling stepped forward in three crisp strides and finished it with a single, decisive slash.

She turned back and shot Wuchen a glare.

"Next time, stop talking."

Wuchen looked unreasonably pleased.

"Alright. Next time you swing first."

"I *always* swing first."

"That works too."

He smiled with such unearned confidence—

like the boy who knelt outside her cave thirty years ago

had suddenly come back twice as shameless.

Lu Ling said nothing more,

only tightened her hold on the ugly bouquet in her arms.

Her mouth stayed sharp, but her heart…was softening, little by little.

* * * * *

The two bickered all the way down the road until they reached the market gate.

Children swarmed them at once, shouting:

"Fairy sister!"

"Sword Master!"

One bold little hand reached out toward the lopsided bouquet.

Wuchen shielded it like it was a priceless treasure.

"Hey, hey—this one I just learned to tie!"

Lu Ling glared at him.

"You're still learning?"

"I am," he said with absolute sincerity.

"Whatever you like, I'll learn."

"I like you silent."

"…I'll try."

The crowd burst into laughter, and the sound rose on the wind, lifting up over rooftops— and higher still into the clear winter sky.

* * * * *

When the year turned old and light grew thin, Lili had finally visited every place she'd ever wanted to see—even the slanted stone slope outside the city, the one she'd once fallen off of.

She climbed right back onto it and jumped twice.

Yu Sord stood below, hands raised, helpless and attentive.

"Careful."

"I'm scared of dying," she reminded him.

"I know."

"But I still want to jump."

"I know that too."

She laughed and when she came down, she fell neatly into his arms.

The three chickens clucked triumphantly, while Little Fira refused to watch at all, dozing under the eaves with golden feathers drooping.

Lili clutched her mirror against her chest,

looked toward the thin gold line on the horizon,

and declared solemnly:

"No more cracking."

A beat.

"Please."

Most things in the world don't obey just because someone says *please*.

But she said it anyway, and saying it made her heart settle.

She had learned to negotiate with the world gently, and the world, somehow, had learned to return that gentleness to her.

* * * * *

That same dusk—

In the Phoenix Palace,

Moony pressed the final seal onto the day's memorials

and looked out toward the blooming crabapple trees.

In her heart, she whispered to her distant mistress:

I'm doing well.

By the riverbank, Yara folded away her embroidery frame and pushed a steaming bowl of ginger soup toward Mo Han.

"Drink it while it's hot."

On Mount Lu Yue,

Lu Ling carried the bouquet, Wuchen carried his sword, and shoulder to shoulder they descended the mountain—still arguing loudly about "whether the ugly bouquet needed a different binding technique."

A thin snowfall drifted down, settling on the sword's spine, and on the crooked wildflowers he had tied just for her.

Farther away, in the distance, the Abyssfall Cliff lay quiet in the thin mist, like a great beast finally asleep.

The ancient fissure had been sewn shut, thread by patient thread, until it finally settled into a thin, gentle scar. When the wind passed over it, the sound changed as well; what had once been a violent roar softened into something quieter, almost like a breath.

The mirror in Lili's arms gave a sudden, soft shimmer, its surface rippling as though stirred by spring water.

She lifted it, and for an instant, the mirror reflected countless scenes, the lantern glow of the Phoenix Palace, a river covered in floating lights, snow on mountaintops, laughter in a marketplace, a hand being held, a bouquet being shoved into someone's arms.

Her nose suddenly prickled.

She reached up to wipe at it, and accidentally caught Yu Sord's fingers in the same motion.

"Did you see that?" she asked.

"I did," he answered.

"Isn't it beautiful?"

"It is."

She muttered, "I like beautiful things the most."

"I know."

"Then I like you too."

Yu Sord didn't reply, only tightened his hold on her hand.

That was how he always was: few words, steady strength.

He didn't need to say me too.

She already knew.

Night wind drifted through the market's oil lamps, and all the flames leaned gently in the same direction.

Someone at the street corner was singing a folk tune, the line *"may every year have a night like this"* echoing as children chimed in off-beat.

The laughter made Lili's chest itch with warmth.

She suddenly turned, toward the mirror, toward Yu Sord, toward the three chickens, Little Fira, and toward her faraway friends who could not be seen, and announced solemnly:

"I don't want to be some Phoenix Lord."

"I want to live."

"I want a mirror, and chickens, and—"

She looked at Yu Sord, drawing out the pause on purpose.

"—and you."

Yu Sord lowered his head and pressed a light kiss to the centre of her brow—a seal as soft as breath.

"All yours."

She leaned sideways onto his shoulder, half a piece of sugar cake still in her mouth,

laughing through the crumbs.

"You'd better give them properly. Missing even one is not allowed."

"I won't miss any."

"Good. Then I can relax."

Down by the mountain foot, Wuchen was getting whacked on the back with a sword spine—

because he had once again tried to talk his way out of a crisis.

On the river, Mo Han set his oar upright against the railing and let Yara sleep against his shoulder.

In the palace, Moony closed the window, lit a small lamp, and moved it beside the bed—as though lighting a path home for someone far away.

* * * * *

Many years later, the archives of Lingxiao added a new page:

"The Liri Mending Method—

not patched with life,

but stitched with the heart;

with the caution of the timid,

accomplishing the courage of the great."

The scribe who copied it down couldn't help scribbling a small note beside it:

"She likes sweets, noise, mirrors, and laughing."

He immediately felt it was unbecoming and hurried to erase it.

But it didn't wipe clean—a faint mark remained on the paper.

In the years after that, children chased three chickens by the market stalls, laughing until they couldn't stand straight; a young student in the academy traced a line in the *Book of Songs*—

"That fair one, on the other side of the water"

The secretly thought of a lone boat drifting across a quiet river.

On the mountain, snow fell, and the flowers were still tied horribly crooked—

but Lu Ling took them every time.

Outside the palace walls, the crabapple trees bloomed year after year;

the old guard at the gate said there was a lamp inside the palace that had never gone out, not many understood what it meant, but those who did were enough.

As for Lili, she often stood before her mirror practicing her "dignity,"

only to collapse into giggles three breaths later when Yu Sord tapped her gently on the brow.

She still got scared sometimes—scared of the dark, of heights, of losing things.

But she had learned how to hold on—

hold on to the mirror,

hold on to the hand reaching toward her,

hold on to a whispered **"please."**

She feared clearly, and she lived proudly.

Far away, the Abyssfall Cliff breathed quietly.

Very close, the four realms rested in peace.

Everyone took their place:

someone kept watch,

someone waited,

someone learned to speak less,

someone learned to speak a little more.

And all of it, finally, was like a repaired brocade, the warp and weft the same, the pattern even richer.

The last lantern was gathered into the basket.

Lili hooked the basket over her arm, lifted her chin, and declared:

"Let's go home."

Yu Sord answered, "Mm."

She added, "—I'm hungry."

He turned his head slightly and naturally took the basket from her hands.

"All yours."

She blinked, then bent over laughing.

"That's not what I meant! I meant all the food is mine!"

"That too."

"Wow, you're so agreeable today!"

"You're very noisy today."

"I'm noisy every day."

"I know."

Behind them, the wind gently closed the city sounds, and the moon paved their path

like a soft silver ribbon.

The three chickens followed with uneven steps,

Little Fira settling onto her shoulder, its feathers warm.

Lili tucked the mirror into her arm, and a quiet, steady thought rose in her chest:

—So this is what 'completion' really is.

Not something earthshaking, just walking a night road not too long or too short, with laughter beside you, with lantern light ahead, and someone answering you with a single, certain word—

"Here."